I'm Locker 145, Who Are You?

Sylvia Gunnery

Cover by
Janet Wilson

YP-91-067

Scholastic Canada Limited

Scholastic Canada Ltd.
123 Newkirk Road, Richmond Hill, Ontario, Canada
L4C 3G5

Scholastic Inc.
730 Broadway, New York, NY 10003, USA

Ashton Scholastic Limited
Private Bag 1, Penrose, Auckland, New Zealand

Ashton Scholastic Pty Limited
PO Box 579, Gosford, NSW 2250, Australia

Scholastic Publications Ltd.
Holly Walk, Leamington Spa, Warwickshire CV32 4LS,
England

Canadian Cataloguing in Publication Data

Gunnery, Sylvia
    I'm Locker 145, who are you?

ISBN 0-590-74039-3

I. Title.

PS8563.U55I5 1991   jC813'.54   C91-094184-X
PZ7.G8Im 1991

6 5 4 3 2 1   Printed in Canada   1 2 3 4 5
                Manufactured by Webcom Limited

HOLY NAME SCHOOL
WELLAND

I'm Locker 145,
WHO ARE YOU?

1

Carla loves Barry

Jon was here

Hi Kelly

Stop writing on this desk

I'm locker 145, who are you?

Jodi Quinn picked up her pencil and scratched *I'm locker 380* next to the question. She didn't know why she'd bothered. She didn't know anyone in this school, and the last time she'd written on a desk, in her old school — about a month ago, in fact — she'd gotten into a pile of trouble. But then it had been more Scott's fault than hers. He kept writing things about her on the desk until finally, in exasperation, she had written *Scott will die* in red marker across his *Jodi kisses dogs*. Mr. MacDonald couldn't help but notice the red marker. Stupid move.

Right now, sitting in science class at Bethune High School — population 1826 — Jodi tried to repress the itchy feeling that she might be fed up enough to miss even Scott. God, she must be crazy.

She didn't look out of place sitting in the third row, fifth seat of room 301, class 10M. Her blonde hair hung straight to her shoulders and her pale complexion was marred by only two pimples — probably the result of the chocolate bars she'd been eating as an excuse for something to do other than stand around and stare at everybody before classes started. Her grey sweater did have the blue crest of her old school on it, but it was just a small one. Most of the kids in her class wore jeans and so did she.

Ms. Blake, her homeroom teacher, had introduced her to two of the "nice" girls in her class the first day, and she had to admit it was a relief to have them help her find the science lab and her locker and all that, but basically they weren't Jodi's type. Not that the bad ones were either. Something in between.

Someone like Brenda from her old school. Brenda, Jodi remembered, was a real, true friend. Like that time Jodi had the pizza party and her parents let them have the house to themselves for part of Saturday night. Jason and Tim had shown up not exactly what you'd call drunk, but obviously having had a few. Jodi's parents would've been furious, so Brenda talked the two of them into going with her to McDonald's. A good friend. She didn't go into shock about things like that. She was good at handling situations that might panic parents without getting all in a flap.

2

God, Jodi thought, she sure missed Brenda.

Not to mention her father — which was why she was in this new school in the first place. She and her mother were living at her grandmother's while her father and her brother, who was ten and knew nothing important, lived at home. Trial separation.

Jodi was more than relieved when the dismissal bell rang and she could go home — home to Nan's, that is. A lot of the students had to take a bus, but she could walk the twenty-minute distance to her grandmother's.

The sharp February wind pushed insolently at her, stinging her nose and cheeks. Her eyes watered, and she let the tiny droplets fall, not bothering to wipe them away. She felt like looking sad. She *was* sad.

The words "trial separation," when Jodi had first heard them, meant more "trial" than "separation." That was what people did when they needed a break — try living apart to see what it was like. It was awful, as far as she was concerned.

And things didn't seem much better for her mother. Last night Jodi had secretly listened in on the extension phone to her mother and father talking long distance. It wasn't that she meant to be sneaky about it. But the phone had rung and she'd rushed to the upstairs one and picked up the receiver just as her mom had answered the one in the kitchen. Perhaps because it was long distance, no one had noticed the change in the sound of the voices as she listened in.

"It's me."

"Oh. How's Teddy?"

The tension on the line was like an archer's bow, taut, ready to fling a piercing arrow at the enemy. And yet these were the voices of her parents. Jodi's heart pounded with fear as she listened.

"Look. When are you going to stop being so stubborn and get back home here? This has gone on long enough."

"Oh, it has, has it? And just what are your criteria for judging that? What's the matter, won't your girlfriend do the laundry?"

"Knock it off, Muriel. There's no girlfriend — "

"Don't try handing me that line!"

"When are you going to take down that brick wall in front of your eyes and see the truth? We've been through all this before. The past is the past, Muriel, and that's where it should stay. There's just Teddy and me here, and you and Jodi should be here too."

"For how long?"

"For as long as you want."

"Or until the next time."

"There won't be a next time. I promise."

"Ha."

"You've got to give me a chance, Muriel. If not for our sakes, then for Teddy and Jodi. Their lives shouldn't be tossed around like this."

"Of all the things for *you* to say!" Her mother's voice was shrill and angry, blaring through the telephone line. "Look who tossed lives around! I

4

didn't leave you on a whim, you know. Really, David, I don't think you realize what you've done. And I won't stand here and listen to you accusing me of upsetting our family! *I'm* not the unfaithful one!"

The clattering of the downstairs receiver against the telephone boomed in Jodi's ear. She stood, holding hers and staring at it. Only a hollow buzz remained. Slowly, she returned the receiver to its cradle. The trial separation, she realized, was not near its end at all.

Moments later the phone rang again. She knew it had to be her father calling back, but this time, instead of picking up the extension, Jodi went to the top of the stairs and sat down where she could hear her mother's voice from the kitchen. It was sneaky to be eavesdropping like this, but she just had to know what was going on. Usually, when she tried to get straight answers, only cover-ups came.

"I had every right to hang up! Who ... Yes, I'm listening ... But ..."

There was a long interval. Jodi strained to hear, somehow, what her father was saying on the other end of the line. He had said he wanted them all to come home. At least that was something. But maybe her mother was right. Maybe he just wanted the laundry done or something like that. Yet, to Jodi, laundry seemed like a pretty strange reason for someone to call long distance and ask someone else to come back home. And he'd said that he didn't have a girlfriend. No one had ever seen this girlfriend anyway. Not that that made it okay or anything, but it couldn't have been such a serious thing if no one had even seen her, and if he said he didn't see her now. Maybe, Jodi thought, if she knew more about just what had happened, she could begin to understand better.

"David, you don't realize what it's like to be me right now." Her mother's voice sounded exasperated, and yet she was not yelling. "You say we've got too much to throw away. Well, I feel like it's already *been* thrown away. What's left for me?"

That question echoed in Jodi's mind and she tried to answer it. She and Teddy still loved their mother in the same way, but maybe it didn't quite count with Teddy living back home. She guessed that it must feel strange for her mother to be sleeping on the downstairs divan rather than in that huge bedroom back home with the blue-flowered curtains and the big window that looked out over the garden in the back yard. The garden. Who'd get it ready when spring came, and when the weeds started, who'd pull them out? And all the stuff in the kitchen. And the paintings on the walls. Just thinking about the details of home brought hot, aching tears to her eyes as she sat at the top of the stairs. She listened to her mother's tired voice.

"I'm afraid to take the chance, David. And I'm angry. I don't trust you."

Jodi's tears slid down onto her knees, wrapped tightly between her arms. She was afraid too. Nothing was normal anymore. Not friends. Not

6

school. Not her bedroom. Most days there was nothing to do at Nan's, and every morning so far, she'd had a thick lump in her stomach and a woozy fear because she didn't know anyone at school. And the teachers were piling on extra work to try to help her catch up with some material she hadn't covered in her old school. It was like punishment for being in a family on trial separation.

Her mother's voice broke into her thoughts. "Yes, I'll try. We can talk then ... Yes ... No, I don't want to talk to him right now. I'm too upset. I'll call him tomorrow night. Don't tell him you phoned me .. I know you are, David ... Yes, I'll tell her. Bye."

Briefly, all was still. The only sound was the TV in the livingroom blaring so Nan could hear it. Then Jodi heard her mother move away from the phone and sit at the kitchen table. She didn't know what to do, so she just sat rooted there on the stairs. She remembered a child's poem she used to read over and over about a little boy who liked to sit halfway down the stairs because he felt like he was in some special place — not up and not down, but some place extraordinary. Slowly she slid down a few steps. But sitting there wasn't really special at all. Her mother was still alone and hurt in the kitchen and the trial separation was still in full force.

* * *

When Jodi finally arrived home she closed the door against the cold and against her unhappy thoughts. She placed her books on the hall table.

"Hi, Nan. What's new on the tube?" Nan was watching her daily soap.

"Hi, dear. How was school today? Did you have any tests?"

Nan always asked if there were any tests.

"No. Not today."

"I made some gingersnaps, and wouldn't you know it, Libby called just when I should've taken them out of the oven and the last batch got scorched and I said to myself, Jodi'll eat them. You know how you like them scorched. Why don't you get some and a glass of milk and come in here and watch the tube with me?"

Jodi laughed a little — not so Nan would really notice, but you just had to laugh about how she picked up slang like "tube" and then used it in the wrong place. She tried hard, you had to say that for Nan. And come to think of it, she'd had Jodi's mother thirty-six years ago. It had been a long time since she'd lived with teenagers, and here was her granddaughter all of a sudden living with her. There was a lot to catch up on.

"It'll be over soon," said Nan when Jodi returned with a glass of milk and a handful of cookies.

Every day after school now, Jodi would watch TV with Nan, not really paying attention — with the soaps you didn't have to — but just because there was nothing else to do. And homework was the furthest thing from her mind. It could wait until after supper.

8

"Jodi," Nan began, patting her granddaughter's knee and looking up momentarily from the television, "I've been thinking."

"Oh-oh. Here's trouble," Jodi teased. But her curiosity was aroused. Nan had a way of stirring your mind when she said that she'd been thinking.

Nan chuckled briefly, then grew completely serious again. "No. I mean it. Muriel's busy, what with her new accounting job, with your father phoning her and with worrying about Teddy. And I don't think we've made enough to-do about you, young lady. You're the quiet one. You come home from school and do your work and watch TV and keep to yourself, so it seems that everything's just fine. But old Nan isn't fooled. I know you've got lots of things on your mind."

It was Nan's blue eyes that killed you. They were so pale they were almost grey, and she had a blue rinse in her silver hair that just about matched them. And she'd get this look in them as soft as boiled icing. It was hard not to get an ache in your heart. And then, of course, there was nothing left but to let the big salty tears ooze up and spill over, which was exactly what Jodi did.

How could she help it? You could only pretend for so long that nothing bothered you, but eventually buried feelings flared like a neon light.

"Oh now, there there," Nan cooed, making a cocoon around her granddaughter, with her arms, rocking, holding her against the itchy wool of her sweater. "You and Nan'll have a big talk. Right now. You'll feel better."

9

Jodi sniffed back a few tears and blurted, "What good's talking going to do? I just miss the old school and Brenda and Dad and even that typhoid-infested creep, Teddy." Jodi had to admit that just beginning to talk made her feel better already. Maybe it was the mention of her brother and the recollection of the gratifying distance between her and his juvenile mind and body that cheered her up. But that was small consolation for all the drawbacks of living in this city so far away from home.

"Mom hardly tells me anything about when Dad calls. She hates him so much. And when I think of what he did, I hate him too!"

"Hate's a pretty strong word, Jodi. He's your father."

"Well he didn't think very much about that when he had that girlfriend. He knew it'd mess up the family. He just wanted to be rid of us, that's all. It's a wonder he kept Teddy — must've thought Teddy would side with him. He probably does too. That creep has the brain of a turnip."

"I'm not saying that a married man should have a girlfriend, Jodi. But I will say that we don't know much about your father's side of the story. There are two sides to a coin, you know."

That was another thing about Nan. She thought in clichés. Admittedly, it made things clearer, but it was a pain sometimes.

"When I first met your father," Nan continued, "long before you were ever thought of, I took to him right away. He had a way about him, I don't know quite how to describe it."

"So does that mean he can cheat on Mom?" Frustration crept into Jodi's voice.

"No, no, no. I'm not saying that. I'm just saying that he'd probably been tempted lots of times. When a woman puts her mind to something, especially a man, she can be pretty tough to ignore."

"You make him sound like some kind of prince charming wearing a white velvet suit and some wicked witch in black snuck up behind him. He wrecked the family, Nan! And that's that!" She was yelling, although she didn't want to. Yelling never solved anything, as Nan would no doubt point out. "I'm sorry I yelled, Nan. But I just can't help it. Dad's gutless."

"No need for language, young lady. He's still your father."

To Nan, any word not found in the Bible was labelled "language" — which, of course, meant "unladylike language." Nan was at least seventy and attacks of raving anger had to be carefully curbed.

"Sorry, Nan. But he is."

"Well, I don't know." This was Nan's signal that the conversation was finished. She heaved a sigh, pursed her lips in careful thought, and got up with forced cheerfulness. "Let's go out into that kitchen and see what we can do about starting supper. What do you say to a lemon pie with Graham-cracker crust?"

How could you help but get a lift when someone mentioned your absolute favourite pie?

Jodi was peeling carrots, mesmerized by the *click-click* of the peeler when Nan, stirring the lemon filling at the stove, turned to her enthusiastically. "Now that's a bright idea I've just had! Why don't we have a party here, Jodi? You can invite some of your new friends from school. A perfect way to get to know them better. We'll make pizzas. I watched them make them on TV one afternoon. Easy as pie."

"But, Nan, I don't know anyone to invite to a party." It certainly was frustrating sometimes when Nan got an idea in her head but forgot to consider all the facts — usually the most important ones.

"There must be some boys and girls in your class that you've talked to in the last few days. I bet they'd love to come to a party."

"Thanks, Nan. But I think I'll pass. Not that it isn't a good idea. It is. But not just yet. Really. I wouldn't know who to ask. I don't even know their names, hardly."

Just the thought of a party was depressing. What would she do? Leave cute little invitations on their desks like in public school that said: *You're invited to a party. Where: My place. When: Friday.* Depressing. Absolutely depressing.

"I'm going to do some homework now, Nan." Jodi couldn't look at one more carrot peel curling into the sink.

"That's fine, dear. You just leave those for me." You could always count on Nan's full cooperation when you mentioned homework. "But I still say a party would be a perfect way to make new friends. You think about it awhile."

12

Upstairs, Jodi closed the door to her room. It had been her mother's room, but now her mother slept in the downstairs den on the fold-away sofa. Nan's room was right across the hall from Jodi's, so she could hear her grandmother's hollow snores late in the night. Her grandfather had died when Jodi was little, barely walking. She had been told many times how sick he'd been for so long. But before he died he'd said over and over that he was ready to die peacefully because he'd seen his beautiful granddaughter. That always made her glow with pride. And when she looked at the sepia-toned photograph in the mahogany oval frame over the buffet in the dining room, she felt an inexplicable closeness to this man who'd held her in his tired lap and said she was beautiful.

But right now, sitting on the marshmallow softness of the old bed with no intention of doing any homework, and still feeling depressed because there was no way she could possibly have the party Nan suggested, Jodi did not feel beautiful. Who was around to think of her as beautiful? And relatives, especially female ones, didn't count.

* * *

"Pssssst." The hissing sound came from the desk behind Jodi in the middle of science class. Mr. Clarrey stood at the front of the room twirling a white ball at the end of a string, round and round so fast that you could hardly see it, then faster still until you just plain couldn't see it at all. He was asking why.

"Pssssst!"

Jodi turned her shoulders slightly and forced her eyes into a painful sideways look, expecting someone to pass something to her that she would then have to pass to someone else. Otherwise, why would anyone be trying to get her attention in the middle of science class?

"Did you write on this desk?" It was the overweight girl whose name was Brenda. Jodi remembered that name because of her friend Brenda, who right this minute was an impossible distance away.

"Huh?"

Brenda was pointing to the writing on her desk. Jodi stared dumbly, then finally understood. Mr. Clarrey had just changed the seating plan, convinced that students did not have new thoughts as long as they were in old seats, or something like that. It all had to do with inventiveness. Whatever his mad-scientist reasons, Jodi was no longer sitting in the desk where she'd written *I'm locker 380.*

"Yes," Jodi replied hoarsely, never really good at whispering.

"Girls," came the inevitable reproach from the front of the room, "if you're putting your heads together in order to solve the mystery of the disappearance of this white ball at certain high velocities, then perhaps you'll tell the class your solution. No? Well let me trouble you to think. With your mouths closed politely." Some teachers sure did have a way with words when they were slicing you up for sandwich material.

14

Finally the blaring sound of the bell brought the twirling ball to a halt, and the students were released from the scientific quest. Now Brenda could speak normally. "Look what's written underneath what you wrote."

Jodi got out of her seat and stood looking down at the pencilled scrawl. *Hi Jodi*, it read. Her heart leapt into her throat.

"It must mean some other Jodi. I don't know anyone here."

"I don't know anyone else by the name of Jodi. And I've been in this school two years." Brenda's green eyes glittered with excitement.

Looking at Brenda now, Jodi realized that she was actually okay-looking. Not a blotch of a pimple. And her smile showed a row of perfect, white teeth. Too bad she was fat, Jodi thought.

"But this is a big school. You can't know all that many people." Immediately she realized the double meaning of her words. "I mean, how could anyone know many people in this place? I've been here almost two weeks and I feel like I haven't seen the same person twice, except every morning in homeroom for announcements."

"I'm telling you, there aren't any other Jodis."

Maybe Brenda was right. Someone had actually written a reply to her. She felt the blood drain a little from her face. The thought of someone snooping around to spy on her to find out her name was a bit scary. Creepy, in fact.

"I don't like the idea of this," she said finally.

"What's so bad about it?" replied Brenda en-

15

thusiastically. "I think it's super-marvellous. I mean, some guy has found out who you are! He must have seen you, he must have watched your locker for hours until you went there, and then he asked around or saw you go into your homeroom, then asked someone in your class. Yeah, that's probably it. And then he wrote your name. He must really like you or he wouldn't go writing your name on the desk. I mean, if he saw you at your locker and thought you were a lost cause or something, well then he'd obviously just not write anything at all. But he did, so that must mean he's interested. It's got to mean that. Isn't that exciting?"

Jodi couldn't shoot down everything Brenda had just said because she might be right, except for one thing — how did she know it was exciting? The guy might be a creep. The way Brenda raved on, you could tell she didn't exactly have the pick of the guys at school. Some unknown person writes a name on a desk and Brenda already hears rockets firing.

"He might be a creep."

"Who cares? It could be fun just to spy around and find out who he is and lead him on or something like that. And then again, maybe he's Mr. W and W."

"W and W?"

"Wild and wonderful!"

Perhaps Brenda might be getting all her ideas from an overrated teen mag, but then maybe she was onto something. It could be a bit of fun, Jodi thought.

16

"What should we do?" she asked, a conspiratorial smile on her lips.

"Don't let on you've read the note. Don't write a reply — yet." A sly grin spread across Brenda's flushed face.

"We need to check out locker 145, right?"

"Wrong. Not 'we.' He knows who you are and he's sure to be keeping an eye out for you, but he'd never suspect that I'm in on it. You just pretend you've never read the note. I'll check out locker 145."

"Okay. But when?"

"Right after school today. He'll have to go to his locker and put stuff in or get stuff for homework. Meet me out by the flagpole."

"Okay. What class do you have now?"

"I've got a spare. You?"

"French. I'd better hurry. Meet you at the flagpole."

"Bye, Jodi."

"See ya, Brenda."

As she rushed in and out down the crowded hallway, Jodi couldn't help smiling. It was exciting, Brenda was right about that. Who cared, anyhow, who locker 145 was? Something was happening other than the same dreary old repetition of going to classes, eating chocolate bars at break, going home to watch the soaps with Nan, and starting all over again the next day. It had been so good just to hear someone say her name and to hear herself say "See ya, Brenda." Just like back home. Almost.

As she waited impatiently at the flagpole,

17

Jodi turned up the collar of her red bomber jacket. It had started to snow a bit and the air was like an icebox. Brenda sure was taking her time about getting here. Jodi studied the guys passing by, watching for odd actions that would tell her one might be locker 145. If a guy was really cute, she imagined him sitting on a chair in his bedroom with his feet up on the desk, calling her on his own phone to ask if she wanted to go to a movie this time or just sit around watching TV at his place. Or if he wasn't cute she thought to herself how, if she got to know him, he'd probably make her split her sides laughing, he'd be so funny. Looks weren't everything. She couldn't stand a guy who thought he was, as Nan would say, "God's gift to women." The only reason a guy like that usually talked to people was so he could practise talking. She hoped locker 145 didn't turn out to be that type.

Then she saw Brenda coming down the front steps of the school towards her with a look on her face that wasn't exactly like Sherlock Holmes' at the conclusion of a murder case.

"Well?" Jodi couldn't wait to find out something — anything.

"Well, nothing," Brenda said flatly. "I waited around like an idiot, pretending to be looking for something in my purse until I couldn't fake it anymore. No show. Maybe he's not here today. Or maybe he left early. For sure he didn't go to his locker, because I was in English class and that's just seconds away from the locker and there's no way he'd get there first and get all his stuff and lock it again and leave. No way."

"So now what?" Jodi couldn't hide her disappointment.

"Tomorrow morning I'll try again. That's all I can think of."

"Hey, I was just wondering. Where do you live? I mean, do you have to catch a bus home now?"

"No. I live over by the Sportsplex. Only a couple of blocks. Why?"

"I live at Nan's, but it's past the Sportsplex. Not far. Why don't you come over and have something to eat or something?"

"I shouldn't, but I will. Eat, that is. Famous last words of a dieter." Brenda shifted her books from one arm to the other, holding them as a shield against the wind. "Let's go."

"You could call your folks from Nan's to tell them where you are," Jodi offered.

"That's okay. I don't need to. Mom and Dad are both at work and it's my brother's turn to start supper this week. So I don't need to be home for a while."

"How old's your brother?"

"Forget it, Cinderella. This guy's no prince. He's in grade eight, has sneakers big enough to sleep a German Shepherd in, and is the human extension of his video game. Borrring!"

Jodi laughed. She wished she had a normal family like Brenda, with parents who lived together and a brother with whom she took turns starting supper. Sounded like a pretty good situation. Doghouse sneakers and all.

2

Brenda had promised to meet Jodi at the cafeteria just before first class. Already the room was crowded with early-morning students scrambling to finish homework before the five-to-nine bell sounded the deadline. She finally spotted Brenda sitting by herself eating a doughnut and drinking skim milk.

"Hi. You have breakfast?" asked Brenda.

"Yeah. At Nan's," replied Jodi, anxious to get on with the investigation. "When're you going to check out the locker?"

"Already did. No luck. But maybe he comes late. Thought of asking someone whose locker is next to his. I dunno. What do you think? Should we let anyone else in on this?"

"No. I'd feel like a dummy. We'll find out ourselves."

"Up to you." Brenda tipped the small carton of milk back to drain it and dabbed at the corners of her mouth with a paper napkin. "Maybe he'll say something else today. You never know. Anyway, we'll soon see. Science is second class this morning. Catch ya later."

"Yeah. Okay. Bye," returned Jodi as Brenda swept her books up into her arms and made her way out of the cafeteria.

Waiting for the end of first class was like waiting for Christmas. Seconds stared her in the face while Ms. Drummond droned on at the front of the class about intransitive verbs.

The way Jodi rushed into science class, Mr. Clarrey probably figured she'd solved the problem of the disappearing white ball, to which she hadn't even given a moment's thought. Brenda was already in her seat, and Jodi could tell from the look on her face that Mr. W and W hadn't left a message.

"Who knows?" Brenda offered. "Maybe he's lying low to see if you'll make the next move. We'll have to do some thinking."

Jodi was disappointed again. It was like going to the mailbox and not getting a letter you were sure would be there. Of course, it was silly to be eager about someone who could turn out to be a creep and who wrote on desks for attention, but all the same, it was an adventure in a dry season of her life. Anything for kicks.

"Should I write something?"

"Yeah. I was just thinking that. Say something that'll force him into a reply."

"Let's see ... What if I just say something like 'How do you know my name?'."

"Perfect." Brenda handed a sharpened pencil to Jodi. "Write."

Jodi obeyed.

"We'll check this out after school."

* * *

When Jodi and Brenda met outside Mr. Clarrey's

class afterwards, he was holding an extra-help class for the grade twelves.

"Maybe we should just wait until tomorrow," offered Jodi. "He probably didn't write anything anyway."

"I can't wait. Drives me nuts to wait." Brenda stared down the hall looking for a brilliant idea. Abruptly, she turned and knocked on Mr. Clarrey's door.

"What're you doing?" whispered Jodi harshly. This could only mean more trouble. She remembered having to copy all those boring lines when she'd been caught writing on desks at her old school.

"Trust me."

Mr. Clarrey opened his door. "Yes, girls, what can I do for you?"

"Excuse me, sir. Sorry to interrupt your extra-help class," began Brenda, oozing politeness, "but did I leave my pen in your class today? It wasn't just any old pen, it was a silver one with my initials that my grandparents gave me and I'm worried sick because I can't find it."

Jodi shaped her face into a look of concern.

"Well, no one has passed in a silver pen, Brenda. But you certainly may come in to take a brief look."

"Thank you, sir. All I need is a brief look."

Jodi waited in the hall, watching Brenda walk boldly down the aisle in front of all those grade twelves. She peered around her desk, even kneeling on the floor to give the appearance of a thorough search for the elusive pen.

"Oh dear," she heard Brenda say, "it's not here, sir. But thank you for letting me in to look. Guess I'll go tear my locker apart for the tenth time. Thank you again."

They were two doors past Mr. Clarrey's room before Brenda spoke. "He replied."

"He did! Tell me. What'd he say?"

" 'I'm smart.' "

"Okay, so you're smart. Nervy is more how I'd describe you. But what'd he say?"

"That's what he said, 'I'm smart.' Those two words were on the desk."

" 'I'm smart' ? What's that supposed to mean?"

"Well, you asked how he knew your name, so he's just answering without giving away anything about himself. This guy's leading you on. Playing hard to get." She stopped and thought for a moment. "I love it!" she finally exclaimed.

"I'm glad you do. It's starting to get to me. I want to know who he is since he knows who I am."

"Somehow we've — you've — got to trick him into talking."

"What could I say? I don't have the foggiest —"

"Pretend you know his name. Act like you're smart too."

"Thanks a lot."

"No, I didn't mean that. You know what I mean."

"What if I write something like 'I know your name too' ?"

"Okay. Tomorrow morning, before classes. Before anyone's in Mr. Clarrey's room."

* * *

The next morning, both girls were already comfortably sitting in the cafeteria when the halls starting filling up with the usual crowds of students standing around talking, walking up and down checking everyone out, or digging through lockers piled high with ancient projects and overdue library books. Jodi's pencilled reply was in its place on the desk in Mr. Clarrey's room.

Science class was third period. "Good morning, Brenda," said Mr. Clarrey with a smile as he set up the overhead projector. "Did you find your pen?"

"Huh?" Brenda stopped abruptly in her rush to check out the desk for a note.

"Yes, she did, sir," Jodi quickly replied, hoping to cover up for Brenda. "It was in her locker."

"Yeah, in my locker. That's exactly where it was. Hidden under my *Roget's Thesaurus* which I hardly ever use so I didn't think it'd be way back there, but *voilà*, there it was."

"I'm glad you found it."

"But now she isn't allowed to bring it to school because her mother says it's a lesson to learn that she almost lost it."

"Yeah. That's what she said. Otherwise, I'd show it to you."

Relieved, Jodi and Brenda continued to their desks. Discreetly, they checked for a note. It was there. It read: *No you don't.*

Brenda looked at Jodi, puzzled.

"How does he know I don't know his name?"

"We've got to try something else."

As Jodi was leaving the room at the end of class, Mr. Clarrey said in his special soft-spoken tone that meant you'd done something wrong, "Could I see you for a moment, Jodi?"

Brenda raised her eyebrows in a questioning look and went out into the hall to wait.

From his desk drawer, Mr. Clarrey took a square piece of wood just small enough to fit comfortably into the palm of a hand, like a bar of soap, and around it he wrapped a scratchy piece of sandpaper.

"I believe you can find good use for this," he said simply. "Do you have a class right now?"

Jodi's face burned red and her heart was squeezing its way up through her throat. "No, sir. I have a spare."

"Well, you can get to the task at hand now, then."

"Yes, sir."

Later, in the hall, she said sullenly to Brenda, "That's it for notes."

Brenda looked even more dejected. "Just when things were beginning to cook."

This was one more disappointment in Jodi's already fouled-up life. It would've been so neat if the guy writing the notes had been someone she'd like — like a lot. They could walk home to Nan's after school. Go places. Skating, maybe. She had brought her skates from home, but who wanted to go skating alone?

All noon-hour she and Brenda stayed in the cafeteria eyeing every single male who came in for lunch. When Brenda got impatient and suggested solving the mystery by going to the office and inquiring innocently about the owner of locker 145, Jodi protested. How embarrassing to have the whole school know she was on the lookout for a mystery man who had written on her desk! If she weren't so desperate for entertainment these days, she reassured herself, she would have shrugged off the whole business in a minute. But, under her current circumstances of absolute, stark boredom, Jodi liked the involvement. Brenda was a lot of fun, besides. At least it was nice to have met her.

"You going to your locker? I'll walk down with you. Have to go to the language lab to make a French tape," Brenda said.

"Sure."

Jodi saw it first, but she thought it was on the locker next to hers. Then Brenda let out a yelp. "A note! It's from him! I just know it!" And she ripped it off Jodi's locker, staring at it like it held the secret to the Oak Island Treasure. "Quick! Open it! Open it! See what it says!"

The piece of scribbler paper had been carefully folded and refolded to the size of a cracker. There was nothing written on the outside. Inside was a pencilled note: *Sorry I got you in trouble. Saw the desk all cleaned off. Figured Clarrey nailed you. Hope it wasn't a big hassle.*

Jodi held the note in her hand, her mind tangled with a zillion thoughts. Whoever this was, at least he was considerate.

"Let me read it. Hey, I like his handwriting. I

26

heard there's lots you can tell about a person by their handwriting. Like if they're conceited or if they have a persecution complex or something. This guy looks nice. And he can spell."

"I'm going to write back to him that I didn't mind sanding the desk. Should I say anything else?"

"Yeah. Ask him who he is."

"Should I put it on his locker?"

"Of course. Where else? And if you hurry, you can do it before classes start. But I gotta go." She turned and started down the hall, then added over her shoulder, "Use your best handwriting."

As she wrote, Jodi had the warm feeling she had found another friend at Bethune High School. Yet a hesitant twinge reminded her that this person was, really, a total stranger.

In between the first and second classes of the afternoon, Jodi walked past locker 145. Her note wasn't there anymore.

Looking down the hall, she could see there was no reply attached to her locker. She wished she didn't feel so disappointed about that.

Standing next to locker 380, however, was Brenda, grinning like a contented cat.

"I left the note on his locker and he got it because I checked between classes. Guess he didn't feel like answering."

"Yes, he did." Brenda's smile grew even bigger.

"What do you mean?"

"Here." She held out a note. "I took it off your

locker when I got here, but I didn't open it. Privacy is sacred. Quick, tell me what he said."

Carefully, Jodi unfolded the small note, trying to picture the guy who had folded it so meticulously. Then she panicked before reading it.

"What if it's just some guys who're doing this to laugh at me? They might be watching us all the time and laughing their heads off."

"Impossible. I saw his handwriting. That was not the handwriting of an imposter. That was the handwriting of a sensitive, thoughtful, handsome, intelligent male who's possibly a terrific dancer."

Jodi laughed as she read the note. *My initials are M.G.*

"Oh, no. Not still playing hard to get." Brenda leaned against the lockers and closed her eyes in exasperation.

"M.G.," Jodi repeated.

"Do you know how many people with the initials M.G. there are in a school this size? I take it back. My revised handwriting analysis is that he is *not* thoughtful. He's driving me nuts."

"Well, maybe next time he'll fill in the rest of his name." Jodi tucked the new note into her pencil case along with the first note, feeling a pleasant stir of excitement. "Tomorrow morning I'll send a real letter."

"What do you mean?"

"I'm going to write a letter tonight. Not just a note. Then maybe he'll say more."

"Sprinkle it with perfume," said Brenda with a sly grin.

* * *

Jodi lay across her bed, surrounded by crumpled scraps of writing paper, and chewed thoughtfully on the end of her pen. What do you say to someone you don't really know? Maybe if he knew too much, he would change his mind about writing to her. So far, she reminded herself, all he knew was her name and what she looked like. Big deal.

Carefully, she reworded and revised her short letter. Finally she lay on her back and held it up to read over one more time: *You know who I am but I don't know who you are. This year my parents decided to try a trial separation and I'm living with my grandmother and mother. The only friend I have here is Brenda. And possibly you. Will you tell me more about yourself? Jodi*

Finally, she let sleep carry her into oblivion, but not without one last delicious thought about this chance for some excitement.

* * *

At the end of first period the next day, her letter was still untouched on locker 145.

"Maybe he's sick today," Brenda offered lamely.

But at the beginning of fourth period, Brenda came rushing down the hallway just as Jodi was going into her math class. "It's gone. I just went past there and the letter isn't on the locker anymore. He's got it!"

When Brenda and Jodi met at noon-hour in the cafeteria, Jodi had not received a reply.

"Give the guy a chance, for heaven's sake," Brenda said. "He's got to think of a good reply to a perfumed letter."

"I didn't put perfume on it."

Brenda sighed. "What's the good of giving good advice?"

Jodi felt that haze of doubt beginning to build again. "Do you think I should've written him a letter?"

"Of course!"

"I mean really. Should I have?"

"And I mean really, of course! What's wrong?"

"I don't know who this guy is. When I think about all the complications of being here instead of home, and of Mom and Dad splitting up, I think that this could be just one more thing I'd be better off without. I'm getting nervous about it all."

"Relax. We're going to find out who he is soon. Trust me."

That night, Jodi sat with Nan and her mother watching TV, but she couldn't concentrate at all. She wanted to unload her big secret onto the two of them — yet she would feel foolish saying, "Hey, guess what. I've been writing notes to some guy I don't even know." That would go over like a bomb.

"I'm going to bed. Started reading a book today and it's really getting good," she said finally. "Think I'll read awhile."

But holding the book in her hands, she only stared at the pages. Was she just a silly kid to get excited about notes? It didn't seem the kind of thing an adult would brag about, and at fifteen Jodi wanted to feel grown up.

The next morning, she heard Brenda's familiar shout and she turned to see her friend running toward her.

Out of breath, Brenda gasped, "I know that M.G. is going to write to you today. I want to be there when you read it. Let's hurry."

"But it's early. He's probably not even here."

"Yes, he is. Hurry."

"But — "

"Come on, Jodi. We're going to find out who this guy is."

"I think the whole thing is silly."

"No, it isn't."

"Why's he being so secretive?"

"He's just having fun."

"I'm not."

"I am. Come on, hurry."

In the dim early-morning light in the hall, the note attached to Jodi's locker leaped out at them.

Reluctantly, yet with a familiar feeling of excitement, Jodi opened the note. It read: *I'm going to phone you tonight at 7:30. Leave your phone number taped to your locker and I'll pick it up later. Signed, locker 145 (M.G.)*

Jodi's pulse throbbed and her face burned beet red.

"Do it! I think this is so romantic!" Brenda, it was obvious, was on a roller-coaster ride of her own. But then again, she had nothing to lose. It wasn't Brenda who would be leaving her phone number for some stranger to pick up. Who knew how often he'd call and bother her if he actually turned out to be a creep?

"I'm not doing it," Jodi said firmly, crumpling the note. "How do I know what he's like or whether or not I want him to phone? If he's so sure he wants to meet me, then why doesn't he just stop me in the halls or somewhere and say who he is?"

"Maybe he's shy," returned Brenda, determined to continue the game. "Maybe he likes a mystery. That's probably it! He's the mysterious type!" She rolled her green eyes in an exaggerated swoon.

"Maybe he's the delirious type," Jodi said flatly. "Who knows what type he is? All I know is it's pretty strange that for days now this guy's been watching me and knows who I am — maybe he's watching us right now — and I'm left in the dark. I don't like it. I'm not going to be led along in this for one second more." She spun the dial of her lock and clicked in her combination while Brenda gawked this way and that to see if perhaps Jodi was right about locker 145 watching them right that very moment.

"I don't think he's watching us," she said finally. "Come on, Jodi. Where's your sense of adventure? What's wrong with leaving your phone number? At least you'll find out who he is."

"Look, Brenda, I'm not going to do it. Drop the subject." She turned away and started down the hall, feeling slightly guilty about talking so harshly to Brenda. But sometimes people just didn't know when to quit. Then, hoping to smooth over things a bit, Jodi stopped and glanced back over her shoulder. "Meet me here after school and we'll go somewhere."

32

"Yeah. Sure. Okay."

"See you then."

"Check ya later."

But Brenda did not move away from the locker. When Jodi was out of sight, she quickly but neatly wrote Jodi's phone number on a small piece of paper torn from the back of her homework notebook and tucked it into the hinge of locker 380.

3

"Your father's coming here on Saturday. With Teddy. He wants to take you to a hockey game and out to supper." Lately, when Jodi's father was the topic of conversation, her mother used what Jodi called her plastic voice, noncommittal and bright, but you could tell she was hurt.

"Will you be going, Mom?" Jodi also pretended to be uninterested in the visit.

"No." She took another mouthful of stew as an excuse not to say anything else.

"Did Dad ask you to go too?"

"Mmhum."

"Then why don't you go? I won't go if you don't go. Who likes hockey anyway?"

"You do, for one." She reached across the table and tangled her fingers in Jodi's. "It's been almost three weeks since you've seen your father and he misses you. Teddy does too."

"I talked to them on the phone." Jodi knew how easily her mother could see through her transparent cool. They were both playing the same game. Why couldn't people just break down and bawl when they felt like it? Every time her mother asked if she was happy being at Nan's, what could

Jodi say? The truth would hurt her mother more. Besides, she was happy about some things. But it just didn't make up for the way it used to be back home before all this mess started.

"It's not the same to just talk on the phone," her mother continued.

"What about you? Don't you miss them?" From the look that passed across her mother's eyes, Jodi knew she'd come alarmingly close to where all the hurt was. "It wouldn't be so bad if you went with us on Saturday."

"When I see your father, Jodi, all I feel is either hurt or angry. It wouldn't be fun, not for me."

There was no getting out of a crying scene now; it was inevitable. Jodi got up from the table and hugged her mother, letting the tears slide. Since they were both having a cry and Nan was out at her church meeting, maybe this was the right time to find out some answers — or at least try.

"Mom," Jodi began tentatively, feeling her own wet tears on her mother's hair, "can't we go back? Are you sure Dad's — " But for the life of her, Jodi couldn't think how to finish that question.

"I'm not sure of anything, Jodi. Your father and I have been married seventeen years. That's a long time. He was bored."

"You're not boring, Mom. And you got a good job as soon as you tried. How could you be boring?"

"Are you unhappy without your dad?"

"No!" As soon as she'd said it, she realized it was a bit too emphatic.

"Maybe this summer you can live with your father for a while. You'd be able to visit your friends back home. Would you like that?"

"I don't know. Sure. Maybe. What would you do? Take Teddy?"

"I thought I might do that. I think I'll go to summer school too."

"School? What for?" To Jodi, summer school meant you'd flunked and you could kiss vacation goodbye as punishment.

"The firm has offered to send me on a three-week investments-counselling course. Be a nice change."

"Will they give you a raise?"

"If I pass."

"You'll pass."

Her mother's smile was a welcome change. Jodi reached for some more milk.

The shrill ring of the phone on the kitchen wall was a rude intrusion. Mrs. Quinn got up to answer it.

"Yes she is," Jodi heard her say. Then she held the receiver toward her daughter, a question mark practically written on her face.

"Hello," said Jodi hesitantly.

The slow male voice that greeted her on the other end of the line was a complete surprise. "Hi, Jodi. It's me. Locker 145."

"Wha — How did you get my number? I — "

"It was on your locker. This afternoon. Where you left it, like I asked."

"Wait a minute. I didn't leave my number, I —" But then it occurred to her, and she pictured

Brenda innocently standing by the locker. Innocently, ha!

"Listen," she continued aloud, her anger spilling out, "I don't know who you are. I did not leave my phone number for some stranger to pick up. I'm not desperate for calls, you know."

"Hold on, Jodi. You sort of started this thing, you know. You wrote back to me on the desk."

"Well, they were just notes. I didn't think about it, I just did it."

"What about that letter? You must've thought about that."

Jodi was beginning to feel cornered. "Well ... I thought you might let me know who you were. But all you do is say you're going to phone me up. Like I'm supposed to be so thrilled when I don't even know you. How did you find out who I am anyway?"

"Easy. I just stayed by your locker and then I followed you to your homeroom and asked a guy in your class."

"Brenda said that was how you'd done it."

"Huh?"

"Oh, never mind. Listen, let's just say this has been a mistake. I don't want you to call me anymore. Goodbye." Jodi started to return the receiver to its hook.

"Hey! Wait, don't hang up!" the boy's muffled voice insisted.

It was hard to be rude with your mother sitting at the kitchen table staring at you the whole time.

"Yes? What do you want?" She tried to show as

much impatience in her voice as she could without being too nasty.

"What's bugging you? I'm just phoning, for cryin' out loud. What's the matter with that?"

His voice, she had to admit, sounded nice. She pictured him as quite tall — maybe her head would come just about to his chin. And he'd have black hair and deep, deep brown eyes. And he'd wear corduroy rugby pants with a striped T-shirt. He'd be about seventeen. But, she couldn't help wondering, if he had so much going for him, why did he hide behind notes and not just walk right up to her and meet her?

"How would you feel if someone called you and knew your name and you didn't have one single clue at all about that person?"

"My name's Mike. I'm in grade eleven."

"And?"

"And — " he seemed to search for something to say. "And nothing else."

"See what I mean? Look, if you want a mystery, why don't you read Agatha Christie? I'm not playing this game."

She hung up. She knew that before she'd get a chance to phone Brenda and give her a blast she'd have to answer some questions her mother was sure to have ready.

"What was that all about?" You had to hand it to mothers — they sure knew how to sum up all their questions in one neat package.

When she had finished explaining the entire situation, including the part about going along with Brenda because life had been pretty boring lately, her mother was starting to act like Brenda.

"He might be a very nice, but very shy, boy."

"Well, I'm not interested in shy boys."

"Don't be too hasty. About Brenda, too. Maybe just sleep on it and when you get to school tomorrow you can talk to her about how you feel. I agree she betrayed a trust, but she did an innocent-enough thing. If the boy calls again, maybe he'll tell you more about himself."

"I think it's time for me to do some homework," Jodi said, allowing the sarcasm to creep into her voice so her mother could take the hint that she was being just a bit too gushy about this boy who might turn out to be a psycho-phoner. As for Brenda, she'd soon be suffering from an earache for the trick she'd pulled.

* * *

Jodi stomped the snow from her sneakers, trying to thaw out the numbness of her toes so that she wouldn't get pneumonia as Nan had threatened when she'd left this morning without wearing her boots. All she wanted to do right now was find Brenda and murder her with a few well-chosen words.

But something was up. A group of students were clustered outside the principal's office and the vice-principal was trying to clear them away.

"Who do you think did it, sir?" one student asked, but no reply was forthcoming.

Did what? Now's the time she needed Brenda,

because she probably knew everything in the greatest detail. The word-blast could wait.

In front of the cafeteria, she met an even larger crowd trying to peer into the room, which was obviously now off-limits. Straining on her tiptoes, she caught a glimpse of what all the trouble was about: the cafeteria had been vandalized. Tables and chairs were upset and most of them looked broken. Something was all over the walls — probably food. Gross!

"Hey, Jodi! What do you think?" Brenda elbowed her way through the crowd, her eyes wide with disbelief and excitement.

"I dunno. It's stupid. What's there to think?"

"Whoever did this stunt is in for it! The police were here already and you can bet they'll be back. Everyone says they think they know who did it but can't prove it."

"When did it happen?"

"Last night. They broke in through the industrial arts lab, but pretty well left that alone. Then they went into the computer lab and stole three computers and a lot of software, and then they got some of the student council money out of the vice-principal's office. I guess they did this to the cafeteria for kicks or something. They didn't steal any food."

"It's stupid," Jodi repeated. How did people figure they could get away with something like this? Any moron who watched television knew about fingerprinting and putting clues together.

"Something like this happened two years ago.

Only we didn't have a computer lab then and they didn't wreck the cafeteria. They wrecked the art teacher's storage room."

Jodi remembered the phone call from the night before and she shifted her books in order to glare at Brenda.

"By the way, *friend*," she said, oozing sarcasm, "since when do you have the right to go throwing my phone number around like it was confetti?"

Brenda's face fell. "Ah — ah — I mean — "

"I know exactly what you mean. You're just in on this for your own kicks no matter who gets embarrassed or who gets mad. I'm mad!"

Talking about it made Jodi relive her frustration of the night before. The guy on the phone had believed she was the one who had left the number for him to find. It was all Brenda's fault!

"Gee, I'm sorry, Jodi." Her eyes were pleading for forgiveness, and you couldn't help but feel that, really, Brenda didn't mean any harm, like Jodi's mother had said. Her pudgy face looked defeated, and it seemed like the awkward smile she was trying to make just wouldn't force itself out.

"You should have thought about it."

"I did. And I thought it wouldn't hurt. What'd he say? What's he like? What's his name?"

"His name is ... never mind. I don't care what his name is and I'm not telling you because this whole scheme has gone too far already."

"Is he a real creep? Is that why you're mad?"

"Of course that's not why I'm mad! I didn't talk to him long enough to find out if he's a creep. Mom

41

was right there, for heaven's sake. What could I say?"

"Did she get mad at you because a guy you don't know called?"

"No. In fact — and this disgusts me — she said he's probably shy and I should give him a chance. You two should get together and form a lonely-hearts club or something."

"Your mother's right! You should give — "

"Stop right there! I told him not to phone anymore and that's that. Let's drop the subject. I'm going to class."

She turned from Brenda and left the crowd still gathered to gawk into the cafeteria.

"Hey!" Brenda called insistently. "Meet you at lunch hour out by the flagpole! Jodi, hey!" Jodi looked blankly at her friend.

"Well, we can't use the cafeteria, that's for sure. So we may as well go to Tony's Place for pizza." Brenda's words were an offering of truce. How could you stay mad for long?

"Yeah. Okay," she replied unenthusiastically, hoping if she remained cool it might teach Brenda a lesson.

"Good. Catch ya later!"

* * *

It was more than the prospect of a large pizza thick with extra cheese and mushrooms and pepperoni that accounted for the galloping pace at which Brenda rushed to the flagpole that noon-hour. Her face was blotched pink and her green eyes glistened with the thrill of having big news to tell.

"Did you see the police at the office this morning?" she asked.

"No," Jodi replied, still trying to maintain an aloofness that would keep alive the guilt in Brenda for giving away her phone number.

"They've got their man, apparently. It's Mike Gidden. He was involved in the break-in the last time, two years ago. Everybody figured it was him. They took him to the office for questioning. Wonder what they'll do. He's seventeen. Is that the legal age to be sent to jail?"

"Eighteen is, isn't it? Who do they think was with him?" Brenda sure had a way of making you get interested in the gossip no matter how boring you started out thinking it was.

"He doesn't hang around with anyone at this school. Probably it was guys he met at reform school. That's where he was before he came here last fall. You'd think a guy would learn."

"What he learned was how to be better at breaking into schools. The police probably won't be able to prove he did it. Questioning doesn't mean much. Let's go get the pizza."

The two girls started across the street, pausing to let a few cars go by before they made the dash to the centre boulevard. Then more cars passed, and suddenly Brenda grabbed Jodi's arm. "Hey! That's him! That's Mike Gidden!"

A lake-blue 76 Ford passed by with dents on top of its dents. The hood was painted with flames as though it were a champion race car rather than the heap it actually was. For some bizarre reason, it gleamed with polish. The guy behind the wheel, in the quick glance that Jodi got of him, looked ordinary enough. He was probably tall, or at least his chin wasn't touching the steering wheel. And he had brown hair, not really curly, not really straight. His black leather jacket was the kind that everyone was wearing these days.

"He doesn't look like a criminal, does he?" said Brenda, staring after the car.

"What does a criminal look like?" Jodi couldn't hide the impatience in her voice. People sometimes thought the dumbest things about what types should look like.

"I don't know. Dirty, I guess. Greasy or something."

"Maybe his lawyer will use that in court. 'Your Honour,' " Jodi mocked, " 'does this young man look like a criminal to you? Where is the dirt? Where is the grease? I tell you, Your Honour, this boy lives a clean life!' "

"Okay. Okay. You've made your point. But I bet he's not a criminal through and through. I just have this feeling."

"You're too emotional. Remind yourself not to be a judge."

"I don't think I'd look good in the wig anyway," Brenda said with a laugh.

They arrived at Tony's Place to find it crowded with hungry students who had the same solution to the cafeteria problem. Luckily, four people were leaving a booth and Brenda claimed it.

"Maybe someone'll have to sit here with us

44

and they'll be wild and wonderful," she said, looking around the room. She certainly was optimistic.

Sliding a slice of gooey pizza from the tray to her plate, disengaging the strings of hot cheese with her fingers, Jodi said, "My father's coming here on Saturday."

"Hey! Neat!" returned Brenda. Maybe it was just the mouthful of pizza that made her gleam with interest, Jodi thought.

"He's bringing Teddy. We're going to a hockey game. Mom's not going."

"Neat! The hockey game, I mean. I love the hot peanuts at the rink."

"Wanna go with us?" As soon as she had asked the question, Jodi realized that it was really a very good idea. Brenda would be fun, and she'd be an excuse not to get too gushy about things with her father. Maybe she could distract puddy-brain Teddy, too.

"You mean it?"

"Sure. Why not?"

"Well ... I just thought that you were mad. About the note on your locker." She looked at Jodi, her eyes pleading. Jodi could imagine her practising this look in front of the mirror to get it just right.

"I won't be by Saturday."

"Great! I'll go!" To celebrate, she chomped energetically into another slice of pizza.

* * *

"My god, Jodi! Come over here by this door. Quick. I don't want anyone to hear this!"

It was the end of the second period of the afternoon and Jodi was just going into her French class when Brenda came racing down the hallway and grabbed her arm in a desperate clasp. Her eyes fairly bulged with horror.

"You're gonna kill me for sure. I don't know why I'm telling you this except if I don't you'll kill me anyway."

"What is it? Brenda, tell me!"

"Locker 145. I know who it is. I just saw him getting his books out."

Unwillingly, Jodi's heart started beating like a frantic drum. The palms of her hands went damp and cold. Whatever it was Brenda was about to say seemed momentous.

"Who is he? What's wrong?"

"What's wrong is that I gave him your number. Oh, Jodi, say you won't be mad at me again. I didn't know, honest!"

Now it was Jodi's turn to grab Brenda's arm insistently.

"Tell me, Brenda!"

"It's Mike Gidden. That's what M.G. stands for, Mike Gidden."

Like a flashback in a psycho film, Jodi heard the slow male voice on the other end of the telephone line, "My name's Mike." She let go of Brenda's arm, stunned.

"What'll we do if he phones you again? He's an ex-con! Your mother'll kill you."

Brenda's art for exaggeration was creating a scene. But she was right. This guy had been in reform school and now the police were trying to nail him for vandalizing the school and for robbery! This could mean big trouble, unless, somehow, Jodi could avoid ever being anywhere near him.

"No big deal," she said finally, trying to sound casual. "I don't even know the guy. And I did tell him never to phone again. So what's to worry about?"

Brenda breathed a sigh of relief that visibly sagged her shoulders. "You're right. What am I getting carried away about? He'll be in the slammer soon anyway."

The shrill metal blast of the bell just over their heads startled them both into nervous, desperate laughter. Time to go to class.

"Hey, stay away from locker 145," Brenda joked. "Catch you later."

"Yeah, after school. Okay?"

"Oh. Forgot. After school I've got a dentist appointment. I'll call you."

"Okay. Bye." Jodi entered her French class just as Mr. Dupont was closing the door.

4

She was not half a block from school that afternoon when she heard a car slowing down beside her and a loud blast of the horn. A quick glance, then she immediately turned, stared straight ahead and quickened her pace almost to a trot. It was that beat-up old Ford with Mike Gidden behind the wheel! He was following her home! Now she'd really be in trouble!

Mike Gidden drove his car just ahead of her, parked at the curb, then awkwardly slithered his body out through the driver's window.

"Hey! Hey, Jodi!" he yelled to her over the roof. "Can I talk to you? I'm the guy who called you. Locker 145."

She desperately wanted to get out of this mess, and right now! If she just ignored him, he'd get discouraged or think she was a snob or something and go away. That was plan number one.

Plan number one failed.

"Hey! Don't be so shy. I'd like to drive you home. What do ya say?"

Shy! This guy wouldn't see a flat *no* if it were painted on his glasses — if he wore glasses, that is. Why was she wasting time thinking of glasses?

Panic was setting in, and plan number two wouldn't come to her at all.

Mike Gidden was back in his car now, following closely beside her and tapping annoyingly on the horn, as if she hadn't heard him in the first place. If anyone saw this guy following her, she'd die!

Blat! Blat! came the rude, insistent sound of the horn.

A hot rush of anger welled up inside her now. The nerve of the guy! Well, there was nothing that said she had to put up with this!

She halted and swung around defiantly. "Leave me alone, creep! Or else I'll walk up to one of these houses and call the police!"

That should do it, she thought as she stomped away.

But instead of driving away, defeated, as she had figured he would, Mike Gidden parked his blue heap again. This time he got out, striding persistently behind her.

"Hey! Wait a minute. What're you talking about police for? What do ya think? I'm some kind of criminal or something? I only asked to drive you home, for cryin' out loud!"

"You *are* some kind of criminal!" The truth, Jodi realized, was easy to blurt out when panic was mixed with downright disgust. Who did he think he was, anyway?

"What're you talking about? I'm no criminal."

"Look — " Jodi stopped and faced Mike Gidden squarely, wanting to end this once and for all.

He was taller than she'd imagined — basketball player's legs. And his eyes were blue, not brown. The red sweater he wore under his black leather jacket looked like a home-knitted one. She remembered Brenda's words, "He doesn't look like a criminal, does he?" and she had to admit, standing this close to him, that he didn't. But even so, there was no way this guy was going to follow her all the way home to Nan's doorstep.

"I know you were in on that break-in at school. The police had you in the office today for questioning. Everyone knows it. It's no secret. So leave me alone. I don't want you around me!"

The look in Mike Gidden's eyes was not what she had expected. After all, insulting a guy who'd stolen from the school and then wrecked the cafeteria might not be the safest thing to do if you liked the shape of your face. But his eyes did not flash with revenge; not even anger. Something else. That something else, Jodi noticed, reminded her of Brenda. It was vaguely like the look Brenda had in her eyes when Jodi was angry about the phone number business. His eyes were ice-blue, but they weren't cold at all. Just now, they were gentle and sorry. That look made her want to apologize, but she decided she'd better not, if she wanted to get rid of him. Only three more blocks to Nan's.

"Questioning doesn't mean guilt," he said finally.

"But they'll prove it. They always do." She started walking, but he wasn't giving up that easily. "Don't follow me!" she blurted, frightened at her confusion now. Why did the guy who wrote those notes have to turn out to be a guy in trouble?

"No law against walking on the sidewalk just because you're here. Besides, I'm not finished talking."

Plan number one was back in action. She quickened her steps and acted like he wasn't there at all. But it was hard.

"Today I said to myself, after the police had me in the office, that things were really lost this time. No one listens to what I have to say. Everyone just thinks about my past and they never want to find out what I'm like now."

Jodi remained silent. This guy wasn't going to soft-talk her with his self-pity. But he kept walking beside her as if he were an invited guest.

"You don't know me." His voice had dropped lower and Jodi found it hard to hear what he was saying. "I figured you might talk to me — because of the notes. I thought it'd be a bit different, that maybe the gossip wouldn't have gotten to you." His words sounded more like questions. He was asking her to talk to him and not believe what other people were saying about him.

Only a block and a half to Nan's and still he wasn't showing any signs of giving up. A new plan was needed, Jodi realized, but she could only think of blasting him with anger.

"Look, I don't know anything about you! I don't know if the things people are saying are true or not! I just don't want you to follow me!" Her voice was edged with frustration. "Now, see that blue house over there? Well, I'm going to walk right up to that door and ask them if I can phone the police to make you stop harrassing me."

"Go ahead."

The simplicity of his reply stunned her. Why wasn't he afraid? Maybe a guy who was suspected of robbery and vandalism thought of harrassment as peanuts.

"Please go away," Jodi pleaded, feeling desperate about how close she was to Nan's with Mike Gidden still tagging along.

"I just want you to give me a chance," he replied, his voice soft and slow.

His eyes had that look again. Funny how a criminal could seem like an ordinary nice guy, Jodi thought.

He still continued to walk along beside her and she was becoming a bit breathless in her rush to get away from him. Nan's house was only a few houses away now. Jodi felt scared. She really didn't want Nan to meet him and it would be a disaster if he found out where she lived. There was nothing to do but keep on walking until, somehow, she got rid of him.

"Look," he was saying now, "when I found out that you were locker 380 and that you were new in school I figured this was my chance to meet someone with no strings attached from the dark ages."

"Dark ages? What are you talking about?" Jodi couldn't look at him.

"As if you don't know."

"I don't."

52

"I got in trouble a couple of years ago. A break-in thing that these guys talked me into." He stopped to pick up a small rock, then began to toss it into the air and catch it, over and over again. "I'd done other things before, but they were only little deals. So I got a couple of months at a reform school for it." The pebble spun up into the air and back down again. "You'd think I had leprosy or something, the way people act." He threw the rock at nothing in particular. "Like you act."

"Well, you should've thought of all that before you got into trouble."

"I was just a kid, for cryin' out loud!"

"Well, what about yesterday!"

"I didn't do that!"

"Prove it, then!" she blurted.

"Okay, I will!"

"Yoo-hoo! Yoo-hoo!" Nan's familiar voice brought Jodi's attention to the fact that she and Mike were now standing almost directly in front of her house. And there was Nan in the doorway, wearing a flowered apron across her roundness, grinning with delight at seeing Jodi and a "friend," and waving a warm greeting for the two of them to come into the house.

"Who's that?" Mike asked.

"Nan."

Again, from the doorway, came Nan's cheery voice, "Come into the kitchen! I just made cupcakes! Bring your friend in, Jodi!"

The two of them glanced quickly at each other, but the same thing was not on both their minds. A sly glint leapt into Mike's eyes.

"He's not — " Jodi began.

"Hold on," Mike interrupted in a whisper. "Let me prove something to you." And before Jodi could close her mouth, which was hanging open in disbelief, he had walked to the front doorway and was shaking hands with Nan like he was delivering a cheque for a hundred thousand dollars. The nerve of the guy!

"Come on, Jodi!" he yelled back.

Nan was practically beaming now. You could tell by the look in her eyes that she had taken to him, and when he carefully removed his shoes and helped Jodi off with her jacket, Nan was sold for sure. It was clearly best just to go along with them and avoid a scene. How could she explain that this "nice boy" was a criminal? It was already 4:30, so he couldn't stay long before it would be time to make supper and then ... . Oh no, thought Jodi, what if Nan invited him to stay? She decided that if that happened, she'd blurt out the whole detailed situation, no matter what kind of scene it caused.

"Are you in Jodi's class?" Nan asked.

"No. I'm in grade eleven."

Jodi remained cool and silent. But Nan didn't notice at all, so intent was she on getting acquainted with this smooth-talker. He told her about his mother and how she had taught him to bake peanut butter cookies when he was eight years old, and how he used to get to the cookie-dough stage and then eat it all because he couldn't wait until they were baked. What a laugh the two of them got out of that tall tale. All the while, Jodi tried to show her aloofness by forcing her face into an amoeba-like blankness. No one noticed.

"Oh goodness," said Nan finally, "look at the time. I must get supper started."

Every muscle in Jodi's back tightened, waiting for Nan's invitation to Mike Gidden to stay.

"I must be going," he said, standing and picking up his glass and napkin and placing them on the counter beside the sink. Such a calculated move. This guy really knew grandmothers.

"Well, it was very nice of Jodi to bring you along to meet me," Nan said. "You'll come again, I'm sure. Jodi doesn't have a lot of friends at the school because she's so new there. Except for Brenda. She's a lovely girl and she sure appreciates my cooking too."

If the Boston Strangler came to the house and ate lots of Nan's cooking appreciatively, she'd welcome him back anytime. It would be a disaster if anyone on a diet came for a visit.

"See your friend to the door, Jodi."

Reluctantly, she went to the front porch while he put on his shoes and his leather jacket. Now that they were alone he winked knowingly, signalling that he'd won.

"She likes me," he said, proud of the fact. "See. She gave me a chance and got to know me a little."

"Well, I'm not going to," Jodi replied, opening the door widely, letting the chill of the early darkness into the porch. "Goodbye."

"You sure are stubborn." He stepped toward the threshold but then stopped and turned to Jodi, his face dangerously close to hers.

She took one giant step backwards.

"I'm not about to kiss you, if that's what you're thinking."

"I didn't think that at all," she said, realizing that her instant candy-apple blush was making her look foolish. "It's just cold here by the door, that's all."

"Relax. You're too uptight. You'll soon find out that I'm not a criminal. I wasn't acting in there with your grandmother. It's easy to be like that when people don't try to bury me under all that reform school garbage."

There was no sense talking anymore, Jodi knew. It only complicated things. He really did seem like a nice guy. But he also might be a very successful con man. "Goodbye, Mike," she said flatly.

For a moment, he didn't say anything, then just shrugged his shoulders. "See you at school." With a bit of a smile, he turned away.

Jodi closed the door in relief. Hoping to go straight to her room to avoid any of Nan's questions, she quietly started up the stairs. No luck.

"Dear?" Nan's voice stopped her like an invisible doorway. "Come into the kitchen and tell me all about your friend."

"There's nothing to tell," she said loudly from her position on the third stair.

"Well, how did you meet him?" Nan wouldn't give up.

"I dunno. He's just at school."

"Why are you shouting from those stairs? Come in with me for a minute."

"I've got to phone Brenda now, okay Nan? It's about some homework she needs because she left school early today to go to the dentist."

"Okay. Okay. I get the message. I shouldn't be prying." A small giggle was barely perceptible in her words.

Jodi continued up to her room, two stairs at a time.

When she hung up the phone, after a lengthy conversation with Brenda, she didn't feel any better. Brenda kept repeating she was sorry. But really, what could she do anyway?

Jodi lay across her bed and stared out into the growing darkness. On her window, she had painted a small scene of a grinning frog on a purple lily pad with a rainbow-like banner overhead. She gazed at it and wondered if things would soon start to brighten up.

Life was getting more and more confusing. First she gets a note from a guy and it seems like it could be fun to find out who he is. Then she finds out and it means big trouble. Then she can't seem to avoid him. Her mother had enough problems of her own without having to worry about a reform-school graduate bugging her daughter.

Jodi tried not to think of Mike Gidden, but his face kept sneaking into her mind. As he'd walked along beside her, his long legs made a stride she couldn't outpace. Actually, it felt kind of nice to have him pay so much attention to her. She'd always liked tall guys, but so far the only boy who'd shown any real interest in her was that moron Scott. He'd been in her class since grade one and was just as boring now as he had been then. What was she doing thinking about Scott, who was back home, and about Mike Gidden, who had to be avoided? She was confused!

Rolling over, she stared up at the ceiling. Back home, she had two mobiles made out of driftwood and pine cones hanging over her bed, so that when she lay on her back and wanted to think about things she'd watch the slight back and forth motion of all the small pieces. It seemed to help her concentrate. Remembering those mobiles now, she grew even more depressed. Nan's place was nice, but it wasn't home.

That phone call she had overheard between her parents certainly wasn't helping much either. It would have been better if she'd just hung up and not listened in at all. Things weren't ever going to return to normal.

* * *

The next day, Friday, Jodi managed to make it through the entire school day without meeting Mike Gidden once. In fact, she avoided any conversation about him. Brenda was discretely silent on the matter. It was clear to both of them that what had started as an innocent intrigue had mushroomed into a mess.

With her father and Teddy arriving the next

day, Jodi had other things to worry about besides Mike. At breakfast that morning, she had sensed her mother's tension too. But when she'd brought up the subject of the coming visit, her mother had given her polyester smile, in her usual attempt to cover her true feelings. No sense trying to talk about it. That might just mean another crying session, and what good would that do? The visit wasn't going to be easy, especially for her mother.

"What's he like?" Brenda interrupted her thoughts as they were walking home after school. Nan had suggested that Brenda sleep over with Jodi for the weekend and Brenda's backpack was bulging.

"Who?"

"Your father."

"He's — I don't know. What do you mean? Do you want to know what he looks like?" It was hard to describe your own father, especially when you used to like him and now you really weren't sure anymore.

"That'll do for starters. Is he tall? Fat? Bald?"

Jodi laughed. Her father had so much blond curly hair that when Afros became stylish he was relieved because finally he could stop trying to manage all those tangles. He used to stand in front of the mirror sometimes after he'd washed his hair and say he'd rather be bald. Once, he put on a bathing cap and looked like some kind of circus clown with bunches of curls sticking out under the bright red cap. One thing about him — he had a good sense of humour.

"He's not bald. And he's about as tall as to here," she said, extending her hand far up over her head.

"And?"

"And he's just a plain father." It didn't do any good talking about him. She was confused about this visit and discussing what he looked like brought back a lot of memories. How could he be the guy in that bathing cap and still have a girlfriend and break up the whole family?

"You're afraid to see him, aren't you," said Brenda softly.

Maybe it was the way Brenda just kept walking and didn't give Jodi a prying stare that made her do it. Maybe it was that stupid red bathing cap. Maybe anything. But Jodi started to cry. And once she started, she just kept on going, with no real sounds, just huge tears swimming out of her eyes and down her face.

Brenda didn't say anything, and they walked along together thinking their own thoughts. Finally, Jodi took out a tissue and blew her nose as a signal to Brenda that she was going to stop crying. It was Brenda's friendship that let her feel free to cry, and it was a relief not to have to answer any questions about it. Why was it that people usually wanted to interrupt a cry by making you explain it to them?

"It was dumb to cry," Jodi said without conviction.

"I'd cry if my father didn't live with us," said Brenda simply.

"Did your father ever have a girlfriend?"

"I don't think so." She looked out to the traffic in a preoccupied way and then turned back to Jodi. "I don't think Mom'd move out if he did. Not that I'm saying your mother was wrong in what she did, but I think Mom'd give him another chance and Dad wouldn't be stupid enough to blow it."

"Maybe that already happened and you didn't even know."

"Maybe."

"Would you get mad at him?"

"Not if I didn't know."

"I mean if you did know he had a girlfriend and your mother was giving him a second chance. Would you still get mad?"

"I dunno. It doesn't seem like something Dad would do."

"Ha!" returned Jodi with a smirk of contempt. "That's what I would've said. That's what Mom would've said too."

"Well, maybe I'd be mad. Or shocked. It's hard to say right out of the blue. But I was just thinking that if he had this girlfriend, and he was sorry and admitted that it was a pretty stupid thing to do considering he had Mom and me and Jeff at home to think about, and if he said that was the first and last time he was ever going to have a girlfriend, then I think I'd only be angry for awhile."

"How could you trust him?"

"I think you could tell if he meant it."

"Maybe he's an expert liar."

"After all the time he's been around, I think we could tell."

"Maybe."

Jodi had to admit that those very same thoughts had crossed her mind in the past month and a half. But her mother sure seemed to have her mind made up. It would have made things easier if they had all talked about it, but it seemed like her parents both thought that she and Teddy were too young or shouldn't know the gory details. Maybe Teddy was too young — he'd always be — but she wasn't. Yet Jodi found it impossible to ask questions that obviously hurt her mother.

"What're you going to say to him when you first see him?"

That was the exact question that Jodi had been racking her brain about for the past few hours. The last time she'd seen her father he was trying to help her pack her suitcase and she wouldn't even look sideways at him. Everything had happened too fast.

Her mother had simply relied on the words "trial separation" for an explanation. She had talked on about how she and Jodi's father still loved her and Teddy, but they felt that their love for each other was not the same. They needed time apart to do some thinking.

The real story came out later, when Jodi's father came home from work and went up to her room where she was packing. She did not actually believe that she was going anywhere — she felt more like a machine packing clothes on an assembly line. She hadn't even phoned her friends to tell them anything.

He came into the room still wearing his coat. He sure looked guilty about something.

"I want to tell you about it, Jodi," he said quietly, like he was in church or something.

"What's there to tell?" She knew that if she tried to say much more, she'd burst into tears.

"Your mother told you she wanted a trial separation, but she didn't tell you why."

"She said something about you weren't sure if you still loved each other."

"It's not quite that simple. Your mother has been hurt — a lot — by me."

Then he told her briefly that he'd had a girlfriend. Jodi had listened, stunned. How could he do such a thing? He was supposed to be theirs — hers, Teddy's, her mother's! How could he be somebody else's?

She hadn't given him a chance to talk. She threw a yelling and crying tantrum and then gave him the silent treatment until she and her mother had left for Nan's. Since then, when she'd talked to him on the phone, she only answered his questions and kept her words to a minimum. On top of all that was that phone call she wasn't supposed to hear. Now she would be seeing him. What could she say?

Brenda's presence in the house helped Friday night go more easily for everyone. Nan even stayed up with them to watch the late movie, but she didn't last long. Jodi's mother seemed in good spirits, although Jodi suspected she was practising cheerfulness for the next day.

Several times during the night, Jodi awoke and stared into the darkness. It wasn't that Brenda was there taking up half the bed or that the

63

fluorescent-pink stuffed elephant she had brought with her was taking another quarter that disturbed her sleep. She was thinking about her father. The still darkness with its mysterious midnight sounds reminded her of waiting for Santa Claus with Teddy, and it even occurred to her that there were things about her brother that she missed. Not many, but some.

Luckily, the morning didn't provide much time for further consideration. They were barely finished breakfast when the familiar beep of her father's car horn sounded in the driveway. Teddy bounded into the house and started to cry right away. That, of course, made their mother cry, and then Nan cried too. With superhuman control, Jodi managed to hold back the flood; but her eyes turned a watery red, especially when her father held her next to his favourite wool sweater, which her mother had knit for him a hundred years ago and which was filled with the musky warm smell of him. He was nervous too, she knew, because his hands quivered slightly along the length of her blonde hair.

"I've missed my little girl," he said against her ear.

I've missed you too, she thought, but she could not let the words out for him to hear.

Teddy ran to hug her, and she hugged him back tightly. They hadn't even hugged the day she'd left for Nan's, so it was obvious that the trial separation was getting to him.

"Dad, Teddy, this is my friend Brenda Cummings," Jodi said in an attempt to lend an air of formality to an otherwise gushy situation.

"Let's go inside and I'll make up some pancakes for you two. You must be starved," said Nan who, as usual, saw food as the solution to everything from boredom to trial separation.

"Hurray!" yelled Teddy. He was back to normal.

Jodi and Brenda got the suitcases out of the car and walked behind her mother and father into the house. Had her parents even said anything to each other yet? Jodi didn't think they had, and yet there they were walking into Nan's like they were visiting for Easter and nothing was wrong at all. Her mother, Jodi realized, sure knew how to cover up emotions.

When Teddy had stuffed himself with enough pancakes to feed an entire starving family, he left the house to find his friend Jamey who lived down the street. They usually played together whenever Teddy visited Nan.

"So what's new with my little girl?" her father asked with a smile. The wistful look in his eyes said he wished it hadn't been so long since he'd seen her.

"Nothing." And really, when you got right down to it, what was there to tell her father?

"Oh?" said Nan playfully. "I wouldn't say there was nothing. What about the new boyfriend you had here this week after school?"

Leave it to Nan to drop a bomb. Brenda's face just about fell into the pile of leftover maple syrup in front of her.

"Now, Nan," said her mother, coming to the rescue, "Jodi hasn't said he's her boyfriend. And, in case you haven't noticed, she hasn't mentioned him since the visit either."

"What's his name?" asked her father.

"Mike." Then, too late, she realized that even mentioning his name was like admitting he was her boyfriend. But she knew her father was only searching for conversation, just as she was. The whole thing was enough to break your heart. There they were with nothing to say except a lot of useless stuff about Mike Gidden, who was practically a criminal and whom no one even knew.

"He's not Jodi's boyfriend," said Brenda. What a friend, Jodi thought, breathing a barely audible sigh of relief. "He's just a guy who hardly knows her. It's no big deal."

"Did you meet him?" her father asked, looking in her mother's direction, almost like he needed an excuse to look at her.

"No. He was gone when I got home, but Nan met him and thinks he's quite a guy."

"I took to him right away," said Nan, squirting detergent into the sink and turning on the hot water.

"Like Brenda said, it's no big deal." Jodi wanted to change the topic but what else was there to say? How's your love life Dad? Who does the dishes every night, you or Teddy?

"Looks like a good game tonight, Dad," she said finally.

"While you talk hockey," said her mother getting up from the table, "I'm going to go over to the office for an hour. I've got to put a few finishing touches on a proposal for a meeting on Monday. I'll be back about noon. Teddy wants to get an Earthquake over at the ice cream shop. Do you girls want to go?"

Brenda didn't need to be convinced.

"Do you always work on Saturdays?" Her father's question was loaded with all kinds of other thoughts, Jodi knew, but exactly what those other thoughts were, she couldn't say. Maybe it was her imagination, but everything so far that he had said directly to her mother seemed to be that way. And her mother was doing a topnotch job of coating her emotions with veneer. She wondered what they would say to each other when no one else was there.

* * *

The hockey game that evening was nothing special. Teddy had dragged them to the door of the dressing room where they managed to get three autographs at the end of the second period. But their team didn't win.

"The peanuts were good," Brenda managed optimistically while they waited in the parking-lot lineup at the end of the game.

"Shall we go for pizza?" asked Jodi's father with exaggerated enthusiasm.

Everyone cheered and then burst out laughing because they were acting so dramatic. Teddy was screaming in her ear and Jodi realized happily how quickly things seemed to get back to normal.

"What about Mom?" Teddy said.

"We'll get her first," said Mr. Quinn. "Where's the best pizza place?"

"Tony's Place, near our school," Brenda replied. "That's the best one, isn't it, Jodi?"

"Sure, I guess so," she answered slowly. She remembered that her mother had said she felt hurt or angry when she was with Jodi's father. So far that day she had managed to stay a safe distance from him. Maybe she should just say her mother didn't like pizza anymore — no, everyone knew that was a lie. Or maybe she could say she was usually really tired on weekends because of so much work at her new job. But, instead of making excuses, Jodi kept silent. Besides, it would be nice to be all together again for a night out, just like back home. She would help her mother avoid any awkward moments — just keep things light and easy.

At home, Mrs. Quinn hesitated a moment, then smiled brightly and agreed to come. It was obvious, as the five of them trooped in to Tony's Place, that not many families came here on Saturday night. The rows of booths were crammed with teenagers stuffing themselves with pizza and talking like everyone was deaf. Quite a few looked up at them as if they were undercover cops ready to bust the joint.

A booth not far from the door had only two

people in it who seemed just about ready to leave, so they waited next to the cash register. Brenda's head swivelled as she tried to see just who was there. Teddy stared at the people eating pizza in a nearby booth, until Mrs. Quinn put an end to his gawking by whispering something motherly in his ear. It worked for three and a half minutes.

Suddenly Brenda shot an elbow into Jodi's side. She tried to whisper, but what came out sounded like a loudspeaker announcement made by a giant with laryngitis, *"He's here! Mike Gidden!"*

"Where?" said Teddy loudly, gawking in every direction.

"None of your business," hissed Jodi, wishing they could all just cancel the plan to have pizza here.

But Mike had also spotted them and he was getting up and walking right over to them as if he were a long-lost friend. It was a tie between Brenda and Jodi for who wanted more to crawl away and hide behind something.

5

"Your booth is ready now," said the cashier.

"Thank you. Let's settle in," said Mr. Quinn, innocently unaware of the catastrophe that Jodi and Brenda felt looming. Quickly, the girls slid into the booth.

"Hello, Jodi," Mike said, grinning as though she'd be happy to have him standing there in front of her parents and her little brother. He sure knew how to put a girl on the spot, just like he did that day in front of Nan's walkway. Well this time he —

Before she could finish her thought, he began introducing himself to everyone, shaking hands with Jodi's father in a grasp that, no doubt, would be impressive. He knew all the right moves, you had to give him that.

"I heard your name mentioned around the house just this afternoon," Mr. Quinn said with a sly wink.

If there weren't so many legs under the table to sort out, Jodi would have given him a kick. All she needed was to have Mike Gidden think she had been talking about him.

"It was Nan who mentioned your name," she said quickly, hoping the tone of her voice expressed cool disinterest.

70

"Would you like to join us?" Mrs. Quinn offered.

Jodi could hardly believe her ears! Her own mother, for heaven's sake, was setting her up for disaster! She shot a desperate glance around the nearby booths to see if anyone from school were watching this.

Brenda managed to find Jodi's foot under the table and pressed so hard that Jodi barely managed to squeeze her foot out from under the painful message.

Teddy slid along the booth to make room for Mike, squashing Jodi. She stared across the table at Brenda and her mother and father, looking for some sympathy.

"I didn't see you at school yesterday," he said to Jodi, leaning past Teddy to look at her.

"I was there," she replied with icy politeness.

Luckily, the topic momentarily switched to pizza as the waiter came to take their order. At least Mike had the decency to refuse to eat with them, saying that he'd already had a pizza with his buddies.

"Those guys you're with are probably wondering where you are," Jodi hinted as the waiter left their booth.

"Naw, not those guys." He had no intention of budging.

"Do you know how many pizzas this place makes in a week?" Teddy asked Mike.

Where did he get such questions? Jodi wondered. But she was thankful the worm brain had come up with something to say.

"Gee, I dunno. Maybe a thousand. Why?"

"Do you know, Dad?"

"I don't actually know, but if it's a guess you're looking for, I'd say Mike's pretty close."

"Mom?"

She looked all around as if she were counting the week's pizza right then and there. "I'd say they make, on the average, a lucky thirteen hundred."

"Aw, you saw the sign," Teddy whimpered, pointing to a pizza-shaped sign over the door.

"You caught me there," said Mike. "Never noticed that sign in all the times I've been here. You're detective material, I'd say."

Teddy beamed at the compliment. Jodi noticed that Mike did have a way of relaxing a situation — although he was the one who had tensed things up in the first place. She could tell that Brenda was warming to his friendliness too, because she'd forgotten about grinding Jodi's foot into the carpet.

The waiter arrived with two very large, very hot, very mouth-watering pizzas and everyone started sitting up straighter and moving things out of the way to make room.

Abruptly Mike got up, almost bumping the waiter in his hurry. "Ah," he fumbled for an explanation, "I've got to go. I just remembered something. Ah — it was nice meeting you people."

Something was bugging him. He was afraid, there was no mistaking that.

"Well, maybe we'll see you again," said Mrs. Quinn.

Jodi looked around quickly, but nothing seemed to have changed. No one had come into the restaurant either.

"Now, I wonder what that was all about," said Jodi's mother.

"Who cares?" replied Teddy. "Let's eat this pizza!"

"It was just strange, that's all," she continued.

"Maybe his friends are leaving," Jodi suggested.

"No," said Mr. Quinn, looking over his shoulder. "But it's probably nothing to worry about." He patted his wife's hand the way he always did when she got worried.

Jodi was surprised that she felt sorry Mike had left. It seemed he'd disappeared into thin air. He hadn't gone out of the restaurant because he would've had to go right past them.

The two platters lay bare in front of them, when Teddy practically screamed, "Cops! Something's goin' on out there!"

Jodi, facing the window, immediately saw what Teddy was shouting about. Two police cars, their red lights flashing eerily in dizzying circles, were right out front.

Everyone was straining to get a closer look and some people crowded through the door to investigate.

"We'd better sit tight until this is over," suggested Jodi's mother.

"Geez, it's a road block or something!" yelled Teddy like he was being paid to keep everyone informed.

73

"Can't you shut him up?" cried Jodi. It was a double embarrassment to have that kid with them.

"Shhh," said Mrs. Quinn. "Let's not have our own scene in here. Teddy, sit down."

An ear-splitting wail from a siren pierced the air as one of the cars swerved out into the street, made a squealing U-turn, and raced after a car that had just sped around the corner. The other police car immediately followed.

"What was that all about?" Mr. Quinn asked the cashier as he paid their bill.

"Looked to me like some problem with a car parked across the street. A beat-up old blue Ford. I've seen it around before."

Fear, like an electric shock, coursed through Jodi's body. That was Mike Gidden's car! The police were after him! She wasn't condemning him now, she was worried for him. It was odd, but she wanted to find a way to help him out of — out of what? She didn't even know why the police were after him. It was too frightening. Why should she even think about him? At least her parents had no idea that he owned that car, and so far Brenda hadn't put two and two together to connect Mike with it either. She'd have to talk to her later, when they were alone in her bedroom.

In the past week, there'd been enough problems to stock her brain for a lifetime, Jodi thought. How much more could happen to complicate her life?

"I've got to talk to you," Jodi muttered to Brenda as they were piling into her father's car.

That was enough to make Brenda a jumping bean of anxiety, since she knew it had something to do with Mike Gidden.

As soon as they were in the house, the girls headed for Jodi's room. Finally, rid of Teddy's nosy persistence, and curled up on the bed in their flannel nighties, they were ready to talk.

"So tell me!" Brenda's patience was as firm as a banana split on a hot July beach.

"The police that were outside Tony's Place?"

"Yeah?"

"They were after Mike Gidden. They had to be."

"But why? He was just in there eating like the rest of us."

"Think for a minute. What kind of car was parked across the street? Where did the police go in such a hurry?"

"After that car."

"And?"

"And what?"

"What kind of car was it?" Jodi was losing patience trying to guide Brenda through these deductions.

"I dunno. It was gone when we came out."

"But the cashier said — "

"Hold it! The cashier said it was a blue car ... a wreck like the one Mike ... Hey! It had to be Mike Gidden's car!"

"Sherlock Holmes would be proud of you."

"Lucky your parents didn't know."

"You can say that again."

"Lucky your parents — "

They both started to laugh, more from panic than from humour. Just then, they heard Jodi's mother coming up the stairs. She was sleeping in Nan's room so that Teddy and Mr. Quinn could share the downstairs den. She knocked on Jodi's bedroom door.

"Come in," Jodi said.

"Just wanted to say goodnight."

"I thought you and Dad'd be up talking for a while," Jodi said.

"Well, we did talk a little," she replied with a sigh that quickly brightened to a synthetic smile. "There's so much to say and really nothing to say at all."

"Yeah," said Brenda thoughtfully.

"Do you understand that, Brenda?" asked Mrs. Quinn. Jodi could tell that her mother wanted to talk.

"Sure. It's like at the end of a big argument, when you've repeated your side so many times and still no one understands, so what's the use?"

"That's a lot for a girl your age to realize."

"You don't know my brother. We're constantly fighting. And I just lose any interest or hope of convincing him that he's a total loser and I'm right."

They all laughed. Jodi was glad that Brenda was there to lighten the gloom.

As soon as Mrs. Quinn left, Brenda started asking questions about Mike. "What do you think happened? Where would he go? Do you think — "

"Hold it! How could I know all those things? I'm as much in the dark as you, you know."

"I wouldn't mind being in the dark with Mike," Brenda said coyly. She picked up her pink toy elephant and placed her cheek against its soft fur, playacting. "You're so strong and handsome, Mike. And your face is so soft."

"Stop that, Brenda. You're crazy!"

"How about you? Are you crazy about Mike Gidden?"

"What? Now, you've really flipped. Did you donate your brain for experiments or something?"

"Oh come on. He's cute. He's trying to be nice. Maybe he's not so bad after all."

"How can you possibly sit there and say that? He's in trouble at school, he's ... oh, what's the use. You know why I can't like him. You're being dumb, that's all."

"All I'm saying is that he's cute and he seems nice. If it was me he was after, I might give it a chance and see what happens."

"What would happen is that you'd be visiting him in jail!"

"Maybe not."

"Or you'd be in jail with him. Brenda and Mike. Bonnie and Clyde."

"Maybe he's telling the truth. Maybe those things he did *are* from the dark caves — "

"Dark ages. He said they were in the dark ages."

"Dark ages. Well, maybe that's true. You've got to admit, he's cute."

Jodi pictured his happy grin and his blue eyes as he sat at their table in Tony's Place. He must have a hundred sweaters, because every time she saw him, he had on a different one. Tonight he'd worn a beige Irish-knit, one that made him look terrific. His easy confidence and his friendliness with her family were bonuses too.

"No sense wasting time on a guy like him," Jodi said. "You could never trust him."

"I'd give him a chance."

"Go ahead."

"It's not me he likes."

"He doesn't like me either."

"What are you? Blind? Anyone can see he likes you. Look at how he was hanging around at Tony's."

"Maybe he has other girlfriends too, or maybe he's desperate because no girls are dumb enough to go out with an ex-con."

"I think he just likes you. You'll see."

"I'm not going to see anything. I'm going to sleep now. Goodnight."

"Sweet dreams."

"Cut it out."

"What? All I said was — "

"We both know what you meant. Now, goodnight, for the final time."

Soon the whole household was asleep, including Brenda's fluorescent-pink elephant.

From a dreamless sleep, Jodi began to stir, although not fully awake. She turned over and her hand struck the wall. When she shifted her nightie became a constricting noose around her legs. A sound had roused her from the depths of sleep — the unrhythmic clattering of small stones against the house just outside her window. Instantly she sat up. Again, several stones bounced against the house.

"Brenda! Wake up," whispered Jodi hoarsely, jabbing her sleeping friend until she blinked open her eyes.

"Whaa?"

"Listen."

"Whaa?"

"Just listen!"

This time some pebbles fell lightly against the window pane. There was no mistaking that someone outside was trying to get their attention.

They crept to the window and looked down through the darkness at a barely discernible form in the yard below. The form was waving a frantic greeting.

Slowly Jodi raised her window, while Brenda and her pink elephant crouched behind.

"Who's there?" whispered Jodi into the chilled air.

"It's me, Mike."

"Oh my god!" breathed Brenda, without even trying to see out the window.

Jodi had no words to reply. A stunned silence followed.

"I need to talk to someone ... to you. Can you come down?"

"Are you crazy? Dad'll hear me. I don't want to

talk to you. You're in trouble. We know because we saw the cops chasing you in your car from Tony's Place. Go away!"

"Wait!" he almost hollered.

If her parents heard him and found out the kind of guy he was, she'd sure be in trouble. This called for drastic measures. "Okay. Brenda and I'll be right down. Wait behind the garage."

"Are you crazy?" Brenda managed to say after Jodi had closed the window again. "If we go out there, they're sure to find out. And then they'll know that I gave him your phone number and they'll never let you speak to me again."

"What do you expect me to do? Let him scream at me from the backyard? We have no choice. Get dressed."

"Are you sure I should go too?"

The look Jodi shot her spoke louder than any explanation. Quickly the two girls dressed and then stood silently, listening through the bedroom door to be sure no one else had heard the backyard intruder.

"Let's go," whispered Jodi.

None of the stairs creaked. Jodi's father was snoring was so loudly that a squeak would have been inaudible anyway. Finally, they were out the front door and walking quickly down the driveway to the garage.

In his jeans and black leather jacket, Mike Gidden was barely visible in the darkness.

"Who do you think you are, throwing rocks at my window and — Hey! How did you know it was my window? What if it'd been Nan's?"

"I doubt if your nan would've painted a rainbow and a frog on the glass of her window," he said matter-of-factly.

"Oh yeah, I forgot. Good thinking."

"What's going on?" Brenda said quickly, unable to wait a moment longer. "Are the cops still after you?"

"They never were."

"Ha!" scoffed Jodi. "You can't try to tell us that. We were there. That blue Ford was yours."

"You're right, the car was mine. And they did chase it. But I wasn't driving."

"Hold on. Start back somewhere where I can follow," said Brenda, shivering in the cold night air.

"While I was sitting in the booth with you guys, I saw some guys that I know — not what you'd call friends — using a coat hanger on my car, which was parked right across the street. I knew what they were up to. That's why I had to split."

"I still don't get it. Where did you go? Where's your car now?" asked Jodi.

"I went out the side exit by the washrooms. And I waited in the alley. These guys don't fool around, so I figured I'd just see what they were going to do with my car."

"But they had no keys. How did they—"

"They don't need keys. Just a wire here and a wire there and you've got it."

"So where's your car?"

"I don't know. I saw the cops arrive. I dunno why they came so fast unless someone reported seeing someone breaking into a parked car. Anyway, then they burned rubber after my car. When things quieted down, I just walked back towards my place, wondering what to do."

"Report them," suggested Brenda.

"Not so simple. Those guys are trying to do something to frame me. I'm not sure what."

Jodi had to admit it was exciting standing out in the inky darkness of Nan's yard hearing all about this, but there was a limit. So far he hadn't said anything about why they were standing around like it was summer-camp storytime.

"I was almost home when I saw them parked in another car about half a block away from the house, just far enough so they could still see my place. Not smart enough to realize I could see them, too. They must've ditched my car and were planning a similar ditching for me. Lucky I saw them before they saw me."

"But why are they after you?" asked Brenda.

"Because they think I told the police on them about the break-in at school last week."

"Weren't you with them?" Jodi asked.

"No, I wasn't." He stopped and looked hard at her, trying to penetrate the darkness with his eyes to convince her he was innocent. But his face was just a shadow cast in her direction.

"Well, who are they? Do they go to our school?" Brenda was hooked and wanted to find out as much as she could.

"No. They don't live around here. They're in this gang. It's a long story."

"Tell us," demanded Brenda.

He looked at Jodi to check her reaction. "Do you want to know?"

Although her better judgement urged her to go back into the house before everyone in the neighbourhood saw them out there in the middle of the night, she, too, was curious to find out more about Mike.

"We don't have time for a long story," she replied. "Can you just give us the basics?"

"When I was fourteen I was hanging around the shopping centre a lot. Nothing else to do. These guys used to be there, too, and at first they'd shove me around — "

"What do you mean? They'd beat you up?" asked Jodi. No one she knew had ever been beaten up.

"Not anything much. Mostly just shoving, or they'd follow me home. But then I guess they decided I was okay or something because they said I could be in their gang."

"What kind of gang?" asked Brenda.

"Just a gang. A bunch of guys."

"But if they shoved you around, then why —" began Jodi, but Mike interrupted her.

"You have to keep in mind that I was fourteen. The gang sounded big-time — what did I know about consequences? All I could picture was walking around with these guys and looking tough. I didn't know they did things."

"Did what things?" Brenda asked.

"Break-ins."

"Stealing?"

"Yeah. First just little things. We got caught stealing a radio from a house, but all that happened to us was we got fines. That is, our parents got fines — we were put on probation. Big deal, I thought."

"But it was still stealing," said Jodi.

Mike just kept on talking. "So then they planned the school thing and I figured it'd be just a break-in like the rest and if we got caught — well, nothing much would happen. It was supposed to be my final initiation."

"Initiation?" asked Jodi.

"Stop interrupting," Brenda said with a hint of exasperation in her voice. "Then what?" she asked, turning back to Mike.

"If I did this school thing, then I'd be equal in the gang. Stupid, eh? But I didn't know they were going to do all that stuff to wreck the school."

"So you got caught," Jodi said.

"Yeah. And this time the judge figured we needed more than a warning. He gave us a reform school sentence."

"My parents'd disown me," said Brenda.

"Dad almost did. But Mom seemed to know it was just a stupid kid move. She was really unhappy, but I think it was her faith in me that made me want to change."

"But that doesn't prove you didn't do it again," said Jodi, unwilling to let his calm, gentle voice soothe her into total trust.

"I know it doesn't prove it. That's what those guys are counting on."

"Huh?" their two voices came in unison.

"They were at reform school. And by the looks of things, they want to go back. They bugged me there, too."

"Why?"

At reform school I played it straight and they knew I was trying to change. I was so scared when they sent me there. The first night some guys tried to get me to join this club."

"What club?"

"It's called Do It Right. The guys in it want to keep doing the same things that put them in reform school, only they don't want to get caught."

"But why pick on you now? You're out. They're out. What's the big problem?" asked Brenda.

"It goes back to last year. The club got broken up after I got there and they think it was me who squealed to the authorities. Ever since then they've wanted to even with me."

"So?"

"So that's why the school was broken into. A frame-up. And I knew it. I didn't tell the cops, but those guys think I did."

"Ahh," came the bright light of understanding from both Brenda and Jodi.

"Meanwhile, we're shivering out here. What for? If Dad wakes up, or Nan, we're in for it."

"I need you two to help me set them up so the cops'll finally believe me."

"Why should we do that?"

"Well, in the first place, because you believe me."

"Wait a minute. No one's said anything about believing you," said Jodi indignantly.

"You must. Otherwise, why would you be standing out here listening to this whole story? You'd wake up your dad and get the cops after me or something."

"I believe him, Jodi," said Brenda.

"Me too," said a shrill voice from beside Mr. Quinn's car. Teddy appeared with the legs of his pyjamas like flannel ghosts beneath his winter parka.

"What are you doing here?" Jodi felt more cornered than ever.

"You guys woke me up. Hi, Mike," he said as if the two of them were meeting on a ball field on a Sunday afternoon.

"I'm going to be in for it now," said Jodi hopelessly. "This mouth will tell all."

"I will not."

"You always do."

"How do you know? You're not at home now. You don't know anything."

"Wait a minute, you two," interrupted Mike. "The fact is, he does know. What's the big deal? We might be able to use him."

"He could get hurt," said Jodi.

"No one has to get hurt. I have a plan and just need a little help, that's all."

"In the middle of the night?"

"No. Tomorrow. I'll go home the back way tonight and those guys won't see me. Meet me tomorrow morning really early, say at seven-thirty, over by the swimming pool entrance of the Sportsplex. If I don't have witnesses, the cops'll never believe me."

"Right on," said Teddy, holding out his hand for Mike to slap it.

"Right on," returned Mike with the appropriate slap.

"I don't believe this. I know it'll mean big trouble. I can feel it in my bones."

"Don't worry," said Brenda. "We'll be there."

"Good. See ya." Mike started out of the yard.

"Yeah. Bye."

"Bye," said Jodi weakly.

"And, you guys?" he said, stopping to face the three of them in the chilly night. "Thanks for believing me."

"We're nuts," said Jodi after they had sneaked back into the house, up the stairs to the tune of Mr. Quinn's cavernous snores and, without a creak, into the bedroom. She hardly slept a wink.

6

Standing out of the wind beside the swimming pool entrance to the Sportsplex, the three of them were beginning to get impatient. It was very cold, despite the bright sunshine of the early Sunday morning.

"Where do ya think he is?" asked Teddy.

"He'll be here," answered Brenda, hugging herself to keep warm.

"Don't count on it," said Jodi. "I think we've all been taken in by a con artist." She felt cheated. Just when she was starting to believe that Mike might really be trying to get his act together and make amends for his reputation, he backed out on them.

"Just give him a chance," Brenda said.

At nine o'clock, when the janitor opened the doors, they had to make quick excuses for why they were waiting there with no swimming gear. It was time to give up and leave. The janitor watched them suspiciously until they were on the sidewalk.

"Well, I guess we got used for joke material," said Jodi.

"Let's wait until we find out his excuse. Maybe something happened." Brenda could work for the U.N., she was so diplomatic.

"Maybe they got to him and killed him!" gasped Teddy, who watched too much television.

"Keep quiet, vacuum brain," said Jodi impatiently. "And don't breathe a word of this to Mom and Dad when we get back to Nan's either."

They walked along, deep in their own thoughts.

"Dad told me something," Teddy said flatly.

No one responded.

"About him and Mom."

"What about them?" Jodi said with little interest.

"He says he doesn't want the trial separation and that you and Mom'll be home soon."

"What makes him so sure? Mom doesn't think that."

"I dunno. He just says."

"Only words."

"But that's what he says."

"Look, Teddy. A trial separation is not a vacation, you know. It's serious. And now Mom has a good job, and she's not sure she can trust Dad anymore. Do you have a clue at all about why they're separated?"

"It's because of a girl. Dad told me."

Jodi could not hide her surprise. "He told you all about that?"

"Yeah."

"Oh."

"She called the house. I talked to her."

"Who?"

"That girl."

Jodi stopped in her tracks, and Brenda turned

to Teddy too. "Wait a minute. Are you telling me that you actually talked to Dad's girlfriend?"

"She's not his girlfriend. I heard him telling her on the phone that it was a big mistake."

"I'll say," muttered Jodi.

"Let me get this straight," said Brenda. "You talked to some woman on the phone and then you heard your father tell her that there was a mistake?"

"Yeah."

"How do you know what mistake they were talking about?"

"I asked Dad when he got off the phone."

"Since when did you qualify for man-to-man talks?" asked Jodi sarcastically.

"Hold on, Jodi. Give the kid a chance. Do you want to know what's going on or not?"

"Look, you two, I heard Dad and Mom on the phone this week and things weren't exactly peaches and cream. They screamed their heads off. If Dad thinks the trial separation is over, then he's dreaming."

"But what if Teddy's right? What if there isn't, and won't be, a girlfriend to get in the way? Would your mother go back then?"

"I dunno. She says she can't trust him."

"I can," said Teddy.

"Easy for you to say. What'd he do to you anyway?"

"He sent you and Mom away."

Jodi stared at Teddy, speechless. Teddy looked her square in the eye. He had a skinny face and enough freckles to camouflage an army tank, but right now his eyes were grown-up. Jodi had worried about herself in a new school and about her mother having to get a job and sleep in the downstairs den, but she hadn't given much thought to Teddy. The little squirt had feelings too. And here he was trying to give her some hope about the trial separation.

"What else did Dad say?"

Like a river held dammed for months and finally released, Teddy's word came pouring out, "Well, he told me he knew he had made a mistake even before Mom found out. He said he wasn't thinking right. But Mom went into hysterics and wouldn't give him a second chance. Then you and Mom went to Nan's. Dad says she shouldn't have done it so fast."

"That's just his side, Teddy."

"Yeah. But that's what he told me. His side is one half at least."

"Well, Mom's side is more complicated because she's the one who's confused. She doesn't know where things stand, and when Dad told her on the phone that there wasn't any girlfriend, she didn't believe him, or at least she couldn't trust him long enough to believe him. That's what she said. That's the other half."

"What'll we do?" The cold was making Teddy's nose run a little, but Jodi decided not to mention it to him. Right now, he was trying to be grown-up. It felt good talking to him straight and not bugging him.

"Hey! I just had an idea. Maybe it'll work and maybe it won't."

"Worth a try," offered Brenda.

"Shoot," said Teddy.

"Maybe you're the one to talk to Mom, Teddy, and tell her the stuff you just told me. Whenever Dad talks to her, she just gets uptight. She might listen harder to you."

"When'll I do it? We're going home today."

"Maybe not today. Maybe phone her up when Dad's not around."

"What'll I say?" Suddenly, his importance shook his confidence.

"You'll know what to say." Jodi pulled his hood down over his eyes, teasingly. "Just tell her what you told me."

"About how Dad said it was a mistake?"

"Yeah."

"About Mom moving away too fast?"

"Yeah."

"Pretend like you're a lawyer presenting your father's case, in a way," said Brenda.

"Yeah, do that." But already Jodi was doubtful. She wanted to believe Teddy herself, but what if her mother was right? What if they went back home and it happened all over again? After all, Teddy was only a little kid and maybe he didn't quite understand what her father had meant when they'd had their man-to-man talk.

"Hope I don't blow this chance," Teddy said.

"I guess you miss your mom a lot," said Brenda, putting her arm across Teddy's shoulder.

He didn't answer, but he stepped ahead a bit

92

so that Brenda's hand slipped away from him. Now that the responsibility of patching up the separation was his, it wasn't the time to treat him like a little kid. As he walked ahead of them, his hands deep in his jacket pockets, Brenda looked toward Jodi and winked. Watching her little brother concentrating on the family problem made Jodi's heart ache. He was such a little guy. Actually, in the middle of a trial separation, everyone seemed so little, so easy to hurt.

After lunch, Brenda, Teddy, Mr. Quinn and Nan played three games of Scrabble while Mrs. Quinn and Jodi each read a book. Half the time Jodi only stared at the open pages, her mind searching for solutions to the questions about Mike Gidden and her parents' trial separation. There was so much to think about.

Obviously, her parents had agreed not to cause any conflict during this visit by avoiding the topic of the separation, at least in front of her and Teddy. But she couldn't figure out when they'd had any time alone to talk.

A funny thing had happened after they got back from the Sportsplex that morning. Not comical-funny, but strange. Mr. Quinn was in the kitchen making breakfast and Teddy started to help him. Nan tied aprons on the two of them and began setting the table.

"Stay out of their way," she joked. "The cooks are busy."

"Since when do you know how to fry bacon?" Jodi sneered at Teddy over his shoulder. "Cute apron, sweetie," she added.

93

"Knock it off," Teddy replied simply. He was changing, she realized. At home she could have sent him into a tantrum with a line like that.

"Where's Mom?"

"We're letting her sleep in. She needs the rest," replied her father as he scrambled the eggs.

That was the peculiar thing — to hear her father talking about doing her mom a favour, like they were all still home, or like it was Mother's Day. He said it so naturally, he didn't even notice it was strange.

By mid-afternoon, it was time for Mr. Quinn and Teddy to begin their three-hour drive home. Everyone helped with suitcases. Nan wrapped muffins and prepared a thermos of coffee and some milk for the trip. Finally, the car was packed and everyone was standing awkwardly in the driveway shivering in the cold and getting ready to say goodbye.

Teddy managed to whisper, "I'm phoning Mom on Tuesday night to tell her the stuff, okay?"

"Sure," Jodi replied. "Don't get dramatic. Just tell her things straight, like you told me."

"I will. I will. You just wait and see."

Jodi noticed that her mother was saying something to her father. He had taken hold of her fingers, but she pulled them away. Then he gave Nan a big hug and started towards Jodi. She let him hug her and ruffle her hair, and then she kissed his cheek, wondering if Teddy really did know what was going on and if his phone call would do anything for the situation.

"You watch out for yourself, little girl," her father was saying. "And don't give that boyfriend of yours a rough time."

"He isn't my boyfriend, Dad."

"I know. Just teasing." His arm was held firmly across her shoulders as he smiled. "But what do you suppose that quick exit was all about last night?"

"How am I supposed to know?"

"Maybe he heard his mother calling," said Brenda, rescuing Jodi from further explanation.

"Well, you two better start on your way or you'll be doing all your driving at night. Teddy, you must have some homework to do when you get back," said Nan.

"Homework? Me?"

"Drive carefully, David. Give Mom a kiss, Teddy. There. Now be good for Dad. I'll phone you this week."

"Maybe I'll phone you, Mom."

"If you like, dear."

"Yeah, I'd like." Then he winked at Jodi and she could hardly hold back a groan. Why did she ever trust this theatrical peanut brain with any information? He'd probably blow the whole thing.

"Let me know if you hear from Mike," whispered Teddy, giving Jodi an exaggerated hug around her waistline.

She returned his hug with a painful embrace that made him yelp.

"See ya, Brenda. Bye, Nan. Good luck with the face lift, Jodi."

"I'm gonna kill you, Squirt."

"There, there. He's just fooling."

"Bye."

"Take care driving."

"Bye."

"Bye."

* * *

Jodi was exhausted. The sleepless nights of the weekend had caught up, so after Brenda went home, she lay on her bed in the quiet of the almost-empty house and fell asleep.

She awoke confused; the charcoal grey of the winter early evening made her think it was morning. Sleepily, she scuffed out of her bedroom to the top of the stairs where the tantalizing supper smells assured her it was not morning after all. When the phone rang at eight o'clock, she answered it in a flash, hoping for some news from Mike. But it was Brenda, wondering the same thing that she was wondering: what was going on with Mike?

* * *

At school the next morning, Jodi wrote a note to Mike, using her math book as a cover-up. She planned to leave it on his locker on her way to second-period French class. That morning she and Brenda had looked everywhere and had waited by his locker until the last possible minute, but he had not shown up.

The note read: *We waited yesterday. Where were you? Meet us by the flagpole at noon-hour.*

Attached to the green-grey locker, the small note looked like a white flag of truce. At noon, and when they checked again at 3:30, the note was still there, untouched.

"Maybe we should phone his house?" suggested Brenda.

"What would we say?"

"Just what you said on the note. That is, if he's there."

"What are you getting at?"

"Well, maybe he won't be home. Maybe something's happened."

"Like what?"

"I dunno. Like those guys might've done something. He did say they were trying to get even and that they were really tough. Who knows?"

"You're exaggerating. This isn't the Mafia, you know."

But Brenda was silent. She probably thought it *was* the Mafia.

"Let's wait until tomorrow and see what happens."

"I think tomorrow'll be too late. If you don't call, I will."

"Go ahead!" Jodi exploded. Brenda's persistence was getting on her nerves and she showed it. "You started this whole thing anyway, when you made that stupid move of giving him my phone number. Some friend!"

Brenda just turned away and began to walk down the hall to her own locker. She didn't try to say she was sorry this time, or plead with Jodi to

97

understand. Watching Brenda's back, her shoulders rounded in the gaudy turquoise and purple sweatshirt she was wearing, Jodi felt overwhelmed with guilt. Why did she insist on treating Brenda so cruelly? It was obvious that she was trying to be a true friend and what did she get in return? Jodi's quick temper.

"Hey! Brenda. Wait." She rushed to catch up, threw her arms around her friend and gave her a big hug, not caring that people passing by might think they were crazy. "I'm sorry. My mouth needs to be sent to reform school."

Brenda laughed and things felt healed instantly.

"You're right," Jodi added, "tomorrow might be too late. I'll phone him tonight. Then I'll call you to let you know what I find out."

* * *

The phone rang four times before someone picked up the receiver. Mike answered, his normally easy, calm voice tinged with tension.

"Hi, Mike. It's me. Jodi."

"Hey! All right!" His voice brightened with surprise and enthusiasm. "You called! I can hardly believe it."

"Well, Brenda and I were wondering about yesterday. And we left a note on your locker today but you didn't get it. So we thought if we called, you'd explain what happened."

"Yeah. Well, sorry about yesterday. I was detained, you might say. And then I thought I

98

might get you in trouble if I called, so I didn't. Today I was at the police station — "

"The police station!"

"Yeah. It's a long story. But I'll tell you the whole thing if you'll listen."

Aware that knowing the whole story could mean trouble for her, Jodi still replied quickly, "I'll listen."

"When I got home on Saturday, it was about three-thirty in the morning. I knew there was trouble because practically all the lights in the house were on. I went in and the cops were there. Everyone looked at me like I was some kind of ghost. Mom was crying. Then Dad started yelling right away, but one cop told him to calm down so they could question me."

"What for?"

"I'm getting to that. My car had been found down at Black Rock Beach on fire at about one o'clock — a guy saw the flames down on the beach at the bottom of the cliff and called the cops."

"On fire! What — "

"Let me finish, Jodi. I'll explain," Mike said, with only a hint of impatience. "The cops traced the car to me and woke Mom and Dad up at about two. Then, of course, they couldn't find me and Mom screamed like I was dead or lying in a ditch somewhere near the car or something like that. But they combed the whole area and couldn't find anything.

"Who did it? What happened?"

"I know exactly what happened," Mike answered confidently, "only no one believes me. They think I did it myself to cover something up or to get insurance."

All this was starting to sound like a story Teddy might make up for a grade five writing assignment.

"You don't believe me either, do you?"

His question surprised her, but she did have some doubts. All she had was his word. And it must have been about two-thirty when he threw pebbles at her window. There'd been enough time for him to ditch his car and hitch-hike back to town. Why should she believe him?

"Well, if you didn't do it, who did?"

"The guys from reform school. They did it to get even with me, but now I'm in even more trouble because they think I'll tell the whole story, which I would if I thought anyone would believe me.

"You should've been at the police station today. Mom kept repeating she'd keep an eye out for me if they'd just put me on probation, and Dad said he'd teach me a lesson or two if I tried anything foolish again. I just sat there like my tongue was on vacation. No sense wasting words, I figured."

"So what did they do?"

"Nothing. What could they do? They have no evidence. But now I'm on probation under the care of my parents. What a joke. If they really cared, they'd believe me."

"How can you expect them to believe you when you did things before? If someone else did that to your car, the police would find out, wouldn't they? You're lucky they let you off."

"Look, Jodi, thanks for calling. But I don't feel in the mood for a lecture. I've got other things to think about now."

Before she could get another word in, he hung up. Sitting there alone in the kitchen, holding the receiver in her hand, she felt a hot rush of guilt. Had she been too quick to judge him? No doubt Brenda would say that she had. But what was she supposed to do — believe every word the guy said like he was some kind of saint? She hardly knew him.

It wasn't easy, though, to dismiss the whole thing, because in some ways she felt like she really did know him — maybe even better than Scott. That was the strange thing. When Mike had answered the phone, the sound of his voice on the other end of the line had set her heart on a double-time rhythm. Was she actually falling for this guy? Probably her heart was just as mixed up as her brain was these days.

She phoned Brenda and, predictably, Brenda sided with Mike.

"Remember in the driveway Saturday night? He looked back at us after we said we'd meet him the next day and he said, 'Thanks for believing me.' Well, I still believe him and I'm going to give him a break."

"What kind of break?" Jodi asked evenly. It would be nice to think Brenda was right.

"You say he's going back to school tomorrow."

"That's what he said. That if he missed school, he'd be in real trouble."

"Well, I'm going to talk to him. Maybe he'll eat

101

lunch with me in the cafeteria. I don't care about the gossip, I'm doing it anyway."

"What if you get in trouble?"

"How can you get in trouble for eating lunch with someone? You make such a big deal of being seen with him, Jodi. Why don't you have lunch with him too?"

Jodi's hesitation expressed more confusion than her arguments.

"You don't have to," continued Brenda, "I won't mind. See you in the morning. Maybe you'll change your mind."

7

She was dreaming about Saturday night. Mike had come to throw pebbles at her window, the gentle scattering of stones invading her sleep. Brenda was beside her, curled up with her large stuffed elephant.

Suddenly, she was wide awake. There were pebbles striking the side of the house near her window and it was not Saturday — it was Monday night! Mike had to be out there again!

She flashed the bedroom light twice to make him stop, and with her housecoat pulled tightly around her, she raised the window, letting in the cold winter air.

"It's me ... Mike."

"I know it's you. What's going on?" she whispered hoarsely.

"I need your help."

"Look, Mike, I know you're in trouble, but how can I possibly help? You're supposed to be on probation. I bet your parents don't know you're out right now, do they?"

"No, they don't. But I had to talk to you."

"Why not phone? It's the normal way."

"You would've hung up. Or given me another

lecture. Listen, all I want to know is if you'll help me. Until I find someone who'll believe what happened, I'm always going to be treated like some kind of criminal. It's driving me nuts."

"You're not the only person in the world who's got problems, you know," said Jodi, exasperated.

"Look, Jodi, I know things are tough with you right now because of your parents. You told me about that in your letter. But the separation isn't your fault. No one's blaming you for anything. No one's watching you every minute to see if you turn into Dracula or something. You've got people who trust you. You're not alone. I am!"

His voice was strained with emotion and had risen too far above a whisper. Someone was sure to hear them.

"Please don't shout. I'll get in trouble."

"Trouble! You don't know what trouble is. You've got it soft with everyone trying to make you happy because they feel guilty they made you move and everything. How do you think I feel? Everyone I know is blaming *me* for messing up *their* lives. No one thinks for a minute how I feel being labelled a criminal for some stupid moves I pulled when I was fourteen. I'm seventeen now. I haven't done one thing to get in trouble since that school break-in, and what've I got to show for it? I may as well be a criminal, for cryin' out loud."

"Mike, stop talking so loudly," pleaded Jodi from her window.

For a moment he didn't reply, then he spoke gently, "All I want is for you to give me a chance to prove all I said. If you helped, maybe I could do it. Maybe I'd get them to trust me finally."

"I can't help, Mike. I'd get in trouble."

In the darkness, he stood silently below her window, close to the house in the shadows. She couldn't tell if he was looking up at her or not. Then, without another word, he left, his footsteps slow and hollow on the driveway.

When she couldn't see him anymore, Jodi finally closed her bedroom window and, with a shiver, crawled back into bed. The warmth from the blankets gradually grew around her and she was glad she was safely in her own bed instead of walking alone down the empty midnight streets.

Where would he go? Probably just back home. That would be the smartest thing, and Mike wasn't dumb.

Restlessly, she tossed in her bed, fluffing up her pillow and trying to settle down to sleep. She kept seeing Mike and remembered his closeness that day when he'd stood at Nan's door to leave. He had embarrassed her when he'd asked if she thought he was going to kiss her. What would she have done if he really had kissed her? Passed out, probably.

She thought about how nice it would be if he were just an ordinary guy at school. They could go out on a date and things would be so simple — no break-ins at school and burning cars, no throwing stones at her window in the middle of the night, no cops chasing him. Why couldn't life be like a Nancy Drew mystery where there were only about ten or twelve pieces and they all fit easily into place? Right now, her life felt like a thousand-piece jigsaw with the key pieces missing.

Before she fell asleep, she decided that it would be best not to have lunch at school with Mike and Brenda the next day. What with living at Nan's and with the separation, her life was already complicated enough.

* * *

But neither she nor Brenda had lunch with Mike the next day. He wasn't at school. By the end of the day, the news was out that Mike Gidden had run away from home. They even had a description of him on the radio, and in Nan's kitchen, just before supper that night, Jodi heard it herself: *Anyone knowing the whereabouts of seventeen-year-old Michael Gidden of ten eighty-four Burbank Drive is asked to contact city police immediately. He was last seen Monday night wearing a black leather jacket, a grey sweater, bluejeans and brown leather shoes. He is one hundred eighty centimetres tall, with brown hair and blue eyes.*

Nan said it was a shame that such a nice boy would do a thing like that. She just couldn't understand it at all. After Nan was settled in front of the TV and Jodi and her mother were alone in the kitchen, Mrs. Quinn said that she felt Mike's disappearance must have something to do with the incident in front of the pizza place on Saturday night.

"Do you know anything about this, Jodi?"

106

"No, Mom. I hardly know the guy." Jodi tried to keep her voice even, neutral, but she knew that her mother could detect the tension. Trying to hide feelings, especially guilt, was a sure way to make them stand out like a flag waving in the breeze.

"If something's bothering you, I want you to tell me, Jodi. I'll help you, if I can."

"There's nothing, Mom. Really. I haven't seen him since we were in the booth at Tony's. Really."

"Mike may be in trouble. I'm sure his parents are frantic with worry. It would be better for him if he were home, don't you think?"

"Sure I do, but that doesn't change the fact that I don't know where he is. I don't, Mom. I'm telling the truth." Jodi's voice rose higher and higher.

"Okay, dear, I know you are. Of course you are. It's such a shame that he's run away. That never solves anything."

Exasperation and tension were shaking Jodi's control. In the next instant, she was blurting out all her unspoken frustration. "Why do you say that? You ran away from Dad, Mom. If running away doesn't solve anything, then why did you do it?"

Tears ran down her cheeks as she saw the hurt her angry words were causing. But Mrs. Quinn held out her arms and Jodi collapsed into them, letting all the pent-up anguish come tumbling out. She cried and cried, as her mother held her in the middle of Nan's kitchen.

"Mom, I'm sorry about what I said. Really. It

was stupid." She blew her nose into the hanky her mother held for her.

"It's okay." She smoothed Jodi's silky blonde hair away from her wet face. "I love you."

Later, in the solitude of her bedroom, Jodi buried her face into her pillow and cried again. She was crying for so many things: for her father and Teddy because they were far away; for her mother who had been hurt so much; for Nan because she thought that Mike Gidden was a "nice boy"; and for herself because she was afraid to give Mike the chance that Brenda was willing to. And now he had run away. She could have told about the late-night visits and about what he'd said to her when she had phoned him Monday night. Maybe that was the biggest reason for the tears now staining her pillow — she was withholding information that might help Mike, but she was too afraid to tell.

She heard the phone ring and quickly sat up in bed, her heart pounding. But it wasn't Mike.

"Muriel," Nan called out. "It's Teddy calling long distance. Did you hear me, Muriel?"

Jodi remembered that this was Tuesday. While her mind was occupied with Mike, Teddy was back home concentrating on his little plot to help patch up the separation. Until now, Jodi had forgotten all about his call. Lying on her bed, she felt too mixed-up and worn-out to even get out of bed to hear what her mother might say after the call. She could hear the easy drone of her mother's voice as she talked to Teddy. She hoped he was doing a good job.

* * *

The next day, Wednesday, Mr. Clarrey was dictating notes in the middle of science class when the vice-principal's voice interrupted over the P.A. system: "Excuse me, Mr. Clarrey, but could you send Jodi Quinn to the office, please?"

"Certainly. Jodi, you may be excused."

Her legs turned to wet spaghetti and her stomach churned. By the time she closed the classroom door behind her, she felt her face burning red with embarrassment and fear. She knew she was being called to the office for something concerning Mike.

Her heart pounded even more when she entered the vice-principal's office. Two policemen, in their stiff uniforms and shiny badges, stood waiting for her.

"Please sit down, Jodi. These gentlemen have come to speak to you about Michael Gidden," said the vice-principal, Mr. MacKenzie. "I'm sure you'll give them every assistance."

"Miss Quinn, we called your home today because we found this on Michael's bedroom bulletin board."

The officer held up the small note with her phone number on it that Brenda had left for locker 145 to find.

"Did you write this note?"

"No, sir. My friend Brenda did. She — we were — we didn't know who he was at the time and it all started when we wrote on a desk." She realized that she probably sounded like a babbling idiot, but she couldn't keep her thoughts organized. She felt like bursting out crying any minute.

"Did you talk to Michael on the phone?" the same policeman asked gently.

"Yes."

"When was the last time you talked to him? I'm sure you know that he's run away and that we're only trying to help him."

"Yes, sir. I called him on Monday night."

She carefully explained to the police all the details of the phone call and of the visit later that night. It was a relief to be telling the truth to someone who might be able to help Mike. Jodi remembered the dejected way he had walked away from her window two nights ago, and she wished she had called him back. Maybe then he wouldn't have run away. Maybe there was something she could have done.

"You've been a great help, Miss Quinn." The taller policeman stood up and smiled warmly down at her, but she could not quell her fear of his authority. "Do you have any reason to think that Michael Gidden may come again to visit you?"

"But ... I thought he ran away. He — "

"Oh, he's probably not gone far. They usually don't the first time. It's important, if he does visit or call you, that you encourage him to go home. His parents are very worried. Before he gets into any trouble, he should go home."

"Trouble? What — ?"

"Well, his friends from the reform school. No telling what they might talk him into."

His words reminded her of what Mike had said on the phone — that no one believed he had nothing to do with the break-in at school or with the burning of his car. Those guys really were framing him. Suddenly, she realized that she was beginning to believe Mike. After all, if he had been guilty, why didn't the police have proof? But, then again, why had Mike run away if he was innocent? Conflicting thoughts bounced up and down in her head like the opposite ends of a seesaw.

As she left the office, the noon-hour bell rang. Jodi was relieved that she didn't have to return to class and the inevitable questioning stares just now. She dumped her books in her locker and walked to the cafeteria to find Brenda. It would be good to talk with a friend.

8

The closer she got to Nan's that afternoon, the more her anxiety grew. Brenda had tried to reassure her that it wasn't the end of the world to be questioned by the police, but Jodi was worried. It must have been Nan who answered the phone that morning when the police called the number on the note. What must Nan be thinking? And what would her mother say when she got home from work? It was senseless trying to hide anything now.

All afternoon at school, people had stared at her like she was in on some secret plot to blow up the place. One guy in her math class even asked her if she was hiding Mike Gidden somewhere! That really made her mad. Some people dreamed up the dumbest ideas in their dust-filled brains!

When Jodi opened the front door, the house was unusually quiet. The TV wasn't even on. She walked into the kitchen and was astounded to see her mother sitting there drinking tea with Nan like it was Sunday afternoon.

"How come you're home?" Jodi asked, although she knew the answer.

"Nan phoned to tell me about the call she

received this morning. And when I called the school — "

"Hey, no one told me you called there."

"I asked them not to. Anyway, your vice-principal said that the police were going to question you so I thought you'd feel better if I was here after school. Do you want to tell me about it?"

"What's there to say?" She knew her mother was only trying to help, but it was hard just the same to sit down and spill out the whole story about the note and Mike's midnight visits and the reform school guys.

Jodi looked at Nan, sitting so quietly, her bluish-grey hair done carefully in small rollers, one hand in her lap and one hand curled lightly around her tea cup. Just looking at her, Jodi felt reassured. If she didn't explain now, the whole thing might become even more of a mess.

So Jodi took a deep breath and told everything she could, regardless of how nutty it might sound to her mother and Nan — even the bit about waiting with Teddy that Sunday morning by the Sportsplex.

Afterwards, things began to seem less complicated. Looking at the kind eyes and smiles of her mother and grandmother, Jodi realized that they believed and trusted her. She started to relax and thought of Mike. No one believed him. For the first time she understood what that really meant, and she knew why it was driving him nuts.

"I wonder where the poor boy is," sighed Nan.

"The police say he's not far. At least that's

what they think because he's never run away before."

"Did he give you any clue at all where he might be?"

"No, Mom. Nothing. They think he might come back here to see me."

"Well, if he does, you just bring that young man in and give him something to eat," said Nan briskly. "Heaven knows what he's been living on these past two days."

Mrs. Quinn and Jodi laughed. Then Nan laughed too, although she wasn't quite sure what the joke was.

Just then they were interrupted by a loud knocking on the front door. Startled, they all stared at each other.

Jodi stood up, aware that all three of them were thinking the same thing — it must be Mike.

Through the small window of the door peered Brenda's unmistakable green eyes.

"It's only Brenda!" Jodi shouted as she opened the door.

"What do you mean it's *only* Brenda?"

"We thought it might be Mike."

"Mike? Why? Did he call? Is he coming over?"

"Slow down. No, he's not coming over. We were just talking about him, so when you knocked on the door... well, we figured it was him. Power of suggestion."

"Hi, Mrs. Quinn. Hi, Mrs. Murphy," said Brenda as she took a seat at the kitchen table. "I guess Jodi told you all about what happened at school."

"We're so worried about that poor boy. If there was only some way we could help," said Nan.

"Yeah. If only," Brenda replied with a heavy sigh. "We had our chance, but it slipped right through our hands. Now he thinks no one trusts him or believes him. What a downer."

For a moment they were all silent. Even thinking hard seemed like a useless exercise.

"What a downer is right," said Nan.

"I wish I'd been nicer to him," Jodi added.

"Don't be too hard on yourself, dear," said Mrs. Quinn. "You did what you thought was best at the time."

"But I was thinking only of myself. I thought he'd get me in trouble."

"And he might have."

"I don't think so now. You trusted him almost right away, Brenda. You weren't afraid to say you'd be his friend."

"Well, I just had this feeling, that's all. I knew he couldn't be all that bad. Something about him ... I don't know exactly."

"Why didn't I see that?"

"Maybe you didn't look."

"Huh?"

"I mean, maybe you looked and only saw what other people told you to see. You didn't give yourself a chance to see him for yourself."

"I took to him right away that day Jodi

115

brought him — I mean the day he followed Jodi home," Nan corrected herself. "He had the nicest way about him. Helped Jodi with her coat like a real gentleman."

"I thought he was just a con artist."

"You've got to give people a chance to prove themselves, I've always said," Nan added, touching the paper flowers arranged in a vase on the table. "No sense in making people wear the past like it was a layer of skin. I like to think of a snake crawling right out of its old skin and leaving it behind. It's almost like a new snake then."

Nan sure didn't know how to be subtle. She tried to act casual as she arranged and rearranged those flowers, but they all knew she was hinting about Jodi's father. Ever since his visit on the weekend, Nan had been doing her best to clear the air about the separation.

"Mike is like that," said Brenda.

"Lots of people are," said Nan.

* * *

Mike didn't come to visit that night as the police thought he might.

All the way to school next morning, Jodi kept imagining what it must be like for him. He'd been gone since Monday night and now it was Thursday morning. What had he been doing? Where was he staying, especially at night when the temperature dropped below freezing? It occurred to her that the guys from the reform school might have done something drastic. Burning Mike's car was bad

116

enough, but at least they hadn't harmed him.

She was deep in her gloomy thoughts as she walked down the polished hallway. Hardly anyone was around yet.

Even before she reached her locker, she saw it, small and white, neatly folded and taped near the combination lock. Running, she grabbed the note and frantically opened it. *I'm getting nowhere. Please meet me tonight at the same spot I told you last Sunday, only fourteen hours later. Bring Brenda if you want.*

He must have sneaked into the school that morning to put the note there. What a chance he'd taken!

For an instant, she held the paper in her hand and considered giving it to the vice-principal. But she remembered what Mike had said about always being treated like a criminal. Would they really believe him? She decided to keep it. Determined to give him a real chance, finally, she started to figure out what it meant: the same spot as last Sunday was the swimming pool entrance of the Sportsplex; fourteen hours later meant seven o' clock in the morning plus — no, it was seven-thirty plus fourteen hours would equal — nine-thirty at night. She was sure Brenda would go too.

* * *

"Why did you have to wear that red jacket and those white mittens?" complained Brenda as she and Jodi waited in the shadows by the Sportsplex. "You stand out like a sore thumb."

117

"Look," said Jodi, "we're not hiding. We're just waiting for Mike to show up. No one knows he's coming here."

"How do you know? Those guys — "

But before she could finish, a slow voice spoke to them, "Hi, you two."

Mike's tall form appeared out of the winter darkness. Even in the weak light over the door, they could see that he looked tired and discouraged.

"Mike!" They sounded like a chorus. "Where were you?"

"Never mind that. Thanks for coming. I wasn't quite sure you'd do it."

"How did you drop off the note without anyone seeing you?" Jodi asked.

"I'm the one who broke into the school a couple of years ago, remember? Anyway, I had to take the chance. I need your help."

"We'll do it," said Brenda enthusiastically.

"Let me tell you first. You can say no, if you think it's too risky."

"Brenda's right, we'll do it," added Jodi. "Give us the details."

"Do — do you mean that, Jodi?" he faltered.

"Yeah, sure. Why not?"

Gently, he raised his hand and touched the side of her cheek. The cool, feathery touch against her skin sent a shiver across her shoulders. He was smiling and his blue eyes searched hers for an explanation for her change of heart. Feeling awkward, all she could do was smile back.

Mike's taut muscles relaxed. "I want to go home tonight. Right after we talk. Then tomorrow I'll go to school as usual. They can't do anything to me just because I ran away from home."

"Well, what should we do?" Brenda couldn't wait to get going with the plan.

"Meet me at school in the morning. Early. All day tomorrow I want to be seen, but not alone. I'll be with you two, or at least one of you, the whole time. That way those guys, if they have any plans, won't be able to do anything. They'll try to wait and get me alone."

"We'll stick by you the whole time," Brenda promised.

"But how's that going to get people to believe you?" asked Jodi.

"That's where the risky part comes in. When it gets dark, I'll walk Jodi home. Those guys'll be onto me by then. They'll probably tail me. So when Jodi goes inside, I'll start going home. Jodi, you'll sneak back out and follow far enough behind so that no one notices. You'll have to watch real close. When they make a move, you run to a house and call the cops. That's the risky part. If you don't move fast, I could be in real trouble. Or if they see you — "

"Don't finish that line."

"If we don't wait until they're doing something for sure, no one'll believe me that they set up this whole school break-in and the car burning. Anyway, that's my plan. What do you think?"

"I think it's brilliant!"

"Easy for you to say, Brenda. You don't have to sneak around in the dark and then bang on some stranger's door to call the cops."

"Look, like I said, you can say no. I know it's risky."

"Wait a minute, I'm not saying no. I'm just saying ... oh, never mind. I like your plan. Let's do it."

"Hurray!" cheered Brenda, and gave Jodi a big hug.

And Mike stretched his long arms around both girls at once. "Thanks."

"Hey, Mike, would you like a two-man escort home?" asked Brenda.

"Sure."

Brenda and Jodi each took one of Mike's hands and the three of them walked out of the shadows together.

* * *

"Hey! There he is!"

A polished maroon car had pulled up to the curb at the high school and Mike was getting out, saying something to the woman who was driving.

"That must be his mother," said Jodi.

"Hi, you guys," said Mike. "Oh-oh, just like I thought." His voice had changed from a cheerful greeting to an ominous groan.

"What's up?" asked Brenda looking in the direction in which Mike had glanced.

He didn't need to answer her. Standing next to an unfamiliar car, large and black like a hearse, were three guys. They looked like members of a

120

comedy act. Two of them were so big they could be halfbacks for any high school football team, but the third was so small that he looked no older than Teddy. All three wore dark navy-blue jackets with hoods, only none of them had the hoods pulled up. They just stood there staring at Mike, Brenda and Jodi, who stood and glared right back.

"That's them, isn't it?" asked Jodi. "What're they going to do?"

"Nothing. Let's go inside. They won't go there. They just want me to know they're around."

"Don't they go to school?" asked Brenda, hurrying along beside Mike on the farthest side from the three guys.

"The little one does, but he'll hook off today."

"He reminds me of Teddy," said Jodi.

"He's seventeen. He's been in about six foster homes and reform school. You should've seen him in there. It was like he had to prove he was as tough as any guy twice his size. And he is too. He wouldn't play sports. He hated being beaten by the stronger guys."

"He sure looks like he's got a chip on his shoulder."

"Wouldn't you if you had only foster homes and no parents?" asked Brenda, as usual seeing the other side of the story.

"I guess he never gave anyone a chance. He always got in trouble no matter where he was or how nice the foster parents were."

"Didn't crawl out of the old skin," muttered Jodi.

"Huh?"

121

"Nothing. I was just thinking out loud. Let's sit over here by this window." For that little guy, she thought, the past must've been just too much to get rid of.

"Don't look now, you guys, but I think we're putting on a concert."

A quick glance explained what Mike meant. There weren't many people in the cafeteria yet, but those who were nearby were preoccupied with the three of them.

"Let them look," said Brenda. "All they're going to see is us talking."

"Does it bother you, Jodi?" he asked.

"No. Why should it?" But Mike was onto something. It did feel funny. For all anyone knew, she and Brenda could've been with Mike on the school break-in. Anyway, who cares what they think, Jodi thought. They're wrong.

When the bell rang for homeroom period, they agreed to meet at break and decide what they'd do at lunchtime. Jodi hoped they'd stay in school instead of going over to Tony's Place — the three guys wouldn't be so cautious there.

But she needn't have worried. The vice-principal solved the dilemma by grounding Mike in the detention room every day until he got caught up on the school work he'd missed. Mike didn't seem to mind.

*   *   *

"I've got a terrific idea!" exclaimed Brenda when she and Jodi and Mike met after school by Jodi's

122

locker. "In fact, I've already called Mom at work and she said it was fine with her. I want you two to come to my place after school and stay for supper. We could listen to some records or maybe play with Jeff's video game. The mini-chip robot has a scout trip this weekend so we're rid of him. What do you say?"

"Great, for me," answered Mike. "I have to check in with the folks. They're being super strict, but I think they'll go along with that."

"I'll call Nan when we get to your house. She's easy."

Outside the school, they looked cautiously around. No black car. No guys waiting for Mike.

But before they were off the school grounds, he elbowed Brenda. "Don't turn around, but a black car is coming past."

"I feel like they're going to poke a machine gun out the window and mow us down," she said through gritted teeth, trying to look like she was smiling.

"Where will they go?" asked Jodi.

"Around the block and back. Don't worry, they'll follow us the whole way to Brenda's. But we want them to do that. How else can our plan work?"

"I'm glad Mom gets home at four-thirty," said Brenda.

9

All along the street in front of them, circles of yellow from the streetlights broke the eerie blackness. It was only 9:45, yet there was a midnight pitch to the darkness. Thick clouds threatened snow and hid the moon and stars. Only a few cars broke the quiet as Jodi and Mike made their way from Brenda's to Nan's. So far, there had been no car following them.

"Are you nervous?" asked Mike.

"No. Well, a little, I guess. What if this whole thing backfires?"

"It won't."

"You're awfully sure of yourself."

"Sure am," he said, laughing. He slipped his hand into Jodi's so quickly that he caught her by surprise. She tried to untangle her hand from his.

"Hey, what's wrong?"

"Well, I ..." But she couldn't explain. For one thing, it embarrassed her. It always did when boys made moves like that. She didn't know what she should do next, so pretending to be annoyed seemed the easiest thing.

"I guess nothing's wrong, then," he returned confidently. "And this has to go." He slid her

124

mitten off and stuffed it into the pocket of his leather jacket, then took her hand again. "That's better."

This time Jodi didn't protest. It felt good to leave her hand in the cool coarseness of his. She knew, though, that her face was burning red and was thankful it was dark.

"I guess if we're holding hands when those guys come along, it'll make things look normal," she said matter-of-factly.

"Yeah," he laughed and squeezed her hand.

"Mike?"

"Yeah?"

"What if they don't try anything?"

"They will."

"I'm sort of scared."

"Don't worry. They won't make any moves until I'm alone and they think you're home. Like I said, these guys aren't stupid enough to try anything in front of a witness. That's why you have to keep out of sight when you sneak back to follow me."

"Yeah," she said, but it was more like a worried moan than the confident assurance she'd meant it to be.

They walked on in silence. A couple came out of a nearby house shouting goodnight to a girl standing in the doorway, the bright yellow lights spilling out onto the snowy lawn. Hurrying across the street, they got into their car and soon were around the corner and out of sight. Again the street was empty, and Mike and Jodi's footsteps were the only sound. The baseball park was ahead, a black and barren hollow breaking into the neat residential street. Jodi was thankful she was walking with Mike, his tall strength security against the darkness.

"Can I tell you something without you getting mad and ripping my head off?" Mike asked.

"Sure, what?"

"I like you. I mean, I like you a lot."

Why was it that if a boy said something the least bit complimentary, all Jodi could think of was a dumb reply? And she did. "I bet you like peanut butter and banana sandwiches a lot too."

Mike burst out laughing and dropped her hand. His laughter echoed. She just stood there trying not to say anything else because it would probably be even dumber than the peanut-butter-sandwich line. But the laughter was contagious and soon she was laughing too.

Finally he said, "You really are insecure, aren't you?"

She hadn't expected that.

"I mean, first you're as cold as ice and you won't even talk to me. Maybe you don't trust any man, especially since your father cheated on your mother."

"How did you — "

"Brenda told me. Anyway, then you finally get convinced that maybe I'm not so bad after all. If it wasn't for Brenda, you wouldn't have gotten that far, I'll bet. Then, when I tell you I like you a lot, you start talking about peanut butter sandwiches. That sounds pretty insecure to me."

"When did you get your degree in psychology?" Her words didn't hide her anger. Boy, he sure knew how to change the mood.

"Hey, hold on. You don't need to get mad, for cryin' out loud. Why can't you look at yourself once in a while? It isn't so bad to be insecure anyway. You're only fifteen."

"Look who's talking. You're only seventeen, you know."

"Yeah, but I've been through more. And besides, I've been thinking a lot about who I am and who I'm going to be. You're too busy being safe."

"Safe?"

"Yeah. That's why Brenda had to leave your phone number that day. You were afraid to."

"Sure I was. Who would blame me? How did I know who this guy was who was writing on the desk? And then we found out it was you, and you don't exactly have a reputation to brag about. Give me back my mitten. My hand's cold."

"I'll warm it." He clasped her hand between both of his, but she quickly drew it away.

"The mitten does a better job." Stubbornly, she held her hand out for the mitten.

"Here. This mitten'll last longer than any guy in your life. No one would stick around long enough for the ice to melt."

He began to walk ahead of her and she rushed to catch up. The deep, hollow blackness of the empty ballfield was a threatening presence beside her now.

Staying just slightly behind to show that she was not giving in to him, Jodi sorted out what he'd

127

said. One thing stood out from the rest. He said she didn't trust men because of what her father had done. Was that really true? It seemed like such a stupid thing to say. After all, how many "men" had she met since the separation had begun? Only Mike. Maybe he was the insecure one. He didn't like to face the fact that a girl wouldn't trust him.

Jodi wished she was safely back at Nan's. How had she let herself get into this mess, walking along a dark street with a boy she hardly knew — one who was in trouble with the police and who was asking her to help him set up three thugs? It was one of the dumbest situations she'd ever gotten into.

"Oh-oh." Mike's voice was a low whisper.

"Wha — " Jodi didn't have time to finish the question. Just at the edge of the light from the streetlamp, coming out of the darkness of the baseball park, were the three guys from reform school. They walked side by side, like a threatening menacing wall. Their faces were hidden by shadow.

"Run," whispered Mike.

But Jodi couldn't move; her legs were like lead posts and her heart pounded fiercely against her chest.

"I said run!" Mike yelled, giving her a push.

She began to run as fast as she could. In a quick backward glance, she realized that Mike wasn't behind her. He hadn't even gotten a chance to start.

Just ahead was a house with a large, brightly

lit verandah. She ran up the steps two at a time, pounding frantically on the door. "Help us! Please, help us!" she cried.

A light came on and she rushed toward it. Inside, cautiously holding back the curtain was a boy, a little younger than Teddy. Then a girl about Jodi's age came to take him from the window.

They were afraid, Jodi realized. It seemed impossible, but they weren't going to come to the door! She knocked on the window but they didn't open the curtain again.

"Oh no," she sobbed. "You've got to help us. You just can't leave him there. They're beating him up." She leaned her forehead against the cold glass of the window and cried.

Then the front door opened just a small bit, the chain lock holding it fast. Jodi rushed over and pleaded, "I need to call the police. Mike ... they're beating him up ... please." Tears rolled down her face and her voice was barely a whisper.

Finally, the girl lifted the chain and opened the door without a word.

"Where's your phone?" gasped Jodi. "What's this address?" She dialled with shaky fingers and, calming her voice, gave the details to the police.

"They said to stay here."

All three went to the window, but empty shadows were all they could see.

Within minutes, a siren echoed into the night and then the flashing red lights of a police car sped past the house. Jodi rushed out and down the sidewalk. The car squealed to a halt and one of the policemen, carrying a large flashlight, ran into the ballfield. The other squatted on the sidewalk beside Mike.

Numb with fear, Jodi stood beside the policeman, her hands covering the look of horror on her face. Mike was lying face down, a small trickle of blood oozing onto the sidewalk beneath him. The policeman gently lifted his head and put his coat under it. Mike was unconscious.

"We'll need an ambulance," the policeman ordered over the car radio. The reply came with a static crackle across the radio lines.

Jodi knelt down beside Mike and put her hand over his. It was warm and sticky with blood. Tears flooded down her face but she didn't both to wipe them away. What if he died? He'd told her to run and had stayed behind to face them alone, so she could escape. His plan to frame them had backfired and now he was lying on the sidewalk, helpless, bleeding. What did it prove? That he was innocent? That he had changed? If he died, it would prove nothing.

"We can't move him," said the policeman, putting his arm around Jodi and standing her up.

It was then she noticed that a crowd had gathered, curious people who didn't know anything at all about Mike. She wanted to explain that it wasn't what it looked like. He wasn't a thug — it was only those other guys. She and Mike and just been walking along when those three, for no reason ... but it would be useless. She leaned against the policeman and cried.

Another siren blared down the street and the

ambulance pulled up, an attendant leaping from the back even before it had come to a complete stop. He placed an oxygen mask over Mike's face while two other men rushed up with a stretcher.

As they lifted him, she could see that his face was badly beaten, and already his features were swollen out of proportion. His body, strapped on the stretcher, seemed lifeless. She took his hand but the attendant motioned her away as they hurried to the ambulance.

"You can come with us," said the policeman kindly. "I think he's going to be all right. These people know what to do. You'll see. Can you tell us how to locate his parents? They'll want to go to the hospital."

Jodi nodded her head and allowed herself to be lead to the police car.

The ambulance started up the street, the scream of the siren fading in the winter night. The crowd began to disperse. Glancing back toward the sidewalk, Jodi shuddered at the small blotch of blood left where Mike had been.

Just then, the other policeman came out of the baseball park leading someone with him. It was the smallest of the three guys. Jodi recognized him immediately and shouted, "That's him! He's the one who started this whole thing! It's him!"

"I finally caught up with him by the bleachers. The other two got away, but this one'll do. He'll talk, won't you, Jimmy?"

"You mean you know who he is?" asked Jodi incredulously.

"Oh yeah. Jimmy's been around for quite a

while. What're you now, Jimmy? Eighteen? Must be."

"Let's call another car over here. We'll send him in with them."

On the sidewalk beside the police car was the young boy and his babysitter.

"Thanks for letting me in," Jodi said.

"That's okay. I hope your boyfriend's all right."

"Me too," said the little boy.

"Thanks."

It was strange to hear someone call Mike her boyfriend, although Jodi did not correct them. In a way, he was.

She rested her head against the back of the seat and sighed deeply. What would happen to Mike? Did they have enough time to — But she couldn't face even thinking about it. All she could do was hope.

* * *

On the stiff chrome chairs in the emergency waiting room, Jodi sat with Mike's parents.

"He was just walking me home when — "

"We know, dear. Don't worry. You've done all you can. Mike's father and I are grateful. We just hope ..." But she couldn't finish. Her tears choked back the words. Mr. Gidden sat silently, one arm tightly around his wife's shoulders.

The main door to the emergency department swung open and Jodi's mother came rushing in.

"Jodi! You're all right! Thank God, you're all right. What about Mike?"

"We don't know yet, Mom. And Mom, these are Mike's parents."

"I'm so sorry. Jodi and I will stay here with you to wait. We're all worried about Mike." She sat beside Jodi and took her hand, holding it restlessly in her lap.

"Thank you," said Mrs. Gidden in a whisper.

"We're sorry our boy got your daughter into this, Mrs. Quinn. It's our fault for letting him out tonight, for trusting him."

"But that's wrong!" protested Jodi in an exasperated voice. "Mom, he's wrong. It's not like that at all."

"Look, young lady," continued Mr. Gidden, "Michael's mother and I have known him a lot longer than you have. He's caused his mother, here, more heartaches than a mother should bear." He brushed his palm against his wife's hand as he held it, sighing heavily. "We've tried our best — but Michael's pattern repeats itself, despite family counselling, despite any of our attempts to — We don't like to say this, but the boy's a hoodlum. He's been in reform school. Perhaps you didn't know that."

"I do know that," Jodi blurted. "And I also know that it was two years ago that he went there. He's different, now. He's changed."

"It's evident that he hasn't changed. If you were a little older, you'd see that. We once believed he could change. He was questioned about a break-in at school only a short while ago. And then he took his car and — "

"But, dear," interrupted Mrs. Gidden weakly, "we don't know for sure that Mike was involved in any of that. He says — "

Mr. Gidden stood up, frustration raising his voice to an angry pitch. " He says, he says. How can we believe what he says anymore? Remember when he said he didn't steal that radio — that first time? And now he's got even this young girl believing his lies."

"They're not lies, Mr. Gidden! You're thinking about the dark ages. People change you know. Snakes can crawl out of old skin and people can change too. Mike protected me tonight. Haven't you spoken to the police? They'll tell you that he was beaten up by three thugs from reform school. They caught one of them."

Her mother had quietly slipped her arm across Jodi's shoulder, not to make her stop talking, but to show support for what she was saying.

Before anyone else could speak, the staff nurse came into the room. "Mr. and Mrs. Gidden? You may come in now."

"Is he — " Mrs. Gidden had not stood up.

"He's as fine as can be expected. But he'll be staying here for awhile. You may come in before they take him upstairs to his room. Understand that he's quite groggy. The drugs and the beating. But we feel sure there's no danger."

"Thank God. Thank God," breathed Mrs. Gidden. "Our boy's all right. We haven't lost him." She leaned into her husband's arms and silently he held her, rocking back and forth gently. "We haven't lost our boy," she murmured again.

Mr. Gidden held the door open. Momentarily, he stopped and turned to Jodi and her mother.

"I ..." he began, but he couldn't finish. On his face was a look of relief mixed with sad regret. Jodi knew that her words had meant a lot to him.

"That's okay, Mr. Gidden. Tell him I said Hi."

He could only smile back.

"And Mr. Gidden?" she added quickly. "Tell him that I like him a lot too."

Then the door shut and she and her mother were alone in the cold sterility of the waiting room.

"Let's go home, dear," said Mrs. Quinn. "We'll come back to see Mike tomorrow. Nan'll be wondering what's happened."

"She'll probably have chocolate chip cookies and milk waiting for us."

They both laughed and Mrs. Quinn hugged Jodi in a tight squeeze that told her she loved her and she was proud of her.

"You said quite a lot to Mr. Gidden about trusting in Mike. Do you believe all that, about people changing?"

"Sure."

"Not just Mike?"

Jodi looked quickly at her mother to see what she'd meant by that. "Sure, I guess so."

"Even your father?"

Suddenly she realized that her mother wanted to give the family another chance. Teddy's call must have worked. That little peanut-brain knew something important after all!

"Sure, even Dad. Besides, I don't have a squirt brother at Nan's to push around. I've been missing that."

"Your father and Teddy are coming down tomorrow. We'll all talk then."

"Is the trial separation over?"

"Maybe." Her mother's sigh expressed her concern.

"I guess it'll still be a kind of trial, huh, Mom? A trial family, sort of."

Mrs. Quinn manoeuvred the car out of the hospital parking lot and they headed for Nan's.

* * *

It was only nine o'clock in the morning, but the nurse allowed Jodi to go quietly into Mike's room while Brenda and Mrs. Quinn waited outside.

"Hi," she said in a whisper.

The face that stared out at her was painfully bruised and distorted. Small lines of stitches criss-crossed on Mike's enlarged lower lip and above his right eye, which was squeezed tight with swelling.

"Hi," he managed but his attempt to smile was cut short. It hurt too much.

"Oh, Mike!"

"It's not so bad." His voice was weak.

"Don't say anything. Here. Nan made a milkshake with real melted chocolate and loads of ice cream. The nurse said you can drink it right now if you want."

She held it out to him but then realized that

136

his right hand was wrapped awkwardly in bandages.

"I'll hold it for you. The two straws can bend, see."

His swollen lips touched the straw and the thick chocolate crept up and into his mouth. Before he stopped, the milkshake was half gone.

"That just about makes this all worthwhile," he said as he dabbed his bandaged hand against the chocolate dripping from his lip.

"Here's a napkin. Let me do that for you."

"Ow!!"

"Sorry! Oh, Mike, I'm sorry. You're so hurt and it's all because of me." She couldn't keep the tears from starting.

"Hey!" Mike struggled with his words. "What're you talking about? It had nothing to do with you."

"You would've run if I hadn't been there. You stayed so I could get away."

"But you were helping me."

"Some help I was."

"And Mom told me what you said to Dad too. Thanks."

"I had to tell him. He had everything wrong."

"And Dad gave me your message."

For a moment she wasn't sure what he meant. Then, in a flash, she remembered asking his father to tell him she liked him. Even though she tried hard not to, she started blushing.

"I bet you like peanut-butter sandwiches a lot," he teased and then laughed. "Ow, that hurts."

"Serves you right."

"When I get these stitches out, I'm going to give you the best kiss I know how."

She held the milkshake straw to his mouth to keep him from saying anything else.

"Hey! Almost forgot. Mom and Dad are going to try to be a family again. Dad and Teddy are on their way down today so we can all talk about it, but Mom says I'll finish out school here and we'll move back in the summer."

Mike reached out and took her hand in his unbandaged one. "That's good news. And we lived happily ever after, almost."

"What do you mean by 'almost'?"

"Well, if you go back home, when'll I see you?"

"Well, I don't — Brenda said the same thing. And — well, Mom said she could come down some weekends and — "

"They won't let me come."

"Yes they will. They trust you now."

"Are you sure?"

"Mom's right outside. I'm going to ask if you can come for a whole week this summer."

"Better start with just a weekend."

"Nope. A whole week."

Moments later she returned with Brenda and Mrs. Quinn sneaking behind her.

"We're not supposed to be here," whispered Mrs. Quinn. "But Jodi said you needed to be told straight from me."

"Oh my god," groaned Brenda when she took a look at Mike's bluish, swollen face.

138

"Thanks for the cheerful greeting," joked Mike.

"I mean — it's not so bad. It's — "

"Save it, Brenda. He's got mirrors," said Jodi.

"We'll all be glad when those boys get what's coming to them for doing this, Mike," said Mrs. Quinn, patting the sheets by his leg. "It's lucky they didn't break anything."

"What's all this?" asked a nurse who looked into the crowded room.

"We're just planning a holiday. Sorry. We won't stay," explained Mrs. Quinn. "We know we shouldn't be here, but Mike and Brenda are coming to stay for a week this summer at our place and we were making plans."

"And we're going to have a party!" said Jodi quickly.

Mrs. Quinn looked at her in surprise.

"It's a celebration."

"Oh, that's nice. A birthday?" asked the nurse, still holding the door open.

"No, not a birthday. Something more special. We're not sure what we'll call it, but it'll be the best celebration we've had in a long time."

"That's nice. That's nice," smiled the nurse. "But for now, you'll have to let the patient rest. If he keeps talking, he'll burst open those stitches."

"I'm keeping my mouth shut," said Mike slyly. "I've got a good reason to get these stitches out as soon as possible." He winked at Jodi.

She managed to keep her blush to a minimum.

A
Cauldron
of
Witches

The Story of Witchcraft

by

Clifford Lindsey Alderman

AN ARCHWAY PAPERBACK
POCKET BOOKS • NEW YORK

For Gertrude Blumenthal,
whose kindly guidance and advice
have helped so much over the years.

A CAULDRON OF WITCHES

Archway Paperback edition published February, 1973

L

Published by
POCKET BOOKS, a division of Simon & Schuster, Inc.,
630 Fifth Avenue, New York, N.Y.

Archway Paperback editions are distributed in the U.S.
by Simon & Schuster, Inc., 630 Fifth Avenue, New
York, N.Y. 10020, and in Canada by Simon & Schuster
of Canada, Ltd., Richmond Hill, Ontario, Canada.

CONTENTS

1 THE AGE-OLD PRACTICE OF WITCHCRAFT   1

2 KING JAMES AND SCOTTISH WITCHCRAFT   14

3 THE "WITCH-FINDER GENERALL"   30

4 MORE ENGLISH WITCHES   39

5 JOHANN SCHÜLER AND WITCHCRAFT
   IN GERMANY   50

6 THE "WITCH" WHO PUT A KING ON
   HIS THRONE   65

7 FRENCH WITCHCRAFT AND WEREWOLVES   83

8 VOODOO AND THE TERRIBLE SECT ROUGE   91

9 OBEAH   104

10 AFRICAN MAGIC AND THE LEOPARD MEN   113

11 THE MATHERS RAISE THE DEVIL IN
   MASSACHUSETTS   124

12 THE SALEM WITCHES   139

13 AND TODAY   161

SUGGESTED FURTHER READINGS   171

BIBLIOGRAPHY   173

INDEX   179

Double, double toil and trouble;
Fire burn and cauldron bubble.
Fillet of a fenny snake,
In the cauldron boil and bake;
Eye of newt, and toe of frog,
Wool of bat, and tongue of dog,
Adder's fork, and blind-worm's sting,
Lizard's leg, and howlet's wing,
For a charm of powerful trouble,
Like a hell-broth boil and bubble.

—Shakespeare's *Macbeth*

A
Cauldron
of
Witches

1

THE AGE-OLD PRACTICE
OF WITCHCRAFT

Most people today believe there are no such things as
witches and witchcraft. Yet there are many who still
cling to the belief. In recent years a number of books
have been published to support the claim that witches
still live.

There have been intelligent people in modern times
who have openly proclaimed themselves to be witches
with magical powers. In wild, remote sections of many
countries, too, ignorant, superstitious people believe in
witchcraft. In some areas of the West Indies there is
evidence that the special forms of witchcraft called
obeah and voodoo are still practiced in spite of strict
laws against them. But as education spreads deeper
into these remote areas, they will doubtless disappear.
In some of the mountainous sections of the United
States, backwoods people believe in "hants" (ghosts).
Even in large cities, there are shops where one may
buy charms, potions and other things used in witchcraft.

Were there ever any witches? Some point to the references in the Old Testament to witches, wizards or sorcerers (male witches), witchcraft, familiars (also called familiar spirits and imps) by which witches were supposed to work their magic through the Devil, enchantments and charms.

The first mention in the Bible is in the Book of Exodus, chapter 22, verse 18: "Thou shalt not suffer a witch to live." This book is the story of the famous Exodus, when the Israelites left their slavery in Egypt to wander for years in the desert until they reached the promised land. Scholars believe the Exodus took place somewhere between the thirteenth and fifteenth centuries before the birth of Christ—that is, somewhere around 3,500 years ago.

In the great European witch hunts and persecutions of the sixteenth and seventeenth centuries, the witch hunters pointed to several places in the Old Testament which said witches must be put to death, as did the Puritans of Massachusetts when the witchcraft delusion spread there.

Do the references to witches and witchcraft in the Old Testament really mean that witches did live in those days? A witch (or, in the case of a man, a wizard or warlock) is supposed to be one who has sold her soul to the Devil. Some biblical scholars are agreed that these references are actually poor or careless translations of the old Hebrew texts of the Old Testament. They say these quotations usually have nothing to do with dealings with the Devil.

These scholars claim that the translation of the word given in the English version of the Bible should be "poisoner" instead of "witch," since there were those in biblical days who professed to be sorcerers and could kill people by magic—that is, by some poisonous potion.

What is known is that for a great many centuries there have been people who claimed to be witches and to do miraculous things. And of the thousands of so-called witches who were put to death in Europe for witchcraft, some undoubtedly claimed to be witches and to perform magic.

It was the way in which the witches were hunted down and condemned that was wrong. It caused the execution of thousands of people who were innocent of any serious crime. It would be difficult, if not impossible, to find a single case in which a crime was proved, without what is called "reasonable doubt," to have been done by witchcraft.

Of those who described themselves as witches, there were different kinds. Sometimes they are called "white witches" and "black witches."

White witches used their arts to heal sick people. They were actually doctors of a sort in days when there were not many real doctors, and wild, rural areas had none. It is true that they usually used certain kinds of "magic" in healing the sick; but at a time when little or nothing was known of medical science, the white or good witches used herbs—or simples, as they were also called—to cure people who were ill.

Many medicines used today originated from plants, roots and trees and their bark, and some still come from them. One example is digitalis, the foxglove plant, used in the treatment of heart ailments. Quinine, one of the best treatments for malaria, originally was obtained from the bark of the cinchona tree, which grows on the slopes of the Andes Mountains in South America. There are hundreds of other medicines,

3

drugs, healing salves and ointments that came first from plants. Today, chemists have learned how to make them artificially in the laboratory.

In Europe, in the tiny rural villages, people—especially old women—used these herbs to cure illness. They were wise in the lore, handed down from mother to daughter, and these cures were often effective. Naturally the sick people who came to them thought their cures were magical, and the witches, as they came to be known, did nothing to discourage this belief, as it brought them more business. Some hocus-pocus had to go with the medicine to make people even more certain that the witches had magical powers.

The witches muttered incantations, used charms and said their customers were bewitched and that they, the witches, could "unwitch" them. They mixed strange and often offensive things in their potions; the chant of Shakespeare's witches in *Macbeth* as they boiled their magic kettle was no exaggeration. Nevertheless, white witches did accomplish many cures, and the "love potions" they mixed for unsuccessful lovers seemed to aid romances.

A "black witch" was a bad witch. These persons specialized in doing harm, or trying to, by using charms, potions, curses, waxen and other images and poison. If someone offended such a witch, she might put a curse on him. Then, if soon afterwards a horse, cow, pig or other domestic animal belonging to the cursed person sickened and died, it was thought to be the work of the witch. Or the cursed person might become lame, sicken and waste away or die suddenly. No one could tell a superstitious farmer or farmer's wife that this was only a coincidence that had nothing to do with a curse uttered by a witch.

These evil witches' services were also available to people who were willing to pay for them. A man might have a serious quarrel with his neighbor. Perhaps he felt the neighbor had cheated him out of some of his land—there were always disputes over land boundaries before court sessions in England—and wanted revenge.

So he would go to a witch and pay her to get rid of his enemy. She would make a waxen image of the neighbor and melt it. Sometimes, especially in Africa or the West Indies, the image would be a doll made of cloth and other materials into which the witch would stick pins.

These image curses are among the oldest and commonest ways of murdering a person by witchcraft. If the curse did not work, the witch could always say that the victim had powers stronger than her magic. But there were so many stories of persons dying under an image curse that a great many people believed in it.

Not only during meetings of witches called sabbats, but at other times the Devil appeared to people, according to what they told when they were examined, tortured and tried as accused witches, as well as in the stories whispered about in many a rural village. When he approached innocent persons, it would be to tempt them to sell their souls to him in return for the powers of witchcraft, money or good fortune.

The number of guises in which Satan was said to appear is almost endless. Often he came as a man, nearly always of very dark complexion, usually dressed in black, tall, sometimes with a black beard. Other descriptions added boots, spurs and a sword and had him mounted on a black horse. Some described his appearance as hideous and saw as many as eight horns on his head. Others saw him with both horns and a tail.

The Prince of Evil was fond of appearing as an animal, often as a goat, which was a symbol of witchcraft. At other times he might be a dog, cat, a horned black sheep, a great horse, even a chicken. He came to one accused witch through a window in the shape of a cat, then changed into a man dressed in red, according to her story.

The black witches were up to other forms of mischief. It was believed they could raise storms to sink ships or destroy crops, cause houses to catch fire, make cows go dry and give no milk, prevent cream from being churned into butter, turn milk sour and dry up wells. In the seventeenth century, if a New England housewife's batch of bread fell flat in her oven or was burned, she would be sure she had felt a little breeze as she opened the oven door to put the loaves in; that was an invisible witch flying in to spoil the bread.

Chiefly in England and Scotland, all witches were supposed to have familiars or imps. It was believed they were given to the witch by the Devil when she sold her soul to him, and that without a familiar she was powerless to work magic.

There were a great many kinds of familiars. They might be dogs, cats, goats, fowls, hares, rats, mice, weasels, toads, all sorts of birds and even people. Some were strange creatures that resembled some animal and yet were different in one way or another, or sometimes like two animals combined.

One witch, under torture, spoke of two queer familiars, one like a fat spaniel with no legs at all, the other a greyhound with a head like an ox. Another told of her rat imps that were shaped like cows, with little

6

horns. All had strange names. There was a mole named Pygine, a dog called Dunsott, a cat, Lightfoot, another cat appropriately named Satan and a weasel named Makeshift. Other names of familiars that came up in witches' examinations and trials included Swein, Rorie, Robert the Rule, Tibb and dozens of others.

A correspondent for an English newspaper in a rural district wrote an article in 1928 about an old woman, in a hamlet called Horseheath, who had died two years before. The country people believed she was a witch and went to her for charms and cures. According to her story, she had sold her soul to the Devil, who made her sign her name in a book and then gave her five imps with which to work magic. Soon afterwards she was seen out walking with a cat, a toad, a ferret, a rat and a mouse.

The witch had to feed her familiars with some of her own blood. She might cut herself and mix some of the blood with the familiars' regular food, or sometimes the imp would suck it from a witch mark. A witch mark was conclusive evidence that a person was a witch. It could be a small pimple, wart or some other small swelling on a person's body, usually hidden from view.

Witches held sabbats to discuss their magic and to worship their master, the Devil. Such groups of witches were called covens. There is much disagreement about covens by writers on witchcraft, but many believe that witches were organized in this way and that a coven consisted of thirteen persons—twelve witches and a leader, supposed to be the Devil.

Why thirteen? It is a number that even today is supposed to be connected with evil or bad luck. Some tall buildings, especially hotels, have no thirteenth floor; the fourteenth comes after the twelfth. A hostess giving a dinner party may be horrified to discover that for one reason or another thirteen people sit down at her dinner table. When the thirteenth of a month falls on a Friday, it is believed to be an especially unlucky day. Some writers say witches' covens always met on a Friday night, and in olden days most ships would not depart for a voyage on Friday.

There are a number of reasons given as to why thirteen is an evil or unlucky number. The principal one concerns the Christian religion, in which Jesus, with his twelve disciples, was betrayed by one of them, Judas, at the Last Supper before his crucifixion. In the Book of Genesis of the Old Testament, Joseph dreamed that the sun, moon and eleven stars bowed down to him. This so deepened the hatred of his jealous brothers for him that they sold him into slavery in Egypt.

There is a tradition about the number thirteen too. Robin Hood and his band of merry men, who seemed to bear charmed lives, numbered thirteen. And even greater figures of English legend, King Arthur and his knights of the Round Table, also totaled thirteen.

In 1941, on a radio program by the British Broadcasting Corporation, a man who claimed to have taken part in an ancient ceremony still held in rural Gloucestershire described it. A circle of twelve small fires were lighted, and in the middle of the ring a large one. Country people came from miles around, he said, to sing, dance and "burn the old witch." Was that ceremony one from bygone centuries in which an "old witch" was actually burned in the big thirteenth fire? If so, thirteen was unlucky for her.

8

Those who believe witches' coven meetings were actually held say they were not always attended by just thirteen witches, but it was always a multiple of thirteen—twenty-six, or twice thirteen; thirty-nine, or three times the evil number; and so on.

The name "sabbats" for these meetings is believed to have come from the old Hebrew Sabbath—the seventh day of the creation of the world, on which the Old Testament says God rested.

The witches' sabbat, or Black Mass, was a mockery of the religious one. It began with the assembly of the witches' covens, always at night, in forests, wild open fields, at crossroads and even secretly in churches.

The stories go that each witch, before departing for a sabbat, took off her clothes and smeared herself with "flying ointment." Then she mounted a broom or forked stick and whisked up the chimney or through an open window, flying to the scene of the sabbat. Sometimes, when a witch was especially favored by the Devil, he would send her a goat, ram or dog, on whose back she soared through the air.

There are several recipes given for the flying ointment. One authority describes three of them.

The first contained hemlock and aconite, both powerful poisons if swallowed, though aconite, in small amounts, is sometimes used in medicine. The famous Greek philosopher Socrates was condemned to death by those who did not agree with his theories, and he was forced to kill himself by drinking a cup of extract of hemlock. According to this authority, even smearing a potion containing these poisons on the body, since it is possible for them to get into a person's bloodstream in this way, would cause the witch's senses to become confused, make her unable to move about easily, affect

9

the heart and cause dizziness and shortness of breath.

The second ointment contained belladonna, another strong poison except when it is used in medicine in proper doses. Rubbed on the body, it could cause a person to become highly excited or delirious. The third ointment had both aconite and belladonna in it, and the results could be like those of the other two.

It is also claimed that witches often drank potions before going to a sabbat, and these too may have given them hallucinations and made them think they were flying. In today's drug-ridden world, people taking certain drugs describe weird "trips" they take while under their influence. And here, in these ointments and potions, is a reasonable explanation for the belief that witches flew to sabbats. Who knows what drugs they may have extracted from herbs and roots as they puttered over such "magical" brews?

Were there sabbats at all? Almost certainly there were, though few people today are credulous enough to believe that the witches really flew to them. As to what went on at sabbats, there are some very queer, eerie and horrible descriptions of them. But many of these accounts were obtained by torture and are therefore worthless. Others came from gypsies or ignorant country people, who may have been drunk or perhaps had vivid imaginations and enjoyed the notoriety they obtained by telling of things they may not have seen at all.

Nevertheless, the scores of accounts of sabbats make it quite certain that such meetings were held.

Once the witches had assembled at a sabbat, so the stories go, the roll would be called and new converts to witchcraft introduced. Then they would all take oaths

10

of allegiance and do homage—sometimes in disgusting ways—to the master of ceremonies, presumed to be the Devil. Next, each would tell what wicked things she had done since the last meeting.

As for the banquet that is supposed to have followed, many descriptions of what the witches ate and drank have been written, most of them obtained under torture. They include testimony that the meat served was the flesh of small children. A magic cake made of black millet seed mixed with the flesh of unbaptized babies was supposed to enable a witch to stand torture without confessing. It is enough to say that all this was probably nonsense.

One of the famous Lancashire witches in England, who was tried and executed in 1612, told of a meeting of witches in the wild and remote Forest of Pendle in Lancashire. This witch, Anne Whittle, described the feast that was served.

"There was victuals, viz., flesh, butter, cheese, bread and drink." She added that "although they did eat, they were never the fuller or better for the same," and that they ate in complete darkness.

After the banquet they danced, usually a folk or country dance in which all joined hands and moved in a circle to the left; sometimes they danced back to back. There was music on the tambourine, violin or pipes, and one witness said the sound was an unspeakable discord interrupted by catcalls. The sabbat then degenerated into an orgy that lasted until dawn drove the witches back to their homes.

One kind of witch or ghost did no great harm to people, but was a nuisance, a very noisy one at that. *Polter,* in German, means a noisy person, and *Geist* means ghost. So a poltergeist, which originated in Germany, is a noisy ghost. Poltergeists are believed to come into people's houses, cause mysterious loud knockings and rappings, make things fly about in the air and do other mischievous and annoying things.

In Ireland, people believe in fairies. They call them the "Little People." Strangely enough, in spite of all the fearful witch hunts, tortures, trials and executions that took place in nearby England and Scotland, witchcraft delusions practically passed Ireland by. There were a few scattered witch trials, but nothing compared with those of Ireland's neighbor islands. As for the Little People, they were, and are, believed to be mischievous little creatures, but not very harmful. Not too many years ago, newspaper stories told how the Little People who lived in the countryside surrounding Shannon Airport were annoyed and resentful over the thunder of airplanes taking off and landing.

Out of all these claims about witchcraft only two things are really clear: that there *were* (and still are) people who professed to be witches and perform magic, and that there were people who did not claim to be witches but were accused, either out of spite or because their ways were peculiar, and were tried, condemned and executed. And everything about the ways in which accused witches were examined, tortured, tried and put to death was wrong. Evidence without any real proof, obtained usually by torture, was accepted that no civilized court would consider today. The horrible tortures by which confessions were obtained and the frightful ways in which condemned witches were executed caused many an innocent person to suffer fearful agonies and horrible death.

To cover witchcraft throughout history and in all the countries of the world where it has existed would be impossible in a book of this size. It will be enough to tell of the principal waves of witchcraft persecution in Europe and America, as well as something of the unusual forms of witchcraft practiced in Africa and the West Indies, and to describe some of the more famous witchcraft persecutions, trials and executions in those parts of the world.

2

KING JAMES AND
SCOTTISH WITCHCRAFT

One night in the fall of 1590, boats filled with dim
figures made their way along the coast of the wide inlet
near Edinburgh in Scotland called the Firth of Forth.
Those in the boats were drinking and merry, and when
they landed at North Berwick, east of Edinburgh, they
came ashore clasping hands and dancing a reel to the
music of a trumpet. They made their way through the
darkness to the door of the Kirk—the Church of Scotland—and filed in.

By that time any Scot could have told that they were
up to no good. The Kirk was as stern and narrow-
minded a religious organization as the Puritan Church
of England, and in some ways more so. Such a rabble
of roisterers had no business in one of its churches at
any time—let alone at midnight, when decent folk were
home and in bed.

Moreover, anyone connected with the Kirk would
have been paralyzed with horror at the scene inside the
church. It was completely dark except for a circle of

flickering candles surrounding the pulpit, where a man in a black coat and black hat who seemed the very symbol of evil stood.

Those from the boats all took seats. Then the mysterious figure spoke: "What have you done? How many have you won over to our organization?"

One by one they rose and told how many they had won over to the side of Satan. Then the figure demanded: "Is the image of the King ready?"

One of the women in the group came forward and gave the figure in the pulpit a waxen image. He took it, muttered an incantation over it and handed it back to the woman, Agnes Sampson, who then passed it among the others.

Meanwhile, the man in the pulpit announced, "King James the Sixth is ordered to be consumed."

Someone asked, "Why do you bear such hatred against the King?"

"By reason the King is the greatest enemy I have in the world."

The group met again in the North Berwick Kirk on Allhallows Eve, better known today as Halloween and long supposed to be a night when witches and evil spirits are abroad. The scene was the same—the circle of candles surrounding the pulpit in the blackness, and the sinister dark figure there before the gathering. After the same opening ceremonies, the leader demanded, "What success have you had in the matter of the waxen image?"

An old plowman spoke up in his Scottish dialect, with its thick burr: "Nothing ails the King yet."

There was a doubtful murmuring in the audience, and the figure in the pulpit quivered with rage over the failure of the waxen image to carry out his pronouncement that its witchcraft must destroy the King.

"How does it happen that our witchcraft can do no harm to the King?" demanded another in the audience.

"He is a man of God," growled the dark man.

But this failure was not the end of the dastardly plot that had been brewing against King James VI of Scotland. Those who met in the Kirk called themselves witches, and they firmly believed the man in the pulpit was the Devil.

Satan (if it was he) set some of these witches to work at other schemes to destroy not only the King but his young bride, the Princess Anne of Denmark. And when the story came out, it seemed to the people of Scotland, who practically all believed in witchcraft, that two of the witches' plans had nearly succeeded.

James VI of Scotland, later James I of England, was a strange character. He was slovenly, piggish in his manner and dirty, with morals of the lowest kind. Some people considered him a fool, but in many ways he was an excellent ruler. Many years after his death an English philosopher described him as "the wisest fool in Christendom."

Like most of his people, James believed in witchcraft and sorcery. Not only did he take a keen interest in it and in hunting out witches and exterminating them, but he was himself deathly afraid of such magic powers.

In 1589, when James was twenty-three, he decided he must marry so that he might have a son to succeed him on the Scottish throne. Arrangements were made for him to wed Princess Anne. In those days a royal marriage was often performed by proxy—that is, a king or prince would send a high-ranking nobleman to the bride's home to sign the marriage contract and stand in for the bridegroom at the wedding. This was done, and James, in England, became the husband of Anne, in Denmark, on November 23.

The new Queen would of course have to come to England. She set sail with a small Danish fleet; but in crossing the North Sea the ships were driven back by a storm and into the shelter of the Oslofjord, one of the great slashes the sea makes into the coast of Norway, and to the capital, Oslo.

King James, waiting expectantly for his bride, learned she had had to take refuge in Oslo. He sailed there at once, and after the royal couple had paid a visit to Anne's home at the royal palace in Copenhagen, they headed for Scotland. As their ships neared the coast a thick fog arose, always a peril at sea— especially in those days, when there were no radar and other instruments to warn a vessel against collision or running aground on rocks near the shore. Nevertheless, the royal fleet reached Scotland safely.

Up to that time no one suspected that witchcraft might be responsible for the dangers to the lives of the King and his new Queen. Then, suddenly, the whole devilish plot burst into the open.

Gellis Duncan, a maidservant in the home of a town official of Trevant, was accused of witchcraft by a neighbor. That was enough to cause her arrest, and torture to make her confess. The Scots were masters of torture when it came to forcing accused witches to tell of their actions.

Gellis Duncan was put to the torture with thumbscrews, instruments that were tightened on the thumbs until the pain grew unbearable. Most people would confess to anything under such agony, even though they knew it would mean an even more horrible death.

Although Gellis Duncan seems to have said nothing about the plot against the King and Queen, she did confess under torture that she had had some dealings with the Devil. And she also accused several other persons she said were also witches—three men and three women. All but one were arrested, thrown into Edinburgh's grim prison, the Tolbooth, and tortured.

One of the three accused women, Agnes Sampson, who had made the waxen image, revealed the fiendish plot against the lives of the King and Queen. Agnes, an intelligent woman, was known as the "Wise Wife of Keith," a village near North Berwick. Grave and matronly, she bore no resemblance to the hag most people think of in connection with a witch.

There must already have been suspicion that the accused witches had been plotting against King James' life, for Agnes was brought before the King and a group of Scottish nobles at Holyrood Palace. James tried to persuade her to confess, but she would say nothing.

"Take her to the Tolbooth and see if she will talk under the torture," commanded the King.

The Wise Wife of Keith was probably tortured with thumbscrews, though the Scots had far more fiendish ways of obtaining confessions from accused persons, such as the iron boot, which could be gradually tightened until it squeezed the bones of a victim's foot into a pulp. At any rate, when Agnes Sampson was brought back to Holyrood, she was ready to talk.

Talk she did, telling such fantastic stories about what had been going on that the King, according to the account he himself wrote of the plot against his life and that of Queen Anne, declared that all of those Agnes claimed had performed such miraculous things were "extreame lyars."

"Believe what I tell you, your Majesty," said Agnes. "I will tell you something that will prove to you that I speak the truth."

And taking the King aside, she whispered to him a private conversation he had had with his bride. James started in amazement and admitted Agnes' words were true.

The Wise Wife of Keith then told how she had first tried to kill the King.

"I took a black toad and hung it up by the heels for three days," she said, "and collected the venom that dripped from its mouth in an oyster shell. Then I kept the shell covered while I tried to get a piece of your Majesty's soiled linen."

"How would you get a piece of my linen?" asked the King, quivering with awe and curiosity.

"I hoped to get it from one of your Majesty's chamber attendants, John Kers," replied Agnes, "since we were old friends."

"What happened?" gasped the King.

"He would not give it to me, so I bewitched him to death," Agnes said calmly, and she added, "Believe me, your Majesty, if I could have had the linen and used it with the venom from my black toad, I could have bewitched you to death in such pain as if you had been lying on short thorns and the ends of needles."

The King, with his deathly fear of witchcraft, trembled.

Why did Agnes Sampson tell the King things that would surely doom her? Because she already knew she was going to die anyway, in a most horrible manner. And her speaking of the bedchamber attendant, John Kers, may explain how she knew what the King had said privately to Queen Anne. There are always eavesdroppers among servants, and the conversation may have been backstairs gossip, known to all the royal attendants.

The Wise Wife of Keith was not finished. "While your Majesty was in Denmark, after going to Oslo to fetch your bride, I took a cat and bound it to some of a dead man's joints. Some of the witches took it to sea and threw it overboard before Leith."

Leith, close to Edinburgh and today a part of the Scottish capital, is on the shore of the Firth of Forth, and the place where the King and Queen landed when they returned from Denmark.

"A very great tempest arose," Agnes Sampson went on. "There was a boat coming to Leith laden with the rich jewels and gifts that were to be given to your Queen when she arrived, but the boat sank in the storm."

Then the Wise Wife of Keith told of the meetings with the Devil and the attempts to take both King James's life and that of Queen Anne.

"Your Majesty would never have come safely from the sea save that your faith was greater than our magic." Agnes concluded. And with that she was hustled back to the Tolbooth to await her trial.

Of the six persons accused by Gellis Duncan, only one was not arrested. He was a nobleman of high rank, Francis Stewart, Earl of Bothwell, the King's cousin and his great favorite. James evidently did not believe the Earl could possibly be plotting against him.

Francis Stewart was as great a rogue as could be

found in all Scotland. He was forever getting into brawls, but the King always pardoned him. However, when Richard Graham, one of the two men who had been arrested, was examined and tortured, he told a strange story about Bothwell. Since Graham dealt in potions and charms, the Earl had sent for him.

Evidently Bothwell was afraid the King might suspect what he was up to, for Graham testified that the Earl had said to him, "I require your help to cause his Majesty the King to like me well."

"I gave his Lordship a potion and told him to touch the King's face with it when he had the chance," Graham continued.

But Bothwell was soon back. "Your potion had no effect on his Majesty," he complained. "Look you, fellow, you profess to deal in magic. The new Queen is about to embark from Denmark for Scotland. I require you to see that her ship is wrecked."

Graham said he replied. "That I cannot do, my Lord, but Agnes Sampson of Keith is a witch. She can perform such things."

What Agnes Sampson did if Bothwell went to see her is not known, but there was the undeniable fact that Queen Anne's fleet had barely escaped destruction off the coast of Norway. Surely, it seemed, after all she had told, the Wise Wife of Keith had had a hand in it. And there was the fog off the Scottish coast.

The five accused men and women were then tried. John Cunningham, a schoolmaster better known as Dr. Fian, came before the court first. He was charged with having dealings with Satan and his assistants, creating the storm that drove the Queen's ships into Oslo, arranging with the Devil to raise a fog that would cause the ship carrying the royal couple to be wrecked on the

Scottish coast and acting as clerk to the Devil at the meeting in the North Berwick Kirk. He was found guilty, bound to a stake on Castle Hill in Edinburgh and strangled, and his body burned.

Agnes Sampson was tried on January 27, 1591. There were fifty-three charges against her. She suffered the same fate as Dr. Fian.

They brought Barbara Napier before the court next, but the jury did not find the evidence against her convincing, and they acquitted her on May 8.

The King was beside himself with fear over all that had come out in the examinations. When he heard that Barbara Napier had been acquitted, he was enraged. He wrote the clerk of the court, telling him it was the royal command that the judge sentence the jury to death. He also ordered Barbara Napier to be strangled and burned. Then he stormed into the courtroom, ordered the jury indicted for "manufactured and Wilfull Errour" and took over the judge's bench himself. When the jurymen fell to their knees, begging mercy, he graciously pardoned them.

Whether he had his revenge upon Barbara Napier is not known. Everything was made ready for her execution. The stake was set up on Castle Hill, and wooden barrels, coal, heather and gunpowder piled around it. But before Barbara could be led to execution, her friends set up a great outcry, saying she was about to have a child.

In such cases it was customary to postpone an execution rather than kill an innocent child before it was born. This was done, but whether Barbara was finally strangled and burned the records do not show, though it seems likely she was.

The third woman, Euphemia MacCalyan of Clifton-hall, was brought to trial June 9, 1591. She fought for her life with all the help she could get. Six lawyers defended her, and the trial lasted four days. The jury foreman was convinced Euphemia was innocent, so he was chased from the courtroom. Even then, the jurors debated all night before they finally found her guilty. The judge was less doubtful, and after all the trouble Euphemia had given him she was condemned to a slower and more agonizing death. She too was burned at the stake, but alive.

Richard Graham was also convicted of witchcraft and sorcery and burned alive at the stake.

From all that had come out in the examinations and trials, it was now evident that the dark figure in the North Berwick Kirk had not been the Devil, but actually Francis Stewart, Earl of Bothwell. He had good reason to be rid of the King, since he might then seize the throne of Scotland because he had royal blood. As for the young Queen, she would have to be out of the way too, lest she have a son to succeed King James.

Bothwell was brought before a secret council of royal advisers and sent to the Tolbooth to await trial. But he managed to escape, and for some years proved to be an eel-like and daring fugitive. He frightened the wits out of the Lord Chancellor of Scotland by going boldly to the chancellor's house, threatening him and then vanishing.

They took away his titles of Earl of Bothwell and Lord Hailes, seized all his property and made him an outlaw. He retaliated with an audacious attack on the royal palace of Holyrood in Edinburgh. Later he attacked another royal palace north of Glasgow. A force sent after him hunted him down and killed his men, but the former Earl slipped away to freedom.

Finally, Bothwell attacked Holyrood Palace again, throwing King James into such mortal terror that he pardoned the rascally Stewart and restored his titles and belongings. Although the Earl had to be brought to trial, he was promptly acquitted of all charges. James believed Bothwell did have magic powers and was willing to humiliate himself in this way so that Bothwell would use no more witchcraft against him.

But the Earl's ambitions for the throne were finished. The Queen now had a son, who was the rightful heir to the crown. Bothwell left England and died in poverty twelve years later in Italy.

It is not strange, after all this, that King James took great interest in witchcraft. His insatiable curiosity caused him to write a book about it, *Demonology,* first published in 1597. It had a powerful influence in stirring the great flood of persecutions, trials and frightful executions in Scotland, England and America in the seventeenth century.

The Scottish Kirk, too, played an important part in the dreadful persecutions in Scotland, just as the Church of Rome was largely responsible for the even greater number of witch hunts on the Continent of Europe.

An accused Scottish witch had little chance of escaping death because of the unfairness of the whole procedure against her. One outstanding instance of this took place in 1629, when a woman was brought to trial in the county of East Lothian, just north of Edinburgh.

"Isobel Young," said Sir Thomas Hope, the prosecutor, "is it not true that twenty-nine years ago you stopped a water mill by witchcraft?"

"No!" cried the accused woman. "I did not do it!

24

The mill just broke down. Any mill will break down."

"And did you not, in this year of 1629, put a curse upon a man of your village, causing him to lose the use of his legs?"

"He was lame before I cursed him!"

Later, the prosecutor argued before the judge that Isobel Young's denials were contrary to the charges against her. The judge upheld him. The Scottish witchcraft law of the time said that confession was not necessary. If an accused person had a general reputation as a witch, that was proof enough. So Isobel Young was convicted of witchcraft, strangled and then burned.

The first notable witchcraft trial, that of the North Berwick witches and involving the plot against King James's life, had a tremendous effect in Scotland. So did his famous book, *Demonology*.

The Kirk does not seem to have wanted to take any blame that might arise from executions following witch trials, although its General Assembly ordered the ministers to search out witches and see that they were punished. Usually the Privy Council of Scotland appointed a commission to investigate a witchcraft case. If there was enough evidence, a court was then convened with a jury of fifteen men, and the commissioners acted as judges. Sometimes, however, the ministers and elders of the Kirk met to draw up charges of witchcraft, and then turned the case over to a civil court to sentence the accused ones. All costs of the trial and execution had to be paid by the accused persons, or their families if they were put to death.

Scottish witchcraft law did make one concession not common in most European countries. As already described in the case of Euphemia MacCalyan, in Scotland an accused witch was permitted to have the aid of a lawyer. Unfortunately, however, most of these wretched people were too poor to afford one.

The Scots made a barbarous science out of torture to obtain evidence against accused witches, since a confession was preferred even though the law did not always require it as proof. They used the vicious methods common in other countries, but they also had their own especially fiendish ones.

A Scottish invention was to put a hair shirt steeped in vinegar on an accused witch. This caused the skin to be pulled off the victim's body.

In 1596, Alison Balfour, who was called a notorious witch, was arrested. In order to obtain evidence, they also seized her husband, her son, her daughter and a family servant, Thomas Palpa.

All were imprisoned and tortured in Edinburgh Castle. Alison Balfour was placed in the "caspie claws," an iron vise used to crush a suspected witch's arms. While she was undergoing this frightfulness, she had to watch her aged husband as they piled seven hundred pounds of iron bars on him. Her son was placed in the notorious "Spanish boots," in which wedges were driven, tightening them until the leg bones were smashed. With Alison's son they used fifty-seven blows to drive the wedges in. Meanwhile, they tortured the Balfours' seven-year-old-daughter with thumbscrews.

As for the servant, Thomas Palpa, he was kept in the caspie claws for 264 hours, and whipped with a lash that flayed all the skin off his back. Though the others were not convicted, Alison Balfour and Thomas Palpa were burned at the stake.

The story of the Pittenweem witches is one of the most

pitiful of all Scottish witchcraft persecutions because of those accused—wrongfully, by a spiteful mischief-maker, as was proved too late—none were convicted but three died because of the horrible conditions of their imprisonment, torture and persecution.

The troublemaker was sixteen-year-old Patrick Morton, who worked for his father, a blacksmith, in the small seaport village of Pittenweem in eastern Scotland. In 1704 a woman named Beatrix Laing asked him to forge her some nails. He told her he was too busy, and she threatened vengeance upon him.

Soon afterward, Patrick saw Beatrix throwing some hot coals into water. He took this as a sign that Beatrix Laing was a witch putting a curse on him, and that he was going to die. He began to feel weak in his arms and legs, lost his appetite and started to waste away. He had trouble breathing, his stomach swelled, he had spasms in which his body became rigid and he would swallow his tongue.

He may have had epilepsy, since some of his symptoms were of that disease. Also, as so often happened in witchcraft cases, his symptoms were probably connected with autosuggestion. He convinced himself so completely that he was going to die that his life was endangered.

Patrick showed marks on his arm where the witches had pinched him, for he believed Beatrix Laing had other witch friends who were helping her. He told who they were, and they were all arrested and imprisoned.

Beatrix Laing was tortured. They kept her awake for five days and nights until she confessed, but immediately afterward she denied everything. The authorities then put her in the stocks—a wooden framework

27

with holes for the arms and legs, set up in a public
place, in which a victim was placed and often enough
taunted and pelted with rotten eggs and fruit or stones.
Next they placed her in a dark dungeon called the
"Thieves' Hole," where she was kept alone for five
months.

However, since her husband was a man of some
influence, she was finally let off with a fine of £8. But
the people of Pittenweem were so enraged at her because they were sure she was a witch that she dared
not go home. For some time she wandered through the
countryside, homeless and wanted by no one, and at
last she died.

Another of the accused persons, Thomas Brown,
met a worse end than if he had been executed. They
starved him to death in a dungeon.

A third accused witch, Janet Cornfoot, was tortured
and confessed, but then, like Beatrix Laing, she retracted all she had said. They were afraid to put her
back in jail lest she convince some of the rest to deny
their confessions also, so they put her in the church
steeple, but she escaped and found refuge for a time in
the house of one of the accused persons.

On the night of January 30, 1705, a mob burst into
the house, bound Janet, beat her and hauled her down
to the seashore. There, in the bitter winter night, they
strung her on a rope between the land and a ship
anchored just offshore, swung her to and fro and pelted
her with stones. At last they brought her back ashore,
beat her again and covered her with a door and piled
stones on it until she was crushed to death.

Not long afterward it was proved that Patrick Morton's charges against the accused people were false—
too late to save innocent Beatrix Laing, Thomas Brown,

and Janet Cornfoot. Nothing was ever done to punish those of the mob who had killed Janet.

A number of estimates were made of how many witches were burned in Scotland, all in the thousands, but about four thousand is considered the closest figure. All this took place in a little over a single century.

3

THE "WITCH-FINDER GENERALL"

In 1644 a forty-year-old lawyer named Matthew Hopkins was living in Manningtree, a village in the county of Essex in southeastern England. He had been born in neighboring Suffolk County, and was the son of a minister.

Matthew was one of the wickedest and cruelest monsters who ever lived. Like most people then, he believed in witchcraft, and was doubtless familiar with King James I's *Demonology*. Since he does not seem to have been doing well in his profession or enjoying it, he invented a new occupation—professional witchfinder.

When Matthew Hopkins took up this gruesome profession, King James had been dead for nineteen years and King Charles I sat on the throne. But the witchcraft persecutions, much influenced by James I's book and by the growing power of the Puritans in England, with their harsh religious beliefs that witchcraft had to be exterminated, were still in full swing. Hopkins saw in this a chance to gratify his lust for cruelty.

Hopkins wrote a book, *The Discovery of Witches,* published in 1647, telling of his experiences in the years 1644 to 1646. In it he told what started him on his wicked career, mentioning the Manningtree witches of the village, who "in March, 1644 . . . with diverse other adjacent Witches of other towns . . . every six weeks in the night (being always a Friday night) had their meetings close to his [he meant himself] house, and had their severall solemne sacrifices there offered to the Devil."

Did he really see this meeting, and were those who attended really witches? They may well have called themselves witches, and Matthew Hopkins may have spied on them. At any rate, some months later he decided to go into the business of hunting down witches. He obtained an assistant, John Stearne, and in 1645 began his new profession.

First he accused Elizabeth Clarke of bewitching a tailor's wife. She was arrested, and for three nights Hopkins and Stearne "watched" her. This was one of the methods he used to detect a witch. The suspected person was placed on a stool, bound if she resisted and observed closely for at least twenty-four hours. During that time she was given nothing to eat or drink. If some insect flew into the room the watchers tried to kill it. If it escaped, this was proof that it was the suspected person's familiar or imp, by which she worked magic through the Devil. Matthew Hopkins was the inventor of this test.

They watched Elizabeth Clarke for three days and three nights. At last, on the fourth night, exhausted by hunger and no sleep, she admitted the Devil had appeared to her.

31

"In what shape did he appear?" Hopkins demanded.

"As a proper gentleman," replied Elizabeth. "He had three imps with him. One was a little white dog with sandy spots named Jamara. There was a greyhound called Vinegar Tom too." She also spoke of an animal resembling a skunk, but Hopkins was later unable to remember its name.

At the trial, Hopkins testified that he had seen these Devil's imps himself, as well as a black cat three times the size of an ordinary one, named "Sacke and Sugar." He said the greyhound chased the cat, but it got away, and the dog came back "shaking and trembling exceedingly."

In her confession, Elizabeth Clarke implicated other women. All were arrested, and their trials, with Elizabeth's, were held at the assize, the county court of Essex, in Chelmsford. In *The Discovery of Witches,* Hopkins wrote proudly that "in our Hundred [a division of an English county or shire in those times] in Essex, twenty-nine were condemned at once, and brought twenty-five miles to be hanged."

Twenty-nine witches—women who had sold their souls to the Devil—hanged at one time! As the fame of Hopkins' success in hunting witches spread, other places began to be uneasy. People spoke of strange things that had happened lately in their own towns or villages. There must be witches about, but who were they? This man Hopkins of Manningtree seemed to have an uncanny ability at smelling out witches. Would it not be a good idea to invite him to come and find who was causing these queer happenings?

In many an English town the authorities decided to ask Matthew Hopkins and his assistant to come there.

Hopkins was glad to oblige. And with his career well launched, he proclaimed himself the "Witch-Finder Generall" of England.

The cost was cheap enough. Hopkins himself boasted of that when he wrote of it: "He demands but 20 shillings a town and doth sometimes ride 20 miles for that, and hath no more for all his charges thither and back (and it may be he stayes a week there) and finds three or four witches, or if it be but one, cheap enough, and this is the greate sum he takes to maintain his Companie with three horses." His "Companie" was himself, Stearne and a female searcher to examine accused women for witch marks.

Twenty shillings was indeed a small sum for all this, even though that amount was worth far more in the seventeenth century than today; but Hopkins was not in this evil business to make money. He loved cruelty, and the satisfaction he got out of seeing wretched people hanged by his own doings was reward enough.

At first Hopkins and his companions roved in that part of England northeast of London, in the shires of Essex, Suffolk and Norfolk. But as the Witch-Finder Generall's fame spread, he took longer journeys.

Hopkins made a science out of witch hunting. He had four main tests for searching out a witch. In the first one, if the suspected witch was a woman, as most were, she was stripped naked and searched for a witch mark by the Witch-Finder Generall's female assistant. If there was any doubt whether something discovered on a person's body was a real witch mark, it was pricked with a pin, needle or a special instrument called a witch-pricker. If the mark did not bleed or the accused person felt no pain, it was proof of witch-craft.

Some marks, like warts, did not bleed easily, nor did the person feel pain when pricked lightly. And examiners like Hopkins had their tricks too. One was to go through the motions—a quick jab, perhaps, that did not really go into the suspected witch mark at all. And some of the witch-pricking instruments had a blade fastened with a spring or some similar contraption, so that when it was applied the blade was drawn back and did not penetrate the mark.

The second test was watching, used on Elizabeth Clarke. After being watched, one old woman confessed she was a witch and had four flies in her room who were her imps. She named them: Ile-mauzer, Pyewackett, Pecke-in-the-Crowne and Griezzell-Greedigut. "No mortal," said Hopkins, "could invent such names."

The third test was even more cruel. The victim was made to walk for hours until her feet were blistered and she was so exhausted she would confess anything. Hopkins also put a man, the vicar of a church in Suffolk, to this test. The clergyman, John Lowes, was nearly eighty years old and, of course, in no condition to stand such a frightful ordeal. He soon confessed he was a male witch—a warlock or wizard.

"I have two imps," he told Matthew Hopkins, according to the Witch-Finder Generall. "One day I was walking with them along the shore and saw some ships sailing off the coast. I commissioned one of my imps to sink one of the vessels."

"What ship was it?" demanded Hopkins.

"She was from Ipswich," the old man said. "I picked her out from the others."

"Did she sink?"

"Aye," replied Mr. Lowes, "she sank at once and fourteen men perished."

34

"What of the other vessels?"

"They paid no heed and sailed on."

Matthew Hopkins, if he did not invent it himself, accepted the ridiculous story without question and without making any investigation before John Lowes' trial, nor did he check the stories the poor old man is supposed to have told of other strange and evil things he had done. So no one knows whether there were any ships or if one did sink, and if so, that it was the work of Satan and his imp—or why none of the other ships came to the aid of the stricken vessel.

Perhaps because he knew he was doomed and was defiant, Mr. Lowes also said, according to Hopkins, "I have a charm that will keep me out of gaol [jail]." If he did have one it did him no good, for he was arrested and quickly condemned. More likely, Matthew Hopkins invented the story to make even more certain the old man would be executed.

On the gallows, when he was hanged at Fralingham in Suffolk, Mr. Lowes denied everything he had confessed and claimed that he was innocent. This is a strange story, and parts of it make little sense, but there is small doubt that the clergyman was one of Matthew Hopkins' victims who were completely innocent. Quite likely his mind was affected by his torture, and this could have made him tell the strange stories.

The fourth test was Hopkins' favorite, and one much used, not only in England but in America when the witchcraft delusion spread there. This was called "swimming" a suspected witch. The poor creature's right hand was tied to the left foot and the left hand to the right foot, and the victim wrapped in a blanket and placed in a pond. If the accused witch floated, it was proof that the water would have none of her and she was a witch. If she sank she was innocent. In some cases a rope was tied to her to bring her to the surface in case she sank, but it did not always work in time. And sometimes, if a suspected witch survived after sinking and was thus proved innocent, they repeated the test, often several times, just to be sure. And of course if the poor victim drowned, her family and friends had the great joy of knowing she died innocent of witchcraft.

Hopkins did not invent the swimming test, for it was used before his time as well as afterward. It had been particularly favored by King James of Scotland and England. True, while he was James I of England, the King began to have doubts about the guilt of some who had been hanged, strangled or burned, but the damage had been done and the murderous persecutions went on after his death.

Matthew Hopkins became so famous that he received invitations to visit towns farther afield and rid them of the plague of witches. He went into Huntingdonshire and Bedfordshire, both north of London, and even to Worcester in the west country.

The Witch-Finder Generall's assistant, Stearne, wrote that about two hundred witches, most of them women, were executed during Hopkins' campaign. In a single day, at Bury St. Edmunds in Suffolk, eighteen condemned witches were hanged as a result of Hopkins' witch hunting. He went into Kent, southeast of London, and sniffed out witches. They confessed they had sold their souls to the Devil for money, but he turned out to be very stingy. They said he never gave them more than a shilling for their services, and more often it was only sixpence or even threepence. For accepting this fortune three were executed at Faversham.

Matthew Hopkins made a mistake when he went to Huntingdonshire in 1646. He hunted down many witches, but John Gaule, the vicar of Staughton, smelled a rat. Strangely enough, this clergyman of the Church of England, the enemy of the Roman Catholic Church, not only believed in witches but declared many popes, friars, nuns and priests had been notorious witches. Yet he wrote a pamphlet in 1646 denouncing Hopkins as a fraud.

"Every old woman with a wrinkled face, a furr'd brow, a hairy lip, a gobber [protruding] tooth, a squint eye, having a rugged coate on her back, a skullcap on her head, a spindle in her hand, a dog or cat by her side, is not only suspected but pronounced for a witch," Gaule wrote.

Hopkins was enraged. He wrote an insolent letter to the town authorities of Staughton, offering to visit there if he was entertained with all the respect and honor he deserved, and provided they were not supporters, like their vicar, of witches and "such cattle." The authorities did not answer.

But Gaule's attack had a powerful effect. Other clergymen came to their senses and spoke out against the Witch-Finder Generall. Hints were made to the judge of the Norfolk Assize that Hopkins himself was a witch.

The Witch-Finder Generall returned to Essex in 1647 to find himself the target of abuse and charges on all sides. He was openly accused of witchcraft. A mob gathered and went after him but he managed to escape.

There are stories that Matthew Hopkins himself was

given the swimming test, floated and was hanged, but they do not appear to be true. However, he did die in 1647, though how is not know. A record in Mistley, near his home in Manningtree, states that he was buried there on August 12, 1647.

His assistant, Stearne, did not agree with the outcry against Hopkins. After the Witch-Finder Generall's death he published a pamphlet defending him and calling him a model of virtue and holiness.

What did this murderous creature look like? A drawing forms the frontispiece of his book, *The Discovery of Witches,* showing him with two of his victims and their imps. It reveals little beyond his dress, the costume of the time, which we associate with that of the Puritans—a high-crowned hat, knee breeches, one of the short jackets called doublets, a cloak and boots with flaring tops that come all the way to his knees. He has been described as a stupid-looking man with bulging eyes, loose lips, a low, apelike forehead, almost no chin, protruding ears and a cunning leer, but whatever he really looked like, the world was rid of one of its most evil men when he died.

4

MORE ENGLISH WITCHES

Witchcraft in England began in the early centuries of its history. Its country people in those bygone days were ignorant and superstitious, and the mixture of races that made up its population all had their ancient legends of witches, sorcerers, fairies and magic. There are records of witchcraft trials as far back as the year 1209, and as early as the tenth century death was the penalty. But as in other European countries, witch hunting reached its peak in the sixteenth and seventeenth centuries.

Strangely enough, during the period before 1563 ordinary persons accused of witchcraft usually got off with light sentences, while accused members of the nobility were in serious trouble. The reason was that, in the case of noblemen, treason was so often involved —plotting against the ruler or government—a crime that was always punishable by death if it could be proved.

A few good things can be said of English witchcraft—

if indeed anything good can be said about it. No convicted witch was ever burned in England. Most were hanged, though a nobleman was usually granted the more honorable death of being beheaded. Nor were there mass executions of the kind that took place in some countries on the Continent of Europe, where hundreds of condemned witches were often burned within a short time. The largest number of convicted witches executed at one time was the twenty-nine hanged at Chelmsford during the time of Matthew Hopkins' witch hunts.

There was some torture of suspected witches in England, but nowhere near that of neighboring Scotland or the countries on the Continent. Estimates of the number of witches executed in England vary greatly, but about a thousand between 1566 and 1685 seems the most reasonable figure.

Perhaps the most pathetic witchcraft case during this time was that of Alice Samuel, her husband and daughter. They lived in Warboys, in the pleasant countryside of Huntingdonshire in eastern England. Mrs. Samuel was seventy-six years old, and she and her husband were poverty-stricken people.

Another prominent resident of Warboys was Robert Throckmorton, a squire, or country gentleman who owned a good-sized estate. He had five daughters whose ages were between nine and fifteen.

This case, known as that of the Warboys witches, was curiously like that of the witchcraft persecutions in Salem, Massachusetts, a century later because children were the accusers of the suspected witches. In November, 1589, Jane Throckmorton, about ten years old, suddenly fell ill of a strange sickness. She would sneeze for a half an hour without stopping, go into a kind of trance with her body so rigid she could not move, then come out of it and shake all over as if she had palsy. Her parents were so alarmed that they sent for two distinguished doctors at Cambridge University, about twenty miles away.

The news of Jane's affliction spread through Warboys. Old Mrs. Samuel was so sorry to hear of it that she called at the Throckmorton house. She was stunned when Jane, seeing her there, cried, "Look where the old witch sitteth! Did you ever see one more like a witch than she is?"

Squire Throckmorton and his wife thought Jane's outburst was due to her ailment, but soon Jane's four other sisters came down with the same sort of malady. And they too said Mrs. Samuel was a witch.

One of the two doctors from Cambridge then declared that the girls must be suffering from some sort of witchcraft. Squire and Mrs. Throckmorton still could not believe that such a kindly, inoffensive soul as Mrs. Samuel could be responsible, but they finally had her seized and brought before the children, who instantly fell to the ground in fits of agony. Even more revealing was that they scratched Mrs. Samuel's hands. It was the belief in England that if a witch could be made to bleed, the person bewitched by her would recover.

The girls again accused the old lady of being a witch. "It is not so!" she cried. "It is all due to their wantonness!"—meaning their wickedness. The truth doubtless was that Jane Throckmorton was afflicted with epilepsy, in which a person often goes into fits, and that her sisters, seeing all the attention she was getting wanted some for themselves and imitated her.

The Throckmortons and others in Warboys now began to think Mrs. Samuel really must be a witch. The old woman was brought back several times, and in each case the girls went into their strange fits. Then, suddenly, the opposite began to happen. The sisters would be tormented, but the moment they saw Mrs. Samuel they would be calm again.

So the old lady was forced to come and live with the Throckmortons so that the girls would continue to be quiet. Jane's four sisters must have been little imps, for they tormented Mrs. Samuel constantly with accusations. They insisted that they could see one of her familiars through which she worked the Devil's magic right in the room, leaping and skipping about. Finally, nearly a year after the trouble started, the wife of Sir Henry Cromwell called on the Throckmortons, since they lived nearby. Lady Cromwell was high-and-mighty, and a vixen too, for when she saw Mrs. Samuel there she flew into a rage.

"You are a witch!" Lady Cromwell screamed. And she tore off the old lady's bonnet, seized her by the hair and snatched out a great handful of it.

"Burn this!" she commanded.

Miserable old Mrs. Samuel dared not offend anyone of noble rank, but she said meekly, "Madam, why do you use me thus? I never did you any harm, yet."

Lady Cromwell was terribly upset. The witch had said "yet." What did that mean? Having convinced herself she would be bewitched, she began to have frightful nightmares and her health failed. Fifteen months later she died.

Meanwhile, the fits suffered by the Throckmorton children returned in spite of Mrs. Samuel's presence in the family. Finally, the old lady pleaded with them to stop—and magically they did.

This did not help Mrs. Samuel at all. It made the Throckmortons sure she was really a witch, and they charged her with it. The startling effect the old lady's words had had in stopping the children's fits put her into such a state that she began to believe she was a witch.

At last she went to Squire Throckmorton. "Oh, sir," she faltered, "I have been the cause of all the trouble to your children. Good master, forgive me."

They brought in the local minister, who urged Mrs. Samuel to confess in public, and she did. But next day, after her agitation had calmed down and fear of hanging had replaced it, she denied everything. Nevertheless she was arrested.

They took her before the Bishop of Lincoln to be examined. The wretched old woman was now so terrified that she not only confessed again to being a witch, but named some of her familiars. By that time the cruel Throckmorton children had accused Mrs. Samuel's husband John and her daughter Agnes of witchcraft.

All three were charged with the murder of Lady Cromwell by witchcraft and tried in the shire town of Huntingdon. Not only were the tales told by the children used as evidence, but several country people flocked in to testify that she had caused some of their cattle to die.

All three of the Samuel family were convicted and hanged.

Another famous witch trial in England was that of the Lancashire witches. It took place in 1612, while James I was on the throne. The scene was one of the wildest parts of England, Pendle Forest in Lancashire, near the border of Yorkshire.

There is little doubt that the two old women accused, both then about eighty years old, one blind, the other going blind, did belong to a coven of witches who met in the dark glades of Pendle Forest. In fact, they were known in the region by their "witch names." The one who had gone blind in 1612, Elizabeth Southerne, was called Old Demdike, and the other, Anne Whittle, by the name of Old Chattox. Old Demdike lived in a place called Malking Tower in the forest.

The reputations of both the women were bad. One chronicler of the time says that in 1612, when she was arrested, Old Demdike had been a witch for fifty years, "a generall agent for the Devill in all these parts," and claimed she had committed many murders and other devilish crimes.

Both Old Demdike and Old Chattox had children whom they instructed in the arts of witchcraft, and Demdike even taught them to two of her grandchildren.

Some strange doings went on in Pendle Forest. There was serious trouble between the family of Robert Nutter, who owned a large estate, and that of one of his tenants, Thomas Redfearne, who had married Old Chattox's daughter Anne. The quarrel was complicated, but Redfearne asked his mother-in-law, Old Chattox, to do away with Robert Nutter's grandson, also named Robert, who had caused the trouble.

One day Old Demdike was going past the Redfearnes' house and saw Old Chattox and her daughter making "pictures" (images) of the younger Robert Nutter, his wife and his father, Christopher Nutter. Soon afterward, young Robert became ill.

He said to Christopher Nutter, "Father, I am sure I am bewitched by Old Chattox and her daughter. I pray you cause her to be laid [imprisoned] in Lancaster Castle."

Christopher Nutter pooh-poohed the idea. "You are a foolish lad," he said. But young Robert still believed he was bewitched. A little later he made a journey to Wales, and while he was returning he died in Cheshire.

It caused a great stir in Pendle Forest, but since Old Chattox was a fellow witch, Old Demdike did nothing about the "pictures" of Robert and the other two Nutters. However, a quarrel soon arose between the families of the two old women. Some clothing belonging to Old Demdike's daughter, Alison Device, was stolen. Later on, Anne Redfearne, Old Chattox's daughter, was seen wearing some of the missing things.

Alison Device was infuriated, and she charged Anne Redfearne with stealing the clothes. But Alison's husband, John, had a terrible fear of witchcraft.

"Do nothing more about this," he warned his wife. "I will take care of it."

And with that he went to Old Chattox and offered to give her a certain amount of meal each year if she would not harm his family with her black witchcraft. The old crone agreed. Later on, however, John Device was unable to make his payments of grain. And soon afterward he died.

Old Demdike, Old Chattox, Anne Redfearne and Alison Device were arrested. Perhaps to escape undergoing an ordeal, Alison accused both her own grandmother, Old Demdike, and Old Chattox. She said she was sure Old Demdike had bewitched a child whose father had refused to let the old woman come on his land in Pendle Forest, and the child had died.

The other three also made confessions. Probably they were threatened with or went through some kind of ordeal, although their "voluntary confessions" were introduced as evidence at their trials. All accused each other of witchcraft and murder, and were put into Lancaster Castle to await trial.

As a result of the "confessions," twenty persons were accused of witchcraft and thrown into the castle dungeon. This caused consternation among the other witches of Pendle Forest and the surrounding countryside. They held a big meeting at Malking Tower on Good Friday in 1612 and made plans to rescue the prisoners.

They decided to kill the jailer at Lancaster Castle, free the prisoners and blow up the castle. They scheduled another meeting to carry out the plot, but a rumor of it reached a justice of the peace, who arrested many of the plotters on April 27, 1612, and sent them to Lancaster. Others who were in the scheme managed to flee to safety before they could be taken.

Ten of the accused witches were hanged, including Old Chattox and her daughter, Anne Redfearne, Old Demdike's daughters Elizabeth and Alison Device and her son James. Two of the others were sentenced to spend a year in jail and appear four times in public in the pillory, similar to the stocks already described except that a person stood instead of sat, and had his hands and head locked into holes in a frame. Old Demdike cheated the gallows by dying in prison before she could be executed. The rest were acquitted.

This is one case where at least the principals seem to have practiced witchcraft. Whether they really succeeded in the murders and other deviltry by means of their black arts is something that will never be known, but they may have used poison to kill those who died.

Among other famous English witchcraft cases, one of the best known is that of the St. Osyth witches in 1582. It took place in wild country too, on the coast of Essex in eastern England. Unlike Pendle Forest, however, this is a lowland region of tidal flats and meadowlands that are often partly submerged at high tide—lonely and desolate, uninhabited except for villages back from the shore lowlands. It was a region for witchcraft to flourish in, and it did in the late sixteenth century.

The chief character in this witchcraft drama was Ursula (or Urseley) Kempe, a woman of bad reputation. She professed to be able to "unwitch" bewitched people, and her neighbors were suspicious of her.

Ursula was also a midwife and sometimes nursed small children as well. One day Grace Thurlow asked Ursula to nurse her child, but was refused. This later proved to be a serious mistake for Ursula, since Grace was a servant in the household of the local judge, Brian Darcy.

Soon afterward, Grace Thurlow's baby fell out of its cradle and died. Grace was now sure Ursula had bewitched the child, but did not, or dared not, do anything about it.

A little later Grace Thurlow had a "lameness in her bones." Convinced that she too was bewitched, she went to Ursula Kempe.

"I will unwitch you if you will pay me twelvepence," said Ursula.

Grace promised to pay if her lameness went away. Sure enough it did, and Ursula Kempe demanded the twelvepence. Grace said she could not pay it. "I am a poor and needy woman," she pleaded.

With that, Grace's lameness returned. She went to

the justice of the peace in the village and charged Ursula with being a witch. When Ursula was arrested, she denied it.

"I only unwitch those who are bewitched," she said. "I learned how to do it ten years ago from a woman who is now dead."

Nevertheless, they put her in jail. Judge Darcy, Grace Thurlow's employer, examined Ursula's eight-year-old son, who was considered a bad boy and who did not hesitate to testify against his mother. He said she had four familiars. She used two to make people lame, and the other two to commit murder. Ursula then confessed it was all true, and named four other women who were involved with her. How the confession was obtained is not known, but from all that happened it would seem that the woman was mentally ill.

Before the case was finished, sixteen persons were implicated. Judge Darcy accepted without question practically everything that was said by witnesses at the trial. He promised mercy to some of the accused witches, but he broke his promise and all were hanged.

Before the witchcraft delusion had run its course in England, there were opponents who spoke out against it, as there were in the case of Matthew Hopkins, the Witch-Finder Generall. Reginald Scott, a gentleman who lived in Kent, believed in witches, but he was outraged at the injustice of the St. Osyth witch trials. He wrote a book exposing some of the frauds that were going on.

Another man who saw through the witchcraft delusion was a clergyman, George Gifford. He wrote two books about it in the hope of ending the punishment of innocent women, since he considered most of the evidence against them to be rubbish. Still another foe of witchcraft, Thomas Ady, denounced the "swimming" of witches, witch marks and other ridiculous methods of exposing witches.

It took courage in those days to write books and pamphlets against the persecution of suspected witches, for such writers made themselves prey for the witch hunters. Yet they did, and their efforts had a powerful effect in bringing the terrible curse of the witchcraft delusions to an end.

5

JOHANN SCHÜLER AND WITCHCRAFT IN GERMANY

It seems strange that a region as lovely as that known in the seventeenth century as the district of Wetterau in south-central Germany should have been the scene of some of the most savage and unjustified witch trials of that time in a country where ferocious tortures and executions were commonplace. It is one of the most beautiful and peaceful-looking parts of Germany. Yet of all Europe, including Britain, the witch hunts, tortures and executions in that country were the most fiendish.

The River Main, rising in Bavaria, twists and turns through the Wetterau region on its way to join the mighty River Rhine at Mainz. The valley is edged on all sides by hills, mountains, forests and hillside farmlands with vineyards and orchards, and the Main flows past the ancient cities of Frankfurt, Würzburg and Bamberg.

Germany was then a loosely tied group of states, a part of the Holy Roman Empire, which at an earlier time had included almost all of central Europe. Each state was ruled by a prince, a lord or sometimes more than one lord, most of them under the domination of the Holy Roman Emperor. Some of the larger places were free cities and towns, however, owing no allegiance to the emperor; the others were imperial cities and towns, ruled by the emperor through the princes or lords of the states where they were located.

Lindheim, in the Wetterau district of the state of Hesse-Darmstadt, was an imperial town. Under the Holy Roman Emperor, who at this particular time in the seventeenth century was Leopold I, Hesse-Darmstadt was governed by a group of men called the *Herrenschaft*. They included Baron von Oynhausen, the High Bailiff or Protector of the Brunswick-Lunenberg district; Hartmann von Rossenbach, the dean or head of the cathedral of Würzburg, not far from Lindheim, and several other noblemen. None of the *Herrenschaft* lived in Lindheim, and they left its government to a chief magistrate named Geiss.

Johann Schüler, a miller, and his wife lived in Lindheim at this time. Schüler had worked hard at his trade, saved his money and bought land, and in 1663 was one of the wealthy and most respected citizens of the town.

Witch hunting had already been raging in Germany for over a century. It had reached its height between 1618 and 1648, during the Thirty Years' War. In Strassburg alone, five thousand witches had been burned in the twenty years between 1615 and 1635. There had been witch trials and executions in the Wetterau district, but they had been banned in 1653, after the war ended.

Thus the citizens of Lindheim lived for eight years without the dread of being accused of witchcraft. But in 1661 the magistrate Geiss went to Baron von Oynhausen of the *Herrenschaft*.

"Lindheim is swarming with witches, your Lordship," he reported.

"How do you know this, Herr [Mr.] Geiss?" asked the baron.

"Curses have been laid upon citizens who have offended the witches," replied Geiss. "Some have had livestock die, others have themselves sickened and died or have been made lame. And the witches have caused much other mischief and wickedness."

"What do you suggest be done about this, Herr Geiss?"

"'The majority of the citizens are much upset and offer, if his Lordship expressed a desire to burn these witches, gladly to provide the wood and pay all the costs."

This was a lie. Geiss was a typical German soldier of the time, brutal, bloodthirsty and greedy. He had fought in the Thirty Years' War and no doubt had done his share of the looting, burning and killing of that long struggle. Now that peace had come, he yearned for more frightfulness.

He saw in his proposal to von Oynhausen a chance for big profits, since the lands and possessions of condemned witches were always forfeited to the government. Geiss expected to get a generous share of this booty.

Fawning upon the baron, Geiss added cunningly, "His Lordship might also acquire much money thereby, so that the bridge as well as the church could be brought into good repair. Furthermore, his Lordship might also have so much wealth that in future his officials might be so much better paid." He was thinking of himself, of course.

Geiss' crafty insinuations about the money to be made from a witch hunt in Lindheim convinced the baron that it would be a good idea. He conferred with the other members of the *Herrenschaft* about it. They too, including the reverend Dean von Rosenbach agreed.

Having gained the permission of his superior, the vicious Geiss appointed four of the lowest, most inhuman scum of Lindheim as his assistant judges (the account in the German language calls them *Blutschaffen*—blood magistrates). They immediately began a savage witch hunt.

No one was safe. Geiss and his murderous henchmen concentrated on wealthy men and women, but since they reveled in cruelty they arrested others, including children between the ages of eight and twelve.

One poor woman, who lived in constant fear of these monsters, always took to her heels the moment she saw one of them on the street. But they caught and arrested her. She was taken to the Witches' Tower, a prison, where the tortures and trials were held. They tortured her until she became unconscious, and soon afterward she was burned.

The burnings were frightful. Usually the condemned witches were chained to a wall about fifteen feet above ground. Below, fires burned, and because the distance was great enough, the victims were like so many fowls trussed to spits. They slowly roasted and were finally charred to death in fearful agony.

Meanwhile, Johann Schüler and his wife escaped arrest, but Geiss had not forgotten them. He seems to have been wise enough to know that the Schülers were such highly respected citizens that he would have to have some very clear evidence before he could accuse them and thus get hold of their wealth.

A sad event for the Schülers took place in 1663. Frau Schüler gave birth to a baby, but it was born dead, something very common then. The couple were grief-stricken, but they had no idea of the horrors the child's death foretokened.

Now Geiss had his chance, and he pounced. First he seized the midwife who, as was usual in those days, had attended the dead child's birth. She was tortured until she confessed she had killed the baby by witchcraft with the help of six other persons.

These six were arrested and tortured. They confessed they had stolen the infant's body from its grave, cut it into pieces and thrown them into a pot in which a witches' brew for a magic ointment was being prepared. But Geiss was not satisfied. He was after bigger game. No doubt he hoped that those he had arrested would implicate the Schülers in the baby's death.

Meanwhile, the Schülers were beside themselves. Johann went to Geiss. "The confessions you have obtained are lies!" he cried. "I demand that the grave be opened so that we can see our little child's body is still there."

Geiss dared not refused. In the presence of himself, the other four judges and Johann Schüler, the grave was opened. The child's body was there, unharmed.

Geiss was enraged. "Keep your mouth shut, Herr Schüler," he threatened, "or I will have you tortured in a way that will make you wish you had!"

Then, since under the law the confession of a suspected witch under torture was accepted as the truth, Geiss burned the midwife and her six supposed accomplices. He still did not have the evidence he needed to accuse the Schülers, but he bided his time, waiting for his chance to strike.

Near the end of 1663, his chance came. He arrested an old woman known as Becker-Margareth, just the kind of person people would believe was a witch. He put her in the Witches' Tower and then sent one of his men to talk to her.

"You must be executed as a witch," the man said, "but if you will make a full confession of all those involved in the death of the Schüler child you will be spared the torture and given burial in the hallowed ground of the Churchyard."

The poor woman, knowing she was doomed, decided it was at least better to escape the torture and to have Christian burial. She accused fourteen persons, among them Frau Schüler.

Geiss immediately had Frau Schüler arrested on suspicion of witchcraft. In the Witches' Tower they searched her and found an old scar on her body. Geiss was triumphant. Ah! a witch mark—undeniable proof that she was a witch.

There was still Johann Schüler to be reckoned with. Since he could do nothing to help his wife, he fled from Lindheim with all possible speed and hastened to Würzburg to see Dean Hartmann von Rosenbach and plead for her life. No doubt Geiss gnashed his teeth when he found Schüler had slipped out of his clutches, but he took his revenge upon Frau Schüler. She was tortured until she confessed that both she and her husband had had a part in killing the newborn child.

The records do not indicate what the dean of

Würzburg Cathedral promised to do for the despairing Schüler, though later on he did warn Geiss to be careful, indicating that he was worried. The trouble was that he and the other members of the *Herrenschaft* had shared in the seized property of the witches Geiss had already burned. If there should be an investigation by the imperial government, all of them might have to share in the guilt with Geiss. At any rate, the dean did not move in time to save Schüler from the torture chamber.

Geiss was lying in wait for the miller when he returned from Würzburg. He arrested him and threw him into the Witches' Tower. It was midwinter, and the wretched man was forced to sleep on the freezing floor without the usual straw for a mattress and without covering. Even his stockings, which might at least have brought some warmth to his legs and feet, were taken from him.

They tortured Johann Schüler for five days before this ironwilled man finally confessed. And torture in Germany was fiendish in its cruelty.

First, the victim suffered mental torture. The torturer (usually the executioner) would threaten the victim with the terrible agonies he would suffer if he did not make an inmediate, full confession. Then the poor man would be shown the instruments to be used.

There were the thumbscrews, the boot and also the ladder, or strappado, to which the accused witch's arms were tied behind the back before he or she was hoisted into the air. Weights were tied to the feet that stretched the victim's body until, if enough of them were added, the person's shoulders would be pulled from their sockets. In another form of the strappado, the victim was hoisted up and then suddenly dropped to within a few inches of the floor. There were eye-gougers, branding irons and a tourniquet that could be tightened on the forehead until the agony would drive the victim out of his mind. Records in one German city tell of an iron chair studded with sharp points. The accused witch was made to sit in the chair and a fire was built under it.

They used the rack on Johann Schüler. It was a large, open frame on which the accused person was laid on his back on the floor. His wrists and ankles were fastened to movable bars at each end of the frame. The bars were then drawn apart by levers and pulleys. Each time the prisoner refused to confess the bars were drawn farther apart. In time, while the agony grew worse, the victim's bones were pulled from their sockets. When Schüler could bear the pain no longer, he confessed and was released. He immediately denied everything he had said. They put him back on the rack until he confessed a second time. But as soon as he was free, this brave man again denied everything.

They got ready to put the miller back on the rack a third time, but the news of his arrest, imprisonment and torture had spread through Lindheim. The tyrant Geiss had executed too many "witches." Who knew who would be next? Friends and relatives of the victims who had been burned organized a mob that set out in the night for the Witches' Tower. They stormed the place and managed to liberate Schüler and several other accused witches before they were driven off.

Led by Schüler, the liberated ones set off for Speyer, on the Rhine above Mainz. There the *Reichskammergericht,* or Imperial Supreme Court, held its sessions. They reached Speyer on February 18, 1664. There was a great uproar when the inhabitants of the town saw the twisted and maimed bodies of the accused persons, especially the women, who had dragged themselves to Speyer over the miles in the dead of winter. The citizens demanded that justice be given these wretched people. A noted lawyer offered to plead their case before the Supreme Court. The judges issued an order that the witch hunt in Lindheim must stop.

In spite of the hostility that had risen against him in Lindheim, Geiss was determined to have Frau Schüler's life, since she was still in the Witches' Tower. On February 23, 1664, he had her burned alive.

The citizens of Lindheim were now so enraged that they rose in revolt early in March and went after Geiss and his associates, ready to tear them to pieces. But the magistrate and the others managed to escape from the town.

When Baron von Oynhausen received the decree of the Imperial Supreme Court, he could do nothing but dismiss Geiss and thus end the witch hunt. Geiss was arrested and brought to trial, but the wicked magistrate was never punished. He pleaded that he had only done his duty and had received only the regular reward for hunting down witches, one-third of the property that was confiscated. He had taken no money that was not his. The other two-thirds of the plunder had gone to Baron von Oynhausen, Dean Rosenbach and the rest of the *Herrenschaft*. And although the men were equally guilty, they were powerful, and this is probably the reason all escaped punishment. But surely if anyone connected with this frightful episode could be said to have carried out the Devil's will, it was not the executed "witches," but the monster Geiss, his infamous assistants and their masters of the *Herrenschaft*.

During the witchcraft persecutions in Europe in the

sixteenth and seventeenth centuries, while only about a thousand people were executed in England, at least 100,000 were put to death in Germany. And the German law required torture of suspected witches. And while condemned witches were hanged in England, in Germany almost all were burned alive.

In Germany, as in other countries, the witchcraft persecutions began because of religion. The churchmen believed the Bible decreed that a witch must not live. In Germany, partly Catholic, partly Protestant, there was little to choose between the parts of the country where each religion was prevalent as to the savagery with which suspected witches were hunted down, tortured and executed.

In most religions there is a Satan of some sort. From the accounts of the brutal, ruthless persecutions that were the result of the influence of religion in Germany, one would think that Satan had indeed obtained a strong hold on the churches and churchmen of the country, and that the Devil had possessed them rather than the wretched victims of witchcraft trials.

Clergymen were seldom the actual witch hunters, however. The men engaged in the evil business were usually public officials or other persons of note. There were counterparts of Matthew Hopkins, the English Witch-Finder Generall, in Germany, including Benedict Carpzov, a learned professor at Leipzig University whose reputation in the law became so great that he was called the "lawgiver of Saxony" and was asked to sit on the Supreme Court of Leipzig to help decide the many complicated cases that came before it for review. Herr Carpzov was a religious man; he never missed a Lutheran church service and boasted that he had read the Bible through fifty-three times.

A just and godly man, one would say. Let us see. He believed in witchcraft, of course, and the extermination of witches—that being the teaching of the Bible, so he thought. He set forth seventeen different kinds of torture that should be used to obtain confessions, and ruthlessly overruled judges of lower courts who tried to obtain evidence in more humane ways. He is said to have signed 20,000 death warrants for the burning of witches. Perhaps this is an exaggeration, but there is no doubt his record was bloody enough.

No part of Germany escaped the great witchcraft delusion of the sixteenth and seventeenth centuries. Practically everyone in the country believed in witchcraft. When large numbers of Germans migrated to America and settled in Pennsylvania early in the eighteenth century, they brought that belief with them. Among the means used to keep witches away was the hex-mark, a circular sign in weird designs placed on houses or barns. Today tourists to the Pennsylvania Dutch country buy replicas of these hex signs to decorate their own houses.

In Germany during the persecutions, the Rhineland section and the area to the east of it was the worst witch-hunting country. Two principalities in that region were ruled by two wicked cousins early in the seventeenth century. One, Prince-Bishop Philipp Adolf von Ehrenberg of Würzburg, burned nine hundred accused witches between 1623 and 1631. His cousin Johann Georg II, known as the *Hexenbischof* (Witch Bishop), burned at least six hundred between 1623 and 1633 in the Bamberg territory.

Rank and wealth were no safeguards in these witch hunts; in fact, money was an object because here too the state seized all the possessions of an executed witch. The six hundred burned by Johann Georg II included many prominent citizens and five burgomasters (mayors or chief magistrates of towns and villages).

A witch hunter to rival Matthew Hopkins was Franz Buirmann, a judge appointed by the Prince-Archbishop of Cologne, on the Rhine. He spent much of his time roving about the surrounding area smelling out witches. In 1631 he paid a visit to three little Rhineland villages, Rheinbach, Meckenheim and Flerzheim. Altogether, these three hamlets had only three hundred households, but after Buirmann's second visit to them in 1636 he had burned 150 "witches" alive.

In Rheinbach, during his visit in 1631, this bloodthirsty fiend singled out a prosperous elderly widow, Christine Böffgen. She had no children and was a generous and highly respected woman. Buirmann had her arrested on suspicion of witchcraft and appointed a court of seven Rheinbach assessors to try her.

Five of them refused to take part in such a ridiculous mockery of justice. But before Buirmann and the other two, Frau Böffgen was blindfolded, searched for witch marks and pricked. Then they gave her the torture of the boot and she confessed. But as soon as they freed her from it she denied the confession. They tortured her again with the same result—she confessed and then retracted it as soon as she was released from her agony. Four times they tortured her, and during the fourth she died, which was probably a mercy. Judge Buirmann then seized her property and wealth.

In the Duchy of Swabia in southern Germany (part of it is now in Switzerland) one of the greatest instances of courage by a suspected witch took place in

1594. There, in Nöordlingen, lived Maria Hollin, who owned the Crown tavern in the town.

In Nöordlingen, witchcraft persecutions were led by the burgomaster, Georg Pheringer, and two lawyers, Sebastien Roettinger and Conrad Graf. In 1630 they burned thirty-two prominent women. All had property which could be seized by these three murderers. The victims included the wives of a former burgomaster, a senator and the town clerk.

Maria Hollin's will to withstand torture to prove her innocence must have been like the toughest, hardest steel. In fact, it seems that she must have survived by some miracle, and no doubt the three witch hunters believed it was the most powerful form of witchcraft.

First, this unholy trio arrested Maria on suspicion of witchcraft and threw her into a dungeon. She remained in this foul, cold, damp, dark hole for eleven months. During this time they tortured her fifty-six times, all in vain. Maria Hollin suffered horribly, but never a word of confession escaped her lips. She was innocent and determined that, no matter what they did to her, she would not plead guilty to something she had not done.

In time, of course, either Maria would have died under the torture or the three brutes would have found some way of convicting and burning her legally. But before that could happen, help came at last for Maria.

She had been born in the nearby town of Ulm, and relatives and friends appealed to the authorities there, with the result that Ulm claimed that since she was a native of that town Nöordlingen had no right to try her. The claim was legally upheld and Maria was saved.

That gave a Protestant minister, Wilhelm Lutz, the

courage to speak out. From his pulpit he thundered: "The proceedings will never end, for there are people who have informed on their mothers-in-law, their wives and husbands, denouncing them as witches. What can come of all this?"

By this time there were enough frightened and infuriated people in Nöordlingen to rise and demand that the witch hunt must stop. The three witch hunters were enraged, but they dared not go on, and the horror that had swept Nöordlingen for four years was ended.

Everyone knows the fairy tale of Hansel and Gretel, who were captured by an old witch who planned to roast them in her oven. An actual case, though far worse took place at Neisse in Silesia, then part of eastern Germany. This time it was "witches" who were the victims, when the executioner there built an oven in which he roasted forty-two women and young girls accused of witchcraft.

As for the more common method of execution, burning at the stake, one of the chroniclers of the time wrote in 1590 about Wolfenbüttel, Brunswick, in northern Germany: "The place of execution looked like a small wood from the number of the stakes." In 1631 Cardinal Albizzi described a journey to Cologne: "A horrible spectacle met our eyes. Outside of the walls of many towns and villages, we saw numerous stakes to which poor, wretched women were bound and burned as witches."

Only one thing could stop the countless witch persecutions of the early seventeenth century in Germany. At last the Holy Roman Emperor Ferdinand II used it. He forbade all seizures of property and possessions of convicted witches. Since his power extended over a large part of the country, he was able to enforce it.

And since the witch hunters were almost always engaged in the savage business for what it would bring them, the witch hunts subsided about 1637.

But later on, after Ferdinand's death, the persecutions flared up again. They did not completely end until 1775, when Anna Maria Schwägel of Kempen, in Bavaria, was beheaded—the last official execution for witchcraft in Germany. Behind her was a trail of bloodstained earth that covered most of the country.

6

THE "WITCH" WHO PUT A KING ON HIS THRONE

She was just a simple French peasant girl who could not even read or write. In her childhood the last thing she ever thought of was that by the time she was in her late teens she would obey mysterious voices that came to her, lead an army that would drive besieging enemy forces away from Orléans, restore a young French king to his throne, be arrested as a witch, be burned to death at Rouen and, nearly five hundred years later, became a saint and have her birthday celebrated as a national holiday in France.

Joan of Arc (or Jeanne d'Arc, as the French spell it), the daughter of Jacques and Isabelle d'Arc, was born in 1412 in the tiny hamlet of Domrémy, smack on the northeastern border of France. Joan's house still stands, restored as it looked in 1412. It is a typical peasant's dwelling of that time—gloomy and massive, with great beams strong enough to hold the heavy slate roof. Inside, the floor was hard-beaten earth, the furniture was scanty and poor, and the walls were blackened with years of smoke from the fireplace.

Through Domrémy a rivulet called Les Trois Fontaines (The Three Fountains), because of its source in three springs, cascaded down the hillside to join the larger River Meuse just below, along its twisting course northward to join the great River Rhine. As a small child, Joan played with other little girls in the meadows along Les Trois Fontaines and the Meuse. But once she was old enough, there was plenty of work for her to do.

In the house she helped with all the cleaning, washing and cooking for the d'Arc family—father, mother, three sons and two daughters. Outside, Joan joined her family in plowing, digging, hoeing, tossing hay and reaping the harvest, and took her turn in tending the villagers' flock of sheep that grazed in the meadows. She grew into an attractive, strong-limbed young girl, with a dark complexion, jet black hair and dark eyes glowing with a radiance that had something holy in it.

There was no school in tiny Domrémy. What Joan learned she got from her mother, and much of it was religion, for Isabelle d'Arc was devoted to the church.

The people of Domrémy, like all French peasants, were a superstitious lot. They believed in fairies they called the "Little People." In former times the had invited the Little People." In former times the villagers had invited the Little People to their feasts and prepared meals in a secret room for them of the choicest food they could cook. But when the village priest began going to the great tree where they were supposed to live to read the Gospel once a year, the

Little People were seen no more. Joan's mother does not appear to have taught Joan anything having to do with witchcraft, but many young girls were told that if they were sinful they might be turned into witches.

France was engaged in a long and desperate war with England and Burgundy. About the time Joan was eleven, King Charles VI of France, who had long suffered from insanity, died, and his son, the young Dauphin, or crown prince, succeeded him as Charles VII. But John of Lancaster, Duke of Bedford, commanding the powerful English armies in France, and Duke Philip of Burgundy had defeated the French, and Henry VI of England was also declared King of France.

One day Joan of Arc fell asleep and had a strange dream in which God commanded her to go to the aid of the Dauphin, who, although he had been proclaimed King by the French, had never been crowned and anointed at Rheims, like all French kings. Joan awoke deeply troubled. What could a simple little peasant girl do to help Charles?

Then one day in that summer of 1426, Joan saw a brightness in the sky and heard a voice: "I have been sent by God, Joan, to help you behave in a good and seemly manner. Be good, and God will help you."

Joan was terrified at first, but the voice was so sweet and gentle that her fears vanished. She fell to her knees and pledged herself to the Lord as long as He wished to keep her in His almighty power.

Later, one day while she was tending the sheep, the voice came again. Dimly, she saw shapes in the sky, one with wings, surrounded by a great choir of angels. It was the Archangel Michael.

"God has a great compassion for France," he told her. "You have been chosen to go to the aid of the young King. You will raise the siege of Orléans and restore him to the throne."

Joan burst into tears. "I am only a poor peasant girl. I cannot even ride a horse, let alone direct a battle."

"Be not afraid, daughter of God," the Archangel Michael replied. "You shall lead the Dauphin into Rheims to receive the sacred unction. You must go to Captain Baudricourt at Vaucouleurs. But the captain will not help you until you have asked three times."

Joan decided she must go to Vaucouleurs, about ten miles down the Meuse. But how? She was sure her family would never believe God had chosen her for a mission upon which the fate of France itself might depend. The village priest would probably think she had been bewitched. She confided her secret to a favorite cousin named Laxart, and he agreed to go with her to Vaucouleurs. They set out for the town and its castle on top of a hill.

Captain Robert Baudricourt, in command of the French royal garrison at Vaucouleurs, was a rich man. When she arrived at the castle's Great Hall, crowded with soldiers, jobseekers and town officials there on business, Joan's mouth fell open in wonderment at its luxury.

She picked out Captain Baudricourt at once. He looked every inch a soldier and knight, with a good-humored expression, though there was a little slyness in it. Joan went straight up to him.

"Captain Baudricourt," she began, "I am here from Messire [a French title of honor, meaning master] with a message for the Dauphin."

Baudricourt was stunned at the sight of this peasant girl, in her drab and work-worn dress, who had the audacity to give him such a message.

"Who is this Messire, and by what right does he give orders to the King?" he demanded.

"Messire is the owner of the kingdom," Joan replied calmly. "He wishes the Dauphin to become King and hold France in trust for him. The Dauphin will soon become King, no matter what his enemies do, and I have been chosen to take him to Rheims to be crowned and anointed."

Baudricourt decided this girl must have delusions. He spoke to Laxart: "Don't waste my time. Send this girl back to her father. A good thrashing will teach her a little sense."

The two travelers left the hall, but Joan was serene. Three times she must ask, the Archangel had told her.

Back in Domrémy, waiting for the chance to return to Vaucouleurs, Joan made the mistake of confiding to a young man who worked with her in the fields: "There is between Coussey and Vaucouleurs a girl who before the year is out will have the Dauphin crowned and anointed as King."

Her false friend could not keep the story to himself. Domrémy was the only village of any importance between Coussey and Vaucouleurs. Who could the girl Joan had spoken of be but herself? And how could such a mission be performed but by a witch? He blabbed the story about the village. People began to mock Joan as she passed.

Joan's parents were horrified. In France, witches were burned at the stake. They decided to marry her off before someone accused her, to make her settle down and forget this nonsense. But Joan flatly refused to marry the young man they selected.

Meanwhile, a new English force had landed and laid

siege to Orléans. The city's military position on the River Loire, almost in the center of France, was most important. The English believed that if they could take it, neighboring French provinces would collapse.

Once again, Joan prepared to set out for Vaucouleurs. In order not to rouse her parents' suspicions, she left Domrémy in her peasant's costume, wearing a shepherd's cloak and taking no baggage. She had a feeling that it was the last time she would see her home.

At Vaucouleurs again, accompanied by Laxart, Joan was welcomed heartily. Captain Baudricourt was convinced she was a fortune teller, and could tell him what lay ahead for the French army; but when she asked him for an armed escort to take her to Charles VII, he hesitated and finally refused. Yet Joan was undaunted.

"Twice you have refused me," she told the captain. "That has caused me no surprise, since my voices have told me I must ask three times. I call upon God to witness that you have delayed too long. The gentle Dauphin has suffered great misfortune, and he will suffer worse if you do not send me to him now."

Baudricourt soon learned it was true. The Orléans defenders' food was almost gone, and a force sent out of the city to attack the English had been repulsed with terrible losses. The captain immediately wrote to the King at his headquarters in Chinon, telling him the story and asking what to do about it.

The answer soon arrived. Baudricourt was commanded to send Joan to Chinon.

It was no easy journey—more than three hundred miles through country infested with robbers and enemy troops. It was decided that Joan would be safer if she were disguised as a man. When they finished cutting her black hair and putting her into a man's clothes, it was hard to tell her from one of the knights' young attendants.

At dawn on February 23, 1429, seventeen-year-old Joan left for Chinon with the cavalcade. Once again she heard the mysterious voice: "Go forward boldly. When you are in the presence of the King, he will receive a sign to treat you well and put his faith in you!"

For twelve days the party rode westward through France, and it seemed that God was close at hand to protect Joan, for the journey was made safely.

Above Orléans they crossed the great River Loire. Avoiding the besieged city, they cut across the duchy of Berry to Chinon, many miles below Orléans. There, lodged at an inn, Joan waited for a summons to the royal presence at the castle.

Charles VII's council feared that Joan was a witch, and that if he put himself in her care his cause would be doomed. Men of the Church were sent to question her. They could find nothing of witchcraft about her, only her simple faith in God. The delegation decided the King must see her.

Supper was over the evening that Joan, who had learned to ride, surmounted the steep hill on her horse and reached the castle. She was ushered into the Hall of State, ablaze with the flaring light of fifty torches. Ignoring the many richly dressed lords in the hall, Joan went straight up to a man dressed in drab clothing who looked anything but a king. She bowed low and embraced his knees, as was the custom before royalty.

"God grant you a happy life, sweet King," she said softly.

"I am not the King," Charles replied. He pointed to one of the magnificently dressed gentlemen of the Court. "That is the King."

"In God's name, sweet prince, it is you and only you who are King," Joan replied.

However Joan may have envisioned him, Charles was a repulsive sight. He had thick lips, a bulbous nose and a swollen face. His eyes were piggish, red and watery, with great pouches below them. His mouth was crooked, he was bow-legged and he shambled when he walked as though his joints were stiff. And Charles was weak, anything but a king by nature. He would gladly have yielded up an enormous part of France to England and Burgundy to end the war if his advisers had allowed him to.

"My name is Joan the Maid, gentle Dauphin," she said. "I have been sent by God to bring help to your kingdom. The King of Heaven sends you this message through me: that you shall be crowned and anointed in Rheims, and shall be His lieutenant, who is King of Heaven and of France."

For all his suspicions that Joan might be a witch, Charles was completely captivated and talked with her for a long time. But one of the bishops at the royal Court felt sure she was one. So they decided to take Joan about fifty miles south to Poitiers. There, in its cathedral, before an assemblage of high churchmen, she was questioned. Again, they could find no evidence of witchcraft.

Cautiously, however, the King's advisers decided to put her to the test of a difficult mission before she was entrusted with the command of a force to attack the English besiegers. Let her first prove her powers by getting food into the starving city of Orléans.

"In God's name," Joan replied to this proposal, "we will put into Orléans as we will, nor will any Englishman prevent us."

Preparations began for the dangerous attempt. They made Joan a standard, a banner of heavy buckram cloth with a fringe of silk. On one side, upon a field of fleur-de-lis, the golden lilies that were the symbol of French royalty, was an image of the King of Heaven seated on a rainbow. In one hand He held a globe representing the world, and the other was raised in a gesture of benediction. Beside him were the Archangels Michael and Gabriel. And in letters of gold was Joan's motto: Jesus-Mary. On the opposite side was a coat of arms, a silver dove on a blue field, holding in its beak a streamer with the words *"De par le Roy du Ciel"* ("In the name of the King of Heaven").

Joan wore a kidskin girdle, a thick, sleeveless doublet, padded stockings and leather shoes. All her clothing had chain mail sewn upon it, and a short kilt of mail extended below the hem of her short skirt. Over all this the maid wore a suit of steel armor polished until it looked white, symbolizing her purity.

Joan's force of some two or three thousand men moved up the Loire on the left bank, across from and above Orléans. There a flotilla of barges sent up from the city were loaded with the precious food.

The English had ringed the city on every side with strong points of heavy timber, protected by outworks or redoubts, all equipped with heavy cannon. Yet, strangely, the enemy made no move as the flotilla went downstream and moved under the protection of the French guns at the Burgundy Gate of the walled city. And at dusk on April 29, 1429, Joan of Arc, mounted on a white charger, entered Orléans.

She had passed her first test. The overjoyed and hungry people of Orléans thought it was a miracle, as indeed it seemed to be.

Joan tried to arrange a peaceful end to the siege. She walked out on the stone bridge over the Loire, on which was one of the English strong points, and called out to the enemy, promising their lives should be spared if they would surrender. The answer was a chorus of catcalls and insults. They called her a witch, and worse. Twice she sent a letter to the English commander, John Talbot. But Talbot was enraged that she had so easily got food into the city and made no reply. He was convinced Joan had done it by witchcraft and was determined to burn her.

"Within five days the siege will be raised," Joan predicted. She went out on the bridge again with a bowman, who sent an arrow carrying another copy of her letter whizzing into the English fortification. To it she had added, "This is the third and last time that I shall write to you."

On May 6 she led the troops out into a fierce battle. In an attack on a redoubt protecting a powerful English fortress, Les Tournelles, the French were hurled back time after time. At last Joan herself seized a ladder, placed it against the rampart and started up. An English arrow zipped from a crossbow and buried itself six inches deep in her chest.

For the first time she was terrified that she was going to die, and she wept like the little country girl she was. But only for moments; then she smiled, seized the arrow and wrenched it out. She was bleeding badly as they carried her back out of range.

The English were elated. It was common knowledge that once a witch saw her own blood her evil powers

74

were gone. But suddenly they saw Joan again, her wound stanched, leading the French once more against the redoubt. They were so stunned that by the time they recovered their senses the French were upon them, and they fled in disorder. And as other strong points fell, one by one, to the French, the English forces finally marched away. The siege of Orléans was over.

Joan of Arc's one thought now was to get the King to Rheims, more than 150 miles to the northeast. She met him at Tours, down the river from Orléans and more than two hundred miles from Rheims. But there the King dallied. His advisers were strongly against a journey through enemy-occupied territory.

Joan had no fear, trusting in the voice from God commanding her to take Charles to Rheims, but some of the King's advisers were insanely jealous of this country maid who had accomplished such miracles. Regnault, Bishop of Rheims, who was also the King's chancellor—a sly, disreputable character with an untidy beard, dirty hair and shifty eyes—kept reminding Charles what the Bishop of Embrun had said during Joan's examination before the relief of Orléans: "She is no more than a flea bred on a dunghill."

New doubts were planted in the King's mind. "God may at any moment withdraw his protection from her," the advisers warned. And Charles began to watch her suspiciously.

At last Joan, with a great sadness in her eyes, said to him, "I shall not last but little more than a year. See to it, my Lord, that you make good use of me in the next twelve months."

One day, when the King was in his privy chamber with his councilors, Joan knocked at the door and burst in. She threw herself at the King's feet. "Noble Dauphin," she cried, "have done with these endless delays! Come quickly to Rheims and receive your rightful crown."

"Joan," said the King, "are you prepared to state what it is that your voices command?"

"Yes, Sire," she replied, "I hear a voice saying, 'Go forward, daughter of God, and I will be at your side to help you!' And when I hear that voice I am filled with joy!"

She was in an ecstasy, her eyes lifted to heaven. And in this the King saw the sign the voice had promised Joan that God would give him. Charles ordered the march for Rheims to start.

Joan, on a black charger, clad in white armor but with her head bare, and carrying a little ax in her hand, led the advance guard of the army of 3,600 men. She bore the coat of arms the King had devised for her—a blue shield with a hilted silver sword on it, and a crown on its point between two fleurs-de-lis.

During the journey there were two bloody battles, in which the English were routed with terrible losses, as well as a successful siege of the rebellious city of Troyes. Then, on the morning of July 17, 1429, the French army marched into Rheims.

There, in the magnificent ancient cathedral where all French kings had been crowned for centuries, Charles took a solemn oath to rule France justly, was crowned as King Charles VII and then was anointed by the Bishop of Rheims with the holy oil used only at coronations.

Joan of Arc, standing beside him with tears running down her face, knelt, embraced his knees and said, "Gentle King, now has God's pleasure been accomplished, Who said I should raise the siege of Orléans and lead you to this city of Rheims to be crowned, thus showing you as the true King to whom the realm of France belongs by right."

Joan did not consider her mission finally accomplished. Paris, the French capital, was still in English hands. If it were taken, all of Normandy would soon fall to France, and gradually English domination of the country would end. And at that time the city was poorly defended and would fall easily.

Instead, the weak King dallied, afraid to assault Paris and preferring to get it by negotiation with Duke Philip of Burgundy, upon whose aid the English foothold in France depended. The treacherous Philip was at the same time bargaining with the English, but he signed a fifteen-day truce, during which Paris was to be handed over to Charles VII. The Duke never kept his promise.

At last, after much marching and countermarching to show himself off to the people of various towns, the King decided to attack. But by that time reinforcements had reached Paris. Joan led an attack on one of its gates, but was again badly wounded. The attempt failed and the King abandoned the siege.

Joan was disheartened and very tired. She begged the King to let her go home and live out her life in retirement, but he refused. Nevertheless, his confidence in her had weakened. Worse, Joan's voices no longer spoke.

Meanwhile, the wily Duke Philip of Burgundy had made a secret alliance with the English. At the same time, he demanded that he hold at least three places as security that the truce would not be violated by the French. All were in the vicinity of Rheims. One, Compiègne, was loyal to the King and refused to give up to the Burgundians.

Joan of Arc decided she must leave the faint-hearted King. Secretly she departed, heading toward Rheims. Along the way, bands of volunteers joined her.

Meanwhile, King Henry VI of England had come to France with the idea of also being crowned King of France at Rheims. But first, the loyal French region around Rheims had to be subdued.

Compiègne was the key town in the English and Burgundian campaign, since it stood directly on the road to Paris. Joan reached it ahead of Duke Philip, who had 4,000 Burgundians, 1,500 English, heavy artillery, battering rams and catapults to hurl great stones against the walls of Compiègne.

Joan had only about two thousand men to oppose this formidable army, which took up strategic positions ringing the city. She saw that her only hope was to make swift raids on different enemy strong points.

With five hundred men, she marched for the nearby village of Margny, held by Burgundian troops. Her men charged up the hill on which it stood, took the enemy by surprise and routed them. It was a daring but futile effort, for now she was trapped by reinforcements the enemy had sent out. But Joan was determined to fight her way back to Compiègne.

"Forward, and we shall have them!" she cried. But many of her men had fled back to Compiègne, pursued by the enemy. Some reached it before the iron portcullis gate of the city was shut down to keep the Burgundians out.

Duke Philip's men then headed for Margny again. Joan was helpless now. She stood out plainly among her few remaining troops in her surcoat of scarlet and gold. The Burgundians surrounded her. An enemy archer grabbed and pulled her off her horse, and she surrendered.

Philip of Burgundy was beside himself with joy. As for King Charles, he did not lift a finger to help Joan. A long captivity lay ahead of her, but all through it the faithless King never mentioned Joan.

Philip wanted to burn her at once as a witch, but the English commander-in-chief, the Duke of Bedford, still smarting over the defeat at Orléans, wanted her too. King Henry VI of England was prevailed upon to threaten to stop the importation of wool from Burgundian-held Flanders into England unless Joan was turned over to the English. Since this would have crippled Flanders' most profitable trade, Duke Philip yielded.

However, the English were forced to pay a tremendous ransom before Joan was handed over to them on November 21, 1430. They moved her from place to place, heavily guarded, until at last, just before Christmas, she was taken to Normandy's capital of Rouen.

At first they put her in a cage of stout planks strapped with iron in the grim castle of Rouen. But fearing she might die under such conditions and cheat them of their gruesome revenge, they took her out, placed her in irons and put her into a bed. At night a heavy chain was padlocked across the bed. Five guards, three inside her room in one of the castle towers, watched her. Their hatred was so great that they mistreated her horribly. One of their favorite amusements was to wake her in the night and say, "You are about to be smeared with sulfur, taken to the stake and burned."

Burning the "witch" was not so simple. The English

were afraid to take the responsibility for it, so they arranged for her to be tried by French churchmen so that any blame would rest entirely on French shoulders.

Joan of Arc suffered the agony of a trial that lasted, off and on, for nearly six months. There were seventy charges against her, including being a "declared witch." They took her into a torture chamber to make her confess she was a witch, but she faced them with such faith and determination that they gave it up. It would be simpler to convict her of heresy—the holding of beliefs against the laws of the Church. For that they could burn her.

At last, on May 30, 1431, she was convicted. They took her from the castle, put her in a cart and hauled her to the Old Market of Rouen. The English were so afraid she might escape that eight hundred soldiers escorted her.

In the Old Market stood three platforms, one for the judges and clerks of the court, the second for the assessors or assistant judges who had voted to condemn her and the third for Joan herself, with two monks and a clergyman who was to preach a sermon.

Joan could look out into an open space where the stake stood, cemented into a base of great stones. It was set unusually high so that the multitude could see her better, to prevent the executioner from controlling the flames to make her death easier and so that the smoke might not suffocate her and kill her more painlessly before the flames reached her.

During the sermon, Joan kept murmuring, "Is it here that I am to die? I fear you may have to suffer much for my death!" Then, on her knees, she said a last prayer. When she had finished, she forgave everyone and said King Charles was not to blame for her death.

Joan's hat, which almost hid her face, was torn off, showing that her head had been shaved. On it was placed a tall cap like a bishop's miter with two devils painted on it, holding up the words, "Heretic, Relapsed Sinner, Apostate, Idolater."

The magistrate who was supposed to read Joan's sentence broke down and could only gesture toward the stake. The cart carried Joan up to it, and she embraced a cross she had asked for.

The executioner then helped her from the cart and up the ladder to the stake and bound her. Then, back on the ground, he and his assistants set fire to the wood piled around the stake.

Smoke rose, and then raging flames that hid Joan of Arc completely. She cried out once as the fire reached her. Then there was a silence until she uttered one last cry—"Jesus!" as she died.

They scattered Joan's ashes on the River Seine there at Rouen. The English were satisfied. The witch who had caused all the trouble was gone.

Was she? The English could not know that their grip on France would soon start to slip, and that in time they would lose it all. It may have seemed that God had deserted Joan of Arc in those last dark hours, but perhaps He had not. Joan had died for France, and France would yet drive her enemies out.

In time, too, the Church would admit it had been wrong. Within twenty-five years her name was cleared of all wrong-doing. Then, in 1875, the heads of the Church in Rome began to discuss sainthood for Joan. Sainthood is not conferred lightly by the Catholic Church. It takes years of searching investigation. Nearly half a century later, Joan of Arc was canonized by Pope Benedict XV on May 9, 1920, as Saint Joan, and her birthday was declared a national holiday in France.

Today, thousands of tourists come to Rouen each year from all over the world to see the spot where a little country girl who was no witch, but had sublime faith in God, was burned at the stake.

7

FRENCH WITCHCRAFT AND WEREWOLVES

Joan of Arc was the most notable accused witch executed in France in the days before the great European witch hunts, although she was actually convicted of heresy. There were other witchcraft cases before Joan's, however. One is remembered because it involved a French King.

Charles VI, father of Charles VII, whom Joan of Arc restored to his throne, was a popular king whose subjects named him Charles the Beloved. But when he became insane, doctors could do nothing for him, and at last his despairing councilors called in several professed witches who said their magic could cure him. Their spells, charms and incantations did not work. Instead, the King's mental illness became worse, and for their trouble the "witches" were all beheaded. In time, Charles VI died, still insane.

During the fifteenth century a good many accused witches were burned in France, and in the sixteenth and seventeenth centuries the record there was nearly as black as that of Scotland and Germany. Some people did profess to be witches or sorcerers, but most admitted their guilt only after agonizing tortures.

In one case an accused witch was not convicted, but through some mistake was burned alive anyway near Laon, northeast of Paris. People were justly outraged when the mistake was discovered, but a noted French judge had an artful explanation. He said the innocent victim's execution was "the secret judgment of God." That, of course, made such a terrible failure of justice all right.

A form of murder by witchcraft, supposed to have originated in Sicily and used there for many years, seems to have reached France also. At least one person there was accused of using what was called the Evil Eye.

Gilbert Fourneau, a stable boy, was charged with putting spells on three women near the town of Bourges. Dressed in rags, he begged in the streets for bread. When two of the women gave him some, he insisted that they break it in half and keep one piece for themselves. One of the women, at least, seems to have died. She felt "snakes crawling over her body"; then she began to swell up so much that in four days she burst.

The third woman, Sylvine Roy, had a different experience with Fourneau. She charged he fixed her twice "with a frightful eye" that caused her to fall down unconscious. This was the Evil Eye.

Fourneau was arrested and put in prison. Sylvine's husband had his unconscious wife taken there. A judge who was present threatened to have the stable boy burned as a sorcerer if he did not cure the woman immediately. By witchcraft, so the story goes, Fourneau brought Sylvine out of her trance.

Restoring one of his victims to life did not help him, even though his accusers searched him for witch marks and found none. Doubtless under torture, he confessed he had made a pact with the Devil. Satan required him to kill three women on a certain day, and he had nearly succeeded. He was quickly tried, condemned and strangled and burned.

One of the most famous names in the story of French witchcraft is that of Gilles de Rais, one of the richest noblemen in Europe and a distinguished military commander. A high-ranking officer in the French army, he was one of Joan of Arc's companions in arms at Orléans in 1429. But he lived in such splendor and squandered his money so foolishly that in time he needed more to keep up his luxurious style of life.

So Gilles tried alchemy, which was not witchcraft but a science that attempted to change base metals like lead into gold. Unfortunately, he made the mistake of hiring assistants who tried to use witchcraft to accomplish the miracle, and Gilles himself was converted to black magic.

When he was arrested, he was charged with enticing young children into his castle, where they were burned, tortured, butchered and cut in pieces and their blood and ground-up bones used to make magic powders.

Gilles was tortured, of course, until he admitted everything, and told all the gruesome details of how he had mistreated the children and then had either cut their heads off or beaten them to death with a stick. A Church court found him guilty of heresy. He was then turned over to a civil court, which found him guilty of murder and ordered him strangled and his body burned.

It must be remembered that Gilles de Rais was convicted only after he had confessed under terrible torture. In spite of all the witnesses against him, there was no real proof that he had committed these dreadful crimes. People often preferred to give testimony rather than to risk torture to get the same evidence out of them. And no doubt Gilles de Rais, a powerful noble, had many enemies.

In the sixteenth and seventeenth centuries, witchcraft amounted to an epidemic in France. In 1571, a convicted magician was executed in Paris. Before he died he said there were a hundred thousand witches in France. Not that many were accused and killed, but far too many were. In 1582, in a single day, eighteen poor wretches were burned at the stake in Avignon, in the south of France. In French King Henry IV's own Basque country, near the border of Spain, a judge Henry appointed to conduct a witch hunt declared that all the region's 30,000 inhabitants were infected with witchcraft. He boasted that in four months he had burned six hundred witches.

However, the most notorious kind of witchcraft in France was lycanthropy—the belief that some persons could transform themselves into gigantic wolves. It was rampant in the sixteenth and seventeenth centuries. There were instances of it in other countries, but it was especially common in France. The lycanthropes were better known as werewolves—or, in French, *loups-garous*. The superstition was brought to America by the French who settled in Quebec, a part of Canada, and for many years the peasants there firmly believed in and feared an attack by a *loup-garou*.

One of the famous werewolf cases took place in 1521 in a wild and mountainous section of eastern France. According to the story, a traveler passing through the region was set upon by a great wolf. He managed to wound the animal with his knife, and it fled. The traveler followed it and saw it go into a hut in a lonely area. He burst in and found a peasant house-wife bathing her husband's wounds.

The traveler reported his experience in nearby Poligny, and Michael Verdung the man who lived in the hut, was arrested. Doubtless under torture, he confessed he was a werewolf and implicated two other men—Pierre Bourgot and Philibert Mentot.

Bourgot confessed under torture that nearly twenty years earlier, his flock of sheep became lost in a great storm. While he was searching for them he encountered three dark men on horseback. One asked what he was doing.

When Bourgot told him, the dark man said, "I will help you if you will serve me as your lord and master."

"If you will help me I will promise to do what you ask within a week," Bourgot replied.

The mysterious horseman agreed, and set a time and place for another meeting. Soon afterward, Pierre Bourgot found his sheep. At the appointed rendezvous he met the dark horseman again.

"I am a servant of the Devil," the stranger said. "You must give up Christianity and swear allegiance by kissing my hand."

Pierre did so. When he kissed the stranger's hand, he found it was ice-cold.

Two years passed, and Bourgot began to regret his

bargain. He started to attend church again. One day Michael Verdung came up to him.

"You are not keeping your promise," Verdung reproached him. "I too serve the Devil. If you will carry out your bargain, I promise you shall be given gold."

Pierre Bourgot agreed. He attended a witches' sabbat one night with Verdung. All those present carried green candles that burned with a blue flame.

During the rites, Verdung said to Pierre, "Take off your clothes." When Bourgot had done so, Verdung rubbed an ointment over his body, and in a trice Pierre turned into a wolf. Two hours later, Verdung anointed Pierre with a second ointment which transformed him back into human form.

In his confession Bourgot told how, by using the magic ointment, he had roamed the wilderness as a wolf.

"I attacked a seven-year-old boy, but he screamed so loudly that I was afraid and ran home, where I turned myself back into a man so I would not be caught," he said. "But later I seized a four-year-old girl and ate her. Then I attacked one who was nine, broke her neck and ate her too."

Philibert Mentot also confessed he had been a werewolf. All three were burned at the stake.

In 1573, in that same region, some peasants rescued a little girl who had been bitten five times by a huge wolf. It was dusk, but as the animal fled, someone thought it looked like Giles Garnier.

Giles Garnier and his wife, Appoline, were poor and ill-tempered hermits who lived in a hut in that area. They were just the kind of people to be suspected of witchcraft. Nothing was done for six days, however, until a ten-year-old boy disappeared on November 15, 1573. Then Giles and Appoline were arrested.

Both were tried at Dôle, though only Giles was convicted. Presumably under torture, he admitted being a werewolf, though on one occasion he said he had killed a twelve-year-old boy while he was in the shape of a man. He did not eat him because he saw some peasants approaching.

Giles said that in the shape of a wolf, he had killed a ten-year-old girl and eaten her. Another attempt failed when three men passed nearby; but on November 15 he had strangled the missing ten-year-old boy and eaten most of the flesh.

They burned Giles Garnier alive at Dôle on January 18, 1524.

In that same part of France, another werewolf case, involving four members of a family—two sisters, a brother and the brother's son—was tried in 1598.

The first to get into trouble was Perrenette Gaudillon, who was known as a queer creature. Doubtless she was insane. One day a young man named Benoît Bidel climbed a tree to pick some fruit. On the ground, his younger sister was suddenly attacked by a great wolf. As Benoît climbed down, drawing a knife, he noticed that the wolf had no tail. As he went for the animal it reached out, seized the knife and stabbed him in the neck. The wolf then fled.

When help arrived it was too late to save Benoît, but before he died he gasped, "The wolf's front paws were hands!"

The enraged peasants of the village immediately decided Perrenette Gaudillon must be the *loup-garou.* They hunted her down and tore her to pieces.

That was not enough to satisfy them, however. The

peasants then seized the other three members of the family. Again, it can only be supposed that they were tortured. Antoinette Gaudillon confessed she was a werewolf. So did her brother Pierre, who said it was the Devil who turned people into werewolves to go marauding about the countryside killing people. He admitted he had killed and eaten both people and animals. Pierre's son Georges also told how he had covered himself with magic ointment that turned him into a wolf.

Of course, these other three of the Gaudillon family were tried, condemned and burned.

All these stories sound fantastic, as they are. The country people in those days were ignorant and superstitious. They fully believed there were indeed many werewolves. Sometimes they probably thought they saw things they really did not. But it seemed perfectly reasonable to the courts of justice that confessions obtained under torture were true.

In that wild, mountainous part of France called the Jura, where these cases occurred, real wolves abounded in those days. No doubt many people there and in other remote parts of France were attacked by them. And it is possible, of course, that demented people like Perrenette Gaudillon may have dressed themselves in wolf skins and attacked people. But there were no werewolves, although even today some people who believe in witchcraft may think there are.

8

VOODOO AND THE
TERRIBLE SECT ROUGE

The story may be true and it may not. It is one of
many told of the dreaded *Sect Rouge,* in the black
Republic of Haiti. At least two writers, one an anthro-
pologist—a scientist whose career is devoted to the
study of man and his works—have described it. Both
lived for years in Haiti, studied its witchcraft and were
not given to repeating stories that were plainly fairy
tales.

This story of sheer terror took place somewhere in
the mountains of Haiti (its very name comes from an
Indian word meaning mountainous country, and some
8,000 of its area of about 10,000 square miles is covered with mountains, with a number of peaks rising
over 8,000 feet high). It was a moonless night, though
the brilliant stars of the tropics were out.

Shadowy figures flitted out of the darkness to an
open space in a mountain valley, south of Haiti's capital of Port-au-Prince. Surrounding the glade were the

thatched houses of the peasants who worked in the sugarcane fields behind them.

In the center of the space stood a silk-cotton, or ceiba, tree. Ceibas are huge trees with enormous trunks that divide toward their bottoms into many much smaller, spreading roots that extend well above the ground. The silk-cotton, or floss, that is the tree's fruit is kapok, the light and buoyant material used to stuff mattresses and life preservers.

Each of the figures who entered the open space carried a straw bag. At last, when about a hundred persons had gathered there, a command was passed among them. Instantly all opened their bags, drew out robes of scarlet and white and put them on. For the time being their heads were bare.

The red color was significant. *Rouge* being the French word for red, the *Sect Rouge* was the Red Sect—and the red referred to blood, human blood. Sometimes its members are called *cochons gris*—gray pigs—and more commonly *zobops*.

Some of those gathered about the silk-cotton tree began a series of weird dances, leaps and songs. Their movements imitated those of wild animals. Then, at another signal, they all took from their bags and put on masks that made them look like cows, dogs, hogs, goats, roosters and hideous demons with tails and horns.

High-pitched little drums began to beat in a strange rhythm. Then a figure in a frightful disguise appeared. He was the emperor of the *Sect Rouge*. Others followed him, including the queen of the sect and its officials and executioners.

To the beat of the little drums, all sang in Creole, a language that comes from French but also has words that stem from Spanish, African languages and the Indian tongue.

At another command, all those in the open space lighted candles and formed a procession. In the middle of the line was a little coffin, ablaze with candles. In a half-dance, half-trot, they moved out into the night along a road that soon reached a crossroads. In all witchcraft, a crossroads is an important symbol. There, according to their belief, lived certain loas. Loas are the gods not only of voodoo, the witchcraft-religious sect in Haiti, but also of the other West Indian witch-craft-religion, obeah.

At the crossroads the procession did honor to the loas who lived there, and made offers of food, drink and money to Maître Carrefour (Lord of the Cross-roads), the chief loa. All prayed to Maître Carrefour to aid them in the grisly hunt for their prey that would take place that night.

Next the procession approached a cemetery. The queen went in first. She danced five times around one of the graves, made a cross on the tombstone with a cheap rum called clairin and placed a candle and a calabash bowl containing blood on top of it. The cross was the emblem of another god, the Baron Cimitière (Baron of the Cemetery), also called the Baron Same-di (Baron Saturday), of whom all lived in terror lest he pick some of them out to die.

Finally the rest of the procession moved into the cemetery. The youngest member of the group was stretched on the grave, and the rest placed their can-dles in a circle about him and danced once around the grave.

Then the queen spoke: "The powers are now joined with the degrees!" The rest closed their eyes so that no one might see where she went as she slipped away into the darkness. Once she was gone, all fled pell-mell in every direction lest Baron Cimitière seize them in his icy clutches. A rear guard of two zobops retreated backwards, brandishing their great cane-cutting knives called machetes to ward off the terrible baron if he moved to take victims.

Well beyond the cemetery the procession formed again and shuffled on to a bridge over a stream. The candle-lit coffin was set down in the middle of the bridge, and more candles were brought up to make it one brilliant glow of light.

The bridge was the taking-off point for the "column." While the officers waited on the bridge, its members faded into the darkness like so many slinking animals. Each zobop carried a cord made from dried and cured human intestines obtained during earlier raids like this one.

For hours the heads of the *Sect Rouge* waited on the bridge. At last the column returned. It brought three men, securely bound and gagged with cords twisted about their throats. They were wretched Haitian peasants who had been foolish enough to be abroad on the roads at that time of night.

Incantations were spoken over these trembling victims. This was supposed to turn them into animals—one cow and two pigs. Thus, when the executioner killed them with swift strokes of their machetes, this was no murder but simply the slaughter of animals ordinarily used for food. And that is how they were to be used, for their bodies were quickly carved up and the pieces distributed among all the cannibals who were members of the *Sect Rouge*. Then, since it was nearly dawn, they went home.

Did the murderous *Sect Rouge* really exist? There is a good deal of evidence that it did, and even that it still does exist in remote parts of Haiti. No one really knows because of the secrecy that has surrounded it. But there have even been reports in recent years that the *Sect Rouge* was able to cover more territory in its gruesome hunts by using automobiles.

These zobops, reputed members of the *Sect Rouge,* were (and possibly still are) the gangsters of Haiti. And as with American gangsters, vengeance can be swift and deadly if one of them talks too much. Stories tell of how a suspected informer would be seized, put into a boat that was rowed well off shore and stunned with a blow from a rock that bruised his skin. A deadly poison, for which there is no antidote, was quickly rubbed into the wound, and the victim tossed overboard. So swiftly did the poison act that before the informer's body struck the water he would be dead.

The stories persist. One concerns a peasant whose life was saved because he did a stranger a small favor. He was walking from one village to another and met a man on the road he did not know.

"Will you give me a cigarette?" the stranger asked.

The peasant gave him one.

"I thank you," said the stranger. "Perhaps some day I will have the opportunity of repaying you."

The peasant went on and reached his destination. By the time he was ready to start back, night had fallen and a journey of several hours lay before him. Nevertheless, he set out.

The hour grew late, and the peasant was still plodding along the lonely road in the darkness. Suddenly a figure loomed out of the night, approached him and cried, "Stop!" The man was naked.

The peasant, knowing about the *Sect Rouge,* had a terrible suspicion of danger as he halted. Could this man be a zobop, a member of the dreaded sect?

The man who had stopped him struck a match and peered intently into the peasant's face. "Was it not you who gave me a cigarette today?" he asked.

The peasant, struck dumb with terror, could only nod.

"You are in luck," said the zobop, "though you are foolish to be walking the roads at this time of night. It is near midnight, and the column will be out. You will soon meet them. Save for me, you would never be heard of again. But since you did something for me, I am going to do something for you."

The zobop had a little bag tied around his neck. From it he took a scrap of paper with mysterious signs and symbols on it, and handed it to the peasant.

"When you meet the main column, don't answer any questions they ask you," the zobop went on. "Just show them this slip of paper and they will let you pass." And with that, he vanished into the darkness.

Only moments later, the peasant encountered the main column of the *Sect Rouge* hunters on their murderous prowl. At the sight of the piece of paper, they let the peasant go on home.

A story is told in Port-au-Prince about a woman in business whose trade was so poor she was scarcely able to live. One day she cried out, "I would become a zobop if only I could be relieved of this terrible poverty!"

One of her neighbors, who was nearby and overheard, looked at her with a strange smile. While of course the needy woman did not know it, the neighbor's husband was a member of the *Sect Rouge*.

That night the woman who had uttered the wish to become a zobop was awakened by the beating of a little drum and singing outside her house. She peered through the keyhole and saw figures in red and white with three-cornered hats, all carrying candles. The frightened woman regretted what she had said and did not open the door. The figures, chanting a refrain with the words. "Aye, aye, zobop, aye, ya, aye," then disappeared.

The next day the poverty-stricken woman's neighbor said to her indignantly. "And me thinking you wanted to join the society to get your business on its feet!"

The poor woman was thoroughly alarmed and pretended she did not understand, but she was in trouble for her careless remark. A little later the neighbor woman offered her a glass containing a liquid. "Drink this," she said. "It is excellent wine."

The other woman was terrified. "I will take it home and drink it," she promised, but when she was inside her house she threw it away. A good thing she did, for the drink was poison prepared by the neighbor's zobop husband. Nor was that the end of attempts to kill her, but she managed to avoid all of them.

The *Sect Rouge* dealt (and still does, some say) in witchcraft, with its murderous rite of supposedly transforming its victims into animals before killing and eating them. Today, intelligent people in Haiti admit it exists but they laugh at the nocturnal rites and say its sinister purposes are a lot of nonsense. Perhaps they are now, but perhaps this was not always so. Presumably the cult performed similar ceremonies when it robbed graves of newly buried bodies. But the *Sect*

Rouge is, or was, only a small society compared with the numbers who practice the witchcraft religion that in the West Indies is largely centered in Haiti—voodoo.

Voodoo is a strange mixture of religions. Originally it was a form of the African witchcraft brought to Haiti in the seventeenth and eighteenth centuries by thousands of enslaved black people. When the Catholic religion was introduced there by missionaries, voodoo took up many of its characteristics. Naturally, the missionaries did not like to see their Christian religion combined with one based on witchcraft; they fought it relentlessly, but could not stop it. Many Haitians saw nothing wrong in going to mass in a Catholic church and then dancing all night in one of the weird and complicated voodoo rites.

Voodoo persists in Haiti even today. It is chiefly the religion of peasants, country people who have little education. From the Catholic religion it has borrowed the priesthood—men known as houngans, as well as priestesses called mambos. Parts of its ceremonies have their origin in the Catholic religion, but most of the rites, and its gods, magic and witch doctors, had their beginnings in Africa.

"Spirit" is probably a better translation of loa, a god, since voodoo does recognize the existence of a true God as some sort of power superior to a loa. The houngans and mambos obtain their supposedly magic powers from a loa who enters their heads while they are in a trance. The person then becomes possessed. It is thought good to be possessed by a benevolent loa, but possession by an evil spirit is greatly feared.

Like the *Sect Rouge,* voodoo holds its meetings at night in a secret place. The secrecy that surrounds everything about it makes it difficult to find out just what takes place, and the ceremonies often differ. Tourists visiting Haiti often witness what are supposed to be actual voodoo ceremonies, but they are usually staged.

Nevertheless, there are descriptions of authentic rites by persons who have lived in Haiti and become well enough acquainted to be allowed to see them. One such account describes the place where the ceremony was held, in which stood an altar and a cage containing a snake, the worship symbol of voodoo. A houngan and a mambo took their places near the altar, and a series of rites took place. First a voodoo "king and queen" both made long speeches. Next, the "queen" got on top of the snake's cage and went into a trance, being possessed by the loa, who spoke through the queen's mouth. In order of age, beginning with the oldest, the people approached and asked the loa to give them what they wanted most.

With that, the snake was put on the altar and all those present made it an offering. A goat was brought in and sacrificed by cutting its throat. The blood was collected in a jar, and the houngan touched the lips of everyone with it, to seal them against revealing anything that had happened. New members of the cult were then initiated, and a dance followed in which all moved crazily to the beat of drums and went into trances.

The trance is the very heart of voodoo. The members say it is because the person is possessed by a loa, but psychiatrists call it hysteria. In the witchcraft delusions that have happened in many parts of the world it has become mass hysteria, spreading from one person to another like an infectious disease, and these people believed they were bewitched and usually tormented or harmed by the witch. In the times of these delusions the great witch hunts, with their tortures and executions, took place.

In voodoo, where it is believed that a loa enters a person's head, the possessed person suffers a kind of hysteria. Such people may go into convulsions and lose control of their movements so that they sway, stagger, tremble, pant, sweat, leap about wildly and act as if they had lost their minds.

Once people come out of trances they remember nothing of what happened to them. This, according to voodoo, is because they were completely possessed by the loa.

A doctor who had lived many years in Haiti, and claimed to be the only white man who fully understood voodoo because he was a member, told a strange story. It illustrates how persons in a trance may be insensible to pain and not be injured by a painful and harmful ordeal.

The doctor told of attending a ceremony in the southern part of Haiti where the people were sure they were beset by an evil loa called Marinette. Strange things had been happening in this village. People had had unusual runs of bad luck. Children had died mysteriously, houses had caught fire and burned, pigs and goats had vanished. The people were sure it was the work of Marinette, and they decided they must be rid of the wicked spirit.

A houngan told them Marinette could be bound and made helpless for seventeen years by means of a fire ordeal. The doctor learned of all this and went to the village, where he stayed with a family he knew.

A girl of sixteen in the family named Apela was one of the nine persons who were to undergo the ordeal.

The doctor watched her intently for any signs that she was being specially prepared to stand the ordeal of fire. He saw none.

The villagers gathered one night on a lonely mountain plateau at the edge of a ravine. There a hole had been dug and filled with pitch pine. Over this a pile of logs was stacked in a pyramid and the whole thing soaked with gallons of kerosene.

Large bamboo flutes called *vaccines* that made a sound something like the bawl of a cow began to play as the fire was touched off. The flames roared up into a raging inferno made more intense by the kerosene and the tarry pitch pine.

The scene in the darkness on the wild mountainside was unearthly. The nine persons who were to undergo the ordeal became possessed by a friendly loa and went into trances. Then, before the spectators, who were in a frenzy of excitement, Apela stepped barefoot into the fire and shuffled over its blazing brands and glowing embers, taking seven slow steps. The doctor scanned her face intently, but it was impassive, with no sign that she felt pain.

Next the eight other possessed persons followed Apela into the fire. Each also took seven slow steps. Then they walked out of the fire, circled it once, went back, took seven more slow steps and continued on, treading back and forth until they had stamped out the glowing embers completely.

After the ceremony the doctor examined Apela's feet closely. There was no sign that they were burned or even blistered. Apela told him: "*I* did not walk through the fire. It was the loa." And thus the wicked Marinette was rendered harmless for seventeen years.

If the story is true, how could it happen? Was it really some sort of witchcraft? Or had the watchers been hypnotized in some way so that they thought they saw the fire-walking? The doctor said no. That Apela and the others felt no pain could be explained by their being in a trance, but how did their feet escape being burned? There is, of course, the possibility that in spite of the doctor's vigilance, Apela's feet might have been treated with some preparation known to the witch doctors, with their expert knowledge of herbs and medicinal plants, that kept her, as well as the other eight, from harm.

Fire walking is known in other parts of the world— among them India, Japan, Tahiti, the Fiji Islands and the island of Mauritius, in the Indian Ocean. There have been cases in which fire-walkers were severely burned, but they claimed it was because they did not have complete faith. And early explorers, traders, trappers and missionaries in North America told of seeing dances in which members of some Indian tribes walked on fire or hot coals.

Voodoo's belief in zombies should be mentioned. In voodoo a zombie is a dead person who had been called back to life, but has no soul. A businessman in Haiti who was asked about them said, "Yes, there are zombies in Haiti and also in the United States."

"Just what is a zombie?" he was asked.

"He is a man who is out of his mind."

But peasants in Haiti think differently. They say these dead people recalled to life do exist and they fear them greatly because they steal and do other evil things.

Voodoo is concerned with witchcraft, but it is also a religion, complicated because of the many African tribes, each with its own religious beliefs and ceremonies, whose members were brought to Haiti as slaves. Although there are other gods in voodoo, loas are the most worshiped of them.

One musical instrument that dominates all the varying ceremonies is the drum. It too came originally from Africa, and in voodooism drumming is a highly developed art. There are many kinds of drums, and their sounds differ greatly. Varying beats or rhythms are used, depending upon the kind of ceremony that is taking place. Much beautiful music has developed from the voodoo drums, accompanied by other musical instruments not commonly used elsewhere. This and the knowledge of herbs in curing illness are at least two good things that have come from the strange witchcraft-religion called voodoo.

9

OBEAH

Voodoo is known and practiced in some other West
Indian islands besides Haiti, but in some obeah or ob
has long been the chief witchcraft cult, and to some
extent is still practiced. From its beginnings it was
especially strong in Jamaica, another of the large is
lands of the Greater Antilles. Obeah too originated in
Africa and was brought to the West Indies by slaves
The name is believed to have come from the wor
obayito in the language of the Ashanti African tribe
meaning a witch or wizard.

Obeah, with its focus upon spells, incantations
charms and potions, is quite different from voodoo. I
place of the voodoo snake as an object of worship, th
spider is of equal importance in obeah.

Obeah can be sinister, benevolent and sometim
comical. The obeah men make all sorts of fantast
claims—that through the gods they can bring good
bad fortune, "unwitch" the bewitched, cure disease
cause it and other ills, discover evildoers, prove th

innocence of the wrongfully accused and save or take away life.

Doubtless the medicine men's knowledge of herbs and medicinal plants often enables them to cure illness, though they surround their activities with all sorts of mumbo jumbo. With their real medicines they use strange materials—the blood of animals, feathers, bones, broken bottles, dirt from graves, parrots' beaks, eggshells and other rubbish.

Most obeah men are a crafty lot. They have more intelligence and shrewdness than the uneducated people who come to them, and they often use it to impress, defraud and overcharge their customers. Fortunately, today's free and independent Jamaica is making great strides in education. New schools are springing up in the interior of the island, and the children of poor peasants have the chance to continue their education in institutions of higher learning. With the younger generation, obeah seems to be on its way out.

The obeah men have many tricks. What is called the Myal dance is an example of how an organized society has been able to "prove" they could restore life to a dead person. Superstitious peasants were invited to attend these dances to show them that this claim was true.

A "victim" was selected from among the Myal men. Beforehand he was given a mixture of rum and a certain drug, supposed to have been made from an herb called solanum. Solanum is a member of the same general plant family as the potato, tomato, eggplant, tobacco and nightshade, a common, vinelike weed with little purple flowers and bright-red poisonous berries that grows in the United States. Solanum is harmless when it is boiled and is used in the West Indies as a substitute for spinach; but mixed uncooked with rum it appears to be powerful indeed.

The dance began with all the mysticism of drums beating a peculiar rhythm, magic signs and symbols and dancers wearing strange costumes. Suddenly the victim staggered and fell to the ground. He did not seem to be breathing, and to all appearances was dead.

The chief Myal man went into a frenzy, uttering wild shrieks and making frantic gestures that created the idea that the man on the ground must surely be dead. Then the leader went away for several hours, leaving the "body" stretched motionless on the ground. When he returned, he had a bundle of herbs. From them he squeezed the juice into the victim's mouth and anointed the eyes and fingertips with it. Meanwhile, he half-chanted, half-howled a song, while the other members of the society circled the victim, stamping their feet.

At last, to the awe of the simple people watching, the herbs' juice overcame the power of the drug. The "dead man" stirred and then got to his feet, very much alive. It was an effective way of showing the miraculous power of obeah.

In the seventeenth and eighteenth centuries, obeah was more sinister than it is today. The West Indies black people were slaves then, and they sometimes used their knowledge of herbs to poison their masters and other enemies.

A French Catholic missionary who went to the French West Indies in 1693 wrote a book in 1712 describing obeah as the slaves had brought it from Africa. He told one story of a slave on the island of Martinique who in two years had systematically poisoned some thirty other slaves against whom he had grudges.

This slave, when he became seriously ill and was on the point of death, sent for the owner of the sugarcane plantation where he worked. He confessed he had killed the thirty-odd slaves, who had died of an unknown disease during those two years.

He had done it by keeping the nail of one finger longer than the rest so that he could scrape off the bark of a poisonous plant and have it lodge underneath the nail. Then he would invite his prospective victim to have a drink with him.

He was fiendishly clever about it, since to avoid suspicion he would drink first from a cup made from the shell of a calabash gourd. Because he suffered no ill effects, no one suspected that before he offered the calabash to his guest he would let the poisoned fingernail soak in the rum. It was a powerful poison, and within two hours his victim would die in convulsions.

There were also attempts, sometimes successful, to poison plantation owners and their families, but obeah was used in other ways to stir up trouble. The peculiar beat of the slaves' African drums could rouse them to frenzied revolts.

Harsh laws enacted in these European-controlled islands checked such practices to a great extent. Drumming was forbidden, as well as assemblies of slaves, and the penalties were severe. As for poisoning, a slave who even attempted to poison his master was guilty of murder and could be hanged, or more commonly burned to death. And in Jamaica a 1781 law decreed that any black person who pretended to have supernatural powers or was caught using any obeah materials should either be put to death or transported out of the island.

A ghastly story of how obeah was used to implicate two greedy peasants in murder on the then British island of St. Lucia, near Martinique, in 1903, is told by a writer on the subject. The two men shared ownership of a few acres of land on which they grew cocoa profitably, and were considered well-to-do. A man from one of the nearby French islands came to them with a story that promised them great riches.

"I am in communication with certain spirits," the stranger, an obeah man, told them. "They have revealed to me the exact place on your land where a great treasure of gold is buried. If you will share it with me, I will point out the place to you."

The simple peasants, overjoyed, promptly agreed.

"First," said the obeah man, "you must give me something of value to prove your good faith. A couple of goats will do."

When this was done, the man led them to the place. "You must dig at night," he told them.

That night the two peasants dug and dug, but they found nothing. They went to the obeah man and demanded their goats back.

"Do not give up," said the man. "The spirits tell me another spirit, more powerful than they are, is pushing the treasure deeper into the earth as you dig. The Devil will not let the gold be taken unless you give me a larger payment first."

They gave him a calf, went back to their digging, excavated a very deep hole and found nothing.

"You have cheated us," they told the obeah man. "Give us back our goats and the calf."

"I am not cheating you," replied the stranger. "The

treasure is there, but the spirits tell me a human sacrifice must be made to recover the gold."

The greedy peasants accepted the story and said they would do what the obeah man demanded. One of the two went to the British island of Barbados. From an old woman there he got hold of a seven-year-old black boy, an orphan. Back in St. Lucia, the unholy trio decided the sacrifice should be made at a Black Mass.

Obeah in the West Indies had absorbed the Black Mass from Europe, where it was a well-known ceremony during the witchcraft era of the seventeenth and eighteenth centuries. It was a frightful mockery of the Catholic mass. The three treasure hunters selected a flat-topped rock near a stream as the sacrificial altar.

A woman who lived on the cocoa plantation suspected some evil was afoot. Although the night was moonless, she managed to spy on the Black Mass and saw everything.

The men took the little boy, bound him hand and foot, laid him on the altar and placed four lighted candles around him. After some hocus-pocus by the obeah man, robed in a white sheet, he butchered the child, ripped out his heart and took it to the peasants' house, where more rites were performed.

The horrified woman ran to a nearby town and summoned the police. All three men were captured and executed.

The obeah worshipers believe in another European influence on their originally African cult—*loups-garous,* as they are called in the French islands, and hags or vampires in English-speaking ones. In France, as already told, the word *loup-garou* is used to describe werewolves, or witches who changed themselves into enormous wolves.

Obeah *loups-garous* are quite different. They fly about at night sucking people's blood while they sleep and are among the spirits believed to live in the great silk-cotton, or ceiba, trees.

It is extremely difficult to keep a *loup-garou* out of a house, since they are believed to be able to get in through the smallest crack. But there is a safeguard. If rice and sand are sprinkled before the door of a house, a *loup-garou* is forced to stop and count every grain before entering the house. And since they die if they are out after dawn, they cannot finish counting in time and must fly away.

Obeah has other strange gods. The Bahama Islands, in years not long past, if not today, were a center for this cult. They had Boomzewooms which hung by their tails from the branches of the silk-cotton trees at night. There were also Chicky-Chasers, who walked on their heads by moonlight with their feet in the air, turned in the wrong direction. They chased people crying, "Hoo hoo!" and biting the necks of those they caught, blinding them for life, according to the obeah belief there.

There were other obeah gods among the Maroons of Jamaica. Originally slaves of the Spaniards, the Maroons escaped to the wild, mountainous interior of the island when the British captured Jamaica in 1655. For nearly eighty years they made life miserable for English planters by raiding and looting plantations. They fought off armed force after armed force sent to exterminate them until in 1734 they signed a treaty of peace. They were given legal freedom and land, where their descendants live today, keeping pretty much to themselves. Their obeah gods were the Duppies, who lived in silk-cotton and almond trees. By just being near a person a Duppy could swell the victim's head to enormous size. But if you drank some tea made from spirit weed, a tropical plant also called manyroot, no Duppy could harm you.

Then there was the Whooping Boy, the ghost of a celebrated cowherd. He was heard only in August, far off, whooping and cracking his whip as he herded his ghostly cows into their pens.

The Three-Legged Horse was not dangerous. He appeared around Christmastime to enjoy himself in the festive parades people held at that season. While he was always disguised in a white sheet, you could tell him by his jumping, leaping gait, and if you looked closely you would see he had two legs in front but only one in back.

A mischief-maker and a plague to the people was the Rolling Claf. His eyes were great balls of fire, and he moved with the speed of lightning all over the wilder parts of Jamaica.

One of the most comical obeah superstitions, though not at all funny to those who believe in it, is the one about shadows. The story is that obeah men, who are evil, steal people's shadows. Without his shadow a person will pine away and die. So the Myal men, who are benevolent, try to catch the lost shadows.

Stolen shadows are caught at night. They are kept in a silk-cotton tree, long regarded with awe and fear by those who practice obeah and believe evil spirits live in them. The person suspected of having lost his shadow is taken there, robed in white. A crowd gathers, and while the Myal men sing and dance, the spectators pelt the tree with eggs and the headless bodies of chickens.

The moment the Myal men see signs that the missing shadow is leaving the tree, a basin of water is brought up to rescue it. The suspected victim is taken home, along with the basin. A wet cloth is put on his head and presto! he has his shadow back.

Like voodoo, obeah is complex and highly secret, and would take a long time to describe fully. But it is witchcraft too, and still practiced to some extent in the West Indies. Yet so is witchcraft today in some remote parts of England, America and other countries.

10

AFRICAN MAGIC AND
THE LEOPARD MEN

It was not night, when most witchcraft is supposed to be practiced, but the broad daylight of afternoon, though the ceremony was held in a dark ravine in a mountainous area in the interior of West Africa.

There a "doll" had been set up, one form of the images used in the witchcraft of many countries to obtain revenge upon an enemy. This was no ordinary doll, but the dead body of a man. He had not died by witchcraft, but of natural causes in a nearby village. He was simply being used as the symbol of another man who was very much alive—a Belgian hunter who had cheated the black natives of that region unmercifully. They had decided they must have revenge upon the hunter.

First they had baptized the dead body and given it a new name—that of their victim. Then they tied it upright to a tree with ropes made of vines, and coated it with tar. In that way it would decay more slowly than if it had been exposed directly to the blazing tropical sun and the rains.

Servants employed by the white hunter while he was in that region had stolen combings from his hair and the parings when he cut his nails. They twisted this hated hunter's hair into that of the dead body, and fastened the nail parings to its fingertips. To complete the image they had dressed the body in a sweat-soaked shirt the hunter had thrown away.

Witch doctors and singers formed a procession to the place where the gruesome figure hung. As the ceremony got under way, drums began a throbbing beat. The witch doctors, in their frightening masked costumes, howled songs of hate; then, as the drums changed their pitch, they began to chant magic incantations over and over.

At last a shriveled little woman danced before the image and sang in a shrill voice. This song was designed to clog and swell the throat of the corpse as it decayed.

The ceremony, which took place in the twentieth century, was seen and described by a white man who had lived and studied witchcraft in various parts of the world, including Africa. He wrote a number of books on witchcraft and related subjects and became a famous expert.

He was able to watch this secret ceremony that would ordinarily never be seen by a white man because he gained the confidence and friendship of witch doctors in Africa.

What did it all mean? The writer was familiar with the ways in which the Belgian hunter had cheated the people of the mountain jungles. The powerful witch doctor who had taken him to the ceremony said that when the throat of the corpse there in the ravine began to swell, the hunter, many miles away at that time, would begin to have trouble in breathing, swallowing and talking. In a month he would be dead.

The writer, aware that a victim of witchcraft must know a curse had been put on him, asked about that. The witch doctor replied that the victim *always* knew it.

The white witness of the affair started the long trek back to the coast, where he had been making his headquarters in Bassam, on the Ivory Coast, then under French control. Two weeks later, still on his return journey, he met an old acquaintance who was taking a load of kola nuts north to be exchanged for salt. This man said the Belgian hunter was on his deathbed. The writer asked what he was dying of, and the reply was that it was *shortness of breath*. He added that some native hunters the Belgian had employed had told the rogue that there was a curse on him.

The hunter refused to believe it until he began to investigate and found out about the hair combings, nail parings and the discarded shirt that had been taken from him. He began to feel very ill, although doctors could find nothing wrong with him.

The hunter then actually became crazed with fear, for he knew the power of such curses. When the writer reached the end of his journey, the hunter had been dead two weeks.

This was undoubtedly another case of autosuggestion, used by those who professed to be witches against persons they wanted to harm or kill. Once the victim knew about the curse it worked on his mind until he was so frightened he became convinced he *was* sick and would die. He then became ill and did die.

Although this incident took place in the present century, so many of the territories of Africa which were formerly under the control of European nations have won their independence that sweeping changes are taking place there. In bygone centuries rich and powerful empires flourished in Africa. There were cities as large as important European ones, with fine buildings and broad streets, connected to each other by a good system of roads.

The Africans of these empires were industrious and highly intelligent. In agricultural regions they had great herds of cattle, sheep and goats, and raised ample crops to feed themselves. Many Africans were skilled artisans. They had learned to smelt iron ore and use it to make tools and utensils, and they also knew how to make brass and work it into useful and beautiful objects. They were expert sculptors and wood carvers; African craftsmanship of this kind is much prized today by collectors and museums.

Like other peoples the world over, the Africans had their myths and legends—and witchcraft. There were many tribes and among them many different forms of witchcraft. When the white traders penetrated West Africa and began dealing in slaves, who were shipped first to the West Indies and later to the American colonies, these beliefs in witchcraft went along with the slaves. Out of this came obeah and voodoo—each a mixture of different witchcraft beliefs, with a great deal added to the original from the teachings of Christian missionaries.

In time the great African empires vanished, like the vast Roman Empire that once ruled most of the then known world. Some of the African empires were conquered by the Moors from North Africa, who crossed the Sahara Desert and penetrated West Africa. Others were victims in bloody wars with less civilized tribes. But witchcraft continued to flourish.

Today a new black Africa is emerging. In the large cities of the new free nations are fine, modern buildings, schools and universities. The old culture continues, with that of the twentieth century added. Nevertheless, there is no more reason to believe that witchcraft in Africa has completely vanished than it has in other parts of the world, especially in wild regions of jungle and mountains.

In earlier times there were good and evil forms of witchcraft in Africa, just as there were in Europe and the New World. Africans lived in terror of the evil kind. There were witch hunts there too, but the treatment of accused witches in Africa was much different from that in "civilized" Europe. Before the white man came, some supposed witches were put to death, but more often they were let off with a fine if they confessed and promised to reform.

There were ordeals, but nothing like the frightful cruelties used in Europe. One favorite method used in West Africa was to give a suspected witch a potion made from the Calabar beans that grow there. Extracts from the Calabar bean are used in medicine, but in any large quantity it is very poisonous.

Accused witches were made to drink some of this potion. Since it made them violently sick to their stomachs, some were able to vomit it up before the poison could have its deadly effect. They were considered innocent of witchcraft. Those who died were witches.

African witchcraft is a fascinating subject, but there were so many different kinds of beliefs, rites and ceremonies that to describe them all would fill a large

117

book. One thing was almost universal in West African witchcraft, however. Female witches were far more powerful than the males, the sorcerers. In some parts of West Africa the tribes believed that only women could work witchcraft.

The beliefs of certain West African tribes in what is today the Republic of Ghana, formerly the Gold Coast, were strangely like those of Europeans in the sixteenth and seventeenth centuries—and of the Puritan witch hunters in the seventeenth. They believed witches met at night in groups—like the covens of Europe and America—and that they flew to these meetings, not on broomsticks or by the use of magic ointments but by traveling along the gossamer cobwebs spiders spin or on the backs of leopards, antelopes, owls and even snakes.

Africa's "white witches" were the witch doctors. A distinguished professor of the University of Ghana, in a lecture in the United States, said that the usual idea of the witch doctor as someone dressed in a terrifying costume and mask, using spells and charms to drive out evil spirits, was false.

The witch doctor, he said, was a master herbalist—an expert in the use of herbs to cure illness. However, although the professor denied it, there seems no reason to doubt that witch doctors did use weird costumes, incantations, charms and the like, along with their healing arts. There are too many accounts of these things by explorers and traders to doubt them all. The witch doctor's mumbo jumbo impressed those who came to him and made them believe in his magical powers—and faith in a doctor or healer is half the battle in recovering from illness.

One interesting aspect of African witchcraft, already

described in the obeah beliefs of the West Indies, is that a person can become bewitched by losing his shadow. The African explanation makes this belief clearer.

In the Nupe country of northern Nigeria it was believed that every person had two souls. One was that of life itself. The other was the "shadow soul." The shadow soul could become separated from a person's body in two ways, during a dream or by an evil witch. The witch could separate her shadow soul from her body and send it out at night to cause misfortune and also to "eat" people's life souls.

Meanwhile, a witch herself was safe from being caught at her evil work because her body remained in her bed. If someone woke her, her shadow soul would instantly return to her. All this, in a somewhat different form, became transported to the West Indies as a part of obeah.

Witch hunts in the Nupe country were conducted by a secret organization of witch finders headed by a person called "the master of the evil spirit."

Before the hunt began, from one to four members of the society would gather secretly, wash themselves with a potion against witchcraft and drink a little of it. They were the "spirits," and at dawn they would appear in the bewitched village.

They wore enormous masks made of a cylinder of white cloth fifteen feet high. At the top of the cylinder was a circular wooden ring attached to a long wooden pole. Under the cylinder and holding the pole, the spirit was completely invisible, but by moving the pole in different directions he could make the mask do a kind of dance.

At dawn the spirits came into the village accompanied by two interpreters, without masks, who told the people the wishes of the spirits. The interpreters carried sticks to drive off anyone who came too close to the masked spirits. The spirits would never work together. One would appear suddenly and then vanish into the bush of the jungle, and another would take his place.

They danced all day in the village. Sometimes they would go into houses to make sure no one was staying away. During this time music would play and old women, shaking rattles in time to it, would dance and sing.

All day excitement and fear would mount among the villagers. After night fell, without warning, one of the masked spirits would stop and bend over a woman (never a man, since the Nupe believed only women had evil powers of witchcraft). This meant the spirit had hunted down a witch.

The interpreters would seize the terrified woman and carry her off into the darkness of the bush around the village. Here she had to go through an ordeal by scratching the earth with her fingers until blood oozed from under her nails. This was proof that the spirits had indeed tracked down a witch.

But unlike the frightful tortures of Europe, and unlike the white witch hunters there, the spirits showed some mercy. The witch could buy herself off if she had enough money and promised to reform. The older the woman, the more it cost, since the old ones were believed to be the most evil.

If the witch did not have the money, she was immediately killed, but quickly and not by the barbarous methods of white Europe. The process of finding witches went on until the spirits were satisfied there were none left in the village. The witch hunts were never held unless there were at least one or two deaths in the village that could not be explained; and the practice no longer exists in the Nupe country.

The great secrecy of the *Sect Rouge* in Haiti has already been described, but compared with that surrounding the notorious Leopard Men or Leopard Society in West Africa, the activities of the *Sect Rouge* might as well have been published in the newpapers. Until fairly recent years, though it now seems to have vanished, it was the most dreaded menace in the wild interior of the region. Yet so little is known of its organization and workings that it cannot be said with certainty whether it was a form of witchcraft, cannibalism or simply a lust for human blood.

That the Leopard Men did exist, in earlier years at least, can scarcely be doubted. A writer on the subject of African witchcraft points to more than four hundred arrests of accused Leopard Men in Sierra Leone between 1907 and 1912. Just how much farther back its existence goes is not known, but there is a record in Sierra Leone of a native executed for having turned himself into a leopard in 1854.

The evidence is plain, however, that the Leopard Men did not actually turn themselves into leopards, although many people in Africa believed they did. The writer who described the troubles in Sierra Leone tells of once seeing a Leopard Man's outfit at a police station. It was a dress made of the entire skin of a leopard. Instead of claws, the outfit included sharp three-pronged knives that could be worn on the hands. There was also a "medicine bag," supposed to make the person who owned it rich and powerful, evidence that suggests witchcraft was involved.

What points even more conclusively to witchcraft is a report of a Leopard Man who was caught dressed in his leopard costume. He confessed, but insisted he could actually turn himself into a leopard. Why, then, the police asked, did he wear the leopard costume? The man explained that he might at any moment be turned back into human form again, and the leopard skin disguise would enable him to escape undetected.

The Leopard Men were more bloodthirsty than the *Sect Rouge* of Haiti. They went hunting for their prey like real leopards, and they killed almost without mercy, apparently just for the pleasure of it. Often, like real leopards, they leaped from tree branches onto the backs of their victims.

One of the worst outbreaks of the Leopard Men was reported from a district of southeastern Nigeria between 1945 and 1947. During that time more than eighty people were found dead with the big jugular vein in their throats ripped open. It was the first time in years that any trace of the Leopard Society had been discovered.

It was always very difficult for the police to tell a Leopard Society killing from that of a real leopard, and so it proved in this case. The victims were always surrounded by the actual paw marks of a leopard. But the police were sure that these murders were not the work of real leopards. The authorities offered rich rewards for the capture of Leopard Men. They put a curfew into effect at four in the afternoon, since the killings usually took place about dusk. From then through the night, people were supposed to stay in their houses.

But some were foolish enough to venture out to their

doom. The killings went on. Hundreds of persons were arrested as suspected Leopard Men, and enough evidence was obtained to hang eighteen men. Finally, the outbreak ended.

Little is heard of the Leopard Society in West Africa today. The laws against such things are strict and well enforced. Yet if, in its great secrecy, it still does exist, it would probably only operate in the wild interior regions.

Witchcraft in general is on the wane in Africa because, particularly among the new, independent nations, education is increasing so rapidly. On the other hand, there is no good reason to doubt that witchcraft still does exist in some parts of Africa, just as it does in other regions throughout the world.

11

THE MATHERS
RAISE THE DEVIL
IN MASSACHUSETTS

Although the Devil was believed to be still at his
malicious work of witchcraft in England in the first half
of the seventeenth century, it was not considered
strange that he began plying his evil trade in New
England at the same time. Since God is everywhere,
why should not His enemy, Satan, be making trouble
three thousand miles across the ocean?

The first known case of witchcraft in New England
appears to have taken place in and near Hartford,
Connecticut, in 1647. Governor John Winthrop of the
Massachusetts Bay colony wrote in his diary during
March of that year: "One of Windsor arraigned and
executed at Hartford for a witch." He did not give the
witch's name, and there is no mention of the case in
the records of the Connecticut colony. Then, in
Charlestown, across the Charles River from Boston, a
husband and wife were arrested for witchcraft in 1648.
When they were tried, the husband, Thomas Jones,
was acquitted.

Like so many persons who were accused of witch-craft, his wife Margaret Jones, was skilled in the use of herbs to cure illness. Because of this, many people came to her, and many were cured. She used none of the charms and magic words other so-called witches were so fond of. Margaret Jones could be called a doctor, though she had no medical training—in other words, a "white witch."

No one claimed to have been bewitched by her. No one charged that she associated with specters or imps of the Devil. No one had gone into a trance or convulsion that could be charged against her. Nevertheless, the authorities in Charlestown decided she must have magical powers and therefore was a witch.

They tried Margaret Jones and her husband before the General Court of Massachusetts Bay, the governing body of the colony. Not only did it make the laws, but its members, as magistrates, were judges. The General Court that tried Thomas and Margaret Jones was composed of Governor John Winthrop, Deputy Governor Thomas Dudley and eight other members, known as Assistants.

Both of the accused witches were examined before the trial. Matthew Hopkins' method of "watching" was used.

"We saw nothing amiss with Thomas Jones," the head of the examiners reported to the court.

"What of witch marks?" asked one of the judges. "Did you find a witch mark on him?"

"None," was the reply.

"And the woman?"

"Ah," replied the examiner, "mark you, your worship, Margaret Jones has magical powers. In the prison we saw her sitting on the floor with a little child in her arms. As we watched, the child ran out of the room. A prison guard set out after it, but before his eyes it vanished."

Another judge remarked wisely, "I make no doubt 'twas one of Satan's imps through which she works her witchcraft. Did you discover aught else?"

"Aye, your worship. A witch mark was found on her body."

Governor Winthrop entered these events in his diary, as well as other evidence brought out against Margaret Jones at the trial. For one thing, the mysterious child had been around before her arrest. A maid who saw it fell ill, went to Margaret and was cured. The accused witch had second sight too—she had foretold things that had actually happened. So said witnesses against her.

In colonial Massachusetts Bay, ordinary citizens were often called Goodwife or simply Goody, and their husbands Goodman. Goodwife Jones was a strongminded woman, and she was infuriated by her arrest. At the trial, Governor Winthrop noted, "she was very intemperate, lying notoriously . . ." and she shouted and raged at the jury and the witnesses against her.

They condemned Margaret Jones and took her to the gallows on June 15, 1648. On desolate Boston Neck, the narrow strip of land that once connected the peninsula of Boston to the mainland, Margaret continued to rage at those who were sending her to her death, protesting her innocence until her words were cut off by the hangman's noose.

Strange things happened after Margaret Jones's execution. Governor Winthrop wrote in his journal that on that very day and at the same hour, a tempest in Connecticut blew down many trees. This was proof, of course, that Satan was enraged because he had been robbed of one of his witches, though the learned governor did not explain why the Devil chose a place so far away from Boston.

As for Thomas Jones, once he was acquitted he had had all he wanted of Boston. He took passage in the ship *Welcome*, then riding at anchor off Charlestown. The ship had eighty horses aboard and a hundred and twenty tons of ballast to make her ride more easily at sea, since she did not have a full cargo.

The weather was perfectly calm, but once Jones was aboard, the ship began to roll uncontrollably and it was feared she would sink. A warrant for Thomas Jones's arrest was hurriedly drawn up, and the moment he was off the *Welcome* all was well once more.

Again, there is no indication that Governor Winthrop, who wrote of this mysterious event in his journal, actually saw it. And if it did happen, it may have been that the *Welcome* was badly loaded. A groundswell, a strong underwater current or tide in shallow water, sometimes causes ships to roll heavily when the wind is calm, and her rolling might have become much worse if some of the ballast in her hold shifted. There is no record of how long Thomas Jones remained in prison, though he does not appear to have been executed for what seemed to be witchcraft.

Late in that same year of 1648, Mary Johnson of Wethersfield, Connecticut, was arrested and charged with "familiarity with the Deuill." She confessed to murdering her own child and to acts of witchcraft. Since she was expecting another baby, her execution was delayed so that the innocent child would not be killed with her, and she was not hanged until June 6, 1650. She seems to have been a poor creature with a bad reputation, and her mind probably was not normal.

Now the Devil shifted his operations up the Connecticut River to Springfield. There, Goodwife Parsons and her husband, Hugh, a rough, quarrelsome sawyer and bricklayer, had a squabble with their neighbors, the Bedorthas. The neighbors retaliated by having Mary Parsons arrested.

The Springfield court found Goody Parsons guilty of starting the trouble and sentenced her either to pay £3 damages or receive twenty lashes at the town whipping post. The fine was paid with twenty four bushels of Indian corn. It caused a bitter feud between the two families, and Mary Parsons was so disturbed that her health failed and it became plain that her mind was affected.

Meanwhile, Hugh Parsons had made a good many enemies by his bad disposition. He quarreled with George Moxon, the Springfield minister, over some bricks Goodman Parsons had furnished for the chimneys of the parsonage, and the very same week Mr. Moxon's two young daughters were afflicted with strange fits.

Hugh Parsons was arrested and charged with witchcraft. His enemies flocked into court to testify against him. Some of the stories they told were ridiculous.

A woman had been making some cornmeal pudding by boiling it in a bag.

"I put it on to boil," the witness said, "and a little later the bag was cut from end to end and the pudding ruined. There was nobody around to do such a foul trick, but soon afterwards I heard a knock at the door and there was Hugh Parsons."

"What did he want?" inquired a judge.

"He didn't say, but I know 'twas to make sure his witchcraft had spoilt my pudding."

"What have you to say to this?" Hugh Parsons was asked. But Parsons could give no good reason for coming to the woman's door.

Witnesses also testified that on the afternoon of the day this suspicious thing had happened, Hugh Parsons had gone into the woods with some other sawyers to cut timber. One of them, Thomas Miller, teased Hugh about what had happened.

"It's all over town about what you did to that pudding," Miller said. "You and your evil tricks—I say it's witchcraft. Aye, you and your wife are both witches. Everybody knows the queer things that've been going on. You've made a pact with the Old Scratch, eh?"

Goodman Parsons answered never a word, but a few minutes later Miller cut his leg with his saw. Hugh Parsons' witchcraft—what else?

While Hugh Parsons' examination was going on, his son Joshua, five months old, died. Mary Parsons then confessed she was a witch and had murdered the child. Even though it was clear she was insane, she was arrested. They sent both Hugh and Mary Parsons to Boston for trial. Mary was very ill at the time, and although she was sentenced to death for murder by witchcraft, there is no record that she was hanged. She may have died in prison before she could be executed.

A jury found Hugh Parsons guilty of witchcraft too, but the case went to the General Court, which reversed the lower court's decision, probably because so much of the evidence was mere hearsay. But Hugh Parsons was taking no chances on falling prey to his neighbors' spite again, for he never returned to Springfield.

It was 1656 before another case of witchcraft occurred in New England. In that year Ann Hibbins of Boston was arrested and charged. The case was strange in several ways. First, not a scrap of evidence on which Mrs. Hibbins was convicted has ever been found. Only Governor Thomas Hutchinson, more than a century later, gave some details in his *History of the Colony of Massachusetts Bay*. Where he got his information, no one knows.

Second, Mrs. Hibbins was one of the most prominent and respected women in Boston. She was the widow of William Hibbins, a rich merchant who had served as an Assistant on the General Court, and had been the colony's representative to the British Government in London.

Third, Governor Hutchinson wrote that when Mrs. Hibbins was searched for witch marks, none were found. He also wrote that when she was first tried before a lower court, the jury found her innocent, but enemies among her neighbors set up such a hue and cry that she was tried again before a higher court, which found her guilty and condemned her to death. She was executed on June 9, 1656. Today, under the Constitution of the United States, a person found not guilty of a crime can never again be tried for the same offense, no matter what new evidence may turn up.

Another witchcraft case in Massachusetts Bay in 1656 was started by malicious gossip. Strangely enough, the woman's name was Parsons also, and she lived in Northampton, only eighteen miles upriver from Springfield.

Goodwife Sarah Bridgman of Northampton, a long-nosed busybody, held a gathering at her house to welcome a friend who had come to visit her from Springfield. As often happens at such affairs, the ladies spent most of the time tearing to pieces the reputations of others who were not there.

The talk turned to witchcraft. "There's some funny things going on over to Parsons'," said one of these ladies. "They do say 'twas Mary Parsons made that little boy's knee sore."

Another snooper cackled, "Aye, and he cried out on Goody Parsons, saying that she did hurt him and would pull off his knee. Mind you, there's witchcraft afoot at Parsons'."

Goody Bridgman repeated this juicy tale to a neighbor who had not been at the gathering. Like all gossips, she embroidered the story to make it sound even worse. "Some that were there said they were jealous [an old New England word meaning 'suspicious'] something isn't right with Goody Parsons," she added.

Joseph Parsons heard the story and had Goody Bridgman arrested for slander in calling his wife a witch. The court ordered Goodwife Bridgman to apologize, pay Joseph Parsons £10 and pay the court costs of seven pounds, one shilling and eightpence.

That disposed of the witchcraft accusation, but not of the feud that arose between the Parsons and Bridgman families. It smoldered eighteen years before it burst into flame again, with most unpleasant results for Goodwife Parsons. In 1674, it was charged that one of the Bridgman family, Goodwife Mary Bartlett, when she died suddenly, had been bewitched by Goodwife Parsons.

Mary Parsons was a forthright woman who had no intention of letting her enemies send her to the gallows. She denied she was a witch; nevertheless, she was sent to Boston for trial. She defended herself so stoutly and the evidence against her, which has disappeared completely, was evidently so weak that the jury found her not guilty. However, the Bridgman family may have felt it had some revenge, since Goodwife Parsons had to endure the discomforts of Boston Prison, a grim and terrible place, for some time before she was brought to trial.

There were a few other witchcraft trials in New England in the middle years of the seventeenth century, but compared to the thousands who were tortured and put to death in the most horrible fashion in Europe, witchcraft in America was a very small tempest in a very small teapot. One historian lists only twelve persons who were executed for witchcraft in New England before 1692.

But by the 1680s two influential and powerful New England ministers, Increase Mather and his son Cotton, were taking a keen interest in witchcraft. Their writings and sermons on the subject and their investigations into it stirred New England into a witch-hunting fever that, while still small compared with those in Europe, was to become famous in American history.

Increase Mather was born in 1639, the son of the Reverend Richard Mather of Dorchester, just outside Boston. After graduating from Harvard in 1656, he became minister of the Second Church in Boston, better known as the Old North, where the signal lanterns were hung that sent Paul Revere on his famous ride in 1775. Increase remained as pastor of this church the rest of his life.

He married Maria Cotton in 1662, and in 1663 they had a son named Cotton. He too became a minister and shared the pastorship of the Second Church with his father. Both the Mathers were brilliant and highly educated men. Cotton entered Harvard at twelve, and when he received his Bachelor of Arts degree in 1678 he was the youngest man ever to attain it up to that time.

Both the Mathers were good men and passionately devoted to their religion. There were cruel men concerned in the New England witch hunts, examinations and trials, but the Mathers were not. Being Puritans, however, the very sound of the word "witchcraft" was horrifying to them. Both became fanatics about it, determined that it must be stamped out forever in New England.

They were familiar with the mischief the Devil was supposed to have stirred up already in the Puritan settlements. In 1648 Increase probably heard his father and mother talking about the witchcraft case of Thomas and Margaret Jones, and perhaps that of Mary Johnson in Connecticut the same year. And he was at Harvard in 1656 when Mrs. Ann Hibbins was executed as a witch in nearby Boston. Cotton Mather grew up to be as fanatical as his father about the necessity for exterminating all the witches of New England.

In 1684, Increase Mather wrote a book, *Remarkable Providences*. It was read far and wide, since the Mathers were now the most distinguished ministers in New England. In the book Increase condemned the use of charms and incantations for curing diseases because those who were thus restored to health obtained it from the Devil. He said a "white witch" who used her magic only to cure illness was as bad as a black one, who worked evil. And he gave accounts of many of the witchcraft cases that had taken place in New England.

Four years later Massachusetts Bay sent Increase to England on an important mission. He sailed on April 7, 1688, as the colony's agent in a vain effort to persuade King James II to restore Massachusetts Bay's original charter, which Charles II had revoked, and thus to make the colony once more a Puritan theocracy—a government under laws based on those of God alone.

Increase was now removed from the scene of New England witchcraft, but his son Cotton was there to fight it. Probably the most famous of New England witchcraft cases up to that time took place in 1688, and Cotton Mather jumped into it with both feet.

The witch hunters of Boston could not have selected a better target than Goody Glover. She was old and poor and had a spiteful temper. Worse, she was one of what Boston called "the wild Irish," and thus one of the Catholics Boston hated, feared, called "Papists" and persecuted. In Boston, which today has so many people of Irish descent that it might be called the Dublin of America, there were a few Irish in 1688.

Goody Glover's daughter was a laundress who did washing for the family of John Goodwin, a mason whom Cotton Mather called "a sober and pious man." The trouble began when the oldest of the four Goodwin children, Martha, who was thirteen, charged the laundress with stealing some of the Goodwins' linen.

The Glover girl went home and told her mother. Goody Glover stalked over to the Goodwin house in high dudgeon and gave Martha a tongue-lashing. Very soon afterward Martha went into strange fits, followed by the other three Goodwin children—John, who was eleven, Mercy, seven, and Benjamin, five.

"Sometimes they would be deaf, then dumb, then blind, and sometimes all these disorders together would come upon them," Cotton Mather later wrote. "Their tongues would be drawn down their throats, then pulled out upon their chins. Their jaws, necks, shoulders, elbows and all their joints would appear to be dislocated, and they would make the most piteous outcries of burnings, of being cut with knives, beat, etc., and the marks of wounds were afterwards to be seen."

They arrested Goody Glover and questioned her, but she would neither deny nor confess anything. Meanwhile, searching the old woman's house, they found several small images or dolls made of rags and stuffed with goats' hair. These well-known charms witches used against their enemies caused the trial of Goody Glover for witchcraft.

"How do you use these images?" she was asked.

"I wet my finger and stroke them," she replied, and showed the court how she did it. The Goodwin children, who were in court, instantly fell down in fits.

"Do you have anyone to stand by you?" was the next question.

"Aye," she said and looked searchingly in the air. Then she shook her head as if puzzled. "No, he is gone. But I do have *one*. He is my prince, and I communicate with him."

That night in the prison a listening jailer heard her reproving the Devil for deserting her in time of trouble. When the trial resumed the next day, a witness testified that a woman on her deathbed two years before had said Goody Glover had bewitched her to death.

While this witness was testifying, her little boy was suddenly afflicted. Word of it was brought to the court, and the witness turned on Goody Glover.

"It is you who are tormenting my child!" she cried.

"Aye," agreed the old woman, "it is because of the wrong you have done me and my daughter."

"I have done you no wrong!" the witness protested.

"Very well, then," said the accused witch, "let me see your child and he shall be well again."

They brought the afflicted boy into the courtroom, and he was instantly cured of his fits.

They condemned Goody Glover to die. Whether the crazed old woman, who doubtless did fancy herself a witch, really, caused these strange happenings is something for a trained psychiatrist to decide.

Before Goody Glover was executed, Cotton Mather visited her in prison to pray and give her spiritual advice, though his curiosity was probably greater than his concern for her plight. At first she would not answer any of his questions, but finally she said, *"They* will not let me."

Fairly aquiver, Cotton demanded: *"They*—who are they?"

"My spirits."

"I advise you to break your covenant with hell, my poor woman," said Cotton.

"You speak a very reasonable thing, but I cannot do it," she replied.

On the morning of November 16, 1688, Goody Glover was hauled in a cart to the gallows on Boston Neck. Before the trap could be sprung, she shrilled: "The children will not be relieved after you hang me!

Others are in it. My daughter . . ." Her voice was cut off by the jerk of the hangman's noose as she was plunged into eternity.

She was right. The Goodwin children continued to be possessed. People who saw them claimed they would flap their arms like so many geese and fly with only their toes touching the ground now and then. They sweated and panted, saying they were in red-hot ovens. They cried out that they were being beaten with cudgels that no one saw, but afterwards the bruises could be seen on their bodies. People seem to have had vivid imaginations in those days.

Two days before Goody Glover was executed, Cotton Mather took thirteen-year-old Martha Goodwin into his own house, watching her queer antics until the following spring. She claimed spirits brought her an invisible horse that she mounted, rode around the room and even rode up the stairs.

In England, Increase Mather was kept fully informed of the Goody Glover affair by Joshua Moody, minister of the First Church.

Cotton Mather was so wrought up over it that he too wrote a book, *Memorable Providences,* published in 1689. In it he set forth three main ideas—that there were witches, how they operated and how witchcraft should be treated. Of course, this book was also widely read.

In time the Goodwin children became normal and were never again tormented. But by then Increase and Cotton Mather, with their books and sermons, had stirred all New England to fever pitch. The Devil was at work there all right, and something had to be done about it.

It would take only one spark to set off an explosion

that would rock the American colonies and go down in history, never to be forgotten. The spark would soon be struck, and Increase and Cotton Mather must take the greatest part of the blame for its beginning, and share a large part of the responsibility for the shameful results. The Mathers, though good and dedicated men, had indeed raised the Devil in Massachusetts.

12

THE SALEM WITCHES

In 1692 Samuel Parris was the minister of the Puritan church in Salem Village, in the Massachusetts Bay colony. The village, today the town of Danvers, Massachussetts, stood close to the larger prosperous seaport town of Salem.

Since in colonial days there were quite a number of slaves in New England as well as the thousands in the Southern colonies, Mr. Parris had two of them. One was a woman named Tituba, from the island of Barbados in the West Indies. She was half black and half Carib Indian, the tribe that Christopher Columbus, on his voyages to the New World, found living in the long chain of islands known as the Lesser Antilles. The other slave was her husband, a full-blooded Carib Indian. If anyone in Salem Village had known his real name it had been long forgotten, and he was called simply John Indian.

Mr. Parris had a daughter named Betty, who was nine years old in 1692. The Parrises had also adopted

Betty's cousin, Abigail Williams, an orphan, then eleven years old. Betty was a sweet, good child, but Abigail was sly, calculating and always up to some mischief—not a good companion for the Parrises' golden-haired, blue-eyed real daughter.

Neither was Tituba a good companion for the two girls, although she gave them tender care. She had brought from Barbados a knowledge of obeah, which her black ancestors had in turn brought from West Africa.

Just how much the little girls learned about sorcery, charms and potions from Tituba is not known, but gradually other girls in Salem Village began to come to the parsonage to take part in secret meetings with Tituba. They were teen-agers, some the daughters of Salem Village families, some servant girls in those households. The oldest was eighteen.

Suddenly, however, the meetings stopped. Little Betty Parris was sick. Just what was the matter with her no one knew, but soon the news spread that Abigail Williams was also ill.

The mysterious ailment spread to the other girls who had met with Tituba in the parsonage. One day Ann Putnam began to do strange things. She muttered to herself, barked like a dog and brayed like a donkey. Then she began to scramble about under chairs and tables, still making queer animal sounds. Suddenly she fell flat on the floor, writhing in convulsions and uttering piercing screams. Her father, Thomas Putnam, saddled his horse and spurred it to a mad gallop towards the home of Dr. Griggs, the Salem Village physician.

Ann Putnam's condition was nothing new to Dr. Griggs. He had seen much the same thing when he had been called to examine Betty Parris, Abigail Williams and two of the other girls who had been meeting with Tituba—Mary Walcott and Susanna Sheldon. He gave Ann the same test and at last shook his head in a baffled manner.

"The evil hand is on them," he declared.

The epidemic went on. The girls who had met at the personage all kept going into the strange fits. Then, for a time, they would be perfectly normal.

Most people in Salem Village were sorry for the "afflicted children," as they were called, though one or two were practically grown up. But a few people said they were faking their odd behavior just to attract attention.

At last Mr. Parris decided something had to be done. He invited the ministers in the surrounding region to come to Salem Village.

The ministers came, and the afflicted girls were brought before them in the meetinghouse. The girls sat perfectly quiet for a time as, one after another, the minister prayed for them. But soon, when the name of God or anything sacred was mentioned, they went into fits, falling on the floor and screaming as if in agony. The ministers had to stop praying because of the noise, but they did ask questions. What or who was hurting them? The girls made no reply. At last the ministers went home, shaking their heads in bewilderment.

Mr. Parris was not finished, however. Considering the mystery, he suddenly thought of Tituba. He remembered that Betty and Abigail had been spending a great deal of time with the slave. Then he recalled that he had seen the other afflicted girls at the parsonage more often than usual. Tituba . . . the West Indies . . . He had been a merchant trading with the islands before he had become a minister. There was witchcraft—black magic known as obeah and voodoo—in the Sugar Islands, as they were often called.

He began to watch Tituba. One day he caught her raking something out of the ashes in the fireplace. When Tituba saw the minister she quickly threw the object to the dog, which ate it.

"What was that, Tituba?" Mr. Paris asked. "What were you doing?"

"Feed the dog, master."

"What did you feed him?"

"Cake, master."

Mr. Parris was hot on the trail now. He finally forced Tituba to confess it was a "witch cake" she had planned to use to cure little Betty.

The minister called his daughter and questioned her sternly until she told him about the meetings. With that, the minister summoned all the girls to the parsonage. All denied that what Betty had told was true, but he persisted until one of the girls broke down and confessed it was so.

"Who else is in it with Tituba?" Mr. Parris demanded.

"Goody Good," replied one of the girls.

Everybody in Salem Village knew Sarah Good. She was a hag with greasy, uncombed gray hair, rheumy eyes and a wrinkled, leathery face. She, her shiftless husband and their children roved about the countryside doing odd jobs on farms. They slept in the haymow until they had finished. If there was not work, Sarah begged for alms and cast-off clothing.

Some people wouldn't have Goody Good around. For one thing, she smoked a villainous pipe, and they were afraid she would set the hay afire in their barns. Some thought she had spread smallpox when one of the epidemics of it that were common in colonial days had raged in and around Salem Village. She was a witch-like woman and, unlike her name, no good.

"Who else?" Mr. Parris then demanded of the girls.

Another one spoke up: "Goody Osburne."

Goody Osburne. That was no surprise, either. Sarah Osburne had not been to church in over a year. She was said to be ill, but some people thought there was something strange about it.

Mr. Parris dismissed the girls and sent for Tituba again. When the slave said she had nothing more to tell him, he beat her until she did tell him much more.

Tituba, Sarah Good and Sarah Osburne were arrested. Since there was no jail in Salem Village, they were imprisoned in the one in nearby Ipswich. Goody Osburne was indeed sick, but they took her along just the same.

There would have to be a thorough examination of the three woman. Witchcraft had been raging for a century or more in the mother country, England, and already Satan had magically flown across the ocean to do his evil work in Puritan New England. Was he now up to his devilish mischief in Salem Village? By all means, if he was, the biblical command would be obeyed and the witches rooted out and exterminated.

Meanwhile, the Parrises had sent little Betty to stay with friends in Salem Town. She soon recovered from the trouble and was not afflicted again.

They held the investigation in the meetinghouse. The "afflicted children" and everyone in Salem Village who could ride, walk or hobble there was present, as well as people from miles around. Two distinguished citizens of Salem Town presided—John Hathorne and Jonathan Corwin, who was a member of the Court of Assistants, high judges of the Massachusetts Bay colony.

John Hathorne, a stern, rock-hard Puritan, did most of the questioning. The constable brought Sarah Good in first.

She was defiant. When Hathorne asked, "Sarah Good, what evil spirit do you have familiarity with?" she spat one word at him: "None!"

"Have you made no contract with the Devil?"

"No."

"Why do you hurt these children?"

"I do not hurt them," she replied. "I scorn it."

Abigail Williams began to writhe and shriek in torment. Ann Putnam also went into a fit.

Mr. Hathorne kept hurling questions at Sarah Good, trying to make her admit she had made a contract with the Devil, but she was not to be trapped.

Finally, Hathorne asked, "Who was it, then, that tormented the children?"

Goody Good gazed searchingly about the meetinghouse. Then she snapped, "It was Osburne."

Witnesses testified that Sarah Good had threatened them when they refused her alms. One couple had taken her, her husband and their brood into their house, but she had been so malicious and spiteful that they turned her out again. A little later seventeen head of their cattle and some sheep and hogs died.

The two investigators decided to hold Sarah in the jail in Boston to be tried for witchcraft. Then they called Tituba to the witness stand. She told them so many weird and wonderful things that she had the spectators sitting on the edges of the pews with their mouths hanging open. She had seen Sarah Good, Sarah Osburne, two other women she did not know and a tall man from Boston tormenting the children.

"Where did you see them?" Hathorne asked.

"Last night at Boston."

Those in the audience looked at each other in amazement and awe. How could Tituba, chained and watched constantly in Ipswich jail, have reached Boston? It would have taken several hours, even on horseback, to ride there and back. Still, everyone knew witches could fly.

Tituba told many other strange things—of familiars Goody Good and Goody Osburne had, or that the slave herself had seen. There had been a red rat, a black rat and a yellow dog with the head of a woman, two legs and two wings. The four women and the man in Boston had taken Tituba to the Putnam house and tried to make her kill Ann with a knife.

"How did you go to Putnams'?" Hathorne asked.

"We ride upon broomsticks and are there presently."

They sent Tituba back to jail and examined Sarah Osburne. She denied everything, but when all the girls stood up and accused her of tormenting them, she did admit she had once either seen or dreamed of seeing a black figure that told her to stay away from the meetings.

"I said I would, and did go next Sabbath Day," Sarah Osburne insisted.

Hathorne had her trapped now. "Why did you yield so far to the Devil as never to go to meeting after that?"

"Alas!" cried Sarah, "I have been sick and unable to go."

They wasted no more time on this woman, who was so plainly a witch. She too went back to jail to await trial.

People in Salem Village were relieved. They thought their troubles with witches were over, but they were wrong. The girls went right on going into fits, shrieking and writhing. People came from miles around to watch them.

Then Ann Putnam "cried out" on Martha Cory, who had laughed at the girls' "afflictions." But the greatest shock of all to Salem Village came when Abigail Williams, in a terrible fit, pulled flaming brands from the fireplace, hurled them about, flapped her arms like a bird's wings and tried to fly up the chimney. They asked who was doing this to her.

"It is Goody Nurse!" she screamed.

People simply couldn't believe it. Rebecca Nurse was one of the finest women in Salem Village, a member of the church since it had first been built in 1673 and piously devoted to her religion. She was now old, deaf and ill. Surely this saintly woman had had no dealings with the Devil.

When they examined Martha Cory, she fought the inquisitors like a tigress. She admitted nothing, but unfortunately her sharp tongue had made enemies who testified against her. They held Martha for trial.

"You can't prove me a witch!" she shouted as she was led from the meetinghouse. They would see about that.

Frail old Rebecca Nurse had to lean on the minister's chair to keep from collapsing when they examined her. Many in the meetinghouse wept while John Hathorne questioned her, although he was gentler with her than with the others.

But both Abigail Williams and Ann Putnam went into fits and accused Rebecca Nurse of tormenting them. So did Ann Putnam's mother, who was not well and probably was mentally ill. She said little children, wearing the winding sheets in which they had been buried, appeared to her and said Witch Nurse had murdered them.

"What do you say to this?" Hathorne asked.

Rebecca lifted her hands in appeal to heaven. "Oh, Lord, help me!" she cried.

They sent her to jail in Salem Town to be tried for her life, a poor old creature who had never harmed anyone.

One other accused witch was brought before the examiners. When Hathorne read the charge against her she stood bewildered, not understanding a word of what it meant. She was Dorcas Good, one of Sarah's children. Dorcas was five years old. They sent her to Boston to be chained beside her mother in the prison there.

More and more "witches" kept turning up. Sarah Cloyce, Rebecca Nurse's sister, was so indignant over what they had done to the poor old woman that when Mr. Parris, in his sermon one Sabbath, declared that every last witch in the region must be hunted down, Goodwife Cloyce got up and stalked out of the meetinghouse.

The "afflicted children" set up a terrible clamor. They said Sarah Cloyce had gone straight to a witches' sabbat in Mr. Parris' own pasture near his house. So they arrested Sarah and sent her to jail.

So many others were accused that the Salem Village meetinghouse was going to be far too small to hold the mob that would surely flock to attend the next examination. They transferred it to the larger church in Salem Town. And this time the deputy governor of Massachusetts Bay himself, Thomas Danforth, was to preside, assisted by five members of the governor's council.

When this court held its session, John Indian was called as a witness against Sarah Cloyce. Like his wife, Tituba, he decided the smartest thing was to admit he was mixed up in witchcraft and accuse others. What he told about Sarah Cloyce and her association with the Devil was so fantastic that she shouted at him: "Oh, you are a grievous liar!" It did her no good, for she too went to jail.

When another accused witch, Elizabeth Procter, was called to the stand, her husband, John, stood up and stoutly defended her. Instantly the girls cried out on him, and both he and his wife were packed off to prison.

One of the girls, Mary Warren, was the Procters' servant. John Procter had given her a stern warning to stop her foolishness and act like a normal person. It seems to have scared her so that she suddenly decided she had been wrong in crying out on the Procters and the other accused witches, and she said so. When the other girls found out about it they screamed that Mary too was a witch. The magistrates in Salem Town hustled her off to jail too.

Another accused witch brought before the six magistrates was Abigail Hobbs. She was a wild creature who roved the woods at night—on some evil mission for the Devil, people now decided. She did not disappoint them. Before the court she freely admitted she was a witch and told tales that made the spectators shudder, accusing several others, including her own father and mother. She and Bridget Bishop, who kept a tavern in Salem Town and had an unsavory reputation, were promptly sent to jail.

So was Martha Cory's husband, Giles. But when it came to the trials, in Giles Cory's case the judges were going to have to deal with someone far different from the others who had already been examined—a man with a heart of oak and a will of steel. But in the examinations his denials did no good, and he too went to jail.

There was a new sensation in the court when one of the accused went free. He was Nehemiah Abbott, who claimed to be nearly a hundred years old. When Hathorne asked the girls if Nehemiah was tormenting them, Mercy Lewis stood up and said positively, "He is not the man." The other girls did not like being robbed of their prey in this fashion, and they demanded that Nehemiah be searched for a witch mark. When this was done, none was found, and the examiners declared him innocent.

Why did Mercy Lewis do this? It may simply have been a bit of cunning. If one accused witch were let off, would it not show that the examinations were perfectly fair, and that an innocent person had nothing to fear?

There were plenty of other victims, however, and all were sent to jail, including another of Rebecca Nurse's sisters, Mary Esty, also a saintly woman, and Susanna Martin of nearby Amesbury. On an early spring day when melting snow had turned the roads into muddy quagmires, Susanna went to pay a call on a friend in Newbury. That visit was going to cost her her life. The "friend" happened to look at Susanna's shoes. They were spotless—not a trace of mud on them. How had

Susanna reached Newbury? How but flying on a witch's broomstick? Susanna went to jail.

Then came the greatest sensation of all. Near Mr. Parris' pasture, Ann Putnam was suddenly seized with a fit.

"Oh, dreadful, dreadful!" she shrieked. "Here is a minister come! What! Are ministers witches too?"

The victim was George Burroughs, who had served for a time as minister of the Salem Village church. He had left to become the minister in Casco Bay, a remote settlement on the coast of Maine, then a part of Massachusetts Bay, and many miles from Salem Village. Yet Ann Putnam insisted she saw George Burroughs there in the pasture, celebrating a sabbat with many other witches.

That Casco Bay was so far away did not stop the witch hunters. They sent word to Portsmouth, New Hampshire, and a constable went from there to Casco Bay. George Burroughs was having dinner, but the constable dragged him off without letting him finish eating, pack for the long journey or say good-bye to his frantic wife and family. In Salem Town they sent him to jail.

Next, one of the richest and most distinguished citizens of Salem Town and his wife found themselves in trouble. Philip English was a merchant who owned a fine mansion, a wharf, a large warehouse and a fleet of ships trading with France and the West Indies. His wife, Mary, made the mistake of going to Salem Village to call on Sarah Cloyce before Sarah was arrested. When Mary heard what they had done to poor old Rebecca Nurse, she was indignant, and said so in no uncertain terms. The afflicted girls heard about it and "cried out" on her. Mary English was arrested and sent to jail in Salem Town.

Philip English used his strong influence to get his wife out, but the best he could do was to have her transferred to Boston Prison, which was less crowded than the jail in Salem Town, fairly bursting at the seams with its horde of prisoners. Mr. English then kept on trying to free Mary, but the "afflicted children" put a quick stop to that. They "cried out" on him, and he too found himself in Boston Prison.

Nevertheless, influential men in Boston were working to save the Englishes. The two prisoners were given better treatment than others there in the grim stone pile, and allowed to attend services each Sabbath, under guard, at the church just around the corner from the prison.

One Sunday, as the Englishes were leaving the church, a milling crowd of men at the door surrounded them. They jostled the prison guards back into the church and locked the door.

One of the Englishes' rescuers cried, "We have horses ready! Mount and ride as if the Devil himself was after you!"

And so the Englishes escaped to live in New York until the New England witchcraft delusion was over. Although the sheriff had seized all of the merchant's property, he started over, and was soon a rich and distinguished merchant again in Salem Town.

At last, with one important exception, all the accused witches had been examined and, save for old Nehemiah Abbott, lodged in jail. The missing witch was the "tall man of Boston" Tituba had spoken of. Who was he? Somehow he must be found and seized.

At last some of the "afflicted children" named him.

The gasp that went up in startled Salem Village must almost have been heard in Boston. Captain John Alden! The oldest son of John and Priscilla Alden, who had come with the Pilgrims in the *Mayflower* in 1620. Impossible! Or was it? The girls were positive. Hadn't they revealed all the other witches who had been tormenting them?

John Alden, tall and living in Boston fitted Tituba's description, just as did scores of other men. He was also a long-experienced sea captain, muscular and ramrod-straight, not looking his seventy years.

When he was summoned to Salem Village, he blew into the meetinghouse like a typhoon. When the afflicted girls were brought in, they were asked to pick out Captain Alden. They hesitated; then finally one girl pointed—to the wrong man! But a meddlesome spectator whispered in her ear, her finger shifted to Alden and all the girls went into fits, shrieking and rolling on the floor in front of him.

It was plain to all in the meetinghouse that Captain Alden, merely by looking upon the girls, had caused them to fall before him, possessed. Alden turned a withering eye on Bartholomew Gedney, who, in spite of being an old friend of the captain's, was sitting with Hathorne as an examiner. "Why don't *you* fall down when I look at you?" he demanded in his sea captain's bellow. "Can you give me a reason?"

Gedney couldn't, but they committed John Alden to await trial. Because of his high standing in Boston, they let him remain in his house instead of prison, though under guard. But Alden had no intention of letting them put a halter around his neck. He bribed one of the guards, sneaked out one morning before dawn and galloped madly for his former home in Duxbury. Good friends there hid him until the witchcraft delusion was over.

Now Governor Sir William Phips of Massachusetts Bay appointed a special Court of Oyer and Terminer to try all the accused witches. Its chief justice was William Stoughton, who had six assistant justices. Stoughton was sixty years old, sour-tempered, with a heart as cold and ruthless as the look on his long, tombstonelike face. He was not married, probably because he had never loved anyone but himself.

The procedure in the trials was much like that of the examinations, and of course the girls were in court to put on their crazy show in case any of the victims should seem about to be acquitted. The accused witches never had a chance of proving their innocence. Stoughton ruled the court like a Roman emperor, and his assistants might as well have stayed home. He accepted only the evidence that would help convict the wretched people who came before the court.

The long-nosed Puritans of Salem Town hated Bridget Bishop, the tavernkeeper, because she liked flashy clothes. She wore her finery to the trial, bedraggled and dirty now from her long stay in jail. That and her defiant air would have been enough to convict her even if there had not been so much evidence against her.

Witnesses testified that an insane neighbor of Bridget's who had killed herself with a pair of scissors had actually been done to death by the tavernkeeper's witchcraft. Two men doing repairs in her cellar said they found rag dolls with pins sticking in them hidden there—the tried and proven witches' device for getting rid of someone. Another witness had awakened one morning to see Bridget in his room, grinning horribly at him. Then—whoosh!—she had flown out through a tiny crack in the window frame.

All this nonsense was swallowed by the court and the jury that found Bridget guilty. Then Stoughton rose and sentenced her, ordering the high sheriff to "take you to the place of execution, and that you be hanged by the neck until you are dead."

Just outside Salem Town a ridge called Gallows Hill rose, its summit rocky and bare save for a few great old trees. On June 10, 1692, horses strained to pull a cart containing Bridget Bishop up the steep, rocky road to the top. An immense crowd had gathered about a ladder leaning against a branch of one of the trees. From the branch dangled a rope knotted with a hangman's noose.

The cart drew up before the ladder, and the sheriff pushed Bridget Bishop off the cart onto the ladder and dropped the noose over her head. A moment later the ladder was snatched from under her.

As they watched the grisly dance of death until Bridget Bishop's body finally hung limp and still, how many in the crowd wondered if this was indeed true justice? How many turned their heads away with a sickening feeling that something was wrong, somehow?

On June 28 the Court of Oyer and Terminer tried Sarah Good; Susanna Martin, who had "flown" from Amesbury to Newbury and kept her shoes clean; Elizabeth Howe of Ipswich; Sarah Wildes of Topsfield; and Rebecca Nurse. All but Rebecca were quickly found guilty. In her case the jury brought in a verdict of "not guilty."

Stoughton stood up, quaking with rage and fixing the jury with a baleful eye. He sent them back to reconsider a few words Rebecca had uttered that tended to incriminate her. After a time the foreman returned to the courtroom and questioned Rebecca about it. By giving the true answer she might have cleared herself in a way that not even the tyrannical Stoughton could have overruled. But the poor old creature was so deaf and so paralyzed with fear that she did not hear the foreman's question and remained silent. And Stoughton had his way. Rebecca Nurse was found guilty and sentenced to die.

They hanged five woman on Gallows Hill on July 19, 1692. When the court sat again, the minister George Burroughs, John and Elizabeth Procter, George Jacobs, Sr., John Willard and Martha Carrier were all convicted and executed on August 19. But then, for the first time, there was a move to save one—George Burroughs. As he stood on the ladder with the noose around his neck he recited the Lord's Prayer.

Someone in the crowd shouted, "No wizard could repeat the Lord's Prayer at a time like this!"

"Save him!" cried another. "Take the rope off his neck!"

Robert Calef, a mysterious enemy of the Mathers, wrote that just as the crowd surged forward to rescue the minister, a young man dressed all in black, mounted on a horse, shouted, "Stay! Let me be heard!" It was Cotton Mather.

"Let me remind you," he said, "that the Devil is never more himself than when he appears to be an angel of light. This man is not what he appears to be."

Whether Calef's story is true or not, the ladder was yanked from under George Burroughs and he strangled.

The Court of Oyer and Terminer sat again on September 9 and 17. It convicted fifteen persons, but only eight of them were hanged. One woman was expecting a baby and was reprieved until the child could be born. Another woman, aided by friends, escaped from jail before she could be executed.

At this point a strange thing happened in the Salem witchcraft delusion. The other five convicted witches were never hanged. Every one of them had confessed to being a witch, including Tituba and the wild woman of the woods, Abigail Hobbs. In fact, no accused witch who confessed to it was executed.

Why? It seems that the authorities kept them alive in the hope that they would accuse still others who had not been rooted out. Possibly Tituba and Abigail Hobbs were cunning enough to realize that confessing was their best chance, and others then followed their example.

The eight who had not confessed were hanged on September 22. Martha Cory was one of them. Next they tried her husband, Giles.

"How do you plead to the charge against you?" they asked the old man. Giles Cory stood there, his jaws set, and answered nothing. They threatened, then coaxed him, but he still stood mute. And it was the law that a person being tried must plead guilty or not guilty. Without a plea they could not try him.

One of the justices who knew his English law remembered that in Europe, for centuries, a person who refused to plead was subjected to *peine forte et dure*. The French words mean "painful and merciless punishment." The balky person was placed on his back, and heavy weights piled on him until his agony forced a plea from him.

They took Giles Cory to a vacant lot near the Salem Town jail and began to pile big stones on his chest. The pain finally forced groans from stout-hearted Giles Cory, but he spoke not a word. At last he died.

The end of all this frightfulness came in a sudden, spectacular way. Governor Sir William Phips, a tempestuous man and former sea captain, whose life story is a strange and thrilling one, had been away in Maine, leading an armed force to stop raids on the forest and coastal settlements there by French and Indians from Canada. He returned to find that his wife, Lady Mary, had been looking into the witchcraft delusion.

She had visited and seen the sufferings of accused witches awaiting trial in grim, cold, damp Boston Prison. And since her husband was away, she had taken it upon herself to sign a warrant in his name, freeing one wretched woman she felt sure was innocent. Governor Phips was outraged that she had used his authority illegally—until Lady Mary exploded a bombshell.

"William," she said, "the afflicted girls of Salem Village, hearing that I released that poor woman, have cried out on me. I am about to be arrested on suspicion of witchcraft."

Sir William gave a roar like a wounded lion. He mounted a horse, charged down on Chief Justice Stoughton's mansion, gave him a tongue-lashing in sizzling seafaring man's language, then galloped to Boston Prison. There he threw the jailer out and ordered all the accused witches released.

And with that the great Salem witchcraft delusion collapsed. It remains only to tell what happened to some who were concerned in it, and to speculate on why it happened in the first place.

Icy-hearted William Stoughton never yielded an inch in his belief that the witch hunts should go on. When Governor Phips ordered him to stop the trials, he stormed: "We were in a way to have cleared the land of them! Who is it that obstructs the cause of justice I know not. The Lord be merciful to this country!"

But others came to realize in time the frightful mistake they had made. It is a mystery, for example, how Samuel Sewall could have sat as one of the justices of the Court of Oyer and Terminer and let the infamous mockery of justice go on. He was a gentleman and a brilliant judge, and he kept an amusing and detailed diary throughout his career that, more than any other record, tells what life in Massachusetts Bay in the seventeenth century was like. It took a tragedy in his own life to make him realize what he had helped to do in Salem Town.

On December 23, 1696, Samuel Sewall's two-year-old daughter died. On Christmas Eve, as he sat grieving in his house, he asked his son to read from the Bible in the hope it might bring him consolation. The boy opened the book at random and read from the Gospel according to St. Matthew: "But if ye had known what this meaneth: 'I will have mercy and not sacrifice,' ye would not have condemned the guiltless."

Those last few words seemed to burn like fire into Samuel Sewall's brain: *". . . ye would not have condemned the guiltless."* Then, before the entire congregation of his church, the judge confessed he had been wrong, and he did penance for the rest of his life.

There were other confessions. Thomas Fish, the foreman, and the other eleven members of the jury that had sent Rebecca Nurse to the gallows signed a public statement saying they had brought upon themselves and the people the guilt of innocent blood. Even Cotton Mather's sleep was plagued by guilty dreams, and he wrote in his diary that he should have used more vigor to stop the proceedings.

Ann Putnam's life was beset by many troubles and ill health, at least partly caused by the guilt that lay heavy on her mind. At last, in 1706, she went to the minister who had succeeded Mr. Parris.

"I do not know why I did those grievous things," she said, "but I must confess my sin before all the people." And she did, on August 25, 1706, before a packed meetinghouse in Salem Village.

As for Mr. Parris, he was soon forced out of Salem Village. A large share of the guilt was his, but the truth was that the guilt-ridden people of the hamlet wanted a scapegoat to ease their own consciences, so they ousted him, to wander from church to church until he died. Little is known of the rest—the other afflicted girls, Tituba, John Indian and the others.

Why did it happen? Psychologists and psychiatrists are pretty well agreed that it was what they call "mass hysteria." The same thing had happened a few times in England. Little Betty Parris' young mind, especially since she was a strict Puritan minister's daughter, seems to have cracked under the strain of the evil knowledge she had gained from Tituba, and for a time she was mentally ill. The affliction then spread, like a contagious disease, to the other girls.

However, there is little doubt that some of the girls, especially the older ones, were spiteful, and that they enjoyed the notoriety that had put them in the spotlight in Salem Village, where life was dull. At times they all seem to have been "possessed," but at others some, at least, knew the terrible things they were doing.

One modern writer had gone so far as to suggest that some of the accused persons *were* witches. Several, like Tituba, Abigail Hobbs and Sarah Good, may have practiced "black magic." But no one, except those who believe that witchcraft did and still does exist, thinks that even these women, if they did profess to be witches, ever did anyone harm with their incantations, charms and potions. And most of the nineteen who went to their deaths on Gallows Hill, as well as Giles Cory and Sarah Osburne, were surely innocent. The reason they died was that practically everyone in New England in the seventeenth century believed in witchcraft.

Strange that the twenty-one who died—including Giles Cory, pressed to death, and poor, sick Sarah Osburne, who died in jail before they could hang her—should have made the Salem witchcraft delusion the most famous of all witchcraft persecutions. Countless thousands perished in Europe—usually in ways far more horrible than the Salem witches, for no "witch" in America was tortured or burned, except for Giles Cory, and that was not to obtain a confession.

It was notorious because it came at a time when witchcraft persecutions in Europe were dying out. Attention was drawn to Salem, and there were so many strange and unexplained things about the Salem witch hunts, such as the acceptance of the unbelievable charges and weird behavior of the afflicted girls by men and women of learning and intelligence, especially the ministers. The historians and students of witchcraft still write and speculate on these things. Probably they always will.

13

AND TODAY

Belief in witchcraft still exists in many parts of the world. Much of what is known of it comes from the West Indies, where voodoo and obeah still flourish in some places, especially Haiti. It also continues in England, whose Puritan and other emigrants brought it to America, probably in other European countries and in the United States itself. In all probability forms of witchcraft still exist in the rapidly shrinking wild interior parts of what was once known as the Dark Continent.

England's most famous modern witch is Sybil Leek. She makes no secret of being one, though in the book she wrote telling of her life as a witch, she makes it clear that she is a white witch, concerned only with doing good through healing. She tells how she comes from a long line of witches, going back to the twelfth century.

She was born in a wild, mountainous section of Staffordshire, in central England, one of the centers of witchcraft and witch hunts in the sixteenth and seventeenth centuries, where she learned witchcraft from her grandmother. She attended the important meetings of a witches' coven called Great Sabbats, held four times a year, including one on Halloween.

Then, when a Russian aunt who was a witch and lived in France died, Sybil was chosen to replace her in the coven the aunt had belonged to. She went through her initiation in a remote place in France, providing evidence that witchcraft still exists in that country.

The ceremony took place in those eerie surroundings before an altar of rough stones. The members of the coven stood inside a circle nine feet in diameter drawn around the altar as a magical protection. Another relative of Sybil's in France, who was also a witch, and a Chinese dealer in antiques were her sponsors.

After incantations for the protection of all had been chanted, the high priest of the coven presented Sybil, first to the high priestess and then to the rest—by their witch names rather than their real ones. Next, containers of water and salt were consecrated. A knife was held close to Sybil's heart as the high priestess explained what her responsibilities would be as a witch. She then took an oath of fidelity and was welcomed to the cult of witchcraft with special dances and incantations.

Soon afterward, Sybil's family moved to a village in the famous New Forest, Hampshire, where witch covens still exist. She joined one, the Horsa Coven, and eventually became its high priestess.

She spent much time with the gypsies who inhabited that region. From them she learned still more about the uses of herbs in witchcraft to add to what her grandmother had taught her. Some of the gypsies' herbs were plants considered as nuisances by most people.

People who live in the suburbs of cities often spend much time and money in getting rid of dandelions on their lawns. The gypsies consider the dandelion one of the most useful of herbs. They say it is especially useful in treating kidney ailments, is good for the liver and is a fine tonic, purifying the blood.

Anyone who has been stung by nettles is apt to keep away from them. But the gypsies use poultices of green nettle leaves to relieve pain. They rub bruised leaves of the weed into their skins if they are troubled with rheumatism. They make tea of nettles to relieve fevers and colds.

Thus, as a witch, Sybil Leek became a healer. She used charms and potions in her work, but with the aid of psychic healing, a combination of psychology and philosophy, along with the keen power of concentration she had learned as a witch.

From far and wide, sick people came to her to be cured of many ailments. She found it difficult and a great strain on herself to treat them. For one thing, many were afraid to put themselves in the care of a professed witch who might be in league with Satan. That fear had to be broken down. Some were desperately ill and feared death, and Sybil had to overcome this feeling in them too.

One day she received a letter from a man in Rotterdam, the Netherlands. He had been told he had only three months to live. Would Sybil come to Rotterdam and try to cure him? He would pay her fare there.

There was no need of that, she wrote him, if he would follow her instructions exactly. He did so, and when she wrote her book she still often heard from the grateful Hollander.

She cured a young man who was supposed to be an incurable drug addict. And even another witch, or sorcerer, who was the leader of a group that practiced black magic came to her for help. His evil powers could not cure his illness. She agreed to help him if he would stop some outbreaks of mischief by followers of black magic. Churches had been desecrated and graves broken into. He promised, and she was able to help him, but in spite of it he returned to the world of black magic.

If all this is witchcraft, surely Sybil Leek is no witch linked with the forces of evil, but an outstanding example of that benevolent kind of witchcraft, a white witch.

Eventually, Sybil became a roving television reporter. Although British television did not favor programs about witchcraft, she did take part in a broadcast filmed in one of the many houses in England that are supposed to be haunted.

She had in her youth become well acquainted with Aleister Crowley, who was once called "the most evil man in the world" and was reputed to deal in black magic. He tried to get her to take up his form of witchcraft, but she refused, though she did attend a Black Mass with him in Paris.

Sybil became well known in England as a witch. When her landlord refused to renew her lease, she came to America. She received a great deal of publicity when she arrived in New York, and found herself overwhelmed with people who wanted her to perform all sorts of miracles for them. She felt disgusted with their lack of understanding in her witchcraft or any

164

knowledge of what it—she calls it a religion—really is. It was always confused with voodoo and black magic.

Sybil then went to Boston, where she found people had a deep interest in her kind of witchcraft. She liked Boston, and especially the Concord countryside outside the city, where she stayed with friends. It reminded her of her own New Forest, and in Concord she took part in the consecration of a small piece of land to witchcraft and predicted that within a few years a coven of witches would hold meetings there. Concord—only about twenty-five miles from Salem!

Sybil returned to England for a time, but finally made up her mind to live in America. She did a good deal of ghost hunting here, some of it filmed for television, and also much work in astrology, in which she firmly believes. She finally settled down in Houston, Texas, with a winter home in Melbourne Beach, Florida.

Sybil Leek's friend Aleister Crowley, another famous modern English witch or sorcerer, was a strange, extremely brilliant man who lived in the first half of the twentieth century. He was a graduate of Cambridge University in England, a poet of distinction and an expert mountain climber. In 1905 he led an expedition that tried to climb the third highest mountain in the world, Kanchenjunga, which towers 28,208 feet in the Himalayas of Asia. It failed when an avalanche buried one of the climbers and two native porters.

Crowley had many enemies, and some of the newspapers did not like him and attacked him. He was accused of dealing in black magic, but he claimed to be a white witch, though he was head of a cult that had some strange and weird ceremonies. And Crowley does seem to have had some sort of unearthly power.

It was his mystic cult that got him into trouble. He bought an old monastery in Sicily and lived there for some time with his followers. Among them was a young poet from Oxford University. At one of the cult's rites, a cat was sacrificed at an altar, and the young poet drank from a cup of its blood. Soon afterward he died, and Crowley and the cult were promptly blamed for it, although the evidence seems to show that the young man was actually the victim of an inflammation of his intestines, either typhoid fever or something much like it. But, as has already been mentioned, it caused Crowley to be called the most evil man in the world.

Another English devotee of witchcraft has become well known. Cecil Williamson calls himself a sorcerer and claims he knows how to bewitch people. He operates a museum in the little English hamlet of Bocastle, in Cornwall, the southwesternmost county of England. It is not far from Tintagel, where the fabled Merlin, King Arthur's sorcerer, performed feats of magic. Among the exhibits is a skeleton supposed to be that of Ursula Kempe, one of the St. Osyth witches hanged in 1582. It lies in a coffin, and by its side are iron spikes said to have been driven into her body to keep her from rising from her grave to haunt Chelmsford, where she was executed.

Mr. Williamson says there are still witches and he has met them, but the real ones are rare and hard to find. As for their flying, he has recipes for some of the ointments witches are supposed to rub on their bodies before taking off.

Mr. Williamson says he can produce spirits by magic—glowing blue forms that gradually take the shape of a human head, sometimes speak and then disappear or float away in the air. Peter Bloxham, who wrote an article about him, published in *The New York Times* on April 19, 1970, did not see this interesting piece of magic performed.

Poltergeists, described in an earlier chapter are the ghosts that cause annoyance with their mysterious shenanigans and are very noisy about it, though they do little real harm. In 1958, in Seaford, Long Island, a family went through weeks of mysterious and frightening occurrences that had all the earmarks of a poltergeist's work.

James M. Herrmann, employed by an airline, his wife and their daughter, thirteen, and son, twelve, lived on a quiet street in this suburb of New York City. One afternoon in February, bottles in the house began to jump about, and their screwed-on tops popped off with small explosions. Some fell to the floor.

This kept on until the family finally called the police. A detective checked every possible cause and threw up his hands in despair. Meanwhile, all over the United States and in foreign countries, newspapers and radio stations reported the story.

Things got worse rather than better for the Herrmann family. The bottles and other containers didn't just continue to "blow their tops." Objects began to fly through the air. A statue of the Virgin Mary eighteen inches high took off and landed twelve feet away, unbroken. A phonograph flew across the room in the finished section of the basement. A bookcase toppled over.

The Herrmanns were driven almost crazy. Not only did the strange occurrences keep on, but they were overwhelmed with people who flocked to stare at the "bewitched" house and to offer their ideas of what had happened to it and how to stop it. Their telephone never stopped ringing.

Dozens of explanations were given. The police detective proved every one was false—and he was in the house when a porcelain figure flew off a table and catapulted for twelve feet. They even tried to explain it as a trick and to put the blame on the twelve-year-old boy, a brilliant student, but there was never any proof that he was the culprit.

Learned professors, and students of the mystic arts called the occult, investigated and had their opinions, but no one ever proved anything. As suddenly as they had begun, the mysterious happenings ended on March 10, 1958. The Herrmanns were never troubled again. If there were such things as poltergeists, perhaps as good an explanation as any might be that one *was* at work in the house.

There have been some similar occurrences in other places in modern days, one somewhat like the Seaford affair in Springfield, Massachusetts, and again no one really knows why.

Witchcraft interests almost everyone. Whether people actually believe in it or are simply fascinated by occurrences like those that have been described and cannot be explained, interest has become intense, especially in recent years. Many books about it are published and successful plays produced. If some of the things reported in recent books about witchcraft are true, there may be as many as 60,000 people in the United States who profess to be witches.

Of these, a good many, no doubt, are true believers in witchcraft of one kind or another, though many others are frauds who claim to practice "witchcraft" for what money it will bring them. Fortune tellers, sham astrologers, tea-leaf readers and "mystics" who hold séances with their table rappings and claims to communicate with the dead still flourish. True astrology, however, is considered by many people to be an exact science and thus not a kind of witchcraft.

Once what was called "second sight"—the ability to foretell the future—was considered witchcraft. Today it is well established that some people are gifted with ESP—extrasensory perception—enabling them to know certain things they have no way of learning by ordinary means. This sense is more highly developed in some persons than others. It is a psychic phenomenon that cannot be explained as the trickery professional magicians use on the stage to mystify their audiences.

ESP is taken seriously by many scientists. Yet if a person were able to predict everything about his future exactly, he should be able, like fabled King Midas of the golden touch, to become fabulously rich. He might trade in the stock market. Knowing which stocks would rise in value and which ones would decline, he could quickly make an immense fortune. The gambling casinos of Europe, Nevada and other places would either have to bar such a person or go out of business.

Probably "witchcraft," in one form or another, will always exist. There will always be people who claim they can predict the future and perform magic by witchcraft.

SUGGESTED
FURTHER READINGS

For a very complete reference book covering witchcraft in all its aspects in Europe and the United States, the *Encyclopedia of Witchcraft and Demonology,* by Rosell Hope Robbins (New York: Crown, 1970), is the best modern work of its kind, compiled from over a thousand reference sources. A scholarly book on the history and practices of witchcraft in general is *Witchcraft,* by Pennethorne Hughes (Baltimore: Penguin Books, 1969).

An authority on witchcraft in England in the sixteenth and seventeenth centuries is Wallace Notestein, author of *A History of Witchcraft in England from 1558 to 1718* (New York: Russell & Russell, 1965).

The Devil's Shadow (New York: Messner, 1967; paperback edition, Washington Square Press, 1970), written for young people, describes the Salem witchcraft delusion in much greater detail than is possible in a single chapter in this present book by the same author. On the same subject, a book for adults, *The*

Devil in Massachusetts, by Marion L. Starkey (New York: Knopf, 1949), is excellent.

Sybil Leek's *Diary of a Witch* (Englewood Cliffs, N.J.: Prentice-Hall, 1968) is the fascinating story of her own life and adventures by a self-professed witch of today. Another book of importance on modern witchcraft, by the noted writer the late William Seabrook, is *Witchcraft—Its Power in the World Today* (New York: Harcourt, Brace, 1940).

BIBLIOGRAPHY

Alderman, Clifford Lindsey. *The Devil's Shadow*. New York: Messner, 1967; paperback edition, Washington Square Press, 1970.

Bach, Marcus. *Strange Altars*. New York: Bobbs-Merrill, 1952.

Barry, Philip Beaufog. *Twelve Monstrous Criminals*. London: Hutchinson & Co., Ltd., 1927.

Bell, Hesketh. *Obeah*. London: S. Low, Martin & Co.

————— *Witches and Fishes*. London: Edward Arnold & Co., 1948.

Bloomfield, Greta. *Witchcraft in Africa*. Cape Town: Howard Trimmins, 1962.

Bloxham, Peter. "The Devil and Cecil Williamson." *The New York Times*, April 19, 1970.

Burt, Henry M. *The First Century of the History of Springfield*. Springfield, Mass.: Henry M. Burt, 1898.

Drake, Samuel Gardner. *Annals of Witchcraft in New England*. Boston: W. Elliot Woodward, 1869.

Earle, Alice Morse. *Home Life in Colonial Days*. New York: Grosset & Dunlap, 1898.

Ewen, C. L'Estrange (editor). *Witch Hunting and Witch Trials*. London: Kegan Paul, Trench, Trubner & Co., 1929.

———— *Witchcraft and Demonianism*. London: Heath Cranton, Ltd., 1933.

Farbre, Lucien (Hopkins, Gerard, trans.). *Joan of Arc*. New York: McGraw-Hill, 1954.

Gallico, Paul. *The Snow Goose*. New York: Knopf, 1956.

Green, Lawrence G. *Under a Sky Like Flame*. Cape Town: Howard B. Trimmins, 1954.

Hale, John. *A Modest Inquiry into the Nature of Witchcraft*. New York: Scribner, 1914.

Handler, M. S. "African Explains the Witch Doctor." *The New York Times*, August 16, 1970.

Harman, Harry E. III and Jeanne. *Fielding's Guide to the Caribbean, 1969-70*. New York: Fielding Publications, 1968.

Hole, Christina. *Witchcraft in England*. New York: Scribner, 1947.

Horst, Georg Conrad. *Zauber Bibliothek oder von Zauberei, Hexen und Hexenprozessen, Dämonen, Gespenstern und Geisterscheinungen*. Mainz: Florian Kupferberg, 1821.

Howard, Daniel. *A New History of Old Windsor, Connecticut*. Windsor Locks, Conn.: The Journal Press, 1935.

Howe, Russell Warren. *Black Star Rising*. London: Herbert Jenkins, 1958.

Hughes, Pennethorne. *Witchcraft*. Baltimore: Pelican Books, 1969.

Hurston, Zora. *Voodoo Gods*. London: J. M. Dent & Sons, 1939.

Hutchinson, Thomas. *The History of the Colony and Province of Massachusetts Bay*. Cambridge: Harvard University Press, 1936.

Huxley, Francis. *The Invisibles—Voodoo Gods in Haiti*. New York: McGraw-Hill, 1966.

Jacob, E. F. *The Fifteenth Century, 1398-1485* (Vol. 6, Oxford History of England). Oxford: Clarendon Press, 1961.

Johnson, Clifton. *Historic Hampshire in the Connecticut Valley*. Springfield, Mass: Milton Bradley Co., 1932.

Jones, J. O. *Matthew Hopkins* (in *Lives of Twelve Bad Men*, ed. by Thomas Seccombe), 1894.

Jones, Louis C. *Things That Go Bump in the Night*. New York: Hill & Wang, 1959.

King James the First. *Daemonology*. New York: Barnes & Noble, 1966 (first published, 1597).

—— *News from Scotland, Declaring the Damnable Life and Death of Doctor Fian, a Notable Sorcerer*. New York: Barnes & Noble, 1966 (first published, 1591).

Kittredge, George Lyman. *English Witchcraft and James I*. New York: Macmillan, 1912.

—— *Witchcraft in Old and New England*. Cambridge: Harvard University Press, 1929.

Lea, Henry Charles. *Materials Toward a History of Witchcraft*. New York: Thomas Yosoloff, 1957.

Leek, Sybil. *Diary of a Witch*. Englewood Cliffs, N.J.: Prentice-Hall, 1968.

Leonard, Arthur Glyn. "Southern Nigeria—Religion and Witchcraft." *Imperial and Asiatic Quarterly Review*, July-Oct. 1907, Ser. 3, Vol. 24, Nos. 47 and 48.

Linton, E. Lynn. *Witch Stories*. London: Chapman & Hall, 1861.

Love, William De Loss. *The Colonial History of Hartford*. Hartford. Published by the author, 1914.

Magoffin, Ralph V. D., and Duncalf, Frederic. *Ancient and Medieval History*. Morristown, N.J.: Silver Burdett, 1959.

Mather, Cotton. *Memorable Providences* (in *Original Narratives of America*). New York: Scribner, 1914.

Mather, Increase. *Remarkable Providences* (in *Original Narratives of America*). New York: Scribner, 1914.

Métraux, Alfred (Charteris, Hugo, trans.) *Voodoo in Haiti*. New York: Oxford University Press, 1959.

Middleton, John (editor). *Magic, Witchcraft and Curing*. Garden City: The Natural History Press (American Museum Sourcebooks in Anthropology, published for the American Museum of Natural History), 1967.

Murdock, Kenneth Ballard. *Increase Mather, the Fore-*

most American Puritan. Cambridge: Harvard University Press, 1925.

Murray, Margaret Alice. *The Witch-Cult in Western Europe.* Oxford: Clarendon Press, 1921.

Nadel, S. F. "Witchcraft and Anti-Witchcraft in Nupe Society." *Journal of African Languages and Cultures,* Vol. VIII, No. 4, October, 1935.

Notestein, Wallace. *A History of Witchcraft in England from 1558 to 1718.* New York: Russell & Russell, 1965.

Oakley, Amy. *Behold the West Indies.* New York: Longmans, Green, 1951.

Parrinder, Geoffrey. *Witchcraft, European and African.* New York: Barnes & Noble, 1963.

Robbins, Rosell Hope. *The Encyclopedia of Witchcraft and Demonology.* New York: Crown, 1970.

Roughead, William. "The Rebel Earl." *Judicial Review.* Vol. 38, No. 2, June 1, 1926.

————— *The Seamy Side.* London: Cassell & Co., 1938.

Scobie, Alastair. *Murder for Magic.* London: Cassell & Co., 1965.

Scott, Sir Walter. *The Heart of Midlothian.* New York: A. L. Burt, no date.

Seabrook, William. *Witchcraft—Its Power in the World Today.* New York: Harcourt, Brace, 1940.

Sergeant, Philip W. *Witches and Warlocks.* London: Hutchinson & Co., 1936.

Soldan, Wilhelm Gottlieb. *Geschichte der Hexenprozesse.* Munich: Georg Müller, 1911.

Starkey, Marion L. *The Devil in Massachusetts.* New York: Knopf, 1949.

Steenholm, Clara and Hardy. *James I, the Wisest Fool in Christendom.* New York: Covici-Friede, 1938.

Stiles, Henry R. *The History and Genealogies of Ancient Windsor, Connecticut.* New York: Norton, 1859.

Strauss, Gerald. *Sixteenth Century Germany, Its Topography and Topographers.* Madison: University of Wisconsin Press, 1959.

Treaster, Joseph B. "Haiti." *The New York Times,* Sept. 27, 1970.

Treharne, R. F., and Fullard, Harold. *Muir's New School Atlas of Universal History*. New York: Barnes & Noble, 1961.

Trumbull, James Russell. *A History of Northampton, Massachusetts*. Northampton: Gazette Printing Co., 1898.

Wendell, Darrett. *Cotton Mather, the Puritan Priest*. New York: Harcourt, Brace & World, 1963.

Williams, Joseph J. *Voodoos and Obeahs*. New York: Dial Press, 1922.

Winsor, Justin (editor). *The Memorial History of Boston*. Boston: James R. Osgood & Co., 1881.

Winthrop, John. *History of New England, 1630-1649* (in *Original Narratives of American History*). New York: Scribner, 1914.

INDEX

Abbott, Nehemiah, 149, 151
Ady, Thomas, 49
Albizzi, Cardinal, 63
Alden, Capt. John, 152
Alden, John, 152
Alden, Priscilla, 152
Anne (queen of England), 16-24
Arthur (king of England), 8

Balfour, Alison, 26
Baudricourt, Capt. Robert, 68-69, 70
Becker-Margareth, 55
Benedict XV (pope), 82
Bidel, Benoît, 89
Bishop, Bridget, 149, 153-54
Bloxham, Peter, 167
Böffgen, Christine, 61
Bourgot, Pierre, 87-88
Bridgman, Sarah, 130-31
Brown, Thomas, 28
Buirmann, Franz, 61

Burroughs, George, 150, 155

Calef, Robert, 155
Carpzov, Benedict, 59
Carrier, Martha, 155
Charles I (king of England), 30
Charles II (king of England), 134
Charles VI (king of France), 67, 83
Charles VII (king of France), 67, 70, 71-72, 75-77, 79, 81, 83
Clarke, Elizabeth, 31-32, 34
Cloyce, Sarah, 147-48, 150
Cornfoot, Janet, 28-29
Corwin, Jonathan, 144
Cory, Giles, 149, 156-57, 160
Cory, Martha, 146, 149, 156
Cromwell, Lady, 42-43

Cromwell, Sir Henry, 42
Crowley, Aleister, 164, 165-66

Danforth, Thomas, 148
d'Arc, Isabelle, 65, 66
d'Arc, Jacques, 65
Darcy, Brian, 47-48
Demonology, 24, 25, 30
Device, Alison, 45-46
Device, James, 46
Device, John, 45
Discovery of Witches, The (Hopkins), 31, 32, 38
Dudley, Thomas, 125
Duncan, Gellis, 17-18, 20

English, Mary, 150-51
English, Philip, 150-51
Esty, Mary, 149

Ferdinand II (Holy Roman Emperor), 63-64
Fian, Dr. (John Cunningham), 21-22
Fish, Thomas, 158
Fourneau, Gilbert, 84-85

Garnier, Appoline, 88-89
Garnier, Giles, 88-89
Gaudillon, Antoinette, 90
Gaudillon, Georges, 90
Gaudillon, Perrenette, 89-90
Gaudillon, Pierre, 90
Gaule, John, 37
Gedney, Bartholomew, 152
Geiss (chief magistrate of Lindheim), 51-58
Gifford, George, 48

Glover, Goody, 134-37
Good, Dorcas, 147
Good, Sarah, 142, 144-45, 154, 160
Goodwin, John, 134
Goodwin, Martha, 137
Graf, Conrad, 62
Graham, Richard, 21, 23
Griggs, Doctor, 140

Hathorne, John, 144-47, 149, 152
Henry IV (king of France), 86
Henry VI (king of England), 67
Herrmann, James M., 167-68
Hibbins, Ann, 130, 133
Hibbins, William, 130
History of the Colony of Massachusetts Bay (Hutchinson), 130
Hobbs, Abigail, 148, 156, 160
Hollin, Maria, 62
Hope, Sir Thomas, 24
Hopkins, Matthew, 30-38, 40, 48, 59, 61, 125
Howe, Elizabeth, 154
Hutchinson, Thomas, 130

Jacobs, George, 155
James I (king of England), 14-29, 30, 36, 43
James II (king of England), 134
Jesus Christ, 8
Joan of Arc, 65-82, 83, 85

Johann Georg II, 60-61
John (duke of Bedford), 67, 79
John Indian, 139, 148, 159
Johnson, Mary, 127, 133
Jones, Margaret, 125-26, 133
Jones, Thomas, 124-25, 127, 133
Judas Iscariot, 8

Kempe, Ursula, 47-48, 166
Kers, John, 19-20

Laing, Beatrix, 27-28
Laxart (cousin to Joan of Arc), 68, 70
Leek, Sybil, 161-65
Leopold I (Holy Roman Emperor), 51
Lewis, Mercy, 149
Lowes, John, 34-35
Lutz, Wilhelm, 62

Macbeth (Shakespeare), 4
MacCalyan, Euphemia, 22-23, 26
Martin, Susanna, 149, 154
Mather, Cotton, 132-38, 155, 159
Mather, Increase, 132-38
Mather, Maria Cotton, 132
Mather, Richard, 132
Memorable Providences (Mather), 137
Mentot, Philibert, 87-88
Moody, Joshua, 137
Morton, Patrick, 27-28
Moxon, George, 128

Napier, Barbara, 22
Nurse, Rebecca, 146-47, 149, 150, 154-55, 158
Nutter, Christopher, 44-45
Nutter, Robert, 44-45

Old Chattox, 44-46
Old Demdike, 44-46
Osburne, Sarah, 143, 144-45, 160

Palpa, Thomas, 26
Parris, Betty, 139-40, 141, 142, 159
Parris, Samuel, 139, 141-43, 147, 150, 159
Parsons, Hugh, 128-29
Parsons, Joseph, 131
Parsons, Joshua, 129
Parsons, Mary (Northampton, Mass.), 130-31
Parsons, Mary (Springfield, Mass.), 128-29
Pheringer, Georg, 62
Philip (duke of Burgundy), 67, 77-79
Phips, Sir William, 153, 157-58
Procter, Elizabeth, 148, 155
Procter, John, 148, 155
Putnam, Ann, 140, 144, 145, 146-47, 150, 159
Putnam, Thomas, 140

Rais, Gilles de, 85-86
Redfearne, Anne, 44-46
Redfearne, Thomas, 44-45
Regnault (bishop of Rheims), 75

INDEX

Remarkable Providences
(Mather), 133
Robin Hood, 8
Roettinger, Sebastien, 62
Roy, Sylvine, 84-85

Sampson, Agnes, 15, 18-22
Samuel, Alice, 40-43
Schüler, Johann, 50-57
Schwägel, Anna Maria, 64
Scott, Reginald, 48
Sewall, Samuel, 158
Shakespeare, William, 4
Sheldon, Susanna, 141
Socrates, 9
Southerne, Elizabeth, 44-46
Stearne, John, 31, 33, 36, 38
Stewart, Francis (earl of
Bothwell), 20-21, 23-24
Stoughton, William, 153,
154

Talbot, John, 74
Throckmorton, Jane, 40-42
Throckmorton, Robert, 40-
43
Thurlow, Grace, 47
Tituba, 139-43, 145, 151,
152, 156, 159-60

Verdung, Michael, 87-88
von Ehrenberg, Philipp
Adolf, 60
von Oynhausen, Baron, 51-
52, 58
von Rosenbach, Hartmann,
51, 53, 55, 58

Walcott, Mary, 141
Warren, Mary, 148
Whittle, Anne, 11, 44-46
Wildes, Sarah, 154
Willard, John, 155
Williams, Abigail, 140, 141,
144, 146-47
Williamson, Cecil, 166
Winthrop, John, 124-27
witchcraft
Africa and, 113-23;
America and, 124-38, 139-
60; Holy Bible and, 2, 8;
England and, 30-38, 39-
49; France and, 65-82,
83-90; Germany and, 50-
64; history of, 1-13; Matthew Hopkins and, 30-38;
James VI of Scotland and,
14-29; Joan of Arc and,
65-82; Leopard Men and,
121-23; in Massachusetts,
124-38, 139-60; the rev-
erends Mather and, 132-
38; obeah and, 104-12;
Salem trials and, 139-60;
Johann Schüler and, 50-
58; Scotland and, 14-29;
Sect Rouge and, 91-103;
today, 161-69; major
trends in, 1-13; voodoo
and, 91-103; werewolves
and, 86-90; white witches
and black witches, 3-6;
"Witch-Finder Generall"
and, 30-38

Young, Isobel, 24-25

Critics' Corner:

"... this book is as much concerned with those falsely accused of witchcraft as with witchcraft itself. The author takes up witch hunting in Scotland, England, Germany, France and the American Colonies, recounting the persecution and killing of many innocent persons. ... He also covers such topics as werewolves, voodoo and *Sect Rouge,* obeah, African magic and Leopard Men and mentions briefly several modern persons who admit being witches. A popular treatment which will help meet the demand for material on a subject in which many young people are avidly interested."
—*A.L.A. Booklist*

"... makes for fascinating reading."
—*Boston Sunday Globe*

Also recommended by: Child Study Association.

About the Author:

CLIFFORD LINDSEY ALDERMAN was born in Springfield, Massachusetts, and graduated from the United States Naval Academy at Annapolis. He became an editor and also went into public relations work in the field of shipping and foreign trade. During World War II he returned to naval service. Mr. Alderman has written historical novels for adults and both fiction and nonfiction for young people. While gathering materials for his books, he has traveled extensively in Europe, Canada, the West Indies and throughout the United States. He lives with his wife in Seaford, Long Island. Mr. Alderman's *The Devil's Shadow: The Story of Witchcraft in Massachusetts* is also in an Archway Paperback edition.

Out of all the claims made about witchcraft only two things are really clear: that there *were* (and still are) people who profess to be witches and perform magic, and that there were people who did not claim to be witches but were accused, either out of spite or because their ways were peculiar, and were tried, condemned and executed. And everything about the ways in which accused witches were examined, tortured, tried and put to death was wrong. . . .

A CAULDRON OF WITCHES
The Story of Witchcraft
was originally published by
Julian Messner.

Kall looked over Aazen's shoulder, squinting. Standing along the shoreline, like dark diamonds against the sun, was a line of men. He recognized them immediately. They were his father's guard, nothing less than his personal retinue. The boys' afternoon of play was over. Guiltily, Kall raised a hand to call them.

A loud whistle cut the air, beating sharply against Kall's eardrums. He never saw the missile's flight, but he heard its impact. The arrowhead and a bit of shaft were just visible through a muscle in Aazen's shoulder.

Dencer's arrow, Kall realized, shocked. He and Aazen had watched and occasionally helped the man fashion the arrowheads into that signature, barbed shape. At the time, Dencer had explained how painful a wound such tips would make, and warned them never to use the weapons for hunting, for it was cruel to cause an animal undue pain.

The cry that burst from Aazen was certainly animal-like, and the impact of the arrow drove him back into Kall's chest.

___

Footsteps stirred Dhairr Morel from the drawings in front of him.

Three small, open arches behind his desk overlooked the central garden of his Esmeltaran estate. Visitors approaching his private office had to pass through the garden on stone walkways or wade among dense ferns and orange trees. He made sure he could always hear them coming. While dust gathered on a sketch of a peridot and opal ring, Dhairr listened, hearing every subtle alteration in the rhythm of that outside world.

"Balram," he said as the man entered the office without knocking. "Well?"

"The house remains secure, my lord," Balram Kortrun replied.

"I am always assured of that, Captain. Was that the task I set for you?"

"No, my lord."

Dhairr smiled faintly. "Then let us come to the point."

"My sources tell me someone plots your death," said Balram.

Dhairr eased back in his chair at the blunt pronouncement, but he was not, in truth, surprised. The surge in his blood came from excitement, not fear. He had always known they would try again.

His hand strayed involuntarily to his throat, where a cordlike ridge of flesh had healed the slash the assassin had given him. Like the carved ivory reliefs adorning the walls of his office, his body told the story of how close he'd come to death.

He looked his captain in the eyes. "Who?"

That was the question that haunted him. His assailants had been faceless walking shadows. To kill them, he'd been forced to sit patiently, awaiting their next strike. Dhairr had waited almost twelve years for this day, but he had not idled in that time. He was well prepared.

He repeated his question, slow and deliberate. "Who comes for me?"

Balram hesitated. "We do not know, my friend," he said, but hastened to add, "Your men stand with you. They surround the house and await any call for aid. No one who enters this house will escape masked . . . or alive."

"They are well trained. I have no doubt. Thank you, Kortrun," Dhairr said. A new thought struck him. "What of Kall?"

Balram shifted, and Dhairr's eyes narrowed. "We believe he and my son are outside the estate, my lord."

Dhairr thrust himself to his feet, his chair scraping stone, but Balram locked a restraining hand on his friend's arm. He ignored the blazing look in the lord's eyes. "Do *not*. I have sent whatever men could be spared to retrieve them, but if the attack comes soon, the lake and environs are the safest places."

Dhairr jerked his arm free and turned away, a clear sign Balram would win the argument. He seldom lost. "However it ends, you will see to him?" Dhairr asked.

"Yes. As you will see to Aazen, if the reverse is true," said Balram.

Dhairr nodded and sank back into his chair, staring at nothing. "Kall has always been defiant—like his mother. There are days . . . nights more than morns," he said, and paused. Another memory flitted before his eyes, but the scars this time were invisible specters. "I should not have sent her away."

"Alytia was a wizard," Balram said flatly.

Dhairr chuckled. His friend—the whole of Amn—predictably reviled the Art. His mirth quickly died. "You have also raised a motherless child. Was it so simple for you, Captain?"

Balram's lips tightened. "My son has never wanted for anything, my lord, and neither has yours." The remark held an edge of bitterness that Dhairr failed to notice. "By removing your wife, you have taken all magic, and the danger that inherently follows such power, from your house and from your son's eyes. Is that not worth whatever deprivation he may have suffered?"

"Yes," Dhairr said, but the familiar conviction did not come. Perhaps it was because he again faced his own mortality.

When he had first known her, nothing about Alytia seemed to matter—not her magic, her defiance, or even her association with the great meddlers of Faerûn. He'd hardly cared about anything save her beauty, her breath feathering his chest in the night, and the child they conceived after a year of such blissful ignorance.

While his son lay wailing in his crib, assassins laid open Dhairr's throat and left him bleeding on the floor of his bedchamber. He'd survived, but his eyes had been brutally opened.

He never learned the identities of the assassins, never knew for certain whether it was hatred of his wife's magic or her dangerous alliances that drove them, but he had taken no chances.

"Leave one alive," Dhairr said, turning his attention back to Balram, "to question."

"I will tell Meraik—"

"No." Dhairr cut him off. "I'll tell them myself. I'm going down."

"Is that wise?"

The lord of Morel house smiled grimly, but his face possessed a gray tinge, a wasted look enhanced by the scar at his throat. "I tire of waiting."

Balram half-bowed as Dhairr swept from the room. He watched through the windows as his lord crossed the garden, heading for the broad arcade that fringed the outer wall.

Stationed along the courtyard and beyond were the house guards, most handpicked and trained by Balram. They nodded respectfully as their lord passed.

The guard captain raised an open palm, surprised at the sweat he felt beneath his leather glove. The slight tremble to his fingers was even more distressing, but he dismissed it as heightened awareness, anticipation of the battle to come.

"You make for a fascinating study, Kortrun. Were you not, I believe I would have abandoned you and your little project long ago."

Balram did not turn at the voice. Soril Angildaen—Daen to those who knew him as a killer—would remain in his presence as long as Daen saw fit, whether Balram acknowledged the man or not.

"Lord Morel prefers soft wine to stronger drink, as the latter leaves his senses dull," Daen continued, unaffected by his companion's silence. He strolled into the room, his fur-capped boots making no sound as he moved to stand next to Balram. "Chessenta's finest fruit-white, as I recall you saying. I believe he keeps several bottles locked beneath an insultingly simple false bottom in this chest." He tapped the box sitting behind Morel's desk with his heel. "You might have shared a bottle, just now."

"We might have," Balram agreed, "and have, many times in the past."

"A noteworthy indication of friendship from Lord Morel, a man who, for the whole of twelve years, has demanded his food tasted for him, and scouts every door for a dagger point. Yet he drinks, uncaring, with you."

"He trusts me."

"Without question. Enlighten me, then; why *is* your esteemed lord and friend not dead?"

"He will be, very soon," Balram assured him.

Daen crossed his arms over a barrel stomach. Balram had no idea how the rogue managed to move so silently while lugging such a gut. He wore a yards-long, gray silk vest tucked snugly into a sash of the same color embroidered in silver threads. His shirt lay open at the neck, exposing pale hairs and a square-cut onyx gem clasped in a silver claw. Balram often wondered if the necklace didn't contain some form of magic. Unlike the rest of Amn, the Shadow Thieves were not known to shy from employing wizards.

"You could have slain him painlessly just then—a quick poison, a mark of mercy. Easier still, you could leave him alive— take his men and join us now, your conscience unfettered by the murder of a friend. Yet you plan this assassination in the same bloody manner as almost caused your friend's downfall twelve years ago. I applaud the irony and your enthusiasm, of course, but you risk much."

With much to gain, thought Balram. Like Morel, he had used his years wisely. "The men I have trained, the men who, if this attempt succeeds, will be assets to your organization," he added pointedly, "have not been tested."

"Ah, unfortunate," Daen agreed. "Men loyal to Balram but not yet weaned from Morel's purse. You have no idea if they will actually be able to betray the man who feeds and shelters them. Which brings up a point close to my heart," he added, as if the thought had only just occurred to him, "and those of my colleagues. How will you be able to survive without Morel's considerable income, should you succeed? The gem road connects his doorstep to Keczulla, and his fortunes look only to increase with the growth of that city. Forgive me, but financially, the jewel-lord of Esmeltaran is a more favorable prospect for the Shadow Thieves than the mercenary, Balram Kortrun."

"I have served Morel a decade this winter. I am not without assets."

"Oh, splendid," Daen chortled. "You have been hoarding the pearls, so to speak. No doubt Morel was willing to pay his guard captain a satisfactory price to keep his family and fortune safe from assassins."

A larger price than Daen would ever conceive, Balram agreed silently. Twelve years of looking over his shoulder had wrought more taints in Dhairr than just paranoia, but that condition had helped Balram's cause the most. Morel had been more than willing to offer his captain the coin and latitude to do as he desired.

More than willing to open his home to a coinless mercenary and his starving son.

The trembling sensation returned to his hands. Balram fisted one on the naked blade of his sword until he felt flesh give. Like the severing of a wire, the tension inside him eased.

You have outgrown Lord Morel, he reminded himself. The Shadow Thieves could offer him more than a life of servitude. They would take him and Aazen into their protection, allowing Balram to expand on the foundation he'd built. In quieter days, he would allow himself to regret killing Morel and his son, even to grieve for them—but not now. Now, he could afford no feeling, no compassion, for the Shadow Thieves—despite Daen's jovial bluster—permitted neither.

If the plan failed . . . no, it would not, not as long as secrecy prevailed. He had warned Dhairr to avoid drawing suspicion, but even on his guard, Morel could not stand against so many. His men would use all caution.

From the window, he had a clear view of the west tower of the estate, its aviary alive with the cries of hawks and other raptors. A guard stepped into view at one of the arched openings. Balram raised a hand.

The guard caught the gesture and slipped into the shadows

of the tower. A breath passed, and the bird cries intensified. When the guard re-emerged, his sword lay bare in his hand, and his face was covered by a dark hood that obscured all but his eyes. In his other hand, he held a flaming scrap of cloth stuffed into a green glass bottle.

Without hesitating, the guard threw the concoction of fire down into the central courtyard, where it smashed against a lattice of wood and climbing roses.

Shouts and smoke immediately filled the courtyard. Balram stepped away from the window. He slid his uninjured hand inside a carefully sewn pocket at the breast of his tunic. His fingers closed around a hard, circular object that seemed to pulse under leather and flesh.

All caution. He repeated the mantra. And if that wasn't enough, well, Daen wasn't the only one who possessed magic.

CHAPTER TWO

Esmeltaran, Amn
12 Eleasias, the Year of the Sword (1365 DR)

Kall couldn't think. He looked desperately to the shore, at Dencer nocking another arrow to his longbow. The other figures were on the move, covering their faces with some sort of hood, fading back into the trees in the direction of his father's estate. Kall could see the tips of its two domed towers in the distance.

Morel house was being attacked from within. His mind fumbled over the realization. Did his father know of the treachery? Was he still alive? The last thought sent a tremor through Kall's body. If Aazen hadn't been there to grab him, Kall would have lurched up onto the rock, running right into death to get back to the house.

"Kall," Aazen croaked, snapping the boy's attention back to the shore. Dencer stood, aiming, but something was wrong. He was taking too long, holding the shot. "W-what's he waiting for?"

Aazen's teeth chattered despite the warmth of the day. Kall held him up, treading water for both of them. "I don't know," he said.

Suddenly, the air whistled again. Kall braced, but the

expected killing blow never came. Instead, Dencer fell to his knees, cradling his right hip.

A horse thundered up the strand of beach, kicking sand up against black flanks. Its rider tossed aside an empty crossbow and drew a short blade as he came.

Dencer had crawled to his feet by the time the rider reached him. Kall could finally make out the man's face. He was one of Kall's personal guardsmen, assigned by his father. "Haig!" he cried.

The rider ignored Kall's shout and swung down from the still-moving mount, sword leading. Dencer hastily blocked with his bow, the only weapon he could bring to hand in time. The sword bit deeply into the wood, cleaving it nearly in two.

Dencer pushed back and thrust the older man off. Haig's attack came in a bull rush, clumsy and imprecise, as if he hoped to finish his opponent off quickly and move on. Dencer dodged a second thrust, at the same time groping with the bolt that had penetrated his armor. His hand fell slack, and he swooned.

Haig pressed the advantage, driving in close for a quick kill, and played right into Dencer's feint. Dencer dropped heavily to the sand on his good side, swept one leg behind and in front of Haig's knees and twisted. The older man bent sideways and hit the ground. In the same breath Dencer sprang to his feet, running full out for the trees.

Haig cursed loudly but did not follow. He sheathed his sword and ran for the water, picking a path across the rocks.

"Haig," Kall cried again when he reached them. "Morel— the house is—"

"Besieged, aye," the man said curtly, hoisting Aazen up in his arms. "Stay behind me." His eyes were on the tree line as they picked their way back to the shore.

"Where is Father?" His heart pounding, Kall knelt on Aazen's other side as Haig laid him out on the beach. "Does he live?"

"He did, when I left him to come for you." Haig caught Kall by the arm and guided him to the arrow still planted in Aazen's shoulder. The man's hands were square and brown. Traces of gray beard lined his cheeks and chin, yet for his age he was easily twice the width of Kall, with muscle as firm as the gauntlets encasing his wrists. He shrugged off a sand-stained cloak and spread it over Aazen.

"Remove the fletchings," he instructed Kall. "Be quick, but do not aggravate the wound."

Kall did as he was told, snapping the feathery ends off an arrow he might well have helped build. The thought jarred him, and his hands trembled.

Aazen was white to the lips. He hadn't spoken. He would be thinking of his own father, Kall realized. An attack on the house would put Balram in the heart of the battle. "What of Captain Kortrun?" he asked. "Does he—"

"Mind your work!" Haig snapped.

Kall flinched and fell silent. He threw aside the fletchings and waited while Haig helped Aazen to a half-sitting position.

Haig looked the boy in the eyes. "This will hurt."

Aazen nodded, his expression resigned. "Take it—"

Before he'd finished speaking, Haig drove his arm forward. From Kall's angle, it looked as if he were trying to wrench Aazen's arm out of its socket, but the sound was nothing like that.

Cold sweat broke out on Kall's arms. He felt like retching. Aazen's body convulsed, but he stayed eerily silent as Haig tossed the bloody arrow aside, unstoppered a vial of milky liquid, and poured it down the boy's throat. His head lolling, Aazen slid into unconsciousness. A trickle of white slid down his chin.

"He'll live," Haig said grimly, putting the empty vial back in his pouch. "He's endured worse."

"What did you give him?" Kall wanted to know, but Haig had already pulled Kall to his feet, and was dragging him to the black horse.

"A healing potion." He mounted and reached down a hand for Kall.

"We can't leave him!"

Haig made an impatient sound in his throat. He hooked a hand under Kall's armpit and hauled him bodily onto the back of the horse.

"Young Kortrun will be safer than either of us," he said. "Now, if you would care to aid your father and fight for what remains of your house, we will ride swiftly and with no talk at all. If you fall off, I will not stop for you." He looked back at Kall. "Do you understand?"

Wordlessly, Kall nodded. Haig had never reproached him like this before. He'd never *spoken* to him at this length in all of Kall's life, though the old man had been a permanent fixture in Kall's memories since he could walk. The common jest, whispered among the guards, was that Haig preferred the company of his horse to that of people and needed no woman to warm his bed. But the subdued old man who'd shadowed his steps on the streets of Esmeltaran was not the same person who sat before him now. Where had the strength and the steel in his eyes come from?

Those eyes raked him from head to foot, noting, Kall thought, his lack of armor. He'd left the pads on the rocks of Lake Esmel with Aazen's violin. Haig reached down and freed a curved shield from where he'd hooked it to the saddle horn.

"Here," he said, thrusting the shield at Kall. "Protect yourself when we get close to the grounds." He shook his head as he gazed at Kall. "Tymora's miracle Dencer was confused. In your smallclothes, with your hair wetted down, you both look just alike."

Kall would have asked what he meant, but Haig dug his heels into horseflesh, and they were away.

CHAPTER THREE

Esmeltaran, Amn
12 Eleasias, the Year of the Sword (1365 DR)

The grounds were deserted. Haig's boots crunched gravel as the big man dismounted in the outer yard. He pushed Kall between himself and the horse. They moved in a line right up to the entry hall. The doors were wide open, and Kall could hear fighting within. Morel's servants—guards who had not turned traitor, even members of the household staff—fought with men in hoods. Kall had counted five such on the beach, including Dencer, and there were more inside without sand on their boots.

"Whatever happens, stay at my shoulder where I can see you." Haig spoke rapidly, reaching for the short sword affixed to his saddle. "I don't know how skilled you are with a blade, but if you get the chance to stick this in something, don't hesitate, do you hear?" When Kall nodded, he went on, "We're badly outnumbered, so remember, this house is no longer your home. It's their ground until we drive them out. Anything is a weapon to that end." He handed Kall the short sword and took a second, broader blade from a sheath. Large emeralds adorned the hilts, marks given to all the blades of Morel, from the lowliest rusted dirk to Balram's elegant long sword—a mark of Morel's success in gems and fine ornaments.

Kall's father scoffed at Amnians who draped their wealth over themselves with no context. Dhairr's gesture to even his lowest-ranking servants had clear meaning: Morel had the means to protect his own.

But he had never planned for an attack from within, an attack that amounted to a betrayal by family. How many of the men in hoods bore emerald weapons? How many would Kall know personally if unmasked?

His chance to find out came when they entered the main hall. Two of the hooded foes darted in from side rooms, as if they'd seen them coming. Haig put himself in front of Kall and ran at both, grabbing up a large Calishite vase from a side table. He smashed the expensive item in the face of the hood to his right while simultaneously batting a raised sword out of his way. Dazed, the attacker fell back, unresisting, allowing Haig to charge forward to engage the foe to his left.

Kall stared at the scene, retaining only the presence of mind to raise his weapon while he watched the old man fight.

Screams filled the air as Gertie, one of the maids, hurtled from the hallway into the crystal display front as if she'd been thrown. Fragile glass panes shattered under her weight. Her hands and arms were bloody when she picked herself up, but she kept running, bolting across the hall. Her usually meticulously combed curls hung loose and wild from her bonnet. A gloved hand snagged her hair, jerking the maid's head back into the doorway to the kitchens.

Kall watched in numb horror as the hand drew a knife in a crooked, horizontal slash across Gertie's throat. For a breath, the young maid's eyes met Kall's across the room. Then she saw the blood pouring down her dress and raised her hands as if she could stop the flow.

Kall charged forward, away from the safety of Haig's back. Instead of engaging the man with the knife, he ran a wide circle. Before the man could realize what he intended, Kall had wedged his sword between the wall and the display front and pulled, levering the heavy glass case away from the wall. Piles of crystal, wood, and glass came down on the hooded man, knocking him back into the kitchen. The last Kall saw of the man was the Morel emerald glinting in his knife, alongside a ruby in a nest of gold loops.

Kall dropped to his knees next to Gertie, but the maid was already dead. Above her ruined throat, her eyes stared vacantly at the ceiling. Kall felt bile rise in his throat, but a glint of gold in the blood pool caught his eye: Gertie's necklace, a small medallion emblazoned with Lathander's sunrise. The assassin's knife had cut it away. Kall scooped it up.

He caught black movement out of the corner of his eye and spun, sending his sword out in a wide, reckless arc. Another hooded figure danced back, Kall's blade swishing across his opponent's stomach to tear fabric if not flesh.

Blindly, Kall followed with a backslash, cutting up and diagonally from hip to shoulder, driving forward in a rush as he'd seen Haig do.

Kall was not a novice to sword play. When he was younger, his father had decided to personally train Kall to fight. Never had the man paid him so much attention. Kall had reveled in it, learning all he could. His skills steadily grew, but his father's interest in teaching waned over the years in favor of seeing to his business and the security of his house. Kall could feel the burn of disuse in his sword arm.

He risked a glance at the old man. Haig had pulled the hood from the foe harrying him on the left. White-gold hair tumbled down a black cloak—Isslun's. She puckered her lips saucily at Haig even as her hand went for the dagger at her belt.

Haig got there first. He slipped the weapon from its sheath and with a grin shoved her away. Immediately, an identical face from the right met him. Aliyea—twin to Isslun—had recovered from the hit with the vase and removed her hood to fight openly beside her sister.

Kall's sword went skittering across the marble floor. Distracted, he'd let himself be disarmed. "Haig!"

Haig hurled Isslun's dagger. The fang buried itself in the hood of Kall's opponent. Kall looked away, sickened, and saw Haig fighting for better position, backing the twins toward one of the smaller rooms off the main hall. "Follow me!" the old man yelled at him.

Kall hesitated. He still didn't know where his father was. The bulk of the fray seemed to be coming from the central garden; Haig was headed in the opposite direction. With a last look at white-gold hair and whirling steel, Kall retrieved his sword and ran for the sunlight, ignoring Haig's voice calling after him.

In the heart of the garden, Kall found his father. Dhairr was alive and fighting, but he bled from several wounds. He straddled one fallen hood and fought two others who pressed him back against the lip of a fountain. This central point irrigated the entire garden; the water had been left to flow freely, turning the terrain off the raised stone walkways into a muddy jungle.

Kall ran down the flooded path, not allowing himself to think as he stabbed the black-robed figure closest to his father. The foe's back arched, and the dying assassin toppled over the side of the fountain, wrenching Kall's sword from his hands. Kall scrambled to get out of the way.

Dhairr looked up in shock to see his son. His remaining opponent backed away, hoisting up a dead comrade. Dhairr spun to see another hood charging at them through the mud, but instead of engaging, this one too, grabbed a body—that of the foe Kall had killed—and started to spirit it away.

"No!" A scream of pure agony and frustration tore from Dhairr's throat. He charged the escaping assassins, but water and wounds slowed him. He could not make the edge of the fountain before his legs gave out. He still grasped his sword in a white-knuckled fist. Kall dodged it and grabbed his father around the waist, gripping and hoisting him up.

"All back! All back!" Dhairr tried to pull away, but Kall held him tightly. Spittle flew from his mouth, and he trembled wildly, slashing his sword at invisible foes. "Guards, to me! Bring one alive, damn you! Bring one alive!"

Bootfalls pounded from the direction of the main hall. Dhairr made an ugly sound in his throat. Kall turned, expecting another enemy, and saw Haig running out to them.

"Father!" Kall stayed the lord's arm as he swung his gaze and blade to the man. Recognition came slowly into Dhairr's eyes, and he lowered his weapon.

"Haig," he said hoarsely. "What happened?"

Kall spoke first. The words tumbled over each other to get out. "Isslun, Dencer . . ." he named them all, describing Aazen's wound and Haig's rescue.

Dhairr had both hands on Kall's shoulders, but he looked at Haig. "How many in total?"

"I can't be certain, my lord," Haig replied. "As it stands, I would trust none of your guard and appeal to the Esmeltaran militia for help."

Dhairr nodded, taking it all in. "Where is Kortrun?"

Boots scraped on stone, and all three of them looked up. Balram stood at the edge of the garden, near the stairs to Dhairr's office. He was watching them, a speculative look in his eyes as they fell on Haig.

"Captain," Dhairr said, relieved. "We were nearly overrun." He noticed the blood dripping from Balram's hand. "Are you all right?"

"I am," Balram said, walking slowly out to them. His sword trailed unsheathed at his side, its emerald winking in the sunlight. "Thank the gods you're both alive." The words held no inflection.

Haig's blade came up, but he stayed at Kall's side. He laid a hand on Kall's arm, as if he might draw him away from his father. "Your captain was one of those who betrayed you, Lord Morel," he said calmly. "Do not trust him."

Dhairr glanced sharply at Balram. "That can't be," he said. "Kortrun—"

"The accusation is fair," Balram replied, cutting him off and surprising a frown onto Dhairr's face. "But you should know its source before you judge." He raised his blade. Haig batted it aside with a clang that was loud in the stillness of the garden. Balram merely smiled and pointed with the sword's tip at Haig's collar. A small silver pin glinted there, barely visible from the folds of cloth. Its crescent moon surrounded a harp and tiny stars. "A piece to rival even your finest work, my lord, if you'll forgive my saying so." His smile melted into a sneer. "We have a Harper in our midst."

"Harper?"

Dhairr started at the sound of his son's voice, as if he'd forgotten Kall was present. Kall stared at Haig, his hand outstretched to the man, too many questions pressing into his throat.

Balram continued, "There are traitors in your house, my friend," he said to Dhairr. "This one, I warrant, is Alytia's work."

"Is this truth?" Dhairr asked. "Speak!" he shouted when Haig hesitated.

Haig met Kall's eyes briefly. "I was asked by the Harper Alytia Morel to see to her son's protection when she was forced to leave this house. I honored her request . . . and continued to do so after her death."

"No," Kall shook his head in denial even as the words sank into him like a cold kiss, through the heat, the buzzing of insects, and the tension of raised blades all around him. His chest seized up. His mother . . . a Harper? Sent away? That was impossible. His mother died giving birth to him. His father told him the story long ago. Haig was confused, he was lying. . . .

Beside him, Dhairr stood in a similar state of shock, but Haig's words did not have the same paralytic effect.

His gaze still on Kall, Haig never saw the attack coming.

Dhairr hit the Harper from the side, driving him to the ground. Haig's skull struck the fountain's edge, and Kall could see the whites of his eyes as he went limp. Dhairr hauled him over and plunged him up to his neck in the fountain, jolting the man back to semi-consciousness.

"Not yet, not yet," Dhairr growled. The sudden outpouring of rage transformed him into a creature Kall did not recognize. Stunned, he fell back a pace.

"Before you die, you will tell me who hunts me!" Dhairr screamed. "Do you hear?" He shook the senseless Harper, plunging him beneath the water again. Haig's hands came up, spasming weakly. "Did Alytia send you to kill me? Is this her revenge?"

"Father, stop!" Kall grabbed Dhairr's shoulder, trying to wrench him off Haig. He pulled, gasping, pounding with his fists, but the lord's muscles were clenched balls of heat and strength. A boy couldn't hope to overpower him.

Kall felt a hand close over his throat, yanking him back. He glared hatefully up into Balram's eyes. "Liar," he gasped. Balram shook him.

"Now, now," he said soothingly, stroking a thumb across Kall's windpipe. "Leave them alone. You and I can entertain ourselves." He raised Kall to his toes. "You say Aazen was injured?" His jaw tightened. "How careless of them. It was supposed to be you. And where is Aazen now, Kall?" Balram asked, his voice rising. "Alone . . . wounded? Did you leave him to die?" He pressed down. Spots clouded Kall's vision. Disgusted, Balram dropped him into the mud.

"He . . . alive," Kall choked. His tongue felt swollen in his mouth. Using one arm for leverage, he dragged himself through the ferns as Balram stalked unhurriedly after him. "Haig!" he sobbed, watching the Harper's body twitch as his father held him under the water for the space of a breath, two, three—too long.

"Father!" Kall screamed as he clumsily dodged a swipe from Balram's foot. "Stop! Help me!"

Balram kicked him in the ribs, knocking the air from Kall's lungs. He tried to curl into a ball, but Balram kicked him again. Kall's arm went numb. He lurched back, reaching desperately, but his father didn't seem to hear anything going on around him.

"If you do not resist, I will tell your father you died defending him," Balram promised, and the reassurance, the sincerity in his voice sent a horrible chill through Kall. He scooped up a handful of mud and hurled it into Balram's face.

The guard captain staggered back, and Kall ran—out of the garden, through the main hall and the double entry doors. He stopped when he saw Haig's horse standing on the track leading from the estate. His ribs burned—hard breathing sent a fire raging over them.

He stumbled to the horse and crawled up the animal's back. It neighed and balked, but eventually settled as Kall draped himself over its back and kicked its flanks. The horse sprang to life, but Kall didn't even glance at the direction it chose. He half-expected a hailstorm of arrows to follow him out the front gates. He buried his face in the horse's dark mane and waited, but he felt only the fire in his ribs and an awful, searing pain in his heart.

CHAPTER FOUR

Esmeltaran, Amn
12 Eleasias, the Year of the Sword (1365 DR)

Balram spat mud. The boy wouldn't get far.

He raised his sword to the east tower, signaling Meraik. The man saluted and disappeared from view.

"Captain." Dencer hurried to him. He cast a wary glance at Morel, who crouched beside the fountain next to Haig's body floating in the water.

"Speak," Balram said, and added pointedly, "Kall yet lives."

"Forgive me, Captain," Dencer said, and lowered his voice. "Haig interfered. My arrow missed the boy."

"And found its way into my son," Balram said grimly.

"Forgive me," Dencer pleaded.

Balram regarded the man for a long time. "Bring my son home to me, Dencer," he said finally.

"I have already seen to it," Dencer said, visibly relieved. "Someone has healed him."

The Harper, Balram thought. "Begin a count of who is dead and who is merely wounded. If you find witnesses, silence them."

Dencer nodded and departed. Sheathing his sword, Balram

went to Dhairr. The lord clutched the Harper's pin in his fist and watched the body float in the fountain. He looked up at Balram like a lost child.

His mind is shattered, Balram thought. This will be easier than I could have hoped.

"Come away, my friend," he said. "It isn't safe for you here."

Dhairr stood unsteadily. He allowed Balram to lead him from the garden, up the stairs to his office. He paused along the way, murmuring, "Kall?"

Balram fixed an expression of sorrow on his face. "I am sorry, my lord. I'm afraid your son was in league with the Harper. I cannot be certain, but he may have helped the assassins gain entrance to the house."

"To kill me. . . ." Morel's face turned ashen. "He is only a boy. The guards—he said they were traitors—"

"A lie," Balram said smoothly. He draped an arm over Dhairr's shoulder and pressed the object he'd been palming into the cloth of the lord's cloak and through, piercing the skin below his collarbone with a needlelike point.

Dhairr stiffened and tried to brush the stinging object off, but Balram held him fast, waiting for the magic to seep into his blood. When he was sure, he drew the object—a small, silver broach set with a square amethyst—out of Dhairr's skin and pinned it neatly to his cloak, as if it were an ornament that had always been there.

He supported Morel the rest of the way up the stairs and into the office, putting him in a chair. He took the one across the desk and waited, watching the magic swirl like winter clouds in his friend's eyes. Abruptly, Dhairr's vision cleared, and he sat up.

"Are you well, my friend?" Balram asked.

"Aye," Dhairr murmured, pressing both palms to his forehead. "What happened?"

"The wounds the Harper inflicted nearly overcame you," Balram said, rising. "I will send a servant in to tend them."

Dhairr touched the drying blood at his shoulder and temple. "The wounds, yes." He looked up at Balram. "I killed him?" he asked uncertainly.

"You slew the assassins who stalked you twelve years ago," Balram assured him. "Be at peace, my friend. You are safe."

"Safe," Dhairr repeated. He settled uncertainly in his chair as Balram strode from the room. When he was alone, he murmured, dazedly, "Kall."

Daen sat at the bottom of the stairway, his legs tucked up against his massive belly like a dam holding the floodwaters at bay.

"It appears you're finally learning, Kortrun," he remarked as Balram stopped and glared down at him.

The guard captain gritted his teeth. "My attempt failed," he said, "as you see."

"Spectacularly," Daen agreed, "but just as well. Now you can get on to the real business."

Had Balram not held the faint hope that the Shadow Thieves might give him another chance, he would have sliced open the fat rogue's belly where he sat. "What might that be?"

"Learning what it means to walk with us," Daen said, his manner turning serious. "How long do you think we would be able to continue our operations if we conducted our affairs in the manner you just displayed?"

"The Shadow Thieves object to the use of assassins?" Balram scoffed. "On what grounds? Morality?"

"Gods' laughter, no," Daen said. "We kill without hesitation . . . and without flair," he pointedly added, "unless the need arises. Only then do we draw attention to ourselves. Violent displays of death-dealing we do not require. We rely on Tethyr for that sort of high entertainment. I don't mind admitting, I despaired of you learning this lesson before it was too late." The rogue didn't appear the least concerned. "But rather than accept failure, you have turned your unfortunate mistake into a venture with promise. Lord Morel is now little more than a corpse, and you are holding his hand, directing him where to turn."

The description, however apt, sent an unexpected shudder through Balram. "And you prefer this . . . state of being?" he asked.

"Absolutely," Daen said. "Morel can keep making his baubles and increasing his fortune; you will continue to siphon the excess to *your* cause and, ultimately, to ours."

Balram pictured the look of childlike confusion in Morel's eyes and suppressed a wave of revulsion. "For how long?"

At that, Daen's gaze hardened. "As long as is required to convince me that you are worth my time and effort. Although, if it concerns you, I believe that Morel will perish of either the magic you used or the afflictions of his mind—perhaps both—long before his years catch up to him."

* * *

Aazen opened his eyes to the slanted wood ceiling of his room. A dull ache was all that remained of the searing pain in his shoulder. Blinking sleep away, he slid to a sitting position and rubbed a hand over the wound. It had closed completely, leaving the flesh smooth—a pink blemish in the surrounding pale.

His room—he was home, in Morel house. Aazen listened intently for the sounds of battle, for wounded cries, but he heard nothing. What had become of Kall and the assassins?

Footsteps echoed on the stairs—the familiar, purposeful tread of his father. Aazen pulled the quilt up to cover his healed wound, realizing immediately it was a useless gesture. Someone—Haig?—had brought him home—washed the blood from his skin. Likely his father had already seen the evidence of the magical potion.

"He cannot fault me," Aazen murmured. "I was unconscious. I was not responsible for what was done to me." He repeated the words like a protective charm. "He cannot blame me."

"You're awake." His father entered the room and perched on the edge of the bed. "Much has happened that we must discuss."

Aazen immediately sat up straighter. His father issued commands. He rarely offered to discuss anything with him, as one man would to another. "Kall and I were attacked at the lake," Aazen said, "by Dencer and men of Morel."

"I know," his father said calmly. "I orchestrated the attack."

Aazen opened his mouth, but no sound issued. He thought his father must be jesting, but by the look in Balram's eyes, Aazen knew he was not. Fear uncurled in his belly like an oily serpent. He swallowed and asked, "Why?"

"To slay Lord Morel and his son, to show our strength to the Shadow Thieves, that we might eventually gain a place among them," Balram explained. When Aazen only gaped, he went on, "I'm sorry I didn't tell you what I intended. I realize Kall is your friend. Dhairr was mine. Nothing about this decision was simple, Aazen, but I am trying to secure our future—*your* future. My actions were justified."

Aazen nodded automatically. He had heard such reasoning from his father before. When he awoke facedown on the floor of his room with a loose tooth or swollen lips, or when his belly burned from lack of food two days after some transgression, the actions were always justified. "Is Kall . . . are they dead?" he asked, striving to keep emotion out of the question. "Haig was with us—"

"Haig is dead," confirmed Balram, "but not by my hand. Dhairr killed him."

"Why?" Aazen hid his horror beneath confusion, which wasn't difficult. Morel, kill an ally? It made no sense.

"Haig was a Harper," his father explained. "Morel has reason not to care for them. Dhairr still lives, but he is no longer a concern. He is under my control and believes his son to be a traitor. Kall, however, escaped. I do not know where."

Relief nearly caused Aazen to swoon. His friend was safe.

"Men loyal to me are searching for him right now," Balram continued. "The boy has seen too much to live." His gaze fixed intently on his son's face. "That's why I need your help, Aazen."

Aazen's fear intensified. "What can I do?"

"Nearly all of your time is spent with Kall. You must have secret places, hidden grounds for whatever foolishness the two of you concoct. Do not deny it," he warned softly as Aazen started to shake his head. "Kall has no other family, nowhere to run except such a place. If we do not find and silence him, if he manages to reach the authorities in Esmeltaran, they will learn what I have done.

"Think, boy," he said, mistaking Aazen's hesitation for a lapse of memory. "You must know a place. We have to hurry. If I am caught, I will be killed."

Aazen frantically searched for a way out of his father's trap. His heart thudded wildly against his ribs. Betray Kall? It was unthinkable. Yet if he didn't, his father would be taken away, and it would be Aazen's fault. "I . . . I know of a place," he stammered.

Balram's face lit with an ugly smile. "Where?"

He would have to tread very carefully, Aazen thought, or his father would sense the ruse. The serpent in his belly threatened to rise up and choke him, but Aazen forced down the fear and guilt. "Near the lake—the Veshpel estate." He named a house that had burned in mid-Tarsakh. He waited a breath and added, as if it were of no consequence, "Many of us go there to explore the ruins."

The spark of triumph in his father's eyes dimmed. "Will it be occupied, at this time of day?" Balram asked.

"Possibly," Aazen said, and in truth, many of the local boys his age spent their free time among the blackened stones. But Kall would not go there for safety, of that he was certain. The estate was too near Morel house and too open to the world. There were better places to hide.

His father was silent, trying to determine the best course to take. Aazen prayed he would let him act, but that decision depended entirely on how much Balram trusted his son. In his heart, Aazen had always believed his father had little faith in him, and so he was surprised—and shamefully warmed—when Balram said, "Then you will have to do it." He nodded, the idea seeming to gain merit the more he considered it. "Kall trusts you. Take my horse. Find Kall in the ruins and draw him out, away from any watching eyes. You need not be the one to slay him," he assured Aazen, squeezing his son's shoulder briefly. "Draw him away, and we will be waiting."

Aazen sat silent a long time under his father's penetrating gaze. This would be the critical test. If he gave in too readily, his father might grow suspicious. Aazen swallowed, hard and audibly in the quiet room. "No."

Balram's eyes narrowed a fraction. "No?"

"I can't betray him, Father." Aazen put a tremor in his voice, a weak, small titter that his father would not be able to tolerate. His father despised weakness. "Please don't ask me—"

The slap blurred the edges of Aazen's vision. His left eye immediately began to throb and water, but the blow had not been debilitating. His father meant only to silence him.

Obediently, he sat, teary-eyed, as Balram rose slowly to tower over him.

"I am asking you, boy," he said, his breath hot and sour on Aazen's face. "I am asking you to help me, to protect me, as I would lay down my life to protect you. Do you hate me so much that you would allow me to be taken, to be killed?" His eyes softened. The hurt crept in. The sight of it made Aazen sick to his stomach.

"No, Father!" he cried, "I don't hate you!" And that was the truth. The only person Aazen hated in that instant was himself. "No, of course not!"

"Of course not," his father repeated, his tone soothing. "You are becoming a man, a loyal son." He touched a large hand to Aazen's head and wiped the moisture away from his reddening eye. "I will bring my horse, and you will ride. Go swiftly, and do as I instructed. In the morning, all this will be a fading memory."

A memory, Aazen thought. If only his whole life could be someone else's memory.

CHAPTER FIVE

Esmeltaran, Amn
12 Eleasias, the Year of the Sword (1365 DR)

Kall swung off the horse. He seemed to fall a long way to the ground. He felt grass under his feet, and mud. In the colored twilight, he gazed up a steep hill speckled with what looked like small swaying firebrands.

The tangerine rose bushes were seasons old and thriving, planted one each in front of a dozen small headstones. The land he stood on belonged to Morel, the burial plots for servants who had died without family in his father's employ. No one passing on the nearby lane would notice the graves, but the expensive flowers—grown for the memory of twelve servants whose names would never be recalled—were sure to be marked by all.

He climbed to the steepest side of the hill, leading Haig's horse up alongside him. Letting go of the horse's reins, he dropped to his knees between two markers. He began plucking at the grass, fingers and nails raking, searching for a seam. His father had shown him the place long ago, but Kall remembered this pair of stones clearly. His father had made him memorize the names: Seth Tarin and Rose Olindrake.

Mud and grass stains covered his hands. It was no good—he'd need something to cut through. Reluctantly, Kall stood and turned to Haig's horse. He felt around the saddle blanket to the bags draped on either side. He found a knife in one.

Movement from behind set every nerve in his body on edge. Kall spun, slashing blindly with the knife.

Aazen caught Kall's arm before he could drive the blade into his neck. "It's me," he said.

Breathing hard, Kall took a long time to focus on his friend and comprehend that he was not some specter from the surrounding graves. The knife fell forgotten to the grass. "What are you doing here?"

Then it came to him in a rush—Aazen's washed-out face, his swollen eye, and the grim set to his mouth. "Your father," Kall croaked. "He—"

"I know." Aazen nodded. Kall mirrored the gesture. It was all the acknowledgment either seemed capable of giving.

"He will kill you," Aazen said. "His men are hunting for you now."

"They don't know about this place," Kall said. He retrieved his knife and started digging.

Aazen scraped dirt aside with his hands. "You don't have much time," he said. He hesitated, looking at the ground. "These won't help you."

Kall's blade found the niche he'd been looking for, and he peeled the grass back, like slipping the lid off a stubborn box. Beneath lay a hollow space lined with wood and cloth. Two bundles of tightly wrapped linen were nestled on top of this, the larger tied with a rope to be worn on the shoulders. He drew them out reverently, as he'd seen his father do when he'd first shown them to Kall.

"I'm going back," he said, glaring into Aazen's skeptical eyes. "If I can just get to Father . . ."

"Your father believes you have betrayed him," Aazen said bluntly. "He is allowing mine to deal with you, in whatever way he sees fit."

Kall's gaze faltered. "You're lying," he said automatically. "Father would never believe I betrayed him."

"He has no say in the matter. Father has Morel under his control. I don't know how . . ." Aazen's mind seized on his healed wound. "Magic, perhaps."

"Magic." Kall's forehead wrinkled. Magic was only a vague concept to him, little more than a fixture in the stories his father used to tell of his mother. Fantastic and sometimes brutal as the tales had been, he'd only ever listened to the parts about the woman herself, soaking up every small detail. . . .

No, Kall thought savagely, thrusting the memories away. All that had been a lie. "It doesn't matter," he said. "I'll go back and free him. I have these"—he clutched the bundles—"they have magic. Father told me. I'll kill Balram!"

The words rang out between them, and Kall sucked in a breath, watching Aazen, hearing the words and their implications for the first time.

He'd just sworn to kill Aazen's father. In one day, their worlds had shattered. Nothing would ever be the same for either of them again.

Aazen said nothing at first, only smoothed the dirt and grass back in place over the hole. He looked up as the sun dipped below the horizon. "You have to leave the city. I was sent out to lead Father's men to wherever you might be hiding. I came to warn you, but I can't stay here. When Father realizes I've put him on a false trail, he'll be tracking me." Aazen stared into the distance, as if seeing something frightening in the dark. "I can't hide for long."

"He won't forgive you. He'll beat you to death and won't know he's doing it," Kall said bitterly. "You have to run."

They had no choice. Aazen was right. If Kall went back now, without his father's aid, he had no hope. It shamed Kall to admit his fear, but stronger than that was the anger, the fury at Balram and all he'd stolen from Kall's family. Balram wanted him dead. The only action Kall could take right now to thwart him was to stay alive.

Absorbed in thoughts and plans, Kall didn't notice Aazen's silence. His friend got to his feet and started walking, out into the dark. Abruptly, Kall realized what he intended and yelled, "You can't go back. You'll die!"

Aazen paused, not looking back. "No. I don't think . . . no. I'm all he has. He cares for me."

Kall's mouth twisted. "How can he? Your father's a murderer."

Aazen said, calmly, "So is yours."

And then, as if it had been waiting, the scene in the garden broke fresh in Kall's mind. He saw his father drowning Haig as the sun shone down and insects buzzed around their bleeding wounds. He'd managed to block it out before, when he'd needed to escape, but Aazen's words conjured the memory effortlessly.

Kall put his head in the grass and vomited. Sweat dripped between his shoulder blades, but he was so cold his fingers were numb. He tried to stand, but the sickness racked his body. Aazen made no move to help him.

"You said . . . you said he was under Balram's control!" Kall spat and wiped his mouth. "Father would never have killed Haig."

"Morel hates the Harpers. My father told me your father had reason to want Haig's death."

"No!"

Aazen looked down at Kall pityingly. "Get on your horse," he said. "Don't come back. Don't come after Balram. I'll have to . . . to kill you, if you do."

Then Aazen went, his footsteps shuffling dully through the grass. Kall sat, frozen in shock, but he didn't call out again. He simply listened, his breath aching in his chest, as his best friend walked away from him.

Finally, his movements wooden, Kall tied the linen bundles on to his back and mounted. He pointed the horse in the direction of the city gates, picking his way in and out of sparse trees, avoiding the open fields of the cemetery wherever possible. After a dozen glances over his shoulder, he left his home behind.

The horse plodded on the road south, and when next Kall opened his eyes, he saw nothing but moonlight on grass and a row of carefully laid stones.

Kall thought he'd turned a complete circle, bringing him back to the same cemetery he'd left earlier that night. No, the stones were different—there were more here, older, and of elaborate design.

He slid down for a closer look, but the family names were none he recognized. A twisted oak overrun by tall grass and brush marked the border of the cemetery. Kall tied the horse to the tree, out of sight, and settled on the grass.

For a long time he stared straight ahead, listening for the sounds of hoofbeats or footfalls that might indicate pursuit. Hearing none, he untied the bundles from his back and clutched them tight.

His empty gaze focused on one of the unfamiliar markers. The name "Alinore Fallstone" was carved deep into the stone next to some kind of symbol. There were more words written underneath the name in a language Kall did not recognize.

He stared at the symbols, at the incomprehensible language, until the words blurred and darkness fell completely over his mind.

CHAPTER SIX

Esmeltaran, Amn
12 Eleasias, the Year of the Sword (1365 DR)

Balram waited at the door to Aazen's chamber. His gaze flicked briefly to Dencer, who'd found Aazen on the road and escorted him home. "Wait outside," he said.

Dencer nodded and shut the door, sealing them off from the rest of the house.

Aazen stood in the middle of the room, waiting, while Balram locked the door and slowly turned. They stared at each other for a quiet breath, measuring, Aazen thought, how much had changed since they'd last spoken in this room.

"Kall is gone?" his father asked at last. He already had the answer, but Aazen recognized what he really wanted to know.

"Kall is leaving Amn," Aazen said. "He knows that to stay is to die. Your secret is safe. I made sure of it," he added, and realized immediately that it was a mistake. He sounded too confident, too powerful, and Balram sensed it.

His father's eyes narrowed and something ugly broke on his calm, inscrutable face. "You made certain. You stood in this chamber and *lied* to me, took my life into your hands. . . ."

"I protected you."

"You were protecting Morel's whelp!" His father took a step

forward. Aazen flinched. He couldn't help it. "You gave no thought to me."

"That's not true, Father," Aazen said quietly. "I give every thought to you, every breath of my life."

"What is it you want, Aazen?" his father asked, his tone altering to curiosity. "You could have gone with Kall. You were clever to lead me astray, more careful than I gave you credit for. I will never make that mistake again," he added, his face darkening. "Yet you returned to me."

"Yes. I want nothing from Kall."

"Why did you come back?"

Aazen would never know why, just as he had never understood the desire that clawed him from the inside. The galling need to please his father, to win approval from this man, this thing who might kill him with a misplaced blow—the need would destroy him one day. He knew that, accepted it, because he could not do otherwise.

He tried to hide the helplessness he felt, but his father saw, and he smiled—a small, satisfied expression. Satisfied because he still had a loyal son, or because he had a pawn he could twist and control? Aazen wondered. Deep down, he knew it was the latter, and for one burning instant, he hated his father as he had never hated anything in his life. Then the feeling was gone, fading to ash as Balram put a hand on his shoulder.

"We will talk more of this later. For now, all that matters is you chose to return."

"Yes, Father," Aazen said. Resignation drained the anger as it had long ago drained the fight out of him. He barely registered the change in pressure at his shoulder, the alteration from affection to purpose—his father's hand slowly turning him to face the wall.

Then there was only pain.

❖

Kall awoke to the sound of a falling tree.

He scrambled up and around Alinore's grave as the sun

disappeared, blotted out by the falling trunk. It struck the forest floor with a deafening thud.

Forest . . . Kall's head whipped around. Trees surrounded him, and in the distance, a cap of mountains graced the southern sky. Haig's horse was gone, and so was the cemetery. All that remained were the bundles he'd been clutching against his chest and Alinore's grave.

Wrong . . . wrong, all wrong. Was he dreaming? Then . . .

"Watch out, you!" A terrific weight slammed him from behind, knocking him to the ground as another trunk fell past his vision.

"That the last of them, by the bloody gods?" shouted a second, muffled voice.

"All clear." The crushing weight fell away, and Kall saw a man peering down at him, haloed by a sea of leafy green. The man's eyes were large and startlingly blue against a dirt-smothered face, and his ears curved as if the tips had been threaded through a needle. On rare occasions, Kall had seen half-elves in Esmeltaran, but never one so large as the figure staring at him now.

"Six young oaks! Six of Nine Hells, that's what you're in for," said the muffled voice again, this time at Kall's elbow.

Kall shrieked as a head burst up from the loose dirt where only a few breaths ago a tree had swayed. A hand followed to wipe the dirt out of a black beard on a pitted, distinctly human face.

"Garavin drew the map," the half-elf said, a bit defensively.

The head and the arm weren't having any of it. "Which you strayed from by a full thirty steps! Look, you." The human's other arm burst up, spraying Kall with more dirt. He flapped a crude drawing in front of the half-elf's blue gaze. "Any more off and you'd have taken the Weir!"

As the pair continued to argue over him, Kall started to slide backward, groping for a weapon, a stick, a rock, anything.

His hand closed on a branch that had been torn away from one of the falling trees. He raised it, and fire licked along his ribcage. Gasping, Kall dropped the branch and fell back, clutching his side.

Immediately, the half-elf crouched over him, his hands probing along Kall's flank. Feebly, Kall tried to push him away, but the man only grinned and muttered, "Cease." His brow furrowed as he examined Kall's wounds. "Get Garavin," he said to his companion. "I think the boy slipped through Alinore's gate."

"Wouldn't be the first," the bearded man grumbled. Instead of hauling himself the rest of the way out of the dirt, the man disappeared back into the earth, pulling his drawing with him.

"What is your name?" the half-elf asked when they were alone. "Who attacked you?"

"Kall," Kall said before he thought better of it. He jerked his head to the south, but kept his eyes fixed on the stranger. "The mountains—they're in the wrong place."

The half-elf nodded. "If you were lying in Esmeltaran's countryside last night, I daresay they are. Those are the Marching Mountains, not the Cloud Peaks. You've come a long way in a short sleep, Kall."

The Marching Mountains—Kall summoned a mental map. He'd crossed the lake, the Wealdath . . . the Starspires, by the gods . . . all those miles. His mind boggled. "How?" he asked.

"My sister's fault, entirely," said a new voice, rough and engulfed by a deep, canine bark.

Kall looked up and saw the animal first, a lumbering bronze mastiff with folds of flesh dangling off its ribs and paws the size of a man's fist. Matching its stride—barely—was a dwarf with skin the color of dead leaves and a full, matching beard that fell nearly to his knees. As the dwarf bent over, Kall could see the hair was as wire-hard as the spectacle frames wedged in front of the dwarf's brown eyes.

The human whose head and arm Kall had glimpsed earlier trailed behind him, dirt-covered and oddly tall and gangly next to the dwarf. In profile, the man's face tapered and curved so prominently that Kall could have hung a cloak from his chin. Gesturing animatedly, he tried in vain to slide his parchment drawing under the dwarf's thick nose. The shorter figure's attention was entirely fixed on Kall.

"My name is Garavin Fallstone," the dwarf said in an oddly formal accent. He extended a hand. When Kall only continued to stare uneasily at the group, a corner of the dwarf's mouth turned up. "Ye need fear no attack from me or any of mine," he said, his voice quiet but still rough as a boot scrape. "Laerin"— he nodded to the half-elf—"would have been about telling ye the same thing, had I not interrupted." He deftly plucked up the human's parchment, folded it, and slid it away in a pocket of his brick-colored vest. "The other here is Morgan, and the dog's Borl. They're not brigands, at least not right now."

"Delvar," Laerin said, as if that should explain everything.

"Means we dig." Morgan glared at the half-elf. "Anyways, some of us dig, and some of us come within a druid's death of slaughtering thousand-year-old trees!"

"Laerin knows the difference between a young oak and a considerably more established Weir," the dwarf interjected smoothly. "No true harm was done. Morningfeast for one more, if ye please, Morgan."

"I'll see to it." Morgan continued to glare at the half-elf as they strode off together into the trees.

"Do ye have brothers?" the dwarf asked incongruously as he took a seat on the ground next to Kall.

A memory of himself and Aazen on the sparkling lake flashed before Kall's eyes. Mutely, he shook his head.

"Neither do I. I took my time growing accustomed to Morgan and Laerin. Ye'll want to do the same." He smiled. "Though I'll make a wager ye give yer parents enough head-aches for ten brothers."

Kall glanced sideways at him. "You're trying to get me to talk," he said.

"Aye," Garavin agreed, still smiling easily. "I'm needing to know if ye have family looking for ye. If so, I can save them the worry and send ye back through the grave—don't mind the expression, it's really a portal. But Morgan tells me ye've been in a fight, and more than a small scuffle. If that's true, and ye've trouble of another sort following ye, then I'm needing to know how many of my diggers to pull out of the ground to defend ye." The smile disappeared, but the dwarf's voice was gentle and matter-of-fact.

"They don't know where I've gone," Kall said. "At least, I don't see how they could."

"Or they would have followed by this time," Garavin said, nodding. "By 'they,' I take ye to mean the trouble and not the family?"

"I have no family."

"I see." Garavin said, as if he'd heard the same raw-voiced statement many times before. "The choice is yer own, then." He pointed to Alinore Fallstone's marker—weed-grown, but in all other ways identical to the grave Kall had fallen asleep beside in Amn. "It's not truly a grave, ye see. I never had a sister, but if I did, I'm relatively certain she'd be appreciating the jest." Kall almost missed the wink Garavin shot him. "As I said, it's actually a portal. There're several hereabouts. A traveler in a rush can fly the Weave all the way to the Great Rift if he uses his head and knows where to set his feet."

"I don't know anything about that," Kall said. "I came here by accident."

"By falling asleep in a cemetery, weeping atop a stranger's grave." Garavin rummaged in a pouch that rode at his hip. He pulled out a vial of milky liquid that Kall recognized immediately. "Most folk of Amn haven't that much sentiment in them, and more's the pity." He held the vial out to Kall. "Drink it all."

Kall took the vial but did not drink. "I wasn't weeping." In truth, he remembered little about the previous night and his sleep, but he wasn't going to admit that to the dwarf. "How did I get here?" he repeated.

Garavin's keen eyes glinted like twin agates. "Drink and I'll tell ye."

Kall shrugged and drained the vial, feeling the warm liquid course down his throat. The fire that had burned in his ribs since the night before gradually began to cool, and Kall took his first easy breath with a sighing pleasure. He stopped, wary, when he noticed Garavin watching him closely.

"Ye're quite trusting," the dwarf remarked lightly.

"I'm not . . ." Kall started, then hesitated, his eyes going dark as they regarded the dwarf.

But Garavin waved away his suspicion. "No, no. Forgive my rudeness. I did want to see to yer wounds, but I have an awful curiosity. If I had a sister, I'm knowing for a fact she would have remarked on it. I found myself wondering what ye knew of the Art, one so young and full of Amnian blood. Yer eyes rounded at my talk of portals, yet ye took the healing potion as if ye knew exactly what it was."

"I know what magic is," Kall said sullenly. "Enough, anyway. I asked how it brought me here."

"So ye did, and my apologies again, for prolonging the mystery." Garavin stood and walked to the false grave, toeing aside dirt and dead branches to reveal a loose circle of stones. "Ye'll have to picture it—the portal in Amn is a mirror to this one, though with a different trigger. I'm guessing about here's where ye were lying." He put a boot in the circle. "Tears are the key to yer mystery—or a few drops of water, whatever's handy. If a body—a living body, mind you—steps in the circle and sheds three or four tears, or a thimbleful of water, the portal will activate, and he'll be somewhere else in the next eye blink." The dwarf smiled, clearly pleased with himself. "Most folk won't be shedding any tears over the grave of someone who never existed, and a good thing, considering how the portal stands in the open. Keeps folk from stumbling into countries they didn't mean to."

"What if it rains?" Kall asked curiously.

The dwarf chuckled. "Ye've an active mind. The portal is sunk beneath the grass blades, so it cannot easily be seen. The rest we leave to luck and hope that no one will be walking about in a cemetery during a storm or crying atop the grave. Ye have the unfortunate honor of beating our odds this time."

Kall crouched outside the circle. From a distance, the stones appeared to be ordinary rocks, but up close, he recognized the same symbol he'd seen carved next to Alinore's name. "Who put the portal here?" he asked. "You?"

Garavin shook his head. "No, lad. I haven't the Art, either. I only drew the map. That's what I do. I make maps and scout tunnels and hunt up knowledge—for myself, and those who need it done."

Kall looked in the direction Morgan and the half-elf had gone. Garavin followed his gaze. "When I need them to, my diggers—those two, and others ye haven't seen—dig. We're always needing more tunnels, it seems." He gave a mock wince. "At times, they dig in the wrong places, but no one's perfect."

"If the portal's a secret, why are you telling me about it?" Kall asked, suspicious again.

"Because yer eyes are asking, and yer mouth will follow once I get ye to the camp for morningfeast, so I thought I should get a head start on the day." Garavin turned, his wide, muscled body rolling like a loaded wagon. "If ye've enemies out searching, it's not wise—for either of us—to send ye through the portal just now. Eat with us, and we'll talk some more."

Kall wasn't sure. He watched the dwarf and the huge dog, which was sniffing around the packages Kall had unearthed in the cemetery.

Garavin whistled, and the dog's head came up. It fell into step beside its master. The dwarf set an unhurried pace through the trees, as if appreciating both the forest and his place in it.

Kall opened his mouth to ask another question, but Garavin, anticipating him again, tossed back over his shoulder, "The forest is named Mir. Ye're breathing Calishite air now."

Kall smelled the camp before they reached the site. The scent of cooking sausages and the sharp, starchy tang of potatoes made his stomach burn.

They broke through a tree line, where the land dipped into a wide-lipped oval bowl of tamped down grass. At the bottom swirled half a dozen people, dwarves and humans in equal number, with more spilling out of a square, two-story hut. The trees curved up in tense green spires around the scene.

"How many are there?" Kall asked as they descended. There were more figures coming out of the hut than seemed possible for it to hold.

Garavin didn't answer but guided him through the crowd. Some of the diggers looked Kall over curiously as Garavin and he passed them by, but most congregated at four large water barrels under the hut's eaves, or took seats on the grass with bowls of sausage and potatoes. All gave way or nodded respectfully to Garavin when they saw him.

The door to the hut was propped open with a large piece of shimmering quartz. Inside, it was dark and humid, and smelled strongly of earth. Ahead of them, Kall could see two ladders poking up into a second-floor loft, which was curtained off. A table and four rickety-looking chairs sat to his left. To the right there was a gaping hole in the ground. More ladders rested against its insides like exposed ribs, descending at least fifteen feet into the ground.

Kall watched as torch- and candlelight bobbed in the darkness at the bottom: more diggers. "What are they doing?" he asked.

Garavin glanced up from the table, where he'd spread out a map. "Forging an outpost, of sorts. Goblins are stirring to the south and east of here, and with Myth Unnohyr hanging above our heads in the north, I—and certain other interested parties—would like to see a wall put between them."

He looked up as a squat, crooked-nosed dwarf appeared at the door. The newcomer's beard was as fair as Garavin's was dark.

Garavin tucked his spectacles away and nodded at Kall. "Take the lad out and get him a bowl, Aln." To Kall, he said, "I won't be long."

Aln jerked a thumb toward the door, and Kall reluctantly followed him out into the yard.

" 'Ere." The fair-bearded dwarf thrust a bowl and a mug of water under Kall's nose. "Eat. We'll be 'ere a while. Fool elf brought down the wrong trees—think an elf'd know better, but ye'd be wrong. Garavin'll be a while patching things up."

Kall nodded, tearing the end off his sausage with his teeth. The meat scorched his tongue, but he barely noticed. He'd had nothing to eat since the previous morning.

Aln eyed Kall as he wolfed down the food. "What of yerself? Are ye staying, then?"

Kall shook his head, though in truth he had no idea where he intended to go. With the immediate threat of pursuit lifted, he had time to think, but he had no gold, no food, and now no horse to carry him. All he had were the items he'd dug up in the cemetery, and he wasn't desperate enough to try to sell them. Not yet.

A shadow fell on either side of Aln as Laerin and Morgan joined them on the grass.

"We were just talking about ye," Aln said darkly.

Laerin gave a good-natured wince. "Feeling better?" he asked Kall.

Kall started to nod, then yelped, "Stop!"

But Morgan had already unfolded the wrappings on the largest of his packages. "Whatever you've got in here's going to rot under these moldy things. . . ." He caught his breath. "Abbathor's hoard," he murmured, drawing out a length of blade.

"Don't speak that name here!" Aln hissed, holding his bowl high as Kall practically crawled over the dwarf's lap to get at Morgan.

"Put that down," Kall snarled, but by now the whole group could see the sword.

The blade was unremarkable, in need of polish and sharpening. But the hilt—veins of platinum ran in swirling designs like a wild river across the guard. The largest Morel emerald lay embedded in the pommel.

"Flawless," Morgan said as Kall tore the weapon from his reluctant hands.

"Are you sure?" Laerin asked, leaning forward curiously.

"Boy probably stole it," Aln muttered.

" 'Course I'm sure," insisted Morgan. "I've appraised more gems than this lot has fingers and toes. Look here, no imperfections." He reached for the sword again, but Kall reacted without thinking, slapping Morgan's knuckles with the flat of the blade.

"Hey, watch it, you!" Morgan half-rose, and Kall scuttled away, raising the blade to chest level. The bigger man immediately took a step back, lifting his hands.

"Stay away." Kall's arms trembled with the effort of holding aloft the big sword. He swung it clumsily between Morgan, who still glared angrily at him, and Aln, who simply looked bored. Some of the camp turned to watch, but most had gone back to their own conversations.

"It's all right, Kall." Laerin stood, and as Kall swung to face him, caught the dull blade in his bare palm. "No one here is going to hurt you, or attempt to take what is yours." He shot a meaningful glance at Morgan. The big man threw up his hands and sat back down, muttering to himself.

"A fine sword," the half-elf said, apparently heedless of the dot of blood that welled between his flesh and the blade. He gave Kall a level look. "Yours?"

"My father's," Kall said carefully. "Now mine."

"Too heavy for you now," Laerin said. When Kall only stared at him mulishly, Laerin casually released the blade. The point thudded to the dirt.

Aln snorted with laughter.

"You need a lighter weapon," Laerin said, ignoring him. "Morgan"—he flicked a hand—"give me your fairer blade."

Morgan looked up from his meal, scowling. "Don't call it that. And if you think I'm giving anything to that little piece of—"

"You owe him," Laerin cut in. "You put your hands where they didn't belong."

"Your self-righteous arse does the same thing whenever it's given half a chance!"

"Fine, then. Shall I tell the boy how Garavin's prying into your own past was rewarded, when we first came here?"

For whatever reason, that shut the man up. He stood, glared at Laerin, and unsheathed a short sword from his belt. He tossed it at the half-elf, who caught it easily, this time by the hilt.

"My thanks. Now." He offered the weapon to Kall, wiping his bloodied hand on his breeches.

Cautiously, Kall placed the priceless sword lengthwise between them. He grasped the hilt of the offered blade and raised it with one hand.

"When you are older," Laerin said, "you will be as tall and as broad as I am. My father was of your blood—thick in the chest and arms. People will think you're a brawler, but you'll be able to wield that"—he pointed a toe at the sword lying in the dirt—"with grace and ease."

Kall nodded, then noticed Garavin silhouetted in the hut's doorway.

"Laerin is correct about yer abilities," said the dwarf. He came forward, lifting Kall's sword from the dirt. "Ye should be taking care of such a precious thing." His eyes closed briefly, as if he were absorbing some invisible resonance from the blade. "It will serve ye more than well . . . but not today," he said, addressing the last part to Laerin.

The half-elf nodded solemnly. Then he bowed briefly to the dwarf, winked at Kall, and left them.

Kall watched him move gracefully around the camp, giving instructions, until he realized Garavin still held his sword. Awkwardly, he took the blade, letting it rest beside him.

"I'm afraid we must put off our talk a bit longer, lad," Garavin said, his brow furrowing apologetically.

Kall nodded, though he couldn't imagine what the two of them had to discuss. Just before the dwarf disappeared inside the hut, Kall said, "I'm not staying here."

Garavin paused and gave a nod. "Then it looks to be a very short conversation."

CHAPTER SEVEN

Forest of Mir, Calimshan
13 Eleasias, the Year of the Sword (1365 DR)

Garavin's diggers worked in shifts of six, with two torch-bearers standing nearby to offer additional light and water when needed. Every few candles the shift would change, but the resting group would stay together in its own cluster, eating, talking, and occasionally shooting glances Kall's way. He ignored them, preferring to spend the time resting and watching.

As night fell, Morgan brought out tin buckets filled with tallow and arranged them in circles throughout the camp. When lit, the bucket candles gave off a peaceful glow like grazing fireflies. The evening meal came next: seasoned bread chunks and ham sliced off the bone by the same man who had served breakfast. The diggers, drawn by the smell of food, gathered again in the clearing, and Garavin joined them, the great dog Borl trailing behind him.

The dwarf chewed a short-stem pipe and had a book wedged beneath one arm. He bypassed the food line, instead heading for one of the few trees in the bowl-shaped clearing.

Large silver-sheened leaves hung around a trunk that looked as if it had been split, long ago, by weight or perhaps by a lightning strike. One half had died, but the other portion thrived. Garavin sat in the space between the living and the dead halves. With his dark, weathered skin, he looked almost a part of the tree, a face staring out of the bark. He smoked, read, and watched the activities of the camp, while the mastiff slept at his feet.

Kall ate with Laerin and Morgan again, listening to them discuss the day's progress, but his eyes kept straying to Garavin. Finally, Laerin nudged him.

"Go," he said simply.

The dwarf did not look up from his book as Kall approached, and Kall wondered if he'd fallen asleep. Then a plume of smoke rose from Garavin's pipe, and his eyes followed. He nodded at the withered bit of stump, and Kall sat.

"Well? What do ye think of my diggers, Kall?"

It wasn't the question Kall had expected, so he said the first thing that came to mind. "They're not like you."

Garavin smiled. "Well, let's suppose ye and I were to mark a map of Faerûn with the birthplaces and travels of all those lads and lasses ye saw today. Ye'd still be about it when winter came, and it would take a lifetime and more to walk in their footsteps."

"They came all that way, just to end up here—to dig?" Kall asked in disbelief.

"Not by intent," Garavin said. "They came because they had nowhere else to go—much like ye, which is why I thought we should be talking."

"I have a home," Kall said. "I never wanted to end up here."

"I understand, and I can send ye back to Amn quick enough," said Garavin, "but that way leads to a quick death, or am I mistaken?"

Kall shook his head. "But I will go back someday," he said, meeting Garavin's eyes.

"I do not doubt ye," Garavin said, acknowledging the vow solemnly. "What I mean to do is offer ye a course for the intervening time. My diggers have been following a generally westward path since Nightal last," he said. "Our work in Mir and the surrounding area will take a pair of years, perhaps more, but once we reach the Shining Sea, I intend to run north for a bit. I could offer ye a place with us now, and give ye the option of leaving us when ye choose. Understand, I'm not in the habit of making this gesture to everyone. I need to keep a certain number of diggers in the company at a time. If I have too many, food will run short. Too few and we're weak on defense. But this way, ye could remain near the place ye're most wanting to be, and learn my trade in the meantime."

"I already know how to dig," Kall said, but he listened.

"This is different," Garavin said. "The first tenday will break yer back. Ye'll hate it, curse it . . . and me, come to think. The second tenday ye won't be able to keep yer eyes open, so ye won't have time to be thinking or cursing about anything—not the past, nor the future beyond putting one boot in front of the other. After that, as ye adjust, ye'll be having nothing but time. That is precious time—to consider yer place in the world and what ye intend to do with it."

Kall didn't need to consider either of those things. He pictured Balram, secure in his father's house, as night fell in the Forest of Mir. He replaced the image with one of himself, plunging his father's sword deep into the guard captain, feeling whatever magic the blade contained slide out, into his enemy. His father would be free—Aazen would be free—and Kall's life could return to what it once had been. Nothing else mattered.

"Why do you dig?" Kall looked at the dwarf, and a glint of green winking from a gap in his beard drew Kall's eyes downward. "What is that?" he asked.

Garavin lifted the object—a pendant—by its chain. Kall recognized the components first: smooth carnelian worked into the shape of a mountain; nestled within it, a faceted emerald shone like a doorway.

"Dugmaren Brightmantle is why I dig," Garavin said. He pointed to the swaying pendant. "Dumathoin guides the shovel."

"Dumathoin." Kall touched the seam, the joining of emerald to mountain, and felt the scratch of electricity run through his fingers.

"I serve the gleam in the eye and the keeper of secrets," Garavin continued, "because in addition to having an awful curiosity, I've dug far enough into the earth to uncover things that should—and shouldn't—be made known to greater Toril. Dumathoin helps me with the sorting out of which is which."

"You hunt knowledge," Kall said, remembering what Garavin had told him in the forest.

"Yes—and secrets. I can find them, and I can keep them. Ye should remember that, if ever ye're needing someone to talk to." He puffed unconcernedly on his pipe as Kall looked away. "If ye do stay, Laerin could teach ye things—they all could, I'm knowing that. But first ye'd learn to dig. That rule never changes."

The sound of raucous laughter at some unheard jest drifted out to them from the camp.

"They're gods, then," Kall said, listening to the forest stir with nighttime sounds. "Dugmaren and Dumathoin."

"Of the dwarf folk," Garavin nodded. "Most of my band is of Dugmaren's mind. They are discoverers—explorers. Dwarf or human, they fit nowhere else, so Dugmaren takes them all."

"Why should a dwarf care what happens to me?" Kall said without thinking, and felt heat rush up his neck. He plunged on. "I don't want to be an explorer. I've got nothing to offer Dugmaren."

"Ye have two hands, and an active mind, as I've already noted," Garavin said. "Even if Dugmaren wasn't interested, I'd still take ye."

Kall refused to meet the dwarf's eyes. "Why?"

"Because at one time or another, we all get trapped in the place ye are now." Garavin leaned forward, his grave face filling Kall's vision. "Do ye know what we do about it?"

Kall started to shake his head, but stopped when he saw

Garavin's eyes twinkling with humor. He caught on and said, in perfect unison with the dwarf, "We dig ourselves out." Kall snorted—not quite a laugh, but something lighter than what had been in his mind. His voice only shook slightly when he said, "I'm going to need a large shovel."

"There ye go." Garavin chuckled, jostling the pipe and sending ashes flying. "Ye'll be fine, Kall."

———◆◆◆———

He slept in the map room the first night. That's what Garavin called the curtained off loft at the rear of the hut. The tiny room was jam-packed with maps, drawings, and rolls of parchment filled to the edges with scrawled notes. In one corner, a cot and blankets were wedged under the eaves, almost as an afterthought.

Kall lay on his back, his nose inches from a ceiling beam, wide awake. For lack of anything to do, he circled the room with his eyes again and again—past Garavin's pipe, left lying on a table next to a comfortable-looking chair, to the oval cut-out window, with Selûne's pale glow filtering through, then back to the beam.

By the fourteenth pass, he was up and at the window, watching the forest. His sword lay on a bench beneath the window, nearly translucent in the moon's glow. The other dirt-encrusted package and his borrowed sword sat in shadow as if in awe of the bright sword.

If anything should happen to me, Kall . . .

That had been his father's commandment. If anything happened, what was between the graves belonged to Kall. The only bit of magic Dhairr Morel would permit in his life, buried deep in the earth.

Kall touched the sword with his knuckle, a light touch, enough to cool his skin on the steel. He felt nothing, certainly not the gentle jolt he'd gotten from Garavin's holy relic. What, then, could the sword possibly contain?

The distant sound of chimes drew Kall from his reverie. The

haunting, beautiful echo seemed incongruous when wrapped around the normal forest noise. Was it a call to worship from some hidden temple? Kall wondered. He'd already witnessed so many things he'd never thought to see. Who knew what this latest mystery might portend?

The chimes came again, closer, and then Kall saw the herd.

The mist stags came into the clearing between the hut and the forest, weaving among the trees like stealthy phantoms. They were the size of spry colts, their pelts steely gray but sprinkled liberally with silver. The bucks' antlers curved inward in conical shapes, and the stags had a wisp of beard at their chins. They ran in graceful, springing motions, as if their feet trod air instead of grass.

A spear tip caught the moonlight as it came out of the trees. Kall sucked in a breath, fearing a hunter stalked the beautiful creatures. He heard the chimes again and realized the sound wasn't coming from the animals, but from their shepherd.

The druid stepped into the clearing, shepherding the bucks. Her gaze lifted to his window, and she stared at him through the dark triangle of her hooded cloak. She couldn't have been much older than he, Kall thought.

The mist stags flowed around her, making small sounds that sounded like alarm. The girl angled her head to listen.

The trees behind her exploded in a fireball.

Heat blasted Kall in the face. He dived below the level of the window, instinctively clawing at his face to feel if he was burned. His skin was warm and slick, but unmarked.

Lurching to his feet, Kall returned to the window, scanning the trees for some sign of the girl, but there was nothing, only the panicked herd scattering in every direction. A tree was ablaze, and there came frantic shouts from inside and outside the perimeter of the camp. The small hut quivered with the pounding of feet on floorboards and ladders.

Kall grabbed his sword and tossed it out of the window. He slung a leg over the curved sill and eased himself out, scraping his belly over the wood. He lowered himself until he hung by his fingertips, then dropped.

Retrieving his sword, he trotted quickly away from the hut, into the chaos of the forest.

She couldn't have gotten far, Kall reasoned as he ducked into the trees. He was so absorbed in trying to pick out her hooded form in the darkness that he didn't see the goblins until they were almost on top of him.

Dark, mottled shapes poked swords out of the smoke. Kall froze, hoping his frantic movements hadn't given him away. There were five of them arranged in a hunting party, torches flickering at its rear. In the flickering light, Kall glimpsed a cracked, filth-encrusted gauntlet wrapped around an equally grimy arm. He dropped into the shadows of one of the huge old oaks and watched the gauntlet pass by.

At the edge of the clearing, the party halted. The lead goblin pointed to Garavin's hut, and the others nodded, shaking their weapons and grunting like two-legged swine. They moved in a haphazard line, with no real leader keeping them in check.

Kall thought he was safe, but the last goblin in line suddenly thrust his torch in Kall's direction, spilling light on his face. An exuberant cry went up, and the goblin broke away from the pack to charge at him. The creature swung the torch playfully, as if batting at an insect.

Kall sidestepped, and felt the heat kiss his ear. He'd never liked fire. He would rather face a thousand deaths by drowning than be burned. When he was seven, he'd tripped and fallen in a dying campfire. The blisters on his hands and arms had been agonizing, and though the scars were mostly healed, he'd lost many of the sensitive nerves in his hands. He would never be a painter or a sculptor, but he could still wield a sword.

He raised his father's blade, backed into the tree, and twisted, putting the trunk between himself and the goblin. He knew he had to run. If he didn't lose them in the trees, they'd simply ring him in until they wore him down.

Kall's toe caught an exposed root. He fell and felt the wind whoosh out of his lungs. The goblin's torch came around the tree, but the creature's laughter was drowned out by pounding feet and harsh breathing that passed close to Kall's face. Their owner smelled of blood.

Panicking, Kall rolled blindly away, and saw Borl leap over him. The jump carried the huge mastiff into the goblin's chest.

The creature put its arms around the dog, clawing, and both went crashing into the underbrush. Borl snarled viciously as the goblin screamed and thrashed. Its torch went out, plunging the immediate area into darkness. The goblins scattered in the direction of the burning trees, confused and terrified by the screams of their comrade.

Kall started to stand and found himself pulled back down by his shirt. He rolled onto his back to free himself and swiped the air, expecting an attack from above. A hand caught his wrist, and he found himself staring into the face of the young girl.

Up close, Kall saw that mottled brown and green paint streaked her face and hands, and her hair was tied back and buried in her hood. Trees and starlight haloed her; she blended into her surroundings like a wraith.

Kall opened his mouth, but she put a tense finger to his lips to keep him silent. He listened, picking up a second set of footsteps approaching fast in the wake of the first hunting party. More goblins, more fire, he thought.

"Are the diggers in the forest?" he whispered around her finger.

The girl nodded, lifting her gaze from him to the trees. Far off, a sound rose over the tramping of goblin feet, an echo like the chanting of a choir at temple. In its wake, a brilliant flash lit the night, casting the area into sharp, blue-white relief. Kall flinched under the power, the nearness of the lightning, but the girl paid it no attention. She stared straight ahead. Her lips moved, but Kall couldn't hear what she said. The entire scene felt like a dream, except he could smell the smoke, the dirt, and the reek of goblin sweat.

The girl stopped speaking, and when she did, a frail mist began to build around them. At first Kall thought it was the fire, but the fog was cool and smelled of an herb he could not place. The mist thickened, drifting against the wind to veil their hiding place. It pushed into the ranks of the marching goblins, obscuring them from view. Panicked grunts drifted out of the cloud, and the druid smiled grimly.

From the underbrush she plucked her spear. It was lighter and sleeker than it had first appeared, with a wicked barbed point. Below the blade dangled a cluster of oak leaves and what looked like tiny silver bells on a cord. Raising her weapon to her shoulder, the girl cast it into the fog. A soft, singing chime echoed within the mist—the same sound Kall had heard from the hut—followed by a solid thud and a goblin scream.

The girl drew out another spear, turned to him, and mouthed something. Kall shook his head to show he did not understand. The girl spoke again, just as silently, and Kall stared at her. Tossing her hood back impatiently, she stood and crept around the tree, using the trunk to guide her steps.

She led him to a large boulder nestled between two more of the great oaks, like a stone in a giant's sling. In the lee of the stone and the trees, they were much less exposed.

The girl wedged two fingers inside a pouch clipped to her belt. She pulled out two cream-colored stones.

Kall was not the expert in gems his father was, but he could tell immediately the stones had no value—they had likely been picked from a riverbed or the forest floor. But she held them as close as Kall had kept his sword. She took his hand, put one stone in his palm and kept the other for herself.

Put it in your pouch, she said. Her sudden voice in the dark startled him. *I forget, sometimes, who bear the stones and who do not.*

"What are they?" asked Kall.

The stones are enchanted to give me speech your ears can hear, the druid explained. *It need not touch your flesh. Only keep it near you, and we can speak.*

Kall slid the stone in his pouch. "Who are you?" he asked.

Cesira, the woman said. *Or the Quiet One of Silvanus, as the Starwater Six—the druids—are fond of calling me.*

Kall jumped, startled, as mist rose around him again, plucking at his waist. Then he saw the antlers and realized the herd had regrouped—and not just the males. The frail mist coalesced under his hand and became a gray-black doe. Without thinking, Kall reached out to touch its fur, but his hand passed right through the doe's lithe body. He pulled back in shock.

Around him, other females appeared from nowhere, some with tiny fawns, all as translucent as the one that stood beside him. Its large black eyes regarded him steadily.

"Are they ghosts?" Kall whispered.

Cesira shook her head. *They are Quessilaren—nearly gone, but for small herds that dwell here and on distant Evermeet. The females run between this world and the Border Ethereal for protection, never belonging wholly to either.*

"Are they dangerous?"

Not at all. They've befriended the wild elves and a handful of us. I and the other apprentices watch over them, when we can. Cesira held up her spear. *When a buck is killed by the goblins, we burn the carcass, but for this.* She let the spear point catch the moonlight. What Kall had at first taken for bells actually looked to be bits of hollowed-out antler.

The chimes they make are as sweet a music as any human will ever hear outside the elf courts, she said. Her expression hardened. *We feel it fitting for the goblins to hear it before they die.*

Kall said nothing, unsure how to react to the passion in the young girl's eyes. Lightning split the sky, turning her skin silver.

Come. Cesira said. *We should move—*

"Look out!" Kall dived at her, crushing his shoulder into the dirt as a hand axe sailed over their entwined bodies.

A lone goblin crashed through the trees after its wild throw. It saw them, helpless in the underbrush, and charged.

Kall rolled off the druid, scrambling to get his sword. He braced the blade as Cesira wrenched the creature's leg, sending it sprawling onto the sword's point. The goblin crumpled as Kall pulled the weapon free, and the pair ran, retreating deeper into the forest.

Wait. Panting, Cesira pulled Kall up short.

"Are you all right?" he asked.

She nodded curtly, but her eyes were wide. *You should wipe the blood from your weapon,* she said.

Kall looked down at his sword. A red stain ran halfway up the blade. He drew it across the grass.

I didn't see the axe, Cesira said.

"I know."

She scowled. *That doesn't mean—*

"I was just as scared," he interrupted, and they gazed at each other in silence. "I want to go back," Kall said. In his heart, he did not mean to Garavin's hut.

She seemed to realize it, and softened. *You can't. That path is closed.*

Her voice was gentle, but the words felt like a slap. Kall's anger returned. "You know nothing about me!" he snapped.

I know much of you, Kall.

"How do you know my name?"

Garavin, she said simply. *Go back to him. Dig holes and make tunnels. It's hardening work, work you'll need. In a year or two you'll be fighting goblins. Dig holes, make tunnels . . .* She paused. *And come to see me, at the boulder.*

"Why?" Kall asked, confused. In the dark and the mist her profile wasn't easy to discern, but he knew she was looking at him.

You helped me, she said. The words clearly came hard to her. *I can help you.*

They didn't speak again. She took him back to the boulder between the trees, so he would know how to find it again.

They found Morgan and Laerin leaning against the rock, arguing.

"If he'd've been some frock-heavy, perfumed Waterdhavian snotling, you wouldn't've thought twice about keeping them!" Morgan accused.

"Yet clearly he's not," came Laerin's gentler reply. He noticed Kall and Cesira, and smiled. "Nor is he quite a boy, after what he's been through. Well met, Kall."

Kall nodded to the half-elf. Cesira climbed the boulder and sat cross-legged atop it.

You're both late, she said.

"Our fault completely," said Laerin. "We lost Kall's trail thanks to your superior forest skills . . . and Morgan dropped the emeralds."

"Found 'em again, didn't I!" Morgan huffed. He reached inside a pouch and pulled something out in his fist. He hurled the object—a small, dirt-encrusted bundle of linen—at Kall.

Kall recognized it at once. It was the same bundle he'd unearthed with his father's sword from the cemetery in Esmeltaran. One end was torn open. Kall could see twin points of green glittering against the white linen: two more emeralds—flawless stones matching the gem in his father's sword.

"You stole them?" he asked incredulously.

Don't let their doltish appearances fool you, said Cesira. *These louts are well known—and wanted—burglars in the finer districts of Waterdeep, Arabel, and gods know where else.*

"Those baubles would have kept us comfortable for several winters," Morgan complained.

"He's right," Kall said, fingering the stones. He fought down his instinctive anger at Morgan's theft and instead looked at Laerin. "Why didn't you keep them?"

"Because you're going to need them," Laerin said. He nodded at Cesira. "They speak, much like your lady's stones."

Kall felt his neck grow warm, but he refused to be distracted by the half-elf's teasing. "Show me."

Laerin took one of the emeralds back, fisting it in the palm of his hand. "Morel," he said aloud. He waited a beat, then raised the stone to his mouth and spoke a handful of words in

Elvish. Kall did not understand any of them. A breath later, Kall looked down at his sword in surprise. The emerald in the hilt glowed, luminous against the platinum veins.

"Touch the stone in your sword and speak your family name," Laerin instructed him.

Curious, Kall did as he said and felt the emerald grow warm. He heard Laerin's Elvish speech coming from the stone, a perfect echo of what the half-elf had said. An instant later, the words repeated, this time in Common.

Friends in the dark.

Kall lowered his weapon. "I had no idea the stones were linked."

"No matter the language, the gems will translate. They have another power," Laerin said. He dropped the second emerald in Kall's open hand. "Anyone who possesses one of the emeralds can locate the other two at any time, no matter the distance."

"Been tracking you since you left the hut," said Morgan.

"What does the message mean?" Kall asked, still watching the half-elf. "Friends in the dark?"

"Means diggers," Laerin said. He winked at Kall.

"Nothing wrong with digging," Morgan agreed.

Kall looked up at the boulder, but Cesira had gone.

"She's rejoined the druids," Laerin explained. "But she'll be back." He pushed off the rock. "We should go. Garavin will be waiting."

Kall held the sparkling emeralds in his hand. The forest was eerily quiet, tense and uncertain in the wake of the goblin battle. In the distance, fires still burned.

It would take a long time, Kall thought, but eventually the forest would look as it had before. Maybe it would be stronger for all the damage it had suffered. Kall wondered if he would see the mist stags again.

Turning, he followed Morgan and Laerin back to Garavin's hut.

CHAPTER EIGHT

Esmeltaran, Amn
2 Eleint, the Year of the Banner (1368 DR)

Three years later, the house looked exactly as he remembered it.

Kall expected to meet the bulk of the resistance at the door, but there was only one guard, a skinny, tired-looking man who stood by the window, with a fist stuck in his mouth to stifle a yawn.

Kall slid around the side of the house, beneath the windows facing the front hedgerows. He came up behind the guard and clipped him on the back of the head with the pommel of his sword. The guard crumpled; Kall caught him under the armpits and dragged him into the shadows behind the bushes.

Returning to the door, he took out the set of lockpicks Laerin had given him and set to work. He hadn't nearly the half-elf's skill, but what he lacked in grace he made up for with persistence. The lock gave way with a click.

Inside the entry hall, lanterns were dimmed for sleep, but Kall knew his house well enough to feel his way. He listened for signs that someone had detected his presence, but he heard nothing.

One inept guard at the door and no stirring in the house—it

was too easy for Kall's comfort. His father would never have permitted such a breach of his private space. A sinking unease filled Kall's chest.

He stepped forward, passing between two twisted columns. He heard the second click a heartbeat too late.

Kall ducked, on the off chance the trap was aimed at his head, but the danger came from below. Metal spikes burst from camouflaged gaps in the marble floor, ringing him in a field of razors. If he'd been standing directly on top of one of them, Kall was certain he'd have lost a foot. A spike caught him in the calf, shearing away his boot like so much meat off the bone.

Kall resisted the urge to jump back, lest he should trigger more of the deadly spikes. Regaining his balance, he began moving forward again, watching the floor for holes. He made it to the other side of the hall without encountering any further traps.

In the shadows beneath the main staircase, Kall paused to listen again. He'd never known his father kept such deadly traps in his own home. Dhairr had always feared assassins—Kall had grown up with nightmares from listening to his father's tales about shadowy, hidden foes—but this? It made his father seem a prisoner in his own home. What other secrets had Dhairr kept from him?

He pushed the thoughts away. He had to find Balram. Someone was sure to have heard the trap go off. He was running out of time.

The back wall by the staircase had only one door. It opened onto the garden between the main house and the towers. He could conceal himself better in the garden than the hall.

Kall listened at the door, hearing a faint scraping sound coming from the other side. He tested the lock, but it was open. Slowly, he eased the door inward a crack.

In the center of the garden, illuminated by faint moonglow, Dhairr Morel crouched in the fountain's dry basin, digging at a jagged crack with his sword. The blade was dull and notched from repeated scrapes across the stone. A shrill, metallic screech filled the air as he worked.

Kall simply watched his father, unable to believe the changes wrought in his visage. Flesh stretched taut beneath his eyes and along his jaw. His lips were colorless and bore ragged crevices and gaps where he'd bitten them too deeply. His hair was thin and coarse, like a wisp broom. It hung past his shoulders and dragged the fountain bowl when Dhairr bent his ear to the crack. His eyes fell on Kall and narrowed.

"Who are you?" he rasped. He flipped his blade up, menacing Kall with nothing more than a blunt edge. "Begone, assassin! You'll not have my family."

"Father," Kall said, taking a step forward. "Don't you recognize me? I *am* your family—Kall, your son."

"Kall," Dhairr repeated, testing the name on his tongue. Slow comprehension broke over his wasted face. "So you've returned. Kall the traitor—have you come back to finish what you started?"

"No, Father," Kall said. "I've come back to free you."

"Lies!"

Dhairr lunged, aiming at Kall's midsection. For all the changes, his father was still fast, and Kall was so stunned by the outburst he almost allowed himself to be impaled upon Dhairr's notched blade. He backed away and tripped, landing awkwardly on his side on the walkway.

Dhairr smiled cruelly. "Don't be careless, Kall. You think I won't do to you what I did to Haig? That I'll show mercy because you're my son? You have no idea who I am, boy."

"You don't know what you're saying—" Kall dodged another swing. His father was still caught in the grip of Balram's spell; he still believed Kall had betrayed him. Kall arched his back, snapping his legs downward in a sharp thrust to get his feet under him. The quick, acrobatic move made Dhairr back off a step, long enough for Kall to bring his sword up at a defensive slant.

"You would fight me with a Morel emerald?" Dhairr slapped

Kall's sword, revealing the matching gems borne by both blades—one steeped in magic, the other caked with dirt. "You were never worthy of bearing that sword." Dhairr sprang again, slashing in and up, trying to get under Kall's guard.

"Father, tell me where Balram is. *He's* the traitor." Kall caught the notched blade and twisted to pry the weapon from Dhairr's fingers. Obediently, Dhairr abandoned the sword and threw his fist instead, landing a blow hard above Kall's ear.

Dazed, Kall shuffled back. His father flipped his sword back into his hands with the toe of his boot. "You're going to lose if you don't fight in earnest. Think carefully, Kall. You either mean it or you die."

Kall shook his head to clear it. "I'm here to kill Balram, not you," he insisted.

"Balram is gone," Dhairr said. "He left me to face my assassins alone, but I'm more than able to weed the filth from my garden."

"Father, please." Kall blocked high and crosswise as Dhairr chopped downward mercilessly with both hands. The impact resonated along Kall's blade to the hilt. Kall was reminded anew of how strong the man could be. Sick as he was, his father was right: Kall couldn't afford to fight the battle halfheartedly.

"You can resist Balram's control," Kall said. He took a step back and to the side, circling Dhairr, waiting for him to take another lunge. He did not. He seemed to be listening. "Balram may be gone, but his evil is still eating away at your soul. Can't you see?" It was a rhetorical question, for Kall immediately took the offensive, bringing his blade in high.

When Dhairr blocked, Kall grabbed his father by the back of the neck and dragged him in close, tangling their blades in a harmless lock. "I've come back to save you." Kall held his father's stubborn, glassy-eyed gaze with one of determination. Let him see. Let him know I'm telling the truth. Kall prayed he could get through.

He shoved his father back, metal raking metal as their swords came apart. Kall followed up with another slash in a broad arc. Dhairr blocked it easily but lost a step, giving Kall ground.

"You're going to be all right." Kall kept swinging and talking, never allowing Dhairr the chance to respond to or deny his words. Slowly, his father's anger gave way to uncertainty. Kall used the advantage, driving his father where Kall wanted him to go. When the backs of his knees struck the fountain's edge, Dhairr fell, his eyes widening in surprise and fear.

Kall ran forward, letting his sword drop to the walkway. He caught his father in his arms before Dhairr's head struck the stone basin. Kall kicked the dull blade out of reach.

Dhairr struggled, but his son stubbornly held on, pinning his arms until the older man stopped fighting. When it was clear he was no physical match for Kall, Dhairr began hurling curses: foul, hateful monologues—that Kall was not his son, that his mother was a godless, murdering whore, that he had no son . . . he had no son.

"Kall . . . Kall," he murmured finally, his voice hoarse. He focused on Kall's face, but there was no recognition. His head snapped from side to side. "Where is my son?" he whispered. "Where is he?"

Kall sat helplessly. For all his father's strength, the man seemed light as air in his arms. He looked small, and very, very old. Kall had no idea what to say to his father, how to answer the imploring look in his eyes. He could only hold him as he slid into unconsciousness.

"You can't save him," said a soft, feminine voice.

Kall whirled, reaching for his sword, but the woman cradled it in her hands. She was almost as tall as he, with a short bob of black hair capping a round face and green eyes.

"A fine blade," she said, watching Kall appraisingly. "I've no doubt he was wrong. You are worthy of wielding it."

"Who are you?" Kall asked, but he recognized the symbol she wore. He'd seen it once before, in this same garden.

"Meisha Saira," the woman introduced herself. Of the Harpers, Kall added silently.

"You're here because of Haig," Kall said, lowering his father gently to the ground. He stood, measuring the woman's intent. He didn't like what he saw. The spread of her feet and the tension in her neck and shoulders gave her away. She was here for a fight.

"I owe you thanks. You've saved me the trouble of subduing his murderer." She looked down at his father with a mixture of disgust and pity. "Not that he appears to warrant great effort, in his current state."

"You can't have him," Kall said steadily.

The woman lifted a brow. "Oh? Was his confession the ravings of a madman, then?"

"The man responsible for Haig's death is Balram Kortrun," said Kall. "My father acted under Balram's influence, and as you can see, he is no longer a threat to anyone."

"He soon won't be," Meisha agreed. She cast his sword to the far end of the garden and raised her empty hands.

Kall got to her first. He grabbed her arm and twisted it, slamming her against his chest with her hand bent at a painful angle against her lower back. "You're not listening," he said in her ear. When she struggled, he wrenched her palm back until she gasped. "If you want justice for Haig, let my father live, and I will get it for you."

"He's no longer your father," Meisha argued. "He doesn't recognize his own son."

"I know," Kall said, swallowing his grief. "What is left of him suffers more than enough."

"Then why not end it? Give him a quick, merciful death."

"No." Kall shook his head. "I won't kill him if there's a chance he might come back."

Meisha fell silent. She relaxed her stance, but Kall kept her hand pinned. "You won't kill him," she said softly. "But are you willing to die to protect what he has become?"

She brought her heel up, clipping his knee. Pain shot up Kall's leg. He released her involuntarily.

Backing away, she flicked a wrist, fingers splayed, and traced a circular pattern with her other thumb in midair. She spoke as she cast. "Will it be your life for his?"

Her eyes blazed red, and Kall thought for an instant they were afire, burning the orbs out of their sockets. The circle she traced filled with flame, swirling in on itself to become a ball of brilliant orange with a blue vortex.

Kall had seen wizards cast spells in battle, and he'd even seen magical fire burn men alive. He'd once accompanied Cesira to the site of a massive spell duel between rival wizards. They'd watched from a protected distance, but after a time Kall's eyes could no longer separate one spell from another amid the devastation.

He'd never seen a fireball form in a wizard's hands at such close range—shaped from nothing, a great ember falling from a god's furnace—never had he seen one directed at himself.

The flames filled his vision as the deadly orb flew toward him. He felt the heat sear his face. Instinctively, he threw up his hands and covered his father's body with his own.

He heard the explosion, but the pain didn't follow. Kall lifted his head and saw the twin, scorching trails marking the path the fireballs had made across the garden. They formed a perfect arc around his and his father's bodies.

"You split them," Kall said, standing. His legs felt shaky. "Why?"

"Curiosity." She dismissed it with a shrug. "Or a test of your convictions. Call it whatever you like, I—"

She tried to dodge, but Kall had her again. He pinned her arms down to her sides. "I appreciate the reprieve. This is just in case you have another of those fire spells ready," he said.

She smiled thinly. "What makes you think I need another?"

Kall felt his skin grow warm. Sweat broke out on his neck, and alarm rose in his chest. He looked down at the Harper. Her skin, pressed against his, was painfully hot.

"Let me go, Morel, or I *will* burn you," she said, her voice echoing with deadly power. "All I want is your father."

Gazing into her eyes, Kall saw she told the truth. Slowly, he slid his other arm around her waist, steeling himself against the intense pain. "If you're willing to kill me for him, get it over with," he rasped.

For a breath, the heat wavered. Kall waited, but then, as suddenly as it started, the burning sensation ebbed. The Harper stiffened, her eyes going wide.

Kall looked up and realized immediately what had cooled the fire. He nodded a stiff greeting to Morgan. The rogue had a stiletto point pressed against the back of Meisha's neck. "I seem to remember telling you I'd handle this on my own," he said, not bothering to hide his irritation.

"Doing a fine job of it too," Morgan snorted. " 'Sides, it was his idea."

Kall released Meisha and stepped back. He looked over Morgan's shoulder, expecting to see Laerin. His mouth fell open when Garavin entered the garden, flanked by Cesira and the half-elf. "You *all* followed me?"

"Not at first," Laerin said. He handed Kall back his blade as Garavin patted Meisha down for weapons.

Cesira knelt next to his father's unconscious body. *We followed your sword,* she said.

Laerin tossed an emerald to Kall, pretending to look abashed.

Kall sheathed his weapon, amazed but still angry at the deception. "You shouldn't have taken it . . . again."

"I shouldn't have," Laerin agreed. "But it was our only link to you. Morgan was distraught at the thought you might get into trouble without him."

"How fares yer father?" Garavin asked, speaking for the first time. He nodded at Meisha. "And what have we here?"

"Garavin Fallstone, meet Meisha Saira," Kall said. "She just tried to kill me."

"Probably won't be the last time," Morgan predicted.

The Harper remained silent, her eyes darting among the new arrivals. Kall went down on one knee next to the druid, who was examining his father. "Can you break the enchantment?" he asked, addressing both Cesira and the dwarf.

Cesira shook her head. *There's magic about him, but whatever the source, it's long spent. The marks it left on him can't be erased with more magic.*

Garavin nodded agreement. "Take him back with us. We'll make him comfortable, and ye can stay with him, Kall."

Kall wiped the fever sweat from his father's brow. "No. I can't be there when he wakes up. Seeing me put him in this state. He believed I was trying to kill him."

You can't mean to leave him here, said Cesira. *You've been waiting three years to save him.*

"Balram's gone," said Kall. "My father is no longer in danger from him. He'll be as safe here as anywhere else."

"And yerself? What will ye do?" asked Garavin.

Lost in thought, Kall stared down at his father's face. He remembered the violence in Dhairr's eyes during their sword fight. "I'll go back with you," he decided. "Gods willing, when my father wakes up, he won't remember any of this. He'll go on as before, when I wasn't here."

"How?" asked Laerin. He took in the damaged fountain, and the garden showing further signs of neglect. "The house mirrors your father's condition. "How long will Morel be able to survive lying vulnerable among the merchants of Amn?"

"Longer than he will if I remain," Kall said. "I'll come back after, to salvage what I can."

"After?" Morgan asked, but surprisingly, it was Meisha who answered.

"After he dies," she said quietly, wincing when Morgan tightened his grip on the stiletto.

Kall nodded. "When that happens, all that is Morel will pass to me. I can rebuild from its ashes." He regarded Meisha warily. "But only if I know my father will not go prematurely to the grave. Will your death be my only guarantee of that, Meisha Saira?"

"If the lass tracked down your father, she might be able to aid ye in tracking Balram," said Garavin. "Might be a shame to be killing her."

But can she be trusted? Cesira asked.

"I can speak for myself," said Meisha sharply. She stared at Garavin, at the symbol around his neck. Kall couldn't imagine how, with a blade at the back of her neck and enemies boxing her in, she could focus on the object so completely.

"If I help you, you'll see that Balram pays for his crime?" Meisha asked, her eyes finally moving from the pendant to Kall's face.

"Whether you help or not, Balram will die by my hand," said Kall. "I promise you."

"Then Dhairr Morel is safe from me," said Meisha. "You have my word."

"We'll be watching to see you hold to it," said Morgan. He took his blade from the back of her neck.

Dhairr stirred, murmuring in his sleep. Kall backed away. "It's time to go," he said, but he lingered in the garden with his father until the others had gone. He put his father's dull blade next to him by the fountain, so he would find it when he woke.

"Forgive me," he whispered as Dhairr twitched in the throes of some agitated dream. "I failed you, but I won't fail our family. I'll come back. I'll restore everything Balram took away and send him to the Nine Hells for what he did to you."

"My son," his father murmured. Kall froze, but Dhairr's eyes remained shut. His struggles slowed, and he slept on, peacefully.

Kall turned away, and saw Cesira silhouetted in the doorway to the garden. She said nothing when he moved to join her, and neither looked back as they walked from the house.

<hr />

Tossing in feverish dreams, Meisha curled unconsciously closer to her campfire. She needed the warmth. She was back in the cold, back in the Delve. Was it calling the fire that had triggered the dream? No, Kall's friend, the dwarf, had done it.

The dream always started the same way—as memory. She could recall every detail with perfect clarity.

The child Meisha huddled in a sullen ball on the floor of the cavern. She stared into the firepit, feeling only a vague sense of unease she could not explain. She'd felt it ever since Varan had brought her to the Delve. It had been three days, but she already felt she'd spent a lifetime out of the sun.

"Are you so determined to be angry with me?"

Varan's voice echoed from the tunnel, but Meisha did not turn to face her teacher. Flames beat down on her shaved skull; heat from the fire made the mud covering her chest crack and crumble. The heat reminded her of highsun in Keczulla, during the markets. The mud had protected her skin from the burning sun, but she didn't need it now—in the dark. She missed Amn, missed the smell and color of the crowds. The Delve seemed unnaturally quiet. Varan preferred it that way.

"Do you imagine, in all Faerûn, you are the only child ever to have been deprived of something—a home, loved ones, a dream?"

Varan sat across the pit from her, his robes pillowed beneath him on the cold cavern floor. Their hem still dripped wet from the water whip spell she'd used on him. "Though you've been blessed with none of those things, Meisha, you have a great gift slumbering within you. I am offering you a home—food and shelter, education, and power. What child would deny such a dream?"

Meisha met his eyes across the pit. Flames surged up between them, the fire reaching the ceiling. Varan never flinched, though the girl swore his beard was singed.

When the fire shrank away, the wizard sighed. "Very well, I concede the battle. Jonal will study water. Fire shall be your element. I cannot deny that flames match your nature. Fire's inherent power will help you survive, until you embrace it for the right reasons."

"What reason is there for hurling flame, except to kill things?" The little girl sneered.

"When you've completed your studies, you will have the answer to that question," said Varan.

"And when I've finished, you'll let me go?" Meisha asked, watching him closely.

"Of course. You are not a prisoner here. The apprentices walk around as they please. You may do the same, but there are rules," he cautioned her. "You're not a Wraith anymore. You will wash the mud from your body and let your hair grow in, though perhaps you'll wear it short"—he rubbed his bearded chin as he regarded her—"to keep it from being singed. Yes, I think that will do. The Delve is my home as well as my fortress, and the caverns are secure, within the confines I've mapped. For your own safety, I ask you not to venture past my wards into the outer caves."

"What's out there?"

"Things you're not ready to see, little firebird," he said.

Meisha bristled at the childish nickname. "I can take care of myself." She looked away and caught movement from the mouth of one of the tunnels.

A small figure stood watching them—a dwarf in dented plate armor holding a large battle-axe. The handle of the weapon was broken, rendering it useless, but the dwarf clutched the remaining piece as if his life depended upon it.

"Varan—" but as soon as Meisha spoke, the dwarf vanished.

Varan smiled. "Did you see something?"

Meisha kept her eyes on the tunnel, but the apparition did not reappear. "Who is he?" she asked, her voice hushed.

"You've seen him before?"

"He watches me," said Meisha. She suppressed a shudder. "I didn't know he was . . . that he wasn't . . ."

"Alive?" Varan supplied. "I believe he is one of the Howlings."

"Howlings?"

"This place was called the Howling Delve, long ago. The Howlings were dwarves—adventurers who made these caves a secret home. They rode on the backs of giant wolves and amassed quite a fortune beneath the earth, or so the dwarven olorns—magic stories—tell."

"What happened to them?" Meisha asked.

"Obviously, they died," said Varan, with a careless shrug, "as adventurers often do."

"Then why are they still here?" The sense of unease tucked around Meisha like an ill-fitting cloak. How could Varan live among ghosts?

"They are only echoes of the past, child," said Varan. "Lingering memories and nothing to fear. My magic can create similar effects."

"How?" Meisha asked curiously.

"Would you like to see? To learn?"

Meisha heard the challenge in the question. She nodded slowly.

Varan reached into a small sack tied around his neck. "You'll see these again when we begin your testing," he said, pulling forth a small, square crystal. "They help me to gauge your progress." He touched one clear surface, spoke a word, and suddenly there were two more figures in the room. The man and child were perfect doubles of Varan and Meisha.

Meisha stared as her mirror image raised a hand and brought it down in a chopping motion. A jet of water rose from the ground and slapped the image of Varan, soaking his robes. The real Varan chuckled and spoke another command. The images shrank and returned to the crystal.

Meisha looked at her teacher. "How long can you keep the memories?"

"As long as I wish," Varan said. "Though perhaps I might erase that one, if you'd care to begin anew?"

Meisha stayed silent, so Varan continued, "I don't expect you to trust me yet, but you can trust this: I am a selfish old man, too curious about magic for my own good. I like to experiment, and I know the value in rearing a fire elementalist, a true savant. You may have a home here as long as you wish, no matter how many hurts you attempt to inflict upon me. I will not send you away. When your training is done, you may go back into the sunlight, if that is what you want." He removed another object from his sack, a small ring, which he handed to her. "When you leave, should you ever wish to return, all you need do is speak the command word on the band. The ring will bring you to the Delve." He leaned closer, so close to the pit she wondered how he stood the heat. "What say you, firebird?" He stretched his bare hand over the flames and met her gaze in another challenge.

Without hesitation, Meisha reached across and touched his wrinkled palm. Pain scalded her arm, but if he wouldn't back down, neither would she.

Varan's eyes shone with approval. "There will always be flame in you, child, for the whole of your life. But it will not always hurt so. Trust me."

Meisha nodded, bearing the pain. She looked over Varan's shoulder and saw the ghost again, watching her from the tunnel mouth. A large pendant hung around his neck with the figure of a mountain inscribed upon its surface. A hole sat in the center where once a charm or gem might have nestled.

What do you want from me? Meisha wondered. If the dwarf was beyond pain, why did he look so afraid?

As if in answer, the memories faded. The child Meisha had gone, and the sleeping Meisha found herself in a place she'd never been in her waking life. Only in her dreams had she been trapped in the stone chamber.

Meisha felt the surge of the campfire in time with her accelerating heartbeat. She knew what was coming, but she didn't want to face it.

This time, the fire was no friend. It held a living presence, awesome and terrifying and buried deep in a stone prison.

The presence, if it possessed a name, never spoke it to her. As far as Meisha was concerned, the creature was the Delve, and the Delve him. No further identity was needed.

She never saw a face, but she could feel the fire emanating from the creature's body—a beast of fire and claws, claws that tested the walls of his prison and the ring of guards on silent vigil.

The dwarves—his keepers. Meisha sensed the beast desired to hunt, but the dwarves kept him sealed inside the cavernous prison. So instead, he hunted them all down, one by one in the vastness. Their screams echoed off the stone as each one fell to the fire-clawed menace. They were still here, trapped alongside him for eternity.

He could slay them again, over and over, but Meisha sensed him growing weary of killing ghosts.

With renewed fear, Meisha thought, he wants to hear living screams.

But the fire beast was patient. His time would come. He could feel it. Until then . . .

"No!" the sleeping Meisha cried out. She watched helplessly through the eyes of the fire beast. He stalked forward and immediately met one of the dwarves. The small figure raised his broken axe in defiance. His pendant flashed briefly, brilliant silver, but the beast flexed his claws and ripped the broken weapon out of the dwarf's hands.

Screaming, Meisha sat up in her bedroll. The campfire flared in one giant stalk that reached almost to the tops of the trees.

Meisha swept an arm out, panting. The flames died, becoming so much smoking wood.

I'd been doing so well; I hadn't had the dream in months, Meisha thought bitterly.

Just when she thought she might be free of the Delve and her master, the memories came surging back like the fire—memories mixing with strange visions. How could she recognize truth from fever dreams?

There was one way, but Meisha would never take it. Her master might be able to explain the dream. She'd never had it before coming to the Delve. The Delve and her master were inextricably linked.

She would never face either of them again.

CHAPTER NINE

The Howling Delve
1 Kythorn, the Year of the Worm (1356 DR)

Twelve Years Ago . . .

When Meisha rolled over in the darkness, she knew she wasn't alone. Lying perfectly still, her eyes tracked every shadow in the small room, seeking a hidden foe.

Her gaze fell on the open chamber door. Meisha knew she'd closed it tightly before going to sleep.

She leaned forward, toward the crack of light filtering through the gap between the door and its roughly worked frame.

In the passage beyond, the dwarf stood quietly watching.

Icy needles crawled up Meisha's back. Every night, she saw him—sometimes passing her in the narrow halls, sometimes in her room, standing at the foot of her small cot.

"What do you want!" she cried, raking her hands through her short hair. "Speak, or leave me be!"

But the ghostly apparition had already vanished. Meisha dropped her head into her hands, fighting the urge to run from the room. She fought the same internal battle every night. She longed to run to the wizard, to demand he return her to

Keczulla, or Waterdeep, or to the frozen North for all she cared. Anywhere that was not the Delve, where she felt buried alive.

A knock at the door made Meisha jump.

Shaera, apprentice of air and one of Varan's older students, came into the room. She cradled a candle in one hand. "Did you call me?" she asked.

"No," Meisha said, her customary sullen gaze snapping into place. "Why would I want you?"

"Why, indeed?" the girl murmured. She walked right past Meisha, ignoring her hissed curses. "I came to leave you this." She crouched next to the cot and spoke a soft, breathy word.

A small column of fire rose up from the floor, floating in midair as if suspended from an invisible wick.

"Just until you learn the spell yourself," Shaera explained. "Always carry a light down here. If nothing else, light frightens the rats away." She smiled encouragingly. "You'll grow used to the Delve. We'll help you."

"You think I need your help to make fire," Meisha said cuttingly. Her eyes rounded, and the flame soared higher, almost touching Shaera's belt.

The girl's smile didn't falter. "He said you were powerful. I'm impressed. But can you make the fire last the whole of the night?"

Color rose in Meisha's cheeks, matching the slow-burning flame. She said nothing.

"I thought not." Shaera paused at the door. "If you get scared again, you can sleep in my room."

"Get out!" Meisha yelled, mortified that the girl had heard her distress. "Leave me alone!"

Shaera nodded and closed the door behind her.

Meisha seethed. Never on her worst night in Keczulla had she cried out, not when she'd been beaten by the Wraiths for holding back food, not when she'd been starving because they'd denied her for a tenday afterward. Through it all, she'd never made a sound.

How dare she, Meisha thought, *how dare she* come into her

room uninvited? What would Varan think of such an invasion of privacy?

She snorted. Varan had probably sent the girl.

"Maybe you'd like the favor returned," she muttered. Her fear pushed aside by anger, Meisha slammed her door and headed for Varan's chambers.

She listened at the doors to each of the apprentices' rooms: Jonal, the water student; Prieces, the earth apprentice. Shaera and Lirna were both air, and shared a room across the passage. Meisha had never bothered to learn beyond their names and elements.

Each room was quiet, the occupants undisturbed by her earlier shouts.

Did none of them feel the unnaturalness of the Delve? Meisha wondered. Or had they been in the place too long? All the apprentices here were at least two years older than Meisha and more advanced in their training. Perhaps they had grown used to the underground setting.

The thought of ever growing accustomed to life without sunlight made Meisha's skin go cold. She rubbed her hands up and down her arms.

That would never happen to her, she swore. She would always crave the Morninglord's touch.

When she came to Varan's door, she hesitated. A thin, green beam of light limned the crooked wooden planks. Enspelled globes, she thought. Varan used them in place of torches to light various parts of the Delve.

She reached up to rap on the wood and felt a tingle of electricity race down her arm: strong magic—dangerous, if she disturbed Varan in the middle of a casting.

The spell glow died away. Varan's muffled voice came through the wood.

"Come in, Meisha."

Scowling, Meisha dragged open the door to the chamber Varan used as a workroom. Her mouth fell open.

"Close the door, please," the wizard said crisply.

Meisha shut the door and turned a slow circle in the chamber, the better for her eyes to take in the writing scribbled on every wall's surface.

She could decipher only a handful of the arcane phrases. Inscribed and illuminated with green light, the writing blurred her vision if she stared at it too long. As if that were not disconcerting enough, Meisha swore she saw the writing move, rearranging itself as she tried to read.

"You couldn't sleep?" Varan inquired, when Meisha continued to gape at the wall of power.

She shook her head. "What is all this?" she breathed, her earlier anger forgotten.

"Some of we poor practitioners still have to rely on spellbooks —the written word—to fuel our Art," Varan explained, "especially when we create new magic."

"Do you often?" Meisha asked. "Create new magic?"

"As often as I am able," Varan replied. "Creation, as I see it, should be the ultimate goal of all who study the Art. That and teaching apprentices are the only ways our magic truly lives on. It matters not if the magic is used for protection or destruction, as long as it exists and can be turned and forged into something new."

"And you think I will be your destructive force," Meisha said, turning at last to regard the wizard.

"I've decided to reserve judgment in your case," he hedged, "as you so often surprise me. But I do not think I will be disappointed, whichever path you choose to take."

He waved a hand, and the light faded from the writing. "So you're having trouble sleeping," he mused. "It may be my stirrings of the Art woke you. In such a confined space, the magic has few places to go. The Delve is old, and the walls are worn with the imprints of old magic and the tread of feet—human and otherwise."

"Why do you live here then?" Meisha asked. With no chair in the room, she settled on the cold floor. "If the Delve is so old, aren't you afraid one day it will collapse?"

Varan chuckled. "From what I've been able to discern, the Delve has withstood far more than an old wizard's spells and come out intact. Now it is my sanctuary. The walls will hold." The wizard shrugged into a thick robe and plucked up a crooked staff as he spoke. "But we haven't solved your problem; you need sleep."

He ushered her out into the hall, spell-locking the door behind them. "When I can't find calm, I work until I'm weary, and I still have a task to finish before I seek my bed tonight. This task will weary both of us, if you'd care to join me?"

Meisha nodded eagerly. Anything would be preferable to returning to her boxlike room in the dark, even with the flame burning all night. The weight of the Delve still pressed down on her, but in Varan's presence the feeling seemed to diminish.

She followed the wizard down a side passage typically forbidden to the apprentices. Meisha recognized the boundary of Varan's wards inscribed on the tunnel wall. They walked right past the sigil, led by the glow from Varan's staff.

They entered a wide-mouthed, bell-shaped chamber that Meisha saw was entirely submerged in water. The cavern's ceiling reflected unbroken across the clear surface of the water, making it impossible to tell where the bottom lay.

Varan released his staff, causing it to hover over the center of the calm pool. "Fresh water source," he said. "Something we're always in need of down here. Close, too, so I'm considering extending the wards."

"So other creatures won't intrude on the watering hole," Meisha surmised.

"Correct—ordinarily—but I've observed this particular watering hole is rarely used by wandering creatures," Varan told her. "Can you guess why?"

Meisha looked at him sharply, at the same time taking a step back. "What dwells in the water?"

"Very good," Varan said, "and to answer your question, *something big.*"

"So I'm to be your bait?" Meisha asked sullenly. She'd

thought Varan would let her attack the thing.

Varan laughed. "Hardly, little one. I am not an ogre, or a Red Wizard, with apprentices to squander—and a waste it would be, for the creature that lives beneath the surface would rend you unrecognizable. Besides," his eyes glinted, "I do not require bait."

"How, then?" Meisha asked, intrigued. The wizard's enthusiasm infected her. She trailed his steps around the rim of the pool.

"First, I'll need your aid." Varan twirled a finger, and his staff inverted, shining the light close to the water's surface. "For all its might, the creature is shy and comes to ground only to hunt. It will need an inducement to reveal itself."

He waited, and Meisha realized he proposed a test. Varan wanted to see how she would solve the problem.

Meisha squatted next to the pool and placed her hands above the water. The words came to her haltingly. She envisioned the words dredged up from the bottom of the pool like so many buried coins, humming with power and warmth. She spoke faster, and the power turned to heat. She felt the glaze of it along her palm, a blown-glass ball she shaped using only her mind.

A bubble popped on the pool's surface. Next to her, a small, blind fish with twisted horns floated to the surface on its side. Another followed, and still Meisha let the heat build. Her calves ached from holding the same crouched position, but she dared not move or risk breaking the spell. Steam brushed her face. She heard another loud pop, and the water churned. Meisha thought it was the spell, but suddenly a fleshy mouth broke the surface of the water, followed by twin webbed claws.

Meisha threw up her hand in automatic defense, realizing she might lose the appendage in her foolishness. Spiky teeth closed around her wrist, but Meisha felt no pressure, no severing of bone or tissue.

With a hissing cry of pain, the creature released her and thrust back, churning water in its wake.

Meisha realized her hand was smoking. She'd burned the creature with her touch.

Varan stepped in front of her when the creature came around to attack again. Filmy eyes dominated the ripples of flesh that made up the creature's head. Below them, the mouth gaped from a nest of four tentacles. The creature's body tapered from a humanoid trunk to that of a serpent or an eel. Meisha couldn't tell from above the water.

Varan's hands traced the air in a scythe-cut. Slashes of light streaked across the chamber, cutting into the monster's flesh. Black ichor shed into the still-boiling pool.

Meisha crawled to a safe corner to watch the grim spectacle play out. She had no doubt Varan would win the battle. He stood so confidently; Meisha wondered if he'd ever lost a duel, with a creature or another wizard. The power he expended seemed immense. Her own spell had drained her completely. The heat she'd created in the chamber, blending with the flashing light, mesmerized Meisha. Her last sight of the mysterious creature was bathed in that light, sharp against the black blood. Her vision dimmed, and she passed out.

When she awoke, Varan knelt beside her, supporting her head. His hard expression softened when he saw her eyes open and aware.

"I feared you would not wake," he said.

"And you would have wasted an apprentice after all," Meisha said faintly.

Varan did not smile at her jest. Gently, he helped her sit up and gave her a long draught from his waterskin.

"You passed every test but one," he said, after she'd collected herself.

Meisha waited expectantly, and Varan nodded toward the pool, which still gave off clouds of steam. The black blood and the creature were gone.

"You tapped too deeply into the fire," he said, "The power overwhelmed you, yes?"

Meisha nodded, for once listening without comment or judgment. Varan was right. She'd felt a depth to the magic, a power just out of reach. She thought if she'd stretched a little bit farther, she might have brushed its source.

"When you're ready, we'll explore how deep the fire goes," Varan promised. "Be patient a few years. If you act too soon, the power may burn you from within, or deteriorate your health, as it has mine."

Meisha looked at him in surprise. She hadn't expected Varan to admit any weaknesses to her. Was it a gesture of trust?

"What was the creature?" she asked, glancing at the water. "Will there be more?"

"I think not," Varan said. "It was a kopru, a sea creature, adapted somehow to the fresh water. He was aged, else he would have been more difficult to kill, I think."

Difficult enough, Meisha thought, as weakness gripped her again. She swayed; Varan steadied her and squeezed her shoulder.

"Are you all right?" he asked.

He was concerned, Meisha thought, and marveled at the notion. No one had ever expressed concern for her before, and now it had happened twice in one night.

"I'm tired," she said, admitting her own weakness.

Varan nodded. "You'll sleep deeply tonight," he said, "and tomorrow."

"But our lesson—"

"Will keep," he said firmly. "I'm spending the next few days in another part of the Delve. You can use that time to recover."

"What part?" Meisha asked, curious. She had only a vague picture in her mind of the layout of the Delve. The upper chambers were laid out roughly in the shape of a spider, with the apprentices living and studying in the main body, protected by Varan's wards from the tunnels branching out on all sides.

Far below them, the testing chambers were arranged and connected like star points. Varan had designed them personally as training grounds for his apprentices. Meisha knew of no other large cavern systems within the Delve.

"Is the way hidden?" she asked.

"Quite well hidden," Varan said, "and magically sealed. I managed to unravel the spells and for my efforts discovered a set of caverns adjoining the testing chambers. In all my years here, I never knew of their existence. They will take several tendays, perhaps longer, to explore fully. I am hoping they will contain something of value to make the effort worthwhile."

"Show me," Meisha pleaded. She didn't like the prospect of spending several nights alone in her room, with only the other apprentices for company. "I could go with you, aid you."

"You could, and I'd be glad of a warm fire, so deep in the earth, but you need to rest. When you've regained your strength, I'll show you the way in, and I'll be glad of your aid."

He touched her shoulder, and Meisha, weary but flush with her small victory in the Art, forgot to push him away.

———————◆———————

Varan's prediction held true. Meisha slept all through the next day and night, rising only to take small meals. Gradually, her energy returned and with it the brush of power, just out of her reach. She left it alone, as Varan had instructed, but she was eager, for the first time, to tell her teacher what she felt.

When she knocked on his door the third day, there came no answer, nor was there on the fourth or fifth. Meisha returned every night, and during the day, when their water supply ran low, she collected bucketfuls from the newly vacant pool.

After a tenday, they began to worry, not just for Varan's safety, but for their own continued survival. None of them knew how to get to the surface without Varan's magic, and they were quickly running out of food.

Meisha and Prieces ventured out into the Delve seeking fresh meat, while Shaera and the rest returned to the training tunnels to search for the wizard and the secret cavern entrance.

When Meisha returned to her chamber, empty-handed and hungry, she saw the green light coming from Varan's workroom.

Running to the door, she felt the same burst of electrical

heat, but this time she ignored it and tried to force the door. The spell lock sizzled along her fingers, hot but not burning. The door was sealed tight.

"Master!" she shouted, pounding on the door. "Are you in there?"

She heard glass breaking and what sounded like Varan's workbench being dragged across the floor. The wizard's voice rang out above the din.

"I'm all right, firebird," he called. "Go back to your room."

"Where have you been?" she persisted, banging harder on the door. "We've been searching the tunnels for you. The food is almost gone."

"I apologize for that, little one, and I've corrected the oversight. You'll find the larder filled, and the next time I leave, you will not be left without provisions."

"The next time?" Meisha cried. "We thought you dead; now you're leaving again? Varan, open the door!"

"Calm yourself," Varan said soothingly. "We will continue your lessons as I promised. I will not be leaving for some time. The objects I brought back will occupy all of my attention for a while."

"What are they?" Meisha asked. "What did you find?"

"Amazing things," Varan said excitedly. His voice drifted away from the door, and she heard more objects being moved around the room.

"Varan," she called. "Varan!"

Light flared through the door, blinding her. When her vision cleared, Meisha heard nothing more from the room. She sensed, without knowing how, that Varan had gone.

She slumped to the floor, wondering what it all meant. Her stomach growled loudly, and Meisha recalled their most pressing need. She headed to the larder, hoping that Varan had indeed stocked it well.

Perhaps, when Varan had sorted out whatever it was he'd found in the caverns, he would show her where he'd been.

CHAPTER TEN

The Howling Delve
11 Uktar, the Year of the Serpent (1359 DR)

She's run off!" Jonal cried.

Meisha opened her eyes, her meditation ruined. Annoyed, she turned to glare at the water apprentice. "What?"

"Shaera," Jonal said. "She's gone beyond the wards, seeking the master's tunnels. She wants to know where he goes."

"Don't we all," Meisha muttered. She began pulling on her boots. "Does Varan know?"

Jonal shook his head. "He hasn't come out—"

"Of the workroom," Meisha finished disgustedly. In the three years since finding the secret tunnels, Varan had squirreled away an unknown number of treasures. He barely left his chambers anymore, for toying with them. "Perhaps it's time to remind him of his responsibilities . . . again."

"But you can't," Jonal sputtered. "If he's in the middle of an experiment, you could be killed."

"We're out of food again," Meisha snapped. "The north wards failed last night, letting in two deep bats and gods know what else we haven't seen. All the while Varan's been tucked away in his nest. It's time someone shook the branches."

The workroom was lit and locked again, but Meisha was

three years older, and Varan had grown careless with his simple magics.

She grabbed the door latch and summoned fire to her hand. Wood disintegrated into black charring, and she dropped the searing latch to the ground.

Meisha burst into Varan's chamber, and immediately saw the glowing circle centered on the wizard's worktable.

Varan stood with his back to her, his attention on an object hovering above the table.

"I'll ask you to repair that door at your earliest convenience, Meisha," he said testily. He moved his hands over the object: a glove that appeared to be made of liquid metal, a shimmering waterfall of steel. "I've grown accustomed to your late night poundings on my door; but what brings you so suddenly and so violently into my room? Risking your own life in the process, I might add."

"Shaera's gone missing," Meisha said. "Jonal says she went beyond the wards."

"Gone exploring, I expect." Varan still hadn't turned around. His shoulders drooped as if he carried sacks of stone, but he maintained the swirling pattern of magic around the glove. "Does Jonal know where?"

"The Climb," Meisha said uncertainly. "I didn't know what he meant."

"You wouldn't," said Varan, "because I have not gotten around to showing the passage to you or warning you that to attempt it is beyond stupidity. Shaera, if she turns up injured, will have taken care of both tasks quite capably."

Meisha, her jaw clenched, stared hatefully at the wizard's back. She fought the temptation to shove him into the bright sphere of his Art. Anything to get his attention for *one* breath, even if it turned out to be her last on Toril.

"Don't you care?" she spat. "If nothing else, she is air. Your training will have gone to waste if she dies!"

Varan made a gesture, and the floating miasma froze in place. Slowly, the orange glow of torchlight replaced the magical light in the room. He turned to face her.

Meisha flinched involuntarily at the haggardness of his face. Gray hairs shed from his beard to litter the front of his robes. Meisha did not know if stress or the force of his Art had caused them to fall out. The magic seemed to be taking him a piece at a time.

May any watching gods smite me if I come to this, Meisha thought. She found herself unable to feel a shred of pity for her master. She was too angry.

For his part, Varan did not seem to notice her fury. "Did you come here to ask for my help, or my permission to go after Shaera?" he asked. He leaned against the table for support. "In either event, I'm surprised at your outburst. You've never shown any inclination of friendship to Shaera or the other apprentices. In fact, you consider yourself superior to all of them."

"Because I am."

"I won't dispute you. But I do warn you: be cautious where you aim your righteous anger, little firebird."

"I don't have time for this," Meisha snarled. "If you won't help me, tell me what the Climb is."

"As you wish."

He told her.

* * *

"The Climb," Meisha chuckled bitterly. She regarded the round rat hole in the wall and the impenetrable darkness within. "More like a long fall."

Varan said hands other than his had tunneled the hole out of the stone. Meisha wondered briefly if those hands had been a dwarf's, and if one of them had carried a broken battle-axe. Varan's mark hung on the wall above the hole, warning the apprentices away.

Jonal stood hesitantly at her elbow. "Do you think it's true?" he asked in hushed tones, as if the wizard might overhear. "Do you believe the tunnel goes all the way down to the testing chambers?"

"And beyond—so he claims," Meisha said stiffly. She didn't know what to believe. She had no idea how far down the testing chambers lay. Varan had always teleported them between the spider and the star, with no indication of the distance traversed. If Shaera expected to find the entrance to Varan's hidden tunnels using the Climb, Meisha hoped she'd prepared for a long journey.

"He hasn't come out of the room?" she asked, though she already knew the answer.

"No," Jonal said. "He hasn't spoken to anyone since you entered his chamber. Will he come out," Jonal asked, "to aid in the search?"

"He will not," Meisha said, "until his experiment is complete. He claims that releasing the magic prematurely could endanger us all."

"Will you wait for him?" Jonal asked hopefully.

Meisha turned a stony gaze on him. The apprentice ducked his head.

"I suppose if I don't return, he'll inquire about our fates eventually," Meisha said, her voice rich with scorn. "Wait for me on this side," she told Jonal, "and do not follow."

Meisha knew her warning was unnecessary. In his heart, Jonal was a coward. He would never enter the dark passage to come after either of them. She saw it in his eyes.

She moved to the tunnel mouth and heaved herself up onto its stone lip. Speaking a word, Meisha blew on her outstretched palm. Her fingers began to glow. The orange light spread down her palm to her wrist. Varan had taught her the spell for light; the variation was her own.

By the glow of her palm she saw the tunnel stretching ahead of her in a narrow tube, and above her in a slender shaft. If Shaera was trying to find the testing chambers, she would have certainly gone forward. Meisha would have to follow, crawling on her belly for gods knew how many feet, and pray that at some point the path widened. She knew it would have to dip down. Far down, if the tales were accurate. And if she were attacked, it would be nearly impossible to mount a defense with spells.

"Lovely," she murmured, and she began to crawl.

———◆◆◆———

Waiting, his claws tense, the fire beast felt the magic coursing through the Delve. He willed it to falter and rage out of control, to shake the caverns and tear his prison apart—it would only take a single misguided stroke of power, and the dwarves' ancient bonds would crumble.

How fragile the structures of mortals were. The beast's fire, his very presence, only served to corrupt the integrity of the Delve further—a consequence of his imprisonment that never ceased to delight him. By the time he won free, the entire stronghold would be suffused with his essence. His hunting ground would be complete, a place of nightmares that merely awaited prey. The beast relished the thought.

Content in his future, the beast settled back into the fire and waited for the dwarves to be reborn into their ghostly existence, so he could hunt again. He did not mind honing his skills.

CHAPTER ELEVEN

The Howling Delve
12 Uktar, the Year of the Serpent (1359 DR)

Meisha thrust herself forward another foot. Her stomach felt raw through her coarse linen shirt. Sweat poured down her face, dripping salt in her eyes, but she kept crawling. The physical discomforts kept her mind occupied. She would endure almost anything to keep the memory of the dream at bay.

The beast of fire and claws. Every time she had the dream, the presence was there, stalking the helpless dwarves. She watched them die over and over again.

Ten more feet, Meisha counted in her head. The stone chilled her flesh, making her lightheaded and feverish.

She pressed her face against the ground. The taste of rock and dirt and something foreign filled her mouth.

A wave of nausea hit her gut. Meisha turned her head to one side and gagged, spitting to clear her mouth of a taste worse than bile. Instinctively, she tried to curl up in a ball, but the tunnel bound her in the shape of a worm.

Meisha forced herself to breathe deeply, to push away the tight fear in her chest.

"You've slept on stone every night for the past four years," she said aloud, just to hear the sound of her voice. "This should not disturb you now."

Perhaps it was because she found herself so far from Varan's circle of protection. She'd always felt more at ease in the wizard's presence. Possibly his magic in some way mitigated the oppressiveness of the Delve.

Not enough, Meisha thought. She ached for the sunlight and the heat, almost as much as she craved the fire inside herself, the power of it. Living in a deep hole in the ground had never stopped feeling unnatural to her.

Was the presence in her dream merely a manifestation of that wrongness?

No, it was more than that, Meisha knew. There was something wrong with the Delve, something Varan chose to deny or ignore. She didn't know which state of mind was the more foolish.

Pushing herself back up to her elbows, Meisha began dragging herself forward again.

Ahead of her, a rock outcrop burst into soft glow. Before she could react, a cold hand closed around her ankle.

A scream ripped from Meisha's throat. The sound echoed down the tunnel. Power flared involuntarily in her mind.

She flipped to her back and splayed her fingertips. Fire rolled down her body, an inch-thick gout of flame that lit up the passage.

When the flames died, the glow had gone, and the only sound was Meisha's ragged breathing. The passage sat empty behind her.

"Show yourself!" Meisha shouted.

The answering silence mocked her. Meisha threw her hands up against the curved stone ceiling, emptying her fear and the fire into the rock. Orange clouds of flame licked along the tunnel in either direction until her anger spent itself.

When the flames grew cold, she regarded the blackened stone above her. Meisha felt some small satisfaction knowing she could leave a mark on the Delve's impenetrable armor.

Reigniting her light source, Meisha squinted into the distance ahead of her, and saw that the tunnel dropped off sharply ten feet ahead of her. She hadn't seen the precipice earlier.

She crawled to the edge and saw a steep, angled drop of roughly fifteen feet. Crawling blindly, she might have fallen over the edge and broken her neck.

Cold sweat pricked her scalp. Meisha closed her eyes and pictured a dwarf's face, for she had no other explanation for her mysterious rescue.

"My thanks," she whispered.

She still had to navigate the steep drop. Feet first, the fall might have been manageable, but Meisha had no way to reverse her position in the tiny space. Shaera, an air savant, would have bypassed the drop easily. Meisha knew few such spells, but would have to learn more, she thought. She'd never trusted magic that did not involve fire. Flame felt natural to her—rendering her body light enough to float down a fifteen-foot drop, did not.

Calling the little-used words to her mind, Meisha cast the spell. Outwardly, she felt no change, but she could sense the release of magic from her spirit, and knew the spell had worked. Still, as she shimmied to the edge of the drop, she felt a hint of trepidation.

She grasped the stone ledge and somersaulted, releasing the ledge before she hit her back against the rock. Slowly, lighter than the stale air in the cavern, she drifted to the floor below.

What seemed like a tenday later, when her feet touched the ground, Meisha sank into a crouch, grateful for the chance to bend her knees. Her spine cracked as she swiveled around to loosen her sore muscles.

By her light spell, Meisha could see the passage angled off to the right, the formerly smooth tunnel walls pockmarked with crags and fissures.

She drew her hand along the ground and found what she had hoped to find. Shaera's footprints hugged the wall. They moved steadily, and Meisha saw no traces of blood or torn clothing to indicate injury. She breathed a little easier as she continued on down the tunnel.

In the quiet, with half her mind alert on the trail and watching for danger, Meisha's thoughts drifted at random. Varan's words came unexpectedly into focus.

You've never shown any indication of friendship. . . .

She'd grown up on the streets of Keczulla, running in packs with other children of the same age and situation: a perpetual state of half-starved viciousness. She would never have risked her life for any of the other Wraiths, not when a loaf of bread was worth killing for. Why *did* she care about the future of a nobleman's daughter like Shaera? Why was Shaera worth risking her life for, when the Wraiths were not?

They had nothing in common. Shaera was refined and educated as Meisha never would be. The girl had never experienced the kind of hunger that was an acid in the belly, blighting any other rational thought.

Perhaps it was simply that Varan *didn't* care. Her teacher had the capacity for kindness; she had seen glimpses of emotion behind his power, but ultimately, the *will* was not there, Meisha thought.

Twice now, she'd been disappointed by those she'd chosen to trust. Yet here she was, groping in the dark after a stupid girl who hadn't sense enough to take a companion on her fool's errand.

Meisha picked up her pace, aware of a downward trend to the passage. At first she hadn't felt it, and if the rate of descent didn't change, she might have miles of tunnel to cover before she reached the bottom.

She stopped briefly to eat cold meat and a biscuit she'd taken from the stores. Before discovering the lower tunnels, Varan had kept a well-stocked food supply that often included fresh fruits and vegetables Meisha had never seen before. She hadn't thought to ask where they came from, until they were gone.

When she resumed her walk, Meisha discovered an abrupt end to the tunnel after roughly twenty feet. The passage fell away again, but this time, instead of being sheer, jagged rocks riddled the drop-off.

Meisha leaned over the edge to touch one of the rocks with her fingertip. Filed, she thought, to a razor edge. She drew her hand back and smeared the dot of blood away.

The architect of the Climb had gone to a great deal of effort to make the descent from the spider to the star as long and as treacherous as possible. If it were the work of the Howlings, to guard their stronghold, how had the dwarves ever traversed such a passage? Surely, there must be an easier way to move between both sets of caverns.

But if such a path existed, Meisha thought, even Varan did not know of it.

Removing a length of rope from her pack, Meisha tied one end around the nearest protruding stone spike. She looped the other end through her belt and slowly fed out the rope as she walked down the slanted wall.

At the bottom of the short climb, she found the remains of the trap.

A pressure plate smeared with blood sat crookedly at the base of the wall. Meisha touched the plate and found it sticky. The trap had triggered recently. She examined the immediate area. Following a line of fissures in the rock, she saw that the release of weight had caved in a false ceiling directly above the plate, spilling a hail of large rocks down on the passage.

Meisha crawled amid the rubble, shoveling stones aside with her bare hands. Dust rose in dry clouds. Her eyes burned and watered. Meisha scraped an arm across them and worked mostly by touch.

Finally, her hands encountered something soft. She uncovered a spill of red hair, and gradually Shaera's upper torso came into view. Blood had dried in a mask over half her face. Meisha put her fingers against the girl's neck and found a beat. Miraculously, she had survived the trap.

The heat from Meisha's hands seeped into Shaera's cold flesh. The girl stirred, moaning when she tried to lift her head.

"Be still," Meisha hissed. She ran her hands along Shaera's spine. "Your back is broken, at least. I don't know how many other bones."

She hadn't expected injuries this extensive. Varan would be able to tend her, but Meisha didn't think she could risk moving Shaera far. Even with magical aid, the jostling would likely kill her.

"What do I do?" she whispered, gazing back and forth down the empty tunnel. She didn't know if she were speaking to herself, Varan, or the ghostly presence that had aided her. In any case, she received no answer.

Meisha sat down beside Shaera, who had lapsed into unconsciousness again. Meisha listened to her breathing in the silence and detected a faint gurgle she didn't like.

"Where are you, Master?" she said. She realized then how much she'd hoped for Varan to follow her. No matter what magical experiment he was juggling, he wouldn't let Shaera die here. For all his selfishness, he was not a monster.

Meisha wrapped her arms around her knees, intending to keep watch. The wizard would come, she was certain of it.

As soon as she allowed herself to relax, exhaustion stole over her. She dozed in fits, tucked between a wall studded with jagged spikes and the pile of rubble.

The only pocket of life for miles, Meisha thought faintly, and a fragile one it was.

<hr />

She roused to darkness and stinging pain in her fingers. At first, Meisha thought it was the cold, but then she felt fur under her hands. Revulsion shook her instantly awake. She chanted the words to bring back her light.

Two rats crawled on Shaera's chest. Meisha swatted them viciously into the wall, impaling one on a spike. Her hands shook as she adjusted Shaera's bloody shirt, covering the ugly bites.

"Forgive me," she said haltingly. She'd forgotten Shaera's

long-ago lesson, that light was the only thing that kept away the rats.

She brushed the hair back from Shaera's face, wondering how long they'd been asleep. The apprentice's eyes fluttered open and looked blearily up at her. She opened her lips a crack, but only air escaped, a thick wheeze that Meisha feared was Shaera trying to breathe through blood.

"Varan is coming for us," Meisha said urgently, even as the light in the woman's eyes started to waver. "Do you hear me, Shaera? You have to hold on a little longer." Her voice quivered; tears burned her throat. "I can hear them in the tunnel. Listen, they're coming down the slope."

Shaera licked her lips and whispered something barely audible. Meisha didn't understand the language, but the rise and fall of the words was familiar—the rhythm of prayer. When the words trailed off, the light in Shaera's eyes went dark.

Meisha sat perfectly still for a long time. Shaera's cheek rested heavy and cold on her hand. Absently, she wiped the blood from the girl's face with her sleeve. She should have done it earlier but hadn't thought to. When her face was clean, Meisha laid the girl's head back and closed her vacant eyes.

"He didn't come."

Meisha heard her voice, but the words seemed to come from far away. Dazed, she rose to her feet. Her movement awoke fresh scurrying in the shadows. The rats waited just outside the pale circle of her light, ready to dart in for a meal.

Meisha stared into the darkness. Fire awakened within her. Heedless of the danger, Meisha reached deep inside herself and found the untouched well of power Varan had warned her about.

She gazed down at Shaera's corpse, half-buried in the rubble. Fire sprang up in quivering columns, forming a protective ring around the girl's body.

Illuminated by the fire ring, Shaera's face appeared peaceful. Meisha committed it to memory, then made a swift gesture with her hand.

The columns fell inward like spokes on a flaming wheel. Shaera's body ignited, the fire burning so hot and fast that it consumed her flesh in less time than it had taken to cast the spell.

When the fire died, Meisha tried to slow her breathing. She quickly gave up. She would not find calm again. Only one thing would satisfy her now.

Kneeling among the stones, Meisha scooped up a handful of ash and put it in one of her empty pouches. Whatever else remained of Shaera would have to stay in the tunnel. Meisha prayed her spirit would find the halls of whatever god or goddess she'd been praying to.

Taking up her rope, Meisha started the long climb back to Varan's sanctuary. She could feel the heat building within her. Darkly, she welcomed it.

<hr />

He was waiting for her. Jonal must have warned him. Meisha made sure he felt the heat before he saw her.

She came around the corner at a leisurely walk. She projected no flame, but she could see Varan's eyes watering as he beheld her. Swiftly, he cast up a barrier against her spell.

"Gods, you are magnificent to behold," he whispered. "You *are* fire."

She didn't answer, only increased the heat. She would burn through the spell shield if she had to.

"Meisha," Varan said calmly, "can you hear me? Are you all right, firebird?"

She stood like a statue. "Where is Shaera?"

"You went to look for her, Meisha. Don't you remember?"

Meisha shook her head from side to side. The air rippled in the wake of the movement. "That is the question you should be asking. 'Where is Shaera?' " Meisha saw the red glow now, the magic radiating in an aura around her. "Say it!"

"Where is Shaera?" Varan said.

"Burnt on a pyre," replied Meisha. "She rests in the Climb

alone." Her voice turned deadly. "I think one of us should join her."

"Do you want it to be you, Meisha?" Varan asked sadly. "Because it will be, if you persist in this. Powerful as you are, you are overwhelmed by grief and exhaustion."

"This is all because of your discovery!" Meisha spat. "Whatever great treasure lies buried beneath our feet that's more important than the lives of your charges!"

"I don't expect you to comprehend it, Meisha," Varan said, "but I thought you at least understood my own nature. I told you I was selfish. My Art is the only thing that brings me joy. You, the other elementalists, are a means to that end. I have no interest in being a father to any of you. The choices you make in the world are yours. The consequences of this, you alone will bear."

He stepped back, dropping the barrier. Moisture sizzled on the tunnel walls.

"Make your choice, Meisha," he offered her. "Use me—as I am using you—to learn what you can, and all Faerûn will be open to you. Or hurl your fire, and I will strike you down, grieve for a day at the horrendous waste of potential, and go back to work." His voice was harsh. "What will it be?"

Meisha's eyes leaked tears that evaporated almost immediately on her cheeks. She closed her eyes and let out a strangled, miserable scream that echoed off the cave walls. Her head snapped back, and she poured her power into the ground. Still, there was no visible flame, but the stone at her feet bubbled, burning through the soles of her boots. The release of power wracked her body; her neck muscles pulled taut.

Varan watched her until gradually the convulsions diminished and ceased. She pitched forward, senseless.

———◆———

Jonal told her later that Varan had gone down the Climb to retrieve Shaera's ashes.

He kept a spell lock—his personal sigil—on Meisha's door

during her long recovery. At Varan's behest, the water elementalist tended her basic needs, but left her chamber as soon as he could.

If the apprentices had not been sufficiently afraid of her before, they were certainly terrified now, Meisha realized.

Shaera had been the only one among them not truly frightened by her power.

When she'd healed enough, she went to Varan.

"Where will you go?" her master asked.

He stood in his workroom, as usual. Meisha stood in the doorway. She refused to enter the room ever again.

"To the Harpers," she said.

"An interesting choice." Varan had cleared the walls of magical writing. The room glowed with torchlight. "Much like wizards, the Harpers are not well thought of in Amn. You'll find them eager to take you, if you can find them, though I wonder if they will understand you as I do."

"I don't see how that matters," Meisha said. Her face was expressionless.

"Perhaps it does not. They may be able to give you what I could not, and that may be enough." He walked to the doorway, and might have touched her, but Meisha stepped back, a warning shining in her eyes.

Varan sighed. "You must let me say good-bye, firebird, and give you some words of caution. If you let the fire consume you, or use it to lash out, the Harpers will never take you. *My* promise to you stands. You have a home here for as long as you need it. You have my ring," he said, looking at her hand.

Meisha closed her fingers into a fist. The gold band pressed into her skin. She'd considered leaving it behind, and part of her wondered why she still wore it at all. She would never return to the Delve, even if the Harpers forsook her, and no matter how badly she might need Varan's sanctuary.

"Farewell, Master," she said.

"Good luck, Meisha Saira." The wizard smiled at her, the same affectionate smile she remembered adoring as a child.

Even now, the smile affected her, made her think he actually cared about her and her future.

Meisha forced herself to turn away, and she didn't look back as he chanted the spell that would send her back into the sunlight.

CHAPTER TWELVE

Amn
1 Marpenoth, the Year of Lightning Storms (1374 DR)

Meisha listened to the rush of the river Vudlur beneath her feet and watched the man stride up the western bulge of the Star Bridge.

He wore tarnished chain mail and a plain but well-kept tunic of mud-brown, with gauntlets and a studded belt to match. Standing easily at six feet, he had broad, muscled shoulders. His hair and mustache were bronze; his skin burned Calishite dark, but his blue eyes belonged in the North. Meisha knew better on both counts. Kall Morel was a son of Amn, and up until a tenday ago, Amn had believed him dead.

"Well met, Kall," she said, extending a hand.

"It's been a while, Meisha." Kall glanced at her bare fingers. "I don't think so."

The Harper smiled. "Still afraid I might burn, even after all these years?"

"Why do you think we're surrounded by water?" Kall leaned against the bridge rail. "I take it you've heard the news?"

"There's talk of little else," Meisha said. "Dhairr Morel's death shocked and saddened Amn, but she is inconsolable to learn his only son yet lives to claim his estate."

"I'm not surprised." Kall turned in the direction of distant Keczulla. "Thank you for making the journey. My father spent his last years in Keczulla. It's the only city where Morel assets survived intact, after the war."

Meisha nodded. In the years after Kall left Esmeltaran, humanoid armies led by two ogre mages—Sythillis and Cyrvisnea, allied with followers of the church of Cyric—had attacked the city and a fair portion of southern Amn. Amn's defenders—Meisha among them—hadn't been able to beat back their armies, and the port city of Murann had fallen to the new Sythillisian Empire. The cities of Esmeltaran and Imnescar had been devastated in the attack, and many of the merchant families lost their entire holdings. In the year since the war began, the humans and monsters had contrived an uneasy truce between them, but Amn had only just begun its recovery.

"You have a long road ahead," Meisha said, "if the froth at the mouths of the Bladesmile and Angathi families is any indication. From the gossip I've gathered, your father had a fair share of outstanding debts, which you've also inherited."

Kall sighed. "Judging by their eagerness, I'd say I have until Nightal to find a way to pay them."

"And what will you do once you manage this miracle?"

"I'll find Balram."

There was venom enough in those three words to fill a hundred rivers. "Yet you've found no trace of him or Aazen since before the war," said Meisha. "Thus far, they have eluded you. They could be dead, and you would never know."

"Balram's a survivor. I'll find him," Kall said. "What I need from you is information about the people who served my father at the time of his death. I don't recognize any of their names or faces."

Meisha was confused. "To my knowledge, Morel could afford little more than a skeleton household staff. They would not be a threat."

"There is also a wizard," Kall said.

Meisha snorted. "Morel, hire a wizard? In Amn? Impossible."

"His name is Syrek Dantane. He hails from Waterdeep and claims my father hired him a year ago for protection. I need to know if this is truth."

Meisha nodded slowly, considering. "Difficult, but I can try. Waterdeep is too large. The most accurate information will come from his time in Amn. Wizards are hard to hide. If he ever acted openly, someone will know of it."

"There's one more thing." Kall reached in a pouch and produced a small object that captured the sunlight. "When I cornered Meraik, he had this on him. He hadn't been in contact with Balram for some time, but he *was* kind enough to point me on the path to finding the rest of Balram's men."

Meisha took the small crystal. Its weight in her palm was so familiar that her skin prickled. The crystal was a mirror of the memory stone Varan had shown her as a child. She turned the crystal in her palm and saw the wizard's mark on the underside.

Why would Balram's man have one of Varan's possessions? Meisha thought. As far as she knew, her master had never sold his creations. To him, they were beyond price.

Meisha's heartbeat quickened, but she schooled her features to reveal nothing. "Beautiful," she said.

"Is it magical?" Kall asked.

"The mark on the base indicates sorcery." That much was truth, Meisha thought. "I can't say what it's used for, but I know someone who might. My former teacher, Varan Ivshar, is skilled in the making and identification of magical items. What makes you think this is connected to Balram?" she asked carefully.

"Just a feeling," Kall said. "Or maybe it's desperation. The trail has gone cold. I have to pick it up somewhere."

"And in the meantime, you've not only returned to the silks and soft beds of merchant nobility," Meisha said, deliberately provoking him to steer the conversation to safer territory, "but you go to salvage the house and fortune of Haig's murderer."

Kall's expression darkened. "Are we going to tread that path again, Meisha? I never lied to you. My father acted under

Balram's manipulation. I place the blame where it belongs."

"As you say. All I see is a murder almost ten winters old and no one to pay the price. I've been waiting a long time, Kall."

"I know," he said. "This crystal may be the key to finding him. Will you aid me?"

"Yes," she said, reluctantly. "I can look into Dantane soon enough," she said. "The crystal will take more time. I'll be in touch when I have information."

"You have my gratitude," Kall said.

"I don't need it." Meisha untied the strings of a scarred leather pouch that hung from her belt and offered it to Kall. "This is for you."

Kall took the pouch. "What is it?"

"Another inheritance—it belonged to your mother."

Kall froze, looking stricken. "How did you find this?"

"I traced her from your description," said Meisha. "She was killed fighting Zhents on the road east of Athkatla, if you're curious. Haig's account of her was accurate. She was banished from Morel's house for her affiliation with the Harpers, and threatened with the death of her son if she tried to return to take him away. So she asked Haig to watch over you. I believe they were either onetime lovers or close companions for him to devote so much of himself to the task. At any rate, the pouch was all the material goods I could find of her. I've been keeping it, for just this sort of parting."

Kall stood in shocked silence, absorbing the words. Finally, he said, "Why are you telling me this?"

"Because you tread in your father's footsteps so readily," Meisha said in disgust. "I wanted you to know the man you're honoring."

"He's my father," Kall said.

"My father sold me for food," Meisha said bluntly. "Blood means nothing to me, unless someone cares enough to shed it on my behalf. *That,* I would be a fool to ignore, as you are a fool to exchange your companions for a life among the merchant fops."

Kall squeezed the pouch in a fist. "I don't want this."

Meisha nodded but didn't take it from him. "Legacies are often that way," she said. "This one is yours. Deny or embrace it as you choose, but you can't change it. Welcome home, Kall."

She turned and strode from the bridge, leaving him with the rush of the river and old memories for comfort.

Overhead, a goshawk cried out. Kall watched its shadow cross the river. A sudden temptation to throw the pouch in the water seized him, but his curiosity proved stronger. He tied the long strings around his neck and tucked the pouch away. His thoughts were full of what he'd just learned. But could he trust it? Could he trust Meisha? Although the volatile Harper had kept her word, never harming his father, Kall knew little about her or her past. Why should she take such an interest in his?

He looked again in the direction of Keczulla and forced his attention to the matter at hand. One legacy at a time, he thought.

Midmorn the following day, Rays Bladesmile would be entering The Thirsty Gnome. Kall merely had to wait for the man to quit the place in his usual drunken stupor.

His first test as a merchant lord, Kall thought as he rode to the city. He'd best not be late to his first business meeting.

CHAPTER THIRTEEN

Amn
1 Marpenoth, the Year of Lightning Storms (1374 DR)

Meisha walked blindly, absorbed in her thoughts. Kall had long left her sight, on his way to Keczulla.

She hadn't been back to the city of her birth since leaving the Delve and Varan's tutelage. As the wizard had predicted, the Harpers were eager to welcome her, but Meisha could feel them always watching, gauging her power and temperament. Without acknowledging it, Meisha had followed Varan's advice and kept her anger—mostly—in check.

The thought of her master and their final parting brought a swell of unpleasant memories to Meisha's mind. Even the company she kept with the Harpers hadn't been able to banish her past with the wizard and his underground home.

She'd promised Kall she would look into where the crystal came from. Meisha clutched the small object in her hand. She'd sooner destroy the magical toy than question its owner. She'd sworn long ago never to return to the Howling Delve.

How she could consider breaking that vow for a man who'd once threatened her life, Meisha had no idea.

Obviously, something about Kall Morel affected her. Maybe it was that night in Esmeltaran, when he'd been willing to burn alive rather than let her get to his father. She'd never witnessed such loyalty. Or perhaps it was what she'd learned of his family in the years since meeting him.

Or maybe it had nothing at all to do with the merchant's son, and everything to do with her own private demons. If she could make peace with her former teacher, perhaps she could move forward. She could feel as if she belonged to the Harpers instead of merely fulfilling a role.

Meisha shook her head in disgust. Keeping her emotions buried had softened her.

She lifted her hand, examining the small gold ring on her finger. She'd never gotten rid of the magical gift—in fact, she rarely took it off.

"I don't want to go," she whispered aloud, surprised at how frightened her voice sounded, "but I don't have a choice, do I, Master?" A part of her still lived in the Delve, whether she chose to admit it or not.

She spoke the command word on the band, and the ring winked with a brief, magical burst. The radiance spread outward to engulf the Harper's entire body.

The sunlight disappeared.

* * *

Meisha blinked the white light from her eyes as the ever-present chill of the underground seeped through her jerkin. Water dripped in a distant rhythm, a sound from her earliest memories of Varan. With it came the familiar sense of intangible dread, a feeling she'd tried to forget in the years since her tutelage had ended.

She took comfort in the fact that she was still in Amn, albeit far beneath the land's surface. Varan had wisely scorned the idea of taking up residence in a populated area. A wizard living openly in a tower or estate would not go unmolested. Amn had persecuted wizards longer than Varan had been alive—for crimes he'd had no part in, but that didn't matter. The people still remembered the plagues, the waves of magical death wrought by practitioners of arcane magic. Amnians were not forgiving, which made Syrek Dantane's presence in Kall's house all the more confusing. What had Morel been thinking?

Meisha pushed the thoughts aside. She had more troubling concerns. She had to find Varan and learn how one of Balram's men came into possession of her master's work.

As Meisha's eyes adjusted to the dimness, she realized the cavern in which she stood was unfamiliar. Her ring should have teleported her directly to her old chamber, unless some magic of Varan's had malfunctioned.

Automatically, Meisha drew a stiletto from her boot and listened. Three of Varan's enspelled stalactites cast a dull glow from the ceiling. By their light, she could see two tunnels branching off opposite ends of the cavern. The only other features of the chamber were two gaping holes: a wide shaft dug into the cavern's ceiling and a deep chasm in the floor directly beneath.

Cautiously, Meisha approached the edge of the chasm and looked down. *Chaareff,* she chanted, and her stiletto burst into flame. The fire licked along the blade to stroke her fingers, but she ignored the heat. Twisting her wrist, she flicked the blade, dropping a tiny ball of fire down the hole. It plummeted quickly out of sight, the last burst of light in some dying creature's eye. The fire illuminated writing on the walls of the chasm, but the script was unlike the markings on her ring. Not Varan's work, then—some other wizard? Either way, Varan must have known they were here.

Off to the side of the chamber lay a pile of rope that looked like it had once been a net. One end was tied to a nearby stalagmite, but the rest was hacked into several pieces.

Meisha extinguished her blade with a word, but at the same time, she found herself bathed in green light. She dived away, landing hard on her elbow just as a circle of light filled the ceiling shaft and shot downward. The green thread briefly connected the two holes.

A portal, she thought. She got to her feet as the first figures dropped through the magical doorway.

There were six in total, but they came through in pairs. Magic slowed their descent, allowing them to twist in midair to avoid plummeting down the chasm. They landed opposite her across the hole.

A woman and five men—one a halfling. Meisha managed to note that much before they saw her. The chasm yawned between her and any close-range weapons, but the woman had a crossbow. She and the halfling stood off to one side. Three other men stood behind them, one in robes with a wand swinging from his belt. Their leader was sizing her up just as she evaluated them.

The wizard drew his wand and loosed a flame arrow, illuminating a black beard curled around thick lips. Not bothering to dodge, Meisha readied her stiletto. The missile streaked toward her. At the last instant she braced herself for the impact and watched the attacking wizard's eyes widen when she simply absorbed the spell against her chest.

"My turn," she said around a plume of smoke, but she had already buried her blade in his abdomen. She turned to face the halfling and the woman.

"Take her alive," said the leader, but Meisha drowned him out with a spell. Her eyes glowed red in the semi-darkness. The woman raised her crossbow, but Meisha finished her spell, thrusting both hands out from her body, the flats of her palms pressed tightly together. A searing jet of wind like the breeze off a coal fire shot across the chasm, slamming into the halfling. The gust lifted him off his feet, driving him into the far wall. The crossbow bolt skittered away across the cavern floor as the woman fell to the ground.

The other men charged, coming from both sides of the chasm. The hot wind stalled them. Meisha ran straight at the dark abyss, the spell sweeping before her in a billowing arc.

She jumped, buoyed up by the wind, clearing the chasm easily and landing on the other side. This caught her attackers by surprise, leaving her only the woman to contend with. She reached out, grabbing Meisha's arm, thinking the Harper meant to run, but Meisha instead dropped flat to her back. Her momentum pulled the woman down. Continuing the movement, Meisha wedged her foot in the woman's abdomen and pushed, somersaulting her backward and down into the chasm.

Meisha started to sit up, but the woman caught the lip of the hole and Meisha's shoulder, dragging her back and costing her the opportunity for another spell. She wrenched free, but the men were pushing through the wind and closing in on her.

Grabbing another dagger, Meisha drove the blade upward into the back of the first man's thigh. He howled in pain and dropped heavily against her. She pushed him away and felt a hot sting at her lower back. Meisha went down with a cry, unable to recover as the leader came in from behind and grabbed a handful of her dark hair.

Meisha felt strands rip from her scalp as he dragged her backward. Stone scraped her skin, and she lost her grip on her dagger. She kicked and clawed until she felt empty air beneath her head.

The leader drew his dagger and straddled her, letting her head and upper torso fall free over the lip of the chasm.

Immediately, Meisha felt the blood rush to her head, her muscles tightening painfully as she tried to balance herself above the abyss. He snatched one of her flailing arms and brought the back of her hand down in a whip crack on a protruding stone.

Meisha screamed, her hand flopping uselessly in her attacker's. He laid the broken wrist straight against her side and waited while the other pair of men helped the woman over the lip of the chasm. She smiled at Meisha's white face.

"Stay still," the leader advised when Meisha tried to move. "See to Warin and Tershus," he told the rest of the group.

"I'm still kicking." Picking himself up, the halfling lit a torch. He bent over the wizard Meisha had stabbed and shook his head. "He's dead, Aazen."

The leader sighed. "Retrieve the chest. They will have it waiting."

When the group moved off down one of the tunnels, the leader turned his attention to Meisha. "If you fight me, I'll stand, and your weight will pull you over the edge," he said. "Your hand is broken. You can cast no spell without great pain. Do you understand?"

But Meisha's attention was drawn to a pool of blood steadily spreading around the man's boots. The sting at her back had been a stab wound. She was bleeding to death while the bastard sat atop her like a king on a throne. Flames blazed in her eyes, an awakening of raw, sorcerous power.

The leader leaned back. Meisha started to slide toward the darkness. She tried to finish the spell, but the strength slowly ebbed from her body, replaced by a numbing cold. She couldn't concentrate. Her spell died half-formed on her lips.

"I might heal you," the leader said, steadying her, "if you answer my questions."

Meisha had the will to chuckle. "If you heal me, I'll kill you."

The man seemed unconcerned. "Who are you?"

Meisha didn't answer. If she timed it right, she might be able to lock her knees around his waist, pull him back into the chasm. She could at least take the bastard with her.

A sharp blow across her cheek forced Meisha's attention back to her murderer's face.

"Varan Ivshar," the leader tried again, and Meisha's narrowing world came starkly back into focus. "So you do know the wizard," the man said, seeing her reaction. "I hoped so."

He knew of Varan. Meisha licked dry lips. "Where is he?" she asked.

The man didn't answer. Meisha squirmed, moaning. The tautness of her muscles would only cause her to bleed out faster. The man eased back, drawing her away from the hole. He knew she was too weak to fight anymore.

"What happened to the wizard?" he asked, watching her carefully.

"I don't know what you're talking about," Meisha said, her expression unfeigned. It seemed to satisfy him.

The man rose to his feet, gazing down at her indecisively. "I'd hoped you'd be able to offer me more," he said. He reached down and his fingers brushed the silver pin of the Harpers. "I don't believe I can justify letting you live." He listened as voices echoed from the tunnel. "They won't allow it."

Meisha waited, expecting him to stab her again, or push her body over the edge with his boot. He did neither, instead turning his attention to the group re-entering the cavern. One of the men carried a large chest held together by rusted metal bands.

"Warin's spell is gone," said the halfling. "We can't levitate the chest. It'll take a bit to secure it by rope."

"You have ten breaths," the leader said.

"Take me that long to tie it off, won't it? Gods only know what'll happen if it falls, Aazen."

The leader nodded but did not look pleased. "You're right, of course." He pointed at Meisha. "Cast the spell, and you will live."

"How did you find this place?" It had taken her years of research to discover the main entrance to the Delve, and then she found it only because she knew there was something there to find. She had never known this portal room existed. Meisha tried to pull herself up to her elbows, to see the man's face by the portal light. His hair was dark and shorn close to his head, as if he'd cut it with his own knife. Fine scar lines peppered a clean-shaven jaw, marring an otherwise attractive face. "Who are you?"

"We're thieves," the leader said.

"What could you hope to steal from a cave?"

"The Delve is much more than a cave. You should have known that, before you entered. Cast the spell."

She lay back and closed her eyes. "I don't know it."

"Very well. I offered you your life."

"Done, Aazen." The halfling tossed the leader the other end

of the rope. He looped it twice around his waist and tied off the end.

Meisha watched him hand a waterskin off to the halfling, who uncorked it and squirted a thick, pastelike substance into his small hand. The skin went around to each member of the group until it was empty, then the halfling tossed the container carelessly toward the chasm. It fell short, landing next to Meisha, but no one paid her any further attention. They were busy coating their hands and boots with the substance. The halfling trotted on the balls of his feet toward the cavern wall. He jumped, his arms outstretched, latching onto the walls like an insect. He scrambled up and across the ceiling, disappearing into the mouth of the shaft. The rest followed in the same way.

The leader came last, climbing slower than the rest and towing the chest behind him on the rope. When he'd ascended to the edge of the portal, the woman braced him as he hauled the chest up. Meisha got her first clear look at it as it passed in and out of the green light. As she'd suspected, the chest was Varan's. What had they done to him?

With the chest secured, one by one the thieves disappeared up into the portal. When the last had gone, the green light faded.

Meisha rolled onto her side, crawling to the closest tunnel. She knew she would never make it out of the chamber, but anything was better than listening to her lifeblood drip down the walls of the chasm.

<hr />

They'd nicknamed him "Dirty Bones," and for good reason. Talal wriggled out from the pile of waste and garbage that had collected at the mouth of the refuse room. He sniffed. Dirty, yes. He didn't mind dirt. But he was starving, too. That concerned him. He'd gladly be called "Fat Bones," but there just wasn't enough food.

"Not my fault. Can't eat garbage." He surveyed the room.

"Plenty of that, but can you live on it?" No. Unquestionably. He'd already tried. His tongue curled at the memory.

Too much thinking, he decided. Time to scavenge. The raiding party had come and gone. He'd counted to make sure there were no stragglers, just as Gadi had warned him. Then came the green light, then silence. It was the same every time.

Talal moved quickly, pulling a mound of wax that only vaguely resembled a candle from behind one of the rocks. He held it out, duck walking along the winding tunnel to the portal room.

Gadi had taught him each step in the process. He paused to listen before entering the room. When he peeked to see what lay within, he let out a whoop of delight. The sound echoed in the vast chamber. Talal clamped a filthy hand to his mouth, his eyes darting over the tops of his fingers. When nothing stirred, he rose to his full five-foot height and practically skipped over to the bodies.

There were two of them—two thieves dead. Warmth rose in Dirty Bones. "Two less to worry about. They'll be thrilled." He would hurry, so he could return and tell them.

"Messy," he muttered as he knelt next to the body of a young woman. Not a tidy kill—like Gadi, he thought—and shoved away all pity for the pretty-faced lass. He went for her boots first, feeling inside for pouches or hidden vials. He drew back with a hiss and raised a bloody finger to his mouth. Cautiously, he tried again, and pulled a pair of daggers from each boot. The lass bristled with them.

He worked his way methodically up her body but found no other treasures. There had to be more, the bitch was dressed too well. . . .

A low groan escaped the woman's mouth.

"Ho!" Talal felt his spine bounce off something hard and realized it was the cavern wall on the far side of the room. He'd slammed into it in his rush to get away from the corpse, which continued moaning.

"The walking dead," he squeaked. "I touched the walking

dead. . . ." He stared at his hand as if the appendage might suddenly turn black and fall off. He wiped it furiously on his breeches. The damned things weren't supposed to come back once they bled that much, were they?

Talal wasn't going to take any chances. He felt around until he found a large rock. Holding it at eye level, he approached the body. Up close, he could tell her coloring was off, but it didn't have the deathly pallor of the other bodies he'd seen. Gadi had been much worse. The woman's eyes were closed, but the lashes fluttered as if she slept.

Talal bent closer and felt a shallow breath brush his cheek. The hairs on the back of his neck stood on end, but he shook away the sensation. "Not dead, that's the problem." Of course he'd known it all along. She didn't look like one of them Shadow Thief bastards anyway. How did she get down here?

"Bad luck, that's how, but we'll fix it . . . maybe." He wasn't any sort of healer, after all. She could die on the way to the camp. But what in the Hells else was he going to do for fun?

Talal tossed away the rock so he could get an arm under her legs. He hauled her up, grunting as blood soaked into his breeches. "If I drop you, Lady, I'm taking it as a sign from the gods this was a bad idea."

CHAPTER FOURTEEN

Keczulla, Amn
2 Marpenoth, the Year of Lightning Storms (1374 DR)

Kall passed through a wide stone archway crowned by a sapphire keystone. The gem inset on the opposite side of the arch, a lighter agate, was not nearly as impressive or flawless, but then again, the difference between districts in Keczulla often hinged upon the worth of a gemstone.

The Keczull clan first gave the city life when it struck iron and gold along the Ridge arm of the Cloud Peaks to the north. Unfortunately for all, the mines didn't last, and a little over a century and a half later, the city was abandoned. It took Pulth Tanislove and his gem mines to bring Keczulla back in 1355 DR. The city had come twice from ruin to prosper in metals and gems, so naturally every aspect of its growth had followed suit, from the four districts: Emerald, Sapphire, Jade, and Agate, to their corresponding wards. The most prosperous families made their homes and businesses in the Mithral and Platinum Wards, and the hierarchy descended from there. Harbor Moon Ward was last in line and made no attempt to put a false sheen on itself. Kall appreciated that, and he suspected Rays Bladesmile did as well.

Traffic flowed around Kall, merchants bearing carts or

wagons of goods packed wheel to wheel on the narrow streets. The ones loaded down with sacks dealt in grain or textiles. Those stacked with chests and lockboxes, their drivers' furtive gazes darting all around—they were jewelers, like Kall. They carried identical bulging rings of tiny keys—one for every box—like the gleaming teeth of a hundred exotic creatures. The jostle of their carts on the pitted streets evoked a discordant jangle that echoed throughout the ward.

The Thirsty Gnome sat just on the other side of the archway. Kall waited in the shade of the building, his eyes straying to a particular set of towers nestled in the center of the Gold Ward. He'd been to his father's house once, just after he arrived in the city, but seeing the structure from a distance like this was equally unnerving.

His father had had the house in Keczulla built identical to the one in Esmeltaran. The gods alone knew why. It certainly wasn't in keeping with the fashions of Amn, which Amnians themselves freely admitted tended to change like light off a gem facet.

"S'only piss an' ale if you try and sell it for three coppers!" shouted a voice from inside the tavern. Kall pushed away from the arch. Lord Rays was right on schedule.

The door to the tavern burst open, and Rays Bladesmile stormed out, the aforementioned ale streaming from his chin.

His eyes barely cleared the depths of their sockets, Kall noted, in a face that more resembled a skull, emaciated and paste white from too much time spent indoors licking the bottom of a tankard. Bladesmile stared angrily around the street as if searching for a fight. When none materialized, he tottered toward an alley, pulling at his breeches' strings as he went.

Kall followed at a discreet distance. He didn't want the inebriated Bladesmile's wrath turned on him.

The roofs of the adjacent buildings overhung the alley in a crooked arch that swallowed light. Aromas of piss and garbage filled the air. Kall stopped at the alley's mouth, waiting in amused silence as Lord Rays added his own offering to the bouquet.

"You wanting to hold it for me, lad?" Rays muttered without looking up.

"Ah, no, thank you," said Kall.

"Hmph. Then what does Lord Morel want here, at the height of a business day? Yes, I know you," he said, at Kall's surprised look. "You can expect all the Bladesmiles to mark your face."

"Actually, I was looking for Rays Bladesmile."

Rays retied his breeches, adjusted himself, and spread his hands in a ready swagger. "Well, you've found him, lad, in all his glory. What can I do for the last scion of Morel house?"

"Just Kall, I think, for meetings in back alleys," Kall said with a laugh. "I sought you out to discuss the debt my father owes the Bladesmiles."

"If that's so, you should have known you'd need to speak to Lord Rhor. The debt was substantial enough that accounting for it and any interest accrued—trust that there'll be plenty to spread around—will fall to him and those immediately under his eye."

"Yes, but I'm most interested in the sums already transferred to your family, the debt repaid in the form of mercenaries," Kall said. "I understand you are still considered the master armsman for the Bladesmile family."

"Gods, you want to talk true business." Rays gave a mock shudder. "Good thing I've already begun drinking. Yes, I'm still head of Rhor's companies, for as long as he deigns to put up with me." He nodded at the inn. "Join me in a bottle, and I might even tell you how much I despise the arrogant bastard."

"Another time, I'd like to hear it." Kall smiled. "Today I'm expected to return to Morel house. I'm hosting a gathering tomorrow evening for some old friends of my father's. Hopefully, by night's end, they will be my friends."

"By that, you mean you hope they won't foreclose on you in the manner of Shilmistan wolves. They're all coming for you, one way or another, and not just the Bladesmiles. Plenty of other families'll turn up claiming 'old' or 'half-forgotten' debts that are neither. They wouldn't mind taking those markers out of a former adventurer turned man of business."

"Then it's fortunate I'm more the adventurer and less the businessman," Kall said. His smile had steel in it.

Catching the look, Rays laughed. "Well, you won't get trouble from me. As you said, your father paid some of his debts in men, and I'll be damned if Rhor didn't cheat him something grievous in that deal. He added a fair number of seasoned fighters to my company. I've seen none finer. No, I've no complaints against your father, no matter what people said about him."

"And these—my father's men—do they serve the Bladesmiles still?"

"They do."

"I see." Kall took in a breath, pausing to consider his next words. "I wonder . . . what a man would have to do to reacquire such fine and *loyal* warriors."

"The price would be high," Rays warned.

"And worth every copper," Kall said quietly.

Overhead, a familiar cry rang out. Kall lifted an arm as the goshawk glided easily between the narrow buildings and alighted upon his gauntlet. "Welcome back," he said.

"Impressive." Rays scrubbed at the black stubble on his chin. "Is she one of Dhairr's?"

"No," Kall said, "but my father's aviary is extensive. I have not taken a full inventory, but I know of at least two goshawks, a peregrine that flies faster than any eye can follow, and others I couldn't identify."

"Do you intend to maintain it, now that you've taken up residence at the estate?" Rays asked, interested.

"I had not considered it," Kall admitted. "Other matters have been occupying my thoughts. Do you have an interest in hunting birds?"

"Not for that purpose," said Rays. "The greater Bladesmiles" —he spat again in distaste—"constantly seek the means to make information travel faster, short of using magic to fuel its steps."

"Of course. I have no doubt my father's specimens could be trained as messengers. If such a service interests the Bladesmiles, I'm certain we could come to an arrangement," said Kall. He went on, "If I may, Lord Rays, I would be honored to have you attend my gathering tomorrow. Beyond the pleasure of your company, I wouldn't mind continuing this discussion in my home."

"In more delicate surroundings?" Rays looked genuinely curious. "Well, lad, if you're brave enough to want me at your table, I accept your invitation and wish you good business." He slapped Kall on the back.

Jostled by the sudden movement, the goshawk let out an ear-splitting shriek and took flight, leaving gouge marks in Kall's leather gauntlet. She soared up between the buildings to glide huffily over the Gold Ward.

The raptor flew gracefully through the wide window of the aviary but came to rest on the ground instead of one of the perches scattered in tiers around the room.

The other raptors screeched in alarm as magic flooded the narrow space. The goshawk's wings twisted vertically, folding feathers and membrane slowly into the flesh of bare arms. Claws shrank into slender, feminine toes, which gripped the cold stone floor reflexively as the change wracked her body. When the transformation was complete, Cesira stood, instinctively reaching out with her thoughts to calm the frightened birds.

Forgive me. I will be more thoughtful in the future.

Cesira had no idea what her true voice sounded like. Mute from birth, she did not know why she could touch animals with her thoughts but not her voice, nor did she understand how Silvanus granted her speech when in animal shape, or heard her spells when she chanted in silence. She had simply accepted long ago that the gods must know the hearts and minds of their followers, and answer accordingly.

Forgive me, she repeated.

When all was quiet, Cesira strode briskly to the door of the tower, which led to a steep flight of stairs. On the landing, she put on the long brown cloak she'd left hanging on a peg earlier that morning. Time to become mistress of the house, she thought, blowing a stray feather out of her tresses.

A servant met her at the base of the stairs—the cook, if Cesira remembered correctly. "My lady," the woman said, curtseying quickly. "I've a message for Lord Morel."

Lord Morel, Cesira thought. Gods help her. She looked the woman over, noting with some relief that she bore the new symbol of Morel woven with ribbon into the collar of her frock: an emerald joined by an elaborate setting to a rather plain-looking stone. The official story was that Lord Morel meant the symbol as a tribute to Keczulla's roots, its rise from nothing to become the backbone of the Morel jewel business. Conveniently, it also bore the enchantment that allowed Cesira to converse with people, making the plain stone in essence more valuable than the emerald. Cesira did not miss the irony. *What is it?* she asked.

"It's from Master Dantane," the cook said, a little uneasily. "He again requests an audience. He wants to know when Lord Morel will be deciding whether he is to stay or go from the house." The woman's tone left little doubt of her feelings on the matter. If the rest of Amn was in the dark about Dantane's profession, it was certainly no secret to the house. "He'd like to speak with Lord Morel as soon as possible."

I'm sure he would, Cesira said. *Please tell him Lord Morel will speak to him just as soon as he returns.*

The woman curtseyed again and hurried away. Cesira's gaze strayed across the hall, in the direction of the other tower. The spire had formerly housed Morel's private offices. At some point it became the wizard's living quarters.

Must they all flock to towers and high places, Cesira wondered. She didn't see the appeal. Then again, she knew nothing of Syrek Dantane or his tastes. That worried her, more than she liked to admit.

CHAPTER FIFTEEN

Keczulla, Amn
2 Marpenoth, the Year of Lightning Storms (1374 DR)

Aazen approached the Contrall Estate from the rear, nodding to Isslun as she strode forward to bar his path. "I need to see him."

"He's waiting for you. We've already heard from the buyer"—she cast a quick glance around the deserted patio—"and the Cowl. We were set up."

"*I* was set up," Aazen corrected her sharply. "And two Gem Guards are dead for it."

Isslun shrugged, unconcerned. "If they cannot identify us, what's the worry?"

"I see your sister took the lion's share of the wits between you," Aazen sneered. "We're starting to attract attention. If this incident draws concern anywhere near the Council's hearing, how long do you believe the Shadow Thieves will continue to support this operation?"

The Council of Six, Amn's anonymous body of rulers, saw to the needs of the land primarily by keeping business running as smoothly as possible between the merchant families—business which would not include an influx of black market magical items, not with two Gem Guards dead in the Harbor Moon Ward.

Isslun comprehended none of that. She pouted, catching her lower lip between her teeth. "If you place so high a value on my sister's wits, perhaps *she* will welcome you to her bed when you grow cold tonight."

"She already has," Aazen said, closing the door on the twin's shocked face.

His father waited in the library. The few books remaining in the tall, narrow room had gathered a thick blanket of dust. For as long as they'd dwelled here, his father had shown no interest in them.

"Are you all right?" Balram asked as Aazen closed the library door.

Aazen felt the abrasions at his wrists where one of the guards had briefly put him in manacles. "Minor wounds. We have a problem."

"I'm aware," Balram said grimly. "A watch commander, Aazen?"

"It was the only way I could see to escape. I took him as hostage. His own men fired the bolts."

Balram nodded, letting it pass. "Jubair was here before you. It seems a member of the Chadossa family approached a contact within the Cowled Wizards concerning a *rumor* he'd heard about black market magic."

"A rumor including the location of the exchanges and the contents of the latest shipment?" Aazen asked.

His father nodded. "So it was Chadossa."

"No doubt the family is having second thoughts about dealing with the Shadow Thieves," Aazen guessed.

"But their son is not."

"What do you mean?"

"Chadossa broke off all contact with us just before their betrayal, all except the boy, the youngest son," said Balram. "He's still buying. There's an exchange tonight. I've left the location up to you. I trust you will be discreet."

Aazen shrugged. "Perhaps he was not privy to his family's intentions. Or they were not aware he was also our client and so failed to warn him. What do you propose to do?"

"I intend to send a message. Chadossa's son will bear it for me, and his sire will learn the price of betrayal."

"You risk the wrath of a powerful family," Aazen warned, but he already knew what his father would say.

"My own family's resources far outstrip any the Chadossas could gather," Balram said confidently.

"And will your *family* support such a bold action?" Aazen dared to ask.

Uncharacteristically, his father waved it off with a chuckle. "Even Daen could not argue with the profit already amassed in this venture. And if Chadossa acts anything like I expect him to, the authorities will never trace the message back to us." His father's expression changed as he looked on his son. "You'll have to deliver the item to him, Aazen." Aazen kept his face neutral.

"Is there no one else?"

"None of the others will touch the broken items," Balram said. "They're afraid."

So was his father, though the man would never admit it. He should be afraid, Aazen thought. Any rational person would be.

"I'll take care of it, Father," he said. "There is another issue."

"What is it?"

"When we retrieved the items, we encountered a woman in the Delve—a Harper."

Balram's lip curled. "They turn up in the most inconvenient places. Did you deal with her?"

"I left her to bleed out, but perhaps I shouldn't have. She knew the wizard. She may have been his apprentice. If so, we could have used her."

Balram shook his head. "Too risky. Secrecy is our best advantage in this, and it's possible she knows another way out. Your only mistake was in not making sure she was dead. We'll take care of that tomorrow."

Aazen nodded. If he had had his way, they would never have returned to the Delve at all. The memories it held for him were not pleasant ones. He still felt it—the distant menace, the sensation of being trapped—whenever he went down there. "What if more apprentices unexpectedly turn up?" he asked.

"As with the woman, they'll find the Delve a place much changed from what it was before," Balram said.

CHAPTER SIXTEEN

The Howling Delve
3 Marpenoth, the Year of Lightning Storms (1374 DR)

Meisha opened her eyes to a blurry world of smoke and stink—the full, cloying smell of sweat and unwashed bodies, broken only by the pungent odor of some kind of herb.

She was still underground, lying on a pallet of blankets. She could make out the uneven rock ceiling by the light of a torch suspended on the wall above her head. Smoke from the brand drifted languidly in the air until it reached the ceiling, then it was swept away like river water to a darkened corner of the room. If Varan's magics still functioned, he must be nearby, Meisha thought.

She tried to sit up and felt pain lance through her lower back. The stab wound was still fresh. She should be dead. Someone must have found her and treated the wound—Varan?

Meisha felt a stiff bandage encasing her abdomen, which seemed to be the source of the herb scent. But she could tell at least some of the bones in her wrist had reknit while she slept. Whoever had treated her had done so with some magical aid, but not much.

She examined her surroundings. The chamber around her

was wide, with a low ceiling that dipped almost to the ground in some corners and fluted upward sharply in others. This place Meisha recognized. She'd made her pact to become Varan's apprentice here, over a pit of flames.

As an apprentice, she'd taken meals here or used the space for study that did not involve casting. Despite the cold and damp of the underground environment, Varan had had the chamber richly appointed. Placed in the center of the room was a round, cherry wood table—with thicker legs than her own—surrounded by soft, wingback armchairs. Two couches with tasseled silk pillows had flanked a bookcase wedged along the wall. All of it had huddled around small fire pits, with Varan's ventilation magic handy to carry the smoke away through one of the carved flues in the ceiling.

But now the chamber was stripped of all furnishing. A sagging length of rope hung around her pallet and held a stained sheet for privacy. Meisha could make out dozens more of the boxed-off areas around the chamber. Distorted shapes moved within them like a complex shadow play. People, Meisha thought—a fair number, at that.

She could hear their voices, sometimes whispering in low tones, other times pitched loudly to carry across the chamber.

"I'm tellin' ye, pick one day for butchering, and we won't have that awful stink to wake to."

"Five toys just today—that's got it, my time's coming up. Always does when yer five times as likely to lose an eye."

"Where's Iadra? Somebody'd best tell her to be puttin' the mark up."

Footfalls tramped on the other side of her sheet. Meisha tensed, but the male voice that drifted over the thin cloth was somehow familiar.

"Tymora's best odds, all I'm saying. Tymora's best odds she don't live through the night."

"You said as much last night," an overly patient female voice answered him. "Return it, please."

"She's not gonna care! You didn't see this blood pool, Har. I pulled her out—no one else was there with her to do the honors. She'd want me to have it."

"Get out of my way, Talal."

"Fine. At least let's nudge her and see—see if she's still kicking."

Hands flung the sheet aside to reveal a pair of large eyes surrounded by a nest of dirty blond hair that had not been combed with anything more elaborate than fingers and spit for many years. The boy couldn't have seen more than two decades of life, and they'd been lean years. His wrists were the breadth of broom handles, and he crouched like a frog, his spindle legs thickening with muscle at the thighs, as if he squatted and crawled more often than he walked. He wore a baggy shirt and breeches. When he moved, the odor wafting off them made Meisha gag.

"It's awake," the boy said, too brightly, as if he were hiding disappointment. "See?" He pointed at her triumphantly, her Harper pin clutched in one dirty hand. "Did that last time. Thought she was dead and whew!" He waggled his fingers and pulled a ghoulish face at the woman who was attempting to push him aside with her hip. "Back to life again." The boy didn't seem to notice the woman's exasperated shoving. "No one dies reliably these days."

Meisha's hand came up, snagging the boy's wrist like a snake after a mouse.

"Ho, there!"

"That's mine," she croaked, squeezing the mouse until the boy dropped the pin on the ground.

"Got 'im worms for wits, but Talal doesn't mean any harm," said the woman. She was much older and not nearly as dirty as the boy. Her hair was stark white in the dim torch-light, and so thin Meisha could see patches of skin through the wispy strands. Her eyebrows had worn away long ago, but she had a quick, affectionate smile for the boy even as she chided him.

"Are you in great pain?" she asked Meisha. The same

pungent herb smell wafted from her hands as she probed Meisha's bandage.

"Only when I move," Meisha grunted. Truth was, she hurt all over, but part of that was from the cold. Despite the blankets piled on and beneath her, the cavern floor was colder than Meisha ever remembered it being. Not all Varan's enchantments were working, she thought, and her heart sank a little. "Who are you?" she asked, stopping the woman in her ministrations. "Where's Varan? What's happened to this place?"

"Easy," the woman said. "One at a time. I'm Haroun." She pointed to the boy. "This one's Talal. Your wound is healing. The knife managed to miss everything vital. Still, you were far gone when Talal brought you in. We're allowed only a small number of healing draughts, and we had to use two just to keep you from death."

"You have my thanks," Meisha said with feeling. She sat up gingerly, and with Haroun's help, got to her feet. "My attackers, do you know who they were?"

"Yes." Haroun's voice was strained. "The Shadow Thieves. They come through the glowing doors once every few tendays— the time varies. They don't want us to know when to expect them. She leaned closer, her milky eyes intent on Meisha's. "Tell me, child, did you come through the doorways? Do you know how to open them?"

Meisha shook her head, and the woman's eyes dimmed. "I came by . . . other means." Before Haroun could ask, she said, "I can't return the same way, but there is a main entrance. It's kept hidden, but I can show you."

Haroun was shaking her head before she'd finished. "No need. That way is closed."

"Closed?"

"Tunnel's sealed off," Talal spoke up. "Bastards caved it in, put something on it when we tried to dig out." He made scooping and filling motions with his hands. "We dig—stays full."

"An enchantment," Meisha said, remembering the wizard

from the raiding party. "Probably activated from the other side of the cave-in. All it would require is a new casting each day, perhaps not even that often." She looked at the boy. "They trapped you in the Delve? How long have you been here?"

Talal and Haroun exchanged glances. "I'll show her," the boy offered, shrugging.

Haroun hesitated, appearing almost upset, but finally she nodded. "Go. She'll need to see the places where it's safe to walk. Show her gently, Talal. Do nothing foolish."

The boy flashed an indignant, "do I ever" look and offered his sleeve to Meisha in imitation of a grand lord escorting his lady. Meisha suppressed a groan, selected the cleanest possible scrap of cloth to grasp, and they were off, weaving among the cubed warrens to a cleared central path that led to an attached passage.

Talal yanked a torch from the wall sconce. He ignored the shouts of dismay from the corner of the cavern subsequently plunged into darkness. "This way."

They walked a short distance down a passage Meisha remembered. It led to a series of carved out alcoves fitted with thick wooden doors.

When Varan had first come to the Delve, he'd used the spaces as storage, but later they became small, private quarters for the apprentices. The wizard's domain was only a small part of the tunnel system. Varan's magic had placed the age of some of the lower tunnels as contemporaries of Deep Shanatar. The wizard speculated the Delve might even have been an outpost of that great dwarven realm.

Talal tugged on her arm. Absorbed in her thoughts, Meisha hadn't noticed when they'd stopped. Framed by a pearly, flowstone waterfall, Talal pointed behind her to a stretch of wall. Meisha turned and blinked.

Numbers covered the stone from floor to ceiling, arranged in neatly ordered columns like a moneylender's account. All were dates, marked with the change of month and the change of year. They ended Marpenoth 3 of 1374 DR.

"Iadra marks a new one every day," said Talal.

"1370," Meisha read from the top of the first column. "Eleasias 20. Four years ago."

"Date we found the entrance. Wish we hadn't," Talal muttered.

"You—all of you?" Meisha shook her head. "Impossible. Varan shields the entrance with magic and places a ward on the perimeter."

A shadow passed over the boy's face. "There was no magic. The way was just sitting there, open as you please. We wouldn't have gone in, but the brigands had started to circle. There were too many of us not to be noticed out in the open."

"What were you doing all the way out here?"

"Running," Talal said.

Meisha waved an impatient hand. "From brigands, yes, but what—"

"No—from Esmeltaran."

"Esmeltaran?" Meisha echoed. Then it hit her: 1370. Meisha didn't need to do the calculation. She knew. "The ogres," she said, and Talal nodded. "You're refugees from the war."

"We were headed for Keczulla when they started shadowing us."

"The men from the portal?" Meisha asked.

Talal actually laughed. "No, the brigands—soft bellies by comparison. There were a lot more of us then. We moved in a group, tight as Tyr's arse. Only thing kept us alive—they didn't want to take on the whole bunch of us. But they smartened up, the longer they stayed with us. Picked off the stragglers, set traps—that sort of thing. We never saw any of the cowardly bastards. Thought we could wait them out in the caves. We should've known something was wrong if damn brigands wouldn't follow us inside."

"Did you explore? Was there anyone living in the caves?" Meisha wanted to know.

Talal hesitated. He swung the torch at one of the alcoves.

Meisha went for the door, but the boy caught her wrist.

"Don't burst in like that!" he hissed. "You want to kill us all?"

"It's Varan, isn't it?" Meisha said. At his blank look, she pressed, "You found a wizard here."

Talal's lip curled. "Pity us, yes."

Meisha freed her arm. "He's the man I came to see—my teacher! He can get us all out of here."

The boy stared at her. "Certainly, Lady," he said, bowing her mockingly toward the door. "You go right on in and ask him to do that."

Dread welled inside Meisha, but she pushed past Talal. The door scraped the stone floor as she wrenched it open, dripping dirt and cold sediment down on her. She ignored it in the face of what lay within.

The room was littered with garbage. Broken bits of junk covered every available inch of floor space, like the aftermath of a child's tantrum. Varan sat in one corner of the squalid room, his back to her, arms moving as if in the midst of a complicated spell. Small, white maggots swarmed over an uneaten plate of meat and bread on the floor next to him.

Meisha slowly circled the rear wall, putting herself in the wizard's periphery so he would know she was there. Varan held an object in his hands, an opaque sphere caged in a knot of iron bands. Within the sphere, tiny lights winked and danced like trapped stars. Wherever Varan touched the bands, the lights would gather, drawn zipping across the empty space to swirl around his fingertips. The collected magic in the room was so intense it hurt Meisha's head to concentrate too closely on any one point. And the Art did not issue only from the sphere.

Meisha uttered a quick word and swept a fanning gesture the length and width of the room. As the spell took effect, the light nearly smote her blind. Most of the intact objects on the floor, with the exception of the food, contained magic—slight in some instances, dangerously strong in others.

"Varan, what have you been doing?" Meisha whispered, but no one answered. She glanced behind her, but Talal had not followed her into the room. He stood, framed in the crack of the half-closed door, watching Varan. His expression showed a mixture of hatred, awe, and fear.

Meisha took a step forward. She felt the boy make a restless motion. Her eyes shot a question at him, and a warning—*don't try to stop me*.

Talal appeared torn. Reluctantly, he stepped into the room, just far enough to whisper, "He won't answer you. He never talks to us."

"What's wrong with him?"

"Lady, you'd need a bucket full of scribes to make that list. Just come away," he pleaded.

Meisha shook her head. "I have to see him." She crept toward the wizard, carefully toeing aside the non-magical debris to make a path.

She knelt next to her former teacher, but he did not stir from his work. He smelled much worse than Talal. His gray-blue robes were stained—Mystra's mercy, in some places charred—and soiled by old urine and waste. Her eyes traveled upward, and Meisha gasped at the gaunt, cavernous husk that the wizard's face had become.

Varan had been aged when Meisha was young, but the man who sat before her was sucked dry, all his energy and vitality gone. His left eye was missing, and the flesh around the empty socket had melted, folding into itself like a pudding. His one good eye stared dully at the wall as his hands moved in a jerky rhythm over the sphere.

Meisha followed his gaze. A rough parchment drawing floated flat against the cavern wall, illuminated by green radiances. On it someone had scribbled—the hand was too spiky to be Varan's—a drawing of the sphere, with notes along the top and sides of the page.

The lights in the sphere flared, drawn to its center. Suddenly, a sound like shattering glass echoed in the room, and the lights went out. Gray mist tendrils flowed from the gaps in the iron bands, curling up sinuously to touch Varan's beard.

The wizard's hands shook, as if the sphere had suddenly doubled in weight. It dragged the old man's arms down, and the mist swirled and dissipated. The sphere hit the cavern floor with a thud that Meisha felt through her knees.

Distaste flickered in the wizard's eye. He pushed the sphere aside and tore the drawing from the wall.

"Broken."

Meisha's head snapped up at the sound of the wizard's voice. "Varan?"

"Hello, little firebird," he replied, but his gaze never left the drawing. Carefully, he tore it into strips of glowing green, flicking each aside like magical confetti.

Relief flooded Meisha at the sound of the old nickname. "Master. What happened to you, to your eye?"

Varan seemed not to hear her. "I broke another one." He selected a brittle piece of meat from the plate and tore off a bite.

"What do you mean, you 'broke' it?" Meisha asked.

"Broken," Varan repeated. "Some of them work, some break. And yet they cling to me, just like you did, firebird. Cling to me, wanting to be fixed. I suppose I'll fix them all, eventually."

"Varan," Meisha said, choking back her revulsion at the white, squirming maggots crawling in the hair around the wizard's lips, "where is Jonal? And Prieces—the other apprentices? Why didn't they aid you?"

"Oh, they're here," Varan said. He patted the small sack he wore tied around his neck. He reached inside and drew out three rings. He dropped them into her cupped hand one at a time. They were identical to the ring Meisha wore, but for the bloodstains.

"Dead?" Meisha couldn't believe it. Three apprentices, and even Jonal, the lowliest among them, bore powerful elemental magic, defenses known only to themselves and Varan. "How?"

But Varan had gone back to his drawing. Meisha picked up

the sphere, but whatever magic it had held appeared spent.

What happened to the wizard? Her attacker's words drifted back.

"Talal, what . . ."

But Talal was no longer in the room. Meisha turned back and found Varan staring at her as if he'd only just discovered she was in the room.

"Firebird, it is good to see you," he said. He lifted a hand to touch her shoulder. The gesture of affection was so familiar it made Meisha's chest constrict.

"Master, how did this happen?" she asked, cupping the melted side of his face gently in her hand.

"This?" Varan twirled a finger in the empty socket. "I believe he took it—or I had to give it away—hard to remember. Bad things are here," he said. Then he shifted the finger, tapping his temple. "But here . . ." He grinned at her. "Gods are at work."

"Oh, Master—"

"I'm glad you've returned, little one. Yes, you can help me fix them—the broken ones." He touched his hand to the wall next to where the drawing had been. His fingers passed through the rock as if it were water, until he'd sunk to the elbow in stone. When he pulled his hand out, he held a second sphere, smaller than the first and copper-hued.

"What is broken, Varan? Where are those coming from?" Meisha asked. She lifted the pouch away from his neck, slipping the rings back inside. "What happened to the apprentices?"

"I told you, they're here. Don't fret." His hand closed tightly over hers. With the other, he stroked her hair.

"But what—"

"I told you." Ancient muscles flexed with astonishing strength, slamming her head into the unforgiving stone wall. *"Don't fret."*

Meisha went down in a burst of red pain and horror. Blindly, she lurched to her back as her teacher towered over her, a terrible, crumbling column of rage and power.

"You should leave now, firebird," he said, his face dark. He murmured something inaudible, and the chamber sparked to life with newly kindled magic. "Leave me alone."

Gasping, cradling her head, Meisha opened her mouth in time to taste fire. The chamber darkened and blurred as if she'd been cast into a deep pool. She could no longer see Varan.

Trembling, Meisha raised herself to her knees and crawled to where she thought the doorway must be. Somewhere along the way the fire went out, but she could smell the smoke of things still burning: rotted meat, clothing, and hair—her own, of course. She slid onto her face and rolled jerkily to put the fires out.

Hands caught her armpits, and Meisha felt herself being dragged out of the room into cooler air. She heard the door grind shut, and Talal's terrified face filled her vision.

"He t-tried to kill me." Meisha coughed on the smoke from her own burnt clothing.

Talal nodded grimly. "The ball. You touched one of his toys. Shirva Tarlarin did the same thing. There wasn't enough of her left to show her husband. You should be dead," he said, half-accusingly.

Meisha shuddered. Her skin was unburned but red and raw, as if she'd stumbled through a bramble bush. "I'm protected—somewhat—against magical fire," she said, lifting a hand to touch her head. "I wish I could say the same for blunt trauma." She looked up at Talal imploringly. "What happened to him? How did—"

"We don't know," Talal said. "He was like that when we found him, but worse—starved nearly to death, and sick. We brought him out of it, but his head's gone. . . ." Talal still gazed at her suspiciously. "You believe me now? That thing isn't your teacher anymore, Lady."

"Then what is he?" Meisha snapped. "What has he become?"

Talal had a quick answer to that. "He's our doom."

CHAPTER SEVENTEEN

Keczulla, Amn
3 Marpenoth, the Year of Lightning Storms (1374 DR)

But of course the family stands happy to extend whatever assistance young Lord Morel may require, provided he understands the weight of the favors his father has already accrued."

"Your point is clearly taken, Lady." Kall bowed to the coldly smiling Lady Rothres and continued his trek across the ballroom.

Absently, he scanned the second floor balcony for Cesira. She was nowhere in sight, but that was hardly a surprise. With its open view of the main ballroom, the second floor was a popular spot, and thus quite crowded.

Kall left the echoing chatter of the ballroom and crossed the dark garden to the tower stairs. The double-arched windows of his father's former offices stood exactly as they had in Esmeltaran, though the current occupant of the tower hardly cared what view he had.

Syrek Dantane stood bent over a table, examining a book that was easily the length of his arm. The wizard had to shuffle a step left and right to read the text.

"I'd love to see the bookshelf that came out of," Kall said by way of greeting.

The wizard did not immediately answer. When he did, he lifted only his eyes from the tome. They were as clear and as blue as Kall's, with a matching sheen of barely concealed hostility.

"I'm sure it would astound you. One actually has to *read* books on a regular basis to appreciate that knowledge comes in many forms."

Kall ignored the insult. "Surely you can agree inscribing a tome that's impossible to lift borders on the absurd?"

"Whatever you say, Lord Morel. In fact, I was just about to gather my absurd bits of lore and be gone from your house."

Kall leaned against the doorframe. "I don't recall asking you to leave. Could be my mind is slipping. We Morels are famous for our scattered wits, you know."

"As it happens, I do," Dantane said. "No, you haven't asked me to leave, but judging from the fact that you've avoided my requests for an audience since you came here, I'm assuming my eviction cannot be far off."

Kall shrugged. "You may be right. Earlier today, I was going to throw you out without a conversation, but I changed my mind."

"What brought about that bit of charity?"

"I have questions about my father."

Dantane gathered his robes about him, perching on the edge of the table. "Ask."

"When did you come to him?"

"Deepwinter. I was traveling through the city and ran into a bit of trouble."

"What kind of trouble?"

Dantane looked irritated. "The kind that comes when ignorance is allowed too free a rein."

Kall smirked. "Amnians are quite vocal about their wizard-hatred, aren't they?" he said.

"Your father was able to intervene on my behalf, although why he took the trouble—"

"Is the mystery I'm most concerned with," Kall interrupted.

"My father hated magic more actively than most."

"So he took great pains to explain to me. Yet, he claimed a greater need drove him to hire me. He suspected someone close was using magic against him. He wished me to find the source."

Now Kall listened intently. "Did you?"

Dantane pushed away from the table. He strode to a locked cupboard in the corner and murmured something. A door creaked open, and Dantane reached inside, withdrawing an object that was unfamiliar to Kall: an ornate silver brooch set with a square, thumb-sized amethyst. "I removed this from your father's person, though its magic was already drained to nothing."

"What is it?"

"Exactly what it appears, but your father's blood is on the pin. That blood bore traces of a subtle mind-altering magic. I've seen similar pieces before. The spells make a person extremely susceptible to suggestion, but only from those they trust—friends or family. For instance, if the lady of the house doesn't approve of the way her husband is using the family finances, instead of throwing a fuss, she can use this to influence him in new directions."

"But the lord would be unaffected in business dealings with enemies and rivals?" Kall asked.

"Precisely. Tailored to fit any Amnian merchant, wouldn't you say?"

"Indeed." So that was it, Kall thought. Magic had tainted his father's blood. "How did my father discover the spells affecting him?"

"He may have noticed when one or both elements of the enchantment began to break down," Dantane said, "the spells . . . and his own mind."

Kall nodded. It made sense. Over time, the enchantment had slowly destroyed his father's sanity. He'd seen it that night in the garden. "When my father hired you, was he . . ."

"Lucid?" Dantane smiled sardonically. "He had stretches,

long enough to keep his business scraping by. I could prolong some of them, with magic. Do you have any other inquiries, Lord Morel?" he asked impatiently, "or may I go?"

Kall considered the man. He knew what Cesira would say if she were here. Dantane was young, tidy with his speech and possessions, but with an unkempt air about his person. His dark hair was too long and shaggy, his eyes perpetually jumpy and fatigued. And he was hungry, Kall thought. He'd watched the wizard poring over his books. The man was too eager for magic to have come willingly to a land so bereft of it. Kall had no doubt there was more to his reason for being here, but whether it had anything to do with the Morel family was what he needed to know.

He knew what Cesira would say. Cesira would send Dantane away without hesitation.

"I want you to watch the party," Kall said, surprising them both.

Dantane raised an eyebrow. "Watch it for what?"

Kall had no idea. "I have no mercenaries, no guards employed to see to the security of the house. You can act in that capacity."

Dantane hesitated. "Lord Morel, you claim a powerful druid as your companion—"

"Yes, but she's fairly intractable . . ."

"—so I fail to see what added benefit I can be."

"You're saying you don't want to continue to receive the impressive mound of coin my father paid?"

"I've seen your guest list, Lord Morel. It more resembles a creditor account. How long will you be able to retain my services once this evening's *festivities* are concluded?"

Kall had no notion of that either. "Start with the party. We'll go from there." On the heels of one problem settled, another occurred to Kall. He took out his mother's pouch, held the strings, then tossed the pouch to Dantane.

The wizard caught it, a puzzled frown crossing his face. "What's this?"

"A task for after the party," Kall said. "Search its contents for any dangerous magic." He still didn't completely trust Meisha.

"And if I find some?" Dantane asked.

Kall paused at the top of the stairs. "Destroy it."

———◆————◆————◆———

Later, Kall sat at his father's desk, his arms folded behind his head as he listened to the muffled sounds of the party going on outside the study. He was still sitting when the door opened, and Lord Marstil Greve stepped inside.

Lord Greve was a handsome man just entering middle years, but his muscles had begun to soften. He wore a jeweled knife at his belt, inset with two gems—one a ruby in a nest of gold, the other a glimmering emerald.

"Lord Morel? I believe we had an appointment," said Marstil.

"My apologies, Lord Greve," Kall said, coming around the desk to offer his hand. "My mind was consumed by other thoughts—old memories."

The merchant nodded. "Understandable. It must be strange to come home after so long an absence. My sympathies on your father's death, he was—"

"Suicide," Kall corrected.

Marstil blinked. "I beg your pardon?"

"My father took his own life," Kall repeated pleasantly. "In this study, as a matter of fact."

Marstil appeared extremely uncomfortable. "I hope you don't mind my speaking with you privately, Lord Morel . . . and speaking plainly," he added, watching Kall's face.

"Not at all."

"Being newly arrived in Keczulla, I'm sure you're unaware that among the merchants of the city, my family is growing in prominence, though we do not have the history associated with the Tanisloves, the Bladesmiles . . . or the Morels." Marstil paused, waiting for Kall to comment. When he was met by bland silence, he continued, "Yet, I have been given to understand that the house of Morel has suffered from . . ." he paused again, and Kall almost smiled. Marstil was searching for a delicate way to say that Morel was a coin toss away from destitution.

Kall saved him the trouble. "Morel would be foolish to ignore an offer of alliance, should it be extended," he said, and Marstil immediately relaxed. "Since we're speaking plainly, I confess my circumstances are such that I'm finding it difficult to pay the daily expenses of a house of Morel's stature, even so far as to be unable to pay the servants' wages or—" he stopped, as if afraid he'd said too much.

"How unfortunate." Marstil's eyes gleamed. He knew he would have the upper hand in their negotiations. "The outcome of this meeting will greatly affect us both, then."

"Oh, I'm certain of it," Kall said. He poured a pair of drinks from a decanter on his desk. He handed one to Marstil. "Of course, it hasn't been terribly difficult to get by, considering my circumstances. Few servants remained at Morel house, even during my father's time. They were all slaughtered by assassins, you see."

The glass stopped halfway to the merchant's mouth. Amber liquid sloshed on his fingers.

"Oh, excuse me, my lord," said Kall. "I filled the glass too full. Allow me to fetch you a towel."

"Yes, thank you," Marstil murmured.

Kall opened a drawer in the desk. He tossed a black cloth to Marstil. The merchant caught it absently, and was wiping his fingers before he realized what he held. He unrolled the silk hood and let it fall between his hands, revealing two crudely cut eyeholes.

"It's not the original, I realize," said Kall. "But it matches my memories closely. What do you think, Lord Greve?"

Marstil dropped the mask and spun toward Kall in one lightning movement. His arm came around, taking the decanter off the desk. Kall dodged, and glass shattered against the wall. Marstil went for the knife at his belt, but Kall locked a hand around his wrist.

"Did you think I wouldn't find you?" he asked, his pleasant tone unchanged. "That I wouldn't know you as soon as I saw your blade? You're a fool, Marstil, a dead fool."

Marstil struggled, but he'd spent too many years away from hard fighting, and Kall was no longer a stripling boy. He held the man without breaking a sweat.

Kall eased the knife from Marstil's sheath and laid it against the merchant's throat, starting at the ear.

"Shall I give you the same death you gave her?" Kall asked. He waited for the man to answer, to plead, but saw only fear and confusion in Marstil's eyes. The bastard didn't even remember the ones he'd killed. "Gertie never saw her death coming, but you will. I'll savor that time, and the pain, until I'm ready to let you go, unless you tell me where Balram is."

"I-I have no idea." Marstil's eyes flicked to the mask and back to Kall's face. There was no lie in them, only terror. "Kortrun and I parted company long ago, when I set out to build my business. Please . . . listen," he said. "I h-have not been Balram's man . . . in years," he stammered, swallowing against the steel at his throat. "I am a merchant now. I've made a family."

"A family," Kall echoed. "Oh, dear. That's the death card, is it? Now I'm required to have mercy." He leaned in close to the man's face. "Tell me, Marstil, do your wife and children know how their father earned his fortune? Do they realize the manse they sleep in at night was paid for with Morel blood? If I tell them that, after I've killed you, do you think they'll forgive me? I like to believe they will." Kall pressed down, and Marstil shrieked. "What else have you got to offer me, Marstil? Please, don't mention your *family* to me again."

"All that I have!" The merchant trembled as a drop of blood ran down the knife's blade into his field of vision. "Whatever you want!"

Slowly, Kall eased the knife away and lifted something in front of Marstil's eyes.

The merchant focused on Gertie's gold medallion, flecked with old blood. "Wh-what is that?"

"The symbol of our new alliance," Kall answered, putting the chain around Marstil's neck. "Your commitment to the service of Morel. The house of Greve is now the benefactor of Morel's servants. They will be paid generously from its coffers, for the whole of their lives, whether they stay with Morel or not, whether the house thrives or burns to the ground. And upon their deaths, every guard, maid, cook, and steward will be buried with the highest honor at Greve's expense. It's not so large a thing to ask, in exchange for your life. Don't you agree?"

Marstil nodded wordlessly.

"Most importantly, you will wear this medallion always, Marstil," Kall said, in a voice of quiet menace. "If ever I see you've taken it off, I will take off your head. You may be assured I will enjoy that far more than I enjoy letting you live."

He stepped back. Marstil fled the study, taking Lathander's sun and leaving his jeweled blade.

Kall followed him out into the ballroom. A lady standing nearby scuttled aside to avoid colliding with the running merchant. She watched his retreating back in consternation.

Kall swept up to her and bowed grandly. "Lady Tanislove," he said, smiling his most charming smile, the one that never worked on Cesira, "might I request a dance?"

———◆———

"Try this one," Laerin suggested, snagging a flute of a bruise-colored liquid from a passing tray. "If you sip it with a bite of cheese, the flavor becomes blueberry tart." He sipped and chewed thoughtfully. "Uncanny."

Morgan wedged a morsel of cheese between his cheek and jaw and took a gulp of wine. "Save a lot of trouble if you just eat the tart." He wrinkled his nose. "Probably tastes better, too."

"Yes, but you have to get in the spirit of things," Laerin chided him. "Tethyrian Blueberry Blush is much more expensive."

"Silly name too." Morgan's eyes were on the crowd. "Didn't know you were a wine snob."

"I am a man of many tastes and talents."

"Good thing shovelin's near the top of the list, 'cause you're knee-deep in sh—"

"Zzar," Laerin cooed, reaching for another tray.

"Careful!" Morgan grabbed a fistful of the half-elf's hair, hauling it and the rest of his friend behind one of the ballroom's marble statues.

"Morgan, why are we hiding, and do I happen to have any hair left, or did you take it all?" Laerin asked calmly.

"Shut it." Morgan pointed across the ballroom, where Kall strode along on the arm of a lady in a green silk gown with fine silver chains encircling her arms from shoulder to wrist. The woman lifted her lips to Kall's ear to whisper something that made him chuckle.

Morgan shook his head. "That'll get him a punch in the bowels—two silver on it."

Laerin sighed. "Cesira would never maim him for flirting with Lhynvor Tanislove. The lady has more sense than that."

Well said. Cesira's arm slid companionably around Laerin's waist, accompanied by a scent that was both flower and herb, exotic and completely removed from the heavily perfumed bodies in the ballroom. *I don't believe you flattering idiots were on the guest list.*

"Ten families seemed a modest number for a welcome home party," said Laerin. "What harm is there in adding two more guests?"

"We didn't come in under 'flattering idiots,' " Morgan grinned. "We're in disguise."

"Obviously, it's working well," Laerin said dryly, but he sobered quickly enough. "We're here to keep eyes on Kall."

"Too many debt-collectors in the room," said Morgan.

Laerin looked at her askance. "Surely you don't object?"

Not at all, Cesira said. *But Kall will—with fervor. I welcome you, so long as you stay silent and invisible.*

"Not two of Morgan's greater talents, but we'll do our best," Laerin assured her. He took a step back, surveying the druid's gown. A wide belt at her waist gathered layers of skirts in subtle shades of earthen red. Worked into the belt's dark leather was the figure of an oak leaf, the symbol of Silvanus. Slashed sleeves revealed tanned arms and matching leather bands encircling each of her wrists. "I'll say this, since I'm certain Kall hasn't thought to," the half-elf said, "these fine Amnian frill-lovers have nothing on you, Lady of Mir."

Cesira inclined her head to hide her smile. *My thanks, O flattering idiot.*

Laerin laughed. "How fares the Lady Morel?"

Her eyes on the swirling crowd, Cesira did not immediately reply. Hired minstrels—she had no idea where Kall had found them—had begun a circle dance, which had drawn many of the guests from the balcony to line up in colorful half-moons across the floor. They were all smiles and good-natured jesting on the surface, but Cesira knew why the merchants were here. They wanted to see if Kall could hold his own among them.

Everything in Amn was a test, a measurement of investment and potential gain. If Kall's manner and surroundings showed promise, the merchant families would give him time to pay the debts of his father. That's why Cesira had agreed to serve in the role of the lady of the house, however much it galled her. She had no intention of letting the wolves eat Kall alive.

She'd directed the servants in gutting and cleaning the house with the same thoroughness she displayed when scourging an army of goblins. The results may not have rivaled the Tanislove estate, but there would be no chink in Morel's armor from this front.

Have you watched them? she asked, nodding to the dancing throng.

"Glaring peacocks, the lot," Morgan said dismissively.

"No." Laerin shook his head. "She means the merchant families."

"What of 'em?"

"They announced them at the door, each according to his station," said Laerin. "I watched them separate immediately, almost as if they couldn't stand to be in each other's company."

Morgan nodded sagely. "Reminds me of my family."

"It's what they prefer you to think. Look." Laerin pointed with his glass to a group of women gathered near the staircase. Their ornate turbans shimmered with glitter dust and bobbed together like a star storm with the force of the women's back and forth whispering. "The younger lass, standing at the edge of the crowd—she's Seyana Veshpel, a niece of Lord Uskan Veshpel—patriarch of his house. I saw her announced last in her family. See how she's treated as such?"

Yet that youngest Veshpel, said Cesira, *so innocently lingering at the edge of the group, stands less than a whip crack from her father, and he from his wife, and she from—*

"Lord Uskan," Morgan said, seeing the pattern emerge.

"So it goes with every family," said Laerin. "A living chain to see and hear everything in the room. Whatever their personal rivalries, good business benefits the whole family."

"Forced loyalty," Morgan muttered, shaking his head. "One of Morel's fine emeralds says in private they're one wrong word from slaughtering each other." He raised a fist, showing three of the Morel emerald and stone symbols between his fingers.

"Where did you pick those up?" asked Laerin, affronted. "I only received one."

Cesira rolled her eyes. *As did everyone at the party,* she said.

"Oh, wait, here's another," Laerin added. He smirked, drawing a handful of glittering green from his pouch.

Wonderful, Cesira muttered. *Now, would you care to point out which ladies you lifted them from, or shall I wait until one of them gives me a look of horror when I try to speak to her?*

Morgan pointed to a woman whose dress was a configuration of red silk scarves fastened in her hair and looping outwards, wrapping down around all the vital portions of her lithe body. "She was definitely one of them."

Thank you, the druid sighed. *I think I can divine the others on my own.*

Cesira slipped away to join Kall just as Lady Tanislove left him.

He's here—Lord Rays, she told him. *He arrived while you were with Marstil.*

"Is he still coherent?"

Barely.

"Wonderful. He'll be much more open to my proposal."

Cesira tapped a slender finger against her chin. *Now, would that be another business venture, my lord, or the systematic murder of Bladesmile mercenaries? I do get the two confused, you know.*

"The latter," Kall said dryly, "but I only intend to murder the ones who prove uncooperative."

You still think one of them will be able to lead you to Balram?

"Somebody knows," said Kall darkly.

As he started to walk away, Cesira took his arm. *Relax, Kall,* she said. *The Morel name demands the merchants treat you as an equal, no matter the breadth of your debt. You have the manner and skills to fit in their world.*

For some reason, the compliment made Kall wince. "What little talent I have comes from my father, and his father before." He grinned. "I'd rather you praised me on my skill with a sword, which you rarely do."

Oh, but I disagree. You make a fine adventurer—a talent inherited from your mother, no doubt, Cesira remarked lightly, waving and smiling at a lady across the room.

Kall sighed, thinking it wiser to ignore the path the conversation was taking. "Where is Rays?"

Cesira pointed across the ballroom to where a man swayed drunkenly against one of the marble statues. He used the brief loss of dignity to make lewd pantomimes with the statue and his body, much to the horror of a group of passing ladies.

The Bladesmiles are among the most powerful and respected

families in Keczulla and greater Amn. Why does this one play the fool? Cesira asked absently.

"His wife died," Kall said, drawing the druid's gaze and a noise of sympathy. "A year ago. He cares nothing for status and position now."

Then perhaps Lord Rays has more wisdom than us all. Cesira watched Kall cross the ballroom, weaving purposely among his guests, on to the next stage of his plan.

Suddenly uneasy and feeling eyes upon her, Cesira looked up at the balcony and met the clear blue gaze of Syrek Dantane.

CHAPTER EIGHTEEN

Keczulla, Amn
3 Marpenoth, the Year of Lightning Storms (1374 DR)

Dantane inclined his head respectfully to the druid. Her eyes registered surprise, but she concealed it quickly.

So Morel hadn't told her he was here. Dantane wondered why. If Morel distrusted him so thoroughly, wouldn't he wish to have the eyes of those he did trust tracking him constantly?

The wizard took a step toward the stairs, when the hairs on the back of his neck stood on end as silent magical wards hummed. The spell was not powerful, but the relative lack of magic in the room made it seem stronger—akin to tolling a bell in a tomb. Had this been a gala in Waterdeep, the resonant hum would have been lost in the greater cacophony of minor cantrips and protective spells.

Dantane looked to the dais. A young woman had stepped forward with a lute. She sang in a deep, pleasing alto, an unremarkable song, but she livened up the show by pausing in the middle of a verse to tell bawdy jokes or humorous stories, always deftly picking up the tune exactly where she'd left off. The crowd gathered, laughing, at the edge of the dais to listen.

Dantane's eyes fixed on the lute. The bard's instrument, or something inside it, was the source of the magic—an illusion, possibly glamour to conceal some defect on the part of the singer. Dantane scanned the crowd for Morel, wondering if he should inform the young lord.

When Dantane spied him, Kall was still speaking to the drunken man. The wizard headed for the stairs, but halted when he saw Kall's face blanch. Dantane traced the room, seeking a threat, but Morel simply stood, as frozen as one of the statues, staring at a spot beneath the balcony. He said something to the drunkard and stepped away.

Fascinated, Dantane watched him walk across the ballroom like a man caught sleepwalking out of a dream. Whatever Morel saw disturbed him greatly, Dantane thought. He couldn't describe all the emotions that passed over Kall's face, but the still, ravaged look, the vulnerability—that interested Dantane, so much so he forgot the lute player and her song.

"Seven—there it is!" The serving table quivered as Morgan slammed his handful of emerald-stone clusters in front of Laerin. "That you can't beat."

The half-elf flashed him a lazy smile. "Darling, must we compete? It's unseemly."

Morgan turned purple, clenching his fists as if he might cram the stones down Laerin's throat. "Empty your pockets. Turn 'em out, or by the gods I'll do it for you!"

Laerin fluttered his lashes. "Now you're just being saucy."

Morgan took a step forward, reaching for a weapon.

"Oh, all right." The half-elf sighed and emptied a pouch of stones next to Morgan's pile.

"Only six!" Morgan spouted triumphantly, as Cesira looked on with an expression of helpless bemusement.

Laerin raised a hand to either side of Morgan's head, and with a flourish produced two more stones from the man's hairy ears. "Your pardon," the half-elf said.

Morgan swatted his hands away, fuming. "Pretty-faced whore's brat—"

Quiet! Cesira hissed. *Hide yourselves. Kall is . . .* As she looked, she realized Kall wasn't headed their way. He'd stopped, frozen next to the drunken Bladesmile. At first Cesira thought he was listening to the bard, but then she saw him staring at something through the crowd.

I've never seen that look, she murmured. She traced Kall's stunned gaze across the room to a corner, where a man stood leaning sedately against a marble column. He ignored the rest of the room, and appeared to be listening intently to the lute player. Broken from whatever spell had smote him, Kall began walking directly toward the man.

"I've seen it," Laerin spoke up, a frown creasing his smooth forehead. "When I first met Kall, he had the same look."

Morgan nodded agreement. "Like he just lost his best friend."

Cesira paled, gripping Laerin's arm. *Aazen,* she whispered.

"Greetings, Lord Morel," said Aazen, as Kall came to stand between him and the dais. He offered Kall one of his rare, genuine smiles. "It is good to see you again."

Kall was at a loss. The man before him was older—and leaner, if possible—than the boy who'd been his best friend. His dark hair was short and shaved. He dressed in black leathers with a cloak of silky midnight blue thrown over one shoulder. The armor was stained, but the cloak pristine—a halfhearted attempt to blend with the throng. Despite the changes, he was still Aazen—a quiet, shadowed young man. Kall had imagined many fates befalling his best friend in the years since their last meeting, but seeing the man grown, greeting him here in his father's house, had never been among them.

When Kall remained silent, Aazen said, "You don't recognize me? I can't blame you. It's been a long while since we spoke."

"Aazen," Kall said, recovering himself. "You haven't changed so much. You were always more adult than child."

Aazen considered. "Yes, I suppose you're right. Are you well, Kall?"

"Well enough, but more than a little shocked to see you here."

"You've been looking for me?"

"Ever since I returned," said Kall.

"Most of Amn thought you dead," Aazen said. "But I doubted it."

Kall grunted. "Thanks. You had more confidence than I did, considering the condition I was in when we parted."

"Yet here you stand, in your house reclaimed."

"Such as it is. Aazen, you know I'm after Balram," said Kall bluntly.

"Of course. I'd be disappointed if you weren't, especially after that passionate speech you gave at our last meeting," said Aazen sardonically. "Have you enjoyed any success in your search?"

"You know I haven't."

"Unfortunately, I don't. My father and I parted company some time ago."

"Oh?" Kall didn't bother to hide his disbelief. "When you left, you seemed bent on staying by his side, in spite of everything. 'Don't come after him,' you said. 'I'll have to kill you, if you do.' "

"I was a child. I didn't know what I wanted." Aazen searched his eyes. "Can you grant me that, Kall? Can you believe I may have found other companions, as you have, or do you think I'll say anything to protect him?"

"I don't know," Kall said. "But I never held any hope or desire to get at Balram through you. I only prayed he hadn't killed you."

"But think, if you'd found me dead, you would have had yet another reason to slay him."

Kall didn't comment. There was too much tension in the room already. "If you can stay long enough, I'd like to introduce you to my companions," he said, changing the subject.

"I've heard many whispers about the beauty of the Lady Morel," said Aazen. "You've done well for yourself, even without my constant looking after you."

"Yes, Cesira is a beauty, and were she mine, I'm sure my manhood would be subjugated to her will within a tenday," Kall said, laughing. "Luckily for me, her affections are not settled on me."

"Aren't they?" Aazen seemed surprised. "Then why—"

"She's playing the part of my wife until affairs here settle down," Kall explained. "Two other friends are looking out for my physical well-being. I'm sure we can find them if we look. They haven't managed to conceal themselves all evening—I don't see why they should start now."

A terrific crash from the dais had both men turning, their hands straying to their sword hilts in a mirrored gesture. The lute player had apparently decided to finish her tune with a flourish, smashing her instrument against the floor. The startled crowd backed away as she crouched to gather the broken bits.

"Lovely," Kall murmured. "The musicians have obviously taken more than their share of spirits for the evening. Excuse me, old friend."

The crowd blocked his path, but Kall could see the woman clearly. She knelt in the center of the stage, cradling a mass of what appeared to be mud and protruding roots that she'd hidden inside the lute. Her gaze was feverishly bright as she stared at the mass.

A wave of trepidation swept over Kall. He was no wizard, but he knew the effects of mind magic all too well. He pushed through the crowd, shouting, "Everyone, stand back! Dantane!"

Shocked gasps rang out as the woman began shoveling the strange mass into her mouth. She swallowed and immediately began to choke, the mass lodging grotesquely in her throat.

Black veins speared out beneath her skin, spreading from her windpipe to her shoulders and up her face. Her tan skin bulged, turning purple-black as her head lolled to one side.

A woman in the crowd screamed and fainted. People tripped and fell over her in their rush to get away. Kall found a gap and jumped onto the dais, his sword raised.

"Laerin!" he shouted.

The half-elf appeared below him, lifting the senseless guest over his shoulder. Morgan stood across the room, herding the crowd to the exit. "We'll get 'em out," Morgan assured Kall. "Cesira's coming."

"Find Dantane!" Kall's gaze remained fixed on the grim transformation unfolding on the dais.

The lute player's flesh rippled and shimmered like a heat mirage, her form lengthening and filling out into that of a young man with shoulder-length brown hair and finely tailored clothing. Kall could not tell his identity, for the black blemish remained on his face and continued to spread, exploding up from the flesh of his arms, legs, and torso as boils and bleeding wounds. He seemed to be filling up everywhere, and the strange, oozing black substance had nowhere to go but through his skin and vital organs.

The thing that had been human lurched up to its legs and swiped with a too-long arm at Kall's face. Kall raised his sword and felt the blade sink into the ooze. The creature howled and pulled back, leaving a trail of black gore that sizzled into the wooden platform.

"*Tarshz mephran!*" came a shout from the balcony, and a spray of electricity yanked the hairs on Kall's arms. Bolts of energy ripped into the creature, spraying black blood in all directions.

Kall jumped back, cursing as drops hit his exposed arm and burned.

Dantane climbed onto the balcony rail and floated to the ballroom floor, his robes flaring at the sleeves as his hands shaped another spell. He aimed the Art directly over Kall's head at the creature. Kall dived behind a harpsichord, pulling its heavy bench over onto its side as a shield when the spell erupted.

Bolts of ice burrowed from Dantane's palms, then streaked across the room to impale the oozing mass. Gore sprayed the bench, burning black pockmarks into the wood.

Kall rolled to his feet behind the creature. He hacked at it, the emerald sword finding flesh that was human and monster and sometimes a bizarre hybrid. The blade penetrated, and what was left of the lute player's voice rang out in screeches of pure agony.

A tentacled arm whipped out from where the woman's stomach had been, catching Kall in the midsection. The blow threw Kall back; he smelled melted leather. He fumbled at his armor buckles, flinching when he felt hands come around him from behind. Fingers pressed flush against the acidic burning.

"Get back!" roared Kall when he recognized Cesira's chanting voice. Damn her, the last thing he wanted was for her to be acid-seared while protecting him.

Steam rose in a cloud, hissing and stinging Kall's eyes, but the burning sensation eased. The druid touched the base of his neck, and Kall felt a faint, humming tingle spread across his skin. It lingered in his ears like the last thrum of a fading song. Silently, Cesira drew away to stand beside him.

You'll have protection from the acid, she told him, *for a time.* She cocked her head, listening to Dantane's chants, watching the measured release of power. *Go now!*

Trusting her, Kall charged in under another rain of bolts, but they seemed targeted only to the creature and sailed harmlessly around him. Tentacles burst at random from the creature's hips and groin—Kall hacked them off, forming a buffer for Dantane and Cesira.

"Kall!" Dantane's voice was thick with magic. "The root in its throat—carve it out. Destroy it!"

Kall risked a glance at the throng retreating from the ballroom. A few stragglers had stayed behind—Lord Rays among them—to watch the horrific spectacle.

Kall yelled to Cesira. "Don't let them see!" The last thing he wanted was for the merchants to witness him butchering the girl, even if she no longer resembled anything human. He waded into the mass of tentacles as the druid backed down the dais's steps, chanting a familiar spell and arching her arms above her head.

The air immediately grew thick and moist. Dense fog billowed from the portal of Cesira's arms, curling around the dais in a concealing bubble that hid Kall, Dantane, and the creature from view.

Behind the vapor wall, Kall wedged his sword in the harpsichord bench and grabbed blindly at the creature with his gloved hands, trusting Cesira's protective spell to hold long enough for him to finish his grim task. He punched into the thing's mouth and felt teeth and tongue give way with a wet crunch.

Kall fought down a rush of bile. Whatever shape it took now, the thing still had a woman's head, and Kall had just rendered it a ruin. Steeling himself, he bore down, ignoring the choking and mewling sounds coming from the monster. When his hand met an obstruction, Kall didn't allow himself to think. He yanked the mass of mud and root straight up.

The creature's head disintegrated around his arm. Kall lurched backward, hurling the root ball across the dais. It landed, writhing, at Dantane's boots.

"Kill it," Kall growled.

Dantane wavered. His eyes followed the movements of the dozens of tendrils branching off the mass, each quivering with something arcane.

"Dantane!" Kall shouted.

The wizard flinched, stirred from his trance. He pointed to the mass and muttered something. Flames erupted from the root ball, consuming it in a flash of blue light and searing heat. Dantane raised his sleeve against the glare and stink. "Done," he said.

Kall strode to the bench, yanked his sword free, and kept moving until the point threatened to slice Dantane's nose in half. "If not for Cesira, I'd be smoking on the floor next to that thing. Mind telling me why you tried to get me killed?"

Breathing heavily, Dantane matched the furious lord's stare.

"I was fighting to prevent the creature from tearing your guests apart. If you've a problem with my methods—"

Kall interrupted, "You've as well as told the whole of Keczulla I'm hiding a wizard under my skirts!"

Dantane hesitated. Something that might have been chagrin came and went across his sweat-soaked face. "I'm not accustomed to fighting under these circumstances," he stammered. "As to the rest"—his white lips thinned—"had I intended you harm, Lord Morel, rest assured, your head would now be in as many pieces as that unfortunate creature."

Kall's grip on his sword tightened, but Dantane didn't back down. "Perhaps you would like me to discern the woman's—or man's—identity?" The wizard's voice sounded smug. "It might prove useful, even vital, to have such information at hand when the Gem Guard come calling about this incident."

From somewhere outside the fog, Morgan's voice rumbled, "Two red inks say he skewers him."

"No bet, I can't see his face," was Laerin's reply.

Kall lingered over the raised steel a moment longer. Abruptly, he sheathed his sword, his eyes still spearing Dantane with hostility. He kicked at the harpsichord bench and jumped off the dais.

The stragglers had gone. Aazen had gone. Kall hadn't seen him leave with the crowd. "Close off the estate," he ordered the servants who'd dared remain within earshot. "Let no one back in except the guard, whenever they turn up." He had no doubt they would. Dantane was right, damn the man again. He had to find out who the lute player was and why she—or he—had turned up at the party with deadly magic.

Could it have been one of the families, attempting to strike at him? It seemed ludicrous, considering their aversion to magic and the rumors flying all evening about his generous-bordering-on-desperate attempts to make restitution among the merchants.

Attempts that might come to nothing after tonight, Kall thought. Fury spiked through him. Amn's retribution for magic use, especially magic that murdered, was second only to the collection of debts among the merchant families. He was about to be buried deep in trouble of both sorts.

CHAPTER NINETEEN

The Howling Delve
4 Marpenoth, the Year of Lightning Storms (1374 DR)

"This was a great idea," Talal said sarcastically as he held the torch around Meisha's body.

The Harper turned, flames catching in her eyes. Talal flinched. "Are you really going to walk at my heel with that thing, or can I carry it?"

"My torch, Lady," Talal said, holding it out of reach.

"Then would you care to lead?" She pointed down the dark, unfamiliar passage.

"I'd care to go back to the warrens!" he complained, handing her the brand. "I showed you the wizard. Haroun says that's enough, and she doesn't even know he tried to kill you."

"You told me your people explore these caves constantly, looking for ways to escape."

"I told you we draw lots for the pleasure," Talal argued. "Stain one stone with berry juice, put the rest in a sack, and choose. Tymora's lucky whipping boy gets a torch, a weapon, and a trip down the tunnel to have his wits smashed all over the place. That's what happened to Gadi."

"He was killed?" Meisha shone the torch down a side passage and listened. She heard nothing but the distant, constant drip of water. When she'd lived here, Varan had always made his apprentices safe, no matter how dangerous the Delve could be. Now the apprentices were dead, and Varan . . .

Meisha suppressed a shudder. Varan had become one of the threats in the dark.

"Smashed, I said. By whatever roams the tunnels outside your wizard's shields," said Talal.

"Varan warned us not to venture outside the wards. Even I don't know what lies at the end of many of these tunnels," Meisha admitted. "You say you've sent someone out already?"

"Braedrin," Talal said, nodding. "Hasn't come back yet. Smash," he murmured under his breath.

"What are these marks?" Meisha pointed to the walls.

"Tells us where people have been," Talal explained. "Means no traps, either."

"Traps," Meisha echoed. A mask of blood and a dead apprentice's face flashed before her eyes.

"Don't know who strung 'em, but they're all over the place. We lost two that way when we first started going out. Pressure spears. Hit you square, one'll take your head clean off. More of Lady Luck's favor, the well-meaning bitch."

Meisha raised an eyebrow. "You've a ready insult for all the gods. Which one do you actually like?"

The boy shrugged, dislodging a scuttling beetle from his clothing. "None of them—easier that way."

"You don't believe in the gods?"

"Believe, yes. But I leave them be, and I wish they'd return the favor." He flicked away the beetle. "Not so much to ask."

"What about after this life? Don't you worry for your soul?"

"Hells, no. I'm aiming to live forever. See how I avoid prancing down dark tunnels with death-seeking sorcerers? I get along fine, Lady; it's the rest of Faerûn that wants to muck me up."

"How many of you are there in the warrens?" Meisha asked, shifting the topic.

The boy spent a moment figuring. "Thirty-eight. We took count of everyone, after the first death, so we'd know names. Forty-nine came into the caves, not counting that bastard Balram and his son."

Meisha stopped short. "The man who trapped you here was Balram?"

"Him and his son, Aazen—not so twitchy as his father, but quiet, scary quiet," Talal said. "Never said more than a few words to any of us."

Aazen. She remembered the name from the cave. The leader who'd stabbed her was *Balram's* son. Meisha tried to take it all in. She pressed her hand against the crystal hidden in her jerkin. She'd almost forgotten it, but now its presence in the hands of Balram's man made perfect, terrible sense.

"I never knew there was a son," Meisha said. "I only knew Kortrun."

Talal's eyes widened. "You *knew* 'em?"

"I've been searching for Balram Kortrun on behalf of a friend." Meisha resumed walking, and after a moment Talal ran to catch up. "They were refugees with you?" Meisha asked.

"We fled Esmeltaran together," said Talal. "When we took up here, Balram—like I said, he was always twitchy—didn't like the Delve or the crazy wizard. We couldn't figure out why he kept going back to the wizard's room, though, if he was so afraid. He'd come out some nights, looking almost sick with whatever he'd seen. Finally, he took his son, said he'd go for help to Keczulla. We all thought he was crazy, but we let him go. No one said so, but we hoped they might make it. We were too damn scared to go with them." Talal stared off into the darkness, thinking. "I guess we're paying for that, too. If we hadn't been cowards, we wouldn't still be here. If we'd've woken up and seen how it wasn't the wizard but the wizard's toys he was interested in . . ."

"But they *did* make it to Keczulla," Meisha prompted.

"And came back with the Shadow Thieves. What a rescue," said Talal sourly. "They made us take the wizard's toys from his room while he slept, then they sealed the entrance to the Delve, trapped us inside. Told us if we took care of the old man, let him be to make his magic toys, they'd come back to collect them. When they came, they'd bring food—meat to butcher, chickens for eggs—clothing, maybe some weapons, if we didn't try to escape—everything we'd need to live."

"So you care for Varan, keep him fed and strong enough to make magic items, and in exchange they give you this existence." Meisha marveled at the complexity of the system, but in reality, the risks and costs to the Shadow Thieves were minimal. What was feeding forty people when compared to the worth of magic weapons, amulets, rings . . . whatever Varan could conceive of in his current state? "You're certain it's the Shadow Thieves?"

"They didn't bother hiding it," Talal said. "We didn't know how they even got in at first, until Gadi tracked them to the doorways. We tried to work them. Gadi said they used some type of key that wasn't a key—he got close enough to see that much."

"Gadi was very brave," Meisha observed.

"My brother." Pride swelled in Talal's eyes, and Meisha's heart twisted. "Runs in the family: brave, stupid—pick one."

They entered a large chamber. Meisha shone the torch high, but the light refused to penetrate to the ceiling.

"I'm going to cast a spell," Meisha said. When Talal didn't answer, she looked at him questioningly. "Is that a problem?"

"No, just . . . not used to being asked, is all." Talal barked a laugh, but Meisha could sense the unease behind his bravado.

"I'll try to be gentle." Meisha lowered the torch, fisting her hands into the flames. *"Mephhisden,"* she hissed.

Fire wound languidly around her fingers and upward into a narrow, twisting column, a length of hemp weaving itself from the air currents. Near the ceiling, it tapered off to a needle point of fire that illuminated the cavern's ceiling and the corpse impaled upon one of the stalactites. Its arms and legs dangled in a spiderlike pose above their heads.

"Braedrin," Talal murmured, recognizing the man's vacant stare. "Pinned, not smashed," he corrected himself.

Meisha wedged the torch between two close stones. The column of fire sparked and twisted, illuminating a pair of over-large shadows with long, triangular tails hovering around the body. "Dragazhars," Meisha said, watching them scatter from the light. "Watch your head."

Talal immediately dropped into a crab crouch, his eyes on the leathery cloaks of the deep bats—night hunters, Meisha noted—which billowed out like dark sails a full seven feet across the cavern's ceiling.

Talal shuddered. "They wasn't what stuck him on that spear."

"No," Meisha agreed. "I'd have to see the body up close to know what killed him."

Unexpectedly, Talal said. "I can get it down."

"The walls are sheer," Meisha pointed out. "Unless you have rope hidden somewhere under that mainsail of a garment . . ."

In answer, Talal pulled a balled up object from under his shirt. Meisha recognized the waterskin the halfling had used and discarded when the Shadow Thieves escaped through the portal. Talal had twisted and flattened the bladder until a small bulge of the magical substance had collected around the mouth. "I've been waiting to try this," Talal said.

Meisha blinked at him. "What about the bats? A moment ago you were terrified of them."

"You'll kill them if they come near me." Talal glanced up from smearing his dirty toes. He appeared hopeful. "Won't you?"

Meisha eyed the floating bats, calculating. "If you insist," she said finally.

Talal stood, balancing on his heels. He trotted clumsily to the cavern wall and placed his bare palms on the stone. He shifted his weight, drawing himself up to his toes and holding the position until he was satisfied the substance would support his weight. Grunting, he hauled himself up the sheer stone wall, moving much faster than the halfling and his comrades had dared.

Meisha kept her eyes on the night hunters as Talal scuttled across the ceiling to the body. He stopped and freed his arms to dangle upside down, using his swinging momentum to carry him to the stalactite. He grabbed the stone tip protruding through the unfortunate Braedrin's chest and hung on with one hand. The other he positioned at the man's back and pushed, grimacing as the corpse slid off the stone into the crook of his arm.

The weight was too much, even for the magic. Reluctantly, Talal let the body fall away into space. Braedrin hit the floor with a loose thud, his arms and legs caught clumsily beneath him. Talal pumped his legs, swinging up to grab the ceiling again. Blood dripped from the stalactite, and the bats began to stir.

Talal turned, heading back toward the wall. The bats glided in a narrow circle and went for him at the same time.

Meisha was waiting. She stroked a hand over the flame column, her eyes widening as if she awoke to a lover's touch. Her irises became rings of fire as she envisioned the shaping, how to use the raw power within her to sculpt the spell.

A pair of arrows—each as long as her forearm—burst from the twisting column and streaked toward Talal. The boy shrieked and ducked his head, but the flame arrows veered away from him to impale the bats. Leather wings caught fire and fell from the air. The bats' tails whipped uselessly against the ground. Meisha watched them smolder as the light died out of her eyes.

Blinking, she felt herself come out of the grip of the magic as Talal dropped down beside her. A ghost of the expression he'd worn earlier—as he watched Varan play with his toy—passed over his face when he looked at Meisha.

The Harper felt a wave of regret. The boy had lived in Amn all his life, and had probably never seen or cared to see Art such as this. "Please don't be frightened," she said, trying to smile. "It's not so worlds-shaking terrible as it all seems."

Talal squatted next to Braedrin's body, his back to her. "Don't they all say that?" he muttered.

He started to say something else, but a tentacle roped him from above, jerking his head to one side.

"Talal!" Meisha bit back the spell that instinctively jumped to mind. She followed the tentacle to the corner, between two rock outcroppings, where a mass of gray, mottled flesh writhed.

With a gesture, Meisha cast the flame rope in the direction of the surrounding stone. The creature wailed at the brightness but did not loosen its grip on the boy.

Braedrin's fate, Meisha thought. A choker, by all the gods, and it had a decent grip.

Talal's eyes bulged as his throat disappeared under layers of spongy flesh. The choker flexed muscles that had no clear definition, trying to yank the boy off his feet, but Talal dug in, the sticky substance keeping him rooted in place.

Looping one arm around the tentacle, Meisha prepared to cast another spell. If she could heat the thing's flesh sufficiently, the pain would make it release the boy. She'd used the same spell to try to escape from Kall, long ago. Somehow, she didn't believe the choker would be as tenacious as the merchant's son.

Her hands began to glow with the weight of the spell. Heat rose to bathe her face and she heard Talal's choked whimpering.

She looked to the boy, afraid she might be too late. Talal's panic-stricken eyes met her own, and Meisha realized he was afraid of the heat. He was choking to death, but he feared her magic more.

Meisha hesitated, then released the spell on a muttered curse. She drew a dagger from her boot. The ropey tentacle was too thick to slice in half, so she brought the steel down overhand into its soft flesh. The choker writhed, releasing its prey and scuttling back.

Talal collapsed on the ground, clutching his throat, and bats poured from a hollow in the upper corner of the chamber.

The light from the flame rope faltered as bats—not as large as the first two, but still impressive—filled the room. Meisha sank to her knees, her back throbbing from wielding the dagger. She felt warm moisture that was not sweat soaking through her jerkin.

Stupid, Meisha thought. She'd reopened her wound. The bats would love her now. Talal was still on the floor, half-hidden by a cloud of dark bodies. Meisha felt the rush of air from leathery wings stir her hair and clothing. Bites stabbed her flesh, a few at first, but gradually increasing as the bats narrowed their attacks. By some luck, the choker faired no better. The bats did not discriminate in their frenzied biting, and choker screams rang out, echoing Talal's frantic cries.

A bat hit Meisha from behind, pinning her on her stomach to get at the source of the blood. Frantically, she rolled, but her vision was all leather and claws. Meisha stabbed with the dagger, making a slit in the creature's wing. Slashing diagonally, she split the leather curtain in half and scrambled free.

She crawled to Talal and rolled the boy onto his stomach. Slapping the bats away, she lay flush against his back. Blood from a dozen bites soaked her as she wrapped her arms around him.

"Close your eyes and don't move," Meisha said against his ear. Without waiting for him to comply, she chanted a spell and prayed the pain wouldn't make her lose consciousness.

The flame column wavered and dropped, falling into itself like a water spike in a dying fountain. Plunging straight down, the fire emptied into Meisha's spine.

The Harper came up with a howl, her back arching. Flames burst from her wound, her eyes, and her mouth, smothering the bats in a blanket of charnel heat. She hoped her body was enough to protect Talal from the upward blast of flame. The oily scent of burning meat filled the air as bats rained around her.

Meisha came down on her back, gulping air that tasted foul but felt sweet on her lungs. Dizziness caused the cavern's ceiling to waver and bend, but at least there were no more bats.

She looked around for the choker and found it huddling out of range of the fire cloud, dangling from the stalactite where Braedrin's body had been. Lambent eyes watched them in the flickering light from the burning corpses.

It was weighing how much of a fight they had left to offer, Meisha thought.

Angrily, she flung out an arm, focusing on her tingling fingertips, gathering power until . . . there, just enough. A tongue of flame sparked from her finger, illuminating her nail with a purple glow. She followed that glow with her eyes as she traced a circle above her head and around Talal's shoulder, past their feet and back up, encasing them in a ring of power only Meisha could see.

"*Trothliese!*" she cried, and fire sprang up where her finger had traced. The ward would last, even if she lost consciousness, but if the choker got brave and crossed the flames or dropped down on top of them, they'd be dead. Meisha hoped the fire and the deep dagger wound would be enough to convince the creature not to risk it.

She lay back, letting the flames from the circle wash over her. Her eyes slid closed. She had no strength left.

She awoke sometime later as if from a fever dream. Sweat poured off her skin, yet she shivered with cold. The ward fire still burned.

"Are you spent?" asked Talal. He was sitting up, his knees drawn under his chin. He looked like a small, terrified boy.

Meisha angled her head to look at him. She smiled crookedly. "Hardly," she replied.

She looked beyond the ward, but the choker was gone. Braedrin's body lay outside the circle, nipped and chewed by the deep bats. His eyelids were gone, making the whites appear huge in his ravaged face.

"I think I can walk. We should get out of here." Meisha

pulled her gaze away from the chilling sight, just in time to see the dwarves walk through the cavern wall.

They came through in silent procession, armed, ringing the fire ward with their own protective circle. There were ten in total, but Meisha's shocked gaze fastened on the leader—a dwarf in dented plate armor, holding a broken battle-axe.

CHAPTER TWENTY

The Howling Delve
4 Marpenoth, the Year of Lightning Storms (1374 DR)

I remember you," Meisha whispered, when the dwarf came to stand in front of her.

He shifted the weapon from fist to fist, and Meisha saw, in the hollow of a hairy throat, a translucent chain, as thin as a cat's whisker. A pendant hung from the chain, with a carved scene depicting the figure of a mountain with a hole in its center.

Meisha had seen a similar pendant around the neck of a gold dwarf scholar, long ago. And before that, around the neck of the ghost that haunted her arrival at the Delve. It was the symbol of Dumathoin.

"Keeper of secrets," she greeted the ghost.

"Bearer of the Harp," he replied. He stood so close, his breath should have stirred the air, yet Meisha felt nothing.

The spectral circle fell back to flank their leader. The dwarves' faces held no expression. Meisha wondered whether they saw her at all. When the leader spoke again, his eyes glowed with faint, silver light. Meisha felt the words scrape against her bones.

"Take the warning."

Wetting dry lips, Meisha rose to her knees, which put her roughly at eye level with the ghost. She felt Talal scuttle behind her, pressing against her back. The dwarf paid him no attention.

"What warning?" Meisha asked. "Who are you?"

The dwarf didn't move or make a sound, yet suddenly Meisha clutched her head. Screams reverberated in her mind. She looked back at Talal to see if he had heard them too, but the boy kept his eyes on the ground.

Meisha waited for the ache between her temples to pass before looking back at the dwarf. "Was that you? What happened here?"

"Secrets at rest beneath the earth stay buried, or come to light, according to Dumathoin's will," the dwarf intoned. "We violated that law and brought the beast upon this plane. Dumathoin charges us to put it right. Take the warning to other secret keepers," he repeated, and swung his axe point level with Meisha's chest. Flames from her ward came up through the blade, casting an orange glow on the spectral metal. He stretched out his other hand in a fist. "Do not venture here."

"What did you—ahh!" Meisha's hand flew to her chest. Coldness spread across her skin. She yanked back the fold of her jerkin where her Harper pin lay. The metal radiated a deep chill; her skin beneath the cloth was red with it. Meisha lifted the pin away from the tender flesh, but the dwarf had lowered his arm, and the cold began to fade.

"Take the warning," he repeated.

Angrily, Meisha shouted, "What warning? We can't take any warning anywhere! We're trapped here, just like you. Unless you can show us the way out, your message won't go ten paces without hitting a wall and splintering into silence."

The dwarf took a step forward. Talal whimpered, clutching at her clothes. "Stop. He'll kill us. He killed Braedrin."

"No, he didn't," said Meisha, shaking the boy off. "The choker killed Braedrin." She looked back at the dwarf. "Something else killed *him*, something else broke his axe. Is that what you want to keep hidden—the fire beast?"

"And the magic that violates the stone," said the dwarf.

Meisha felt Talal stir behind her, but he kept silent. "Varan's tinkerings?" she asked.

"Magic builds upon magic, layer by layer, century upon century, until it is too bright and terrible to comprehend. We collected the power here, and the power brought the beast. It was not our intention, and now we must pay for our crime. We must keep him bound."

"That's where Varan is getting his components," Meisha realized. "The secret caverns are yours. All those years ago, he found one of your bolt-holes. He created an extra-dimensional pocket to get to them, and now he's plundering the magic *you* left behind to make his toys."

"The gathering power will wake the beast. He seeks release; the walls are breaking down. Soon he will be free."

"We can't subdue Varan without risking him bringing down the whole cavern system," Meisha said. "We need help." Take the warning. She grasped her Harper pin as an idea began to form. "Your power affected this," she said. "Can you affect the same object, at a greater distance? Can you push your power through the earth?"

"I can," the dwarf said. "There will be a price."

Meisha didn't like the sound of that, but she didn't see any other way. "The closest person . . ." Gods, she thought, when I tell him it's Balram, he'll come running. He won't know what to make of this. "It will have to travel over many miles," she told the dwarf.

"What are you doing?" Talal wanted to know.

"Sending a message," said Meisha.

———— ◆◆◆ ————

"What is it?" Kall asked.

Kall and Dantane stood over the wizard's worktable while Dantane sifted through the charred remnants of the magic that had killed the lute player, Dynon Chadossa.

"Whatever the outcome, the magic's intended effect was to create an illusion, something to make the boy appear and sound as a woman to conceal his identity," Dantane said.

"I spoke with his family privately this morning," said Kall. "Lord Chadossa, as far as I could tell, appeared genuinely baffled. He was unaware his son even enjoyed music, let alone possessed a talent for bardcraft."

"It would appear Dynon didn't want his father to know about his shameful hobby," Dantane observed as he dug out one of the charred roots for closer inspection.

"There's no profit in bardcraft in Amn, not if you're the son of a wealthy lumber merchant," said Kall. "The boy must have realized his family would be subject to ridicule if word got out that he spent his nights plucking a lute instead of helping his father challenge the Bladesmiles for their stake in the lumber trade. He'd've done better building instruments instead of playing them."

"The punishment will be much worse now that he's been killed employing a magical device—a faulty one at that." Dantane tossed the root aside and went for another.

"There will be no retribution from the families," Kall said. "Chadossa has seen to that."

Dantane raised an eyebrow. "Oh? Amn has suddenly developed a forgiving nature when lives are threatened by horrific wizardry?"

"The family officially reported Dynon missing as of this morning. A search is underway, but the outlook is unfavorable. The Lady Chadossa is sick with grief, or so I'm told," Kall said, his voice flat. "The body of the lute player is being reported as an unidentified human female, as many witnesses can attest."

"You know it's Chadossa's son. Chadossa knows."

"Yes, but in the lord's words, 'sullying his family's name with magic won't avenge the boy's death.' An investigation into where he acquired such dangerous magic might, but Chadossa seemed uninterested in that suggestion," Kall said bitterly.

"What did he offer you in exchange for your silence on the matter?" asked Dantane.

Kall looked away. "A substantial loan—enough to cover my remaining debts—with next to no interest attached. He was most . . . generous."

Dantane looked impressed. "Then your worries are over. You can reestablish your father's business in a season. Many blemishes on your name will be forgotten in the wake of such a feat."

Kall shot the wizard a withering glance. "I will keep my silence, but I didn't take the deal, as you knew I wouldn't."

"How would I know?" countered the wizard, appearing genuinely surprised. "Any merchant family in Amn would welcome Chadossa's offer, and if I'm not mistaken, your goal is to count yourself among their elite. I know nothing of your motives or character, nor do I care to learn. If you wish to impress someone with your nobility, seek out your lady. Oh, but I forget," Dantane said, sneering, "She only pretends to be yours, as part of your ruse. Go to the friends who watch over you, then, if you can root them out from their hiding places."

Kall bristled. "You speak outside your experience, Dantane. Tread lightly where my friends are concerned."

"Of course, Lord Morel." Dantane offered a mocking half-bow. "Perhaps, if you feel the need to prove something, you should avenge the boy's death yourself. You obviously want to, since Chadossa will not. My only interest in the matter is how long you can continue to pay my salary, and since you refused Chadossa's offer, the answer to that is clear. Fortunately for you, *this*"—he rustled the ashes of the lute player's bane—"interests me greatly. Its age alone makes it worth a fortune Dynon Chadossa could not have hoped to have lying about."

"How old?" asked Kall, setting aside his anger for the moment.

Dantane held up the tendril he'd been examining. "I was wrong. These aren't roots. They're threads. The ones which remained intact after the burning are made of some type of ore.

The item is not plant-based, and no wonder. I'm only estimating, but some of the components appear to be over a thousand years old." His voice rose excitedly. "But there's more. There are layers here, magic from multiple casters who may or may not have lived in the same century. It's as if I'm unraveling a tapestry put together by different weavers. I'm going to attempt to identify the layers. If I can do that, I might be able to determine where the magic malfunctioned, turning the boy from a woman to a monster." He gestured for Kall to move aside. "You'll want to observe from a safe distance. If whatever affected Chadossa's son tries to attack me as well . . ."

Kall's sword hissed from its scabbard. "You'll have a quick death," he said.

"I was going to say I'll need your aid to break free," Dantane said sourly, "but I've just now reconsidered. Stand back."

Reluctantly, Kall moved to the far side of the room and stood near the window. He rested his sword point down in front of him and leaned against the wall, waiting.

Dantane knelt on the floor, placing the remnants of the item in a prepared circle of symbols drawn in chalk lines on the floor. His fingers moved, stiffly at first, gradually gaining speed and dexterity. Steepling his thumbs, the wizard pressed the backs of his fingers tightly together in a rough imitation of one of the symbols on the floor. The corresponding mark burst into a blue radiance. The wizard continued to gesture, and each of the symbols in turn lit to join a strange, pulsating dance around the charred item.

Kall raised a hand against the sting of the blinding light. If Dantane succeeded, he wondered, then what? Chadossa's own family didn't care what had caused Dynon's demise. Why did he? Was it simply because he'd had a taste of Dynon's life—because he'd known the father who gave nothing of himself, except his name, to his son?

He'd never known Dhairr, not truly, Kall admitted. As a boy, he'd craved the man's attention, but eventually he'd accepted the fact that Dhairr was content only when building his jewel empire and plotting against invisible assassins. Kall knew nothing about the man's past or how he'd met Kall's mother, Alytia.

He had to believe there was more to what he felt than a sense of neglect. His and Chadossa's stories were common enough among the merchant families. There were certainly worse fates than being born to an uncaring father.

Kall thought of Aazen, and wondered if his friend truly had managed to escape his father, or if he was still trapped in Balram's unyielding grip.

Wingbeats sounded behind Kall, and the scrape of talons on stone as a hawk landed in the open window. A moment later, Cesira stood beside him. Her familiar presence bolstered him.

What is he doing? Cesira asked, nodding at Dantane.

"Either divining the secrets of an ancient magic or preparing to blow the tower apart," Kall answered, as the light brightened to a blinding intensity.

Cesira's eyes narrowed. *What is the second magic originating from?*

"The second—what?" Kall swung toward her sharply.

Cesira pointed, but Kall saw it—the second blue glow reflected in her eyes. Twin rectangles of light outlined Dantane's cupboard on the far side of the tower.

"Dantane!" Kall shouted. He started forward, but Cesira grabbed his arm.

Do not, she said. *You could injure him.*

The point quickly became moot as the light from the circle soared upward in one explosive beam, trailing shattered symbols and throwing Dantane flat on his back. The wizard stared vacantly at the tower's ceiling as the wild magic ripped it apart. Support beams and planks flew into the empty sky. At the same time, the glow from the cupboard burst from its confines, blowing the cupboard doors off their hinges.

In a darkness lit only by columns of ancient, glowing stone, the fire beast stirred, awakened by the brutal release of power. It came from within the Delve and without at the same time, strong enough to awaken him from his forced sleep.

The beast sensed he had slumbered a long time, dreaming strange dreams of dark chambers filled with whispering mortals. They lived and scurried about like rats above his head, rats ripe for hunting.

In the beast's dream, his fire and claws were gone. He was a one-eyed wizard surrounded by bright power. He'd used the human form, and wielded magic he'd never known before to strike at someone—a woman. Where had she come from? She was a threat. She'd come too close to his secret. The beast had tried to eliminate her, but *he* interfered—the wizard.

Now that the beast was awake, he started to remember. Rage burned tracks of fire in the stone beneath his feet. He remembered the one-eyed wizard who had maimed him. Was it his power that had awakened him? Had the fool undone his own spell? No—it was the dwarves. The magic clearly had their mark upon it.

The realization brought the beast fully awake. He stood, muscles flexing, and filled the narrow chamber to its ceiling. The ancient columns reacted slowly—too slowly—and the creature remembered that the columns were not columns at all. The dwarves were still here, silent watchers hoping to keep him contained by the will of their pathetic god.

Not anymore, the beast thought. He let out a satisfied howl that shook the stone foundations. He dived at the nearest dwarf and bit it in half, his massive jaws tearing its spectral limbs.

He remembered the taste of dwarf flesh, the sound of dwarf screams as he ate each one alive. He found the sound as pleasing now as he remembered. The wailing of the pitiful soul was lost, and the beast turned to face its comrades.

He was free, and soon he would have living prey to hunt. He had the tools; all he needed was the opportunity.

Kall tackled Cesira, pressing her beneath him as wood and stone rained down around them. He gritted his teeth as splinters embedded themselves in the flesh beneath his collarbone.

He looked out of the bare hole where the ceiling had been. Debris struck the earth at least ten feet out from the tower in a destructive ring, slicing through the Morel colors flying on the opposite tower.

Kall looked across at Dantane but couldn't tell if the wizard still breathed. Kall started to rise but fell back again as the light from the cupboard shot across the room, seeking release in what was left of the confined space. It struck the tower wall but did no discernible damage. Kall gave silent thanks. If the light had punctured the wall, the resulting explosion would have caved in their skulls and buried them in stone. Instead, the beam thickened and began to take shape—a humanoid shape, to Kall's eyes. He could make out little else in the dust-choked room.

Cesira raised a hand and clasped his shoulder. *Dantane,* she said, and Kall nodded, keeping his eyes on the shape.

Kneeling beside the wizard, the druid probed his wounds with careful fingers. At her touch, Dantane blinked his eyes open, focusing on her blearily. He seemed beyond speech.

Kall positioned himself in front of the pair as a dwarf figure stepped out of the dust and into the sunlight that now poured through the roofless tower. He was half Kall's height but easily his equal in girth and stride-length. The dwarf carried a broken battle-axe and a visage completely devoid of expression. His body passed through furniture and debris as easily as if he walked through dust. His boots made no sound, and left no footprints on the stone.

"Greetings, Kall."

Kall startled so badly at the sound of the voice he nearly dropped his blade. The ghost's lips formed the greeting, but the voice that came from the dwarf's throat was not the deep grating of the mountain folk, not at all like Garavin's steady rumble.

The voice was female.

The voice was Meisha's.

Kall turned, daring to take his eyes off the spirit to look at the cupboard. Cesira followed his gaze, and her eyes widened.

The magical light had incinerated his mother's pouch. It had also consumed any mundane items the pouch might have contained. All that remained was Alytia's silver Harper badge, standing up on end. The light emanating from it shone straight out to the dwarf's form like a banner in a high breeze.

Kall looked back at the specter. "Meisha?" he asked. He couldn't believe it. "What is this?"

There was a long pause, but just as Kall started to ask another question, the dwarf spoke again. "I don't have long, and I can't answer the questions crowding your tongue, so listen well to what I can tell you.

"I need your aid, Kall," the ghost continued with Meisha's voice. "I'm trapped in the Howling Delve with a group of Esmeltaran refugees. They escaped the siege, the same one that drove your father out of the city those years ago.

"The Delve is a stronghold long inhabited by my master, Varan Ivshar. Its location is underground roughly twenty miles southwest of Keczulla, but that information will do you little good. The entrance to the Delve has been hidden and sealed magically, by agents of the Shadow Thieves."

Cesira caught her breath in surprise, and Kall muttered a curse.

"The only way in or out now is a portal used by the Shadow Thieves, a portal that leads to somewhere within Amn. I'm asking you to find the door in, if you can, and come to get me. The Shadow Thieves are after magical items. There's a warehouse worth stored in the Delve, and they're putting considerable manpower behind removing and selling them on the black market."

The message paused. "There's something else down here, a beast of fire. I haven't seen it, except in nightmares, but my friend the ghost says it's worse than the Shadow Thieves. I think . . . I think it might have done something to Varan, as well—changed him. I can't be sure.

"The only thing I can tell you about the portal is that the dwarves probably used it when they were still alive. Varan's markings aren't on it. The dwarves used the Delve as a stronghold, so they must have had the portal connect to a major city, a place to sell what treasure they collected. Keczulla is closest, but it could just as easily be Athkatla or Murann, gods forbid." There was another short pause. "If you receive this message, come soon, Kall. I need eyes, and blades, and whatever else you've got. It's not just the Shadow Thieves, old friend. When the Shadow Thieves come, Balram and his son come with them."

The dwarf fell silent. Kall took an unsteady breath. Indeed a thousand questions swirled in his thoughts, but he forced his lungs to work instead. He addressed the messenger. "Can you speak?"

The ghost seemed to focus on him for the first time, but he said nothing.

"Who are you?" Kall asked.

The ghost lowered his battle-axe. Kall got a good look at his hands and realized the dwarf had lost parts of multiple fingers. They flexed against the wooden handle.

"I have given my warning," the dwarf said simply. "By Dumathoin's command."

"Wait!" Kall cried, but the ghost had already gone. With him went the brilliant light, and as the clouds of swirling dust began to settle, the full extent of the damage to the tower was revealed.

The ceiling was obliterated. Boards and blocks of broken stone littered the floor. Most of Dantane's equipment was destroyed.

Cesira had her hands over a deep wound in the wizard's throat. She murmured a prayer, and soft, yellow light spooled from her fingers. The physical manifestation of the spell covered Dantane's bloody gash, closing and mending the tender flesh.

"Is he going to live?" asked Kall, when she'd finished.

A dry wheeze answered him as Dantane spat a clump of dirt and blood on the stones. He coughed again, and Kall realized the wizard was laughing. The humor looked ghastly on his bloodstained lips.

"This house . . . is a tragedy—a treasure. You are cursed, Morel." Dantane hacked more blood, shuddered, and began to breathe normally. "I've explored Netherese ruins and never encountered such a clash of the Art. Mystra in her humor leads me to power in the most magic-barren country in Faerûn. I shall never doubt the Lady again."

Cesira helped Dantane to a sitting position. *It appears you've given him an epiphany, my lord,* she said.

"Wonderful," said Kall. "I'm delighted someone's enjoying this."

Do you think it's genuine? Cesira asked.

"The message? Yes. And if Balram's involved . . ."

"So you'll be going after her?"

These last words were from Dantane. Kall looked at the wizard, at his torn robes, and the shambles of the room. "Why should that concern you?" he asked. "I would have thought you'd be lamenting the loss of your workshop and demanding restitution from me."

"Oh, I'll get to that," Dantane assured him. "But if you're going into the Delve, I'm coming with you." Before Kall could protest, he said, "Consider that the beginning of your restitution."

"Why?" Kall wanted to know. "Is it just for the power you smell, Dantane? Pity you didn't learn a lesson just now, when it nearly killed you."

"You're hardly in a position to judge me, Morel. Kindly refrain." Dantane wiped the blood from his mouth, but his gaze never left Kall's. "The magic tempts me greatly. I don't deny what I am, the power I want. But there's something else—and this will interest you both." He sifted through the rubble until he uncovered his ruined magic circle. "The incoming message disrupted my spell, so I could not identify young Chadossa's magic item, but it hardly matters anymore. The Art is identical. The spells came from the same source. They collided and became wild magic. If you find your sorcerous friend, you'll find the cause of Chadossa's death."

"The Shadow Thieves," said Kall. "Balram." And Aazen.

Kall remembered his friend's words as Aazen watched the lute player sing his last song. *Can you believe I may have found other companions?* Kall never dreamed Aazen would number the Shadow Thieves among his friends.

"Now we know the reason the Chadossas didn't pursue a murder investigation," said Dantane. "The family has been dealing in dangerous magics through the Shadow Thieves. Chadossa can't have that information known to the general public. For myself, I want to find the source of the power I felt, and I would be more than willing to help you take it from the Shadow Thieves."

Kall wondered in whose hands the magic would do the most damage. "Do you have contacts in the city? Wizards?"

When Dantane hesitated, Kall snapped, "Speak. You want power—come to the Delve and take all you want. If your speech about ancient magic is true, that should be more than fair compensation for risking your friends' identities. I'm no threat to them, especially not after this explosion, which was likely witnessed by half of the Gold Ward. The merchant families will have taken my head long before they get around to your friends."

Dantane didn't disagree. "You'll let me choose my reward— for myself and my contact, should he agree to aid us?"

"If Meisha allows, so do I, just set up the meeting. Find someone who knows about this portal."

Dantane nodded and left them. Kall waited for the echo of his footsteps to fade before rounding on Cesira. "You're staying silent in this?"

No, said the druid, surprised. *What's angering you, Kall? Surely not the loss of a tower or Dantane's greed?*

Kall shook his head. "I sent her," he said, "to her master. I sent her right into Balram's hands."

Meisha is more than capable of seeing to herself, and this is larger than Balram, said Cesira. *You heard Dantane. There are forces at work neither you nor Meisha could have predicted.*

"It was the same with Haig, my father, and Aazen," said Kall, as if he had not heard her. "I couldn't save them. Now Meisha may die. And Aazen . . ."

You believe he's involved? Cesira asked.

"Yes, and I'm afraid I'll be forced to put a blade through my best friend to accomplish what I must." Kall had prayed, nightly, that it would not come to that. He prayed Aazen had escaped, or if he hadn't, that he would let Kall save him from his father's shadow. Merciful gods, shouldn't Kall be allowed to save at least *one* of those closest to him?

An image of Meisha flashed before his mind, drawing his deliberations to a close. "Dantane will find the portal," he said.

Yes. Cesira nodded.

"Setting up the meeting will take time."

Time enough to send a message of your own? Cesira asked, crooking an eyebrow.

Kall nodded. She knew what he was thinking. She nearly always did. "I want to know more about this Howling Delve." And if they were going underground, who better to aid them than a digger?

He cupped the sword's emerald between his palms and called out in his mind. His voice traveled across miles and mountains, to reverberate with the sword's sister stone. The gem graced a new weapon, a weapon that was not of Morel house, and yet the owner was no less than family to Kall.

CHAPTER TWENTY-ONE

The Earthvault
5 Marpenoth, the Year of Lightning Storms (1374 DR)

Garavin Fallstone strode back and forth on a patch of empty air before a large expanse of cavern wall. He held up a taper that had burned down to threaten his thumb and had coated his arm in a waxy cast. He noticed neither circumstance, and continued to read the historical record etched deep into the stone.

The runes were inscribed with the same care and precision taken by a Candlekeep scribe, and Garavin should know. He'd been such a one, though it seemed like a lifetime ago: a scribe, a digger—Deepwarden for his clan. Garavin had worn many mantles, but all of them felt at home in the Earthvault.

The cone-shaped cavern rested far beneath the Marching Mountains. Mages of Shanatar, the ancient kingdom of the shield dwarves, had created it centuries ago. The vault was, to Garavin's mind, the most impressive archive to be found outside Candlekeep's doors. From the lowest point, where only worms burrowed, to the highest ridge, the history of the shield dwarves and their great realm unfolded for any of dwarf blood—and *only* those—to read.

Far below Garavin's boots, a tawny mastiff with stiff joints slept on the cavern floor, next to an account of the beginning of the shield dwarves' shattering war with the duergar. Garavin's satchel and maul rested against Borl's haunches, but the mastiff didn't notice when the emerald in the weapon's handle began to glow. Only when the stone hummed with gathering power did the dog stir and leap to its feet, and that was more the fault of the huge elemental being that appeared out of the air.

The powerful earth dao, keeper of Earthvault lore, spoke in the Dwarvish tongue.

"What magic do you bring, Garavin Fallstone, once son of Sorn? You disturb the stones."

"My apologies, Diuthaizos," Garavin said, bowing respectfully as he floated to the floor. "The Art will do no harm. I will take it above, so as not to offend."

Nodding regally, the dao floated away, but kept one wary eye on the dwarf and his companion.

Garavin sighed and picked up the glowing green maul. "Well, this trip is looking to be shorter than expected." He touched the emerald with a crooked finger. "Wonder what the boy wants now, eh?" But he smiled as he said it.

<hr />

The meager apartment had thick walls. That was the only quality Aazen could recommend about the place. Situated above the vacant storefront of Eromar's Tailoring, the pair of rooms had frigid floors in the winter and rats scuffling in the walls in the summer. Aazen's music drowned them out, yet did not carry to the street. He had a cot in the corner with a blanket and a sheet, a chest of drawers, and a washbasin. He had few personal effects to store, save his violin, so the tiny space suited him well.

At peace, lost in his music, Aazen fumbled the bow in a discordant screech when the Cowled Wizard came up the stairs.

Jubair Ardoll looked far too nervous to be a proper wizard,

but perhaps it was the secretive nature of his organization that bred the look of rabbit-wariness in his eyes. He wore a large black pearl earring in his left ear and was bald but for two unattractive strips of shorn hair arching over both ears. Most folk assumed he was a former Nelanther pirate. Dressed as a pirate, obviously he must be so. Amnians were not much on imagination unless it earned them coin. They had little notion of his real occupation as his fellow wizards. Dressed as a wizard, obviously he must be so and nothing more—certainly not an agent of the Shadow Thieves.

Aazen watched impassively as Jubair raised a hand in greeting, then immediately stumbled back with a cry of pain, nearly falling down the steep stairs. A line of blood appeared at each of the wizard's ankles, dribbling down to stain his gold-threaded slippers.

"Watch the wire," Aazen suggested.

Jubair stepped over the invisible trap, hurling a stream of curses any pirate would have envied. "You might have warned me, you sick bastard."

"I wanted to finish my song," Aazen said, removing the violin from his chin.

Jubair glared at him. "Is your father insane, lad, or merely cow-eyed stupid?" he said without preamble. "The Cowls haven't stopped murmuring about the incident at Morel's party. It's all I can do to steer their eyes away from the streets."

"I wonder why you bother," Aazen said, sliding the violin back in its velvet-lined case. "As my father predicted, Chadossa is not pursuing the matter. No evidence points to us. It was simply an unfortunate mishap. These things happen when dealing with arcane magic," he said, "as any Amnian will rush to assure you."

"And you know as well as I the horse dung that drips from merchants' mouths," Jubair said, his face reddening. Magic intolerance was one of the few things that could stir the man to anger. "The thing's face *melted*, Kortrun, is what they're saying. They had to scrape it off Morel's floor."

"I take it, then, the Cowls will not let the matter rest?" Aazen asked, "despite your best efforts?"

Jubair rubbed his pearl between two fingers, looking ruffled. "There have been inquiries. I've managed to convince most of them to let me look into the matter, but I have to give them something, a scapegoat preferably. You have to tell your father—get him to see reason. If he continues to act recklessly, the whole operation could be exposed. That will be you and me," he said, flapping his hands in the air between them. "Daen won't go down for this, but he'll see that your father does."

And soon after, his corpse will be cooling on my floor, Aazen thought, but he didn't speak the sentiment aloud. "I'll talk to him. We'll have something for you soon."

Jubair nodded, appeased. His gaze fell on Aazen's instrument. "I didn't know you played," he said, eyeing Aazen curiously.

"Mind the other wire on your way out," Aazen replied, putting the case away in the bottom drawer of the bureau.

Jubair looked stricken. "The other wire?"

"I set it at neck level. Most people who enter my rooms uninvited end up with an extra air hole in their throats," Aazen told him. "Fortunately, you're smaller than most. Don't find me here again, Jubair," he said over the wizard's outraged sputtering. "This is my private space, away from my father, away from the Cowled Wizards, and away from the Shadow Thieves."

Still fuming, Jubair maneuvered his body carefully across the threshold in a half-crouch. "Do you truly believe any place is private from Daen?" he scoffed, his eyes alight with taunting amusement. "The Shadow Thieves are your family now, except they're larger, more dangerous, and more vindictive than most. If you didn't want that, you shouldn't have signed on alongside your father."

I had no choice, Aazen thought. He remembered the Harper down in the Delve, the woman he'd allowed to bleed to death because the Shadow Thieves—his father—demanded it.

He thought of Kall. He knew his friend had survived

the battle with the broken magic item. He hadn't been worried about Kall's safety, but he regretted the incident had to happen in Morel's house. It would have been better if he had not allowed Kall to see him. His friend surely suspected his involvement in the murder. More than that, if Kall decided to pursue the matter, he could pick up the trail far easier than the Gem Guard or the Cowls. If he suspected the trail might lead to Balram, Kall would follow it to the Abyss and back. No, the Cowled Wizards didn't concern Aazen. Kall was the threat to fear.

Aazen wondered if he should mention to his father just whose roof Varan's broken toy had ended up under. Doubtless he would find the irony upsetting. No. Balram would find out soon enough. Then he would tell Aazen what to do about it. Aazen had no doubt that if it became necessary, his father would make him deal with Kall and his allies personally.

I have no choice, he repeated, speaking to Kall in his mind. He reached again for his music.

* * *

The Silver Market was held, appropriately enough, in the Silver Ward in the Jade District; it was also called Selune's Market, for it took place at night during the warmer months. The market was the Jade District's answer to the Jewelers' Quarter, where the largest concentration of jewelry in Keczulla was made. But Selune's Market was fast gaining a reputation as the place for up-and-coming merchants. Whether it was jewelry, loose gems, or elaborate, jewel-bedecked clothing one wished for, the Silver Market was the place to spot new talent and possible future competition.

Dantane rounded a corner, weaving between two comely lasses in low-cut gowns who offered him trays of sugared peaches.

Cooking vendors had set up stalls along the ends of the avenues, so that you couldn't cross one street onto another without being intoxicated by the scents of fresh fruit and spices.

Dantane crossed a back alley and froze as a group of gray shadows detached themselves from the buildings. Wraiths, he thought in disgust. He had no time for this.

Keczulla knew its share of poverty. The wealthier merchant families contributed generously to providing homes for orphaned children, as a way of showing off their vast fortunes, but some youths could not be tamed by civilization. These half-feral children, the Wraiths, roamed the night markets in packs, stealing food and purses largely by surrounding easy marks and overwhelming them with sheer numbers, plucking, biting, and scratching until the unfortunate soul gave up and surrendered any belongings of worth.

Their bodies were emaciated, smeared in mud to protect them from the sun. They shaved their heads with crude knives to keep away lice. Sometimes their appearance alone was enough to have folk fumbling at their purse strings.

Dantane was not impressed. He turned to the encroaching maggots and hissed a spell. His hand glowed brightly, spitting sparks that hissed as they struck the mud-covered bodies. The Wraiths halted their charge and scattered to the far sides of the alley. No matter how hungry or desperate they were, none of them wanted to battle a wizard.

Eddricles waited for him beside one of the beer wagons, scowling fiercely when a plump-faced man tried to offer him a sample. He stood examining a belt strung with multiple gold chains. He wrinkled his nose critically.

"Paint is never going to conceal the fact you've only gold enough to make half a belt. I suggest you reduce the number of chains—twelve is hopelessly gaudy—or sell belts to starving ladies." He tossed the belt back at its red-faced owner and rounded on Dantane. "I detest charity work," he said, by way of a greeting. "Speaking of which, you, my boy, are fortunate I'm in a good humor. Walk with me, but not too close. I don't want anyone to think I like you."

Dantane reluctantly fell into step beside the moneychanger. It was said Eddricles could determine the value of a gem without the aid of a glass. Dantane suspected the man's extraordinary vision was due more to the fact that he was also a wizard, but he'd never asked Eddricles to confirm or deny the theory. In the moneychanger-wizard's presence, one tended to listen, plead, or weep. Dantane listened.

"The next time you send me a missive, please don't bother to include the words: magic, portal, sorcerers, or Morel—gods, especially Morel. Do you know what they're saying about the whelp?" He didn't bother to let Dantane answer. "They say he employs a wizard, a wizard who murdered a bard at the man's own party and blew the top of one of his towers off." He whirled abruptly, forcing Dantane to sidestep. "Do you happen to know what fool wizard is begging from Morel's table these days? What a bountiful feast it must be!"

"No one knows who I am," Dantane said calmly, speaking for the first time.

"They'd bloody well better not!" Eddricles stormed. The normally aloof moneychanger was as agitated as Dantane—and perhaps the whole of Faerûn—had ever seen him. "You and Morel have been rutting all over the lives of respectable wizards in this city. We haven't been able to meet in safety since Morel returned."

Eddricles and several other Keczullan wizards met often in secret to share magic and discuss their craft without threat of molestation. Dantane knew they feared their own activities coming to light in the wake of Morel's string of tragedies.

"I did not murder the bard," Dantane said as they resumed their walk. "And you should know the woman was not a bard, nor a woman at all, but a powerful merchant's son, one who dabbled too deeply in magic he did not understand."

"Hells, Dantane, you've just described every young family in Amn. They're all delving into business they shouldn't be."

Dantane scowled. "I was not aware the merchants or the Council of Six made any exceptions where their hatred of magic was concerned."

"Oh, they don't, and neither did those young hotheads like

the one you scraped off Morel's floor. Not at first. When the corpses were still cooling from the plagues, the families who'd lost all were ready to grab any wizard and tear him to pieces. Likely some of them did too. Publicly, the grudge against the arcane still stands. But much as Amn would like to live in a comfortable, xenophobic nest, wider Faerûn encroaches. The Sythillisian Empire is a reality, and the truce will never last. Amn needs power and allies, and these allies will scoff at the notion of a society fighting wars without using killing magic—as well they should.

"But more than that is the inevitable cycle of time. These young merchants and their children are fascinated by the things their parents have forbidden them. It will be many more years before the plagues are forgotten, but I wager you're seeing the start of it right now, with these magic items."

"Do you know where they're coming from?" Dantane asked as they passed in the shadow of a dressmaker's tent. "The magic items? Are the Shadow Thieves running the operation?"

Eddricles considered the question. "If the items are as powerful as you claim, the Shadow Thieves had better have a hand in their distribution. They may be extortionists and cutthroats, but at least they have the resources to handle such magic."

"Not this time, if the debacle at Morel's party is any indication," said Dantane. "What about the portal?"

Eddricles laughed loudly. The sound was disconcerting, as if he lacked sufficient practice in the action. "Do you think me an idiot, boy?"

Dantane wisely kept his silence.

"Do you believe I will give you information on one of the best-kept secrets of one of our most powerful merchant families without the guarantee you'll make it well worth my while?"

Eddricles pulled Dantane to one side of the avenue, where the crowd was sparse. He hustled the wizard close by the collar of his robes and spoke rapidly into his ear.

Dantane listened and nodded. "It can be done. I've had assurances from Morel."

The moneychanger rolled his eyes, clearly not happy, but he nodded agreement. He spoke again, softly, so Dantane had to strain to hear him. He managed to catch the most important word, and his eyes widened.

"Bladesmile."

CHAPTER TWENTY-TWO

The Howling Delve
5 Marpenoth, the Year of Lightning Storms (1374 DR)

Meisha came awake to total darkness and hands pressing her upper arms. She struck out, found a human throat, and dug her fingers into it. She heard a ragged cough and the smell of garbage hit her square in the nose. She relaxed her grip and heard Talal hiss, "Sune suck me, but you're a mean one."

"Why is it dark?" she asked. "I left a candle burning."

"I blew it out. We have to move, Lady," he said urgently, pulling her up from her pallet. "Don't," he hissed as she began chanting a spell. "No light. No damn fire. Give me your hand."

He took her down the passage out of the warrens toward Varan's chamber. Meisha could see a faint line of light beneath the wizard's door. "Where are we going?" she asked.

"Shh! They're coming," Talal whispered.

"The Shadow Thieves?"

"Them—Balram too. And his son. One big, happy clan again."

Meisha stilled. "Both of them? Why?"

"To make sure you're dead. We have to hide you. If they find out we kept you alive . . ."

"Wait." Meisha caught his arm, stopping him in front of

Varan's chamber. "You said they never go in here. They're afraid of Varan."

Talal shook his head so vigorously Meisha felt it through his entire body. "He'll attack you again. They'll find your corpse, and it'll still be bad for us. Come *on!*"

"I won't touch anything. I won't disturb him." Voices drifted out to them from the warrens.

"They're gathering everyone together," Talal said, fear rising in his voice.

"Then we're out of time." Meisha hauled the door open. Ambient light from the room cast shadow pits on Talal's pale face. "I'll be fine," she promised. She reached out to ruffle his hair playfully, because she knew it would annoy him.

The boy darted away, snorting. "Oh, sure, rip my throat out then pet me like your lap dog. Don't fret, Lady, my manhood's unscathed. If you're going to do this, give me your boots before you go in."

"My what—why?"

"Just hurry!"

Rolling her eyes, Meisha pulled the buckles loose and braced herself against the door as Talal yanked off her thigh-length boots. Her stockinged feet instantly went frigid when they touched the floor.

"You're welcome," she muttered as the boy darted off down the passage in the direction of the voices.

Meisha pulled the door shut, sealing it securely from the inside. She stood a moment with her ear to the wood, listening for approaching footsteps, but she heard nothing. Taking a deep breath, she turned to face the room and whatever doom might await her.

Varan was asleep. She'd looked in on the wizard from behind the door a handful of times since coming to the Delve, and each time he'd been awake and active, building his mysterious items. She'd never seen him at rest.

He lay in a half-slump in a corner, clutching sheafs of parchment in limp fingers, far away from the pallet Haroun had made for him. Meisha suspected he worked himself into exhaustion and simply collapsed wherever he happened to be sitting.

His pile of magic items had been depleted. Talal or one of the others had collected the tribute.

Moving along the wall, Meisha sat down a safe distance from the wizard. His breathing was deep and regular, but his arms and legs twitched erratically, like a dog in the throes of some disturbing dream.

"What are you seeing, Master?" she whispered aloud, knowing he could not hear her. "What is tormenting you?" Was it the fire beast? Meisha had always sensed a wrongness, a feeling of malevolence lurking at the edges of Varan's underground sanctuary, but remembering the ghost's warning and her own strange dreams, she felt the sensation intensify a hundredfold.

And now the Shadow Thieves were here. Meisha ran a hand down her back, over the ridge of healing flesh. She hadn't been strong enough to take them on when she was whole. She had no chance now. All she could do was pray to the Lady that Kall had gotten her message. The ghost had said only that he would deliver it. He hadn't appeared since to confirm or deny its receipt.

Sighing, Meisha traced a circle in the dirt and sediment in front of her. "*Chareff.*" The familiar power kindled—the first spell she'd ever learned.

Always have a candle for the rats, Shaera had chided her.

She placed the tiny flame in the circle. Meisha lay down on her side, curling around the fire so she could watch Varan sleep.

He continued to toss and turn fitfully. Meisha bit her lip as she felt power stir anew, magic awakened by the wizard's violent trembles. It called to the sorcerous power within her, raking over her skin like hot coals. She shuddered.

Then why not end it? Give him a quick, merciful death.

The memory came out of nowhere, the words biting at

Meisha's heart. The woman who'd spoken those words to Kall was unrecognizable to her now. She had no desire to be reminded of the person she'd once been.

"Kall," she whispered, feeling tears sting her eyes as she remembered the young man who'd stood defiantly in her path and watched his death smolder in her eyes. "I understand now."

She could never kill Varan. Even had she the magical might, she had no will for the task. Not when there was a chance he might be saved.

She closed her eyes against the memories, retreating instinctively into a meditative trance. Varan had taught her that, as well. She would need to conserve as much strength as possible for what lay ahead. She'd been wrong—she couldn't rely on Kall getting her message. Something had to be done to get the refugees out of the Delve before Varan became any more volatile. For if the fire beast didn't kill them all, Meisha knew, deep in her soul, Varan would.

⟡

Haroun walked beside Talal to the front of the warrens, where the refugees stood herded together. The crowd stood tense and wary, fighting desperately to keep the guilt off their faces as Balram questioned each about Meisha.

"I don't remember you." Balram held the back of his hand to his nose as he spoke to Talal, but the boy only grinned innocuously.

"I was smaller when you were here last, sir," he said. His voice was chipper and polite, as if he were trying to sell Balram goods on a street corner. "Cleaner too, I'll warrant."

Balram didn't answer but looked back to where Aazen leaned against a wall. "You're sure she was a Harper?"

Aazen shrugged. "She wore the pin. I left her body beneath the portal. Only the bloodstain remains."

"I see." Balram grasped a fistful of Talal's dirty hair. He didn't pull or shake the boy; he simply held the tender strands straight out behind his left ear, sifting them through his fingers. Talal stiffened, and the vacant smile on his lips slid away, replaced by a taut line as fear battled with anger.

Aazen waited. He'd been on the receiving end of this punishment when he was younger than Talal. He knew what would happen if the boy displeased his father.

"What did you do with the Harper's body?" Balram asked. "These people—your friends—say you're a scavenger. Did you scavenge her corpse? You don't look like a vulture, though you're filthy enough to be one." He leaned closer, still holding Talal's hair. He sniffed, wrinkling his nose in disgust. "Your breath stinks of refuse. You'd eat your own droppings, wouldn't you, if you thought they'd nourish you. Did you eat the Harper too?" His eyes gleamed wickedly. "Are you so very hungry? But that's ungrateful. Don't we feed you well enough down here—provide for your every need? Only an animal eats its own leavings."

"I didn't eat her," Talal said. His voice trembled with suppressed rage. "I took her boots." He pointed to his feet.

A pair of brown leather boots bunched up awkwardly around his knees, straps and buckles dangling. Scorch marks from old fires bruised the leather.

"They're hers," Aazen said. "I remember sitting on them."

"Oh-ho." Balram chuckled. "Straddled her like a two-taran whore, did you?" He clucked his tongue. "Isslun will be disappointed in you. Or is it Aliyea?"

Talal stirred. Balram snapped his hand straight out from the boy's head without looking away from Aazen's face.

Talal screamed out in pain and fell to his knees. He clutched at the patch of bare, bloodied skin behind his ear. Tears streamed from his eyes.

Haroun started forward, but Aazen caught the woman's arm, roughly drawing her back. "You will only worsen the pain," he hissed in her ear.

She glanced up at him, surprised, but kept her silence.

Balram calmly sprinkled bits of loose hair over Talal's whimpering form. "It certainly sheds like an animal. What a mess you are." He crouched down, snagging Talal's chin. "If you're truly the heartless vulture, why should you care what insult I give the Harper?"

"I don't care," Talal said through gritted teeth.

"Oh, but it seemed like you did, just then. The look on your face was terribly affronted. I'm warning you, boy, if you value these people's lives, you will give me truth. Where is the Harper?"

"We brought her here!" Talal shouted. Jerking away from Balram, he climbed back to his feet and stood defiantly before the gathered Shadow Thieves. Behind him, the refugees, though far greater in number, stood in stunned, terrified silence while Balram regarded the boy.

"Why?" he asked.

"We tried to heal her," Talal said, calmer now. He wiped his running nose as blood dripped down his neck. "So she could help us escape."

A collective tremor went through the crowd, but still no one spoke.

"Did you expect we wouldn't try?" Talal asked mockingly, his eyes daring Balram to come at him again.

Balram smiled. "I wouldn't have expected an animal to speak so boldly. Yes, I knew you'd try. Were your efforts rewarded?"

Talal shook his head. "She died during the first night. We didn't want to waste our last healing draught on a lost cause."

"Really?" Balram sounded impressed. "What little mercenaries you've become . . . that is, if you're not little liars. Where is the body?" He raised his hand again, tracing the air alongside Talal's head.

The boy refused to flinch. "Follow me," he said. "I'll take you to her."

<hr />

She awoke to a hand softly brushing her cheek. Meisha opened her eyes and saw Varan staring down at her.

Her hands were numb from being pressed against the cold floor. She clenched them into painful fists to keep from throwing herself away from Varan, but he merely sat before her, one hand endlessly shuffling his papers, the other resting on her skin, as if he had forgotten he'd laid it there.

Slowly, Meisha uncurled her body and slid out from under his hand. She came to an unsteady sitting position against the wall, still too close to the unstable wizard for comfort.

How long had she been meditating? No, that wasn't true, she thought, berating herself savagely. Meditation had turned to sleep, and a deep one. That had never happened to her before, not unless she willed it. Had Varan used some magic to make her sleep? The thought was more than unsettling. Meisha knew what he could do to her when she was awake and aware. It was frightening to contemplate what he might have done to her while she was helpless in sleep.

Helpless in sleep.

Meisha stood up so quickly that Varan looked up from his reading. His smile struck her with a profound chill. "You're dreaming, m'dear. Back to sleep now, child. There's a good girl." He resumed his shuffling.

Meisha slid back to the floor quietly, but her thoughts raced. Even in his current state, even asleep, Varan had sensed her presence in the chamber. He may have been confused about who she was or how old, but he knew *someone* was there with him. Of course—it should have dawned on her long before now.

Varan had known all along when the refugees were in his chamber. They shouldn't have been able to take his discarded magics from him without his consent, not while he could still cast spells—and she'd had painful proof that he could capably defend himself. But according to Talal, he'd never attacked any of them, until Shirva Tarlarin and Meisha herself, after she'd picked up the banded sphere. Meisha looked around the room for the item, but it was gone, taken in the last delivery to the Shadow Thieves. Varan didn't seem bothered by its absence.

Why, then, had he attacked her? Perhaps there had been another reason behind his violent outburst. Perhaps he'd killed Shirva Tarlarin for that same reason.

She watched Varan for a long time, but his face registered nothing and offered her no clues.

Meisha jumped at the sharp rap on the door.

"It's just Talal," Varan muttered without looking up from his papers.

Meisha's mouth slid open and shut, but she had no time to marvel at Varan's flashes of lucidity as the door opened a crack and Talal wiggled through.

"What happened to you?" Meisha demanded, seeing the dried blood on the boy's neck and shirt.

"Lost some hair," was all Talal would say. His hands shook slightly as he ran them through his dirty locks. His eyes were bright, hard chips of stone, but he smiled as he reached for her hand. "Still alive, I see. Good. Come with me. You'll like this."

Curious, Meisha followed him out into the corridor and down the passage he'd tried to take her through before. It arched away from the warrens and back up a tunnel in a rough horseshoe, emptying into a circular chamber bounded by steep flowstone sides. Scattered about the floor were piles of small- to mid-sized stones.

Meisha stepped around Talal to see at a better angle and realized the piles were arranged in tidy rows. A group of men with shovels scooped rocks onto a high mound at the back of the chamber.

"They're graves," Meisha said, counting the fallen and coming up with the exact number—plus one—of refugees Talal said had died in the Delve. Her gaze returned to the fresh stone pile.

Talal followed her eyes. "Like it? One of 'em's yours. We dug it the night I brought you in," he explained, and had the good grace to look sheepish. "You know—just in case. After you mended, we kept it for when they came back. Oh"—he kicked off her boots and held them out—"you can have these back. Don't fit me anyway."

"They believed I was dead?" Meisha asked, suspicious. "On sight of a grave alone?"

Talal exchanged grinning gazes with the circle of digging men. One of the men winked at Meisha. "Not at first," the man replied. "But Talal told 'em we'd dig you up, 'yes sir, right away sir—it'll only take a few days with these little stick shovels you give us, sir.' " The digger laughed heartily.

"So we started in," Talal said, frowning as he fingered the newly naked skin behind his ear. "We actually dug up Shirva. Aazen left with half the men and the latest shipment when we started digging, and Balram didn't linger to look beyond that she was female and recently dead. It's just like before," he said, looking at Meisha. "Balram hates the Delve, everything about it makes him twitchy. It was all he could do to be down here smelling us."

"Bloody cowards," another man said. He spat on the ground.

Meisha smiled at Talal. "You have my thanks," she said. "You've saved my life twice now."

The boy jerked his shoulders, but he was blushing fiercely. "Nothing to it, Lady. You get us out of here, Tymora puts us in balance." He added quickly, "The bitch."

"We have to talk about that," Meisha said, looking at the gathered men. "Get everyone together, if you will. We can't wait for Kall to find the portal. We have to try to escape on our own, and the only way out is through the Shadow Thieves." There was restless murmuring among the men, but Meisha ignored them. "According to Talal's brother, at least one of them has the key to activate the portal. We're going to take it from the next party that comes through the door."

Eyebrows soared around the circle of diggers, but Talal grinned, slapping an arm around Meisha's neck. "What'd I tell you, boys? She's going death-seeking again. That's our Meisha."

When the diggers had dispersed back to the warrens, Meisha pulled Talal aside. "I need to know about Shirva Tarlarin," she said.

Talal looked surprised. "What about her?"

"Do you know which of Varan's items she touched that set him off? Was anything found near her body?"

Talal thought for a moment. His eyes clouded. "She had one of his strings," he said finally. "From his neck sack."

"His neck pouch?" Meisha asked. She hadn't expected that. Then she remembered the rings. She'd put the apprentices' rings back in Varan's pouch at the same time she'd been handling the sphere, just before Varan attacked her. Had Shirva Tarlarin touched the pouch too? "Is that why he killed her?" she wondered aloud.

"Don't know, but the string was wrapped around what was left of her fingers. I think he"—the boy swallowed—"near as we could tell, he bit some of her fingers off taking it back."

A mental picture of Varan attacking a woman with only his teeth made Meisha light-headed. She felt Talal steady her with a hand to her waist. "Why would he do it?" she asked. "He keeps nothing of great magic in there. What is he hiding?"

CHAPTER TWENTY-THREE

Keczulla, Amn
5 Marpenoth, the Year of Lightning Storms (1374 DR)

Cesira stood in the ruined tower, watching through one of the arched windows as Dantane, Morgan, and Laerin rode toward the estate.

Kall came to stand behind the druid. He lifted a hand as if to touch her long hair, but her tresses stirred in the wind, blowing out of his grasp.

You never asked me, Cesira said, turning to face him. *You didn't ask me to stay behind.*

"I was afraid you'd say I was a damn fool," Kall said with a laugh. "I thought I'd try an indirect approach to get you to do my bidding."

As if you've ever had a problem convincing me of anything. And you've always been a damn fool. Getting some years on you doesn't change anything, she said. *Why do you want me to stay here? Even my charms—though considerable, I grant you—won't be enough to save Morel's name. Amn has seen through all our pretenses.*

"It isn't for that," said Kall, frowning. "Don't you think I would rather have *you* at my back down that snake hole than Dantane? Now which of us is the fool?"

Then why?

"Because Balram won't stop us from entering the portal. He'll find out about it, and he may put up a token resistance, but he wants us to get in. And once we're inside, he'll come in after us and bring all manner of Hells down on our heads. He'll want to kill us all underground, where no one will see, then go about his business."

Cesira laughed shortly. *You fill me with such confidence, my lord. I may faint from it,* she said.

Kall shook his head. "I'm not worried about a fight with Balram in the Delve. But if he tries to seal us in, if Garavin's plan to get the refugees out fails, we need someone on this side who can blow that sealed entrance apart. You're the only one I trust, and the last person I ever wanted to ask to do this." He took her hand, folding her fingers around a small emerald.

Cesira looked at him questioningly. He showed her his sword. It rode at his hip as always, but the emerald in the pommel had gone. When Garavin took his gem down into the Delve, she could use her magic on the link between them to locate the hidden entrance, bypassing any concealing magic laid on the tunnel.

"Take rooms at an inn somewhere in the better districts," said Kall. "Garavin will use his stone to call you, if something happens." He grinned lopsidedly. "Believe me, if something goes wrong, we *will* call. I'm not too proud to ask for a rescue if I can't dig myself out of a hole."

But Cesira frowned, refusing to be distracted by the jest. *Take rooms at an inn? Why would you ever think I would agree to hide, Kall? What are you protecting me from?*

Kall hesitated. "This house won't be safe. When Balram finds out who's coming after him, he may send men here."

And?

"And if he does, they'll be out to destroy whatever is left of Morel. No loose ends this time. Balram won't allow it."

Then I hope he won't be too disappointed to find the lady of the house here to greet him.

Kall's eyes narrowed. His lips moved, but no sound came

out. *What was that, my lord?* Cesira asked teasingly. *I am the one who lacks speech, remember?*

Kall put his hands on her shoulders and squeezed, fighting the temptation to throttle her. "I said, you're a stubborn, arrogant wench."

And you're a blind pig's arse, Cesira threw back, *if you think I'm running away to hide.*

"I can't have him get to you." Kall tried to steady his voice. "I won't let it happen."

Kall . . . Her anger gone, she seemed as much at a loss as he.

If anything happened to her, Kall realized, it would be the end of everything. He'd begun to build a new life the night he'd been hurtled through the portal to Garavin's camp. Now the ashes of his old life threatened to destroy everything he'd come to cherish.

Kall stepped back, kneeling before Cesira. He lifted a hand toward her. "Come here. I want to show you something."

Hesitantly, Cesira placed her hand in his palm. His fingers wrapped securely around hers. He guided her to the floor, splaying her hand beneath his against the rough wood. "Do you feel that—that catch?" he asked.

Cesira nodded and pressed. The false floor slid back to reveal a slender nook, no wider than their two arms but just as long. Arrows filled the pocket. Dust covered their fletching, but the points were still sharp enough to kill.

"My father feared attackers from every direction, even before Balram's magic took his mind," said Kall. He felt calmer now, and oddly detached as he spoke of the past. "He had dozens of these caches hidden throughout the estate. I don't think I've managed to find them all, but there are weapons and traps—some of them wickedly ingenious. I've written the locations down, along with instructions for how to set the traps. Morgan and Laerin were very helpful in that area, as I'm sure you can imagine. You'll want to go through everything step by step so you can remember where they are without looking for them."

Cesira watched his face as he spoke. *You knew I would insist on staying,* she said.

"Yes."

The druid forced a smile. *Perhaps,* she said, *after all this is over, you'll return to Mir with me? Unless, after you pull off your heroic rescue, Meisha decides to make you a Harper.*

Kall groaned, a little of his old humor returning. "Gods forbid. Being a merchant was difficult enough."

"Ye don't need to be harping, anyway," echoed Garavin's voice from the stairwell. He appeared at the door, grinning. Morgan, Laerin, and Dantane trailed behind in the stairwell. "I've seen ye dig, and that's fine enough work for any man."

"I didn't think I'd ever be able to stand upright again, after that first day," Kall said with a mock wince.

"Ah, well, that was all part of my plan. Bent over, ye could hear me better. Young people are too tall for their own good—makes it harder for them to listen."

Did you find what you needed? Cesira asked the dwarf.

"Aye, but it came at a high price." He wagged a finger at Kall. "This little adventure had better hold my interest, young one," he warned.

"Trust me," said Kall, clapping the dwarf on the shoulder. "If Meisha's message is any indication, it's long past time the Delve's secrets were brought to light. Dumathoin will approve."

"And Abbathor's fury will be unleashed," said Garavin.

"What do you mean?" asked Dantane.

"Meisha's Howling Delve is named for a dozen or so dwarf venturers who fell to the sway of the god Abbathor," said Garavin. "The Howlings worshipped Dumathoin first, but greed corrupted them. They were banished from their clan and went into exile."

"Into the Delve," said Kall, "and into business with Amn. According to Dantane's information, the ancestors of the current Bladesmiles made a substantial and secret fortune buying magic weapons and item components from the Howlings. They made the exchanges through a portal that connected the Bladesmile estate with the Delve."

"Until the day the portal went dark on dwarf heels and never lit again," said Dantane. "The Howlings disappeared and so did the supply of magic. Subsequent Bladesmile generations locked away the portal and removed its keys. If they couldn't make money off it, they didn't want their name associated with arcane magic. Except now the portal's been reactivated."

"By the Shadow Thieves," Kall said, "in a quiet, no-questions-asked arrangement with the Bladesmiles." He looked at Garavin. "We hoped you could tell us what this 'beast' is."

"I couldn't say, but Abbathor and Dumathoin have long been enemies. One is forever trying to draw faithful away from the other. Abbathor won a plump victory with The Howlings, yet this ghost ye spoke of wore Dumathoin's symbol—with the gem sundered from the mountain. I'm suspecting the two gods are still at war over the Howlings. It could be on account of the beast the sorcerous lass hinted at—a prize for Abbathor, surely, and a secret Dumathoin wants bound to the earth. When we go down there, we'll be caught in the middle of the fight."

"Standing between two dwarf gods is not the most appealing place to be," Kall conceded.

"While we're speaking of that," Garavin said, "have ye given any thought to what ye'll do when ye encounter yer friend?"

"I don't know." Kall had avoided thinking about what he would do if Aazen came down into the Delve after him.

If he's made his choice, Cesira put in, *You won't dissuade him, not after he's spent so long under Balram's hand. He won't be the friend you remember.*

Come with me! Kall remembered shouting, in vain. He had escaped and was given a new life with comrades to walk beside him and to protect him when needed it, because they counted him as a friend. Aazen had had nothing but pain.

Kall couldn't forget that ultimately, without Aazen's help, he never would have had the chance at the life he enjoyed now. Balram would have killed him before it all began, if not for Aazen. Kall would never know how much that small betrayal cost his childhood friend, but he'd seen the scars on the boy as early as seven years old. He knew Balram's fury was immeasurable.

"He gave me a chance," Kall decided. "I'll give him the same."

Garavin nodded, and something that might have been approval lit his eyes.

Is the magic Rays gave you sound? asked Cesira, changing the subject.

"According to Dantane, it is," replied Kall. He held up a large bloodstone, deeply green in color with red flecks. Rays's item, bought at a high price, would transport them to a similar gem located in the portal room at the Bladesmile estate. All they had to do was take care of whatever guards weren't drawn away by Rays's distraction and get the portal key.

"Once we're in, the Shadow Thieves'll be nipping at our heels." Garavin turned his maul over in his hands. "We'll have to be hoping we're not strolling into a maze to find yer friend."

"Then it's fortunate we have the Sword Coast's foremost expert on caves and tunnels in our party," said Kall, grinning.

"Ah, the flattery of the very young and foolhardy knows no bounds," Garavin sighed. "Here I thought ye brought me along for me battle prowess."

"We'll be needing lots of that too." Kall placed the bloodstone on the floor in the center of the tower. "Dantane, you and I are first," Kall reminded the wizard. "Light spell ready, in case we're headed into the dark?"

"Yes," the wizard replied. Kall hesitated. "Slaying spell ready, in case we're headed into certain doom?" he asked hopefully.

Dantane made a gesture that had Laerin clucking his tongue. "Get on with it," the wizard snapped. Kall put his hand on the gem, leaving room for Dantane to do the same. "The rest of you, wait for a moment, then follow." He looked at each of them in turn, his gaze resting last and lingering on

Cesira. "Remember what I told you," he said, all trace of humor gone. "Please."

She nodded, not speaking.

The gem pulsed, veiling the tower in a red haze. Cesira blinked, and Kall was gone.

A moment passed in silence. Laerin tossed a gold danter into the air. A circle of six tiny stars winked on its foreface as it fell. Morgan snatched it out of the air, juggling it with nimble fingers.

"Told you," he said smugly.

Laerin sighed. "No tearful parting, no farewell kiss," he said, putting his hand on the bloodstone. "Cesira, my love, I'm going to have a talk with both of you when we return."

Cesira blew him a kiss as he and Morgan disappeared.

Garavin knelt next to the gem, gripping the mastiff by its thick collar.

Watch over him, Cesira said.

"Like as not, he'll be the one watching me, but I take yer meaning. Ye take yer own care, lass," Garavin said. "The last thing he wants is for ye to be hurt by his enemy's hand. He wouldn't recover from that blow."

Cesira shook her head. *Balram is my enemy too. I don't know if killing him will resolve anything for Kall.*

"But ye're willing to find out?"

Eager, said the druid.

CHAPTER TWENTY-FOUR

The Howling Delve
5 Marpenoth, the Year of Lightning Storms (1374 DR)

"Maybe you killed them all," said Talal hopefully.

Meisha stood in the center of the cavern where they'd found Braedrin's body. Her eyes were on the ceiling. Her arms dangled loosely at her sides.

Talal held her shirt and boots. She wore only her leather jerkin, bound tightly at the waist by her belt, and her breeches. Her lips curved as Talal fidgeted. "You're welcome to wait with the others," she offered.

"Cowards, all of 'em," Talal said, pitching his voice to carry down the passage where Haroun and the others stood ready.

"One step at a time," Meisha said, closing her eyes. "They're taking their fates in hand. They're already terrified to be defying the Shadow Thieves."

"Terror?" Talal sniffed. *"Terror* will be when my clothes fall apart or get burned up standing too close to fire-crazed sorcerers. I'll be tromping around here naked before I beg that bastard Balram for more clothes."

"Gods forbid," came Haroun's voice from the passage.

"Just you keep that in mind while you're clinging to the walls out there!" Talal bellowed.

"Settle down," said Meisha. "I can hear them. Get ready."

"Nets up," Talal called down the tunnel. "Even if you do get them to fly down the right hole," he said, "how do we know they won't just chew through the ropes and get loose, maybe in the warrens?"

"I treated the ropes with poison," said Meisha. "It isn't lethal—not even painful—but it'll taste awful to the bats. Besides, we only need to funnel them to the cavern off the portal room. As long as that net holds, we'll be fine. Get down!" she shouted as black shapes began to pour from the hole near the ceiling.

Talal hit the ground as deep bats filled the chamber. He watched Meisha step back, cross her arms over her chest, and burst into a pillar of flame.

* * *

Kall passed through the portal and started to fall. He reached out blindly, his hands sliding down rocks, but there were no handholds. He fell into empty space.

Abruptly, his back and buttocks hit something solid. He flung his arms behind to catch himself, but they kept going, flailing in midair until something else caught his armpits and held him securely.

Panting, Kall looked around. Dull green glows revealed an expanse of hemp net stretched taut across a circular chasm. His legs and arms dangled through gaps in the net. All was quiet but for the swaying and creaking noises made by his weight against the rope. Beyond the chasm lay a large expanse of cavern, with tunnels adjoining either end. The tunnel in front of him was clear, but an identical, crudely fashioned net draped the one behind him.

Kall looked up and saw a mirror of what lay below him; but the shaft in the ceiling was clear of obstruction, lit by green radiances from the active portal. He watched, transfixed by the unusual perspective, as one by one his companions plummeted through the light and down the shaft.

Kall braced himself as they hit the net. Each impact jarred his back and shoulders. The net strained under their weight. Garavin's hound howled as it tried to disentangle its legs from their painful positions.

"We need to get off this," Kall said, noting the frayed ends of the rope looped around three nearby stalagmites. "The rope won't hold all of us."

"Meisha didn't mention a death trap'd be waiting for us," Morgan said.

"This was probably her work." Kall helped Garavin lift Borl out of the tangled ropes. "Without it, we'd be at the bottom of the chasm."

"Still could've warned us," Morgan grumbled.

Kall waited until they were all off the net. Using his sword, he hacked the ropes free from the stalagmites. The net sailed down into the darkness.

"The Shadow Thieves will have ways to avoid the chasm," Dantane pointed out.

"Now they'll have to use them," Kall said. He turned to Garavin. "What about it, old friend? Are we in the right place?"

The dwarf examined the cavern walls, clasping his holy symbol reflexively. "Aye, lad," he said. His voice sounded unnaturally thick. "We're here." He turned to look at Kall earnestly. "Dumathoin is here too."

Kall and Laerin exchanged glances. "What do you mean?" asked the half-elf.

"Where do ye feel most at peace, Laerin—closest to yer god?" asked the dwarf.

"In Erevan's grove or Dugmaren's tunnels," answered Laerin.

"This is Dumathoin's place," said Garavin. "But it's been tainted."

"He's right," said Dantane. The wizard closed his eyes. He appeared to be listening, though Kall detected nothing breaking the stillness but the distant sound of water. "There's some sort of distant aura in effect."

"Meisha's master lived in the Delve," said Kall. "Could it be some latent magic of his?"

"I don't think so," said Dantane, "not unless her master was of another plane."

"Meisha was trained as an elementalist," said Garavin. "Might be there's links to the elemental planes here."

"Kall," Morgan said abruptly, "we're not alone."

Kall turned. A child stood in the opening of the clear tunnel, watching them with wide, fearful eyes. Her face was pale and thin, almost emaciated. Kall took a step toward her, but she darted off down the tunnel.

"The refugees," said Laerin. "Do we follow?"

Kall nodded. "Light two torches. Keep your weapons out but down. We have to find Meisha."

"Kall." Dantane pointed to the other tunnel branching off the chamber. The net strung over its mouth glistened in the torchlight. A thick, mucuslike substance dripped from the ropes, collecting in black puddles on the floor. "Something's coming."

Kall heard it—the sound of air rushing up the too-narrow tunnel. Next to him, Borl growled from the gut, shifting agitatedly. "Get away from the net," he snapped as Dantane bent to examine the black drippings.

The wizard ducked away as a leathery wing swiped at him. Twin lines of needle-teeth bit down directly in front of his face. The bat screamed as the black substance filled its mouth and foamed. It fluttered back against a wall of a dozen or more creatures just like it. Their wings tangled in the small space, causing them to snap indiscriminately at each other.

"The Shadow Thieves?" Laerin said. "Or are these meant for us?"

"I don't know," Kall said. "But we're not going that way. We follow the girl." He looked at Dantane. "You have the portal key?"

Dantane touched a pouch hidden in his robes. Within, he'd placed the oblong stone that activated the portal from this side of the Delve. Rays had kept his word.

"It will be safe," Dantane said.

Kall nodded. He and Laerin led the way down the open tunnel. Dantane, Morgan, and Garavin brought up the rear. Once out of the spell light of the portal room, the tunnel became stygian. The torches cast a glow in front and behind their group but made the air close and smoky. Kall couldn't imagine being trapped in the enclosed space for any length of time, as the refugees had been. It would have driven him mad.

The passage turned, weaving in a snakelike pattern for several yards without changing direction. Laerin pointed to the ground, where scuffed imprints of bare feet were clearly visible, even in the wavering torch light. "She won't be hard to track."

Frowning, Kall held up a hand for the group to pause. He listened. "Why don't we hear her running?"

"Maybe she's hiding," Laerin suggested. "We won't hurt you, little one," he called out down the tunnel.

Far off, Kall thought he heard a whimper. "Let's go."

The tunnel angled gradually, and at an intersection, Laerin guided them to the right. The tunnel dipped, forcing them to crouch and move single file.

"She's smart," said Morgan. "She knows we'll catch up to her on open ground. She's looking for a mouse hole."

The passage turned again, and finally Kall could stand upright. He shone the torch ahead and stopped, holding back Laerin and the others when he saw the girl.

She stood at the cusp of a second intersection, as if unsure which path to take. She swiveled her head to look back. Her eyes widened when she saw Kall, and she started to dart away.

"Don't!" Laerin shouted, springing forward.

The girl flinched. Kall saw her foot slide forward and heard the pressure plate click. The half-elf's sharper vision had seen the trap even in the shadows.

Laerin snagged the girl by the waist and pulled her to the ground beneath him. Above their heads, a spear burst from a hole in the tunnel wall, shooting across the intersection to ricochet off stone.

"Are you all right?" Kall asked. He started to move forward, but Laerin held out a staying hand.

"Let Morgan check the intersection first," he said.

Kall gave Morgan the torch, waiting while the rogue checked the walls and floor for more spear holes. Laerin kept a protective arm around the girl, but Kall saw him wiggle his eyebrows and whisper something to her that made her laugh. After that, her face lost much of its fear. The scene reminded Kall of how easily the half-elf had drawn *him* out, when he'd been a frightened boy in Mir.

He turned to Dantane. "We can't take time to check all the walls. We need a barrier."

The wizard considered the tunnel wall where the spear had originated. He touched the stone and began a clipped chant.

A chill breeze funneled down the passage, tugging at Kall's hair. Dantane's breath fogged and the veins on the backs of his hands turned a sickly yellow-blue. The red flesh beneath his fingernails bled white. All of a sudden, he stopped speaking and slapped the wall with his open palm.

The sound was that of an ice-covered branch cracking against stone. Kall half-expected the wizard's hand to shatter, but it did not. A sheet of ice spider-webbed from his fingers, the frozen strands shooting down the tunnel and thickening, filling in the gaps until the entire wall shone white.

"That should hold anything that comes from the wall," Dantane said.

"Floor's clear," Morgan added, helping Laerin to his feet.

"Can you take us to Meisha?" Kall asked, crouching in front of the girl. Her eyes shifted to the torch in his hand, and Kall chuckled. "That's her—fire."

The girl nodded, and Kall set off again, keeping her just behind his hip as they walked along the passage. The tunnel stayed straight, and at the end of it, Kall didn't have to ask if they were close. He could see by the moisture dripping from Dantane's ice wall.

They entered a deep chamber with a high ceiling. A pillar

of brilliant flame stood in the center of the room, lighting it to every corner. Meisha stood within the fire column, her hands clasped together against her chest.

"She's killing herself," breathed Dantane in fascination.

A hearty snort echoed in the chamber. "Not hardly."

Kall turned to see a boy of about eighteen or nineteen enter the chamber from an adjoining tunnel. He was as thin as the little girl, but his eyes held no fear, only defiance as he stared Kall down. "She just finished herding the last of 'em," he said. "Who're you?"

"Friends," said Meisha. The fire died away, leaving the Harper's skin sweat-slicked and flush. "Well met, Kall."

"Meisha." Kall held out his arm, and she clasped it gratefully.

"I see you brought the whole army," Meisha said, greeting Morgan, Garavin, and Laerin with a nod. Her eyes fell on Dantane and widened with curiosity. "This one's new."

"Meisha Saira, meet Syrek Dantane." Kall waited while Dantane bowed politely to the Harper. "I wish I could say that was the extent of the party, but the Shadow Thieves will be coming behind us."

"That's what the bats are for," said Meisha. "We didn't know if you'd be able to find us. We planned an ambush."

"We'll need it." Kall looked at the boy. "Is this one trustworthy?"

"Likely more so than your wizard," the Harper answered, grinning when Dantane flushed in irritation.

For his part, Talal bristled with all the fervor of his nineteen years. "Trust me not to catch on fire, without so much as a warning," he muttered.

"Talal saved my life when I came down here," Meisha explained.

Kall nodded approvingly. "Then I owe him my thanks as well. Go get the others together, Talal," he said. "Not here—we'll gather them in the entrance tunnel. We need to know where the seal is."

Talal took off back the way he'd come. "What are you

planning?" Meisha wanted to know, but Kall shook his head.

"You'll see. Garavin and Dantane have it worked out. Meisha," he said, pulling her aside, "where is your master, Varan?"

Meisha's eyes were stone. "Varan is dead."

"Dead? But your message . . ."

"Oh, he still breathes," she said harshly, "and his mind functions, on some level. But there is no heart in his eyes, no passion driving his actions, unless you consider madness a sustaining emotion."

"How did it happen?" Kall asked, shocked. "How did the Shadow Thieves overcome him?"

"It wasn't the Shadow Thieves. They exploited Varan's condition to get their magic items, but they didn't put him in his current state. I don't know how it happened, but now all he can do is sit in a room and make deadly magic."

Kall took it all in. "So Chadossa's illusion, the black market in Amn . . ."

"The what?"

"A piece of broken magic that twisted a boy into a monster. It came from the black market." Kall's expression darkened.

"And they got it from Varan," Meisha said. "As far as I can tell, some of his creations work, some are . . . broken, and run wild. But they're all dangerous, as long as the Shadow Thieves have them."

Talal's voice broke in as the boy came barreling back into the chamber. "They're on the move," he said breathlessly. "Every one of 'em." He noticed Meisha's stricken face. "What? What's wrong?" He frowned at Kall, as if knowing instinctively he was to blame.

"I'm fine, Talal," Meisha said, forcing a smile as she looked at him. "Are you ready to bathe in the sunlight, Dirty Bones?"

He sniffed. "Ale is what I'm aching for. Keep your water and sunshine."

"We'll use Meisha's bats as distractions," Kall said as they filed in to the tunnel. "Can you let them out safely?" he asked, looking at the Harper with concern.

"I'll take care of it," Meisha said.

She retraced Kall's steps quickly to the portal room, while the others headed for the main entrance.

Careful to avoid the bats, Meisha placed her hands against the poison-treated net and called the fire. The power, simmering dangerously close to the surface, answered immediately. There was no flame, but the ropes began to smoke where her palms touched them. She waited a moment to make sure the hemp would burn, then ran back to the opposite tunnel.

She slowed, wary, when she saw Dantane waiting for her.

"What was that spell?" he asked curiously.

"It will slow-burn the net away," she said. "Between the fire and the poison, the bats will have worked themselves into a fine furor by the time our friends arrive."

"You're an elementalist," said Dantane, "and a sorceress. Have you learned to bypass spells completely, turning your raw power into whatever form you will?"

Meisha pulled on a loose end of rope left dangling by the tunnel mouth. A third net unrolled from the shelf of rock above the opening; poison slathered these ropes too. "No," she said. "The power would burn my organs from within if I tried."

"How can you be certain, if you've never experimented?"

"Because my master knew his craft. He trained all of his apprentices the same," she said, "before they were murdered—before my master was driven mad and sealed in a lightless prison to make toys for a man I would trade my soul to slay in the most terrible of ways."

She turned, and Dantane took a step back, disturbed—perhaps for the first time in his life—by the kindling power in the Harper's eyes. They shone red—raw, blistering wounds in a face ravaged by grief.

"Yes, Dantane. I am a fire elementalist," she said. "The best Varan Ivshar ever trained. And I intend to burn down the Shadow Thieves, even if it means suffering the fate I just described."

Behind her, bats flooded the portal room.

"How many are left?" asked Balram, when Aazen entered the house.

"Four that I know of," said Aazen. "There may be more. My contact said that when Kall departed for the Delve, he left behind the lady of the house and a handful of servants. She should not be mistaken for a helpless chatelaine," he added. "She is a powerful servant of Silvanus."

But Balram didn't appear to be listening. "So Kall Morel has come full circle, back to the kingdom where he almost lost his life." He looked at Aazen. "Now you see what comes from leaving tasks unfinished," he said, as if Aazen were a boy sitting for a lesson. "The thorn has grown into a dagger, pressing at our throats."

"Forgive me, Father," Aazen offered, but there was no passion in the words.

"The past is done," said Balram. "We will deal with what remains of Morel's house and then we will never have to think of him again. Take men down to the Delve," he instructed. "Kill them all." He gripped Aazen's arm when he would have walked away. "I mean *all,* Aazen. The Delve is due for a thorough scouring."

"What about Varan?" Aazen asked. "Without his caretakers, he will eventually starve himself, or die of sickness, if his magic fails."

"After you've killed Kall, bring the wizard to the surface," said Balram. "The portal is no longer secure. We will continue the operation above."

"You can't be serious," Aazen said. "Varan will not allow us to take him from the Delve. His magic is there. Whatever his diseased mind is planning, is *there.* He needs to stay in the Delve."

"Use the Harper," said Balram. "You said she knew him. Use her to get him to cooperate."

"He is mad," Aazen said clearly, trying to make his father see reason, "and the Harper is dead."

Balram's lip curled in a mocking sneer. "You don't believe that any more than I do. They must have switched bodies on us. Why else would Morel be seeking the portal, unless he had been somehow warned of our connection to the Delve? The Harper bitch is alive. The tunnel rats are hiding her, and now they'll pay the price for their betrayal. After you've secured the wizard, kill her and seal the portal. We have no more use for the Delve."

Aazen didn't know what to say. "Is this my death sentence, then?" he asked bluntly. "For betraying you as a boy and allowing Kall to come back to torment us? For that you're sending me into the Hells, hoping I won't return?"

Balram seemed genuinely taken aback, which gave Aazen a strange bit of comfort. "Never, my son," he replied. "I send you because you are the only one I can trust to see this done." He put both hands on Aazen's shoulders, as he'd so often done when Aazen was a child. The gesture had always come across as equal parts comfort and threat. "With the Shadow Thieves at our backs, we need never worry about failure, about weakness, ever again. They are our family now."

Family, Aazen thought, remembering Jubair's words. What exactly did his father mean by likening the Shadow Thieves to blood? Oh yes, Balram had power now, such as he never had before, but they weren't free to act by any stretch of the imagination. Daen oversaw all Balram's actions, approving or denying his plans as he saw fit. Whom Daen answered to, Aazen did not know, and neither did Balram.

The Shadow Thieves wove a complex web around their organization, relying on anonymity to protect their power bases. At least, when Balram had served Morel, he knew where his superior's authority began and ended. How much control could they truly have over their own lives if they didn't even know the identities of their masters?

"Do you have such strong faith in your family?" Aazen said, aware even as he asked it that the question had multiple layers.

Balram took his meaning. "I would trust them, and you, with my life," he said without hesitation.

Aazen nodded. "Then I'll see to the Delve," he said, "and to Kall."

Balram watched his son's retreating back. He said, pitching his voice low, "I've already arranged to send a second party."

Daen stepped into the room, taking a seat on one of the dusty sofas. His bulk had diminished somewhat over the years, but any rumors that the Shadow Thief's heart was in any way failing him found themselves quickly and brutally squelched. "You believe he will betray you again, after all this time?"

"Once was enough," said Balram. "I'll not be blinded to him again."

"Ah, but you can't beat the lad into submission anymore," Daen pointed out. "And if he discovers you don't truly trust him, it may send him over the edge. This course of action may come back to bite you at the heel, my friend. How can you hope to stop him if he decides to go his own way?"

"By using any number of my other sons or daughters," Balram replied. "Those I've trained for a decade and more."

"The Shadow Thieves will support you," Daen agreed, "but that one is your blood. I wonder if you can forsake him so casually?"

"We'll see," said Balram.

In truth, Daen did not care whether the father or the son prevailed in this, yet he sensed in Aazen a fascinating strength: the ability to survive, even to thrive, under the most unique and terrible strain. The boy had lived in a hole in the ground and in the countless Hells of his father's making; yet he'd come out whole, or nearly so.

Daen had recruited runaways and child-cutpurses barely surviving on the streets, but most hadn't lived long and none ever knew who held their leads. Aazen had known that murderers and thieves protected him ever since he was a boy. He was a child of the Shadow Thieves, if such a thing existed. Daen didn't know if that meant a long and prosperous career within their ranks awaited Aazen, or a quick death, but he decided it would be fascinating to find out. Through experience, Daen had learned to pay close attention to the people who fascinated him, whether they were intelligent, greedy, sane, or mad. The ability to read people, to judge their actions and worth, was what made Daen so successful at what he did. And the Kortrun family had made him a very rich man indeed.

<hr />

Dantane trailed behind Meisha as they caught up to the others. Ahead, the passage widened into a chamber comparable in size to the portal room. The path dead-ended abruptly in a wall of loose dirt and rubble.

"This is where we came in. No need to fetch shovels," Talal said sardonically.

"Boy's right," said Morgan. "You won't be tunneling through that, not with magic on it."

"I'm not disagreeing," said Garavin. He scratched his thick sideburns as he eyed the wall. "Though he might relish the challenge."

"Who?" asked Talal.

The dwarf grinned at the boy. "Ye'll see." He handed Dantane a tightly wrapped scroll sealed in green wax and bearing the imprint of an open hand lying upon an anvil.

Kall recognized the seal of the Fallstone clan. As a boy, he'd seen it depicted on several documents in Garavin's map room.

Dantane unrolled the parchment and read for several breaths, nodding as if he'd seen similar text before.

"Clear enough?" asked Garavin.

"You're certain you can control this?" asked the wizard. "There's no time to construct a summoning circle."

"It's not a summoning in the traditional sense," said the dwarf. "More like a calling. He may answer or not, as he prefers, but he's never denied me before."

Dantane's eyes moved rapidly over the text. Finally, he let his hands fall to his sides and closed his eyes. He murmured what might have been a prayer under his breath, opened his eyes, and began to read aloud from the parchment.

This time his voice carried, booming unnaturally across the chamber. A tremor of unease went through the refugees. Kall motioned to Talal to keep them still.

The echo of Dantane's casting seemed to stick in the walls, building to a steady rumbling Kall could feel in the stone itself. The air felt thick, as if he were breathing rock dust or sand instead of air. The cavern seemed to grow smaller around them. A single rock in the center of the cavern swelled in size before his eyes, expanding to fill the chamber, forcing the refugees back against the far wall. A few of the people cried out or tried to run, but there was no room. A boy standing near the front of the crowd stumbled and went down on his knees. A foot scuffed the side of his face as he tried to stand. He fell again, harder.

"Cease!" Kall barked over the rumbling, and his voice, too, seemed eerily magnified. The crowd quieted, and Kall helped the boy to his feet.

Kall turned again to look at the rock, expecting it to have returned to its normal size as the disorientation cleared. It hadn't. It had, if possible, gotten larger, and now appeared to be breathing. Slow inhalations and exhalations like the wind through a long chimney flue were punctuated by a deep moan coming from somewhere beneath the thing.

Kall had listened to Garavin tell stories of the delvers, beasts friendly to the dwarves. The slablike tunnel dwellers were as large and as cumbersome as boulders, and this one was no exception. Moving by inches and trailing a stain of sticky fluid, the delver made its way to where Garavin stood with one boot propped on the rock pile.

The dwarf put out a hand—in greeting, Kall thought; but Garavin laid his palm gently across the ridges and slopes that might have passed for the thing's face and bowed deeply, his holy symbol falling against his nose.

The low moan came again, and Garavin nodded as if in answer to a question with no words. "A poor way to wake, to be sure," he said, in tones of sincere regret. "We would not have done so, if our need was not great, Iathantos. Dumathoin has asked, and so I must ask ye to aid us, for ye're the only one who can."

The delver fell silent. Kall looked around at the refugees, but they, too, were quiet, riveted in awe or horror at the exchange between the dwarf and the huge, living stone.

Finally, the delver shifted its great body, shuffled backward a step, and moaned again. Garavin inclined his head in response.

"My thanks." He pointed to the base of the rock pile, and the delver came forward again, engulfing the space with his bulk. There was a sharp cracking and a sloshing release of sizzling liquid. The stones turned dark with wet, and the delver began to burrow into the cavern floor.

Garavin walked back to the group, shaking his head, but he was smiling. He laid a hand on Talal's shoulder, guiding the boy to where he could see the churning as the delver took the stone into itself.

"He'll tunnel ye out, and do it gladly," the dwarf explained. "He absorbs minerals from the stone to nourish himself, and being that we're close to Keczulla, this rock is richer in them than most. That, and his loyalty to Dumathoin, made him answer our call."

"But it's not a dwarf," said Talal. "Not even a person. Why would it serve a dwarf god?"

"Because it thinks and understands like any other sentient creature," said Garavin. "It may take him longer, and he may never aspire to the intelligence of two-legged folk, but he's capable of despair and loneliness, and of needing to combat those emotions."

"Then why doesn't it have its own god?" Talal pressed. "Someone who understands *him*."

Garavin met Kall's eyes briefly, and Kall knew what he was thinking. Talal's questions were not unlike another cautiously stubborn boy's curiosity. "He might have," the dwarf allowed, "I only know he serves Dumathoin for the same reason I do: to keep the secrets of the stone, and to bring the rest into the light, whether it's gems and gold, fossils of history, or—"

"Us," Talal cut in, his expression thoughtful. "Down in the dark, where no one can see." He touched the patch of naked skin on his head. "Balram thought he could keep us a secret."

"But Dumathoin would not have it so," Garavin said. "Sooner or later, all secrets come to light, whether we want them to or not."

"Will they be safe?" Kall asked Garavin, watching the delver work.

"Yes. Iathantos will protect them. He's given his word," said Garavin. "If any Shadow Thief gets past us, they won't care for the fight they'll find waiting."

"What's he mean?" asked Talal, looking to Meisha for an explanation.

The Harper appeared torn. "We have to leave you now," she said, shaking her head when Talal opened his mouth to argue. "The Shadow Thieves will have learned about Kall's rescue party by now. They'll be coming, and we have to meet them. An all-out assault will give the creature time to tunnel deep enough to cross the boundaries of the enchantment."

"Once you're outside, head for Keczulla," said Kall. "The delver will take care of any guards outside the entrance, but I doubt there will be any. They don't expect you to escape that way. Use my name at the city gates."

"Ignore it when their visages pale and they soil themselves," said Morgan.

Kall glared him into silence. He slipped a ring off his finger and handed it to Haroun. The emerald and stone, in its gold setting, was the first symbol of his new status. Garavin had made it for him long ago using Cesira's enchanted speaking stone.

Haroun slid the ring onto her thumb. Her eyes swam with tears. "How can we thank you?"

"You saved my life," Meisha said. She looked at Talal, but the boy was shaking his head mutinously.

"I want to stay with you," he said, "for the fight."

"Ha," Meisha said. "You don't mean that, not when you're scenting freedom at last. No"—she shook him playfully by the shoulder when he tried to protest—"No more death-seeking for you, little Dirty Bones. We'll follow you out once we take care of the Shadow Thieves."

Morgan and Laerin filed back down the tunnel. Dantane and Garavin followed. Meisha took one last look at Talal and Haroun, who stood apart from the rest. Haroun had a firm hand on the boy's shoulder.

"They'll be safe," Kall said.

"I know." Meisha allowed the others to get some distance ahead of them, then she clasped Kall's wrist to slow him. "Balram's lived too long, Kall," she said fiercely, "taken too much. It's time to end him. You promised me."

"Meisha, I'm sorry about your master—"

"Don't," Meisha cut him off. "When I saw him sitting in that room . . . you can't imagine how it felt." She caught her breath and looked at him sharply. "No, that's wrong. You can imagine. You've seen it before."

He nodded grimly. "Rage blocks all reason. You'll do anything to fix things. You'll forgive him any terrible thing he's ever done." Kall touched his sword hilt. "I'll keep my word, Meisha." He pointed to the tunnel. "Let's go get Varan."

CHAPTER TWENTY-FIVE

Keczulla, Amn
5 Marpenoth, the Year of Lightning Storms (1374 DR)

Cesira heard the servant calling her from the foot of the stairs. Since the explosion, none of them had dared venture into Dantane's tower. While the druid appreciated having a place where her privacy was guaranteed, she'd come to the tower for a very different purpose.

The stones formerly connected to the tower's ceiling were chipped and broken, forming rough crenellations. The tower had become her battlement—Cesira perched on one cloven stone in hawk form, gripping the ruined surface with her sharp talons.

The servant had come to tell her about the party approaching the house, but Cesira's keen eyes had already spotted them on the road.

Cesira spread her wings and let out a cry, just to hear her voice echo into the twilight. She glided to the floor and transformed, standing barefoot in the center of the ruined tower as her vision gradually returned to its human limitations. She strode to the stairs and called down to the servant.

Show them in when they arrive, she said. *After that, you're dismissed for the night and the day to follow. Tell the others.*

"My lady?" was the man's timid, confused reply.

Lord Morel and I will not be in residence, Cesira said. *Go quickly.*

"Yes, my lady."

My lady, Cesira repeated to herself. Gods help her. She had to get out of Amn. The audience she was about to endure would be her last in this wretched city, she vowed.

If she survived it.

The screams of night hunters greeted Kall's ears as he waited outside Varan's chamber. "Hurry, Meisha," he said.

"We're coming." Meisha stepped out into the passage, guiding the old wizard by the arm. He stumbled on legs unused to walking, but Meisha steadied him, whispering to him constantly, coaxing, encouraging, as one might handle a child—or a wild beast.

"Unwelcome," Varan murmured as they walked. "Unwelcome, unwelcome you all are. You've never died before, none of you . . ." He snagged Kall's arm suddenly. "But you will," he hissed.

Gently, Meisha disengaged Varan's hand and wrapped it around her arm. "Be easy, Master. We will bring you more work, more magic."

"Broken," Varan muttered. He lowered his gaze to his feet as he shuffled forward. "I'll fix them all eventually."

The net was still draped over the end of the tunnel when Kall and Meisha arrived. Laerin and Morgan lay flat on their bellies before it, watching the battle in the portal chamber. Dantane and Garavin waited some distance behind.

"How many?" asked Kall when Morgan crawled back to them.

"Dozen and a half," said Morgan. He did not sound pleased. "They fight good."

Laerin was equally subdued. "Your friend is with them," he said. "The man from your party."

Kall nodded. He should have been prepared, but it still felt as if he'd been hit with a fist. For a moment, he found himself at a loss as to how to proceed.

"The whole room's like a bottle. Meisha and the wizard can fill the room with killing," suggested Morgan, "before we set a foot inside."

"But it gives the boy, Aazen, no time to explain himself," Garavin said.

"Some of us are more concerned with not getting murdered," said Dantane coldly. "If we act now, I can fill the room with lightning before they slay all the bats. It will buy the refugees more time as well."

"They're bound to have magical protection," Laerin pointed out. "A wizard of their own, at least."

"Dantane will single him or her out," Kall decided. "But Garavin's right. I want to talk to Aazen." Dantane cursed, but Kall ignored him, addressing Meisha instead. "That's how it's going to happen. After I'm through, you're free to fill the room with fire, just leave Varan here. He'll be safe enough."

Meisha nodded. Kall watched her guide Varan to a protected nook down the tunnel while the others gathered at the tunnel mouth. The sounds of battle were fading.

Kall drew his sword and sliced away the net. A pair of men saw him coming through. They raised bows, but a voice barked out, "Hold!" before they could fire.

"My thanks for that," said Kall amiably as Aazen pulled his sword free of a deep bat's body. He wiped the gore across the creature's furred chest. "For a moment I feared you'd come to kill me."

"We've come for the wizard," said Aazen. "Give him to us, and your companions can leave unmolested."

"And the folk who've been plying your father's newest trade for these last years? What will their fate be?" Kall asked.

"Does it matter?" Aazen countered. "My only interest now is Varan. Let him go, Kall. He is too far gone to care what company he keeps, so long as he is allowed to continue his work. He'll be safe with us."

"Too many people have enjoyed your father's version of 'safe' over the years, Aazen," said Kall. "Yourself included. We both know neither of us is getting out of here without fighting our way out. Your father sent you to kill me."

"Yes," said Aazen.

"He's done it before. But you couldn't betray me then, and I don't believe you'll betray me now. Why not come with me this time, old friend?"

"You still don't understand," said Aazen. "My choice was made a long time ago. I cannot disobey my father. He is all I have."

"You had me!" Anger and long-buried resentment sparked to life within Kall. "You could have started a new life. You could have escaped him."

"As you escaped your father?" Aazen said coldly. "Where has your freedom—the freedom I won for you—brought you, Kall? Right back to Amn and the arms of the merchants, right back to the edge of death, only this time, I won't be there to save you."

"It's not the same."

"Oh, but it is," said Aazen bitterly. "Our deeds are unforgivable, I grant you. I have no illusions about my life. But your father was as ruthless a murderer as mine."

"No."

"His actions sprang from the same darkness of heart. Why do you think friendship blossomed so easily between them? They were two similar creatures who came into conflict with one another."

"My father was nothing like Balram!" Kall spat.

"He was brought down, crippled long before death, but if he'd been left unchecked, his cruelties might have come to rival Balram's. Yet you've devoted your life to avenging him and restoring what he lost through his own folly. You never gave half so much thought to Haig's legacy, did you? How terrified you must have been to even face his memory."

"You know nothing of Haig."

"But I know you, Kall. You stand before me in a cage as

complex and binding as my own, and you have the gall to promise to free me?" Aazen laughed. "We are both trapped. We can only claw at each other from our prisons. The loser in this contest may end up being the fortunate one."

"Is that the way it's to be, then?" said Kall sadly. "Is that what you truly want, Aazen?"

The question seemed to stir his friend, and for a breath something faltered in Aazen's gaze. Kall took a step forward, but Aazen recoiled, falling behind the men with bows. "Kill him," he said clearly.

At close range, the arrows were a blur. Kall only saw the twin jets of flame. The missiles burned up in mid-flight.

Meisha materialized next to Kall, her eyes red as she stared down the bowmen. His friends appeared in a swarm as Dantane's invisibility cloak fell away.

Garavin swung his maul, smashing aside the bows. Their bearers fell back out of reach of the massive weapon and broke their protective flank around Aazen. Borl ran alongside his master, snarling and herding them into a corner of the room.

Morgan and Laerin fought side by side with swords and daggers. They formed a rough wall for Meisha and Dantane to cast spells behind while Kall separated from the group and chased after Aazen.

Two heads of white-gold hair met him as Isslun and her twin crowded him from Aazen's other side.

"Never turn down two at once," sang Isslun as the twins attacked in unison. She slashed high, almost lazily, aiming for Kall's throat. Her sister ducked under the strike and came up in a burst of speed at his guard.

Kall crouched, sweeping aside Aliyea's blade. "How you survived the years since our last meeting"—he came up under her sword, forcing her to follow him back to his feet—"is a mystery." He danced to one side, spinning so that Isslun was between him and Aliyea's attack. "They've been hard years, though, haven't they?" he taunted. He slashed his sword in a mimic of Isslun's strike, tracing the line of a white scar running along the woman's jaw. Isslun flinched, and Kall came at her. He shifted his grip, changed the direction of his swing and cut a much deeper line across Isslun's stomach. She let out a shocked gasp, clutching at her abdomen.

Aliyea shouted her sister's name in rage. She drew a dagger from her belt and hurled it over her sister's shoulder as Isslun crumpled to the floor. Kall spun away, but the fang sunk into his arm, and pierced through to the other side of the muscle. Pain ran a fire trail up his arm. Kall dropped back, kicking out with his foot to sweep Aliyea's legs out from under her as she charged him. She fell, but she grabbed the dagger hilt protruding from Kall's arm as she went down.

Kall felt muscle tear when the blade came free sideways, carving a hunk of flesh from his arm. Aliyea's eyes glinted maliciously as he cried out from the pain. She gripped the dagger with both hands and raised it above her head.

The dagger burst into flame. Aliyea's eyes widened. She released the burning weapon with a yelp of pain. In one movement, Kall snatched it out of the air, turned, and plunged it through a gap in her armor. The fingers of his maimed arm came away blistered from the fire. His stab wound bled liberally, making him lightheaded, but he had no time to bind it. The cavern swirled with fighters, far more of them foes. He jumped to his feet and over the twins, making his way to Garavin, who stood closest.

Near the rim of the chasm, the dwarf danced atop the ring of stones encircling the pit, swinging his maul angle-out, like a pendulum, to keep three Shadow Thieves at bay. Despite his heavy tread, the dwarf moved among the rocks as if he strode through mist, using his weight to lever the maul.

In the end, two of the men leaped forward. The man to Garavin's left swung a light flail in imitation of Garavin's maul.

Garavin feinted toward him but broke to the right, striking the second man a quick, snapping blow across the kneecap. The man's leg went out, and he was down, scrabbling on the rocks to keep from falling into the pit.

The distraction allowed the dwarf to focus on the flail. The spiked ball wrapped around the handle of his weapon. The chain cinched tight.

Instead of grappling with the larger man, Garavin relinquished his weapon to keep his footing. The man yanked his maul away. Garavin clasped his holy symbol and mouthed a fast prayer. The triumphant smile disappeared off his opponent's face. The maul turned upright, floating in the air as if held by invisible hands.

The man gaped at the rotating weapon. The maul shot out over the chasm, dragging the flail chain and its owner with it. The thief lost his grip on the weapon and pitched headfirst into the dark.

Garavin snagged his maul and the flail before they fell, turning with both weapons to the second man on the rocks.

He brought the maul around as the man swung an axe blade in a reverse chop aimed at Garavin's chin. The dwarf blocked the blow, but the weight of both weapons was too great, and the impact of the axe drove him back hard. He skirted the lip of the chasm. The axeman lunged forward to try to force him the rest of the way into the pit.

A blast of hot air caught the dwarf from behind, pushing him forward. He smashed the maul through the axeman, clipping his opponent in the ribs. Bones cracked audibly, and the man fell back. Garavin threw a quick salute skyward, where Meisha hovered above his head.

The cavern's ceiling was alive with aerial battle. Dantane and Meisha flew around each other, using stalactites for cover as they engaged the Shadow Thief wizard and his two protectors—a younger man and woman who appeared to be apprentices. Their hands moved in frantic, mimicking circles, weaving spell-shields for their master.

Meisha hurled her last two stilettos. The blades caught fire as they spun through the air. One burning missile caught the woman in the thigh, forcing her to break rhythm to put out the flames licking her robes.

"Dantane!" Meisha cried, but the wizard was already casting. With one palm atop the other, his fingers flush in a rough X shape, Dantane yelled, *"Krevatcya, dannan shae!"*

The woman let out a desperate shout, but she couldn't get the spell out in time. A ball of black energy formed under Dantane's hands and streaked down to hit the other wizard in the chest, ruining whatever spell he'd been preparing. Instead of dissipating, the black energy mass crawled along his skin, trailing electrical sparks that singed his robes. The wizard tried to claw the ball off, gasping when his hands met a jolt of painful electricity.

Meisha spared Dantane a glance, but the wizard wasn't looking at her. He'd paused to witness the effects of his own spell. The black energy sizzled along the wizard's flesh. Dantane seemed detached, analytical as he watched it.

Thumb-sized teardrops of flame appeared, one above each of the fingers of Meisha's open palm. She murmured an incantation, and the flames began to spin in a circle like tiny stars. They shot across the cavern, peppering the wizard's apprentices with tiny firebursts. Protection spells flickered and peeled away as the wizard continued to grapple with the dark, killing energy.

Meisha grabbed the stalactite for leverage and swung around the base. She started to drop down and felt a painful coldness shoot up her leg. Whirling, putting her back to the stalactite, Meisha saw another thief crawling along the walls, his hands and feet covered with the same sticky climbing aid Talal had taken from the halfling. He held a barbed whip in one hand and a blade between his teeth.

Meisha put a hand over her thigh where the whip had ripped away cloth and flesh above her boot's cuff. She was in the crossfire of the wizard and the whip-wielder now, and the man's whip obviously bore some type of enchantment, for her leg was rapidly going numb with the cold.

She looked below. Morgan was nearest, but he bled liberally from a gash across his eyebrow. He ran below her to aid Garavin.

Her mind worked rapidly. Meisha pointed at the man on the wall, holding her arm out almost perpendicular to her body, affording him an easy target. He took the bait.

The whip snapped out, circling her arm, driving its barbs in deep. Cold spasms shot up to her elbow. Meisha clenched her teeth against the pain and called the fire. She prayed it would be enough to siphon off the cold. She pictured the whip in her mind—the shape, the coil of rope and spines when it lay at rest, then up, into human hands, ready to strike, to steal her life-force . . .

Fire filled her veins, coiled out from her trembling finger. She sent a jet spiraling along the whip's length, all the way up the thief's arms. The fire whip slashed across his face, leaving a red line between his nose and his ear.

The man shrieked and raised his hands to his face. His grip on the ceiling faltered, and he fell to dangle above the tumult by his legs.

Meisha did not linger to see if he would drop. Her arm fell uselessly to her side, aching with the pressure of a thousand needles. She pushed off the stalactite with her good leg and flew to a corner, putting her back to the wall for some cover.

The battle below was growing more and more desperate. For all their skill, they were outnumbered. Where was Dantane?

Then Meisha saw him, flying up from the ground. He intercepted a stream of missiles from the wizard, who'd managed to rid himself of the black energy but not its effects. The electrical ball had burned his robes away at the chest, exposing singed hair and blistered skin. His face trembled with rage. Dantane smiled and cast another spell.

"Dantane!" she cried.

"Are you all right?" the wizard asked when he flew up to join her. He came in at an angle to examine her leg.

"Forget it," said Meisha. "The arm's worse. I can't cast, not for a while."

"We don't have that long," Dantane replied. He rummaged in a pocket of his robes.

"We're not going to make it." Meisha leaned her head back against the wall. She was sweating. So hot. . . .

Dantane pressed a vial between her limp fingers. "Drink this. Stay here," he said. "I'll get to Kall."

Meisha started to ask what that would serve, but she saw something across the cavern that stole the breath from her body.

Talal, clutching one of her boot daggers—she hadn't even known it was missing—was sneaking up behind one of the men fighting with Laerin. The half-elf saw the boy in time to check his own swing, a blow that would have cleaved through his opponent's skull and likely taken Talal's head as well.

"Fool," Meisha whispered, a sob in her throat.

White-faced and shaking, the boy reared back and stabbed the Shadow Thief. The boy wasn't strong, but he had four years of pent-up hatred and grief driving the blow. Meisha didn't see where the blade penetrated, but the man stiffened. Blood trailed from the corner of his mouth. Laerin danced to the side to avoid being borne to the floor with the body. He was just in time to catch Talal as he, too, pitched forward unsteadily. Laerin pushed the boy behind him.

<hr />

Across the cavern, Kall saw Dantane flying toward him. He pulled his blade out of a Shadow Thief and moved to meet him, but another figure rose up in the wizard's path. Kall stepped aside, expecting Dantane to hurl a spell at the fool. Then he saw the tattered robes, the wild hair. . . .

"Varan!" he heard Meisha shout, but the din of battle reduced her cry to nothing.

Dantane saw the wizard too late. He tried to pull up, but flew straight into an invisible wall. The impact sent him reeling backward. He lost control of the flight spell and fell to the cavern floor at Varan's feet.

<hr />

The fire beast howled in triumph. In his mind's eye, he forced the wizard to crawl to the man lying prone on the ground.

Bring them, the beast thought. He bore down on the link between his mind and the wizard's, pressing mental tongues of flame against Varan's will. He enjoyed reducing the wizard to little more than a dog, herding his prey to exactly where he wanted them.

Embrace our bond, the beast cooed, and heard the silent screams of the wizard trying to resist the mental command. *Join me, and witness power unimaginable. I know your thoughts. Isn't that what you've always wanted? Who would deny such a dream?*

The wizard sobbed pitifully, and the beast reached out to stroke him again with fire and claws. He gloried in the ensuing screams, as the wizard went to carry out the beast's will.

———————◆———————

Kall broke into a run, heedless of the danger. Cold dread welled up inside him. He swept aside a blade that came at his flank and kept going. He was almost to Dantane when pain exploded in the back of his neck.

Kall went down in a protective crouch. He swung around and saw the halfling reloading his sling. Aazen motioned the halfling back and stepped to block Kall's path. Behind him, Varan rolled Dantane's unconscious body over, feeling inside the wizard's robes. He removed the portal key and turned. Kall saw his face clearly for the first time.

Varan looked terrified.

Kall sprang up. He raised his weapon to cut a path, but Aazen was there, his blade ringing off Kall's enchanted sword. "I need him alive," Aazen said, shoving Kall back.

"He'll kill us all!" Kall swung the blade high, angling it at his best friend's head. He did it without thinking, putting killing force behind the blow.

Aazen ducked, maneuvering to attack from Kall's wounded side. Kall twisted and blocked, but was forced to retreat a step away from Varan.

"That's it, Kall," said Aazen, stalking forward, inviting Kall to continue his attack. "This is exactly how I need you to be."

Kall swung again, bewildered. Had Aazen gone mad as well? "Meisha!" he shouted. If she could get Varan's attention, get through to him, they might have a chance.

Varan took the key and crawled to the dark pit. Tears streamed from his good eye, and he clutched the empty socket, making pitiful mewling noises as he moved.

"Please, don't!" Varan cried as he approached the edge of the chasm. He stared down into the dark, his terror magnified by whatever he saw. "Don't make me!" He grabbed the pouch at his neck, as if to tear it away. His hands locked into claws around the bag, and he screamed. With a violent motion, he reached inside the pouch and pulled out something small and black. Fumbling, he pressed the object against his empty socket.

It was an eye, Kall realized, but it was no human orb.

Black, with thready gray veins bulging from the sides, the eye was too large for the space Varan intended. Kall watched, sickened, as the wizard forced the organ into place with a howl of agony.

Varan lifted the stolen portal key in his other hand and slammed it down against the rocks. Words of power, dredged up from some unwilling place deep inside him, spilled out into the darkness.

The cavern began to shake in great, wracking tremors. Light flared, a halo that burst from the chasm, momentarily blinding everyone in the cavern. Meisha tried to fly, but a falling stalactite struck her out of the air. The blow knocked her senseless. She dropped, straight toward the pit.

Kall saw her fall, saw her body disappear into the green light. He cried out in wordless grief that manifested in a jarring blow against Aazen's sword.

She was gone, Kall thought. He hadn't been able to save her after all.

Grief melted into rage. Kall batted aside Aazen's unresisting blade and knocked him to the floor. For a moment, he fought the urge to keep going, to run his blade through Aazen's heart.

"Kall!" Morgan cried.

Chest heaving, Kall tore himself away from his friend's prone body and ran for the chasm. The cavern was still shuddering. The tremors seemed to come from deep below ground. More stalactites and rock shook free of the ceiling and dropped in a deadly rain. He dodged a spear that plunged to the floor where he and Aazen had just been fighting. Aazen had gotten to his feet and was looking to his own remaining men, issuing commands Kall could not hear over the rumbling.

Kall made it to Dantane. He hauled the wizard up into a sitting position. Varan had collapsed on the stones.

Dantane opened his eyes. They widened—he grabbed Kall by his uninjured forearm. " 'Ware!" he cried.

Kall reversed his blade, stabbing backward blindly, but Garavin was already there, using his maul to pluck a Shadow Thief off his feet like a rag doll.

"We have to go!" the dwarf shouted over the rumbling. "The place'll come down on our heads."

"Tunnel's blocked!" called Laerin from the far side of the cavern. He held Morgan by one shoulder, Talal the other. They limped across the room to join the group. The Shadow Thieves left alive had ceased their attacks in light of the greater danger. "It'll take a while to clear it."

"We don't have any time," said Kall.

"It's another portal," Dantane said, pointing to the glowing green halo, which had formed over the chasm rather than the shaft above. "The wizard wanted someone to go through it."

"Like Hells," said Morgan. "I say we go back through the shaft—take our chances with the Shadow Thieves."

Kall stared down the chasm. "Meisha's down there," he said. "She may still be alive. The rest of you use the key to activate the other portal once I'm gone, but I'm going through this one."

Garavin called Borl to his side. "I'll take my chances with ye," he said simply.

"As will I," said Laerin.

Morgan spat. "Don't be believing him!" he said. "He's just doin' it to make me look bad." He faced the portal reluctantly. "Let's go then, if we're goin'."

Kall helped Dantane to his feet. One by one, they stepped off the stones, into the green light, until only he and the wizard remained.

"What about him?" asked Dantane.

Kall knew he meant Varan, but Kall stared across the room at Aazen. He'd gathered his remaining forces under a protected shelf of rock near the blocked tunnel, but even that meager cover was cracking, coming apart like the rest of the cavern.

"He's on his own," said Kall. "So are you, Dantane, if you leave now."

The wizard shook his head. "I haven't gotten my reward yet. I go with you."

"Suit yourself." They stepped off the edge, into nothingness.

CHAPTER TWENTY-SIX

Keczulla, Amn
5 Marpenoth, the Year of Lightning Storms (1374 DR)

Balram stepped into Morel's main hall. He felt as if time had reversed itself. Suddenly he was back in Esmeltaran, his men at his side, seeking Morel's death.

But the setting had changed, and it wasn't Morel or his son who faced him from the top of the ballroom staircase. A woman stood there, wrapped in a hooded cloak, her face painted in forest colors. A long spear rested comfortably in the crook of her right arm. She looked like a savage carved from stone—beautiful and cold—staring at him as if she craved his death.

"Lady Morel." He bowed in greeting, allowing his men to fan out across the hall. If she was intimidated by the show of strength, her expression did nothing to give it away. She walked down the stairs, her soft boots padding against the wood. She stopped on the first landing.

"Might I have the pleasure of knowing you?" Balram asked when she said nothing.

Certainly, sir, she replied, but Balram could not hear her voice. He could only follow the movement of her lips to make out her words. She tipped her spear horizontal and threw. A soft, singing chime filled the ballroom. The spear impaled the man standing just to Balram's left, one who'd been taking slow steps toward the base of the stairs.

Keeping his eyes trained on the woman, Balram bent to see that the man was dead. As he did so, his eyes fell on the druid's spear. Tied among its decorations was the emerald-stone symbol of Morel. When Balram's fingers brushed it, the woman spoke again. This time her voice rang out clear across the hall, making Balram startle.

I am Cesira of the Starwater Six, Quiet One of Silvanus, and the lady of this house—she inclined her head stiffly—*and the doom of Balram Kortrun.* She glided back a step and pressed her hand to the banister rail in a certain spot.

Balram's eyes widened in shocked recognition. Gods, she couldn't know the locations of the . . .

"Fall back!" he cried, much too late.

The floor tiles running down the center of the hall creaked from years of lying stationary, but the trap still functioned.

Spikes exploded from the floor, catching the men behind him in a deadly hedge. Two went down as the sharpened edges burst through the backs of their legs. The rest managed to leap away, but the trap had cut them off from the exit.

Balram turned to the stairs, but Cesira had climbed back to the top. She stood behind the balcony rail, a second spear resting on her shoulder.

"You won't get out of here alive, bitch," he snarled at her. He motioned to one of his men, who began moving along the outer wall, smashing lanterns and spilling oil in streams across the floor. Fire licked up in tall pools. "You'll burn with this house, if we don't get to you first."

Then by all means, Cesira said, holding out her arms, *Come to me.*

The fire beast exalted in his find. Magic raged wildly above his head, fueled by the mad wizard and their mental link.

The mortals were scattered throughout his domain. He

could smell them leaving their imprints on the Delve in a complex web, moving, trying to find each other.

The woman of fire and one other—they were closest to his former prison. The beast dismissed them at once as too easy. Let them have a start on the game. He relished the challenge of two well-prepared magic wielders.

His senses drifted outward. Two more were near the thoroughfare, and a larger party was across the bridges—but wait. The beast picked out the scent, distantly, in the Howling burrow. Four fighters, moving stealthily—deeper into the mazelike tunnels constructed by the dwarves.

There lay his hunt, a chase through the labyrinth to claim the first of his prizes.

The beast rumbled in satisfaction. He stretched his lean muscles and began to run, tracing the faint scents to their source.

<hr />

Meisha felt as if her bones had been dashed over rocks. Perhaps they had been. She felt a hand prod her shoulder and hadn't even the strength to fight it off.

"Meisha."

Dantane's face swam into focus. The wizard leaned over her with a vial in his hand identical to the one he'd given her in the portal room. "Drink," he said, putting the glass to her lips.

Meisha drank, and gradually felt the strength returning to her aching arm and leg. The magic faded, leaving only a dull pain. "Where are we?"

"We came through a second portal," Dantane said. His voice sounded odd, uncertain. "The chasm in the floor. I found you not far from where I appeared. I don't know where we are, but you need to see something."

"What is it?" she asked.

Dantane hesitated. "I believe it's you."

"What?" Meisha sat up, gazing over the wizard's shoulder. She recognized where they were immediately. The circular chamber was crowded with pedestals of rock rising up four, six, sometimes ten feet into the air, separating the chamber into various levels. Two exits lay at opposite ends of the room. At the ends of those tunnels would be similar testing chambers.

"The star," she murmured.

Meisha suddenly realized they weren't alone. She looked up at the shortest pedestal, where a child stood. She was bald but for a dark fuzz beginning to sprout from the top of her head. She waved her arms in the motions of a spell. Below her, a man in well-kept robes watched her casting with a critical eye.

Varan—but not the mad wizard trapped in the Delve. This Varan was whole, and appeared much younger. For Meisha, seeing the little girl was like seeing a ghost.

"We're in a testing chamber," she said, for Dantane's benefit. "Varan designated one for each apprentice, arranged like the points of a star. When I was here, these caves could only be reached through Varan. He teleported us down."

"You didn't know the portal led down here?" asked Dantane.

"No. I didn't know *Varan* knew of the portal," she admitted. "The markings on it don't match his sigils. Perhaps that was how he discovered the secret tunnels," she murmured, half to herself, "through the portal."

"There are more caverns?" Dantane prompted. "Do you know where?"

"Varan said they adjoined the testing chambers somehow. We looked, as apprentices, but the entrance was magically concealed. I suppose it's possible, now his other magics are breaking down, that the connecting passage has been revealed."

"So we'll have to explore each chamber," Dantane said. "Our companions might be there, or in the other tunnels." He looked at her. "Do you know what they contained?"

Meisha laughed humorlessly. "Whatever great Art the Howlings saw fit to store. You were deposited in the wrong place, Dantane, if you seek treasure down here."

The wizard grimaced. "Such seems to be the course of my life," he said.

Meisha stood up, her eyes drawn back to the phantom image atop the pedestal. She watched, fascinated, as the air in front of her double seemed to split in two. Out of the breach came the head of a being that only vaguely resembled a human. Hairless, outlined in white flame, it stared at its summoner curiously. Though she felt no heat, Meisha recalled well how the air around the creature rippled with burning. It was the first time she'd ever interacted with a fire elemental.

The scene blurred and faded, leaving them alone in the chamber.

"What was that?" asked Dantane.

"A memory," answered Meisha, "from soon after I came to the Delve. I was a Wraith—half-feral—in Keczulla, when Varan found me. He took me on as an apprentice because he sensed my talent. I remember when he brought me down here to converse with the fire elemental. I could *feel* it burning, just like I burned inside. It's part of every savant's training, to recognize how their spirit matches the element they've chosen. With proper training, eventually, the spirit melds with that force and becomes part of it," Meisha said, her voice oddly hushed.

"Is that what you aspire to?" Dantane asked, "to join with the fire and become as an elemental creature?"

She glanced at him. "It's what every savant wants."

"But do you?"

Without answering, Meisha stood up, her eyes scanning the floor where the phantom images had been. "There." She bent down, lifting a small piece of glittering crystal from the floor. "The source of the memories," she explained.

"Your master's work," Dantane said, impressed. "He has great power."

"Obviously, not enough," Meisha said, "or he failed to follow his own teachings."

Had Varan recorded all his past sessions with his apprentices? she wondered, and if so, how many crystals, how much Art would be required for such a task?

"Why do you despise him so much?" Dantane asked. "He awoke the power in you. Without it, you might have died a Wraith."

"I know," Meisha said. "He cared about me, as much as he was capable of such feelings. He offered me magic and a place in his world, but I couldn't accept it."

"Why not?"

"Because if I hadn't possessed that power and if Varan hadn't sensed it, he would have passed me by on that street without looking twice. It was the power that fascinated him most, not any of us. And yet, I still wanted to love him."

"Then why did you come back?" Dantane asked. "Why help him now?"

"Because he was right. He was the only one who understood me, and I still love him for that," Meisha said bleakly. "That bond—the one I see reflected in Kall's group—I've known nothing like it, not since the night Shaera left the candle in my room."

"Shaera?"

"It doesn't matter." Meisha waved the memories away. "She's gone now—they're all dead—and Varan is not the master I knew."

"What about the boy," Dantane persisted, "the one who followed you?"

"Talal," Meisha said, and something inside her constricted. She'd avoided thinking about the boy. "Talal is . . . he has no scrap of magical power in him, and yet I find myself wanting to mentor him, in life, if not in the Art. It's strange. Then, in the next breath, I remember what I am and what I could do. When I remember, I want to put him as far from myself as I possibly can."

"It seems he would choose otherwise," Dantane observed.

Meisha shook her head grimly. "I pray that choice doesn't bring about his doom," she said, "if it has not already."

She touched the crystal, and the phantom Varan appeared again, drawing Meisha's attention back to the pedestals. This time the apprentice was not Meisha, but a young man with short blond hair cropped in a bowl shape.

"Prieces," Meisha said. "The earth savant. I've never seen this."

The young man appeared pale and drawn, even by the blurry magic illuminating the memory. His gestures were not as crisp as the child-Meisha's had been. His arms weighed heavily with fatigue, but he pressed on under Varan's encouraging gaze.

The earth elemental crawled up from the ground opposite Varan, but it was bigger—twice as broad as the creature Meisha had helped to summon. The force of its arrival shook the cavern, knocking Prieces from the pedestal. Varan reacted instantly, throwing out a spell to keep the apprentice from injuring himself. He didn't see the earth elemental smash the pedestal Prieces was standing on in half. Stone shards flew, striking Varan in the back. The wizard turned, intending to banish the creature, Meisha thought, but the thing rose up, crashing headfirst into the ceiling. Cracks fissured through the stone, and the chamber, unstable from all the tunnels carved in one place, began to come apart.

The elemental thrashed wildly, seeking release. It picked up the shattered pieces of the pedestals and threw them. The flat portion hit the wall and fell back, crushing Prieces beneath it.

Meisha cried out and ran forward. Dantane caught her arm. "It is an illusion. It isn't real," he hissed in her ear.

"But it *did* happen," Meisha whispered. She watched helplessly as Varan shouted an incantation that blew the stone aside, into the earth elemental. The force of the spell knocked the creature backward off its massive feet, giving Varan time to levitate Prieces to safety, but it was too late. The body of the unfortunate apprentice hung limply in the air, his neck broken.

Varan turned, chanting a spell that finally banished the elemental. The wizard collapsed to his knees next to Prieces. Stone continued to fall, but he erected a magical barrier that deflected the falling rock.

"Look there," said Dantane, pointing across the chamber.

The back wall of the cavern had completely caved in, revealing another set of passages that curved and split off in the darkness. Within them, a light burned, but Varan was oblivious to it.

"Is that another testing chamber?" asked Dantane.

Meisha shook her head. "There should be nothing behind that wall but solid rock."

They watched the strange light grow brighter, and as the rumbling gradually ceased, another sound filled the silence—the *tap-tap* of what sounded like rain on a campfire.

The light flickered and went out, but only because an object had passed in front of it, a swift, blurry movement not unlike the fire elemental.

Not rain, Meisha thought, as the thing coalesced, taking on shape and substance, but claws.

Dantane gasped when he saw what the walls had imprisoned. "Impossible," he said.

<hr />

Laerin hauled Morgan to his feet. The rogue's boots skidded on a pile of bones. Morgan regained his footing and cursed a loud, long streak that echoed down the tunnel.

"See how you corrupt the children," Laerin tutted, shooting a wink at Talal.

Talal didn't share the humor. He was still on the ground, shards of broken bone digging into his knees.

"Where are we?" he asked. He dislodged an oblong skull from a pile. "What are all these?"

"Animal remains," Laerin surmised, taking the skull from him. "Wolves of great size. They all died here together."

"In pieces," Morgan said. His head perked up. "Quiet."

Talal listened and heard the echo of footsteps. Swiftly, Morgan picked up the remains of a battered rib cage and smashed it into the face of a Shadow Thief as he came around the corner.

The thief went down, and Morgan put his boot on the man's neck.

"Brittle pieces." Morgan sniffed. He cast away the shredded bone cage.

"Is he harmless?" Laerin asked. The squirming thief was trying to reach a dagger clipped in his boot.

Morgan pressed harder, until the man choked. "As kitten teats." he grinned.

"Let me talk to him." Laerin squatted next to the thief. "Where are the others?" he asked calmly.

"Your friends or mine?" the thief rasped. He spat blood in Laerin's face.

The half-elf wiped the dripping red trails. "This one's as lost as we are," he told Morgan. "Have you ever been down here before?" he asked the man.

"No," the thief said, for he couldn't shake his head under the weight of Morgan's boot. "We've never been in these tunnels."

"Think Meisha knows about this place?" Talal asked hopefully.

"Maybe, but I wouldn't wager on finding her soon," Morgan said, "if this place's as vast as it seems." He pointed to three tunnels splitting off the cavern, all stretching an indeterminate distance before branching again.

"We'd better start looking," Laerin said. "Let me scout ahead."

"What do we do with him?" Talal asked, indicating the thief.

"Trap trigger," Morgan said cheerfully. "We'll move faster that way, with him testing the path ahead of us."

"Clear," Laerin declared, trotting back up the passage. "Narrow, but more likely to be free of traps. These caves are buried too deep to be heavily protected."

"Cheerful thought for this one," said Morgan, dragging the Shadow Thief to his feet. He shone his last torch over the walls. "Not one of these tunnels looks to be sloping *up*. They're all going deeper underground. Anything look familiar?" he asked, nudging Talal.

Talal shook his head. "Where do you think the others are?"

he asked, though he feared the answer. He'd seen Meisha fall down the chasm.

"Portals malfunction," said Laerin. "When that happens, they can deposit a person off the mark from where they intended to appear—a few feet, a mile . . ."

"Into a wall," Morgan muttered, and Talal's heart wrenched.

Laerin squeezed his shoulder and sent Morgan a quelling glance. "The portal is old," he said, "but I believe it to be sound. We'll find them."

"I suppose more of them damn shadow mongrels got scattered about, too," said Morgan.

"That might be a blessing," said Laerin. "If they followed us and are separated, we may have a better chance of overcoming them. Speaking of which . . ." The half-elf drew his dagger and prodded the Shadow Thief in the back. "Hearty congratulations," he told the man, "you're taking point. Stray too far ahead and you'll find my blade between your shoulders."

The thief nodded curtly, and the group set off with him and Laerin leading.

The first tunnel bent to the right, then bent back on itself so sharply that the way was impassable for even Talal; they had to backtrack to the second tunnel.

Morgan made slash marks on the walls with a crusty piece of chalk to show where they'd been.

The center tunnel connected three larger chambers. A blackened firepit in the center of the first room suggested a kitchen; fragments of rotting wood might once have served as furniture.

"Living quarters," Laerin said. "If the Howlings did dwell all the way down here, they lived sparsely."

"The tunnel's are defensible," Morgan said. "Long bottlenecks, mazelike. And if the portal's the only way down, they can dig themselves in cozy if they have to."

"I have a hard time believing the dwarves would rely on magic alone to move them through the earth," said Laerin. "It's not their nature."

Talal gazed down the third tunnel. The passage spilled into a long, narrow chamber. Chipped and sheared stalagmites formed stone benches. A dozen men would have fit comfortably in the room, Talal thought, but the benches squatted close to the floor to accommodate shorter legs.

At the back of the room, situated in front of another tunnel, a wide altar rose up from the floor. Spiky writing was etched deep into the stone, but a crack cut a jagged line down the center of the monument.

Talal watched Morgan and Laerin examine the writing. The half-elf's lips moved as if he could read the words. His face creased in consternation.

"What does it say?" Talal asked.

The half-elf cocked his head. "The script is Dwarvish, of course. It's an altar to Abbathor, the dwarf god of greed."

Talal knew nothing of the dwarf gods, not enough to blaspheme them, anyway. He would have to ask Meisha about Abbathor.

The thought of the Harper sent an unexpected stab of pain through his chest. *If she's alive, she's safer than you are,* Talal told himself. *He* was the fool. He'd had the opportunity to escape and see daylight again, but he'd wasted it worrying over a fire-twisted Harper he barely knew.

His thoughts shattered when a sharp blow cuffed the side of his head.

"Watch him!" Laerin shouted, and the half-elf was suddenly in front of Talal, shielding him with his body.

Dizzy and in pain, Talal heard Morgan grunt and, a breath later, the sound of a body dropping on stone.

Laerin's arm caught his. "Are you all right?"

Talal wiped blood from his temple where the Shadow Thief had struck him. "Second time they've roughed up my head," he mumbled.

Laerin grinned. "Luckily you keep nothing important up there." His face sobered. "Forgive me, I should have been watching him more closely." He turned to Morgan, who was wiping blood from his sword. "Dead?"

Morgan nodded. "Hope you were done questioning him."

"I was," Laerin replied, taking one last look at the altar. "A pity Garavin isn't here. He would have wanted to see this."

They headed for the tunnel at the back of the temple, but Talal stopped abruptly. His head still felt fuzzy from the blow. He wondered if he were imagining things. "Did you hear that?" he asked.

Morgan and Laerin continued ahead of him. "Keep up," grunted Morgan.

"It sounded like . . . rain."

They moved past an intersection of four tunnels. Laerin choose to keep going straight, but the sound persisted just at the edges of Talal's hearing. He wondered why the half-elf couldn't hear the steady beat, water against stone.

Talal glanced behind and saw movement in the darkness of the intersection. "Look at that!"

Laerin turned, following the streak of Morgan's pointing torch.

A dwarf ran into the intersection. He was bald, dressed in plated armor that should have creaked loudly in the stillness. His short legs skidded on the loose dirt, but he caught himself with a hand on the ground. He half-turned toward them, and Talal gasped.

The entire left side of the dwarf's face was gone, exposing white skull and a length of jawbone. Torchlight flickered off the shadows and hollows created by the missing flesh. No one could be that injured and live. The dwarf was dead, Talal thought, just like the one he and Meisha had encountered in the upper tunnels. He was dead, and he was running. None of the other ghosts had run, and none had looked at Talal with such terror-filled eyes.

The dwarf regained his feet and plowed on down the tunnel. The sound of rain drew closer.

"Talal," said Laerin, drawing his sword, "Run. Down the passage—now!"

Talal felt the half-elf shove him hard. He stumbled and fell, unable to take his eyes off the intersection. Fear crawled along his body. A breeze passed over his skin, bringing heat and a scent that made his eyes water. The tunnel suddenly felt humid. Steam pools rose up from the floor, and the sound of rain became a sizzling.

Talal crushed his eyes shut, and time seemed to slow, as if he were experiencing everything from a great distance. He opened his eyes in time to see a shape pass through the intersection, filling it utterly with weight and light. The timeless silence shattered, sundered by a roar that filled the caverns, knocking Morgan and Laerin to their knees.

Talal covered his ears and screamed, but he could not hear the sound of his voice over the terrible roar. Morgan and Laerin crouched beside him, shielding him with their bodies and weapons. They, too, seemed incapable of movement.

The beast's head looked vaguely like that of a lion. A full, red mane streamed out behind it, stained with black ash from an ember fire. His body, as it stretched into the tunnel after the dwarf, filled the length of the intersection. Huge, muscled haunches tapered to four black-clawed feet that scraped furrows in the stone. The rain sound was the sizzle of the demon's claws, constantly burning where they touched the earth.

Talal watched, transfixed, as the creature drew his head out of the tunnel. In his jaws struggled the dead dwarf. The beast bit through its shoulder, and the dwarf's screams were as loud and pitiful as any living being's. It was the screaming that finally galvanized them.

Morgan grabbed Talal by one arm, Laerin by the other, and they ran down the tunnel at breakneck speed, careening around corners at random.

Morgan cursed liberally. "What the bloody piss and Hells is it?" he shouted.

"A demon," said Laerin grimly. "Meisha's beast. The doom of the Howlings."

"A jarilith," said Dantane as the phantom image of the creature stepped into the chamber. "A tanar'ri—a hunting beast from the Abyss."

The demon leaped at Varan. The battle that ensued was horrifically beautiful to watch. Varan hurled spells that ravaged the left side of the creature's face, removing the jarilith's eye. Enraged, the demon sprang forward, curling around the wizard. The jarilith raked his claws sideways along the wizard's flank.

Varan retreated, trying to heal himself with a cracked potion vial, but he bled from dozens of small wounds. He grasped the demon's lost eye and chanted. The words spilled out, booming with power, and it seemed he would complete the magic before the beast could launch another attack.

But the demon charged, tangling with the release of the Art. Tremors shook the cavern, and suddenly, Varan clutched the left side of his face. His mouth twisted in agony.

Horrified, Meisha watched the flesh beneath Varan's fingers blend together and melt, becoming a hideous mirror to the jarilith's ruined visage.

The demon tossed his head in renewed frenzy, as if some invisible foe were attacking him. Clawing the stone, the jarilith fell back into the caves from whence he had come. Varan followed, crawling on his hands and knees, one arm clutched awkwardly against his face. He did not have to go far. The demon collapsed, unconscious or enspelled. Meisha could not tell which.

When the scene faded at last, Meisha saw the breached wall, just as the vision had rendered it. Empty.

"The demon's awake," said Dantane.

"I don't understand," Meisha said. "Why did he do it? Why did he stay to fight?" He could have escaped, come back when he'd recovered from Prieces' death and the battle with the elemental, Meisha thought. Why had he fought the demon in his weakened state, using magic to merely put it to sleep?

"What was that spell?" asked Dantane.

Meisha had no idea. "It seemed to allow him to control the demon, at least in that moment."

"Through a mental connection," said Dantane, nodding. "It requires a focus. In this case—"

"The jarilith's eye," said Meisha, and the truth dawned on her. Varan hadn't been weakened or desperate when he'd cast the spell. He'd known exactly what he was doing. "Watching gods, he couldn't have wanted to keep it alive," she said.

"For curiosity's sake," Dantane affirmed. At Meisha's revolted expression, he added, "Fueled by arrogance, I grant you. Your master saw a new vehicle to test his spells and acted accordingly, believing his will would be enough to overcome the jarilith. He discovered differently, to his doom. The spell drove him mad."

Dantane's voice was coldly matter-of-fact, but he was right. Meisha accepted the truth, though it filled her with a profound anger and disappointment in her former teacher. "Are they still linked?" she said. "Is that why Varan opened the portal and cast us down here? Is the demon fighting him for control?"

"Fighting him, fighting the dwarves," said Dantane. "There may be hope for us and your master, if that's the case."

"But if the demon escaped from Varan's spell, why is he still down here? Why has he not tried to get to the surface?"

"Can't you feel it?" Dantane asked. "The demon's aura? It's everywhere."

Meisha nodded. "I've felt it ever since I was a child. I still wake at night blanketed in the dread and the cold. I just never had a name for it before. What does that have to do with the demon's escape?"

"He doesn't want to escape," Dantane said. "From the dwarves, yes, and from Varan's control, but the Delve has been absorbing the demon's essence for a century or longer. The Delve has become part of him—the ideal hunting ground. I suspect all the demon wants is something worthwhile to hunt."

"Through Varan, he's gotten everything he needs," Meisha

said bitterly. "All he has to do is pick us off one by one."

"An appealing fate for the Shadow Thieves that may have followed us," Dantane said. "In fact, without the demon's interference, we might have died at their hands."

"Astounding how the gods sort matters out," Meisha muttered. "This way," she said, leading Dantane on to the next testing chamber. "We have to move quickly. We don't know where the demon is now."

As with the other chambers, raised rock platforms dominated the next room they entered, but the entire back wall of the cavern had gone, plucked from the surrounding stone like a cork from a wine cask. Darkness, impenetrable by her spell light, stretched down a long passage Meisha had never seen before.

"A permanent tunnel of darkness," Dantane said. "Small wonder your master concealed this entrance. There will be traps and wards, unless he cleared them himself."

"Let's hope so," Meisha said. "We'll have enough to worry about when we find the jarilith." She took stock of her weapons. Her stilettos were gone, but she still had one dagger. Fire crackled in her mind. "Ready?"

Dantane nodded and stepped forward. They were almost to the mouth of darkness when they heard the demon roar.

<hr />

Talal didn't look back. He knew the creature had turned to pursue them. He could hear the sizzle-click of his paws hitting the stone. The beast's huge strides would have overtaken them immediately if the passage hadn't kept making sharp corners.

Morgan swung around a bend and came up short, shouting, "Too narrow!"

Talal fetched up behind Laerin. He saw the bigger man wedged between two slabs of stone. Beyond lay an open chamber.

"We can't go back!" Laerin shouted, before he plowed into Morgan from behind.

Morgan's tunic ripped as Laerin's weight pushed him through the narrow gap. The half-elf followed, and Talal, grateful for once to be the slightest, had no trouble slipping through the crack.

In the chamber beyond flowed an underground river.

Talal stopped and stared at the black water darting with shadows under the torchlight. The river rushed from a fissure in the northwest corner of the room, flowing out through a wishbone shaped crack at the opposite end. On the other side of the water, the cavern dead-ended.

Morgan crouched at the river's edge. He splashed handfuls of water on two wicked slashes across his chest where the stone had cut into his flesh. "That's got it," he wheezed. "Game's over before it began."

Talal looked at Laerin. "We're trapped," he said. "Maybe if we double back—"

A loud keening drowned out the rest. Talal went down in a protective crouch, while Laerin and Morgan turned to see what had made the sound.

Curved claws raked the stone, stabbing through the gap in the rocks. Stone chips flew, and the smell of brimstone filled the chamber.

Every coherent thought fled Talal's mind. Rationally, he knew the demon couldn't penetrate the layers of rock, not quickly, but all he could hear were the claws shearing away the stone.

"Get in the water!" Morgan shouted to be heard over the awful sound. "Swim to the other side!"

Talal backed away—he'd never liked water—but Laerin dragged him into the river, and soon he was forced to swim.

The current threatened to pull him down. Talal fought it, but it took Morgan's strong arm to haul him out on the other side, else he would have been carried away.

On the opposite bank, the sound of the river muffled the demon's claws enough to allow them to talk.

Morgan, his hair dripping in lanky strands around his

exhausted face, said, "Figure it drove us in here?"

Laerin nodded. "I probably cracked a pair of your ribs, pushing you through that gap. He's wearing us down."

"Not much need for that," said Morgan, "once he corners us."

"I don't think he'll do that yet," said Laerin. "He's just stretching his legs. He knows we'll get out of here." The half-elf pointed to the wishbone in the wall. "That way."

Talal blanched. "We don't know how far the river runs, do we? That thing won't need to kill us if we drown first."

"I'm willing to bet there's another chamber nearby," said Laerin. He looked at Morgan. "What do you think? Can't be much longer than that sewer tunnel in Waterdeep."

"Least the water's cleaner," Morgan said. "I think I got enough breath in my lungs."

Talal couldn't believe what he was hearing. They were all lunatics.

"Give me back the fire-woman," he muttered.

"Sorry," Morgan said, "Fire can't go where we're headed." He inverted the torch he carried into the river.

Instantly, Talal went blind. The oppressive darkness of the Delve closed in around him. He felt Laerin's hand on his shoulder, prodding him toward the rushing water. Reluctantly, Talal waded back into the frigid river and let the current snare him.

Treading water, he felt the downward sweep to the wishbone just before his shoulders brushed rock.

For a moment, Talal panicked. He braced his hands on either side of the passage, resisting the water's pull with all his strength. He didn't want to drown. He'd end up a blue corpse in the dark, and no one in Faerûn would care.

"You can't fight it forever," said Morgan's voice in his ear. "But you can go on your terms."

Talal forced a steadying breath into his lungs. Calmer, he closed his eyes and remembered how it was to feel his way in the dark. He'd done it before. He could do it underwater.

Cautiously, he let his hands slide down the stones, following the curve of the wishbone.

Pretend it's a lass's legs, Dirty Bones, and stop your whining.

The water closed over his head.

Froglike, Talal swam with the current. He kept one hand above his head to brush the stone ceiling, searching for air. The river propelled him forward at a quick pace. He sensed Morgan and Laerin beside him now and then, though he could see nothing in the dark. The water dragged at his shirt. Talal stripped it off and left it for some deep-dweller to find.

Ten feet farther Talal's shoulder banged against something rough and unyielding. Talal hoped it wasn't alive, or if it were, that it couldn't swallow him. He kicked sideways and realized the river bent, angling off to his left. He had no choice but to follow the path.

His lungs began to burn. Unconsciously, he let a tiny gasp of air escape. The respite was brief, however, and the burning sensation that followed was excruciating.

Kicking feebly now, Talal allowed the river to carry him. His hand dragged limply across the unbroken rock ceiling. He felt no gap, no magical pocket of air to save him.

The muscles in his abdomen convulsed. His body demanded air, and in its absence was willing to drag in lungfuls of the killing water. Talal clutched his midsection, trying to hold in his last gasp.

His hand slid off the rock. Talal spasmed, sucking in a freezing cold breath. His lungs suddenly felt heavy. His muscles contorted in agony. Then the pain went away, and the cold, and Dirty Bones went to sleep.

He awoke vomiting water.

Talal heard Morgan cursing and felt the big man's arm supporting his chest as he emptied the river from his body.

When he could breathe again, Talal looked around. They

were in another tunnel, but he could hear the river somewhere behind him. Morgan must have carried his body a short distance before reviving him. Talal had thought himself dead. He shivered violently at the memory of his near-drowning.

Laerin offered a hand to pull him to his feet. "We can't linger here. The creature will follow the river and fence us in again if we don't keep moving."

They moved off down yet another tunnel, but Talal trailed behind. His legs felt rubbery, and his lungs still ached. The only thing that kept him moving was the presence of the demon's frightening aura, steadily building behind them. Every time they came to an intersection, Laerin changed their direction and increased his speed. Soon they were running again. Behind them, the sound of rain echoed in the tunnels, drawing closer.

"Keep turning!" Laerin shouted as they ran. "Outmaneuvering is the only way. If it catches us, there won't be any room to fight. We'll be running through a forest of razors."

Laerin skidded down a short, steep incline. At the end of the slide was a vast chamber that opened wide and dipped into a crater. Stalagmites, arranged like a maze, rose from the floor like trees, forming dense clusters throughout the room. Two paths led from one side of the chamber to the other.

"Help me," said Morgan, grabbing Talal by the waist.

"Let go!" Talal kicked air in a futile attempt to win loose, but Morgan's grip was solid. Laerin came up on his other side, snagging his foot. The half-elf went to one knee and hauled upward, tossing Talal bodily into the air. He landed hard on his stomach on one of the higher platforms. The breath whooshed out of his lungs.

"Stay there!" Morgan hollered when he rolled to the edge. The echo of another roar—so damn close!—and the sound of claws raking stone reached Talal's ears. He fought the urge to curl into a ball.

"Not enough," said Laerin. "The demon will smell him before it gets into the room."

"Suggestions welcome," Morgan growled. "Stand or run?"

Laerin regarded the two pathways through the chamber. Each led to a separate exit. "Split up," he said finally. "We'll each take a path. The boy can run along the top. With luck, it'll only be able to chase one of us. Talal can follow the other into the tunnel and hopefully find Kall."

"Awful lot of luck and hope in that plan," said Morgan, his face white.

Laerin smiled grimly. "We work with what we have," he said. He looked up. "Do you understand what we're going to do, Talal?"

Talal swallowed. "I got it," he whispered.

Laerin met Morgan's gaze steadily. "One more bet," he challenged softly. "Let it be a race."

Morgan grunted, but his grip faltered as he reached in his pouch and dropped two gold coins on the ground. "A race, then."

"Two danters?" Laerin whistled. "Heavy price."

"Seemed appropriate."

A deafening crash sounded nearby, but they felt the demon's approach long before they heard his claws again.

Morgan jerked his head. "Go."

Talal crouched near the wall, ready to jump to the next stalagmite cluster. He watched Morgan and Laerin take off at a sprint down their separate corridors. He glanced at the far tunnels, willing the pair to reach them before the demon caught up. He could feel the demon coming closer. Brimstone scent crawled over his skin, into his clothes.

"Run," he whispered, "run, oh run, oh run." He chanted it like a prayer, the closest he'd ever come in his life to crying out for divine intervention. But to whom would he implore? There were no gods left that he hadn't blasphemed. None of them would believe an abrupt conversion to the faith. Talal almost smiled at that, but he was too deeply sunk in despair and the horror of the demon's aura.

Talal suppressed a whimper when the beast entered the chamber. For a long, terrible moment the beast just stood there, then he raised his head and looked straight at Talal. Talal wanted to run, heedless of the consequences. He held himself down, scratching his nails against the stone until they bled. If he ran, the beast would kill him. Talal sensed the demon testing him almost teasingly with his powers. He squeezed his eyes shut against the awful fear.

Then it was over. The demon passed by, charging down one of the corridors. Talal opened his eyes and forced himself to stand, to watch the beast run down his prey.

From his viewpoint, above the scene, Talal saw which corridor the beast chose. The figure running before the demon—so small in comparison to the beast—never had a chance. At the last moment, he turned, his weapon brandished, and fell beneath hundreds of pounds of burning muscle.

The demon came down on the sword, howling in rage and pain, raking the body beneath him from shoulders to calves. At the same time, the beast's jaws closed on his victim's neck, snapping it with one careless jerk.

Bile burned Talal's throat. So much blood, and yet the demon ran on, trailing red prints down the passage on his hunt.

Talal didn't stop to grieve. He bolted for the other tunnel.

———————◆•◆———————

Kall opened his eyes when the green light faded. Garavin and Borl stood over him. He must have blacked out from loss of blood during the transition through the portal. The dwarf was binding his arm. His holy symbol hung away from his neck, brushing against Kall's bare flesh. Kall felt the same brief, warm jolt he'd felt years ago from the relic.

"Thought I'd lost all of ye," Garavin murmured as Kall looked around. The three of them were alone in a smaller version of the cave they'd just left. The circle of stones sat to his left, but there was no chasm in the floor or shaft above. The room was dark, but for lines of dim light shining through a pair of doors at the end of a narrow passage.

"Where are the others?" Kall asked, panic rising inside him.

"They didn't come through," said Garavin. "Or they ended up somewhere else."

"Is that possible?"

"In this place, who's to say? But if this other portal is old as the Delve, and what with the wizard's magic disturbing the cavern, it may have malfunctioned and scattered us about. The others should be close by, if that's the case."

"We have to find them and get out of here," said Kall.

He headed for the light. When they drew closer, Kall realized the double doors ascended over two stories up the rock. A winch was attached to the doors to pull them open.

"I wonder if the dwarves built this," said Kall.

"Only way out," said Garavin.

They took hold of the crank together and pulled. The mechanism ground with age and neglect, but turned after a moment of coaxing. The doors ground against stone, the sounds echoing loudly in the passage. When the doors were half-open, Kall signaled Garavin to stop and peered out through the man-sized opening.

"Gods above," Kall murmured in awe.

Kall stepped out onto the narrow stone bridge that extended just beyond the double doors. Garavin and Borl came to stand beside him. A memory surfaced, of meeting Meisha on the Star Bridge outside Keczulla. The markings on this bridge were strikingly similar, except there was no roaring river beneath his feet, only an endless, black abyss stretching off in both directions.

Below and above, more bridges joined two steep rock walls divided like the parting of a great, barren sea. On both sides, tunnels honeycombed the walls—some were open, others secured with doors similar to the ones they'd just passed through. Blocks of a strange, clear substance obstructed three doors; they seemed to writhe and twist within the confines of the stone portals.

"What are those?" Kall asked.

Garavin looked where he pointed. "Gelatinous cubes," he said.

"Amazing," Kall murmured. For as far as he could see, there were only the tunnels and the rock walls, and the bridges over the abyss. It was as if they'd stepped into an underground labyrinth. They had only to choose a door.

Morgan whipped around the corner and stopped, listening. Had the demon passed the chamber by or gone for the boy, despite their efforts? He dragged his blade out of its sheath. The tunnel lay open and inviting before him, but Morgan turned his back on it. As good a place as any to make a stand, he thought, much as it pained him to let the half-elf win a bet.

Rocks showered his hair from above. Morgan swung in an upward arc but checked the blow just in time.

Talal came skidding down the stalagmite to land next to him. He paused long enough to grab Morgan's arm, towing him along.

Morgan pushed the boy away. "Keep going," he hissed. "I'll hold it off."

"He's dead," Talal cried, plucking stubbornly at the thief's tunic. "We have to run, we have to . . . he'll kill us. . . ."

The boy was hysterical. He didn't know what he was saying. Morgan turned back to the room. "Come on!" he shouted wildly. "Come at me, you bastard!"

"Shut up," Talal squeaked. "He'll come back. We have to . . . have to go."

But Morgan's feet refused to move. His mind worked sluggishly: the half-elf . . . Morgan hadn't heard it. He'd heard nothing. What kind of thief was he, what kind of partner, not to hear when the job went wrong?

The stupid half-elf had always been faster than him. "Legs like twigs, but he moved like he weighed nothing," Morgan babbled. He tried to make the boy understand. "He should've won; we *never* let each other win. The arrogant bastard should be halfway back to Keczulla by now."

Talal moaned in despair. "You're crazy. That thing's going to kill us both, and it'll all be for nothing!" He pushed, but Morgan grabbed him roughly.

"Listen to what I'm telling you!" Morgan shook the boy by the shoulder, ignoring his whimper of pain. "We'll meet up with him at the next intersection. He'll be there, waiting, and then—"

His head snapped to the side. Stars filled the corners of Morgan's vision. He looked at Talal in bewilderment. It slowly dawned on him that the boy had punched him in the jaw. He raised a hand; Talal flinched. Tears streamed down his thin face.

Morgan blinked several times to clear his head. Calmly, he forced all thoughts of the half-elf to a dark corner of his mind. Later, after he had spilled enough blood, he would take them out and examine them.

He grabbed the boy by the collar, pushing him toward the tunnel. "Run fast, little mouse," he growled. "Or we're all meat." At Talal's uncertain expression, he said, "Don't worry. I'll be right behind you."

CHAPTER TWENTY-SEVEN

The Howling Delve
5 Marpenoth, the Year of Lightning Storms (1374 DR)

Aazen tensed when he heard the distant howls. He raised a hand to halt the party, surveying what resources he had left.

Isslun and Aliyea were still above, probably slain. Tershus was there too. Falling rock had obscured Aazen's last glimpse of the halfling. The rest of his party had either been slain by Kall's group or separated by the journey through the portal. Aazen had only five left with him. One of them, Kiliren's apprentice, had to be half-carried due to his wounds. If he didn't succumb, Aazen was tempted to leave the man, especially in light of what he intended to do.

"Straight ahead, torches low unless absolutely necessary," he said. "Kall is nearby."

"Whatever's down here's killing them already," said Bardle, shifting his weight against the man supporting him. "We should wait to see if any survive."

"If they do, we may never find them again in these tunnels," said Aazen. "We could wander down here until we starve, or until whatever made that noise finds us. Kall—or one of his group—had to have come through the main portal. To find the way out, we go to him."

Bardle laughed, drawing uneasy glances from the men standing near him, but the apprentice's eyes were wide, delirious with pain and blood loss. "You're a fool, Kortrun. You want to find your friend. Balram knew you wouldn't be able to kill him."

Aazen stopped, his expression frozen. Slowly, he turned and walked back to the man. He lifted his sagging head by the hair. "What an interesting observation. Please enlighten me. What is my father planning?"

Bardle coughed and tried to shake his head, but Aazen held him firmly.

"Very well." Aazen removed his hand and pressed his knuckles into one of Bardle's open wounds. The apprentice howled and thrashed, but Aazen pressed him back with his other forearm. "What is his plan?"

"Another party," Bardle choked out. "I overheard my . . . master speaking of it. He was communicating with Daen magically. If you betrayed us, he was to send word to the other party."

"Thank you." Aazen removed his hand, wiping his bloody fingers on Bardle's robes. The apprentice collapsed against the tunnel wall, sliding down to the floor.

Aazen's thoughts raced, but his eyes stayed on the men surrounding him. They kept their faces averted, their expressions schooled to reveal nothing of their thoughts. And why should they? They were well trained and knew that Aazen, traitor or not, was the best hope they had of getting out of the caverns alive. But how many of them had known? How many of his "family" plotted against him?

"We go on," he said at last. When one of the men moved to lift Bardle from the floor, Aazen shook his head. "Leave him. He'll slow us down. Scout ahead, but do not be seen. We follow Kall's party." he paused, looking at each of them, making them meet his eyes. "Unless anyone else has objections they'd like to voice?"

They had none. The scout started to move away down the

tunnel. He turned a corner, and Aazen saw him stop and take a jerky step to the side, as if he'd lost his footing. The man behind him moved forward to steady him.

"Wait!" shouted Aazen.

The scout fell sideways. A triple line of gashes ran vertically from his chest to his bowels. The ribs and organs in between were mauled. The scout had died before he knew what killed him. The man behind him cried out as he was yanked forward, around the corner into the darkness. This time Aazen heard the swish of claws passing through air and smelled the unnatural fire reek.

Grabbing the man nearest him, Aazen dived into one of the narrower tunnels off the main route, one they'd decided not to take for fear it would dead-end or become impassable. He heard the screams of his men, of Bardle trying to remember the words to a spell as the horror overcame him.

"Keep moving," Aazen snapped to the man he'd saved. He did not look back.

* ◆ *

Cesira lay on the floor, her vision encompassing all of an inch-tall gap between the storeroom door and the ground. Her forked tongue passed over her fangs, touching wood and tasting dust. At last, she saw the shadows of feet approaching. The lock rattled, and the footsteps retreated. Scant breaths later, a loud crack echoed in the dark space as a foot connected with the door, busting the old lock and splintering the doorframe.

A man poked his blade in among the stacks of linens, searching for a place a human woman might hide. He failed to notice the snake lying parallel to the threshold.

Cesira struck once, and then again, sinking her fangs into the flesh behind his knee. The man cried out, falling forward into the closet.

The black snake slithered away as the man's legs, sticking out into the dimly lit hall, began to twitch from the poison.

"Meisha once told me Varan believed the Delve to be an outpost of Deep Shanatar," said Kall. He looked out over the vast expanse of cavern. "I suppose this confirms it."

But the dwarf shook his head. "This *is* Deep Shanatar, lad."

Kall lifted an eyebrow. "I don't believe your memory for maps has failed you," he said. "So I don't have to remind you that we are not where Deep Shanatar should be."

"Who says so?" argued Garavin. "I'm telling ye—and having studied far longer than ye've been alive, I should know—we're in Shanatar, and I'm guessing a part of it that's never been known. An outpost, maybe, but a grander one I've never seen."

"Kept a secret, even from Iltkazar?" Kall asked, naming heretofore the only known surviving kingdom of Deep Shanatar. Garavin had told him stories of the place long ago. "Why does one build a secret outpost?" he asked. "Unless they're doing something other folk might not approve of?"

Garavin looked at him. "Yer point?"

"You dig strongholds for people who have secrets or who want to protect knowledge. Is it possible the dwarves did the same here, with magic? Did the Howlings, and by extension, Varan, stumble upon that work?"

"If they did, it was all tainted by the Howlings' greed when they turned to Abbathor." Garavin said, shaking his head sadly.

"Why are Abbathor and Dumathoin fighting over such a small group of souls?" Kall asked.

"Because the Howlings are fighting," Garavin replied. "These gods of the Morndin Samman, our pantheon, are forever locked in struggle. The Howlings are olorns, stories that become symbols. Whichever side wins in this will gain more than souls."

"They gain a victory in lore," said Kall, understanding. "Your stories will reflect the redemption of the Howlings from their greed. Dumathoin's power grows."

"And his children would rejoice," said Garavin.

"Are the Howlings powerless in this? If they seek redemption, why do they not renounce Abbathor and ask Dumathoin's forgiveness?"

"Because they made a pact with the god of greed and accepted his blessings and aid. That gives Abbathor power over the Howlings that isn't easy to forsake. Dumathoin can only intervene so far as to hold them between life and death. For the rest, they must atone."

"But Meisha's master disrupted that process," said Kall. "So her message—the dwarf's warning—was also a cry for help."

"Issued to one who might carry and keep a dangerous secret," Garavin affirmed, "and risk everything for the sake of a friend. Meisha was wise to seek ye out."

Kall did not voice his doubts on that score. "And do you think it's a coincidence that I count among my friends a devout servant of Dumathoin?" he asked instead.

Garavin smiled. "Little in this world is a coincidence, lad." He nodded up and down the abyss. "Which door?"

"I don't think it matters," said Kall, "but whichever we choose, we can't lose track of *these* doors." He looked back at the open portal. "That's our way back to the surface."

"The Shadow Thieves are sure to block it," Garavin pointed out. "If they haven't already. Might be we'll have to find a different exit."

Kall didn't need to tell the dwarf how monumental a task that would be. Their odds of surviving long enough to collect the others and find the way out seemed slim indeed at the moment.

"We could call out," he said finally, "from the bridge. The echo will carry down at least a dozen of these tunnels. If they're nearby, one of them might hear us."

"As could any number of beasties foraging in the tunnels," Garavin said.

Kall nodded. "Better to encounter them in the open than a bottleneck in a tunnel, where traps may be waiting to spring."

"Agreed," said the dwarf. He drew his maul out and cradled it in both hands.

Kall strode to the center of the bridge. His bootsteps echoed in the vast chamber.

Thousands of feet must have trodden these bridges, Kall reflected, a testament to the forgotten legacy of the dwarves, and far grander than all the merchants of Amn above. The enormity of such a lost existence humbled Kall.

He raised a hand to the side of his mouth. "Meisha!" he shouted. The Harper's name carried far down the cavern in either direction. "Laerin! Morgan!"

He shouted until his lungs ached. Nothing stirred in the vastness.

Kall turned back to Garavin, seeking a new suggestion, when Borl began to bark furiously. The dog pushed his head between the stone slats of the bridge.

Kall looked down. Thirty feet below, Talal ran from a tunnel in the opposite wall onto a bridge, so fast and stumbling so much that he nearly toppled over the edge. Sheer luck kept him upright as he plowed across.

"Morgan!" Kall yelled as the tall man came out behind Talal. "Up here!"

Neither slowed. Morgan flung his head back and hollered, "Stay there!" Spinning, he flung a dagger at the tunnel mouth. The throw broke his stride, and the normally graceful thief fell sprawling on the bridge.

Kall saw Morgan's dagger stick to the hilt, and his eyes traveled upward in horror to see the demon. The beast stalked onto the bridge, his four legs spread to block any possible retreat. Blood ran from his mouth all the way to the stone. Crouching down, the demon leaped into the air, springing toward Morgan.

The Howlings' penance—Meisha's beast, with blood-soaked claws—and Kall's friend, lying helpless on the bridge without Laerin to back him up.

"No! Gods of stone damn you!" Kall shouted. He vaulted

over the rail and dropped, curling his body and praying he could hit the beast in mid-spring. If nothing else, he would take the demon over the side with him.

They collided in the air. Kall felt the heat, the blast of brimstone, before he even touched the demon's hide. He landed flat on the beast's back, surprising him and driving him aside of his intended target. The demon's claws raked for balance; his hindquarters fishtailed back and forth on the bridge, trying to shake Kall off.

Kall felt blood on his hands. They were covered with small wounds ripped open on the spines sprouting from the demon's back. And he burned. He felt slick blisters form on his palms and remembered the sickening smell of his campfire burns. If the nerves in his hands hadn't been dulled, he wouldn't have been able to withstand the pain.

The demon reared onto his hind legs. Kall slid off his back to the walkway. He no longer needed to worry about taking the attention off Morgan. The demon's smoldering, malevolent gaze was firmly fixed on Kall. The beast lunged at him, his claws poised to rake whatever exposed flesh they could find.

Kall had no space to maneuver or dodge on the bridge. Without really considering it, he jumped over the rail and off the bridge, plunging straight down again. Reaching out, he caught the bridge's stone ledge. The sudden, snapping weight jarred his shoulder, nearly wrenching it from its socket. Kall gritted his teeth and reached up with his other hand.

The demon hit the bridge where Kall had stood and turned, coming back for another attack.

In his peripheral vision Kall saw Morgan on his feet, climbing a rope Garavin had tied onto the upper walkway. The dwarf fired his crossbow at the demon. Dangling from the rope, Morgan threw another dagger.

The demon hardly seemed to feel the stings. The beast shook out his long, red mane and stalked Kall. Up close, Kall could see a fresh piercing wound had rent his abdomen, but the maimed socket where his eye had once been was an old wound.

Hatred emanated from the orb that still functioned. Kall felt it as a creeping fear that worked its way up his spine, threatening to paralyze him.

The beast was playing with him, trying to shake him loose from his perch without an effort. Blood dripped from his fangs onto Kall's face. When Kall didn't move, the beast stepped back, and a veil of darkness descended around them.

Agony exploded in Kall's injured hands. Sickeningly, he realized the demon had sunk his jaws into the backs of them.

With a shout of pain, Kall let go, and found to his horror that his hands were impaled, tangled in the thing's mouth. Curling his legs, Kall kicked out against the bridge, away from the demon's face. The demon's hot breath was a furnace of filth and rot. He pulled his hands free, and then he was falling.

He passed out of the globe of darkness in time to see a shower of magical bolts streak above him, into the sphere. Kall prayed the magic came from Dantane, that the wizard would be able to save the others.

He looked beneath him, but all the bridges were out of reach. He plummeted past the last one and down into another, greater darkness. His vision failed as the light from above faded. His ears filled with rushing air, then suddenly, nothing. His descent came to an abrupt halt.

Kall waited for his bones to shatter against the stone. His chin struck his chest, mashing his tongue between his teeth, but other than that small pain, he felt whole.

Groaning, Kall rolled to his stomach. A wave of vertigo swept over him as he realized he was staring into the bottomless chasm, suspended by some invisible string. Pumping his legs, he felt the fly spell propel him upward.

Dantane, he thought, or Meisha. Could it be she survived? Trepidation warred with giddy relief that the Harper might still be alive.

Kall put his boot against the cavern wall and pushed off, hurling himself back to the battle.

When he emerged into the light, his suspicion was confirmed.

Meisha and Dantane stood on the bridge with Talal between them. Meisha saw Kall coming and motioned to the demon, which stalked cautiously down the walkway toward the group. The globe of darkness had gone, and Dantane continued to hurl spells, but the demon kept coming, measuring the wizard's strength.

Kall flew up from beneath, his sword leading. He slashed along the demon's flank and kept going, up out of his reach. On the bridge, the advantage was temporarily theirs. As long as they could stay out of the demon's reach and resist his aura, they could fight. If he managed to herd them back into the tunnels, they were mice in the snake hole.

A massive, clawed paw struck out at Kall's face. He flipped over backward and came from beneath with his blade out straight. He stabbed for the demon's chest, but he dodged away.

Kall pulled out of the roll and floundered, losing precious time as he righted himself. His grasp of the flight spell was tenuous at best. He took a claw to his shoulder for his mistake, a wound that burned down the length of his arm.

Kall circled under the bridge and came up in a burst of speed, hoping for surprise, but the demon was gone. Weary of the wizard pricking at him, the beast chose to charge down the bridge to the spellcasters and Talal.

Dantane threw out a hand as though to ward off an attack. In response, a wall of thick stone sprouted from the bridge, growing like a blunt spike to intercept the demon's charge. The demon slammed into the wall, shaking the entire bridge, but the spell held firm.

"The rope!" Kall yelled up to Garavin. He grabbed the dangling end and flew over the wall. The demon continued to pound and claw against the barrier. He would wear it down quickly, Kall knew.

He floated down, putting the rope in Talal's hands as Garavin retied it from above. Meisha flew beside him, helping the boy scramble to the relative safety of the upper bridge.

"He's breaking through," said Dantane. The wizard weaved on his feet, drained by the force of all the released Art.

"You have to keep him on the bridge," said a new voice.

Kall reacted instantly. He swung his sword with all his strength.

Aazen's blade caught it. Steel sang loudly in the cavern.

Kall cursed. Now they were pinned from both sides.

Aazen lowered his weapon, motioning the man behind him to stay back. "I'm not going to kill you at the moment, Kall," he said.

"A pleasant fact to know," Kall remarked, keeping his sword raised.

"At least not until the demon is dead. Get to the other bridge," Aazen said, addressing his man.

"No. Over there." Kall pointed to the closest walkway below, well out of range of his friends above.

Aazen nodded, and the thief tossed a grappling hook out over the chasm. Aazen remained with Kall and Dantane.

"I will guard the wizard," he offered.

This elicited a sardonic laugh from Kall. "How generous of you."

Aazen waved a hand impatiently. "We have no time to argue. Fly and work that sword while you have the opportunity."

"He's right," said Dantane unexpectedly. "Go."

Kall shook his head. "Don't trust him."

"I do not," Dantane snapped. "I'm not as blind as you. But he has it aright. Go, while you can."

Kall's gaze remained on Aazen, silently promising what would happen if he betrayed them. He stepped off the walkway, allowing himself to float in the air. He turned, flying toward the disintegrating wall.

He landed on the top in a skid. Using the spell to aid his balance, Kall slid down the opposite side. He brought his sword down vertically just as the demon came at the wall again. This time the demon couldn't dodge, and his blade sheared into the beast's ribs. Kall twisted aside, expecting an immediate retaliation, but the demon fell back, surprised, favoring his side.

Kall pressed, stabbing him in the haunch, anywhere he could reach, using his sword as leverage to propel himself back into flight.

Recovering, the demon followed and struck out, snagging Kall's leg with a massive claw. The demon dragged him back down to the ground. Kall felt the claws penetrate his boots, burning, adding to his other wounds.

Not enough, Kall thought as he felt himself rolled onto his stomach, his arms trapped beneath his body. He would run out of fight—they all would—long before the demon was finished.

"Keeper of knowledge—sever the link."

Garavin turned from the battle at the sound of the voice, compelled by a force impossible to resist.

The ghost of one of the long-dead Howlings stood before him, spilling silver light from the sockets of his vacant eyes. Garavin looked involuntarily at the light, and the symbol at his throat began to burn. He heard the voices of the others, screaming at Kall, screaming for Garavin to help him, but the dwarf stood frozen. Couldn't they see him? Even Borl wasn't reacting. How could they not see?

"Dumathoin," Garavin spoke, in a voice rigid with awe. He slid to his knees. "Lord Under Mountain, we cannot defeat the demon. Aid us, please."

The god's essence spoke through the ghost. "Secret keeper, call to him." The avatar reached out to touch his forehead. "Show him."

Tears spilled from Garavin's eyes, hissing as they touched Dumathoin's holy symbol. He felt the power grow inside him, and he knew what form it would have to take. "I understand, Lord Under Mountain. I obey."

Kall felt Dantane's energy spells reverberate through the demon's claw, knocking the beast off balance. Whether it had any effect other than to incense the creature, Kall didn't know, but he used the distraction to crawl out from under the demon's bloody paw and free his sword. Gripping the blade, he realized the vibration wasn't coming from the demon.

The magic came from his sword.

No more than a tremor at first, the sensation grew, until Kall had to hold the weapon with both hands. The empty space where the Morel emerald had been was filled with a silver light that outlined the blade. Accompanying the light, the vibrating hum sounded like music. Then he heard, within the song, Garavin's voice.

"Banish the demon, Kall."

The dwarf's voice pierced his temples. Kall shook his head to clear it and to deny him. "You have to get out of here, back through the portal. If we stay, he'll slaughter us all," he said.

"Listen to me, lad." Garavin's voice shook him, unrelenting. "Ye can wound the thing a thousand times, but his link to this world has to be severed. He's holding onto it desperately. As long as he's sure it's safe, he can kill us all at his leisure. By Dumathoin's will, Kall."

"Kall!" This time it was Meisha, shouting to him from the bridge. "The eye, Kall! The empty eye!" the Harper cried.

Kall swung his sword around. It seemed to have grown heavier with the weight of Garavin's voice coursing through the blade. He flew into the demon's path, angling to its left. The jarilith didn't need eyes to find him, but the beast turned anyway, running alongside Kall, using the points of his spines as defensive weapons.

Kall pulled back, sucking in his gut. He didn't trust his armor to hold, and wasn't surprised when he heard cloth and chain rip. His cloak, caught against his flank, tore into two ragged slits.

My hands are already ruined, Kall thought, so . . .

Reaching out, Kall grabbed a handful of red and black mane

and pulled, hoping to wrench the beast's head around.

He might as well have tried to turn a statue's head.

The demon jumped straight up, pulling Kall with him. His grip shaken, Kall fell onto his back on the walkway. He managed to hold onto his sword, but the weapon still vibrated painfully in his hands. Its guard wedged against the stone bridge, allowing him to see the silver light clearly. Movement reflected within it like a mirror, showing the demon as he turned and jumped again, intending to finish his prey while he was out of the air.

Bringing his arms and legs in close to his body, Kall swung the humming blade around until the demon filled the reflective surface, and all he could feel was heat, a great waterfall of it coming down on him. The blade's edge crossed his center of vision then thrust back, deep into the demon's empty socket.

His sword ripped out of his grasp, and the last thing Kall heard before the fire buried him was the demon's roar, a scream that sounded almost human.

———◆·◆·◆———

Varan screamed, clawing at the punctured eyeball. He tore it out of its socket and cast it aside. The Shadow Thief guarding him skittered back a step in revulsion.

Crying, the wizard flopped onto his back. His breath hissed erratically in and out of his lungs. Blood that was not his own ran from his ruined eye socket. After a moment, he raised his hands to wipe the moisture away—blood from one eye, tears from the other. He began to laugh, a relieved, hysterical sound that echoed through the caves and brought the other thieves running.

"What happened?" asked Geroll.

"Don't know," said the guard, taking another step back just to be safe. "He just started screaming, then pulled out his own eye. Crazy bastard looks almost happy about it."

CHAPTER TWENTY-EIGHT

The Howling Delve
5 Marpenoth, the Year of Lightning Storms (1374 DR)

Kall felt the weight of the demon come down and knew the battle was over. He prayed the spines would impale him and end his life quickly. If they did not—panic rose sickeningly in his throat—he would burn to death from the demon's flesh.

A silver light filled the cavern, blinding him, but the killing weight did not follow. Kall blinked the brightness out of his eyes and strained to see. Running feet came across the bridge toward him. Dantane's wall had come down. The wizard and Aazen were coming to him, but neither wore looks of fear or alarm. If anything, their expressions were confused.

Kall rolled onto his side, still shocked at his ability to do so. A few feet away, his sword lay on the walkway.

The jarilith was gone. There was only a small puddle of blood left on the bridge. Either the demon had fallen from the bridge, or Kall had truly severed his link to this place.

"He's gone," said Dantane, echoing Kall's thoughts. He knelt beside Kall to examine his wounds. "You need healing, or you're going to die," he said.

Kall laughed. Pain flared in his abdomen. "No need to spare my delicate feelings. Tell me the truth."

"Kall! Dantane!" cried Meisha from above them. "It's Garavin!"

Garavin—his voice had cut off sometime during the flash of silver light. Kall used Dantane's arm to haul himself to his feet. Light-headed from wounds and the terror gripping his heart, he flew unsteadily to the upper bridge. Dantane flew beside him.

Out of the corner of his vision, Kall saw Aazen looking past them, up to the double doors Kall and Garavin had come through. Green portal light spilled out through the doorway. Aazen motioned to his man on the opposite bridge.

Let them go, Kall thought. Dantane was right. He wasn't in any condition to fight.

He crested the stone lip, and all thoughts of Aazen deserted him.

Garavin lay prone on the bridge. Meisha and Talal crouched beside him. The dwarf clutched his holy symbol in his hand, his eyes fixed and staring at nothing.

Kall bent, trying to pry the symbol loose, but stopped when he felt the latent heat. "What happened?" he demanded.

"It was the ghost," said Talal. "The one from the room, where we found Braedrin's body. Meisha's messenger. I saw it touch him. I don't think he's breathin' at all."

"Garavin," Kall said, taking his friend by the shoulders. There were no visible wounds on the dwarf's body. "Wake up. Wherever you are, we need you back here." He held his maimed hands in front of the dwarf's vacant eyes. "Look at this. See what a wreck I make of myself when you're not here?" His voice cracked. "By the gods, you'd better not be dead." He leaned close and spoke in the dwarf's ear. "There are too many ghosts down here already, old friend. Please."

Kall thought he heard a shallow push of air fill his friend's chest. Garavin's bloodshot eyes slid closed, then opened again, and something of a presence returned. Kall breathed a quiet prayer of thanks. "Can you hear me, old friend?" he asked.

"He's gone," said the dwarf, looking beyond Kall to something unseen. His voice held a sadness Kall had never heard before.

"Who's gone?" Kall asked quietly.

"Dumathoin," replied the dwarf. Beside him, Meisha drew a startled breath, but Garavin's attention was on Kall. "He's gone, and so are the Howlings. Their penance is done."

"Is it safe to go now?"

Garavin nodded. "Best to leave it all to the dust, lad." This time he did look at Meisha. "And take the warning to other secret keepers. This Shanatar doesn't exist."

The Harper nodded, and Kall stood up. Garavin touched his hands and stomach and began a healing prayer.

"As soon as we can move, we're getting out of here," Kall said, feeling the pain of his wounds diminish. When Garavin would have tended other hurts, he gently pushed the dwarf away. "I'm all right, old friend. Save your strength."

"To what fate are we escaping?" spoke up Dantane. When Kall turned, he pointed to the double doors. "Your friend is gone through the portal."

"Could be an ambush waiting for us up top," said Morgan. He sounded as if he did not care either way.

"Or the portal malfunctioned again, and they could be sitting anywhere in the Delve," said Kall. He thought of Cesira, back at the estate. "We don't have any other way out."

While the others gathered themselves, Kall went to Morgan, but the thief remained subdued. He would not meet Kall's eyes.

Kall tried to speak, to confirm what he hadn't been able to acknowledge when Morgan had run onto the bridge without Laerin, when he'd seen the fresh blood on the demon's claws.

"Is there . . ." Kall cleared his throat and tried again. "Is there a body?" Morgan paled, but it was Talal who answered.

"There's nothing you'd recognize," he said, shuddering at a memory he could never be rid of. "Your friend's gone."

Kall nodded, but inwardly, the rage was so profound he thought he might burn from it. Was this what it was like for Meisha, he wondered, to be filled with fire and anger so consuming it swallowed his thoughts? To think that his friend, who loved the light, the road, the open air—that this should be his tomb. . . .

"Kall."

Kall blinked. For a breath, he'd thought it was Cesira's voice—impatient, always commanding, but with an underlying softness she tried to hide. He looked up, but it was Meisha who addressed him.

"There might be another way out," the Harper said. "The Climb. It should lead all the way to the portal room."

Kall met her eyes and saw the reluctance there. "What aren't you telling me?"

"We might all die in the attempt."

"Of course." Kall looked around the group and received answering nods of assent. They were with him. "Let's go," he said. Cesira's face was still bright in his mind.

I'm coming.

<hr />

Marguin slid around the corner, using a mirror the size of her thumb to see that the way was clear. Elsis came behind her with an arrow nestled in the curve of a fully drawn bow.

"We know you're here, Lady," Elsis sang out mockingly. He tipped a silver candelabra off a side table onto the floor. Flames licked at the expensive woven rugs, sending up charred fumes. "The longer you hide, the more painful it will be when we catch you."

Movement from one of the doorways caught his eye. Elsis trained his bow on the spot, but it was only Marguin's reflection in a mirror on the opposite wall.

The house was too damn quiet. There were so many rooms that connected to other rooms without spilling back into the main hallways. The bitch could be leading them around the house, and they'd never know it.

Catch this, breathed a voice at his ear.

Elsis swept the bow in an arc and released. The arrow did not have far to travel. Less than two feet away, it splintered through Marguin's armor near the base of her spine. The woman made a small, pitiful cry and dropped in front of him. Elsis fumbled another arrow from his quiver and nocked it, but he did not hear the voice again. He was alone in the hallway with Marguin's body curled at his feet.

------- ◆ ◆ ◆ -------

Cesira watched the man with the bow scour the hallway. She didn't have enough spells to run him out of arrows, but she was more than willing to disquiet his search. Murmuring a word, she cast the ghostly whisper again. This time, his arrow shattered a mirror.

Crouching low, Cesira crept back to the servants' stair. Two down—more if any from the downstairs trap were still incapacitated. Still too many, she thought, plenty enough to box her in, and there was no sign of Balram. He must still be in the main hall. He wasn't going to make it easy by coming for her himself. Going to him would be beyond foolish.

Cesira tried to recall how many weapons and traps remained. Not enough to take out all of them at once, but if she could get a clear path to the garden—yes, it might work. Or she might die carrying out her plan.

"You were right," she said, holding Kall's emerald to her breast. "I'm an arrogant, stubborn fool." She'd underestimated Balram and the Shadow Thieves, and now she was hopelessly outnumbered. "Time to even the odds."

------- ◆ ◆ ◆ -------

Aazen came through the portal, appearing on the rocky rim of the cavern floor before a circle of drawn weapons. The thieves saw Tarthet's body clutched in Aazen's arms but did not lower their steel. If anything, suspicion grew in their eyes.

"Where is Morel?" The man who addressed him was Geroll, one of Daen's men.

"Food for a demon, when I left him," Aazen lied. He settled the dead man on the floor and drew Morgan's dagger from his back. He'd picked it up on the bridge just before they'd entered the portal room. Tarthet might have corroborated his story. Aazen would never know. "Does the wizard live?" he asked.

"If you can call it that." Geroll nudged the unconscious Varan with his leg. The wizard did not stir. "He's been like that ever since he lost his eye."

"His eye?" Aazen echoed, then he saw Varan's empty socket. So that was the link. "Perhaps it's best. Now we can safely remove him from the Delve."

Geroll nodded carefully. "Call the others back," he said to the man nearest him. "We have what we came for." He looked at Aazen, clearly reluctant to relinquish the authority he'd thought would be assured by Aazen's treachery. But he had no proof, and to accuse Balram's son without it would mean his death. "Balram will be expecting your report," he said finally.

"Of course." Before Aazen could issue an order, the portal in the shaft above his head flared green, and Tershus dropped through, wounded but alive. The halfling saw Aazen and ran right up to him, ignoring Daen's men completely.

"You'd better come," he said breathlessly. "It's your father."

Aazen stiffened. "What about my father?"

"He took a group of men to Morel house. They haven't returned, and there've been reports of fire in that section of the city."

Aazen grabbed Tershus by the arm, digging in until the small man yelped. "Bring the wizard," he said.

"What about the portals?" demanded Geroll. "We can't leave them open."

"My men and I were separated," said Aazen. "If you wish to eliminate any hope of them returning alive, by all means, close the gates. I'll be happy to explain your decision, and the manpower lost, to Daen."

He didn't wait for the man to formulate a reply. He shook the halfling in his grip. "Bring the wizard," he repeated. "Now."

Tershus pulled away, his eyes wide at the alteration in Aazen's demeanor. But for Aazen, the feelings that coursed through him were familiar, shameful, and completely unsurprising to him.

His father was in danger. His father—who'd sent these Shadow Thieves to kill him—needed his son. And Aazen ran to answer that need, as he had always done, as he would always do, for as long as Balram was alive.

* * *

Cesira knelt on the floor by the stairway, preparing to change form, when the bolt struck her. Her leg gave out, and she sprawled. Twisting, she pressed her back to the meager protection of the pillar at the landing.

Below her, Balram lowered his crossbow, a weapon he hadn't been carrying when he'd entered the house. "You are far more fetching in that shape than any other, my dear," he called up to her. "And you are not the only person outside the Morel family who knows where the master of the house kept his toys. Come down, and perhaps I'll show you a few Kall doesn't know about."

A generous offer, my lord, Cesira replied. She bit her lip against the pain in her leg. *But I'm afraid I must decline.* Shadows stirred in the upper hallway, and Cesira heard footsteps coming, running toward their voices.

She risked a glance down to the hall. She couldn't see Balram, but there was, as she'd hoped, an unobstructed path to the garden. The question remained, how many crossbow bolts would she take getting there?

Elsis's shout from the hallway decided her. She could not outrun arrows *and* bolts.

Elsis came around the corner, his eyes widening in surprise when he saw her just sitting, exposed, at the top of the stairs. Cesira grabbed a knife from her belt and threw it, forcing him to duck back around the corner.

Standing unsteadily, she found her balance and flipped forward over the stair rail, hanging from her fingers. She swung out feet first and let go, landing in a painful crouch on the first floor. Her eyes tracked the room for Balram—corner pillar; there you are.

She jumped before she heard the twang of the crossbow. Her feet left the floor at the same time her hands came down. She pushed off, into a forward roll, and the bolt struck wood somewhere above her head. Free in that breath, she sprang up and ran, ran as she used to run with the mist stags in the deepest parts of Mir. Her leg was on fire, but she ignored the pain.

She hit the doors to the garden, flung them open, and the third bolt slammed into her back, driving her forward. She felt the tip scrape a rib and resisted the urge to scream. She would not give Balram, a man who reveled in pain, the satisfaction of seeing hers.

Cesira stumbled into the garden, breathing night air and taking in her first—and possibly last—glimpse of the cloudy sky since her vigil on the tower. She ran through the garden's heart, calling silently as she went. In her mind, she screamed their names with her true voice, a voice only the wild beasts could hear.

Sparks flew as an arrow skittered off the stone fountain. Distracted, Cesira tripped and fell to the walkway, striking her head against the ground. To the side, she saw Elsis and another man with a lantern step into the garden alongside Balram.

"So many memories from Esmeltaran," Balram remarked idly. He reloaded his weapon as he approached. "An empty garden, a dry fountain, and finally an end to the Morel family."

He stepped onto the walkway. "What form *would* you care to die in, my lady?" he inquired politely. He raised the crossbow. "The woman . . . the beast?" His lips curved. "Or are they all the same?"

All, my lord, the druid gasped as a rush of wind filled the garden. *We are all bitches with sharp claws.*

Balram felt the wind and looked up in time to see the birds—Morel's hunting raptors—descend on the garden. Balram snapped his crossbow up, aiming for Cesira's heart, but the flock absorbed the bolt. The night filled with wings, talons, and the high, shrill cries of incensed animals.

Balram took a step forward, but the swarm only increased the closer he got to the druid. A sharp pain burst from his ear, ripping up into his head. He touched the side of his face and found the earlobe gone. Blood dripped down his neck.

"Back inside!" Elsis cried. "Get back!"

"No, damn you!" Balram grabbed the lantern from the other man's hand. He waved it in the air, batting aside the large bodies. The lantern broke, sending birds up into the sky aflame. Balram threw up his other arm to protect his eyes, but he felt scratches and bites all over his body.

Through the violence, he saw Cesira—once helpless at his feet—now with her eyes changing shape and color. Her arms joined the mass of wings, and for a bizarre breath she was a hybrid of woman and bird. Balram swung the lantern again, charging forward, but she was already gone, transformed and carried away by the flock.

❖

Meisha had never seen the bottom end of the Climb, but her research since she'd left the Delve told her it should be there. Still, it took her a while to find it. She'd only traversed a portion of it in her search for Shaera—a search that had ended in tragedy. Now she had to lead an entire group to safety through the treacherous passage to the surface—if it still led all the way to the surface. Damn the Howlings anyway.

Kall stood at the base of a tunnel that slanted upward until it was almost vertical. Stone platforms jutted from the walls to form uneven rungs.

"I'll lead," Kall said. "Meisha and Talal come behind me, then Dantane and Garavin. Morgan, take Borl and bring up the rear."

"Slow going," Dantane commented, "with a dog and an injured dwarf."

"Then we go as slowly as necessary," Kall said. He pulled himself up onto the first stone ledge.

Meisha floated globes of shimmering fire ahead and behind them, so they would be unencumbered by torches. She could see nothing of Kall beyond his boots and the tail of his cloak, but she could sense the urgency in his movements.

"What will you do once we reach the surface?" Meisha asked. "Aazen and the Shadow Thieves will be long gone."

"Cesira," Kall said, hauling himself up another rung. "They'll be going for the house. I have to be there."

"And Varan?" Meisha asked.

"The Shadow Thieves will have him," Kall said. "They won't give him up easily."

Neither will I, Meisha thought.

Below them, Garavin succumbed to a fit of coughing that echoed through the shaft. Kall stopped the group.

"How are you doing, old friend," he called down.

Morgan answered him. "He's spitting some blood, Kall. That silver light messed him up bad."

"Hang on just a little longer," Kall said. "We're almost out of this shaft." He closed his eyes and murmured a prayer to Dumathoin.

Don't forsake your servant now.

Kall looked up. He could see an obstacle ahead. He motioned for Meisha to send a fire globe up so he could see.

"Son of a god's cursed whore," he hissed under his breath.

Staring him in the face was a rusty shield floating in a cloud of viscous fluid. The fire globe drifted higher. Kall could make out the edges of a gelatinous cube suctioned to the walls of the shaft.

"Is it alive?" Meisha asked. She touched the oozing substance dribbling down the walls.

"Alive or dead, it can still suffocate us, depending on how far up the shaft it reaches," Dantane said.

Kall leaned closer to the cube. The slime distorted the objects within—relics of the creature's last victims—but he could make out enough of the stone handholds inside the cube to pull himself through.

"Morgan, I need your rope," he called down.

Morgan unhooked an end of silk cord from his belt and tossed it up to Kall. Tying one end of the rope around his waist, Kall handed the other to Meisha.

"When I pull the cord in three quick jerks, it means I've reached the other side," he said. "The next person uses the rope to climb up. We pull Garavin and Borl up last." He looked at Talal. "Big breath," he told the boy.

Talal muttered, "Already drowned once today, why not twice?"

"Hold it in tight," said Kall, "You don't want a lungful of what's up there. You won't come back from it."

Secured by the rope, Kall positioned himself in a crouch on the stone ledge and thrust up from the knees, into the gelatinous cube.

Sound and light instantly disappeared. Kall tried to lift his arms, but it was as if someone had attached sandbags to his muscles. His muscles burning and stretching with the effort, he gripped the next rung and climbed.

His face brushed something hard that felt vaguely like fingers—a lost gauntlet, perhaps, all that was left of one of the cube's victims. Kall would have shuddered, if his muscles could have responded to the impulse.

His lungs burned. The rough stone grated against his injured hands. They would be raw and bleeding again soon. With a desperate shove, he broke through the slimy surface and hit his chest against a stone platform.

Coughing and spitting slime, Kall hauled his lower body out of the cube and onto the stone platform. He lay on his back gasping for a moment. His entire body was saturated with slime, but at least he could breathe air again.

Kall wiped his eyes clear and saw darkness, illuminated faintly by Meisha's fire globes drifting below. The light filtering through the cube cast eerie green glows on the walls.

Gathering the rope about his waist, Kall pulled until it came taut three times. He hoped Meisha's slighter weight would make the climb easier.

A tense moment later, a cap of black hair broke the surface, and Meisha crawled up beside him onto the stone ledge.

"What a wonderful experience," the Harper said, flicking the substance off her fingers. Slime plastered her hair to her forehead, and her eyelashes stuck together in dark clumps.

The others followed slowly, until only Garavin and Borl remained. It took the combined strength of Kall, Morgan, and Dantane to haul the pair through the cube, Borl with his muzzle and nose tied shut with cloth. By the time the dwarf was clear of the creature, he barely breathed. Kall quickly unfastened the cloth that kept the dog from breathing in the slime, then turned to Garavin.

"Help me clean him off," Kall ordered. "The slime will corrode his skin if it's left alone."

They laid the gasping dwarf down onto the stone platform. Garavin dredged up a grin for Morgan as the thief tried to wipe away the slime.

"Laerin would be chuckling if he could see ye playing nursemaid," the dwarf said.

Morgan offered one of his halfhearted grunts. "Don't get used to it," he said.

"All right, finish up," Kall said. "We have to keep moving." He pointed to a tunnel angling away from the shaft. "Level ground, Garavin," he said. "Easy going."

"If it lasts." Dantane said, always the voice of dissension. He nodded to the dwarf. "He won't make another climb like this."

"I'll be looking after myself just fine, young one," said Garavin sharply. He got to his feet unaided, but leaned heavily against the tunnel wall.

Kall exchanged a glance with Morgan. Garavin never lost patience with anyone. For the taciturn dwarf to do so now frightened Kall more than a little.

"We'll rest here," Kall said. "Dantane's right. We don't know how long any of us will last if we encounter another long climb."

The others moved away to give the dwarf some room. Kall guided his friend back to a sitting position and settled beside him.

Garavin leaned heavily on him for support. When he looked at Kall, his pupils had dilated to two piercing black holes surrounded by a mound of wrinkles. He seemed to have aged a decade in the space of a moment.

"What happened, Garavin?" Kall asked, keeping his voice low. "Was it really Dumathoin on the bridge?"

The dwarf closed his eyes and breathed. The rough wheeze was barely audible. "It was . . . a power I've never felt before, lad—or could ever hope to feel again."

"Did the power consume you from the inside?" Kall asked urgently. "Can you recover?"

"I think so," said Garavin. "To live on—feels like Dumathoin's plan for me." He looked at Kall. "But we—none of us, have the guarantee of living through this passage."

"Don't worry, I'll see to that," said Kall.

Across the tunnel, Meisha listened with half an ear to their conversation, and used her remaining attention to direct the light globes down the tunnel to scout ahead.

"Stay back here, Talal," she called out to the boy, who'd wandered halfheartedly to follow the globes. She heard the scrape of feet on stone and Talal's voice, echoing back to them.

"The tunnel slants down!" he called out. "Spikes on the walls, but the bottom's clear."

Through her exhaustion, the words came to Meisha sluggishly. Spikes on the walls.

Memories of her own trek through the caverns came rushing back from a buried place in her mind.

With an incoherent shout of warning, Meisha came to her feet. She ran in the direction Talal had wandered, knowing even as she skidded down the slant that she would be too late.

The boy's foot touched a pressure plate identical to the one Shaera had encountered on her ill-fated journey farther up the

Climb. Meisha heard Morgan shout as the thief recognized the danger, but her eyes were only on Talal.

She pushed off, using the slanted stone for leverage, hurling herself into the boy. They crashed together to the floor as rocks rained down on them.

"Meisha!" Kall shouted, but his voice was lost in the hail of battering stones.

Meisha heard Talal screaming in her ear. She felt the impact of the stones against her back, smashing ribs and bruising flesh.

"No," she whimpered, when Talal's screams abruptly cut off. She felt the boy go limp in her arms. In Meisha's mind, all she could see were Shaera's dead eyes, all she could hear was the prayer to an unknown god the girl had whispered in the dark. Talal had no one to watch over him. He was alone in the dark.

Shaera's blood-covered visage . . . Varan's ruined eye . . . Laerin's blood on a demon's claws.

Something inside Meisha broke. Without thought or hope, she called the fire.

Flame blazed from her eyes, her mouth, from every wound torn open by the falling stones. Meisha's pain disappeared, replaced by raw burning—a heat that should have incinerated her body but did not. The fire did not even singe her clothes. Instead the flames shielded her, casting away the falling stones or burning them to smoking blisters before her eyes.

Meisha had never experienced this kind of release. The power within her swelled, and for the first time in her life, she felt nothing could harm her. The fire consumed all, taking thought and emotion and turning the world black inside her mind. Safe in the flaming cocoon, she could exist as one with her element and never have to feel the pain of the world again.

Is that what you want?

Dantane's words echoed in her mind. "Yes, oh yes!" she screamed, crying tears of black flame.

Let me stay this way, always.

"Meisha!"

She heard the voice near her ear, frightened but insistent, distracting her from her paradise. Meisha tried to ignore it. The fire beckoned her, seductive and soft, a lover's touch that banished all her memories. She did not even recognize the voice calling her.

"Meisha."

Hands gripped her shoulders, shaking her and sending waves of cold through the inferno. Meisha shuddered at the icy touch.

"Go away," she snarled, hearing the flames in her own voice. "Leave me be!"

The hands shrank back, and for a moment Meisha thought they would retreat. Then she felt the slap across her cheek, sharp and brutal. The hands shook her again, harder.

Meisha reared back, prepared to burn her attacker to cinders, when she heard the choked cry of pain. The voice spoke her name again, this time in anger.

"Meisha—stupid, flame-kissing Harper—have done!"

Meisha opened her eyes. The flames drained out of her body, leaving her weak and quivering. She collapsed on top of Talal, who squeaked in fresh agony.

"How many ways are you trying to kill me!" the boy screeched, pushing her off and scrambling away.

"You're alive," Meisha said wonderingly. "The cave-in . . . I thought it had killed you. It killed her—Shaera."

"Is she all right?" came Kall's voice from somewhere above her head.

"Babbling something, but I always knew her mind was addled," Talal said. The boy snorted, but his eyes were filled with concern when he looked down at her.

"How?" Meisha asked.

"Your fat bulk shielded me from the worst of it," the boy said, grinning. "Got a nasty bump, though." He touched his head and winced. "Your back's going to have some pretty scars on it."

He reached under her arms and felt for broken bones as Kall and the others approached.

Meisha caught Talal's wrist and saw the blistering burns on his palm. Her eyes filled with misery. "I burned you," she said bleakly. "I could have killed you."

"You could have killed us all," said Kall, as Garavin knelt beside her and muttered a prayer. "But you didn't."

Meisha looked at Dantane. She felt the dwarf's healing wash over her, closing the worst of her injuries. Talal was right, she thought. Some of the scars would never heal.

"I felt the power," she told the wizard. "The element. I *was* fire. I wanted it so badly."

Dantane nodded, understanding, but Talal scoffed. "Showing off was what she did," he said. "Boom! That's all you sorcerers are about."

Meisha touched the boy's wrist. "Thank you for telling me when to stop," she whispered. This time, moisture trailed down her cheeks rather than fire.

Talal's face scrunched up at the sight of the tears. He looked more panicked than he had when she was on fire. "Get me out of here, Lady, and we're even. Sune's teats, I swear this is the last time I'll ask."

"Can you continue?" Kall asked her.

With Talal's aid, Meisha got to her feet. "I can," she said.

He nodded. "Let's go, then. There's still a long climb, and the Shadow Thieves are waiting."

CHAPTER TWENTY-NINE

Keczulla, Amn
5 Marpenoth, the Year of Lightning Storms (1374 DR)

When Kall emerged from the Bladesmile estate and saw the black cloud hanging in the sky above the Gold Ward, he didn't realize it was alive. He'd been on guard for a Shadow Thief ambush, but the portal room, both in the Delve and the estate, was deserted, the gates active and waiting. He'd been certain it was a trap, but there was no sign of the Shadow Thieves or Varan.

When the black cloud shattered, the birds scattered throughout the city, some dropping from the sky impaled with arrows, others on fire, reeling wildly in the air like dying phoenixes. Kall knew at once where they'd come from.

"Take Garavin to Waukeen's temple," he told Morgan and Talal. The dwarf still walked in a haze, his strength depleted. Kall didn't know how long it would take for him to recover from his experience. "Meisha, Dantane. Come with me." He offered no other explanation; he simply ran toward his home.

He was almost to the line of dark hedgerows that led up to the main entrance when Meisha and Dantane caught up. With surprising strength, the Harper yanked him down behind the hedge while shadows moved in front of the burning house.

Kall grabbed her by the front of her jerkin, both in fury and to steady himself. "If you're not going to help me," he snarled, "get out of my way!"

Meisha glared at him. "Clearly you've forgotten whom you're speaking to," she said, nodding to the house. "They have Varan. I will merrily tear your home apart to find him if it pleases you, but I would rather not die until Balram is writhing safely in the deepest Hells." She leaned close. "I have held myself in check; now you will do the same. Remember your promise, Kall."

They held each other's gaze, and then, jarringly, Kall's face split in a grin. "Fine—tear the place apart. But clear a path for me first. Remember the garden?"

* * *

The guards stationed at the double front doors were shocked when they saw Balram and his two companions re-enter the hall, bleeding from scores of scratches and bites. At the same time, light—bright as a bonfire blaze—filled the vertical windows aside the front doors.

"What was that?" asked Balram, one hand covering his bleeding ear.

Elsis ran to the window. "The fire must have spread faster than we anticipated," he said. "The hedgerows are ablaze."

"What?"

The guard pointed to the twin lines of fire burning up to the carriageway.

"Bloody gods," Elsis murmured, flinging one of the doors open to get a better view. "What is that?"

He saw a man striding up the path. His cloak was torn apart, his armor soiled with blood, and his hair and skin were scorched by fire. Yet he walked as if the fire itself propelled him forward. A rush and roar sounded in the distance, and a woman stepped onto the path behind him. From her hands, a ball of fire bloomed and exploded down the walkway, chasing the man hungrily.

Elsis watched, his mouth agape, as the flames closed in, and still the man walked forward. He didn't even glance over his shoulder, though the heat must have been unbearable.

Just before the flames reached him, the woman made a gesture with her hands, pulling her palms apart and spreading her arms wide.

The fireball split. Each half streaked aside the man and past him, exploding in Elsis's face, driving the guard back into the doors and through. The front of the house collapsed, folding in on itself as the structure absorbed the brunt of the explosion. The rubble buried those of Balram's guards not consumed by the fireball.

Kall mounted the steps and crossed the shattered threshold of his home. He saw Balram come out from behind one of the pillars, bloodied and flush from the fire.

Kall noted the bites and scratches. "I see you've met my wife," he said.

Balram did not speak. His gaze flicked to Dantane and Meisha as they flanked Kall in the doorway.

"Welcome home, Kall," said a voice from the doorway. "Now step forward."

Kall smiled. "Am I to be forever finding you just over my shoulder, Aazen?" he asked.

Aazen stepped around them, kicking aside glass and debris to make a path. He half-led, half-dragged Varan in the crook of one arm. In the other, he held a long dagger at the wizard's throat.

Meisha stiffened, but Kall motioned her and Dantane to step forward ahead of him. He kept his back to them and his eyes on Aazen as they moved fully into the hall. "You're a hard man to find, Balram," Kall remarked as Aazen circled around to join his father. "And I've been looking for you a long time."

"I'm flattered. But you shouldn't have come back," said Balram. "Now all this will end in much the same way it began. Except this time"—he touched Aazen's shoulder, and the look of paternal pride in his eyes sickened Kall—"my son *will* kill you."

Aazen lowered the wizard to the floor and handed his father the dagger. Balram took the blade and settled it back against the wizard's throat. Aazen drew his sword.

Meisha took a step forward, but Balram pivoted so she could see the folds of Varan's skin lying atop the steel. "Move again, and my hand will slip," he promised.

Dantane drew her back. They stepped aside as Kall and Aazen approached one another. To the surprise of all, it was Kall who moved in first, banging his blade off Aazen's with a loud ringing.

"You're not hesitating, Kall," Aazen said, swinging through the parry. "Won't you try to convince me to stand down, to help you kill my father?"

Kall blocked a low thrust. "I told you I would never use you to get at Balram. I asked you to turn from the Shadow Thieves. You'll never be able to trust them."

Aazen drew his blade back, following up with a snapping kick aimed at Kall's midsection. Kall dodged, but caught the brunt of the kick against his bound arm. The pain teased stars from the corners of his eyes.

"I trusted you," Aazen said. "No matter what mischief you convinced me to take part in, you always looked out for me. In your house, I was safe."

"But you trust your father more, because no matter how twisted his love, you believe blood will never betray you," Kall replied.

"Yes." Aazen blocked a flurry of short attacks and reeled when Kall surrendered his advantage to strike with his fist. The punch glanced across Aazen's throat. He folded into a defensive crouch, but Kall followed, forcing him to move back and block while he choked for breath.

"But it's you, Aazen, who loves him beyond reason. He's buried you so deep in his control you don't know the way out. I thought I could convince you to come with me, but I lost you that night in the cemetery, didn't I? I didn't even realize."

"Shut up," Aazen said, whipping his sword around and

biting Kall's arm again. The pain was brilliant, but it was still nothing compared to being burned by a demon. Kall stepped into the move, allowing Aazen to deepen the wound. In doing so, Kall put himself right in Aazen's space. Aazen pressed the attack, oblivious. He believed Kall would weaken, favor his arm, and retreat.

Kall batted Aazen's blade aside, flipped his own blade to his off-hand, and grabbed Aazen by the throat, lifting him bodily from the floor. Blood streamed down Kall's arm, but he held on, pressing his fingers in under Aazen's jawbone until his sword fell from his hand.

"Aazen!" Balram cried, and for the first time there was real fear in his voice.

"Kall, stop!" yelled Meisha, who saw what he intended.

Kall ignored them both and released Aazen. His friend dropped, falling onto Kall's angled blade. Aazen grabbed Kall's shoulders to keep himself upright. Kall held him steady. He leaned forward and spoke against his friend's ear, but he meant the words for Balram.

"He was always faster, more graceful, when I was all limbs and bone. Laerin taught me better. A half-elf taught me how to beat him." He slid the blade from Aazen's stomach. "A dwarf taught me how to live."

He stood up, but Balram's eyes were fixed, horrified, on his son. "Aazen," he whispered. The knife went slack in his hand.

Kall reacted, closing the space between him and Balram with speed that would indeed have made the half-elf proud. Kall's sword, wet with the son's blood, found the father's heart with no fight at all from Balram. Kall drove him back and off the ground, drawing the knife away from Varan's throat.

Balram's body hit the ground in a pool of the spilled oil. The latent flames from Meisha's fireball touched the puddle and ignited, and Balram joined the fire that slowly consumed the wood skeleton of Morel house.

Kall backed away, making no move to put out the flames. He took Aazen's arms and slung his friend's body across his shoulders. Dantane lifted Varan, and Meisha took Varan's other side as they headed for the doors.

"This way," said Meisha. She waved an arm and the flames covering the door folded aside, boiling in orange swirls. The group slipped out through the small opening into the outer yard.

"Dantane," said Kall, laying Aazen down on the grass.

Glassy-eyed, Aazen watched in resigned silence as his lifeblood soaked the green lawn. The scene reminded Kall of that day on the Esmel shore, when Haig had saved Aazen's life. Those boys were long dead, Kall thought. "Hurry," he said.

Meisha took Varan, and Dantane handed Kall his last vial. "You should have killed him," the wizard said impassively.

"Garavin would have been disappointed if I had." Propping Aazen against his shoulder, Kall poured the healing potion down his friend's throat. Aazen choked on the concoction, but Kall held his mouth. "Swallow, damn you. You're not gone yet."

Aazen swallowed. Selûne's light reflected in his eyes as he stared upward. Gradually, they cleared and swiveled around to focus on Kall. "I thought you had done it," Aazen said hoarsely. "I thought you'd killed me."

"I would have been returning the favor," Kall pointed out. "You tried to kill me."

"I had to," said Aazen, sitting unsteadily. He stared over Kall's shoulder, through the gap in the front of the house. His father was in there. He would never come out again. It took a moment for the gravity of that truth to sink into Aazen's soul.

He looked back at Kall. "If I didn't make you fight in earnest, you couldn't have won," Aazen said. "I would have killed you before you got to him." He paused, remembering. "But I never thought you would use me that way. I didn't think my father could be so distracted."

"He loved you," Kall said, "as much as he was capable. You were right about that."

Meisha looked at Aazen incredulously. "You *wanted* Kall to win," she accused him. "You wanted him to—"

"Kill me," Aazen said. "Yes."

"Gods, why? If release was what you wanted, why didn't you kill Balram yourself?" she demanded.

"He couldn't," said Kall. He wiped his blade on the grass and resheathed it. "No more than I could accept that my father murdered Haig by his own will and took my mother from me. He was right. We were both in a cage. He wanted me to win."

"When did you figure that out?" asked Aazen.

"After we fought in the Delve," Kall said, "I suspected. I knew it later, when the portals were unguarded. I should have known long before."

"Why didn't you kill me?"

"Because you wanted to be free of Balram. Your death wasn't necessary."

"Free," said Dantane, looking at Meisha. "To face justice?"

Aazen shook his head. "To return to the Shadow Thieves."

"No," Kall and Meisha said, almost as one. Dantane smiled.

"You will still answer for the refugees in the Delve," said Meisha, "for Varan."

"And for you," Aazen said, looking at her. "I did try to kill you. I thought I had succeeded. But now *you* of all people should want me to go free."

Meisha laughed scornfully. "The excuse would have to be profound," she said.

"Balram is dead. The Shadow Thieves' work in the Delve has been compromised, but Varan is alive, and they will not give him up easily," said Aazen. "If I return, I can report his death, and you will be free. Keep me for your Harper friends and there will be no safe place for you and the mad wizard."

"The Harpers are more than capable of protecting their own," Meisha said, "and no bond of friendship holds me. I need nothing from you."

Aazen smirked. "And will the Harpers welcome a mad,

dangerous wizard into their fold?" he asked. "You know there's only one place for him now, and if I don't go back, he'll never be able to get there. It's your choice."

Kall imagined Meisha's inner struggle. He fought his own feelings on the matter, but he wasn't surprised when Meisha finally nodded. "I accept," she said reluctantly, and added, "on the promise that if anything happens to Varan—if he is attacked, kidnapped, or suffers a mysterious 'accident' in his bed at night, the Harpers will come after you." A red glow suffused her skin, or perhaps it was just the reflection from the burning house. "And I will be leading the way."

Aazen nodded. "You, on the other hand," he said to Kall, "will be much harder to convince."

But Kall shook his head. "Go your own path," he said. "I won't hinder you, but choose any way but the Shadow Thieves. I spoke the truth. You'll never be able to trust them."

"I know," said Aazen. "And so they will never have a hold on me. I claim no love . . . or friendship," he said pointedly, "and so no one will ever control me—*ever again*."

The conviction in his voice, the look in his eyes struck Kall with sadness. "True love doesn't control," he said.

"Of course it does," said Aazen. "Love and friendship are flawed emotions. They can be twisted, manipulated, as we've both experienced. Never again," he said. Then he added softly, "You've found better companions, Kall. Keep them."

When Aazen walked away, Kall did not cry out for him to return. For a second time, he watched the darkness swallow his friend, but this time Kall was not alone. Meisha and Dantane stood on either side of him, and later, Morgan, Talal, and Garavin joined them. They stood, silhouetted in the light of the fire, until the Gem Guard came.

CHAPTER THIRTY

Keczulla, Amn
8 Marpenoth, the Year of Lightning Storms (1374 DR)

The following days saw widespread rumors. Whispers said the fire that consumed the estate had killed Morel's heir and an undisclosed number of assassins. A surprising public statement from the Bladesmile family partly fueled the rumors, reporting that all Morel assets were now in the care of Rays Bladesmile, per Kall Morel's request. The furor arising from the announcement, combined with Kall's disappearance from the city, led to rampant speculation about the fate of the Morel line. Many believed it to be extinct at last.

Kall was content to let the speculation drift where it may.

Garavin rode beside him as they left the city behind. "Has there been any word since that night?" he asked.

"No," Kall replied. "But I'll find her."

"And ye're sure she's alive?"

Kall gripped the gem from Garavin's axe in his gloved palm. "I'm sure."

They rode in silence for a while. Kall glanced down at the dwarf. "I like your new ornament," he said, pointing to a gray streak running through the center of Garavin's beard. "Distinguishes you—channeling a god, and all that. Lucky for me, it hasn't made you insufferably self-righteous."

Garavin laughed. "If ye mean because I haven't argued against Meisha's plan, ye're wrong. I think Dugmaren would approve, even if Dumathoin does not."

"Oh? Why so?"

"Because as much as Shanatar needs protecting, there's another school of thought says it needs to be explored, its magic understood. Otherwise it gets misused, as the Howlings misused it—as the Amnians suffered from what they didn't understand."

"Some would argue—myself included—that a mad wizard is the last person to take on such a task. Truth, old friend—should he really be allowed back in the Delve?"

"Yes," Garavin said without hesitation. "He's been touched by a god and a demon, and still he's trying to find his way back. That's what the lass believes. As long as there's hope, she can't give up on him, just as ye couldn't give up on yer father or Aazen."

"I left Aazen to the Shadow Thieves," Kall said. "What good can that possibly do his future?"

"Nothing," Garavin said, unwilling to lie to his friend. "But ye set his mind and heart free from his father, something he couldn't do for himself. He'll find his way on his own. Whether ye approve of his path or not, ye can't change him. Ye've yer own course to follow now."

"And you're coming with me?" Kall asked, trying to make it sound casual.

Garavin wasn't fooled. "Aye, lad, I'm coming, if only to see ye don't get trampled on by that wizard and the Harper firebrand."

"I'm hoping Morgan and the boy will mitigate some of that," Kall said, though he privately wondered if he weren't setting himself up for a world of hurt when he finally did track down Cesira, with a fire-loving Harper, a thief, an orphan, and a rogue wizard in tow. He suspected Dantane's motives for joining the group had everything to do with Meisha's desire to take a leave from the Harpers and come along, and not any real concern for Cesira.

He looked up at the sky, but there were no birds today. The clouds threatened rain. They would be soaked by the time they got on the road, but Kall didn't care. His path, now that he'd found it, spanned Amn, the Sword Coast, to the frozen North if necessary. Whichever road led him to Cesira, he would follow it gladly.

"Where are we meeting Meisha?" Garavin asked.

"Outside the Delve," replied Kall. "After she takes Varan home."

Meisha guided her master back to his pallet in the small workroom. With a word, she lit newly placed torches along the walls, flooding the room with warmth.

Varan did not seem to notice. He sat right down and reached into the wall, pulling out fresh tools and components as if from nowhere.

Meisha suppressed a shudder at how comfortably he fell into his old routine. Now that she knew just what his hands touched —what ancient power—was she doing the right thing?

"I'll be back to look in on you," she said, hoping some part of him heard her. "Between visits, someone else will come to take care of you. You won't be alone."

Varan made no reaction, so she turned to go.

"Fixed."

"What?" Meisha asked, turning back to him.

Varan held up an object: a small, square disk that seemed to be made of fluid metal. "Fixed now, firebird," he said confidently. "I'll fix them all."

"Eventually," Meisha said. She smiled a little as Varan's face blurred in her vision. "Fix them all, Master. Maybe when you do, you'll find your way back to me."

Talal waited for her in the hall. Meisha's anxiety, deep as it was, couldn't hold under the boy's shy grin. "Ready?" she asked.

"More than," he said. His eyes fell on the pouch in her hand. She'd removed it from Varan's neck. "He let you take that?"

"The demon's eye has been destroyed," Meisha explained. "The jarilith—and in turn Varan—only ever guarded it because it served as the link to Varan and to this plane. That's why he killed Shirva Tarlarin and attacked me—to protect the link."

"What will you do with it?"

"Give it to Dantane. He needs payment for his contract in Keczulla, and he wasn't able to salvage any magic items from the Delve. I offered this, and whatever's inside." But she'd removed the apprentices' rings. They now rode on a chain around her neck.

Talal looked disappointed, but he didn't say anything.

"You don't like him," Meisha guessed. "Dantane."

"I don't trust him," Talal countered. "Neither does Kall," he added.

"Kall trusts him. He just doesn't like him," said Meisha, smiling.

"Why not?"

Meisha shrugged. "Maybe because Dantane was able to relieve Kall's father from his enslavement—if only for a little while. It was something Kall couldn't do. I think it chafes him a bit, though he'd never admit it." She glanced sidelong at him. "I still don't know why you're coming with us," she commented.

The boy shrugged. "Nothing better to do," he said.

Meisha raised an eyebrow. "There will be more battles," she said.

"How do you know?"

"There always are," she said dryly. "And more magic, more fire. I know you're afraid of it."

Talal nodded. They walked on in silence, and were almost to the tunnel entrance when he said, "But I'm not afraid of you."

"Oh." Meisha felt the warmth grow inside her, a heat that didn't burn. The feeling was so alien she didn't quite know what to make of it.

Was this what she wanted, an existence somewhere between fire and cold, between anger and love? And if so, how could she ever hope to maintain such a delicate balance? Varan hadn't been able to teach her that skill. Maybe Talal and the others could.

They stepped into the sunlight, where Kall and his party waited.

EPILOGUE

Keczulla, Amn
10 Marpenoth, the Year of Lightning Storms (1374 DR)

Aazen wasn't surprised to see Daen waiting for him at the Contrall estate. Daen stood in the library behind his father's desk, pouring two glasses of wine.

"I've been awaiting your report," Daen said, regarding the hole in Aazen's tunic curiously. "I assume you encountered some trouble?"

Aazen reached for one of the glasses. "My father is dead," he replied. "The operation can no longer continue."

"I suspected as much." Daen didn't seem the least moved to hear of Balram's demise. "But we'll go on."

"You're not upset," said Aazen, draining his glass.

"Not at all. The profits from Balram's venture were exceptional, and the planning and intelligence behind the initial scheme equally so. True, his loss is a blow, but you are alive, and not the traitor he believed you to be. I received great things from Balram. I expect no less from his son." He saluted Aazen and drank. "In fact, I believe you'll come to mean a great deal to our organization in the future. That is, assuming you still wish to walk with us?" He smiled faintly at Aazen. "Or should I be upset about something?" he asked.

Aazen set the glass back on the desk with a soft clink. "You should perhaps be concerned that I've poisoned your drink," he said bluntly.

Daen didn't immediately react, until Aazen held up his open palm. Wired to his middle finger was a small vial, no larger than a thimble. Daen opened his mouth, but Aazen went on, "To answer your question, yes, I still desire a place among the Shadow Thieves—your place, specifically."

Daen grunted. "You're bluffing. Do you truly believe we don't have ways of dealing with poison?"

Aazen shrugged. "In that case, we'll talk tomorrow, when the time for an antidote has passed."

"Wait." Daen's bravado slipped a fraction when Aazen turned to the door, but he tried to appear more interested than upset. "What do you want?"

"To know more about my 'family,'" Aazen said. "I want to know how far your web reaches and who controls my fate."

"None of us know that," said Daen. When Aazen started to turn away, he chuckled. "Kill me if you like, but it's the truth, and the not knowing serves us all well. You're clever, but you're still a babe, Aazen. You need my guidance." Daen had returned to patronizing, the master to the student. "I can help you."

"Can you?" asked Aazen. "Because I tire of having my fate dictated by others. I told Kall the Shadow Thieves would not control me, and I will keep that promise."

"What is it you want, then, to rule us all?" scoffed Daen.

But Aazen was perfectly serious. "Yes. And you will help me, Daen, or you will die painfully tomorrow. Which will it be?"

"Oh, you're a dead little fool," said Daen serenely, but he nodded. "I'll help you, as long as it serves me to do so. For now, I have no choice, if I want to stay alive. But if I get the chance to kill you—"

"Agreed," said Aazen. "We'll take things one day at a time. As long as you impress me, Daen, I promise you'll stay alive."

Daen's jaw tightened—the first visible sign of anger Aazen

had ever seen from the man. "Where shall we begin?" Daen asked.

"The lowest point in the web," Aazen said. "Every Shadow Thief under your command. We'll work from there." Were he to lead them someday, he would need to know every member of his new family. He was looking forward to meeting all of them.

PHILIP ATHANS

The New York Times best-selling author of *Annihilation* and *Baldur's Gate* tells an epic tale of vision and heartbreak, of madness and ambition, that could change the map of Faerûn forever.

THE WATERCOURSE TRILOGY

BOOK I
WHISPER OF WAVES

The city-state of Innarlith sits on one edge of the Lake of Steam, just waiting for someone to drag it forward from obscurity. Will that someone be a Red Wizard of Thay, a street urchin who grew up to be the richest man in Innarlith, or a strange outsider who cares nothing for power but has grand ambitions all his own?

BOOK II
LIES OF LIGHT

A beautiful girl is haunted by spirits with dark intentions, an ambitious senator sells more than just his votes, and all the while construction proceeds on a canal that will alter the flow of trade in Faerûn.

BOOK III
SCREAM OF STONE

As the canal nears completion, scores will be settled, power will be bought and stolen, souls will be crushed and redeemed, and the power of one man's vision will be the only constant in a city-state gone mad.

"Once again it is Philip Athans moving the FORGOTTEN REALMS to new ground and new vibrancy."
—R.A. Salvatore

PAUL S. KEMP

"I would rank Kemp among WotC's most talented authors, past and present, such as R. A. Salvatore, Elaine Cunningham, and Troy Denning."
—Fantasy Hotlist

The *New York Times* best-selling author of *Resurrection* and The Erevis Cale Trilogy plunges ever deeper into the shadows that surround the FORGOTTEN REALMS® world in this Realms-shaking new trilogy.

THE TWILIGHT WAR

BOOK I

SHADOWBRED

It takes a shade to know a shade, but will take more than a shade to stand against the Twelve Princes of Shade Enclave. All of the realm of Sembia may not be enough.

BOOK II

SHADOWSTORM

Civil war rends Sembia, and the ancient archwizards of Shade offer to help. But with friends like these . . .

September 2007

BOOK III

SHADOWREALM

No longer content to stay within the bounds of their magnificent floating city, the Shadovar promise a new era, and a new empire, for the future of Faerûn.

May 2008

Anthology

REALMS OF WAR

A collection of all new stories by your favorite FORGOTTEN REALMS authors digs deep into the bloody history of Faerûn.

January 2008

RaVeNLoft
the coveNaNt

RaVeNLoft's LoRDs of DaRkNess Have aLways waiteD foR the uNwaRy to fiND them.

Six classic tales of horror set in the RAVENLOFT™ world have returned to print in all-new editions.

From the autocratic vampire who wrote the memoirs found in *I, Strahd* to the demon lord and his son whose story is told in *Tapestry of Dark Souls*, some of the finest horror characters created by some of the most influential authors of horror and dark fantasy have found their way to RAVENLOFT, to be trapped there forever.

LauReLL k. HamiLtoN
Death of a Darklord

CHRistie goLDeN
Vampire of the Mists

p.N. eLRoD
I, Strahd: The Memoirs of a Vampire

aNDRia caRDaReLLe
To Sleep With Evil

eLaiNe beRgstRom
Tapestry of Dark Souls

taNya Huff
Scholar of Decay

October 2007